Passing Through Darkness

© 2019 by

Malcolm McKenzie

Second Edition

I0642976

The World of Passing Through Darkness

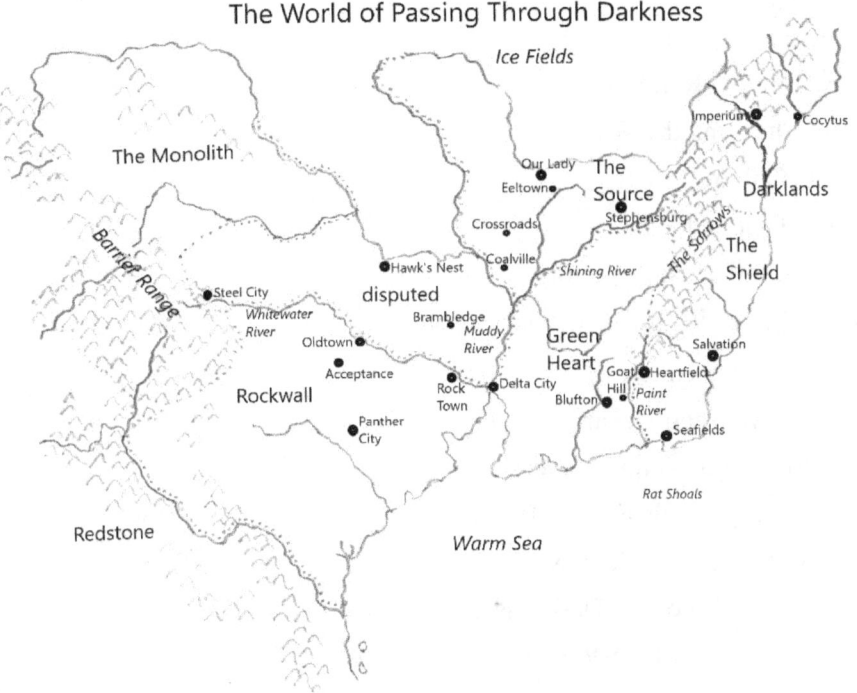

Contents

Book One - Born in Darkness

"We must pass through the darkness, to reach the light."
Albert Pike

1. On the Flow

"Gah, you stink!" Luco grunted as I stepped into the Hole.

I shrugged and smiled ruefully. "Yeah, I hit a gas pocket."

We all stank, of course. Everyone and everything on the Flow stank. Hundreds of years under the scorching sun had boiled away much of the landfill's surface stench, but the Flow was dozens of yards deep and miners were constantly uncovering new layers. Inside the mass of garbage were sealed bubbles of methane, the ferment of rotten fruit, old diapers, dead rats. Hitting a gas pocket was a bit like having a skunk explode on you.

The Hole was carved into the cliff wall on the west side of the Flow. It was cool and dark, and the wind usually carried the reek away from it. But everyone in the Hole was a miner, and all miners stank.

"Find anything good today?" Luco asked.

I teased him a bit, opening my sack and rummaging inside. "A plate, pretty good shape." Solid stoneware, with only a tiny chip and an inch-long crack that, with proper care, shouldn't grow to the point of breaking. "About twenty feet of copper wire, nice and thick." Useless to me, unlike the plate, but we got good prices for copper.

I let a smirk play across my lips. "A watch..."

Luco's eyes lit up. He loved watches. "Mechanical?" he asked eagerly.

"Battery," I said. His face fell.

"You dog squat," he said, without heat. He would have traded me just about anything I wanted for a mechanical watch. Battery-powered, this one was worth no more than the scrap value of the steel. We had no way to replace the battery, though they were everywhere in the Flow. They must have been trivially easy to make in the old days, but they were all dead now and I had never found anyone able to make a new one.

Luco chuckled at my little practical joke. The humor on the Flow had seemed cruel to me when I first arrived two years ago, but it had grown on me over time. Like the stink. I doubt anyone could ever get used to the reek of a gas pocket, but the background stench was no more than a mild discomfort. Less so than the autumn sun.

"You taking that to the forge now?" Luco asked.

"In this heat? I'll wait until it cools off a little out there." Most of the other miners had gotten off the Flow by noon. I had only stayed to excavate the pocket and let the sun and wind carry away some of the smell before I tracked it into the Hole - not with any great success, apparently.

"Hey, blackeye, c'mon over and have a drink," Joran called from the bar. I left my sack on the floor near Luco's table and headed back, deeper into the darkness. Joran handed me a rough clay mug of beer, enough alcohol in it that you didn't have to worry too much about where the water had been or if it had been boiled long enough.

The clinging orange dust of the Flow coated all of us, masking my gray skin and white hair. Except for the solid black of my eyes, I could have passed for an ordinary man. "Blackeye" was not a polite term, and Joran had told me very frankly that he despised the Select - which was a common enough prejudice. But he had been unfailingly kind to me since my arrival. The miners were a rough, strange crew, but then it seemed to me that people were pretty odd everywhere - part of the human condition, even for those of us that others might not consider quite human.

There was food as well as drink in the Hole, but my credit was running low and in our unspoken, informal tally of such things, I now owed Joran a beer. The copper and steel I had salvaged were worth something even though they hadn't yet been melted down, and no one would accuse me of mooching... But I didn't like to owe anyone favors.

"I'm heading up to the trading post," I announced to the Hole in general, nearly a dozen individuals who mostly weren't listening and didn't care. "I'll swing back around tonight after I hit the forge."

"Why don't you stay a while, Minos?" asked Luco. "You said it yourself - it's hot out there."

"Yeah, but we could probably use someone else on watch up top," I replied, which was usually the case. And in all honesty, my gray skin was better suited to the sun than most anyone else's. I picked up my sack, pushed aside the hanging, and was back in the blaze of the early afternoon.

Just because my skin didn't burn didn't mean I cared for the heat. The path up to the trading post was a gravelly track worn into the western wall of the Flow, leading from the Hole in the direction of the City. A slippery scree of little brown stones on dry, orange dirt, every shuffling step and thrust of my walking stick sending up a small cloud of dust. It would have made sense to cut steps, but it had been like this when I'd arrived and it hadn't seemed appropriate for a newcomer to suggest changes. Over the years I'd gotten used to it.

Kala was half-asleep in the shade of a rough square of cloth stretched between four posts. A couple of dolls, some toys, a small stack of plates, knives, spoons, and forks were set out on and around the table in front of her. Bulkier and more valuable items were stored in a cave deep in the back of the Hole where they were less exposed. A large hunting knife was stuck into the ground by her chair - for defense, although she'd sell it if someone offered a good price. As expected, there was no one else up here.

To be honest, Kala wasn't my favorite person, and standing watch over the trading post was a tiresome chore. But there were always people in the world who found it easier to take something by force than to earn it, even if the only thing to steal was the result of someone else's garbage picking. It was better for us to have a couple of watchers topside just in case. Especially if our people minding the store were willing to sell their own weapons.

"Hey, Minos," Kala murmured, eyelids still half shut.

I nodded. "Kala." Shading my eyes, I scanned the horizon. To the north, I could barely make out the topmost spires of the dead City looming miles distant. To the east lay the wide, meandering desolation of the Flow. And the featureless plain of the Low Furnace stretched off to an infinite horizon to the south and west. Nothing moved.

I turned in a little circle, trying to think of something useful to do. Pieces of brick, shards of concrete, and bits of plastic surrounded us, but none of it had any use. Metal, wood, and anything else of value had long since gone into a forge, ours or others'. The tide of human civilization had receded in the Age of Fear, drawing back into the great cities, building walls around them to keep danger at bay. The remains lay scattered like broken shells on a beach, the miners on the Flow picking over the rotting remains like crabs.

Here the City had died as well, generations ago. The very tops of towers of glass and steel in the distance were all we could see. The City had outlived its suburbs and then devoured them because people had felt safe inside its walls. Now its corpse endured unspoiled because we feared what might remain within them.

The cities had built up within those walls, towers reaching for heaven. Until the power went out. No one wanted to climb a hundred floors worth of stairs. And some of the things that lived on those abandoned floors weren't friendly.

Staring at the dead City wasn't accomplishing anything, so I picked rocks out of the cactus patch. The prickly pears were the only things we could make grow. Last year there had been an attempt at corn, but the sun had killed it. The cacti could survive nearly anything. Some of the miners swore by the sweet juice from the fruit and leaves. I hated it, but it was better than nothing.

The stones and bricks from the cactus patch went into a wall that surrounded it, which to some extent kept lizards, rabbits, mice, rats, and raccoons at bay. Or at least gave us a better chance of taking them out with a slingshot as they climbed over, adding some protein to our diet. As the cacti grew and reproduced, or someone ambitious dug one up from elsewhere and transplanted it into the patch, we enlarged the wall with the stones we dug out.

An empire of cactus. Still, it was life, and it might well prove more lasting even than the empire of garbage our forefathers had left us.

Shifting the debris out of the ground into the wall had taken less than two hours, even with frequent stops for shade and a drink of the disgusting cactus juice Kala kept in a clay pitcher. Kala herself had not gotten out of her chair during that time. She had a long, lean, athletic figure that had been much admired by Alben, the previous headman of the miners. Alben had left not long after my arrival, offered a position as foreman on a large farm to the southeast. Panther City was raising levies again, and men were leaving the farms for the military, where at least you were pretty certain to get fed. There were opportunities. As a proven leader of men - even garbage miners - Alben could have had a non-commissioned officer's rank in the armies of Rockwall had he wanted it... But he'd said he was too old and too wise and that war was a game for the young.

Dorren, our new headman, held Kala in lower esteem. She knew it but didn't change her behavior. Either she couldn't, or she thought it best to laze while she could. It might not be such a bad philosophy.

I wouldn't have minded lazing myself, but that was not a luxury a Select could afford. Instead, I picked my way back down into the Flow to get a compost bucket. The cacti did fine on their own, but the compost helped. And besides, the smell would annoy Kala but she wouldn't be able to complain.

My skin might not burn, but I was soaked in sweat by the time I got the bucket back up the cliff side. For all the rest I'd gotten, I might as well have gone back out onto the Flow to dig. When I was finished spreading the bucket's stinking contents on the cactus bed, I was done for the day. I lay down on my back in the dirt next to Kala's chair and fell asleep.

The sun was beginning to go down when I woke. Kala was already gone. It was rare enough for travelers to stop at all at the trading post - it was unheard of so close to dark. There was no safe shelter from the night within hours of us. I wondered if Kala had actually carried all the goods down herself. That would have taken a couple of trips. She had probably gotten someone to help.

North in the direction of the City, the forge's fires glowed orange in the twilight. It was a good time to get my scrap melted down. Dodd would still be working, but it wouldn't be as infernally hot inside as during the day.

The City lurked dark and skeletal on the horizon. Its original name had been abandoned in the Age of Fear, when superstition cursed with ill luck all names used before the Fall. Even personal names had changed. In our fallen world, to be named "John" or "Mary" invited unidentified, unspeakable disaster. The City had come to be called Acceptance before it died. Now it was nothing but broken steel bones and crumbling concrete flesh, its name remembered only by those of us who picked out a living like scavengers on its rotting refuse.

There was another mining camp further north on the far side of the Flow, closer to the City. Rumor had it that the pickings were richer there. The leavings of the Last Days were a fertile ground for metals, technology, and other goods that were now difficult or impossible to make. Thus our life on the Flow. But none of us here were tempted to get closer to the City. Things still lived there - perhaps even things like humans, though anything a human could quickly and easily salvage had long since been stripped away. We had all heard stories of shapes seen moving in the City's towers, glimpsed by those who had dared to approach the walls - gaunt, four-legged shapes with strange proportions...

slouching, shambling things... rats the size of wolves were the least of the City's horrors if Alben was to be believed.

In my travels I had seen no sign that the Darkness had reached this far into the southwest, but if it was anywhere, it would be in the City. It didn't pay to take chances with the Darkness.

You could hear Dodd's hammer halfway down the Flow. Inside the forge, the pounding made the bones in your skull vibrate. He was beating out something that looked like a shovel head on the anvil. Fenn, his assistant, was heaping trash onto the fire. It didn't burn as hot as coal or even wood, and it stank, but we had plenty of it.

Dodd couldn't hear me coming over his own hammering, but he noticed when Fenn stopped stoking the forge. The smith slammed his hammer down a few more times on the shovel blade, turned it over critically with the tongs, gave a little sigh, and plunged it into a bucket of stagnant water to cool. It wasn't fine work, but it would serve its purpose.

"What've you got for me, Minos?" His voice was rough and gravelly from a lifetime of breathing smoke.

I held up the loop of copper wire. He grimaced at the rubber coating. "Of all the things I burn in this place, I swear rubber is the one I just can't learn to abide the smell of." He paused and reflected. "Well, and dung, of course."

"Goes without saying, I think."

He nodded. "Speaking of dung, what happened to you? Gas pocket? You smell like you fell in the compost pit."

It was my turn to nod. "Yah, pocket, and I hauled a load up to the cactus patch."

"Kala sleep all day again?"

"I can't speak for all day - pretty much the whole time I was there."

Dodd grunted and pulled the shovel head out of the water, tossed it into a corner. "One of these days she won't wake up to get inside and the Darkness'll get her. And the worst thing is, it wouldn't be much of a loss."

I didn't believe the Darkness would find her even if she spent the night alone at the post. Other things might, though. What I said was, "Ah, she's probably safe enough. I doubt the Darkness has any use for her either."

He smiled at that, a flash of teeth in his cracked face. "Got anything besides the wire?"

I held up the watch. Fenn's eyes widened. "Mechanical?"

If Dodd had ever had the knack of fixing delicate things, decades of pounding iron into shape had robbed him of it. Fenn had an artist's touch, though. He could even mend a tiny spring. Watches fascinated him as much as they did Luco.

I shook my head. "Battery."

Dodd spat a little gob of black phlegm. "Guess there's about a knife blade worth of steel in there anyway." He tossed the watch in his hand. "Does the finished knife sound like a fair trade for the copper and the steel?"

I had a knife, but the one Dodd made would be better, and I could trade the other. "Done," I said.

It was fully dark by the time I headed back, but I could see well enough by the moonlight. The pale glow bleached the orange dirt to gray. Torches near the Hole cast a ruddy light that painted the ground red and black with fire and shadow. With the dead City squatting to the north, I felt briefly like a damned soul in a particularly arid and smelly part of hell. I shivered, though it was still warm. I wasn't religious, but even the thought of hell was invoked cautiously after the Fall. The Darklands far to the northeast, with their demon inhabitants, were infernal enough that the concept wasn't purely metaphysical.

My place clung to the cliffside between the forge and the Hole. I had two good sections of pipe sunk a couple of feet into the earth. With the cliff edge as my back wall, I had sheets of corrugated tin on two sides and the roof, anchored to the pipes. The fourth wall needed work - it was a sheet of plastic, nailed to the roof at the top and weighted with rocks at the bottom, and it served as both wall and door. Someday I would find something better.

I had told Luco and Joran I would be back to the Hole, and while it was dark it was still early... It would still be safe enough, but I was tired and not feeling social.

Each of the pipes had a bracket holding a torch dipped in grease, and I lit both before I went to sleep. The Darkness didn't like open flame. I'd never seen it this far west... but it didn't pay to take chances with the Darkness.

The next day the temperature was beginning to dip down into the bearable range, even at midday. If we were lucky, we would have a couple of months of pleasant weather before winter's freezing wind scourged the Flow. Winter on the Flow was worse than summer. It didn't stink nearly as much, but the cold was far more dangerous than the heat, and the garbage froze hard as rock. Food would become hard to come by. Animals retreated into their burrows, and the farmers' prices for their stored surplus went up at the same time our productivity went down. We'd be living mostly on whatever we'd squirreled away.

So autumn was a good time to dig. I'd gotten an early start with half an hour of kata, unarmed and with my walking stick. I would have rather slept in, but the day was too fine to give me any excuse. The rest of the morning had not gone so well. Dolls with no heads, some cracked glass bottles that had broken when I dug them out. I'd found a machine which I had at first thought to be a treasure trove of salvageable steel; it had turned out to be chrome-colored plastic instead. There was a sort of wheeled, rectangular chest made of some kind of flexible, lightweight, woven synthetic. One of the wheels was cracked but it was otherwise intact. I couldn't figure out what to do with it but it seemed a shame to leave it there.

I gathered the glass into my sack, getting two tiny slivers stuck in my hands. It could be melted down and reused, but wasn't worth much - fresh glass was easy enough to make from sand, and the world had sand in abundance. I put the sack in the rolling chest and zipped it shut. At least I hadn't hit another gas pocket.

As a result, no one had much to say to me, good or bad, when I plopped myself down next to Luco in the Hole.

There was the unlabored quiet of a room full of tired men and women. "Nice day today," Joran said after a time. There were nods all around, but no comments.

The character of the silence changed abruptly when the hanging pulled open, silhouetting a tall woman in the sunlight.

"Prophetess," someone breathed.

I'd heard the term before, though I'd never seen her. A girl from one of the farming villages southeast of the Flow, she'd decided she was called by the Universal Church's God to save the world. Or something like that. She'd been preaching around the Flow for months but hadn't visited us before.

Luco got up and pulled out a chair. "Have a seat, Prophetess. There's beer, and Thassa's got a pot of water boiling. There's stew on, too, I think. It's" – he looked toward Thassa in the kitchen.

"It's stew," said Thassa. She was a decent cook, but you were generally better off being a little vague on the ingredients.

The girl let the hanging fall back into place but didn't sit. "Thank you for your generosity. I'll have a cup of water, please. But I didn't come to eat or drink."

"Of course, Prophetess. We'd, uh, be thrilled to hear you explain God's Word, but you know how it is, we do have to be getting back to work." Luco summoned up an unconvincing smile.

With the light no longer behind her I could see our visitor grin broadly, her eyes twinkling. "I didn't come to preach either." Her smile widened as people tried to smother sighs of relief. "It's time for me to move on - the Lord is calling me away from here. I've come looking for an escort."

We exchanged glances. Most of the miners had never been more than a few miles from the Flow.

"Escort to where, Prophetess?" Joran asked.

"Stephensburg." Capital of the Source. It must have been nearly a thousand miles to the northeast.

Now the silence was deafening.

She looked around, trying to read faces in the darkness. "There's not much I can offer... Really just that it needs doing."

Most of the crew looked a little guilty. They were almost all Universalists. Some brave, pious soul should have volunteered to shepherd a spiritual leader of their faith, even a self-declared spiritual leader. But no one did.

No one would have volunteered in her home village, or in the places she preached, either. Or she wouldn't be here... begging.

"I'll go," my mouth said. I had no idea where that came from. "If you don't mind the company of a Select." That part sounded more like me, or would have if the tone had been petulant and sarcastic. The note of sincerity rang out of place on my tongue. Luco and Joran were staring at me.

I shrugged. "You guys have been great," I said, "But you know, over the past two years I've come to realize this place just doesn't smell that good."

"Oh, hell," Luco said, "If I were you I would have left a year ago."

"Never could figure out what you were doing here in the first place," Dorren rumbled from the back, "Though we've been glad to have you." I hadn't realized he was in the Hole. "But you go up north with the Prophetess, you may be Select, but people like you die up there."

"I'm pretty sure people die everywhere, Dorren," I said.

"You sooner than most, smartass," he snapped. He had a point. Select could live a very long time, but sarcastic, smart-mouthed Select weren't likely to do so. Nor were Select who left the safety of a place like the Flow to escort a self-proclaimed prophet halfway across the continent. The Darklands lay that way, beyond Stephensburg. I'd come west to escape the demons and the Darkness. This would take me the exact wrong direction.

But I'd liked the way her eyes had twinkled when she'd laughed at herself.

Of course, the Universal Eucharistic Church had, over the years, found unpleasant things to say about the Select. So the choice might not be mine to make.

"I'd be pleased to travel with a Select who is willing to accompany me so far," she said. "And your name is?"

"Minos," I said, and stood up. And that was how it was decided.

It had taken only minutes to say my goodbyes to everyone that mattered - I would catch up with Dodd and Fenn on our way out. It took only minutes more to gather everything I intended to take with me - a warm cloak, canteen, knife, flint and steel, whetstone, compass, frying pan, slingshot, and three ten-weight silver coins. I added a couple of small knickknacks I'd collected over the years that were light and might be valuable in trade. A tarnished silver ring with a slightly chipped stone in it, a pair of scissors from which I'd polished the rust, a little porcelain cat trimmed with a thin, flaking layer of what looked to be real gold. And a handful of oil-soaked torches, wrapped in plastic.

It looked like I wasn't going to be replacing the door to my shelter after all.

The woman who called herself Prophetess was traveling light as well. Now that I could see her clearly in the daylight, I looked her over from the corner of my eye. She wore a billowing, hooded tunic over long pants and sturdy leather boots. Like me, she had a walking stick, though hers was longer, nearly as tall as she was. And she was not a small woman, the top of her head reaching my eyes - and though I might still have some growth left in me, I was Select, and none of us are short.

In the bright sun I thought her exposed skin was pale under the dust of the Flow. Her hair was a dirty brown... although how much of that was its natural color and how much actual dirt was hard to say. She had crossed the Flow to reach us here, and no one in this part of the world bathed very often.

Her eyes were gray but expressive, not hard or cold. The eyes and her smile made her instantly attractive. Was that why I had impulsively decided to accompany her? Yes, probably. Still, I suppose there were worse reasons to risk your life.

"And what takes us to Stephensburg, Prophetess?" I asked as I shouldered my pack.

"We have to get there before Yoshana." She looked down, it seemed to me oddly hesitant for someone on a mission from God. "If she gets there first, it may mean the end of... everything."

The end of everything certainly sounded ominous - our world was fallen, but it was the only one we had. Of course, it stood to reason that prophets were supposed to traffic in dooms and apocalypses. But, "Yoshana? The Overlord Yoshana? Isn't she dead?"

Prophetess scoffed. "We've heard she's been dead before. More than once. Although this time..." she paused. "This time she may actually have died. But if she did, she's risen. And she's saying she's returned with a message from God."

Another shiver ran through me. Yoshana's armies had overrun much of the Green Heart, my home before I'd fled. The thought of the Overlord's legions at my back had taken me this far west. I'd slept easier believing she was gone. I kept my tone nonchalant. "Ah. And it offends you that she's using your faith for her own purposes."

"Maybe. A little. But what's a lot more frightening is that she may really believe it."

Well. Religious war had touched off the catastrophe leading to the Second Fall. Maybe this truly would be the end of everything. If so, a farm girl who believed herself a prophet seemed like an unlikely savior of the world, but who was I to judge?

Racing against time to keep an undead Overlord from destroying the world. How hard could it possibly be? I forced a smile and started off to the north, walking stick in my hand and pack over my shoulder. "Then I guess we'd better get going if we're going to stay ahead of her. At least it gets me off the Flow."

Thad was watching over the trading post, carving designs in a wooden rod. He was good at it, with a steady hand, an artist's eye, and the patience for detailed work. "Prophetess," he said as we came up the track from below. He nodded to me. "Heard you're leaving."

There had only been a handful of minutes for that gossip to beat us up to the post. I was briefly amazed. Then again, there was little news on the Flow, and the arrival of a prophet and departure of a miner, all in one day, was about the most excitement we were going to get short of a bandit attack or an outbreak of cholera.

I quickly took in the table, the same goods laid out on and around it as yesterday. "No one, huh?"

"Not yet."

There was a good chance that "not yet" meant "not at all." Most of the farms that traded with us were a few miles south of the Flow or a few miles northwest, beyond the wasteland that surrounded the City. The farmers would generally rise with the sun and be here by noon so as to be home well before dark. The only thing likely to stop after mid-day was a long-distance caravan, and those were rare.

Thad knew what I was after. "So no food," he added.

For traveling we would want something that lasted and packed a lot of energy into a small space, like pemmican. But on the Flow we had neither berries nor a reliable source of meat. Days or even weeks could go by without getting a successful shot at the critters that raided the cactus, and they usually went into Thassa's stew.

There were rats on the Flow, of course, but you had to be truly desperate before you ate rats that lived on garbage. That was asking to get sick, no matter how much you cooked them. The cats that ate the rats were a better bet, but they were clever and hard to catch. Besides, most of us liked the cats.

"Take some leaves." He nodded toward the cactus patch.

I dug the little porcelain cat out of my pack. Thad waved it away. "You've put more time into the patch than most, and that cat's worth a lot more than a few leaves. Just take 'em."

I shook my head and set the cat on the table. I didn't like to owe people. Thad picked the cat up, turned it over, and handed it back to me. "Just take the leaves or I'm gonna bust your face. You're hurting my feelings."

The cactus leaves weren't really Thad's to give without taking something in trade. Maybe he was speaking for everyone else, maybe he wasn't... but he really might take a swing at me if I annoyed him.

"Thanks," I said. I cut off four leaves and handed two to Prophetess. We sat in the shade and plucked out the needles. I had a little roll of cloth in my pack and used it to wrap up the larger spines.

"Do you have a use for those, or do you just like sharp things?" Prophetess asked.

"If I can find a reed, and some cotton, I can make a blowgun and use them for darts. Might be able to take a bird, or something bigger if we can find a rattlesnake for the venom."

"That's a lot of if's," she smiled.

"Waste not, want not."

She turned to look back at the Flow and her smile faded. "Yes."

"So where are you headed, Minos?" Thad asked.

"Stephensburg," I answered without thinking. Then it occurred to me that Prophetess might not want me advertising her destination if she was really trying to stop a resurrected Overlord. I shot her a quick look, but she didn't seem upset.

"That's a hike," Thad said. "Think it's started getting cold up there yet?"

"Nah, I wouldn't think so. Might be by the time we get there, though."

He nodded. We sat for a couple of minutes, but there didn't seem to be anything more to say.

"We'd better get going before we run out of light," I said.

"Yup. Careful on the way." He looked uncertainly at Prophetess. "Uh, go with God."

"Thank you. May his blessings be upon you," she said.

Thad's face brightened a little and he waved at us. I had to chuckle as we started north. I doubted she was really a prophet, or that there was such a thing, but the girl seemed to be able to brighten people's day, and that was worth something in itself.

Not only could we hear Dodd's hammer halfway down the Flow - to be truthful, you could probably hear it from one end to the other if you listened. There wasn't a lot of other sound. As we got closer, I could tell that two hammers were ringing - Fenn would be beating out iron too, then, rather than stoking the forge, fetching fuel, or any of the countless other tasks his apprenticeship required.

I hoped Fenn's growing skill with the hammer didn't rob him of his delicate touch with the tiny, intricate treasures we sometimes found. That would be a shame.

They were both absorbed in their work and didn't hear us come in - not surprising, over their banging at the metal. It was a miracle either of them could still hear at all. I was a little more surprised they hadn't noticed the change in the light as I opened the door, but I suppose the shifting glow of the forge flared and ebbed... or maybe they were just too busy to be distracted by us.

Prophetess and I waited patiently. It wasn't wise to interrupt someone with a red-hot bar of metal in one hand and a twelve pound hammer in the other.

Dodd noticed us first. "Ah, Minos!" he exclaimed. "And the Prophetess. An honor. Stopped by to say goodbye?"

"Not a lot of secrets in this place, are there?" I laughed.

"We're garbage miners, Minos. It's not like there's a lot of excitement. You're not from here, but most folks around this place know your business before you know it yourself. You know what they say in Redstone – 'a small town is one big hell.'" He looked at Prophetess. "Begging your pardon."

She smiled. "I grew up on a farm where privacy wasn't a word in our vocabulary and I tried to convince people who'd seen me in a diaper cloth that I've been called by God. I know what you mean."

"Speaking of hell," Fenn waved apologetically to the forge, "Can we get you something to drink? We have water and, uh, water."

It must have been at least thirty degrees hotter inside the forge than outside, enough to drive the temperature from cool to sweltering. I wasn't sure what they were burning today, but it didn't smell good - which only made the small, hot space seem that much more close and confined. One side benefit, though, was that there was no problem boiling water, so it was safe and abundant. If it hadn't been, Dodd and Fenn would have dehydrated within an hour.

The water was warm and tasted both of soot and metal - but Prophetess still thanked Fenn as if were the finest drink she'd ever tasted. His eyes lit up and he beamed.

"So you're going north?" Dodd asked. "Know your route?"

I looked at Prophetess and she blushed furiously. "The Lord tells me where to go. He doesn't give me a road map."

Dodd shot me a look. It might have said "you're crazy" a little more clearly if he'd stuck out his tongue and made a little circle around his temple with his finger - but only a little.

I shrugged. "You know I'm from southeast of here. Northern geography isn't my strongest point." I had never discussed my origins in any detail, but you didn't gain acceptance in a small community like this without telling people anything at all. "I figure we head northeast until we hit the Big Muddy and try to get passage on a steamboat."

"And when you hit the forests west of the river? If the Darkness doesn't get you, the things it's infected will."

That was a bit of an exaggeration. The Darkness would be no thicker there than it had been in the forests in the southeast of the Green Heart where I had been born. It was dangerous, but hardly a death sentence. At least not to a Select. Prophetess would not be used to dealing with it, though.

So, "What do you suggest?"

"Well, you know I'm from Redstone, so I'm hardly an expert on the northeast either. But if it were me, I'd head straight for the Whitewater and take a boat to the Muddy. Whitewater dips south before it meets up with the Muddy, so it's a bit out of your way, but you're on water almost the whole way and I've never heard of the Darkness venturing onto water. Don't think it can."

I doubted that. The Darkness had certainly crossed the Big Muddy itself, so water was not an absolute barrier to it. And the Darkness was far from the only thing we had to worry about.

"Aren't they still skirmishing along the Whitewater?"

"Pfft. They've been doing that for longer than I've been alive and don't figure they'll stop after I'm dead. Rockwall and the Monolith both want that farmland too much and neither of 'em are going to hold it."

Which was true enough. Too much of Rockwall was desert and too much of the Monolith was mountains - the fertile belt between the Whitewater and the Red River was an irresistible temptation to both states' ambitions. When Panther City raised its peasant levies, most of them went to die pursuing Rockwall's northern claims. I suspected the inhabitants of that disputed land mostly just wanted everyone to leave them alone. The semblance of order the nation states imposed probably wasn't worth having armies trampling your fields every spring - certainly not when they just passed through, again and again, without ever bringing a resolution.

"Thanks, Dodd. We'll make for the river."

It occurred to me that I was speaking for the person in charge of our mission. "If that's all right with you, Prophetess."

She nodded. "Seems reasonable."

"We'll need to come up with some way to pay for passage."

"I'm hoping to appeal to their better natures," she smiled.

Right. "As we head east of here most people are going to be Reborn until we get into the Source. They've certainly got a tradition of traveling preachers, but I'm not sure they're going to do any favors for a Universalist prophet."

"Then I'll row the boat, shovel coal, or do whatever needs to be done to buy passage," she said flatly. "The Lord will provide. He never promised to provide a first class cabin. If you read your Bible I don't think you'll find many of the prophets enjoyed any luxuries. I'm not expecting any different."

"As long as we don't get swallowed by a whale," I said. "I don't care for fish."

"Funny enough, whales aren't actually fish," Dodd remarked, which I had known full well. Prophetess didn't seem amused. I let the subject drop.

"Anyhow, you'll be wanting this," the smith said. He handed me a folding clasp knife, its wooden handle inlaid with intricate copper scrollwork - clearly Fenn's craftsmanship.

"You can't have had time to make this out of what I brought you yesterday," I said.

"No, but I had something like it in mind, and this is on hand. Unless you want to wait a few days until I can finish the other, but seems like you're set to go now."

"Yes, I mean we couldn't wait, but this –"

"Minos," he said, "you're not a bad kid, but you need to learn to say 'thank you,' be grateful, and shut up."

There wasn't much to say to that but "thank you," so I said it and shut up. I shook hands with Dodd, which hurt - the smith was a strong man, but I think he knew his own strength perfectly well and was crushing my fingers just to make some sort of point. Then he slapped me on the shoulder, which also hurt. Fenn's grip was gentle, as was his smile.

We stepped back out into the cool wind coming down from the north, and I was instantly chilled from the drop in temperature. "So, off we go," I said. I shrugged. "It's funny, but I think I'll actually miss this place."

Prophetess cast a sad backwards glance. "They're good people," she said, "But waste is a terrible thing to mine."

2. The Edge of Acceptance

The massive landfill that was the Flow occupied a dry riverbed that started just southwest of Acceptance and meandered southeast toward Panther City. I had originally planned to travel due north, skirting the City's western edge. The land was inhospitable, the border of the desert called the Low Furnace. But it was safe, with excellent visibility. I had thought to keep the barrens to our west and grassland to our east as we worked our way north. But Dodd's advice would turn us immediately east instead, making our way to Oldtown on the Whitewater to take ship to the Muddy.

That meant crossing to the eastern edge of the Flow from our camp on the western side. It wasn't a dangerous undertaking, but it was slow. You watched your step in unfamiliar parts of the Flow. Most of it had compressed over the centuries into a solid surface, but there were still thin crusts that wouldn't hold a person's weight. Stepping through one of those was likely to burst a gas pocket, and if you were really unlucky you might land on something sharp - and dirty. Cleaning the wound with alcohol we distilled from the prickly pears would generally take care of infection, but it wasn't pleasant.

Prophetess wisely prodded the ground ahead with her staff, raising tiny puffs of orange dust. We skirted the half-buried corpses of plastic carts. Prophetess tapped one.

"Nothing to be done with these?"

"Oh, no. We can use just about anything. If you melt the plastic down and mix it with sand, you can make pretty decent building bricks out of it. But it's not the most valuable stuff in here by a long shot - not really worth it. And this is getting pretty far away from where we do most of our digging."

We trudged on a bit farther. "So what brings a Select to mine garbage in the middle of nowhere?"

I shrugged. "Over the years, we've learned it pays to spread out. Makes it harder for anyone to kill us all in one fell swoop. Been tried, you know. We're not the most popular people in the world. I think it's the eyes." I smiled tightly, blinking my black eyes. Lots of animals had black scleras, but in a human it was somehow viewed as sinister. "Traditionally we're supposed to take off on our own at thirteen."

I looked suspiciously at a depression in the ground in front of me and poked it with my walking stick. A hole two feet in diameter cracked open, venting an odor of rotten eggs and worse things. We gave it a wide berth.

"My parents started getting nervous when Yoshana's legions pushed into the Green Heart. Not that Yoshana seemed to hate the Select more than she hated anyone else. But then the Hellguard turned on her, and we know the demons don't like us."

I was watching the ground in front of me, but it seemed that Prophetess' eyebrows went up.

"I know a lot of people don't see any difference between us..."

She shook her head. "No, no, the Books of the Fall are clear that the Select and the Hellguard are... separate."

"But related, yes? That's what they say."

She stopped and faced me. "Aren't you?" And then, before I could get angry, she blushed red as a beet. "I mean, both the Select and the Hellguard were... changed. Made."

"I was born from my mother, same as you. I don't know exactly where the Hellguard came from, but I'm pretty sure they weren't born like you and me. I know the church says the Select and the Hellguard caused the Fall –"

"No, that's not it. Not caused." She cocked her head. It was hard for me to tell exactly what was in her expression. Was she sad? Apologetic?

"Saint Arvan wrote that the Select and the Hellguard walked abroad in the land, a sign of what was to come. Not a cause, but a - a symptom. A manifestation." She winced. "I'm sorry, I didn't mean to offend you."

I waved my hand. "I'm not offended." And I really wasn't. "Tell me, how does a girl growing up on a farm get to be a prophet?"

That probably hadn't come out right. Now it was my turn to apologize. "I don't mean... It's just, isn't that a lot of religious theory for someone who grew up on a farm on the edge of the Flow? You know, discussing manifestations?"

To my relief, she smiled. "My mother wanted me to have an education. Be literate, at least. All we had to read was the Bible, the Books of the Fall, the Catechism of the Church... And Father Jem down in Noble was always easy to talk to. Well, until I told him the Lord was speaking to me. I think then he decided I was a nut."

I burst out laughing, clapped my hands to my mouth.

"Verily I say unto you, no prophet is accepted in his own country," she said. "Maybe especially if people are used to seeing you milking goats at the edge of a garbage dump."

"I don't know," I said, "I hear they were tough on that carpenter's kid in his home town too."

Her face froze over in an instant. "Don't do that."

And now I was in familiar territory with a girl - having offended her without understanding how. "Huh?" I said stupidly.

Her expression softened. "Sorry. But there's only one Lord. Making the comparison - well, it's blasphemous."

Hadn't she just been the one making that comparison?

She stared at the ground for a moment, then met my eyes. "I've had a lot of people ask me who I thought I was. If I thought I was the Second Coming. Believe me, I don't. At best, I'm the voice crying in the wilderness. Sorry I'm so sensitive about it. The truth is, it's not easy. The Bible says God chooses his prophets carefully and gives them strength when they're weak. So I can't doubt that. But sometimes I do."

I had nothing helpful to say. So I put my hand on her shoulder.

She smiled and said, "So, we'd better get moving. One thing that's pretty clear is prophets need to walk where they're going like everyone else."

On our side of the Flow there was a lot of open space between our camp and the handful of grubby farms to the north. As we clambered up the eastern side of the gorge, however, we found ourselves within spitting distance of a settlement. The City came further south here as well. There was another mining camp just north of us, but I'd had enough garbage for the day - maybe for the rest of my life if I was lucky.

Or not so lucky. The rest of my life might not be very long.

"Spitting distance" was an exaggeration. A hundred yards or so separated us from a low, weathered wooden fence that marked the edge of the cropland to our east. The nearest farmhouse was another hundred yards beyond that.

A dog trotted up to the other side of the fence and barked at us, more curious than challenging. I breathed deeply and slowly and called out, "Hey, buddy." I had learned to control my breathing and heart rate around dogs, and they generally tolerated me now. There was something about the Select they didn't seem to trust, and if I allowed myself to reciprocate their suspicion I could send them into a fury of barking and snarling with no more than a dirty look.

Past the dog, two small children were picking rocks from beneath the stubble of last month's wheat harvest. One of them shouted "Mom!" But like the dog the little girl seemed more curious than concerned. It was broad daylight, and there were only two of us.

I had crossed plenty of farmland uninvited when I'd come west, but since we'd been seen it was only polite to wait at the fence. So we did.

Less than a minute passed before a stout, middle-aged woman came around the farmhouse and made her way toward us. She waved us in long before she reached us. She had a pitchfork, which she might have been using for any number of things - including deterring unwelcome visitors.

The fence was more of a notional boundary than an actual barrier. Not even waist high on me, it consisted of two rows of rails between posts set perhaps seven feet apart. It was hard to imagine any kind of animal that wouldn't be able to go over, under or through it. I supposed it might serve to pen in an unambitious cow or sheep. It was no defense against predators, whether on four legs or two.

"Come on in, Scout won't bite," the woman called. The dog danced around us, several yards away, as Prophetess and I swung ourselves over the fence. "Most useless fool guard dog on God's green Earth," she continued.

The children fell in behind her as she approached. "I'd heard there was a Select working on the Flow," she said. "Hadn't really believed it." She looked Prophetess up and down. "You aren't Lemard and Dassy Carter's daughter from down toward Noble?"

"Yes, ma'am," the girl answered.

"Ah, then, you'd be the one who's, ah..."

I thought about volunteering the word "crazy" but for a wonder managed to keep my mouth shut.

"Yes, ma'am," said Prophetess.

The woman considered us for a while. The children were still behind her, maybe a bit put off by my appearance. The dog had stopped barking and was sniffing at my backside, which I imagined smelled about the same as everyone else's.

"Well, you'll likely be on the road to somewhere, then?"

We nodded.

"Sorry that I don't have any supper ready yet to offer you," she said. "Rendel and the oldest boy are out to the woods hunting a bit. They should be back before dark, though, if you want to wait. We could put you up with the children, Miss Carter, and you'd be welcome to the barn, Mister?"

"Minos," I said. I wasn't sure whether I was being offered the barn because it would be improper for me to sleep under the same roof with Prophetess or because they didn't want a Select in their house. I decided to make an effort and take the more favorable interpretation.

"I expect you will be wanting to stay, with it getting late now?"

It was early afternoon. There were hours of daylight yet. I said something to that effect.

She shook her head. "They say there's drelb in the woods. Rendel's having a look as I say, but I've told him I don't want him out after dark. They say the Darkness is on the move."

I highly doubted there were drelb this far west, except perhaps further to the north. When Yoshana's legions began to cross into the Heart, we'd heard every kind of rumor you could imagine. In that case at least it was true that Yoshana brought the Darkness with her, but the panic had outpaced her troops by weeks and miles. I'd seen it in places I'd passed through on my way here - sometimes the farther from her armies, the worse the reaction. A filthy, slow-witted vagabond had been beaten to death, mistaken for a drelb by people who had obviously never seen one. Townsfolk had decided that a strange, lonely adolescent boy had been possessed by the Darkness and burned him alive.

I smiled politely. At least I thought I did. "You don't believe me, young man, but there's strange lights in Acceptance at night and I've seen strange shadows moving across 'em."

Well, sure. Everyone knew you didn't want to be in the City at night. There was a reason we mined for steel in the Flow instead of trying to pull rebar out of the broken hulks of Acceptance's buildings. A lot of the farming communities were built in part from the ruins of the City, but only from what their ancestors had hauled out in the daytime. Diseased wolves, giant rats and maybe some degraded paleo gangs weren't at all the same thing as drelb or the wraiths of the Darkness, though.

Still, it didn't hurt to get whatever information we could. "We're headed to Oldtown. Anything to worry about on the way, do you think?"

The woman considered. "The Oldtown road should be safe enough. Might be bandits, of course. If I were you I'd take the old section trail out east of the lake, then head due north for the road. That's how most folks round here do it when they've got call to head that way. There's a sort of a fishing lodge at the southeast corner of the lake. You'll want to stop there for the night."

"That's not that far from here, is it? I'd thought to make it farther."

"It's a good fifteen miles, young man, which is all you'll do before it gets dark. And after that you've got twenty miles on the northbound trail through the woods to the Oldtown road, and you do not want to do that at night. My mother always told me you Select were supposed to be too smart for your own good. I can't say I ever understood that, but maybe she meant you don't have a whole lot of common sense."

I really wasn't going to snap at her and say something spiteful. I really wasn't. But Prophetess smiled and said, "Well, if he had any common sense he wouldn't have agreed to escort me, so I for one am grateful for it."

And the farmwife laughed and Prophetess laughed and the farmwife said she figured we should take some fresh baked bread with us, and we were all great friends. Okay, so they had both called me an idiot and laughed at me, but I wasn't upset about that. Well, not more than maybe just a little.

The children had lost all interest once the conversation turned from exciting things like drelb. Any interest a Select held for them was apparently dispelled by learning I was a moron. They were back to picking rocks out of the field instead - it had amazed me in my limited time on farms that no matter how many times you plowed a certain patch of ground, there were always more rocks in it.

"Rocks," I muttered. "Dumb as a bag of 'em, that's me." I trailed along behind Prophetess and her new friend as they chatted.

We continued on our way soon enough, and the warm, fresh bread we chewed on lifted my spirits. Ego loses out to a full stomach most days.

The dusty section road was just as orange as the Flow, as indeed the cleared soil of the farm had been. I was a bit surprised anything grew in it. The bones of the City stretched out to the north, more visible here. The afternoon sunlight winked off shards of glass and stained the bleached concrete golden. A dead zone several miles wide extended between the northernmost farms and the City's wall, now crumbling. Everything between had been stripped, scavenged, at first to go into that wall, later into the villages built outside it. Any usable metal, wood or stone had long since become walls, homes, carts, what have you. People didn't venture into the City itself.

Acceptance had probably been abandoned over a hundred years ago near the end of the Age of Fear. A pair of small rivers that had watered it had dried up, leaving behind only dust and the gorge that had become the City's dumping ground - the Flow. There had been nothing to support the concentration of population. Of course, Panther City, capital of Rockwall, had survived without a navigable river or any other obvious natural advantages, but that was generally attributed to sheer cussedness.

The wheat had been harvested in every field along the road, leaving nothing but stubble. A few cows and sheep were grazing in it, most contained by the same sort of fence we had crossed before - so apparently they did serve a purpose after all. I was a little surprised there was no more impressive barrier. They might not get drelb here, but it would be odd if coyotes, wolves or mountain lions didn't sometimes go after the sheep. On the other hand, the chain link fences from before the Fall were mostly rusted junk by now, and they were much harder to make than the simple wooden construction the farmers used. Some villages in the Green Heart used log palisades, especially near the border with the Shield or in the foothills of the Sorrows, but that was probably more trouble than it was worth here. I supposed the occasional lamb being taken didn't merit the effort.

The farmwife had given us skins of small beer to go along with the bread, and those made the dusty road quite bearable. With no obstacles in our way we made good time, and the shadows were just beginning to get truly long when we sighted the fishing lodge she had mentioned.

It sat at the southern tip of a lake that stretched several miles to the north. And as she had said, the woods grew up around it - thick stands of evergreens that reached well over a hundred feet into the air. This was familiar territory for me - the hills of the eastern Green Heart were thick with pines - but stopping for the night didn't seem like such a bad idea after all.

And speaking of stockades, one was taking shape around the inn, itself a solid log construction obviously built from the local timber. The wall seemed designed to start at the water's edge, forming three quarters of a circle open to the lakeshore. The builders must have shared Dodd's belief that the Darkness couldn't cross water. The construction remained unfinished, the two wings not yet meeting in the middle. Presumably a gate would go there, which would require more engineering than simply sticking sharpened poles in the ground.

For the moment, an overgrown dirt track led through the open space to the building. Tree trunks meant for the palisade, some already trimmed, lay in the yard.

The lodge was a two story structure surrounded by a roofed porch. Small, roughly glazed windows were set at regular intervals. It was nothing fancy, but it was solidly built.

A bearded man, his hair just beginning to show touches of gray, was lighting an array of torches outside. "Evening," he said, not taking his eyes from his work. "Room's forty-weight in silver a night for the both of you, supper and breakfast included."

"The Lord has called me to Stephensburg," said Prophetess. "It would be a blessing if you supported us in that calling."

The man moved to another torch, still not turning to look at us. "The Lord stays for free. Everyone else pays."

I had hoped to make it farther than one day's walk before we needed to use my meager stock of trade goods, but then again, that porcelain cat was going to break soon anyway. I opened my pack, but Prophetess set her hand on mine.

"If generosity doesn't move you, how about simple profit? Are all your rooms taken? You'll make nothing if we walk on, and it's getting late. A discount is only reasonable."

The man turned to us for the first time, a small smile on his face. "You'll sleep in the woods tonight if you walk on, and they say there are drelb out there. Almost certain to be something in the dark you don't want to meet. So who has more to lose, you or me?"

I shrugged and pulled the cat out of my pack. The innkeeper took a step closer and squinted at it. "Gah, that's an ugly thing and no mistake! What would I want with that?"

"Oh, come on," I said, exasperated. "That's real gold on it. Probably." I looked around at the pile of logs. "Or I can help you put up that palisade."

His smile widened. "First good offer I've heard from the two of you. I'll have your work on the wall until it's time to sleep, and your friend that's been called by God can help in the kitchen." He turned to Prophetess. "Assuming God taught you how to do anything useful?"

"I can peel potatoes, wash dishes, milk cows... If you find that useful," Prophetess said frostily.

"That'll do. I'm Oren. Welcome to the Trout Trap, and make yourself right at home in the kitchen. Your Select friend here can put his muscles to use for me."

Prophetess proceeded inside. Oren stepped to the pile of timber and tossed a hand ax toward me. I could have stepped forward to catch it, or back to let it land on the ground in front of me. I opted for the latter.

He gestured at the stacked trunks. "The two on the right there already have the limbs off and the ends sharpened. You can start doing the same to the others."

Twenty minutes later, the sun was almost down, and I was finding cutting by torchlight even less pleasant than dealing with the sun in my eyes.

"Not very good at that, are you?" asked Oren, looking critically at my handiwork.

"If you'd rather, I can dig holes for them instead. I've spent the last two years digging. More my area of expertise these days."

"That'll do," he repeated. So he gave me a shovel, and I went to work. I'd gotten off the Flow after two years, and I was still digging holes.

When the first hole was deep enough, we hoisted one of the finished logs between us and maneuvered it into place. I steadied the bottom while Oren used a long leather strap to pull it upright. He was a solidly built man and I was doing no more than half the work, but sweat was pouring off me despite the chill air by the time we were done.

"Right, let's get the other one up," he paused for a gasping breath, "And we'll call it a night."

"I'm not sure you got forty-weight's work out of me," I said.

He grinned. "No, but I don't think you have forty-weight. And I don't want that ugly cat of yours. And your friend's right, the place won't be full. The grain wagons have gone out and come back. And who knows, maybe it will earn me a reward in heaven. Or at least a few hours less in hell."

Speaking of hell... "Do you really think there are drelb out there?"

He leaned on a trunk. "I haven't seen any, but folks coming through swear they've seen big things moving in the woods. Might just be deer, or we've always had a few black bears in here. Or might be drelb. The Darkness is out there, that's for sure."

"You've seen it?"

"Me? No - God forbid. Who sees it and walks away untouched? But stands to reason, doesn't it? Demons pushing into the Green Heart... If it wasn't in these woods before, it'll be here soon enough."

There were almost a thousand miles and the bulk of the Green Heart's army between here and the Hellguard, so I wasn't particularly convinced by his reasoning. There was no point in arguing, though, so I went back to digging instead, and he resumed trimming tree limbs.

We grunted and heaved and wrestled the second sharpened log into place. The torches Oren had set around our work area flickered, casting shadows in the pines and sending up billows of smoke. The innkeeper and I looked out into the dark forest, then looked at each other.

"I think that's enough," he said.

I nodded. I was tired. And I was willing to bet that the movement we saw in the trees was no more than shadows, wind and woodsmoke... but it didn't pay to take chances with the Darkness.

Inside the lodge was warm and comfortable, smoky from the fireplace and torches but with a high ceiling that kept the air from becoming stifling. Most of the first floor was taken up by a large common room, with guest rooms around the outside of the second story, ringed by an interior balcony.

A woman, of an age to be Oren's wife, served me a bowl of hot stew and a mug of beer. Both were good.

"The young lady went up to bed already," she said. I nodded - my mouth was too full to talk. "She's a nice girl," the woman added. I nodded again and kept eating. She opened her mouth, shut it, scowled at me, and walked away.

Strange. I suppose when you live alone in the woods, you get a little odd.

Hah. No, I was not actually that oblivious. But I had no intention of doing anything to hurt, offend, or insult the honor of - the girl whose name I didn't even know. Miss Carter. Prophetess.

In any case, at this point I was tired, full, and had no intention of doing anything at all besides sleeping. I asked which room was ours, got the answer - with another scowl - and headed upstairs.

The room was dark, but enough torchlight filtered in from outside that I could see Prophetess was asleep. On the only bed. The only - small - bed. Suddenly the attitude from Oren's wife was becoming clearer.

I shrugged. I had slept on worse things than a wooden floor. And I was tired enough to sleep on an anthill.

I wrapped myself in my cloak, pillowed my head on my pack, and closed my eyes. I turned over, then turned again. The floor seemed to be unusually hard, even by the standards of wooden floors. I put my back against the wall, which was cold, but helped me feel more comfortable.

At least until Prophetess started snoring.

Every hour or so I would wake up, sore and cold, and look at the bed, and judge how much room there was. And then I would think of the scowl on Oren's wife's face, and I would roll over and try to go back to sleep.

3. The Oldtown Road

I was stiff and tired in the morning. I didn't do any warm-up exercises or kata, and instead wrapped myself around a plate of bacon in the common room. That made me feel much better. My parents had taught me that morning exercise gave you energy for the rest of the day, but the only thing I ever enjoyed about morning exercise was the times I allowed myself the luxury of not doing it.

Prophetess was in excellent spirits, and why shouldn't she be, since she'd had the bed to herself?

Our labor had earned us not only room and board, but also washrooms with buckets of hot water. After scrubbing and rinsing myself, I was once again gray, rather than orange. It would have taken too long to wash and dry our clothes, but I was able to shake off a lot of the dust. My rough linen tunic and pants were back to something like their original dirty white color - though still a dirtier white than they'd been when new.

I had been right about Prophetess' skin - it was pale, a color that reddened and freckled in the sun rather than tanning. Her hair was a light brown. Her clothes and boots, now also cleaner, looked much like mine. Dyes weren't a luxury either of us could afford.

We said goodbye to Oren and his wife, hoisted our packs, and headed for the northbound section trail. The trees thickened around us immediately as we turned onto it, a mix of deciduous and conifers that spread above the road and filtered the light into a greenish haze. The trail itself, over twenty feet wide originally, had been narrowed to a dozen in most places by the encroaching foliage. Only a few hundred feet along the way a particularly aggressive oak had somehow managed to grow right in the middle of the path. Gashes worn in the bark of the nearby trunks showed that some of the wagons had a hard time navigating around it as they came through.

Prophetess' eyes darted from side to side. "Too many trees," she muttered. "How can there be so many here?"

It was strange to see so much green only a few miles from the desolation of the Flow. "Nature's tough," I said. "If there's water, something will grow." I pointed ahead. "See, mist off the lake." Not yet burned off in the morning sun... or maybe it would last all day under these trees.

Prophetess stopped dead. "Are you sure that's just mist?"

I stared at the softly drifting cloud.

"The Darkness is - dark. Yes, it can hide in mist, but I'd be pretty surprised to see it doing that way out here in the daytime."

She still had a skeptical expression. And she still wasn't moving.

"Look. The Darkness could be here - and it doesn't pay to be careless around it. But I grew up just south of the deep woods in the Sorrows. Go up into the foothills there, and it's a totally different world. The Darkness is so thick in places there that it comes together, coalesces... Some of the wraiths are so concentrated the people up in the Sorrows worship them as gods. There's nothing like that here."

"And you've seen those god-sized wraiths up close, have you? So the tiny little clouds we get out here are nothing for you to worry about?"

"No," I snapped, "I haven't seen them up close, and no sane person ever would. But I've seen the Darkness and know what it is, which is more than anyone I've ever met on or around the Flow could honestly say."

"It's a good thing I have you protecting me, then," she said. Still not moving.

Why was she mocking me? Just because I was implying she and everyone she knew were rubes who were frightened of their own shadows?

You Select were supposed to be too smart for your own good, the farmwife had said. She thought it meant we didn't have any common sense. Maybe it meant that when you're genetically engineered to be smarter, stronger, tougher and longer-lived than anyone else, you didn't make any friends by pointing it out. Or even implying it.

I took a deep breath.

"I'm sorry," I said. "You're right, of course, the Darkness is dangerous anywhere. But I do have some experience with it. In the kinds of concentrations I've heard about here, it would hardly ever come out in the light. And in those quantities, it can't take you if you close your mind to it, and it's afraid of fire - which is why we've got torches."

She looked me in the eyes. "So you're saying there's nothing to worry about in these woods."

Well, maybe not exactly. But, "At least I'm saying it's safe to walk through that mist."

She shrugged and began marching forward again. "Easy for you to say," she muttered. But she went straight into the mist without hesitating. "I've heard the Select are immune to it."

The patch of mist was only twenty feet across and we came through it unharmed.

"Well," I said, "Some of the Reborn claim we can't be possessed because we don't have souls. And of course the Josephites say we're already damned. But some of the Select mercenaries that fought for the Green Heart against Yoshana found out the hard way that the Darkness can kill us the same as anybody else. My bet is it can possess us too. Might be a little harder, but I'm not going up into the Sorrows to find out."

Prophetess stopped again, putting her hand on my shoulder. Again she looked into my eyes for a long moment, then turned away, shaking her head. "I can see most people's souls in their eyes," she said. "Not you, though."

I summoned up a twisted little smile. "Maybe the Reborn are right, then. Nothing to see."

She shook her head again, more violently. "That's not it."

"They do say the eyes are the windows to the soul, but we Select prefer tinted glass."

She snorted, punched me in the shoulder, and started walking again.

Say what you want about the woman, but she had an arm on her. And sharp knuckles.

It was only an hour later when we broke out of the trees and the trail began its gentle climb up to the bridge over the Rock Town road. It was a crumbling concrete span over a weed-choked ribbon of asphalt eighty feet wide, but Prophetess was so clearly happy to be out of the trees that we stopped to eat a nasty prickly pear leaf.

In the bright sunlight it was hard to imagine the Darkness existed anywhere in the world. Behind us the woods seemed less forbidding, farther north the trees thinned abruptly as we got farther from the lake. The Rock Town road stretched wide and inviting to the east, but that meant a three hundred mile walk. We would be heading that way, but the easier route was to go another dozen miles north and head for Oldtown instead - only a hundred miles, and then passage on a boat down the Whitewater.

To the west - if we had gotten here an hour or two earlier, would the morning sunlight have set Acceptance's surviving windows ablaze, a shining reminder of its former glory? Because now, with the harsh light of the sun above it, the City's distant towers looked like nothing more than the bleached concrete corpse of the Last Days.

Maybe it wasn't so hard to remember the Darkness existed after all.

On the far side of the bridge, a huge, low structure bulked to our left. It might have been a church or meeting hall at one point, but the stands lining the road suggested it now served as a market. The cleared area around it was given over to little plots of fruit and vegetables, and pig pens. Lots of pig pens.

We smelled the pigs before we saw them. The creatures stank in a way cows and sheep never did. Not enough to seriously turn the stomach of someone who had spent two years mining garbage, but still not something you wanted upwind of you.

As we came abreast of the stands, two of the swine came trotting out and snuffled at us. They were an off-white color, under the mud and orange dust, and they were huge. Each must have weighed over five hundred pounds. Although theoretically contained by the same sort of fence we had seen on the farms further south, I strongly suspected they could break through if they put their minds to it. They looked at us with their little piggy eyes and one let loose a series of piercing squeals.

I'm not too proud to admit I moved toward the other side of the road. So did Prophetess.

A woman emerged from the building, wearing a dress much the same color as the pigs, and not much cleaner. "Oh, hush you noisy things," she bellowed. I assume directed at the hogs, not us.

It might have been a bad assumption. She regarded us with what must have been the most insincere smile I'd ever witnessed. "Well! A pleasure to have visitors. On the road to somewhere, are you?"

I refrained from saying "obviously."

"Off to Rock Town? Or Oldtown perhaps? Or maybe headed south to Panther City, I'm thinking. In any case, my young friends, I'm sorry to say there's bandits about on the roads. Now, I'm not meaning to pry into your business, or offer advice as may be unsought after or unwelcome, but it seems to me a young couple like yourselves," and she raised her eyebrows a bit, "might be well served to have a bit of something to defend themselves. Now I've a lovely crossbow that I could let you have for only five hundred-weight."

It was all I could do not to choke. I found it vanishingly unlikely that this hole in the middle of nowhere housed a crossbow worth five hundred-weight. Nor did we have five hundred-weight in silver or the equivalent to spend.

"Thank you," I managed, with what I hoped was a straight face, "but I think we're safe enough."

"Not for me to say yes or no, my young friend. And I mean nothing by it, I'm not one to judge. But a pretty young woman and a Select traveling together, there's some as might not look kindly on that."

"The lady is a prophet of the Lord," I said coldly, "and I am her protector."

I thought I kept my tone level, but both hogs grunted and squealed, dancing nervously sideways.

"Shut it, you fat slabs of bacon," I snarled at them.

I swear the things growled at me. I'd never seen a pig growl before.

Prophetess gently laid a hand on my arm. "Let me chat with the nice lady," she said.

I glared at her but backed away, and the hogs subsided.

"I'll defer to my escort in matters of weapons," she said, "but we could surely use some dried fruit and jerky if you have it."

"Of course, of course," the merchant oozed. "I have some lovely dried apples and pears for ten-weight a pound, and jerky for twelve."

Prophetess shook her head sadly. "Coming up through Noble they were selling at two and four."

The woman gasped and clutched her heart. "By God, child, the apples must have been rotten and the meat gone to worms for them to sell at that price. No, I don't have the heart to sell food of such a poor quality. But for you, I could let you have two pounds of pears and two pounds of jerky for forty."

I crossed to the other side of the road and leaned against the remains of a fence. I should have known that Prophetess, growing up on a farm, would know how to negotiate for produce.

She joined me soon enough.

"How did you do?" I asked.

"Three-weight a pound for the fruit and six for the jerky."

I nodded approvingly. "Nicely done."

She looked away, then met my eyes. "More flies with honey than vinegar and all that."

I grimaced. "I'm not normally so grumpy. Really. But when someone calls me an abomination at the same time she's trying to cheat me, it kind of sets me off. I may be a symptom of the Fall, but I don't need some bigoted, greedy shopkeeper reminding me of it."

I cast a backwards glance over my shoulder as we walked away. The merchant had already headed back inside, but the pigs were still at the fence. I swear the nasty things were glaring at me.

We were well past the lake now, and it was getting dry again. There wasn't much going on to either side of the road once we got past the pigpens.

"She didn't really call you anything that I heard," Prophetess said.

"Trust me, when someone says 'I'm not one to judge,' her friends with clubs and torches aren't far behind. You may think there's a distinction between being a cause and a symptom of the Fall, but that nuance is lost on a lot of people."

We walked on in silence for a while. After a time, she said, "You talk about the Fall but you don't really believe in it, do you?"

"Sure I do. It just means different things to me and to you. To me it's the fall of civilization, not a fall from grace. The first Fall was the fall of Rome, not the fall of Adam. The Second Fall is a useful phrase - it can mean whatever you want it to."

I thought for a little bit. I was probably going to offend her again, but she'd started this conversation. "I thought the Bible said we were supposed to be saved. So I've always been a little confused. By your definition, how could we fall again?"

"Salvation is made available, not forced on us. God doesn't wave a magic wand and poof, we're saved. We have free will. We can always choose not to take the hand He reaches to us. In the Second Fall, our society chose not to be saved. So I think your meaning of the phrase and mine aren't so different after all."

"Isn't that a pretty broad brush to be spreading the tar with? Our whole civilization rejected salvation?"

"It's the original sin. Pride. Willfulness. Taking it upon ourselves to remake creation with the Darkness, the Hellguard..." She stopped and looked into my inscrutable black eyes. "The Select."

I shrugged. "Is it immoral to believe we can make improvements?"

The sweep of her arm encompassed the pigpens, the withered trees, the ruins of the City, the Flow beyond. "Were we good enough stewards of what we were given to believe we should try to improve on it?"

Two years mining garbage made that particular point hard to argue.

There wasn't much to see as we continued north to the Oldtown road. Farther from the lake, nothing grew but scrub oak and patches of beige prairie grasses. There seemed to perhaps be farms off the road, but we didn't see signs of life.

We covered the distance in good time and with little conversation. I had thought - and feared - that a prophet would be more talkative, but she was comfortable in silence.

The section trail met this road as an underpass, thick with weeds. It looked like something might live in there - maybe something like pheasants, that I could try to take with my slingshot. Or maybe something bigger - that might regard us as edible. It didn't seem worth the risk of finding out.

Instead we trudged up the embankment to the Oldtown road. "Almost there," I smiled.

"Already farther from home than I've ever been before."

"Seems like that calls for a celebratory meal."

We gave ourselves a break from the prickly pear leaves and started in on the jerky and dried fruit instead. The small beer we had gotten the day before had just enough alcohol in it to travel well.

It was sunny and warm and my stomach was pleasantly full. We had an easy three day walk on a paved road that looked pretty much intact.

So of course I had to go shoot off my mouth again. "You know, we've got a thousand miles to go and I still don't know your name. I'm not planning on just calling you Prophetess the whole time."

She blushed. "I set my name aside when the Lord called me. I feel he's called me to renounce myself to do his will."

So insisting that people refer to her by a title was a show of humility? I couldn't see it. And I wasn't smart enough to let it go. "How about if I call you Tess?"

I grinned. She returned a blank look. "You know, the Prophet, Tess?" Her expression didn't change. "It's a joke, see?"

"I understood it," she said. "I just didn't think it was funny."

It's strange the way people have a limited sense of humor when you ridicule their deeply held beliefs. I still couldn't drop it, though. "Suit yourself, Tess."

She didn't speak to me for hours.

So I was in a foul mood when we heard hoofbeats and saw the dust cloud approaching on the road ahead. Normally I would have gotten off into the bushes to see what was coming and avoid trouble, but at that moment I was nursing the sort of sullen bad temper that felt like a confrontation might cheer me up.

Don't have a whole lot of common sense, the farmwife had said.

The cloud resolved into a group of five riders, heavily armed and armored, moving at a leisurely trot - a pace I had always found agonizingly uncomfortable in my limited experience riding. They wore steel cuirasses over leather armor, and each carried a sword and bow. Their faces were sun-creased and determined. But by the time I could see them clearly I had no fear they were bandits. That didn't quite mean there was nothing to fear.

Their identifying characteristics were the naphtha-filled packs on their backs, connected by a hose to a sort of lance resting in a stirrup holster. They were fire wardens, Rockwall's peacekeepers. Their role included patrolling against highwaymen and enforcing Panther City's will in the provinces, but their true calling was keeping the Darkness at bay.

No one else would carry the naphtha-throwers. They were the best possible weapon against the Darkness, but mortally dangerous to their users. An errant leak and a spark, and weapon and warrior would go up together like a torch.

All bore the sign of the cross on their breastplates. Fighting the Darkness was a holy calling for every religious faith. The leader, who was likely a deacon of the Universal Church, had a massive iron crucifix on a chain around his neck. As they came closer, their horses slowed to a stamping walk around us. I could see the others had mystic runes etched into their armor and talismans hung from their saddles. None of those adornments looked like orthodox Universal symbols to my untrained eye, which should have annoyed the deacon. But maybe he was willing to excuse anything that made his troops more comfortable with the cargo of burning death they carried. I certainly wouldn't begrudge someone who strapped a canister of naphtha onto his back any superstitious crutch he found helpful.

Fire wardens were hard men. Sometimes bigoted. They were disciplined, but you never knew if they might be in a foul temper. They weren't likely to beat me just for being a Select abomination, but they certainly could. I wished I'd had the common sense to get into the bushes. That farmwife was looking smarter every day.

"How is the road ahead, Brother?" Prophetess asked the deacon.

He pulled his horse to a halt. It snorted loudly but stood more placidly than most warhorses among unfamiliar people. I suppose you wanted a calm animal without much imagination if you were going to be confronting the Darkness. In fact, the level-headedness of a donkey or mule might come in handy, although I suspected they were too smart to approach the stuff.

"Clear enough on this side of the river, ma'am, though I'll not speak for the other if your path takes you beyond Oldtown."

His eyes traveled up and down Prophetess, shifted to me, and did the same. "We've heard a rumor of bandits on the road but seen nothing. But then that's usually the way of it. You two should have no trouble if you keep to the daylight."

One of his troops hawked and spat in the dust, but if that was meant to be a comment he didn't elaborate on it.

The deacon ignored him. "There's a village about fifteen miles on. Probably a good enough place to stop."

The soldier spat again. Unless he had a serious cold, it was a comment.

The deacon gave him a distinctly dirty look this time. Somebody was courting latrine duty. "There was a death," the deacon conceded. "It may not be the happiest place right at the moment."

"Yeah, and that's the only thing wrong with it," muttered the disgruntled trooper.

The village wasn't sounding like the best option. "What kind of death?" I asked. "And where's the next place on the road?"

The deacon snorted. "Big, tough Select. I thought you people were supposed to be hard enough to handle anything."

I shrugged. "Mostly we're smart enough to stay away from things that might kill us. Whatever killed the person in the village, for example." I looked over the warden's armor and array of weaponry. "I don't have four heavily armed friends, so sometimes discretion is the better part of valor."

He looked at me contemptuously. "The man died of pneumonia. So unless you think disease is spread by evil spirits, I don't think going in unarmed is going to put you at a disadvantage."

"Fair enough," I conceded. Although from the corner of my eye I saw the trooper spit again. How did he stay hydrated on the road?

"You gave last rites, I imagine?" Prophetess asked.

"Too late for that. He was dead by the time we got there. They're Reborn anyway, so not my concern."

Prophetess frowned. "Wouldn't it have given them some comfort for you to say something? As a representative of the Church? Even if it's not their church?"

The deacon hauled on the reins. His horse danced, kicking up dust. As it stutter-stepped around us the soldiers turned and started away. "My job is to patrol the road and eradicate the Darkness. A dead man in a village isn't my job unless the Darkness got him, and it didn't. Good luck, ma'am. Hopefully your brave Select will keep you safe."

A spiteful, juvenile part of me thought a pebble from my slingshot might be usefully applied. But I couldn't decide which horse's ass to aim for - the one the deacon was riding on, or the one doing the riding.

In any case, I was a little more mature than that - and Select did survive by discretion, not by antagonizing patrols of fire wardens.

"Come on, Tess, let's go," I said. "Your brave Select will keep you safe." So maybe I wasn't more mature than that after all. Prophetess rolled her eyes at me, but showed just the smallest smile.

A muddy little creek bubbled up from somewhere, running parallel to the road. The dry grasses and occasional scrub oak gave way to cattails and low-lying ferns. Within a mile, the creek swung south and a dirt trail followed it off the highway. A few dozen yards down the track stood a small cluster of stands much like our trading post on the Flow, ragged canvas awnings stretched over roughly hewn tree limbs.

The shelters were empty now - as were the ruins beyond them, although those had been abandoned for generations, while the shelters were recent. We followed the trail into the remains of the fallen buildings. Rot had set in, wood turned soft and flaking away, bricks fallen where mortar had crumbled over the course of decades or centuries. But the place had not fallen through neglect, or even the natural devastation of storms. Rough, splintered timbers still showed the signs of axes and rams. Although countless years of rain had soaked them, I could see where fire had blackened most of the structures. There wasn't an intact window in sight.

I poked at the little craters in a door frame where high caliber bullets had left their distinctive traces.

Other buildings had been demolished altogether, in some cases leaving nothing but foundations and bits of corroded plumbing behind.

"What do you suppose happened here?" Prophetess asked.

I shrugged. "Who can say? But if I had to guess, I'd think the original town here was sacked by the paleos during the Age of Fear. The village the fire wardens were talking about must be further along. That creek probably gives them some irrigation for farmland. They would have stripped this place for construction materials."

Sure enough, once we cleared the ruins we could see a cluster of frame houses ahead, built around a rough stockade. Plots of tilled earth separated by low stone walls and lines of stubby trees radiated out around the village.

"Good guess," Prophetess said.

"Not the first time I've seen it. The paleos mostly went south where it was warmer, so a lot of the country I passed through on the way here from the Green Heart went through something like this."

She was nervous again. "Did you see, you know..?" Once again, it sank in that this self-appointed prophet was just a country girl who had probably never been more than ten miles from the Flow.

"Actual paleos? You know, I never have. Not many left these days. Once they started getting infected with the Darkness, you can imagine they got even less popular. Thank God they're mostly exterminated now."

"That's not something you should say. They're still people. They're still God's creatures."

"They're just barely people, and trust me, the feeling is more than mutual. Other people may have their doubts about the Select, but when the paleos rejected technology, they lumped us in the same category of demons as the Hellguard. The difference is, a bunch of idiot savages in loincloths with clubs who want to go all the way back to nature aren't much of a threat to a Hellguard. They can do quite a bit of damage to a family of Select, though. They killed a lot of my people in the Age of Fear, Prophetess. A lot."

I don't suppose the smile on my face was very pleasant then. "If you want evidence of divine justice, it's the fact some of those idiots went into the Darklands. If you don't have the technology to reliably make fire, and you're the kind of moron who believes going back to being a hunter-gatherer is a good idea, you're a pretty easy target for the Darkness. It's a shame they went and spread it as much as they did - they got a lot of innocent people killed and pretty much destroyed civilization. If you want to lay the Fall on someone, lay it on them, not on the Select or even the Hellguard. But at least they mostly got what they had coming."

"That's a lot of hate."

"They deserve a lot of hate. And that's the great thing about not being a Universalist, Prophetess. I'm free to hate people that deserve it."

According to the fire wardens, the villagers weren't Universalists either. The Reborn had most of the same doctrines, though, so they shouldn't just casually murder travelers. But the Reborn tended to be even less tolerant of the Select than were the Universalists, and I'd found that a lot of the religious principles of love and brotherhood were rarely if ever observed by the faithful.

As we got closer, I could see that the village followed a familiar pattern. The older houses, weather-beaten and covered with vines and lichens, huddled up against the timbers of the stockade. During the Age of Fear, citizens would have built within easy running distance of the fort - right after the destruction of the original town, people would probably have lived in barracks inside the stockade itself. More recent construction was farther out, with space for vegetable gardens. Some newer houses stood in the center of the surrounding fields, as much as a mile from shelter. Even with the threat of the Darkness and bandits, these were safer times.

Although I noticed that the palisade looked very well tended. Sometimes I had seen them rotted or with timbers stripped for other construction. Not here, though.

There was no one visible in any of the outlying buildings, but we could clearly hear sounds of life from within the stockade walls. I was pretty certain I heard sobbing, which made sense if someone had recently died. But the hairs on the back of my neck still twitched as though I could feel someone taking aim at me.

"Maybe we should pass on," I said. "They may not want outsiders intruding on their grief."

"And they may want comfort. We can only ask. The worst they can do is say no."

I wasn't at all convinced that was the worst they could do.

But I was just the bodyguard. I shrugged, worked the stiffness out of my shoulders under my pack, and gripped my walking stick a little tighter.

The gates to the compound stood wide and unguarded. But as we passed through, I noticed that there were well-maintained steps up to a firing platform ringing the inside of the palisade, with crossbows and buckets of quarrels pre-positioned.

It seemed like the entire population of the village must have been crammed into the center of the stockade. There was a huge open space within the walls, the only building of any size a large, two-story wooden structure with a cross-topped steeple at the far side, likely serving as both church and last defensive redoubt. In the center of the courtyard a hundred people clustered around a trestle table with a still body resting atop it. At the fringes of the crowd the men, women and even children stood somberly, but the people at the center were sending up a wailing that could fracture stone.

"Still not too late to walk away," I muttered. But of course it was, because Prophetess was already edging into the group.

I was tall enough to see over most of them. The corpse looked to be a middle-aged man.

"What happened?" Prophetess asked the young woman next to her.

The woman, shorter than Prophetess by six inches and shorter than me by a head, turned to the unfamiliar voice. She frowned just a bit when she didn't recognize Prophetess, then did a double take when she took in my gray skin, white hair and black eyes. The frown deepened. If things went very badly, this was the kind of situation that could lead to running away while hoping no one was a good shot with those crossbows.

Prophetess had a kind of sad smile that conveyed empathy without words. I couldn't have generated it if I'd had a week to practice in front of a mirror. In the end the villager reacted to that instead of to me.

"Last winter he cut his foot with an ax. Got infected and never healed right. When he got sick last week it went straight into his lungs. Every time he coughed you thought he was going to die. Jaslyn, that's his wife, went into Oldtown for medicine, but I guess too late. Or they sold her swamp water in a bottle. Who can say? Last night he wouldn't stop coughing and blood came out. This morning he was dead. Jaslyn and the boys are pretty raw. She'll do all right. The boys are big enough to help with the fields. But he was good to her and the boys, even though the oldest wasn't his."

The woman's mouth snapped shut like a trap as she realized she'd divulged the widow's private business to strangers. Prophetess just nodded and began to work her way through the press of bodies.

"Oh boy, here we go," I muttered.

The question was whether I should stay close to protect her, or stay back so she wasn't associated with me. In the end, I hung back. That honestly seemed like the wisest choice for keeping her safe - but I have to admit the thought of cramming myself into that circle of humanity made my skin crawl.

When Prophetess reached the center, she leaned over and spoke to an old woman heavily wrapped in shawls despite the warmth of the afternoon sun. That lady looked Prophetess over, nodded curtly, and whispered in the ear of the middle-aged woman doing most of the sobbing.

The woman snuffled loudly, stared into Prophetess' face, then threw her arms around my companion.

"Dammit," I spat, bringing my walking stick up to open my way through the crowd. Then I flushed as I realized the woman was embracing Prophetess, not attacking her. Fortunately, everyone around me was too focused on the drama up front to pay any attention to me.

Prophetess patted the woman's back and stroked her hair for a while. When the widow - I assumed that's who it must be - finally let go, Prophetess turned to the corpse. Placing both hands on his forehead, she spoke in a clear, musical voice.

"The Lord will renew your strength. You will run and not grow weary, you will walk and not grow faint. You will rise on the wings of eagles."

Something to hope for in the next life, certainly. All that was going to happen to the dead man here on earth was that worms were going to eat him. I supposed that if a bird ate the worm, a little bit of him would be flying like an eagle.

One of the reasons I preferred not to be religious was because if there really was a hell, my attitude pretty much guaranteed me a close acquaintance with it. Unless God had an amazing sense of humor.

Once again, though, Prophetess had worked her wonders. The widow had taken her hands and was thanking her.

It seemed like hours that Prophetess was in the circle of villagers. I stood at the outer edge, watching, largely ignored. Which was fine with me, compared to most of the alternatives I could imagine.

Prophetess had become a minor celebrity. Apparently there was no Reborn minister to be found in the area closer than Oldtown, and a boy sent to fetch him had not yet returned. So the self-taught farm girl from the edge of the Flow was the closest thing to a spiritual guide available.

We were taken to the village headman's house - they had no inn. There, too, all eyes were on her while I was mostly ignored. Sometimes people would look over at me with the sort of perplexed curiosity with which they might regard a six-legged dog. I had to suppose they didn't get many Select here. But they were polite.

Evening turned to night, and some sort of local wine that was only about half fermented was passed around. Prophetess drank more of it than I did. The stuff didn't seem to be very strong, and she had a good head for it. Still, I preferred to stay alert - or as alert as I could stay after walking all day.

"Those crossbows," Prophetess said. "Minos thought the old town had been attacked by paleos a long time ago. Do you still have problems? With paleos?"

If I'd been a little closer I would have kicked her under the table. Although it was too late by then.

The headman just laughed. "No, no. Not so long as anyone here can remember. But never hurts to be careful, eh?"

Well, that was true enough. It never hurt to be careful.

It must have been after midnight when the headman's youngest daughter was evicted from her bed to make room for Prophetess. I slept in the stable - at my own request. There was actually a half-hearted offer to make room for me, but I preferred somewhere that felt a little more defensible. Just in case. The villagers had been nothing but kind, but I was still thinking about those crossbows in the firing platforms on the walls. Maybe I should have stayed closer to Prophetess, but I had the feeling that anyone or anything that made an attempt on her would try to take me out of the picture first.

There are certain strange truths of the human body - even the Select variant of the human body. For example, sometimes no matter how tired you are, if you start turning something over in your head, you can find yourself completely unable to rest.

On the other hand, sometimes no matter how paranoid you are, sleep takes you like the wind blowing out a match.

I woke up alive and unharmed the next morning to find light creeping in through cracks in the stable wall and roosters crowing at me. I stretched for a few minutes inside the stable with two donkeys observing me incuriously. I opened the door, blinked in the light, and sneezed. For some reason sudden exposure to sunlight sometimes did that to me. Select weren't supposed to have allergies, certainly not to light - but nobody's perfect, even those designed to be.

I crossed the dusty yard to the headman's door, stepping around a cluster of chickens scratching for worms. I could faintly hear voices inside. I hesitated a moment, then knocked.

"Come on in." A woman's voice. I pushed the door open and stuck my head inside. The kitchen was just to the right of the door, and Prophetess was frying little slices of potato. The headman's oldest daughter was peeling more.

"Morning, Minos."

I was a little embarrassed that the woman I was supposed to be protecting had already started making breakfast before I woke up. "You're up early," I said. "I figured you'd sleep in. Late night last night."

"Farmers are up with the sun."

So were garbage miners, usually. I couldn't think of anything clever to say so, for a wonder, I said nothing.

"You want some potatoes?"

I did. They came fried with strips of onion and pork fat. Not necessarily the healthiest thing I'd ever eaten, but it tasted very good.

More family members drifted in while I was eating, including the headman himself.

"Thank you for your hospitality, Mister Tanner," I told him.

"Berrel and Jaslyn Paxton are good people. Well, Berrel was, I mean." He looked over at Prophetess, still at work on the potatoes. "Still is, I suppose, his soul, that is."

I couldn't help but be amused at how much people worried about offending her, as if she were some sort of ecclesiastical authority who could excommunicate them. If the Reborn could even be excommunicated. I was pretty sure they couldn't.

We lingered longer than I would have preferred, but we had ham, apples and onions in our packs when we left, and fresh small beer in our water skins.

We also had an escort. Three young men from the village headed out to the road with us.

"Keep you safe on the way," the one named Tal laughed. And indeed, they all wore swords. Prophetess chatted and laughed easily with them as we walked, but I was glad when two hours later they turned off the main road to stop at an outlying farm where, they claimed, the finest butter, apple pie, and wine in the entire region could be found. Not in that order of importance.

"You weren't very sociable with them," said Prophetess. Which was true enough. I hadn't spoken more than a dozen words. I grunted, not wanting to break my streak.

"It was nice of them to come with us and keep us safe from bandits. The fire wardens said there had been rumors, you remember," she added.

"Oh, I don't doubt it," I said. I looked over my shoulder to make sure our companions had vanished from sight and earshot. "And I suppose in one sense, traveling with them might have been the safest place to be. Better on this side of those swords than on the other."

Prophetess stopped in the road. "You're not suggesting...?"

"Farmers carry all sorts of sharp things that come in handy for self defense. Axes, sickles, pitchforks. Maybe a bow to take game, and a good knife is always useful. But a sword has a definite purpose, and it isn't farming. Those firing platforms for the crossbows back at the village looked pretty well prepared, too."

"I can't believe they're thieves."

"It can be a good income supplement. The village is close to the road, but far enough away it's not too obvious. If someone does suspect and try to do something about it, they shut the gates and plink with the crossbows."

Prophetess shook her head. "I still can't believe it. So we walked right in... And spent the night there..."

I shrugged. "Yes, but you also guaranteed they wouldn't bother us on the road. So on balance, I'd say the good deed was rewarded."

For some reason that seemed to annoy her again, so I let the subject drop. I couldn't be sure, either. But whatever the truth of my suspicions, we made it through the rest of the day unmolested.

We passed a large inn early that afternoon. A line of vendors' stalls edged up to the road, forming the near side of the inn's huge, dusty courtyard. We had enough food, but traded what little gossip we had from the road for a couple of mugs of small beer.

There was a lull in traffic these days, with wheat and apples recently delivered to Oldtown. The fire wardens we had seen the day before had been the inn's only recent guests. It was conveniently located an easy day's walk from Oldtown, we were told, but there was another one closer.

And so we pressed on to that one, reaching it as night was beginning to fall. I was just starting to regret the decision not to stop at the earlier opportunity when we saw the welcoming glow of torches and lighted windows shining through a copse of trees.

The inn was a tight, snug, warm wooden structure, and the food was surprisingly good. And the innkeeper was happy to take my little ceramic cat in payment for two rooms and board.

And so, well-rested and well-fed, the next morning we set out on the final leg of our march to Oldtown. We would take ship down the Whitewater, then up the Muddy. The hard part was over.

4. Crossing Over

The next morning we started late and set a leisurely pace. As we crested a low hill, the sun glinted red on a rusted, skeletal structure stretching twenty feet above the surface of the broad roadway. An overpass loomed behind it, but they didn't seem related.

"I've seen these before," I remarked, "But I have no idea what they are. It's too small to be a bridge, and it doesn't go anywhere."

Prophetess shrugged, eloquently conveying the phrase, "Don't know, don't care," with the tiny movement of her shoulders.

"Funny that no one's salvaged it. It's a good chunk of iron." I tapped a bolt thicker than my thumb anchoring the structure into cracked concrete. "Hard to get out, but you'd think it would be worth it."

Prophetess shrugged again.

And then we were at the top of the hill, beneath the span of intersecting road that no longer led from anywhere to anywhere else, and I found that I didn't care either. Oldtown spread out in front of us.

Why it was called Oldtown I couldn't say. It was clearly a pre-Fall city, a tightly packed mass of ancient buildings climbing into the sky. There was nothing to suggest it was any older than the ruins of Acceptance, though, or anything else nearby like Panther City or Rock Town. Of course, Oldtown wouldn't have been its original name before the Fall, any more than Acceptance's would have been the dead City's.

Oldtown's south side was wedged into a bend of the Whitewater. The buildings massed larger on the north shore, a great bulge of packed construction protected by a wall. The northern shore needed that protection because it fell into the disputed zone between Rockwall and the Monolith, but we had no business there.

On this side of the river someone had actually put some thought into the layout. Apple orchards and the stubble of harvested wheat fields spread west, upstream from the city's sewage. Downstream, south of town, were the hog farms and factories. We were approaching from the southwest and, even from several miles away, the smell made it pretty evident the factories ran on the methane from the pigs' waste.

Fortunately, the wind carried the stench away from the city, so it actually faded as we got closer. All very well planned. Not so good for the towns downstream, of course.

"That's strange. Lots going on this side of the river, but nothing at all on the other side," Prophetess said.

She was right. The south shore teemed with people, horses, and carts. There was no sign of life outside the northern wall, and not much inside it on the far bank of the river.

"Not our problem," I replied. Perhaps the eternal, low-level war between the Monolith and Rockwall had heated up. Or the Darkness had inched farther into the southwest. I had no desire to find out. I was grateful for Dodd's suggestion that we take ship here and avoid the disputed lands to the north.

Oldtown had been fortified on this side of the river as well, but in the relative safety of Rockwall it had spilled far beyond those boundaries. We were well in among the shops and homes of the city's outer fringes before we came to the wall. It was impressive enough, a concrete barrier twenty feet high and six feet thick that must have been built during the Age of Fear. The gate we came upon was guarded, but the sentry was sitting on a bollard and didn't challenge us. His head came up when he saw I was Select, but even that novelty wasn't enough to bring him to his feet.

Outside the wall the construction looked recent, the low wood and brick structures of our fallen age. There were remains of older buildings, of course, but those had largely been scavenged or converted. Inside the wall, buildings reached for the sky like the giant, skeletal hulks of Acceptance, but these were living. At least to a point. I wondered whether floors hundreds feet above street level were truly in use. That was a lot of stairs. There were ways to power the pre-Fall elevators, but they were expensive... and I wouldn't relish hanging a hundred feet up in a metal box held aloft by machinery that had gone for centuries without proper maintenance.

In the east the upper stories of larger buildings had been destroyed. Walls, floors and windows were removed to expose the rooms to the sun... and make them less hospitable nests for the Darkness. Here people were perhaps less concerned with that, and justifiably so. Still, you wouldn't have gotten me into one of those upper stories at night.

I hadn't spent much time in the larger cities of the Green Heart, and of course Acceptance was dead and shunned. So I felt like a bit of a rube as Oldtown's towers rose gigantic around us, higher than the tallest trees.

I had hoped that at least Prophetess would be terribly impressed with the city and I could feel a bit more sophisticated by comparison, but she didn't indulge in any gasping or gawking. Instead, she simply asked, "So where are we going?"

Which was an excellent question.

"Riverboats will be down by the river," I observed.

She rolled her eyes at me but made no further comment as we proceeded deeper into the city, heading vaguely east.

There were plenty of people we could have asked. Oldtown was as alive as Acceptance was dead. Vendors in stands or pushing carts sold apples, chunks of brown meat on sticks, fried dough, unpleasantly thick beer. Shops at the ground floors of the hulking buildings had every possible variety of goods and services - clothiers, barbers, metalworkers selling everything from pots to swords, apothecaries who might or might not know more about medicine than the barbers.

It wouldn't be fair to call the noise overwhelming. Oldtown was a large city of wide avenues, and obviously far emptier now than in its prime. The calls of the vendors and the clatter of hooves and wagon wheels were nowhere near as oppressive as the clangor inside Dodd's forge, for example. But compared to the silence of the Flow or the emptiness of the open road, it was an assault on the senses. Including what was left of my sense of smell. It seemed like every horse in Oldtown felt compelled to void its bowels within range of our noses.

And I had never much cared for crowds. Situational awareness was easy when there wasn't much moving around you. When you were surrounded by people, there was a fine line between the level of paranoia that made you jump every time someone stepped out of a shop and the obliviousness that let your pocket get picked. Or let a rock hit you in the head.

Not that people threw things at Select all that often just on general principles. But you never knew. Someone muttering "stinking blackeye" under his breath might be only a couple of drinks and a loose cobblestone away from trying his aim.

So, ironically, Prophetess was more at her ease than I in this unfamiliar city.

We had little left to trade, so rather than buying lunch from a cart or stopping at an inn, we ate apples and jerky as we walked, our pace now leisurely. With the sun beginning its descent into the west, the shadows made it easy enough to keep to an easterly course toward the river. I guessed, based on no particular evidence, that the docks would be toward the southern edge of the city, so we kept vaguely south as we moved east. Three bridges crossed the Whitewater, and we followed the occasional wooden sign for Southbridge.

My guess seemed a good one. The buildings and their inhabitants coarsened as we neared the river. When I started hearing profanity so creative I couldn't understand it all, I figured the docks must be near at hand. Prophetess walked a little closer to me, which was pleasant, although I had to shift her to my left side to leave room for swinging my walking stick... if the need happened to arise.

Still, despite some muttered comments about both Prophetess and me - quite different in nature - that we both pretended not to hear, we reached the docks uneventfully.

My concern began to grow, however, when we emerged into the open loading area along the river. There were goods piled high in crates, barrels, sacks, baskets. There were longshoremen in great plenty. There were long, flat-bottomed barges at anchor.

But nothing was moving.

The longshoremen sat or lay on the sacks. The smell... the smell of a working port is never pleasant. Food rolls out of sacks and rots before anyone can bother to do anything about it. Rats breed, live, die, and go about the full range of their digestive processes. Occasionally so do the sailors and longshoremen. But this was different. This smelled like everything on the docks had been there just a little bit too long. And it wasn't hot enough for that to happen quickly.

We headed for a barge whose gangplank was guarded by a man who looked neither particularly drunk nor particularly villainous. As we came up he made a half-hearted swing with his staff at a huge, black rat climbing a mooring rope. The rat dodged easily, bared its teeth in a gesture that seemed more contempt than anger, and scurried onwards.

I pulled out my slingshot, fitted a smooth stone, and let fly. It missed the rat by three inches. If the creature even noticed it gave no sign.

It would have been a pretty impressive gesture if I'd hit the beast, but a moving rat at thirty feet isn't an easy target.

"We're looking for passage to Rock Town. In spite of what you just saw, we can make ourselves useful aboard ship," I said.

The sailor snorted. "If you can kill an army with that thing, you can have passage in the captain's cabin and half share in the cargo. Otherwise you can sit on your -" he looked at Prophetess and changed his phrasing slightly, "On your backside here like everybody else while our cargo rots around us."

"Why's nothing moving?"

The man's eyebrows went up. "Are you blind, stupid, or every little bit the backwoods hicks you look?"

"With those options, I'll take the last."

He snorted again. "Well, the short of it is the Principalities hired in Hawk mercenaries to raid all along the Whitewater. Guess they figure if they make the border miserable enough, maybe Rockwall will give up its claims in the Breadbasket."

Prophetess looked at me blankly.

I sighed. "You remember I asked Dodd whether they weren't still skirmishing on the Whitewater?"

She nodded.

"Apparently they are. The whole stretch of land north of here, all the way up to the Ice Fields, between the Muddy and the mountains, that's all disputed between Rockwall and the Monolith."

I looked at the sailor for confirmation, and he nodded. I continued, "The Principalities are three little city-states at the edge of the mountains. They're independent, but they usually do the Monolith's dirty work. There's blood ties in the aristocracy there. It sounds like this time, though, they've brought in the Hawk's Nest to raise the stakes."

The sailor spat. "Those Hawks will do anything, as long as someone promises there's money in it and it doesn't make any damn sense."

Prophetess continued to look blank. I said, "The Hawk's Nest is another city state in the Breadbasket. The ruler there - do they call him a prince?"

The sailor shook his head. "Nah, it's some funny long word. Like hegemon or autarch. Something meant so's you think he isn't a stupid, conniving thief who got where he is by poisoning his relatives."

I had to grin. "So, as you can maybe tell, people aren't too impressed with this fellow. He mostly seems to be good at getting the Hawks into pointless fights. The Hawks field a big mercenary army, but they always seem to wind up in battles they can't win, or where they don't get paid. The Green Heart called them in during Yoshana's invasion, but when the demons turned on her and the invasion fell apart, the Heart said the Hawks hadn't done anything and refused to pay. So the Hawks wound up marching halfway across the continent for nothing. Of course, they made up for it by foraging their way through the Green Heart on the way back, which didn't make them any friends."

"Well, and that's the thing of it," the sailor said. "The Hawks are flipping idiots, but it's no fun when you're on the receiving end of it. They've got the Whitewater shut down 'til Rockwall brings an army up. All the farmers on the other side of the river crammed themselves into the city 'cause they figured it's better to lose your farm and stock than to lose your wife and daughter. And now the Darkness has got into the city on the other side so the bridges are sealed. Half our crew's stuck on the other side and I don't know if the fire wardens will let folks back across even if the river was to open."

Prophetess looked alarmed.

"Are they sure it's in the city?" I had seen this before. Whenever there was war and panic, fear of the Darkness spread faster than the Darkness itself.

The sailor looked grim. "I saw it myself. They cornered a man taken with it on the far bank. You know it can't cross water."

Or at least the person thought to be infected couldn't swim. But I nodded.

"They caught him and burned him right there. I saw it come off him."

"You saw smoke...?" It was the usual proof. The Darkness would spill out of its victim rather than burn with him. But the Darkness looked enough like smoke to salve many guilty consciences.

"Smoke don't move against the wind. This did. I've stoked the furnace on a barge, and I know how smoke moves, the way it can eddy in a wind current around the river. This wasn't smoke."

I looked at Prophetess. "This complicates things. If the river's shut down, we're back to crossing on foot and heading straight northeast through disputed territory until we hit the Muddy and get into the Green Heart or the Source. But I hadn't counted on raiders being in our way."

My gut tightened a bit at the thought of the Darkness as well. It had been years since I'd actually seen it. If it had truly infected a refugee population… the Darkness flourished where fear, rage, or lust ran high. While I had read the Books of the Fall, I didn't believe that the Darkness was the physical manifestation of sin. But sin did seem to provide it a fertile breeding ground. The desperation of a sealed city crammed full of refugees would be the perfect place for it to grow.

The miners on the Flow believed that Acceptance had been abandoned because it had no natural waterways, agriculture, or much of anything else to sustain it. That was probably true. But cities had also fallen during the Age of Fear because they had been overrun by the Darkness.

The fire wardens had sealed the bridges to save the southern city. They might be willing to destroy the northern side if it came to that.

This might not be a safe place to be at all - especially for a Select.

Prophetess' expression said she didn't think the city was looking like a safe place for a farm girl from the middle of nowhere either.

I muttered a thank you to the sailor and we moved away.

"This doesn't look good, Prophetess," I said. "We're not getting a ship here anytime soon. If the Hawks are harassing river traffic, they'll probably be hitting any fords or bridges for miles up and downstream, too."

"We didn't see any troops outside the north wall when we were up on the hill," she said.

"Why actually put your soldiers in range of Oldtown's artillery if you can accomplish the same thing by burning farms and shooting at riverboats? The Hawks aren't the brightest military minds in the world, but they're not complete idiots."

I realized too late that I might have just suggested that Prophetess *was* a complete idiot, but she didn't take offense.

"So how do we get across?"

"I'm not sure we do. We've got no good way to know how far up or down the river the Hawks are attacking. I guess we could walk down to Rock Town, but that's over a week, and no guarantee we could find a ship there either. The Hawks could be raiding on the Muddy itself. We could get to Rock Town and still sit for weeks waiting for Panther City to send troops. And if we're racing Yoshana…"

Prophetess shook her head. "I can't wait that long. Yoshana's marching on Stephensburg already."

"How can you be sure of that?"

"I'm sure."

I puffed out my cheeks and blew air. "If you can't wait, and we can't cross… I don't know. Maybe we give this up. Go home." I had to admit that the option of not crossing through a war zone to oppose the will of the world's most infamous Overlord had some appeal.

"You can go home if you want, Minos. I can't do that."

"Can't God pick someone who's a little closer to the goal? And doesn't have an army in the way?"

"He picked me."

The funny thing was how she said it with no trace of ego or pride. She didn't sound like a self-promoting charlatan, or even a self-deluding lunatic. She sounded like someone who had been given a hard task that she didn't relish but couldn't turn down.

I didn't relish the task either. Suddenly Yoshana loomed much more real in my mind. The Overlords used the Darkness as a tool. Every Overlord was terrible. But Yoshana was a legend among her own kind. She had wrested the crown of the Shield from its previous master, then launched a lightning assault on the Green Heart. Only betrayal by her demon allies had stopped her.

She was supposed to be dead, fallen on the battlefield. Prophetess said she was back and on her way to the same place we were going. It was hard to think of a worse idea than trying to beat our generation's most formidable Overlord general to her goal if there was any chance we might not get there first. Walking into Yoshana's jaws to oppose her plans was no way to ensure a long life.

"Fine, then. We'll go across." Even though self-deluding lunatic still seemed like the most likely explanation for Prophetess' quest, escorting a pretty girl through deadly peril had a lot more upside than mining garbage. It just had a lot more downside, too, associated with the "deadly peril" part.

I set off walking briskly south along the river. Prophetess broke into a brief trot to catch up. "What are you doing?"

"Like I said. Going across. You pointed out there aren't any troops besieging the city. Over Southbridge and out the city gate on the other side is probably the safest way."

She grabbed at my arm. "But the Darkness is in the city."

"Yep. So we'd better get out while it's still daylight, don't you think?"

As it turned out, we didn't get out while it was still daylight. At least not the same day.

As soon as I made up my mind to go, naturally Prophetess decided that she needed to go to mass first.

"By the time we find a church, and they have a mass, there's no way we'll make it out of here today," I complained. "It's not like they have masses every hour. Do they?"

"No, but some things are important. If we're going to be walking through the wilderness, it hardly seems like I'll have another opportunity any time soon."

Did God pick his prophets for their capacity to be annoying? Admittedly, the Bible suggested that might be the case. But still. "You just finished telling me you're an appointed - anointed - whatever - prophet of God on a holy mission. Why on earth would you of all people need to interrupt that mission to go to church?"

"I of all people most desperately need to go to church."

Thanks to our gray skin, Select don't flush the same way other people do. We just turn darker. My skin might have matched my eyes by the time I got through gritting my teeth and said, "Fine."

Although Oldtown's citizens were mostly Reborn, we found a Universal church easily enough. But the next mass was shortly before sundown, hours away.

That gave me plenty of time to sit around and stew about the fact that we were going almost unarmed into disputed territory, with mercenaries and a rumored infestation by the Darkness. Our options for weapons weren't good, though, and we didn't have the money for any of them. A rifle or even a musket would have been nice, but in addition to the gun itself I would have needed to buy as many shells or musket balls as I possibly could, since no one could be bothered to standardize calibers this far west. I couldn't afford the weapon in any case. Even a bow was beyond our reach. Over time I could make one, but that was time we didn't have, and a reasonable supply of arrows would take as long to make as the bow itself.

I would have to trust in my slingshot and hope I didn't need to hit any rats with it. I spent some of our spare time wandering around collecting rocks of a promising shape and density.

Prophetess said, "I'm a little surprised by the slingshot. I expected something more lethal."

I shrugged. "It's easier to carry and take care of than a bow. And the ammo's a lot simpler - it's no easy thing to true up and fletch an arrow, and trust me, every straight dowel left from before the Fall got turned into an arrow and shot into something a hundred years ago. Rocks don't take a lot of work. You give up range and power, but it's good enough for wild turkey or coyotes. I had friends who said they could take deer with a slingshot, though I can't say I've ever tried."

"I was thinking more about defending ourselves than food."

"Don't underestimate how unpleasant it is to take a rock to the head. Just ask Goliath."

She smiled. "So you're counting on the Lord to guide your hand?"

"I'm traveling with a prophet, aren't I?"

It should go without saying that I did not join Prophetess at mass. The Universalists and the Reborn weren't actively hostile to the Select, or not as much as the Josephites, but I was still just a bit concerned I might be ejected by force if I entered a church. Or that I might burst into flames.

Instead I alternated between sitting on the church steps and searching for more rocks in a small, empty park nearby. There being a limit to how much weight of slingstones I wanted to carry with me, I began to replace my more lopsided inventory with better shaped options, and after an hour I had a bag full of nearly spherical ammunition.

This part of the town seemed little trafficked, and I saw few people on the street. At one point a curious dog trotted over to see what I was up to. I controlled my breathing and greeted it with a raised eyebrow. It sniffed at me indifferently and went away.

Dusk was just beginning to darken the sky when a lamplighter came by, touching a flame to oil-filled streetlights spaced at close intervals. The cost of the oil would add up, but that would be a small price to keep the Darkness at bay.

Not that it really would, of course. The Darkness avoided open flame, but could hide in any shadow - or, for that matter, spread in broad daylight. But the lamps made people feel safer, and in the end, that was worth whatever the oil cost them in taxes.

And despite the situation on the other side of the river, on this side people did still seem to feel safe. A handful of worshippers trickled out of the church with Prophetess, and seemed in no great hurry to rush home despite the coming night.

"Let's find a place to sleep," I said, and she nodded.

In retrospect, it was a shame we didn't spend that last, safe night in Rockwall in luxury, or at least in comfort. But we didn't. We found no inn that was interested in accepting trade goods, and our stock of silver was tiny. In the end we secured one room the size of a prison cell with a single bed. As on that first night by the lake, Prophetess slept on the bed while I lay cold on the floor. The less said about the quality of my sleep the better.

5. The Other Side

The sun was bright and the air was crisp. The guards holding the bridge shook their heads in wonder, or perhaps disgust, but made no attempt to stop us from crossing. They did point out that they wouldn't let us back over if we changed our minds. And one of them called me a fool, but that went without saying.

The barricade was improvised, but effective - a hedge of wooden fencing, spiked with nails and bristling with pikes and lighted torches. There was no gate. We had to climb over - carefully. Trying to get across in the other direction, with the guards shooting crossbows, jabbing with pikes, and slashing with swords, would be virtually impossible. And there was a fire warden in the group, ready to unleash burning death on anyone or anything trying to force its way across.

The sun was just as bright as we stepped off the bridge, but the air was thick with tension, as if the city were holding its breath. It was amazing how on the south shore, daily life was proceeding unaffected, while here you could literally feel the desperation in the air. My pulse quickened uncomfortably and my guts knotted.

There were few people on the streets, and those within sight of the barricade threw angry glares at it before looking away. No one was massing to storm the barricades yet, but if the Darkness was really spreading, that would change. And whether it was or not, the citizens of Oldtown believed it. Windows were boarded up, torches were out in broad daylight, and citizens were on the street only in groups. Generally at least lightly armed.

When things got bad enough, there would be riots. Or people would abandon what had been the safety of the city, risking the Hawk armies beyond the walls. Or the fire wardens would burn the place to the ground. Or all three.

The dread of the Darkness had destroyed trade during the Age of Fear. The economy of the continent had never recovered. It wasn't just technologies like the legions of dead batteries we found everywhere on the Flow. The mistrust that remained hampered exchange. The specialized goods the ancients had enjoyed were beyond our reach. Even something as simple as a pencil was difficult to make today, though we found them strewn so liberally through the garbage that they must have been almost free before the Fall. That was the attraction of the Flow, the reason the bones of the Last Days were picked so clean. Sometimes the discarded refuse of the past was a priceless treasure in the present.

This far west the fear of the Darkness was less, but the distance between cities was greater. And so the world always hung on the edge of hunger, fear, and poverty.

Getting lost in my thoughts was safe enough on the Flow. Not so here. I didn't recognize the press gang for what it was until the leader's hand had closed on my arm.

"You're a big one, blackeye," he said, breath stale in my face. "You could do us some good on the walls."

A brass medallion on a chain around his neck might have been some kind of badge of office. There was nothing else to suggest he had any authority, except maybe the short sword hanging at his hip. And the two burly thugs with nail-studded clubs flanking him to either side. The leader was a big man, tall and heavy-set. He stank of wine, but that didn't make me think he'd be easy to fight. And I didn't know how fast Prophetess could run.

I smiled in what I hoped was an ingratiating way. "I'd love to help, but I have a commitment to escort the young lady here."

"We can take care of her," one of the thugs smirked.

"I figure it'd be better and healthier all around if you did your civic duty and helped out on the wall," the leader said, not taking his hand off my arm. "Soldiers are patrolling inside the city now, 'cause of... it."

He wouldn't name the Darkness. "Someone's gotta go on the wall in case the Hawks attack. That's you."

I took a deep breath. "The lady is a prophet of the Lord," I said. "Sent to do his will and robed in awesome power."

I'd read that phrase somewhere and always wanted to use it. "Stand aside or you'll know the might of the Lord's staff, passed down from Moses himself."

"Huh?" The man stared at me stupidly.

I locked my black eyes on his, unblinking. "I'm not saying she'll turn you into a frog, but I hope you like the taste of flies."

"He's crazy," said the thug who hadn't spoken before.

"On your own head is the doom if you stand in our way."

The men looked at each other uncertainly. One smacked his club into his palm, but the other elbowed him.

"Oh, get the hell out of here, you crazy blackeyed freak," the leader snarled, pushing me away. "We don't want nuts on the wall anyway."

A minute's walk later Prophetess glanced over her shoulder to make sure they weren't following, then said, "Moses' staff? Turning them into frogs?"

"It worked, didn't it?" I smiled, pretending my knees weren't trembling.

"My brave protector, threatening our enemies with some fairytale mockery of my faith," she snorted.

I stopped. "Well, alternatively, I could have gone with them to the wall. Or I could have gotten into a fight with them and someone, either me or them, would have wound up on the ground bleeding. This seemed like a better option."

For a wonder, that actually shut her up.

I never knew if the Darkness was truly in the city or not. But we traveled the five miles to the East Gate of northern Oldtown without further incident. And like the guards at the bridge, those at the gate were perfectly willing to let us out - but made it very clear we wouldn't be getting back in. And very much unlike the city gate on the south shore, this one was closed, locked, barred, and manned by a double handful of alert and well-armed soldiers.

It shut behind us with a thud and a clash of bolts and braces sliding home.

Also unlike the way we had come in, there was no construction beyond the protection of the city. The road outside rose up to the gate, forming a concrete bridge over a muddy ditch that might have passed for a moat if it rained enough.

Past the ditch, a scattering of abandoned wood and thatch stalls clustered in forlorn clumps on either side of the cracked pavement. I suspected it was only a matter of time before the guards cleared them out, before some overly aggressive band of Hawks decided to see if they could scavenge the wood to set the gate on fire.

Stretching out in front of us, weeds choked the ruined foundations that were all that remained of this part of Oldtown, houses and shops that had once stood outside the wall. As in Acceptance, bricks and stones had gone into the city's defenses during the Age of Fear, wood into its furnaces. But the foundations remained, making the land unsuitable for crops. So, ruins. A few still stood, perhaps serving as homes for the farmers who had worked the empty fields beyond. Those too were abandoned now, the farmers inside the walls.

Out beyond the remains of the buildings, the harvested stubble of the fields stretched as far as the eye could see, the cracked, pitted and weed-choked roadway running through them.

"We need to get off this road," I said. "There may not be any soldiers right around here, but people can see us for miles."

"No better in the fields," Prophetess said, which was true enough. That barren ground rose and fell in rolling hills devoid of trees. A Hawk army could be just over the next rise, out of sight now but impossible to escape if we blundered into it. The road was broad and flat, an overgrown median the only cover.

I pointed east. "We might as well make for those trees," I said. "They're the direction we want to go anyway, and at least we won't stick out against the skyline so badly." A good part of the way there we would be in the ruins, which offered a bit of concealment for us. Of course, they also offered cover for anyone lurking in ambush. The same went for the trees themselves.

There was no way forward without risk, now.

"Swallow hard, take a deep breath, and trust in the Lord," Prophetess said.

"I thought he helped those who helped themselves."

"That's why I hope you're better than you look with that slingshot."

There wasn't much to say to that so I swallowed hard, took a deep breath, and we headed for the trees.

Trees are wonderful. Wonderful for shade, nuts, all sorts of things. Wonderful for hiding in. Hiding travelers… and mercenaries… and the Darkness.

This was no ancient forest, I told myself, not like the endless stretches of pines that blanketed the Sorrows and sheltered masses of Darkness so concentrated that the surviving natives feared and worshipped them as gods. Yet the oaks loomed huge when we reached them, a hundred feet tall and more, the largest too wide for Prophetess and me to have joined hands around them. There was tall grass between the edge of the fields and the trees, but underneath their branches the oaks had blotted out most of the plant life. Acorns littered the ground.

"What is that?" Prophetess pointed at a mass of webs coating a branch twenty feet up. "And there?"

More of the webs clung like nests among the trees.

She took a step back. "What kind of spider does that?"

"Not spiders," I said. "Web worms."

"Worms?"

"Sure. Nothing to worry about." Better than spiders, anyway. I hated spiders. Though the nest-like webs, crawling with worms, were undeniably hideous.

"And we're going in there?" Prophetess asked.

"Sure," I said. I gestured to the acorns. "Those are good eating."

She frowned. "Really?"

"No. But you can live on them if you boil 'em long enough. And where there's acorns there's squirrels, and those are pretty good eating. A little stringy."

"I don't see any squirrels."

"Well, it's not like they're going to come running up to us. But they're in there."

She took a step forward, then stopped again. "Does the Darkness infect squirrels?"

"No, the Darkness does not infect squirrels." Although how would you tell if it did? The image of an angry little squirrel, seething with evil power, squeezed a chuckle out of me as I walked past her and in among the trees.

The idea stopped being funny about three paces into the woods.

Dammit. I had crossed half the continent two years ago, younger, smaller, and weaker, and never once worried about being set upon by Darkness-infested rodents. Now, as I listened to rustlings that might have been wind or light-footed animals, I couldn't think about anything else.

We didn't talk. We were too busy keeping our eyes and ears open.

Half an hour later I knocked a squirrel off a tree with my slingshot. It looked like any other dead squirrel, in other words, like a rat with a fluffy tail. Somehow the tail made it much more appealing and I felt vaguely sorry for killing it. And it was only after I walked over to the little corpse that I wondered how Prophetess would feel about murdering adorable forest creatures.

That worry evaporated when she unfolded a clasp knife and started to skin it. I should have realized that farmers are rarely sentimental about animals.

The raw meat raised a question, though. Did we dare to cook it? I had come to discard the notion of Hawks hiding in the woods. Why would they? There was no opposing army north of the river. But how far away could they see smoke rising from the trees? Pretty far.

"We'd better wait until night to start a fire," I decided.

"Won't anybody who can see the smoke during the day see the fire at night?"

"Not from as far away, I don't think. These woods are pretty thick. Besides, it won't hurt to have a fire going at night. There might be wolves or mountain lions, and it should keep them away." And, hopefully, it would keep away worse things as well.

So the bloody squirrel carcass went into my pack and we trudged on.

It wasn't hard going in the trees. With little scrub underfoot, roots and hummocks were the main obstacles. The web nests continued, but were far enough above our heads that we didn't risk blundering into them.

There was no stream visible, but ground water must have lain near the surface. Every now and then our boots would squelch in a damp spot. Not surprising - the trees were getting water from somewhere, and we were no longer close to the Whitewater.

The forest alternated with stretches of tall grass. As nervous as I was in the trees, I found that I dreaded leaving them. We were hideously exposed on the plains.

This disputed land was dangerous in ways that Rockwall was not. It wasn't just the Hawk army, which would almost certainly steal everything we owned but would probably let us live. The paleos had not been exterminated here. They would certainly kill me on sight, and likely as not eat us both.

When we reached the grassy sections, we loped across to the protections of the next stretch of forest. Once I put my foot in a hole and nearly fell, but fortunately escaped a twisted ankle.

I took another squirrel and a rabbit with my slingshot. We didn't see anything larger while the sun was in the sky, although I heard rustling beyond my line of sight that sounded like it was made by something bigger than a rodent.

The sky was turning golden through the tree branches. We found a stream, and I filled my frying pan with water.

"Might as well stop here," I said. "I can boil us up some acorns and the water at the same time, and we can cook the meat."

Prophetess nodded agreement and began collecting acorns from the ground, where they lay in amazing abundance.

She was six paces from me when a patch of weeds in front of her exploded.

She screamed. I whirled, tripped over the rocks I had gathered to make a fire pit, and fell on my backside.

A pheasant shot into the sky, wings a blur in the dusk.

I fired a rock at it but didn't even come close.

"I thought you grew up on a farm?" I said.

"Not the same thing chasing chickens and having something jump out of the woods into your face," she snapped.

I have to admit my heart didn't stop pounding until I was halfway done lighting the fire.

Full dark fell quickly. No more than twenty minutes after the fire was lit, it was the only light to be seen but for the stars we could glimpse through the treetops.

The rustlings beyond the edge of sight didn't stop with the setting sun. If anything, they seemed to get closer. Prophetess and I crowded the fire.

I tried to think of something encouraging to say, but my tongue failed me, not for the first time. The best I could come up with was, "There's going to be worse than this to face if we really have to confront Yoshana."

Prophetess just nodded. "I know."

"I never actually saw her," I went on, "But her troops were moving into the Green Heart when I came west. The stories about her... Well. You can't believe all of them, but she's an Overlord, and I'm willing to believe she's the most powerful one anyone's ever seen. People said she could control the Darkness as well as a Hellguard."

"They say she's half Hellguard herself."

"Well, by definition. That's what the Overlords are. Half human, half demon."

"They say... they say the human half is Select."

I nodded. "I've heard that too. People said that's why she was so much stronger than the other Overlords." I paused. "But I thought she died. I heard she took a spear all the way through the chest."

"I know," Prophetess repeated.

She said, "You hear all kinds of things. Even on a farm in the middle of nowhere. That she made a pact with the devil to return. That she was so evil hell couldn't hold her. Maybe she wasn't really dead at all - people were wrong, or lying."

Her eyes were focused somewhere far away. "But that's not what the Lord says to me. He says she was dead and she rose again. That she's formed a new army. That she says she's seen the face of God. And that she'll destroy the world."

A shiver went all the way through me, though the air wasn't cold. "You said that before. But, sorry if I get this wrong, don't you believe the end times will come someday? When God separates the sheep from the goats, and all that? Maybe that's now. So why are you trying to stop it? Not that I mind," I hastened to add. "This may not be the best of all worlds, but it's the only one I've got."

Prophetess looked me straight in the eye. "If Yoshana isn't stopped... when God separates the sheep from the goats, there may be no sheep left."

"You're saying she'll kill everyone who stands against her."

"No. I'm saying she'll corrupt everything around her until no one stands against her at all."

That was a cheery thought. So how much more so was the idea of racing to confront that?

Prophetess seemed almost to read my mind. "Why did you come, Minos? I truly appreciate it, but it's dangerous, and you don't believe what I do. You came all this way to get away from Yoshana, and now you're going right back toward her."

I could have said I'd follow a pretty girl anywhere. And I did find Prophetess very attractive. But that wasn't it, or at least not all of it.

"I suppose I've always wanted to follow someone who believed in something. Even if it's not something I believe in myself."

She smiled. "There are worse reasons."

We each ate a roasted squirrel. I would have happily eaten the rabbit too, but decided we should smoke the meat and restock our dwindling supply of jerky.

It's an unfortunate fact that no matter how long you boil acorns, they're still just not very good. We ate them anyway.

I wouldn't say I was full, but my stomach was no longer growling by the time we were done. I was starting to bank the fire when we heard the howl.

It wasn't right on top of us, but it wasn't that far off either. And I was pretty sure the one that followed didn't come from the same source.

"Wolves?"

"More likely coyotes. But could be wolves, yes."

"Not - ?"

"Drelb? I'm pretty sure they don't howl. But wolves would be bad enough. They don't usually attack humans. Unless they're really hungry. Of course, there's no good way to tell how hungry they might be." Although if they tried to eat us that would be a clue.

So we stoked up the fire and set watches. Prophetess took the first, and began a long, muttered litany of prayer. Maybe under other circumstances that would have been relaxing, but as it was, neither of us got much sleep. Especially when we began to notice the eyes among the trees, reflecting the firelight.

It was a miserable night. I was never going to complain about sleeping on a nice, level floor inside a secure building again. It seemed like there was always one more stick or rock under me, however many I removed. Even wrapped in my cloak, the side of my body facing the fire baked while the other side froze.

And those eyes had watched us all through the night.

Had it been this bad when I had come west two years ago? Objectively, surely it had. I had been younger, smaller, weaker, more vulnerable by any realistic measure. My life with my family had been considerably more comfortable than life on the Flow, so the comparison should have seemed even worse.

Maybe it was that now I felt a need to do the job I had taken and protect Prophetess, which meant not heading up the nearest tree when a wolf got too close. I had done that before. Or maybe Prophetess' fear of the Darkness was rubbing off on me. Maybe I was intimidated by the thought that we were going straight into danger, returning to face Yoshana, whose abstract threat I had fled before.

Maybe it was just that as you grow older, you lose the idiotic sense of invulnerability that comes with being young.

There were paw prints in the soft earth no more than thirty feet from the fire. From the size, they looked like wolf tracks. I didn't share that with Prophetess.

Wolves weren't the worst possibility. There were bigger things out here. And some of those climbed trees.

In the cool light of dawn the forest looked harmless enough. There was cover, shade, water, food. Still, I found myself tracking the sun's progress through the branches as we made our way northeast.

Sometimes we could make out the ruins of buildings through the trees. We didn't approach them. They might have held useful supplies... or they might have held other things.

Around noon I said, "I think we should be clear of any fighting by now. I have to admit I'd like to start looking for somewhere to spend the night out of these woods."

Prophetess let loose a nervous peal of laughter. "And I have to admit if you'd wanted to spend another night in these woods I was going to take off on my own."

As best I had been able to tell, the forest stretched out in a line pointing northeast, roughly parallel to the road. Logic suggested that if we headed north, we would eventually come to the road if the woods didn't give out before then. With the sun directly overhead, I went by what little sense of direction was left to me, checking myself against which sides of the trees seemed to have the most moss on them.

At least an hour later, Prophetess had a look on her face I was interpreting as, "Are these woods ever going to end?" Although it could also have been, "Do you have any sense of direction at all?"

Another hour after that we finally began to see gaps in the trees and stumbled out into an endless sea of waving grass. The open space with its infinite sight lines had seemed like such a threat only a day before, but now we grinned as if we'd found salvation.

I shaded my eyes with my hand and stared to the northeast. "I think I see something up there. Farmhouse, maybe."

We didn't have much left to barter with, but there was generally plenty of work to do on a farm in exchange for food and a roof. We started off eagerly, a new spring in our step.

The prairie grass was so high, the building remained little more than a black shape until we hit the cleared stubble of the fields around it.

That was when we realized there would not be much shelter to be had.

Although it was still nearly half a mile away, I could make out the blackened timbers and gaping holes where there had been a door and windows.

"You stay here," I said to Prophetess. "Keep your head down below the grass."

She sank down without a word.

I approached in a crouching lope, popping up occasionally to scan the horizon.

I needn't have worried. The fires were long since burned out, and the crows and flies were at work. This had happened days ago. The death was old enough that I didn't even have much trouble keeping my gorge down, although I was flushed with more than exertion when I got back to Prophetess.

"Was it soldiers?" she asked.

"Not impossible, but... no. I don't think so. They would have left more."

"What do you mean?"

"The bodies aren't... whole, Tess. And I don't think it was wolves that were at them."

She just stared at me.

"The paleos aren't above cannibalism when they're hungry."

She shook her head, angry and disgusted. "That doesn't make any sense, Minos. I know you hate the paleos, but why all of a sudden, right now? It seems a lot more likely…" She stared out at the burned farmstead. "It seems a lot more likely the Hawks killed these people, then animals got at the bodies."

"The paleos are hunter-gatherers. By definition. They live hand to mouth. The Hawks could have pushed them out of their hunting grounds on their way through. Made 'em angry, made 'em hungry." I almost spat, but wasn't sure what would come up. "It doesn't matter. This is no place for us to stop."

Prophetess shook her head again. "Something needs to be done for those people there."

"There's nothing left to do for them."

"They need burying. There are things that need to be said."

"You don't want to go over there, Tess."

The look on her face screamed "idiot" more loudly than if she'd shouted it in my face. "Of course I don't."

But she went anyway.

I suppose she prayed for them. It wasn't until I heard the sound of a shovel breaking ground that I joined her behind the remains of the house. Tears were streaming down her cheeks, but she was making good progress. I found another shovel in a shed, only a little darkened by smoke, and joined her.

I think, left to myself, I would have rolled the bodies into the shallow graves with the shovel. But Tess lifted the smallest one up and set it gently in the hole, oblivious to the not-quite-dry blood that smeared her tunic. I couldn't do any less.

After we covered the graves with earth she said some words. I could have made a comment about a God that let things like that happen. But for a wonder, I actually kept my stupid mouth shut.

We walked away without looking back and without another word, although Prophetess cried softly for a long time.

6. Driven Out

We didn't go back to the woods, even with the danger of the plains so clear to us. While Prophetess might think the Hawks were responsible for the massacre, I was convinced it had been paleos, and they would be very much at home in the forest.

We walked along with the trees to our right, but saw nothing else in that sea of grass until the sun went down. When it did, we sank down into the concealing stalks and ate dried fruit and smoked meat. We didn't talk at all. Prophetess went a distance away to pray, but when she returned she lay down very close to me, facing the other way. It was cold, and dark, and somehow it seemed like the right thing to do to put my arm around her and cover us both with my cloak.

She didn't pull away, and we fell asleep like that.

The next morning I woke up stiff, sore, cold, and damp. Dew had accumulated on us during the night, and while the ground looked smooth as a tabletop from a distance, it was thoroughly lumpy once you got to know it up close. We decided to continue north until we came to the road. We would be obvious on it, but the idea of another night in the woods or huddled in the weeds had no appeal, and somewhere along that roadway there would be a settlement.

As it happened, we found the settlement before we found the road.

The first thing I saw was a drift of smoke on the wind. That could be good or bad. Smoke could mean a town, or the cook fires of soldiers… or the dead remnants of a farmstead slowly returning to ash and dust.

Prophetess and I exchanged looks. She shrugged and, without speaking a word, we headed in that direction. As we got nearer, we began to make out the tops of short trees. Still I was surprised when we emerged from the grass to find ourselves suddenly at the edge of a huge expanse of cleared fields, rows of apple trees separating them into pie slices.

It was a strange shape for farmland, round rather than square, which would make it harder to plow. I suspected the reason was the same as for the tall palisade of sharpened stakes we could now see at the center of the pie - it was not safe here, and the circle of cropland marked the farthest distance anyone was willing to stray from the protection of the walls.

The smoke was rising over the palisade. A lot of smoke. That wasn't the scattered wisps to be expected from some cooking fires and a smithy. It was a thick, black column.

"That doesn't look normal," I said. "I think we should go around."

"They may need help."

"Anyone who can torch a town that size is more than we can help with." The stakes in the palisade must have been twenty feet high, and the wall looked to be at least a half mile in circumference. Unlike the bandit village we had visited in

Rockwall, there were no buildings visible outside - no one here had been willing to forego the wall's protection. How much protection it actually offered was debatable at this point, of course.

Prophetess was already walking through the harvested field.

"Aw, for the love of…" I sputtered. "At least keep to the trees so we don't stick out so much."

So we approached among the apple trees, which grew in double lines with a grassy space between. The oddly shaped orchard gave out well before reaching the wall, and then we had to work our way around the cleared space toward the north, as there were no doors on our side. I could see a spur of the road coming in from the northwest, and that must lead to the gate.

There was no real cover, other than to move from one row of apple trees to the next. At this distance from the wall, a hundred yards or so separated each row. We jogged from one to the other. I kept my slingshot out and a stone in the pouch.

Our fourth such move brought us within sight of the gate. It was open, but a guard with a crossbow stood to either side. There was no sign of battle.

The guards hadn't noticed us yet, and I put the slingshot away. It was no match for a crossbow, and I didn't want to give anyone an excuse to put a bolt into me.

"Well?" Prophetess asked.

Well what? This was her idea. "Those guys look like they belong here. People sacking a town don't generally post sentries like that. I have no idea what's going on with the fire, though." The column of smoke continued to rise unabated.

"Let's find out." She started toward the gate.

"Let's not," I muttered, but it was too late. "Here we go again." It was a wonder she had lived this long.

The guards were alert enough to spot us at a good distance - not difficult as we approached across the open field. They didn't raise their crossbows, which was a good sign. But the one nearest to us waved his hand in a shooing motion.

"Ah, get along. The last thing we need now is more gawkers. That worthless excuse for a storyteller is bad enough."

Prophetess and I both stopped and stared at him.

"Go on," he snapped. "Beat it."

I was just about to take Prophetess' arm and turn around. One thing Select learn quickly is if someone tells you you're not welcome, it's a good idea to listen.

But of course Prophetess was talking instead. "We don't mean to be any trouble. We've just come up from Rockwall. We had to spend a night in the woods and yesterday we found a farm where everyone had been killed. We're tired and scared and we're just looking for a place to stop."

The other guard spoke up. "Ah, Frek, I don't think they're here to snoop like that Dee guy. And the Darkness is out there. We should let the girl in at least. You don't want her on your conscience."

Oh, sure. Let the girl in. Let the Select get taken by the Darkness.

"You want to let them in, you go tell the sheriff," Frek growled.

"Fine." The second guard stomped off. Fortunately at the last second he resisted the temptation to throw down his crossbow in disgust. The weapon was spanned, and with my luck it would have gone off and shot me in the face.

Frek glowered at us in silence. I suppose that no more than five minutes passed before the other guard returned, but it was long enough for the suggestion that we just walk on to die stillborn on my lips at least a dozen times.

The sheriff proved to be a block of a man in a leather jerkin with a shortsword at his side. An inch shorter than me, he probably outweighed me by fifty pounds, and it didn't look like fat. He looked from Prophetess to me warily but without outright hostility.

"I don't mean to be inhospitable, but Brambledge isn't receiving visitors," he said, his voice low and rough. "You see that?" He pointed at the column of smoke. "We're burning the miller's daughter today."

"What?" Prophetess' voice was an octave higher than usual.

"The Darkness took her. There's nothing else for it. She nearly killed Quilla Farr. Quilla's lucky she didn't lose her left eye, and she'll never be a pretty girl again."

I wouldn't normally be the one to interject here, but few things got farther up my nose than a bunch of ignorant peasants burning someone because they mistook a quarrel for demonic possession.

"No disrespect here, sheriff, but can I guess the girls were, uh, romantic rivals?"

He gave me that look the Select sometimes get, as if I were some kind of talking dog. But he answered evenly enough. "Sure. Wennit, that's the miller's girl, she's always wanted what Quilla had. That's Reeve Hansen, you know."

"So, again no disrespect, that doesn't necessarily sound like possession by the Darkness if one of them scratched the other's face."

The sheriff blew out his cheeks. "Yeah, you'd think that, wouldn't you?" He began to unwind a wrapping on his left biceps.

The four parallel gouges in the flesh were each half an inch wide and at least half that deep.

"That look like a scratch to you? Damnedest thing is it hardly bled at all. Hurts plenty, though."

No human could carve out chunks of muscle like that with her bare hands.

"That Dee fellow says the Darkness wouldn't have infected me through the wound, says that's not how it works. Can't say I'm not a little worried, though."

I shrugged. "As far as I know he's right there. It can penetrate intact skin just fine. If it wanted to infect you, it wouldn't need to go through the wound."

"Still think it's not the Darkness?"

I shook my head.

"But to burn her…" Prophetess said.

"You think anyone wants to do that? Everyone in this town has known her since she was born. There's no other way to get it out."

And that was true. Once the Darkness took a host, it wouldn't leave until that host was dead. The Darkness feared fire, and would avoid open flame. But experience had shown it couldn't be bluffed out. It would dig into the host, going deeper to avoid the fire, until the body was lifeless. Only then would it try to flee.

"With God all things are possible," Prophetess said.

Frek snorted loudly. "Is God going to walk into town and cast it out?"

"No," said Prophetess. "I am."

"You've done this before, have you?" I murmured as Sheriff Rolf led us to the town's tiny jail.

"The Second Book of the Fall describes exorcism," Prophetess replied.

"But have you done it yourself?"

She was silent. "Always a first time for everything," I muttered. "Including being torn to shreds or possessed by the Darkness."

We passed the town square, where helpful citizens continued to pile more wood onto the bonfire. The stack of logs was four feet high and the flames leapt a dozen feet above that. We came no closer than ten yards, but the heat poured off in waves even at that distance.

"It's the damnedest thing," the sheriff said. "This was finally a year when everything was going right. Not too much rain, not too little, no hail. Good harvest. Guess it was all just too good to last." He gestured at the blaze. "We're going to, uh, do it just at noon. Figured that was our best chance to keep it from getting away after. We've been building up the fire since dawn. Getting it as hot as we can. No one wants her to suffer."

Not that there's a pleasant way of burning to death. The scorching air radiating from the bonfire made it all too easy to imagine flesh charring.

"Say there," a voice came behind us.

A scarecrow of a man was hurrying toward us, arms, legs, and tunic flapping like a man-shaped bundle of loosely jointed rags.

"Are you the ones who are going to cast the Darkness out of the miller's daughter?"

Prophetess nodded. I kept quiet. I wasn't going to be casting anything out of anyone.

"I'm Doctor John Dee. Master of the occult sciences."

Frek's comment about "that worthless excuse for a storyteller" made more sense now.

"Doctor... John... Dee." I drew it out. If my eyebrows had gone any higher they would have been lost in my hairline. "That's a bold name. Most people would think it's bad enough to use a given name from before the Fall without claiming that particular one. If memory serves, John Dee was one of the greatest charlatans of his age."

The man smiled. "Truly they say the Select are learned..." his smile broadened, "But have not learned quite enough to find wisdom. My namesake was a master of philosophy, of the intersection between science and witchcraft. I have devoted my life to the study of the Darkness, which lies at just that intersection."

I was still searching for a reply to that when Prophetess said, "We're wasting time. I have a task to do."

As she started off again, I was displeased - though not surprised - to find that Dee was tagging along.

"Do *you* know how to cast out the Darkness?" I asked him.

"Why, no," he replied. "That's why this will be such an instructive experience for me."

The jail was a squat, wooden cylinder, fifteen feet in diameter and not quite as tall. It might have started life as a grain silo before being given a new purpose. Three broad steps led up to a stout oak door, banded with black iron, pierced at head height with an iron grate and barred from the outside.

The sheriff slid the bar aside and swung the door open, revealing one interior room split in half by a wall of iron bars. The half closest to us contained a table, a chair, and a cabinet. The other half contained a bench, a water jug, a chamber pot, and a figure huddled on the floor, wrapped in heavy chains of the same black iron.

"Did you have to chain her like that?" I asked.

The sheriff handed me a tangle of rope from the table. It had split into two strands. The break didn't look like it had been sawn or cut - it had simply come apart. "Nothing else would hold her. I checked the chain this morning. It's starting to wear through too, but it'll last long enough."

"We'll need torches," I said. "If it does come out it's not going to be happy. And it's going to be looking for someone else to infect. Or kill."

Rolf jogged to the bonfire and returned with three burning brands, giving one each to Dee and me and keeping one himself. "I'll watch from outside. No offense, and appreciate what you're trying to do. But we can't take the risk of you getting infected and breaking out."

I had to admit that made sense. "What about you?" I asked Dee.

"I believe I will be best positioned to observe and expand my research from outside as well."

And that made perfect sense too.

And then the door was barred behind us, and Prophetess and I were alone in the flickering torchlight with the girl. And the Darkness.

"Wennit?" Prophetess said softly.

The figure on the ground unfolded and rose to its feet, amazingly gracefully for someone whose ankles and wrists were shackled together. The girl was dark-haired and pretty, maybe a bit older than Prophetess or me. Her face was smudged with dirt and her clothing was torn in places, but she looked perfectly healthy - free of the cuts and bruises that someone would get if they struggled while being put in chains.

"Can you come a little closer?" she asked, shuffling right up to the bars.

I put my free hand on Prophetess' shoulder, holding her in place. "Very bad idea."

"Can you let me out?" asked the girl.

"I'd like to let you out, Wennit," said Prophetess. "You just have to let go of the Darkness."

The girl threw herself against the bars. The chain linking the manacles on her ankles and wrists kept her from reaching through, but she slammed herself into the iron three times. The bars rattled in their frame. The cell had probably been built to hold obnoxious drunks who needed to sleep it off - I wondered exactly how strong it was.

"You don't care about me!" she screamed. "You're just like all the rest of them! None of you care about me!"

I had lost my grip on Prophetess' shoulder, and she took a step forward. I hadn't dismissed the idea that she was a deluded fool, but she had more courage than I did. It was all I could do not to hammer on the door and scream to be let out.

"We care about you, Wennit. God cares about you. If you embrace him, you can cast out the Darkness."

"You care about me?" Her voice was wheedling again. "Then come closer. You and your big, strong Select. Do you love me? Then come and embrace me yourselves."

There was a fierce hunger there at the end, repulsive and yet somehow seductive.

"Wennit, you need to embrace God. He's reaching out to you. Embrace him and let go of the Darkness. Let God's light burn the Darkness from you."

"Burn me? That's what you all want to do, burn me!"

"Everyone here loves you, Wennit, but they're afraid of the Darkness in you. You have to embrace God and cast out the Darkness. They're afraid you'll hurt other people. You hurt Quilla, and the sheriff. You don't want to hurt anyone like that again, do you?"

"That bitch Quilla? She deserved it. She took Reeve from me, and no one cared. No one cares about me, just about her. I'll make her pay for it. Nobody cares what I want. But I'll make you care!" She slammed herself into the bars again.

I pulled Prophetess back. "I don't think you're going to be able to get it out if she's not going to help you," I whispered.

"It's the Darkness talking," said Prophetess.

"Not completely, I don't think. Maybe she wouldn't say those things without it in her, but I bet she'd think them on her own."

Prophetess took two more steps forward. "Wennit, God sent his own son to save us. He's reaching out to you. You just have to grasp his hand. But you have to really try. God reaches out, but we have to take hold of his hand. If you do that, the Darkness has no power over you."

"God's never done anything for me. Nobody's ever done anything for me."

"God loves you. Everyone here loves you. No one wants to hurt you."

"They want to burn me!" she screamed. And then, softly, "I'm scared."

Tears began to trickle down Prophetess' cheeks. She stepped up to the bars and took Wennit's hands. My grip closed so tight on the torch that the wood cracked, but I didn't know what to do.

"Let God in, Wennit. There's no fear in the Lord. The light of the Lord casts out all Darkness. Let in the light of the Lord."

"I'm scared."

"He is love, Wennit. In his name I cast out the Darkness. Say it with me." In a voice of command I'd never heard from her, she repeated, "Say it with me, Wennit. God is love. In his name I cast out the Darkness."

"I don't... God is love. In his name I cast out the Darkness," the girl murmured.

"Again! God is love. In his name I cast out the Darkness! There is no Darkness in the light of the Lord. There is no fear in the light of the Lord. In his name I cast out the Darkness!"

Prophetess repeated the command, over and over. And Wennit followed her, softly at first, then more loudly. Prophetess began a litany of what I recognized as her Universalist prayers, and the girl repeated those as well.

Prophetess abruptly gripped Wennit's shoulder with one hand, placed the other on her forehead, and bellowed, "In the Name of the Father, and the Son, and the Holy Spirit, I cast you out!"

"Oh, crap," I breathed. Because it was coming out.

A cloud of what looked like smoke rose off the girl. It hovered for a moment in the air above her, then, before I could even think of moving, encircled Prophetess.

"The body of Christ is in me," Prophetess cried. "There is no place for you here!"

For a moment the cloud hovered, then darted toward me. I waved my torch at it in a panic like a child trying to shoo a bee. The cloud dodged the flame, drew up toward the ceiling, and then streamed out through the grate.

Seconds later the sheriff slid back the bar and opened the door. I staggered into the sunlight.

"It took off into the air," Rolf exclaimed. "It's gone."

On the floor of the jail Prophetess and Wennit leaned against each other, holding hands through the bars, each dissolved in tears.

"Extraordinary! I've never seen anything like it," Dee was repeating for the third or fourth time.

Needless to say, Prophetess was the most celebrated person the village had ever hosted. A religious pilgrim is one thing. A religious pilgrim who can actually cast out evil, saving lives and souls, is something else entirely.

I was trying to wrap my head around it. "It wasn't a very big cloud," I said, mostly to myself. "The girl must have been weak, but Prophetess had enough strength of will to overpower it."

"The Darkness preys most readily on the weak, that's true," Dee said. "But it's most dangerous when it possesses the strong."

I had no idea what that comment was supposed to imply. Somehow it came across as a thinly veiled jab, although I couldn't say why other than that the self-styled philosopher just rubbed me the wrong way. I had the feeling that if the cloud had possessed me and driven me into a murderous rage, Dee would have been the first to go.

We were squatting with the townsfolk on the ground around the bonfire. With no humans to be burned anymore, the fire had been banked and used to roast pigs and sheep instead. I was a little disturbed by the imagery, but not so much that I wasn't eating.

Wennit had offered up tearful apologies to Sheriff Rolf and Quilla. The sheriff had waved it off, blaming his wounds on the Darkness and the hazards of his profession. Quilla had been less gracious - her acceptance of Wennit's weepy, clingy contrition had been sullen and half-hearted at best. That was maybe not so hard to understand. Wennit was now a minor celebrity herself, the woman who had survived the Darkness. Quilla was just a girl with four huge scars gouged into her face who would never be pretty again.

Prophetess was surrounded by admirers, from the miller whose daughter had been saved to the mayor of the village. I was stuck with Dee.

On closer inspection he seemed older than I had first thought, nearing middle age. He was tall and lanky, dressed in a motley assortment of rags that would embarrass a garbage miner. I was again vaguely reminded of a scarecrow.

A talking scarecrow. He didn't seem capable of shutting up. His evident fascination with Prophetess didn't sit terribly well with me either. I wasn't certain that interest was entirely academic.

"At least we're getting a good meal out of all this," I mumbled around a mouthful of pork. "Hopefully we'll get reprovisioned too. We need to be on our way tomorrow," I added meaningfully.

"Of course, of course. I must imagine that a holy pilgrim like our Prophetess has a vital undertaking guiding her, eh?" He grinned. "And of course it will be my pleasure to accompany you - I daresay I know this territory like few others. My pleasure to help in any way I can, and what an opportunity to learn from each other, eh?"

Oh, dear God, seriously? Just because I don't believe in you, is that any reason to torture me?

7. On the Run

I hadn't argued. I had merely suggested to Prophetess, in the mildest terms, that hauling around a babbling, middle-aged fraud of an occultist might not contribute to our speedy progress. I hadn't used those words - at least, not exactly those words.

She had disagreed. And I had been forced to admit that I was not familiar with the land this far north. Dee assured us that he was. I didn't particularly believe him, but I wasn't going to call him a liar to his face. I suppose the silly bugger must have come from somewhere.

The following morning saw us on the road, our packs loaded with smoked meat, dried fruit, fresh bread, and small beer.

"…fascinating to observe it first hand," Dee was saying, or continuing. I wasn't sure he had stopped speaking since our meal the day before. He might have kept talking in his sleep.

He kept pace with us easily with a strange, loose-jointed stride. He was a tall man, between Prophetess and me in height, but gaunt. His constant babbling didn't interfere with his walking, although I couldn't tell when he had time to breathe. But he carried a pack larger than mine, and walked without the aid of a stick.

"While of course doctrine would tell us that the Darkness is the physical manifestation of sin, to actually see it confronted and defeated by faith, well, the experience is unique, not so?"

Exasperated, I interjected, "The Darkness isn't the physical manifestation of anything. It's a technology gone wrong. It was made by men just before the Fall. I'm pretty sure sin has been around a lot longer than that."

"Well, just so, my Select friend, in the narrowest sense. But here, you see, you myopically focus on the physical and fail to consider the metaphysical. Yes, the Darkness is human creation, but in a real way so is sin itself, not so? The Darkness is the product of the original sin, pride, man's arrogance and disobedience, yes?"

He raised his eyebrows at Prophetess, and she nodded.

"And of course you can see how in the village the young lady's sins, her lust, her rage, were manifested through the Darkness. Closing the circle, as it were."

"All that you're really saying is that the Darkness was created through a bad decision and people make bad decisions when they're infected with it. You might as well call it the physical manifestation of stupidity."

Dee chuckled. "Do you really think the girl's actions under the influence of the Darkness are best characterized as stupid? Or as evil?"

I grunted and held my peace. Dee was goading me into saying foolish things just to contradict him. There was no sense falling into that trap. What he chose to call the Darkness didn't change what it was.

Waving grasses stretched to infinity on either side of the road. Under that bright morning sun, it again seemed strange that the Darkness could lurk anywhere in the world.

Although I could imagine other things in all that grass.

Prophetess had dropped behind. I glanced over my shoulder and she was keeping pace, but a few yards back, suddenly looking tired and drawn. She had been quiet all morning, although I had assumed that was just because Dee let no one else get a word in edgewise.

I slowed until she caught up with me. Dee continued ahead, still talking.

"Are you all right?"

I was shocked to see a tear run down her cheek.

"Hey, hey, you just faced down the Darkness itself! What's wrong?"

"I don't know if I can do it again," she said, her voice tight. "It was all I could do back there not to run away screaming. How am I supposed to face Yoshana? Yoshana isn't some girl possessed by the Darkness - Yoshana *commands* the Darkness. Maybe God chose wrong."

Even to an unbeliever like me, that suggestion seemed blasphemous on its face. I was just barely clever enough not to say that, though. But I was puzzled. "You said Yoshana was claiming she's been reborn into the service of God," I said. "How would she square that with using the Darkness?"

Dee's voice interrupted. "Does not the psalm say, 'even the darkness is radiant in his sight?' That's how, my friend. Yoshana says she has harnessed the Darkness itself in the service of God. In fact, while her followers mostly call themselves the Knights of Resurrection, she has named her army the Darkness Radiant."

We were all stopped in the middle of the road now, and Dee was giving me a penetrating look that suddenly didn't seem foolish at all. "You have to realize, my young Select friend, if you're going to confront Yoshana... she's not just so much stronger than you that she can kill you with an errant thought. She's *smarter* than you are too."

I frowned.

"No offense, my friend, but Yoshana is considered the greatest military mind of our age. She's so dangerous not because of her command of the Darkness, though that's lethal enough. But every Hellguard has that mastery, and many other Overlords come close. No, she's dangerous because of the intellect behind all that power. Manipulating the raw power of the Darkness, manipulating forces on the battlefield, manipulating the emotions of her followers - she's without peer at any of them. I don't know what you have in mind to oppose her... but it had best be something of surpassing cleverness."

I looked at Prophetess. I didn't have any plan at all, let alone a clever one. She looked stricken.

"Well, I'm sure you'll think of something," Dee said.

We had plenty of time to think of something. We walked down that road for days, an endless, wide ribbon of asphalt stretching between scrubby woods and abandoned ruins. Of course, it might have been easier to think if Dee had ever stopped talking.

The man had an endless accumulation of facts - or at least thoughts - on an endless array of subjects. And an endless capacity to expound on them.

On religion:

"The irony is that with the breakdown in trade, religion coalesced rather than splintering. Before the Fall there were dozens of organized religions, many of them not even Christian. But now, except for the Descendants and a few other isolated sects - and the paleos - only the Universalists, the Reborn, and the Jospehites remain. I must say, it was a richer world before."

On the Darkness:

"While I can see how a strict rationalist might reject the metaphysical significance of the Darkness and view it simply as a tool gone wrong, you must surely agree that it is both a result of Man's worst impulses, and an expression of them."

On the Select:

"While I of course must defer to the native expertise, as it were, of one who is himself Select, my research indicates the gray skin, white hair and black eyes are entirely accidental. Before the Fall, the parents of the Select could select, so to speak, any combination of skin, hair, and eye color for their offspring. The neutral coloring the modern Select exhibit is a base, a primer if you will, onto which the desired appearance could be imprinted. But with the loss of the imprinting technology, the base color has become the Select's only color. And now it stands, forgive me, as a sort of mark of Cain to illustrate the folly of interfering with God's design."

That last would probably have offended me if I hadn't become numb long before. But while Dee didn't speak in a monotone, he was certainly monotonous.

He talked while we walked. He talked while we stopped to eat. He talked while we made camp at the side of the road. I was mildly surprised to find that he didn't talk in his sleep.

To be completely fair, he didn't speak constantly. He was perfectly willing to listen to others if he felt they might expand his store of knowledge. But if no one else was talking, he seemed to feel obligated to fill the void.

The days blurred together, an endless march down that road to the accompaniment of his voice. It must have been on the fourth or fifth day that we were passing through the ruins of a large town or small city. Unwalled, it had probably fallen when the Age of Fear began. Devastated skeletons of building stretched past the limits of sight on either side of the road. There was only the mildest change from his lecturing tone when Dee announced, "Oh, I do believe that's going to be a problem," and pointed down the road behind us.

Three figures had broken from the cover of a concrete hulk of a building a hundred yards away and were loping in our direction. Between their lank, matted hair, the poorly cured hides they wore, and the wooden spears they carried, I had no doubt what they were even though I had never actually seen their kind before.

"Paleos!"

I fumbled my slingshot and a stone out of my pack. The paleos began to whoop as they came closer - wild, inhuman sounds. One slowed to a jog, fitted his three-foot javelin to a second, shorter stick, then let the spear fly.

"Quite ingenious, the spear thrower," Dee remarked. "No technology to it at all, but you see how by effectively lengthening the man's arm it imparts far more speed and distance to the projectile."

The wooden spear hurtled by over our heads.

"Not much for accuracy, though," Dee added, somewhat sadly. He'd wanted it to be more accurate?

I sighted down the slingshot and caught the nearest paleo in the forehead with the rock as he charged. He went down on his face in the road.

"Amazing the advantage of a simple piece of rubber," said Dee.

"Are you going to make yourself useful or just stand around and observe?" I snapped.

"Oh, observe, I should think," he replied. "Do you know, at their best the paleos can be quite gracious hosts to a storyteller. Unfortunately, the Hawks moving through their lands hereabouts have quite disrupted their hunting, and I suspect they've gotten hungry. And when they're hungry they can be rather… unpleasant."

"They're going to eat us?" Prophetess demanded.

"Unfortunately, I wouldn't bet against it."

I fired another rock at the next paleo and missed, possibly distracted by the prospect of shooting the storyteller in the mouth.

The savage hurled his spear at me. It was a crude thing, not even a straight piece of wood, and it wobbled past. Of course, his aim wasn't helped by the fact that I threw myself to the ground.

He screamed an incoherent challenge and pulled some sort of club from a leather belt at his waist. It looked like it might have been a bone. I didn't examine it closely as he charged and swung.

I was back on my feet, bringing my walking stick around. Years of kata were good for this, at least. I pulled the blade free of its wooden sheath and met his wrist with a rising Flowing Water strike.

Despite its basic shirasaya fittings, the sword within was by far the most expensive thing I'd ever owned. The steel was strong, and sharp. The paleo's hand spun away in the air. He was just starting to look surprised when I reversed the stroke and brought the blade through his throat.

The last of them, the first to have flung a spear, was closing on Prophetess. He had dropped the spear thrower and poked at her with a second javelin, hopping at her like some kind of demented frog. She batted the strike away with her staff and gave ground.

Honor didn't even begin to be a consideration for me. I took five long strides to circle around him and stabbed him through the heart from behind.

That left the one I had hit with the sling stone. David and Goliath notwithstanding, I doubted I had killed him. That would be easily remedied, though.

He was just starting to lever himself onto his elbows when I reached him. He looked up at me, and I could see the angry, pink goose egg of a welt my stone had left starting to rise on his filthy forehead.

I took a step past him to get a better angle on the back of his neck. The look in his eyes would have passed for resignation in a higher being.

"No!" Prophetess screamed at me.

I held my stroke and glared at her. Blood pounded in my temples. "What do you mean no?"

"You can't just kill him in cold blood."

"It's a basic principle that you don't leave people who want to kill you alive behind you," I snapped. "Failure to observe that principle leads to death."

Dee had come up as well. "I must say, Prophetess, the logic is sound."

The paleo had flipped himself onto his back. The dirty bastard actually laughed. "Do it, troll," he said.

"Not really the best way to plead for your life, you piece of subhuman trash. I've been called a lot of nasty things over the years, but 'troll' is a new one. We'll put it on your tombstone."

"The word is actually 'trol,'" said Dee, incapable of stopping his lecturing even in the middle of a fight to the death. "Short for 'control.' The paleos believe all civilized people - that is, city-dwellers - seek to control the world and thus are evil. Ah, I must say, they believe that of the Select most especially."

"Control, controlling, controlled," said the paleo. "Slaver and slave."

"That's not completely different from the doctrine of the Fall," Prophetess murmured.

"Yeah, except correct me if I'm wrong, but I don't think Universalists eat people who disagree with them."

The paleo barked out a laugh again. "Ah, won't eat. Waste the flesh when you kill me. No worry. Wolves and crows will know better, trol."

I let out a breath I seemed to have been holding forever. "So you think he should live, Prophetess? You think I was wrong to take care of his friends back there? They would have killed us."

"They would. I don't doubt this one would have too. But he's also a child of God, and it's not for us to take him out of this world if he doesn't force us to."

I must still have looked mutinous.

"If not for him, Minos, for you. Murder is a stain on the soul."

Dee chimed in, of course. "They do say the rules of war are for the benefit of those who follow them, not for the benefit of their enemies. So that one may fight monsters without becoming one."

"I'm pretty sure that's not how that saying went." I sighed. "Fine."

I brought my right foot up in a cross kick, smashing my boot down on the paleo's kneecap. He screamed as the bone shattered.

"He's alive. As long as his friends don't eat him now that he's crippled. And he's not going to be following us anymore."

Dee looked somewhat horrified but miraculously kept quiet. Prophetess opened her mouth, took a good look at my face, and said nothing.

We left the paleo choking back sobs of pain. Part of me thought I should feel bad, but I didn't.

We stopped only long enough for me to clean the blood off my sword and use a bit of the oil soaking my torches to touch up the blade. Whatever the stories might say about steel hungering for blood, the reality was if you didn't get it off right away your weapon was going to be coated in rust the next time you pulled it out.

We were all quiet. I knew I had upset Prophetess, but I certainly wasn't going to apologize for doing the right thing. But while I was well accustomed to silences, this one was an echo of discomfort. I almost found myself wishing for Dee's chatter.

"I must say, my Select friend, your skill with the blade is impressive. Is it true that you all study war?"

Almost.

I sighed. "A lot of Select wind up as mercenaries. I suppose we're suited for it, and we're hardly welcomed in most other professions. And it never hurts to be able to defend yourself when you're as unpopular as we are. So most of us study the basics - personal combat, tactics, strategy. Even if we never use it."

Prophetess spoke up. "I hadn't thought... back in Oldtown, when the guards were bothering us..."

"You thought I was a coward? You thought I didn't know how to fight? Were you happier then, or now? Most Select do know how to fight, Prophetess. But we generally prefer to run away."

The opportunity to run away came soon enough.

We had eaten a subdued lunch and were walking again when the whooping started up behind us. This group of paleos wasn't hiding in ruins or tall grass - they were jogging up the road behind us. There must have been at least a dozen. They were still nearly a mile back, but gaining quickly.

"This is what happens when you leave someone alive to tell them which way we're going," I muttered.

"Maybe if we'd been kinder to him he wouldn't have told them which way we were going," Prophetess retorted.

I grimaced at her. "Can you ask the flying pigs that live in your world to swoop down here and give us a ride?"

"Normally I'm the first to enjoy the clash of wits, the cut and thrust of the beatific against the pragmatic," Dee said, "But might I suggest in this case we save our breath for running?"

Say what you will about the paleos - and I for one had almost nothing good to say about them - but they can run. Even though they had been at it longer than we had, they continued to catch up.

"I fear," gasped Dee, "that we must take to the woods on our right."

And in fact we were nearing a thick stand of trees.

"That makes no sense," I panted. "They'll just follow us in, and they'll catch up even faster in there."

"Ah," Dee replied, "but they won't."

"Why not?"

"They're afraid of the drelb."

Say what you will about Dee - and I for one had almost nothing good to say about him - but he knew something about paleos. We were forced to drastically reduce our speed once we got in among the pines, but there were no sounds of pursuit.

"I don't suppose they're afraid because of some primitive superstition in their feeble, savage minds?"

"I fear not," Dee answered. "I'm given to understand that there are in fact drelb in here."

I could have said something about going from the frying pan into the fire... but considering that the paleos were most likely planning to kill us and eat us, there really weren't any worse options. Even drelb. Drelb would probably kill us and eat us too, but at least there was a chance we wouldn't run into any.

The forest was thicker and darker than any we had seen. It was beautiful in a way, pine giving way to birch and oak as we made our way deeper. The leaves on the deciduous trees were turning but had not yet begun to fall. But it was not hard to imagine that leafy dimness might be haunted by monsters. Except for the twittering of birds and the crunching of our own feet through the undergrowth, the silence was tomb-like.

Maybe not the happiest analogy.

We paralleled the road. My goal was to stay far enough inside the woods that the paleos wouldn't come in after us, while staying close enough to open terrain that we could run for it if we were set upon by drelb. I had no reason to think the creatures wouldn't come out of the trees, except that the paleos seemed to think the road was safe.

Great. Now I was relying on murderous savages for strategy.

We stopped for lunch when I judged the sun was directly overhead. The bread was no longer fresh but it was neither hard as a rock nor moldy, the meat and fruit were good, and the remaining small beer hadn't yet started to taste too much like the leather water skins. We were far enough from the road that we could see no trace of it, just the barest thinning of the trees at the edge of sight. I didn't want to make it easy for the paleos to track us.

"Do you suppose they'll just give up and go away?" I asked.

"I doubt it." Dee shook his head sadly. "The paleos are very patient people. They're clever, too, whatever you may think. They know the direction we were going. They'll most likely assume we're doing what we're doing and wait for us to come out. I would expect they've got scouts spread up and down the road, since they can't know exactly how fast we're moving."

I sighed. "And we'll have to light a fire at night, which will tell them exactly where we are." I looked from Dee to Prophetess but saw no sign of a brilliant idea illuminating either face. "We'll have to head through the woods. Try to get out the other side. Do you know how far it is?"

"More than a day, I'm afraid," Dee said. Prophetess turned visibly pale. "I do tend to agree that it's the only way," the occultist added. "On my own, it's perhaps possible I could talk the paleos into letting me live, despite their obvious grumpiness, but in the company of a Select? No, I'm afraid they would certainly kill us."

Dee was annoying, but he clearly did possess at least some useful information. He was slowly starting to grow on me… like a wart or similar annoying, itchy infection. Still, I was about to suggest that he was welcome to try his luck alone with the paleos when he stood up and cheerfully announced, "So, I suppose we'd best get going, eh?"

The forest remained beautiful as we drew deeper into it, but every shadow under a bush now loomed sinister. Every rustle in the leaves might be a drelb. If there was a pause in the birdsong, we stopped and anxiously scanned the trees to see what could have caused it. I constantly fought the temptation to unsheathe my sword.

We tried to head east as best we could. A short time later, I spied something looming through a gap in the trees. We stopped and stared.

"Some kind of building," I said.

The structure was a low, squat pile of cinderblocks, overgrown with vines and weeds. Still, it seemed solid. Dee, Prophetess and I exchanged glances.

"It's shelter," Dee said.

"For something," I snapped. "You said there were drelb in here. What if that's where they live?"

We exchanged looks again, and gave the building a wide berth. It took an effort of will not to look over my shoulder as we left it behind.

After a couple of hours we came to a steep-banked ravine running roughly parallel to our path.

"Do we follow it?" Prophetess asked.

"It's going the direction we want, and following it we'll be sure we aren't going in circles. It's a good source of water. And I wouldn't think the drelb would cross it, so it puts something safe on our north side." I paused, and gave in to the urge to look back the way we'd come. "The downside is if they come from the south, we're pinned against it."

"Why wouldn't you think they'd cross it from the north?" Dee asked mildly.

I considered the sloping, tree choked sides. "It's not exactly hospitable terrain…"

"Could you get up the banks?"

"Sure, but…"

"Then so can a drelb."

"Running water…" I began, aware even as I said it that I was retailing a belief I myself regarded as rank superstition.

"Surely you don't believe that? Men or any other creatures infected by the Darkness can cross running water as readily as anyone else. I would hardly have expected you to put any stock in that sort of folklore."

"Let's just go across it," I muttered. "I think it bends southward anyway and that's not the direction we want to go."

None of us had any difficulty climbing down and back up the other side. The banks were soft earth and moss-slicked rocks, but gnarled trees provided plenty of hand-holds. The water at the bottom was clear and inviting, so we refilled our skins.

We left the ravine behind us, heading north and east. Too soon, though, the shadows were lengthening, and long before night truly fell we settled in a small clearing and began gathering firewood.

"They do fear fire, don't they?" I asked Dee.

"Oh, I'd certainly think so." I was so used to his voice that I mentally filled the silence that followed with the words, "If not, I highly doubt we'll survive the night." But he didn't actually say that.

Dead wood was plentiful, and our fire was huge. Dee carried a pot not unlike my frying pan, and we used both to boil the water we had taken from the stream. I could have gone hunting or foraging, but felt no inclination at all to venture away from the camp.

Dee chattered away long into the night. For once, I was thrilled with the distraction of his voice. Eventually we agreed to set watches, but for hours after sundown none of us slept.

The result was predictable. I awoke with a start from a terrifying dream - the paleo whose knee I had shattered screaming at me from a pit of disembodied mouths. Reality was not much more reassuring. I found myself surrounded in a white mist. The horror of the dream, which had receded for a moment, rushed back. Where was I?

As my heart slowed I recognized our clearing. The light filtering in through the fog meant it must be morning, but how long after dawn I had no idea. Dee and Prophetess were both asleep. I wasn't sure whose watch it was supposed to be. But we had survived the night.

I went a little ways into the woods, relieved myself, and returned to organize our camp. Some of the logs on the fire still smoldered fitfully, but the damp had almost completely extinguished them.

Dee and Prophetess woke as I was clattering around with the pots.

"Ah, good thing that you had the watch," Dee remarked.

"I'm not sure I did. If I did, I slept through it until about ten minutes ago."

We looked at each other guiltily and shrugged. A military organization we were not. In any case, we had survived the night uneaten. Maybe the paleos really were just superstitious. That was a heartening thought as we packed up and tried to decide on the right way to go in the clinging morning mist. Visibility was no more than a hundred yards, and the sun was a vague brightness in front of us.

Either we hadn't done a very good job of orienting ourselves or the ravine curved back north. Whatever the case, we ran into it again within half an hour. This time we decided we might as well follow it. The mist still had not burned off, and the danger of walking in circles was now very real.

Keeping the ravine at our right, we made decent progress. The edge of the world was circumscribed by the white haze, trees looming out of it ahead of us as if newly created.

From somewhere behind, beyond the edge of sight, we heard a long, low, moaning roar. I suppose if you had to render it in words, it would be something like, "drrreeeelllllbbb."

Thus the name.

"Run!"

We crashed through the sparse undergrowth. I tripped over a tree root, caught myself on my sheathed sword, staggered two more paces and fell to my knees on a rock. The first moment was dominated by surprise. Then the pain started. I was probably bleeding, but I was going to be bleeding a lot worse if I didn't get moving. I hauled myself to my feet and continued on.

But even with the seconds I had lost, I realized I was still ahead of Prophetess. Growing up near the Flow, she had no experience on this kind of broken terrain. Her breath was coming in ragged, terrified sobs as she struggled along twenty feet behind me.

"Ah, dammit," I growled.

Dee was vanishing into the mist ahead, dodging obstacles as if he had been born in the woods.

"Come on!" I shouted. I found that terror was an excellent pain suppressant as I put on a burst of speed.

And then Prophetess slipped.

It was less a scream than a loud squeak as she went down.

You know what they say - you don't have to be faster than what's chasing you. You just have to be faster than the slowest person in your group.

The drelb called out again, closer. In that moment, with the unseen horror closing in for the kill, the urge to flee grew overwhelming. There's something to be said for living to fight another day.

"Ah, dammit," I repeated as I stopped and turned.

There's also something to be said for being able to live with yourself if you make it to that other day.

When I got back to where Prophetess had fallen, she had already pulled herself back to her feet. Though her clothes were damp and stained with dirt, she seemed unhurt.

But by then a dark shape was already visible through the mist.

It came at an ungainly lope, a hunched gait that should have been slow but covered ground with shocking speed. When it saw us waiting, the monster stopped and reared to its full height, again voicing that wailing cry that seemed equal parts rage and despair.

The beast was big. And hideous. It must have stood a head taller than me, but was bulky far out of proportion to its height. Short, bandy legs supported a long, massive torso. Pale skin sagged in heavy folds, with mangy patches of hair that thickened at its waist and extremities. The face was bestial, mouth elongated into a fanged snout. Stubby fingers ended in huge, hooked claws, but a malign intellect burned in its small, black eyes, and it carried a heavy tree branch as a club.

It waddled toward me and roared again. I pulled my sword clear. In retrospect, the paleos had not been formidable opponents. They had been short, and scrawny, with inferior weapons. The drelb was another matter entirely. But I figured it would still bleed if I cut it.

It bellowed one last time, huge teeth bared, then dropped to all fours in a shambling charge that ended with it rearing over me, swinging the tree limb.

There was no running away now, so I stepped forward instead and used the same Flowing Water cut I had employed against the paleo.

The force of the drelb's arm slamming into my blade drove me to my knees, but the steel did its job. The club hit the ground a foot from me, the monster's paw landing a pace farther away.

I could cut it, and it would bleed - except it didn't.

I was just starting to regain my feet when the other hand swung around and caught me on the side of the head. At least I suppose that's what happened. All I really knew was that one moment I was getting up and the next I was lying on my back six feet away. I had a good view of the stump of the drelb's right wrist. No blood came out. Instead, a black cloud bubbled from the wound, sealing it. The monster roared and took a step toward me.

"Hey!"

It whirled, quick for its bulk, to glare at Prophetess. She hit it in the nose with her staff.

The beast howled and swung at her, only to remember mid-strike that its right hand was missing. It looked down in puzzled anger and she smacked its nose again.

I scuttled on my backside to retrieve my sword and sheath. The drelb was eying Prophetess uncertainly. It must have been five times her weight, but it was visibly shaken by the loss of its hand, and maybe even more by the stinging blows to its nose.

I got to my feet, blade extended in front of me. "Get behind me," I said. She didn't waste any time doing so. "We're going to back up to the ravine," I said, "and then we're going to go down the slope, and then we're going to run."

We suited actions to words. The drelb growled deep in its throat but came no closer. By the time we felt the earth sloping down behind us, the swirling mist was beginning to hide the monster. I sheathed my sword and we slid down the bank in a rush into the stream below.

"Let's stick to the water for a while," I gasped. "If it hunts by smell, it might lose the trail and not know where we come out." Plus we found that we could splash along at a good pace over the slick stones.

We didn't look back, and I fervently wished the Darkness-infested abomination was growling a final curse over its shoulder and hoping never to see us again either.

Somehow it didn't surprise me when a mile later we emerged on the south side of the ravine to find Dee waiting for us.

"Nice of you to stay around and help," I snapped. Even though I had myself come within a hair's breadth of bolting and leaving Prophetess to her fate.

The occultist just smiled easily. "Come now, you can hardly believe I'm the sort to battle drelb. You seem to have come through it quite nicely, considering. Though I suppose that must hurt." He gestured to my face.

"It didn't until you pointed it out." Which was true. Once he mentioned it, my right cheek began to throb. I probed it gingerly. "What's it look like?"

"Much as if you'd been hit in the face by a bear, which is hardly surprising. Quite a bruise, and four scratches. Nowhere near as bad as that poor girl back in Brambledge, though. You must not have made it very angry."

"I'd just cut off its hand. It seemed pretty annoyed."

Dee shrugged. "Interesting. Perhaps the Darkness really does avoid the Select, though I'd never believed that myself. Or perhaps it simply doesn't operate in the drelb as it does in humans."

"When I cut its hand off, the Darkness came out instead of blood and sealed the wound."

"Fascinating. Perhaps it builds on the notion of a bear's invulnerability."

Prophetess said, "That's the second time you've said 'bear.' Why?"

Dee's eyebrows went up. "Well, because that's what the drelb are, of course."

I snorted. "I've seen bears. They had more hair and didn't carry clubs. That wasn't a bear."

"It's the closest the Darkness can come to turning a bear into a man," Dee said. "The Darkness is a construct of mankind, and seeks out man to bond with. If there are no humans at hand, it will settle on a reasonable approximation. Such as a bear. The beast's hair falls out, it tries to use tools… it would be rather pathetic if they weren't so very hostile. And, as you noted, difficult to kill."

I thought of that wailing cry and was surprised by a swelling of sympathy for the animal I had fought.

Sympathy was still playing second fiddle to fear, though.

"Do you think it'll follow us?"

Dee considered. "It might be reluctant to try the ravine with one hand missing. And bears do hunt by smell, so going through the stream was clever. I think we may have seen the last of that one." He paused. "That doesn't mean there aren't more, of course."

With that thought in mind we followed the ravine east as fast as we could go without stumbling.

8. Finding Religion

It was with a huge gasp of relief that we emerged from the woods late in the afternoon. We made camp atop a low hill a quarter of a mile from the tree line. More forest loomed against the darkening sky to the south and east. We weighed the possibility of nearby paleos or Hawks against the risk of drelb coming out of the woods and opted for a small fire. It would be visible from a huge distance, but hopefully would deter wild animals and the Darkness - or mixtures of the two.

As she so often did, Prophetess withdrew to pray as soon as we finished eating. I suppose I was a little resentful. I would have liked to speak with her in the aftermath of that awful day, but instead her solace was with the Lord. Or whatever religious phrasing she would use to explain the fact that she'd rather sit around talking to herself than to me.

Dee must have seen something in my face and, being who he was, he had to poke at the wound rather than letting it be. "Unusual, I suppose, for a prophet to have a Select bodyguard. To my knowledge few of the Select confess the Universal faith. Unless you are an exception, of course?"

"Um," I said, and shook my head. It seemed like the response best designed to discourage conversation. Not effective at stopping monologue, though.

"Particularly interesting since Yoshana also counts a Select as her principal lieutenant."

"Like I said before, most Select have some military training. It's pretty common for us to serve as bodyguards." I saw a chance to both change the subject and possibly learn something useful from Dee's endless lecturing. "What else do you know about Yoshana that might be helpful to us? I know what everyone does, but I left the Green Heart when her invasion started, so I have to admit I'm no expert."

"Ah." Dee stared into the fire, apparently captivated by the rising sparks. For a moment I thought he might actually be at a loss for words, but he quickly proved me wrong. "You know Yoshana was not just the supreme military commander, but also became the dictator of the Shield."

I nodded. "Sure. It was pretty common knowledge she deposed Karst about a year before the invasion. If by 'deposed' you mean 'killed with her bare hands.'"

"Just so. Interesting story, that. Karst was a consummate master of the Darkness himself, despite having less demon parentage than a full-blooded Overlord. Rumor has it that they had dueled to a stalemate, each trying to turn the Darkness against the other, when Yoshana ended it by snapping his neck. The lesson in that, of course, is that whatever game you're playing, she doesn't play by the same rules you do. Something to bear in mind."

So besides her natural advantages, Yoshana would cheat. That was encouraging.

"She's always tried to avoid direct force-on-force conflict if she can," Dee continued. "She thinks it's wasteful. She always prefers deceit."

There was something to be said for that - in fact, Sun Tzu, history's greatest master of strategy, had said it.

"She outsmarted herself with the Hellguard, though. Karst had always courted a relationship with them. For generations the Shield stood between the Hellguard and the Green Heart - thus the name - even though the Shield's Overlords are themselves half demon."

"That part I know. I am from the Heart, remember."

"Yes. Well. So, then you also know that Yoshana continued Karst's alliance with the demons. For centuries the demons have been confined to the Darklands - ice to the north, sea to the east, mountains to the west. The Shield was the plug bottling them up to the south."

"Did I mention I'm from the Heart? I understand the basic geopolitics behind the invasion. The Hellguard backed Yoshana's armies and they rolled over us like a wave. We lost Gateway, Heartfield, Seafields... everything between the Salt and Paint Rivers. My family lived on the other side of the Paint outside Goat Hill, but they sent me away as soon as Heartfield fell. My father said once Seafields fell and Yoshana had access to a real port, there would be no stopping her."

Dee glowered at me a bit for interrupting but continued undaunted. "Just so. But then the demons turned on her. We can't truly know why, but I've heard the Hellguard wanted to press forward, using Yoshana's forces as shock troops. But Yoshana has always been careful with her men. She ordered the army to pause and consolidate its gains. But the demons weren't interested in keeping her force intact. They wanted it expended in the assault. When she wouldn't push on, they turned many of her Overlord commanders against her. There was still a good deal of resentment over her coup against Karst. And the demons played to the Overlords' ambition. They promised them satrapies in the conquered lands. But while Yoshana fought to retain control of her armies, her two top lieutenants, Grigg and Roshel, joined the Green Heart defenders and stopped the demons at the Paint River."

He paused and shook his head. "There's some confusion there. Some say Grigg and Roshel had left her even before the demons turned against her, that they didn't support the invasion at all. Whatever the case, they rallied partisans to the Green Heart's defense - including quite a few Select, I've heard."

Dee looked at me quizzically. It was easy enough to guess his thoughts. I had wondered the same thing. Would my parents have joined the battle against the demons? They had not made the military their profession like so many other Select, but they were both trained in the art of war. And with the battle lines drawn at the Paint, they would literally have been defending their home.

Had they fought or fled? If they had fought, had they lived or died? I had put that thought aside for two years. They had sent me away, to survive. To continue the line of the Select. Though they had loved me - because they had loved me - they had told me not to return.

I shook my head. "Our minds aren't linked, you know." Supposedly the Overlords and Hellguard could actually use the Darkness to communicate with each other over considerable distances, though no one had ever suggested they could bridge the hundreds of miles that separated us from the Green Heart. "I've had no news but the vaguest rumors from there."

Dee nodded in what I might have taken for sympathy from a less self-absorbed individual. "Well. In any case, Yoshana and her loyalists joined the forces led by Grigg and Roshel and dealt the demons a crushing defeat. Killed the Overlord general who had supplanted Yoshana, then exploited the confusion to catch a whole corps of the Hellguard forces in a pincer movement and tear it apart.

"No one's quite certain what happened next. By many accounts, in the confusion of the battle, one of Grigg's own partisans stabbed Yoshana by mistake. What everyone agrees on is that she died."

"If I remember right, Yoshana faked her death at least once before when she was organizing her coup against Karst. You said it yourself, deception is one of her favorite tools."

"The spear pierced her heart from behind. The blade thrust out through her breast and she died." Prophetess had rejoined us at the fire without my noticing.

"How can you know that?"

She just shook her head.

"Indeed. That is consistent with the accounts I've heard," Dee said. "And I hardly think this was a ploy, because I can't see what cause of hers it would have advanced. With her slain on the battlefield, the partisan forces and her Shield loyalists collapsed. Many were absorbed into regular Green Heart units. Others just dispersed. Until..."

"Until she rose, reborn from the Darkness," Prophetess said.

"Yes, well, there is a belief that the Darkness preserved her life essence until it could heal her body. But the version she has put about is that she was raised by God himself." He looked sidelong at Prophetess. She nodded.

Dee continued, "She claims that with her resurrection, God showed the way to turn the Darkness to his ends. As the psalm says, even the Darkness is radiant in his sight. She began to gather the remnants of her army back together - as I said before, calling it the Darkness Radiant. Although her troops seem to prefer the term Knights of the Resurrection."

He paused and considered. "That was in the spring. Around the Easter season, in point of fact." He looked at Prophetess again to see if she would react to that, but she kept silent. "She's been making her way across the Green Heart the whole summer, attracting followers as she goes. Mostly veterans. So far I gather they've largely managed to live off the land, but I have to think they're going to need a patron state to keep them supplied."

"That's why they're going to the Source," I said. "She's looking for a sponsor for whatever crusade she's planning to launch." I let slip a cynical little chuckle. "You really don't see how dying benefits her?"

"What do you mean?"

I poked at the fire with a stick. Another shower of sparks rose into the sky. "Before she was just a general who had lost her command. Now she's a prophet."

Prophetess nodded decisively. "A false prophet. She may be the antichrist of Revelation."

Dee stared. "Ah. Well. She is, in the end, only human. Even if she is an Overlord."

"And don't many scholars believe that John the Divine was speaking of the Roman Emperor Nero when he named the antichrist?" Prophetess shot back. "Isn't the Darkness the work of human hands? The fact she's human doesn't mean she can't bring about the corruption of the world."

The occultist's mouth opened and closed like a fish's.

"Just because she grew up on a farm doesn't mean she's stupid, Dee," I laughed. It was about time for someone else to be at the receiving end of Prophetess' unexpected insights.

"I'm sure no one meant to suggest I was stupid, although people do say the Select think they're smarter than everyone else," she retorted.

My mouth snapped shut again. You'd think I would learn not to open it.

But I spoke again anyway. "The question is, how does this help us stop her?"

"The only way you stop lies," Prophetess said. "With the truth."

She stared into the fire. "Although it would be really helpful if we got to Stephensburg first."

We picked up an overgrown trail that was probably the remains of an ancient road as we continued east. I hoped that this close to the Muddy, the area would be more settled and the risk of encountering paleos and drelb would be lower. I was wrong about the settlement, but we weren't set upon by savages or corrupted bears.

Then the trees gave way and the river spread dully gleaming in front of us, so wide the trees on the far bank were a blur of green half a mile away. It was as brown as its name suggested, the current dragging along branches, leaves and soil as it slowly but inexorably ate away at its banks.

Yoshana was somewhere on the other side - if Prophetess was right, heading to the same place we were.

"There's a saying that if you stand by the bank of the river long enough, eventually the body of your enemy will come floating by," I said.

Prophetess looked puzzled, then scowled. "That's a stupid saying."

"I'm pretty sure it's from Sun Tzu. Counseling patience."

"Still stupid," Prophetess declared. "If we stand by the bank of this river long enough, eventually Yoshana's armies will sweep over us and we'll be converted or killed."

She had a point. Of course, racing to beat Yoshana's armies to Stephensburg so we could defy her seemed like an even better way to get killed.

I didn't say that, though.

Getting there, at least, should be a simple matter. I was pretty sure we had hit the Muddy above the fork where it split to the northwest and northeast. Dee agreed. All we needed to do was follow the bank south until we reached the fork. There it should be easy to find a boat going upriver to the east. The eastern fork would take us to within a few days of our destination. It would be slow going against the current, but no worse than walking, and the boat wouldn't stop for the night.

Just a question of finding that landing.

The sun was starting to set and we were looking for a good spot to make camp when we saw firelight in the distance ahead.

"Should we go take a look?" asked Prophetess.

I thought out loud. "Could be a town. But if it is, they may not let us in at night. Or it could be the Hawks. They might be happy to see us, but it's hard to imagine we'd be happy to see them."

"Maybe. But I'd rather not spend another night out here."

I had to laugh. "If you're not going to listen to my answer, why ask the question?"

She had no reply to that, but we kept walking, so that was another argument I lost by default.

It wasn't a town, but the ruins of one. Old ruins with new inhabitants. An array of campfires sprouted among the fallen buildings.

We stopped a few hundred yards short of the encampment. I waved the others back and moved forward through cattails. My night vision was better.

I was back quickly. "They've got sentries out, but it's not a military camp. It's mostly women and children."

"Refugees," Dee said.

"I think so. It should be safe enough if we don't spook them."

We approached slowly, trying to look as unthreatening as possible. Prophetess and Dee looked about as harmless as you could imagine - each was tall but thin, with nothing at all warlike about them. As for me - I stayed a little bit behind the other two.

"Hallo the camp," Dee called when we were within fifty yards of the nearest sentry. He was a boy about my age, big but armed only with a pitchfork. He gripped it in both hands and shouted, "Who's there?"

The sentries had torches set around their positions to protect themselves from the Darkness, but as a result they were night-blind and could see nothing outside the little circle of firelight.

"We are simple travelers. I am a historian and teller of tales. My companions are religious pilgrims."

"Come into the light where I can see you."

As we reached the ring of torches the sentry started, stepped back and poked his pitchfork in my direction. "Hey, he's Select!"

"Why, just so," Dee agreed easily. "The Select travel like the rest of us and have the same needs for food and shelter. As it happens, he is the protector of the young lady."

The boy's brow furrowed. "I don't think the Reverend's gonna like this."

"Well then by all means take us to him, and we'll let the man decide for himself."

The sentry nodded his head once. "Sure. Come on with me," he said, and abandoned his post to lead us deeper into the camp.

"If it's going to be any trouble we can just keep walking," I said, but he ignored me.

"Surely it's better to spend the night around a nice, safe, warm fire," Dee said. "After all, the worst that can happen is they turn us out."

My pulse was quickening and adrenaline was starting to flow. I looked for conveniently shadowed paths out of the ruins. "That's not the worst that can happen. In case it had escaped you in your travels, some people don't like the Select very much."

"I'm sure the Reverend will be perfectly reasonable," Dee said soothingly.

"Abomination!" the Reverend shrieked, pointing a quivering, bony finger at me. "Loris, you fool, how could you allow this perversion among us?" The man's bulging, blue eyes swiveled to skewer the sentry who had accompanied us.

The boy paled, stammered, then turned accusingly to Dee. "He said they was religious pilgrims."

"Does 'I told you so' seem about right?" I muttered.

"Shut up, Minos," Prophetess hissed.

The refugee camp centered on what had been the town square. The Reverend had taken over a largely intact building of bricks and columns that might have been a town hall, or maybe just a post office. Bonfires burned brightly in the square, and many of the refugees had set up ramshackle tents in no particular organization.

Apparently the Reverend had just finished some sort of address to his flock when we arrived. Very obviously he was not pleased to see us. With "us" more specifically meaning "me."

"And it did not occur to you to wonder what sort of vile rites this creature might follow? 'Religion' does not mean 'true religion,' Loris. Aren't our misfortunes enough without further tempting the Lord?"

A small crowd was beginning to gather. This was probably more entertaining than most of the Reverend's sermons. Nobody seemed overtly hostile yet, but "stone the infidels" rolls off the tongue pretty quickly and we were seriously outnumbered.

"What is the nature of your troubles, Reverend?" asked Prophetess.

"Who are you to ask, woman?"

She considered the question for a moment. "Just a humble servant of God trying to do his will as best I may."

He blew air contemptuously. "Strange company in which you do it." Still, a little bit of the fight went out of him. He looked older, then, and tired. His face was lined, and his hair was white. If he had brushed or combed it, it wasn't recently.

"The Hawk's Nest let fly its birds of prey. I suppose you know that." We nodded. "The armies made their way south by different paths. The autarch has not so much one army as different bands of cutthroats, each with its own captain. Word came to us that Black Keorg's troops were marching toward our town.

"Of all the Hawks, he's the worst. As soon burn a city as pass by it. A judgment of the Lord, to have Keorg's locusts descend on you. The iniquities of our town fathers brought it down upon us. I saw the Lord's vengeance and gathered up those who would hear me and we fled, not even looking back lest we be struck down like Lot's wife.

"I led our people to the river. South of here stands a bridge, which by God's grace is still passable. I thought we would cross out of this forsaken wilderness into a better land, in the Source. They say Stephen is a righteous man. But his sentries turned us back. Not interested in taking in vagabonds, they said." His mouth worked like he was planning to spit. "I might have reasoned with them, but they told us that hell's whore Yoshana had marched her legions up through the Green Heart and was making her way up the eastern river through the Source. I'll not settle where that demon has corrupted the ground with her passing."

And the grapes were probably sour anyway. I exchanged looks with Prophetess. Yoshana was not only ahead of us, but in our path.

"But winter is coming, and we have only what we brought with us."

"How many are you?" asked Prophetess.

"A hundred and a bit more. Most in the town would not listen and now lie dead, I'm sure."

There was no way for a hundred townfolk to live off the land in the winter. The Reverend might or might not have saved his flock from the Hawks, but if they stayed here he had doomed them for certain.

"So what's the plan now?" I asked.

The look he gave me for daring to speak could have cut glass. "Now the Lord provides, abomination. Your kind never understood God's providence, but it is infinite."

I really should have just shut up - something of a recurring theme in my life - but any sympathy I had for his plight had evaporated. Funny how being called an abomination can do that. "So to be perfectly clear, you think God wants you to sit here until you starve?"

"God's plan is not for you to know!" he thundered.

"I've got a real live prophet here, let's ask her," I snapped. Putting my foot all the way into my mouth after Prophetess had so carefully avoided that point.

"Blasphemy!" His face was turning all sorts of interesting colors. White had rapidly shifted to red, and was now moving on toward purple.

I shot a quick glance around to see if anyone was about to brain me with a stick yet. Thankfully, they seemed to just be watching the show. So far.

Dee, who generally personified the phrase *discretion is the better part of valor*, inexplicably piped up. "In fact, Reverend Sir, I've seen the lady cast out the Darkness with my own eyes."

The Reverend's mouth opened and then shut. His eyes narrowed. "So. A false prophet in the company of a cursed race, with her herald to go before her to announce her lies." He turned in a circle, taking in his followers. "You see, truly the end times are upon us. The Book of Creed said it would end so. Even now the servants of the Darkness Radiant walk among us." He spat in the dirt. "On your way to join your mistress Yoshana, hellspawn? You'll find no souls to take here."

Now the crowd was starting to look ugly. People nodded their heads and grumbled agreement, angry expressions on their faces.

While I was taking a deep breath and considering our options for getting out of this with our skins, Prophetess decided on a different approach.

She took two steps forward, putting her nose within a foot of the Reverend's face. "You're wrong. And you're a fool. You are the servant who hid away the talent his lord gave him, because he was too fearful and too stupid to do his master's will. The Lord has commanded me to oppose Yoshana. If you heard him you would oppose her too instead of cowering. Now you've consigned not just yourself but your people to the darkness."

She turned too, taking in the crowd just as the Reverend had done. "A week's walk to the southwest is a walled village called Brambledge. Their harvest was abundant this year. I cast the Darkness out of the miller's daughter there. Go to them and tell them I sent you, and they are to take you in. They will do it."

She stuck her face even closer to the Reverend's. "You can lead your people there as a shepherd should, or you can stay here by yourself and rot. It's for you to decide if you're the good shepherd, or just the hired man who flees when the wolf comes."

And with that she turned her back on him and pushed her way through the crowd. Dee and I hurried after her.

We hadn't gone fifty feet when the boy Loris and two others caught up with us. I loosened my blade fractionally in its sheath, but he said, "Can we go with you?"

"Why?" asked Prophetess.

"If you're going to stop Yoshana, you'll need help. And we want to do something, not just hide away like you said."

Prophetess smiled. "And *that's* how the Lord provides. Get your things."

As the three boys hurried off, I said to her, "Aren't those people going to have trouble with the drelb? There might be more in that forest."

She shrugged and kept walking. "We all have our bears to cross."

9. Choosing the Way

"So I'm guessing you still don't want to just give up and go home," I murmured to Prophetess.

She gave me a dismissive smile. "It would hardly be fair to disappoint Loris, Doral, and Hadal just because Yoshana is in our way." Those being our three new friends. My immediate impression was that none of them was the swiftest sheep in the flock, but they were young and strong and enthusiastic. If they had also been veteran soldiers, and we had several thousand more of them, we would have made a formidable challenge to Yoshana's armies.

"We can't just follow her up the river," I said.

"No," she agreed. "I think we should go north, try to get around them."

That would take us closer to the ice sheets with winter coming on. Still, we should make better time than an army, and there was merit in the idea.

"If we went farther north we could go to Our Lady," I suggested. "They could help us decide what to do." Which I hoped would be to turn back.

"I know what we need to do."

The sanctuary at Our Lady was the seat of the Universal Church in what was left of the known world. For Prophetess to suggest that she didn't need the direction of her own church seemed presumptuous, if not blasphemous.

She put her hand lightly on my arm. "There's so much I don't know. But what I have to do - that I know. That, he's told me."

We walked on a bit. "You certainly seemed very definite with the poor Reverend," I said.

She snorted. "I'm not going to have some fool Reborn question my faith."

I was taken aback. "That's a little harsh, isn't it? You believe in the same God. I didn't think there were that many differences in doctrine."

Bad move.

"Ah," interjected Dee. "There are in fact centuries of doctrinal differences and quite a bit of accumulated animosity. In brief, perhaps the most obvious distinction is in the belief of the literal transubstantiation of the eucharist..."

Fortunately I was tired enough to stop listening. We made camp half an hour later in a clearing near the water's edge.

"... but building on the role of the priest or minister as intercessor between the supplicant and the divine, there is of course the rejection by the Universal Church of the Books of Jome and Creed as canonical Books of the Fall, which..."

"Yes, exactly, Dee. Now let's get a fire built and set a watch."

Dee looked disgruntled. "Surely Huey, Dewey, and Louie can take care of that for us."

"Who?"

Dee's look of disgust deepened. "I was referring in a jocular way to… oh, never mind. It's not funny if you have to explain it."

Hard to argue with that.

Hadal, Doral, and Loris - or Huey, Dewey, and Louie, according to Dee - treated Prophetess with all the reverence due to… well, a prophet. It was a little odd. As impressed as Dee was with her, in his case the fascination really was academic. For me - I wasn't quite sure how I felt. But it was nice to have someone else make the fire and take watch, which they did.

"Let me take that pack for you, Prophetess," Doral offered the next morning. Hadal and Loris looked upset that they hadn't thought of it.

That seemed like a bit much. "Tess has been carrying that pack for five hundred miles," I said. Was I really petty enough to revert to that nickname just to demystify her? Yes, evidently I was.

Six eyes glared daggers at the Select who dared speak for a prophet of the Lord.

"Tess can carry her own pack," Prophetess said with a smile. "Tess can also speak for herself."

Why did I keep starting this kind of exchange if I never won? Maybe Select really weren't as smart as we thought we were.

Five miles later Loris finally worked up the courage to ask her, "Why does the Select call you Tess?"

"It's his little joke," she answered. "The prophet, Tess."

Loris frowned. "That's disrespectful."

"It's kind of funny, though," she said.

The crippled paleo was laughing at me. I couldn't imagine what he found amusing. His two dead friends were lying next to him, lifeless eyes glaring at me accusingly. But he just kept chuckling and pointing, even though his left leg was at a completely unnatural angle.

"What's so funny?" I snapped at him. "Want me to break your other knee?"

He lifted his arm higher, waving his finger. I abruptly realized he was pointing *behind* me.

I didn't want to turn, but I did.

The seething mass of Darkness was shaped roughly like a man. Somehow, a ragged cluster of sharp, white teeth floated where a mouth would be. Red, flaming eyes narrowed as they swept me with deepest contempt.

"I am Yoshana," it said. And reached for me.

That was all the sleep I got that night.

"You're up early, Minos," Prophetess said, hours later. I growled something incoherent and took another swipe of the whetstone down my blade. If I was going to keep killing people for her, I might as well be good at it. Until someone or something stronger got me instead.

She gave me a long look and turned away. We broke camp efficiently enough and continued north. I drifted to the back of the group, and Dee fell in beside me. "Fascinating, our friend's ability to draw followers," he said. "Most of the biblical prophets were solitary, though the greater ones, such as Moses, or perhaps even Jesus or Mohammed -"

"Why don't you go lecture Huey, Dewey, and Louie," I snarled. "I'm sure they could use the instruction."

Dee looked hurt, but moved ahead without another word.

Annoying as the man was, snapping at him felt like kicking a puppy. But the dream had put me in a foul mood, and it looked like I was going to take it out on everyone around me.

And why shouldn't I? A cross-country trip with a pretty girl was not improved by the addition of a windbag occultist and three illiterate oafs stricken with religious fervor. I had killed two people and crippled a third, all of whom undoubtedly deserved it, but I was still having nightmares about them. I'd been insulted, chased, and pummeled. And now we were charging madly forward to thwart the plans of the greatest warrior of the modern age, because a mildly insane farm girl thought she could talk to God.

The fact that I'd idiotically volunteered for it didn't make me feel any better.

Still, the sun was bright, and the day was cool and pleasant. Pines began to crowd the shoreline as we moved north, but it was still easily passable. If there was anything in the woods, it must have decided that six of us made an unattractive target.

Slowly I began to feel that I should apologize to Prophetess and Dee. I sensed that I had been unreasonable, or at best uncharitable. And only a couple of hours after we started, we could make out a bridge across the river. In short, I was beginning to feel better.

Until we got closer.

"You're not planning on crossing that!" I burst out.

"Look at the river, Minos," Prophetess replied. "It's starting to turn west ahead of us. Who knows how far it'll take us out of our way if we don't cross now."

"I can guess how far it'll take us out of our way when we fall in and get swept downstream - those of us who can swim."

The structure couldn't possibly have been intended as a bridge, although I couldn't imagine what else it was. It was simply a pair of rusted metal tubes, each two feet across. A web of wires strung from two gigantic towers suspended it over the water across the river's huge width.

"Maybe we're supposed to crawl through the tubes?" Doral asked.

That seemed like an even worse idea than walking over them.

"They're sunk into the ground," I observed as we reached the end of the span. "Even if we wanted to wedge ourselves into a tiny, dark, mile-long tunnel that might be filled with who knows what, there's no way in."

"Not much more than a quarter mile across here, I shouldn't think," Dee said.

It was true enough that the banks were much closer here than they had been farther south, but even a quarter mile balancing on a pair of tubes seemed excessive.

"I still don't think this is a good idea."

"Look on the bright side," Prophetess said. "If it's not meant to be crossed, it's probably not guarded on the other side."

Not meant to be crossed was putting it mildly. The tubes came straight up from the ground before turning at a right angle nearly a hundred feet in the air. Metal rungs went up the sides of both tubes, suggesting a ladder, but they were badly rusted - some all the way through. I set my jaw and climbed, careful not to look down. Why did the person who thought this was a bad idea - and who was also afraid of heights, if truth be told - have to go first?

The group had decided that as a Select, I was both the heaviest and the strongest. So if the ladder could support me, it could support anyone, but if it broke, I had the best chance of hanging on while dangling by one arm.

I suspected that as a Select, I was simply the most expendable.

A hundred feet was a lot of ladder with a pack on my back and my sword shoved uncomfortably through my belt beneath it, where I had hoped it wouldn't interfere with my climbing. About halfway up I got careless.

"Dammit!"

A particularly corroded rung gave way under my right hand. I swung out backwards for an endless heartbeat, left hand and feet slipping, then righted myself. I clutched the ladder for a few trembling moments before I realized my hand was bleeding. I stared at the ugly, jagged stump of the rung above me.

"Let's hope that famous Select immune system resists tetanus," I muttered.

"Are you all right, Minos?" Prophetess called from below.

"I'll live." Probably. For a while. "Watch the rung here - it snapped."

Of course, the fact that the ladder below had held for me didn't necessarily mean it wouldn't break under the next person. I briefly entertained myself by picturing Dee with lockjaw. I had to imagine that after a couple of hours of being unable to speak, his head would explode from the pressure.

I reached the top without further incident, only to realize that had been the easy part. The bridge stretched in front of me. Was it really only a quarter of a mile? It looked a lot farther now. Through the foot-wide gap separating the two tubes, I could see the ground below and the expanse of the river in front. There was a sort of metal mesh platform stretched over the tubes, but the thin wires from which it was woven were in worse condition than the ladder, probably more of a hazard than walking on the round tubes themselves would have been. Heavy cables supported the bridge, with thinner cables at regular intervals creating a kind of railing - but those too were heavily rusted, and some had already snapped, hanging loose like giant cobwebs.

"Are you all right, Minos?" Prophetess repeated.

I didn't want to look back, or down. I nodded my head, although she probably couldn't see it, and started forward.

"Select are disciplined. Select don't have phobias. Specifically, Select aren't afraid of heights," I whispered to myself. Unfortunately, whoever else might have believed that, I didn't.

A quarter mile, if that's really all it was, is still a long way when you're on a rusty metal bridge five feet wide and a hundred feet in the air. I could hear the others following, metal ringing behind me. I still didn't look back. Or down.

I was trying to find something else to think about. Unfortunately, halfway across I began to wonder what this bridge had been intended to transport. Not people, certainly. What would move through those tubes?

Legend said the Darkness could not cross water, but clearly it had crossed the Muddy. Maybe it had help? At some point would the Hellguard have wanted to bring it across? Might they have built a pipeline to take it over the river, disappearing into a hidden tunnel on the other side, shielding it from daylight?

And if so, was the pipeline still in use?

I stopped dead as I visualized a river of the Darkness rushing an inch below my feet.

Logic said that even if the tubes were flooded with the Darkness, the wisest course was to keep moving to get off the bridge as fast as I could. But on the other side of the river were Yoshana's armies, already in our path to Stephensburg. Whether the Darkness was beneath me or not at this very moment, I was charging straight into it.

Why had it seemed so much easier to cross the forests on my way west to the Flow, so much harder as I came back east? *Because this time I was going the wrong way.*

People like you die up there, Dorren had said.

"Minos?"

Prophetess' voice was close behind me now. I looked down. The river rolled along below. The fall would be survivable, and I could swim. I could float back down to Rock Town on a raft, and walk from there to the Flow in relative safety. An end to this fool's errand.

Prophetess had three protectors now - four if you counted Dee - and certainly didn't need me. Taking a quick dive off the edge of the bridge would be very briefly harder than going forward, but vastly safer and easier in the end. I rested my fingers on the rust-browned cable to my right. There was no reason not to go over.

Except that I had said I would take her to Stephensburg.

I shook my head. "You really are an idiot, Minos," I murmured under my breath. And walked on.

No one fell off the bridge or the ladder. In fact, I was the only one who took any injury at all in the crossing. Once I was safely back on the ground I cut a strip off my tunic, wrapped it around my hand, and hoped for the best.

It probably says something horrible about my character that I would have felt a lot better if someone else had gotten hurt, or at least lost their pack.

This side of the river looked much like the other, except that here the red, gold, and brown leaves had already begun to fall with the coming of autumn. It seemed that there was a bit more of a chill in the air as well.

Prophetess had been right - there was no sign of guards, or any other form of human presence. The lack of people didn't make me feel any more comfortable about the purpose of those tubes, but in the bright sunlight it felt silly to voice my fears. When Hadal and Doral decided to fish from the sandbar jutting into the river beneath the bridge, I didn't object - although I watched the rusted span from the corner of my eye.

Either they were amazing fishermen, or the most gullible fish in the world made their home around that sandbar. Half an hour after they cobbled together improvised fishing poles from sticks, we had enough bass to easily feed us all.

Dee patted his belly and belched contentedly. "Fresh fish, a warm fire, bright sunlight, and good company. What more could a man ask for?"

"How about all of this at our destination without a hostile army in our way?" I snapped.

Dee just smiled lazily. "Where's your sense of adventure, Minos?"

Easy for him to say. Judging from past experience, "adventure" meant I fought monsters and savages while he ran away.

I swallowed that comment and confined myself to, "My sense of adventure is saying we should get moving while there's still light. We're lucky that Tess was right about the bridge not being guarded, but somehow that gives me a feeling this might not be a healthy place to be at night."

I glared at the tubes. Nothing horrible poured out, but they say a watched pot never boils. I really didn't like the idea of this one boiling behind my back.

I stood up. "Time to go."

Dee looked wistfully at the fire. "It's nice and warm here," he protested. "And there are fish."

"And the longer we stay here the colder it's going to get. Let's get moving."

"And where exactly shall we go, O sage guide?" He waved his arm expansively, taking in the tree-dotted grasslands stretching east from the river.

I pointed. "Stephensburg is that way." And I started walking through the grass.

There was no road to be found. The grass gave way to a thin forest, carpeted with fallen red and gold leaves. An hour later we found another river blocking our path.

"Oh, for..." I muttered. The water was only forty feet across, a trivial barrier compared to the Muddy, but just as impassable without a bridge.

"Think we can ford it?" Loris asked.

"You have any idea how deep it is?" I retorted. There was almost no current, but the water was a stagnant, dirty brown. The bottom could have been three feet down or thirty.

"So what do you suggest?"

I shrugged. "We need to go north anyway. Might as well follow this thing until we find a bridge."

Miles went by and we found no sign of a bridge. We did see a beaver dam.

"You're not seriously thinking of crossing that?" Prophetess blurted as I stopped and considered the accumulation of sticks.

I had to laugh. "You made me cross half a mile of metal tube that might have had the Darkness flowing through it, but you won't cross fifty feet of beaver dam?"

"The Darkness?" Her face went white. "What makes you think that?"

Doral, Hadal, and Loris crossed themselves and looked around fearfully.

"I don't know it. But those tubes were for transporting something, and it wasn't people." I shrugged. "It's behind us now."

"Then let's get it farther behind us," said Loris. His feet were on the dam before he turned and looked at Prophetess. "Please?"

She nodded. "Let's go."

The land began to fold into rolling hills on the other side of the river. Sundown might come upon us quickly if it caught us in a valley, and our shadows were stretching a dozen feet in front of us when we crested a rise and sighted the town. It was not so much walled as that a ring of buildings had been joined together with brickwork, streets sealed up to leave only one entrance that we could see. The buildings' lower windows had been bricked up as well, and lights blazed in the upper stories even though it was not yet dark.

I could see the telltale signs of ruined foundations stretching far past the wall, but the land had mostly been cleared and given over to fields. This town must have shrunk back within its walls hundreds of years ago, at the very beginning of the Age of Fear.

"Place looks like a fortress," Loris muttered.

"What do you s'pose they're afraid of?" asked one of the others. To be honest, I had a bit of trouble keeping straight which was Hadal and which Doral.

"The Darkness," I answered. "It's thicker the farther east you go. Who knows what else. If they let us in, we may not have to find out the hard way."

Maybe I had spooked myself, but it seemed that the sun was racing to the horizon behind us as we made our way through the stubble of harvested corn to the town's gate. It was a massive thing, wood barred with iron, and even as we approached, it began to swing shut.

"Hello the town," Dee called. We quickened our pace.

A guard in a leather jerkin appeared. The light from a half dozen torches set in the wall cast shadows on his angular face. Under his heavy brows, his eyes looked as black as mine. He turned and over his shoulder snapped, "Telmar!"

A second man came out, taller than the first. He held a huge, lighted torch, long as a spear. I heard Prophetess draw a sharp breath.

"That's not right," she hissed.

I looked more closely at the torch. It was a pole seven feet long, with a massive, brass crucifix atop it. At the base of the cross was a vessel that must have contained oil, because flames licked up from it over the metal. Fire spread across the limbs of the crucified Christ, creating a disturbing impression of motion.

Dee shrugged. "Common enough here in the Source. Fire and cross to ward the Darkness away. These people are Universalists like you, Prophetess."

"We don't set the Lord on fire."

He shrugged again.

We had stopped a dozen yards from the gate. As the sun slipped below the horizon, the looming buildings in front of us only looked more forbidding. With its massive walls and single entrance, this place would not be like the refugee camp - once we went in, there would be no easy way out.

But the idea of spending the night outside the walls appealed even less. I started forward.

The burning cross came down and jabbed toward my face like the spear it resembled. Two long paces away I could feel the heat coming off it.

"What are you doing here?" demanded the first guard, stepping forward. I only then noticed the short sword at his side. His hand was on it.

"We are simple travelers," came Dee's smooth voice from behind me.

"Travelers from where?" snapped the guard.

That was the question. How hostile were these people to foreigners? There was a gate on this side of the town, so someone must be expected to use it. My eyes flicked around. We had approached from the southwest, but a road came in from the north. Had the guards seen us coming? Could we claim to be visitors from the next town up the road?

I had to laugh at myself. We didn't know what that place was called, or if it even existed. It was hard to imagine a less convincing lie.

"Across the river," I said.

"There's nothing across the river." The second man, Telmar, stepped forward and thrust the flaming cross closer to my face.

"God, he's Select!"

The guard's sword was drawn. I shifted my grip on my walking stick. If I was reading his stance right, I could take the swordsman's hand off as I unsheathed my blade. The burning crucifix could be a formidable weapon, but two steps would take me inside the man's guard and then he should be easy to finish. Or, if I misjudged, I would be dead in a few seconds.

"He's my bodyguard," Prophetess said. She stepped forward, her body between me and the swordsman. Who was guarding whom? "It was God's grace that brought me to him. Without his help I would have been killed by the paleos and the drelb we fought to reach here."

There was a collective intake of breath from Huey, Dewey, and Louie. We hadn't told them about the paleos or the drelb.

The swordsman looked impressed. But the other's face only hardened more. "So you've been exposed to the Darkness, and now you bring it here?" He waved the cross, the flames describing a circle in front of my eyes.

"No one here is infected," Dee said. "In fact, the lady is a holy woman. With my own eyes I saw her cast the Darkness out of one of its victims."

The guard barked out a hard laugh. "The only people who command the Darkness are Yoshana's legions. So are you a fiend or a fraud? Either way, you can spend the night outside and be on your way without troubling us."

We were not having a lot of luck with that story. Dee should probably stop telling it.

Prophetess was slowly turning red. I set my hand on her arm. "Let it go. The last place we want to be is in a walled town where we're unwelcome. And it wouldn't be the first time I've been turned away from a gate."

"It's the first time for me," she said tightly.

"You get used to it." You didn't, really, of course. My blood was still pounding in my temples, and I still felt the urge to pull my sword. But that wouldn't accomplish anything except get some people killed - probably including us. We outnumbered the guards, and I could quite possibly deal with both of them myself. But they would have a lot of friends inside. Some of those were probably watching.

"We won't trouble you further," I said, and turned north.

"No. You won't," snapped the man with the burning crucifix, and holding it high, he turned his back on us and marched through the gate. The other gave a brief, almost apologetic shrug, then followed.

We made camp in a field north of the town, within sight of the walls. There was no wood at hand to make a fire. I hoped this close to the walls nothing would molest us.

The night was dark and moonless. To the south, firelight flickered in the town's slitted windows, casting ominous shadows. Above us the wind chased clouds across the stars. It was colder than it had been on the west side of the Muddy, or perhaps it was just that we were moving north and winter was approaching.

I could hear Dee's teeth chattering as we lay down in our bedrolls.

"It would seem only prudent to huddle together for warmth," he muttered.

That set off a debate. We were all cold, and everyone could see the wisdom of his comment. But as far as Huey, Dewey, and Louie were concerned, Prophetess was a holy icon. It would be a sort of blasphemy to huddle up against her.

In the end, Dee was placed on one side of Prophetess, on the theory that he was old and harmless; I didn't think he was that old or entirely harmless. And I was placed on her other side, apparently based on the idea that I wasn't quite human, so it was a bit like her curling up next to a dog. I was offended, but I got to sleep next to her so I wasn't going to complain.

"It's also strange but true that when huddled together, warmth is shared more efficiently if the group is unclothed," Dee commented.

And then he let out a sharp grunt as Prophetess elbowed him in the ribs.

So no, neither that old nor that harmless… but a woman who could face down the Darkness could take care of herself.

"I'm not looking forward to more of that," I grumbled as we broke camp the next morning. Even sharing warmth, it had been a cold and uncomfortable night. And as winter set in, food would begin to get scarce.

"If we continue north we should find a major road east to Crossroads," Dee said. "That's as much of a trade route as is left in our world - there should be inns."

"We're almost completely broke," I pointed out.

"I've never yet found a place where I couldn't trade a story for a meal and a bed," he replied. He paused a bit. "Of course, I'm not sure about the rest of you."

"We could be traveling players. You can be the narrator, Prophetess can be the damsel in distress, I can be the villain, and our three new friends can be… oxen?"

"Ah, haha, you jest…" We looked at each other. It wasn't the worst idea I'd ever had.

As it turned out, we had no opportunity to test the idea. The road wasn't completely overgrown with weeds, suggesting it saw some traffic. But there was no sign of a town, a village, or even an isolated inn. The rolling hills were lightly wooded, the land less threatening than it had been west of the river. But in the end, it was no more hospitable.

I wounded a pheasant with a rock, but it flapped lamely into a thick copse of trees and vanished. We were almost out of food, and I heaved a sigh and waded into the woods, hacking at underbrush with my sheathed sword. But the bird had vanished.

Close to nightfall we passed beneath an underpass and found its shelter supplemented by a wooden lean-to, a single wall of crooked planks braced at an angle by a pair of timbers. A stone-lined fire pit was the only amenity. A tiny stream nearby showed why this site had been chosen.

We gathered wood and boiled water and shared out what was left of the food. With fire and shelter, we were far more comfortable than we had been the night before.

"I don't suppose there's any more food?" Hadal asked wistfully. None of those boys looked like they missed a lot of meals. They weren't fat, but each was solid, with the slight softness of someone who's never spent time starving.

I glared at him.

"I didn't think so," he sighed.

I sat next to Dee. "How well do you actually know this area?"

"Well, in general terms, I'm certainly well acquainted with the geography of the entire continent, and the Source in particular. If you wish me to reduce that encyclopedic knowledge to the raw specifics of this particular, forsaken tract of land…"

"You've never been here before and have no idea where we are."

"Erm. I would think we're about a week southwest of Crossroads. But much sooner than that, once we find the road I mentioned before, we should begin to encounter regular settlements."

"How long until that road, do you think?"

"Oh, I should hope not more than another day."

It was more than another day. The next morning dawned colder than the last, and the temperature dropped as the day went on. Whether it was because of the coming winter or because six people made more noise than two, we saw few animals. The only one that came close enough to kill was a skunk, which glared at us as if daring me to pit my slingshot against its tail. We moved on.

I'm reasonably sure we could have found something to eat if we'd taken time to split up and hunt, but we preferred to push on. It wasn't until the sun was falling that we realized that had been a mistake. We found another shelter almost exactly like the first at the side of the road and gathered acorns to boil for soup. They were just barely better than nothing. Maybe.

At noon the next day I asked Dee, "Any chance we missed that road of yours?"

"Oh, no, I shouldn't think so," he answered. "As I recall it's anchored at the western end by a trading town."

"Not, by any chance, that town that didn't let us in?"

"Erm, no, I think not. That is… no. No, a town that thrives on trade would hardly be so inhospitable."

"Unless, for example, something had changed recently. For example, the Darkness Radiant passing through the area."

"Ah. Well. An interesting point." His brow furrowed in thought. "Still, I think not."

I sighed. "I suppose if we hit the ice sheets we'll know we've gone too far."

"Exactly," Dee said, brightening.

With that dubious reassurance in mind, we gave an hour of the afternoon over to foraging. That netted us two scrawny squirrels, a double handful of frost-burned, slightly overripe blackberries, and a bundle of cattails that Doral swore were edible.

The cattails were easier to chew than boiled acorns, but that was about all that could be said for them. The berries made me wish we had found them a month earlier when they would still have been good. The squirrels we saved for night, when we would hopefully be able to make a fire.

"If the Lord's going to provide, couldn't he provide a big, fat cow that would die of a heart attack when it saw us?" I muttered.

"Don't presume on the Lord's mercy," Prophetess rebuked me. "Although that cow would be nice."

"Maybe a nice wild hog," said Hadal.

"Do you have a boar spear?" I asked. "Because I don't. Those things are mean. If we find one we're more likely to spend the night sitting in a tree than roasting it."

"Then what are you going to use to kill the cow?" he demanded.

"That's why I want it to die of natural causes at our feet, remember? If I'm hoping for things, I don't see why I should hope for things that are realistic. If God can provide mana from heaven, he should be able to deliver a cow with a heart condition."

I shot a look at Prophetess to see if she was offended, but she seemed to be lost in thought. Possibly daydreaming of steak.

No cow presented itself that day. Nor did a town. The shelters seemed to have been positioned assuming a steady pace without stops. It was dark by the time we found the next one. The lean-to here was more exposed than the others. We hadn't seen an overpass all day.

The shelters were angled to block the wind from the northwest. In the night a frigid gust swirled around from the east and blew out the fire. I woke shivering in the dark. Somewhere in the distance, wolves or coyotes were howling. Maybe they were cold too.

Wolves would be a problem if they were hungry enough, although I didn't think they would attack such a large group. A force of six was enough that wolves, drelb, or even paleos would likely steer clear of us. But numbers wouldn't protect us from hunger or the weather.

I couldn't quite make myself get up and gather more firewood. Instead I drifted in and out of an uncomfortable sleep for the rest of the night.

The next day dawned colder still. In fact, "dawn" was something of a misstatement. The sun wasn't visible at all - only the lighter gray of the lowering sky told us it was up.

Of course, it could get worse. Of course, it did.

Around midday a dark, gray wall appeared in our path a mile away, stretching up into the sky. We stopped and stared. It was moving toward us.

"What is that?" demanded Prophetess.

I'd seen it before. "Rain."

Five minutes later I was soaked through and as cold as I had ever been. "We might as well have swum up the Muddy," I shouted over the pounding drumbeat of the water. "We wouldn't be any wetter, and we'd be warmer."

"Not funny!" Loris shouted back.

And it really wasn't. If the rain had been any colder it would have been ice. It came down in an almost vertical sheet, but with just enough wind behind it to blow the stinging drops into our faces. For the first few minutes we pushed into a shambling trot to see if it would pass as quickly as it came, but when it didn't, our pace slowed to a sodden, dismal trudge.

Prophetess murmured under her breath, over and over. I thought it was a prayer, but when I got closer, I could just make out the words. "I'm cold. I'm cold."

"It can't keep this up for too much longer," I said, hoping that like the occasional torrential rain on the Flow, this one would blow through quickly.

But it didn't. We were all shivering, our clothes far too wet to retain any heat.

"Let's get into the trees," Loris suggested.

We staggered off the road, wading through standing water in a little gully at the side. Waist-high grasses lashed at us. But the trees were thin, and their autumn leaves were falling away under the force of the water. There was no shelter there and we returned to the path. Doral slipped and fell heavily as we climbed the slight embankment, and Hadal and Loris had to help him up.

The surface was now awash, turning holes and ruts into deep pools that could catch at our feet. Stepping in them couldn't make us any wetter, but risked turning an ankle.

Trying to find food was hopeless. Not that it mattered. Hypothermia would kill us before hunger did. Yoshana wasn't even going to be a factor.

Eventually the rain slowed from a torrent to a drizzle. The wind picked up further, though, whipping stinging droplets that were almost ice into our faces and stealing the heat from our bodies. My ears and toes had stopped hurting. I knew that was not a good thing. Prophetess and Dee were both shivering uncontrollably - as the rain let up I could actually hear their teeth chatter.

If the temperature dropped below freezing I wasn't confident we would all survive the night.

"Hold up there!"

I raised my head and was stunned to see a tall iron gate in front of me. Not more than a dozen paces away two figures bulked huge in the misty spray.

"Please," Prophetess croaked. "We need shelter."

"Well, I daresay," said one of the figures. "You look like drowned rats."

"Don't be cruel, Tarm," said the other. "Welcome to Opportunity. Come forward and be recognized."

"I t-t-t-told you so," shivered Dee, though for once the smugness of his words was overshadowed by the simple relief in his tone.

Up close the figures resolved into two men of average size, made large by broad-brimmed leather hats and ponchos. Each held a spear casually in one hand.

"A Select," said one, and I tensed. But he only added, "Don't get many of you through here. Where are you coming from?"

I was too tired to even think of lying. "Rockwall. Across the Muddy. We've been on the road for weeks. Haven't had a decent meal or a bed in days. Tried to stop at a town a few days south of here but they wouldn't let us in."

I instantly regretted my rambling, but the guards nodded. "Not real hospitable in Coalville. No worries here, friend. Just give me your arm for testing, and you can go in and get warm."

"My arm?"

"Yeah." The nearer guard pulled a knife from his belt. "Got to test for the Darkness."

"What? We're not infected."

"Didn't say you were, friend, or I'd be poking you with the spear instead of the knife. But rules is rules. I don't know how you do things in Rockwall, but here we test for infection before we let people inside the walls. It's not personal, you know. Not just strangers get tested. Our own folks after they come back from traveling too."

Any other time I might have argued. But there was no fight left in me. I extended my arm and rolled up my soaking sleeve.

The guard made a quick cut on my forearm, not deep. The blade was sharp and my flesh was numb. I barely felt it. He watched blood ooze out for a couple of seconds then nodded his head, satisfied.

"What does that prove?" Prophetess asked.

The guard looked at her as if she were simple. "The Darkness will close up a wound like that."

"Always?"

I thought of the miller's daughter in Brambledge, free of cuts and bruises despite being chained and thrown in a cell, and the instantaneous healing of the drelb's paw.

"I dunno, I suppose a Hellguard or Overlord maybe could control it, let themselves bleed if they wanted to," the man said thoughtfully. "But we've got bigger problems if there's Hellguards or Overlords outside." He stopped, struck by a sudden thought. "You're not with the Darkness Radiant, are you?"

I choked out a laugh that turned into a cough. "Does it look like it?"

"I suppose not."

The others submitted to the test without complaint, and the guards opened the gate.

"There's inns just inside, either side of the street. Over by the east gate they're a bit finer, but these ones down here are cheaper - don't see as much trade, you know."

I nodded thanks and started forward.

"Oh, and three doors up on the right is an outfitters. Don't know how much further you're going, but you'll need better gear if you don't want to freeze."

We picked the first inn on the right, a ramshackle wooden structure with a faded sign that appeared to portray a juggling rooster, simply because it was the first one we passed. I let out a sigh of relief as I crossed the threshold. Inside it was dim, smoky, and stuffy - and warm, and dry. A fire crackled in the hearth, and our whole group was soon crowded around it.

I bartered my silver ring and steel scissors for a large room that the six of us would share. Dee offered an evening of storytelling in exchange for supper and breakfast. The innkeeper, a short, fat, greasy man, was eager to trade gossip, especially once he decided it was true that we came from the wilds across the great river.

"Rumors may be the only trade goods we'll be having for the season," he grunted. "Don't reckon much else'll be coming out of Crossroads for a time."

"And why is that?" Dee inquired around a mouthful of stew.

"Why, Yoshana's army's marching on the city, that's why," he announced, pleased with the drama of his declaration.

Prophetess' spoon clattered on the table.

"We had heard she was following the river," Dee said quietly into the silence.

"Ah, that she was, but Stephen sent an army down the river to meet her. So she shifted north and avoided him. Naught worth speaking of between her and Stephensburg now, so they say. A neat maneuver, but then, I do suppose it's hard to outflank the Darkness itself." His tone conveyed only admiration, no dismay at the fact that the legions of the world's most infamous Overlord now marched on his nation's capital.

"We could go back to the river," I suggested hesitantly.

"And be at least a week behind," Prophetess retorted. "No. We have to continue north, get around her that way." She took a deep, shuddering breath. "The Lord's hand is in this. I must pray and seek counsel at Our Lady."

I opened my mouth to point out that had been my idea and then, with a great effort of will, shut it again. Dee beamed at me. "And that," he said with all the pride of a doting father, "is the beginning of wisdom."

10. City of Refuge

Our host informed us that Our Lady was at least a week to the northeast, more likely two with the winter coming. We were completely unequipped for another two weeks. We needed furs, oiled leather outerwear to shed the rain, provisions. The outfitter next door was more than happy to provide all of that - except that we had nothing to offer in trade.

Dee and Prophetess each promised the burly, bearded man immortality after their own fashion. Dee swore the merchant and his business would be celebrated in story and song. Prophetess was eloquent in seeking his support for her divine mission.

The outfitter was completely unmoved.

"I see no path forward - or back, for that matter," Dee murmured as the three of us huddled over a table back at the inn. "Under normal circumstances, we could have hired out as guards and laborers on a caravan to Crossroads. But now no one's going east, there's no trade north at this time of year, and commerce to the south with our inhospitable friends in Coalville is sporadic. I'm afraid we're stuck here - we'll need to find some sort of employment until trade resumes."

Tears of frustration started in Prophetess' eyes. "We can move faster than Yoshana's army, Dee, but not if we're not moving. There has to be a way. We'll search the city. There must be someone we can persuade to take us north or give us the supplies to go ourselves."

My stomach churned. By any sane measure, the option I was considering was idiotic. What I was contemplating, for a cause I didn't believe in, would be an outrage against my heritage.

So, if it were done, it were best done quickly.

"I'll be back," I muttered, grabbed my walking stick, and left the inn.

Dee and Prophetess gawked at me when I returned twenty minutes later laden with gear.

"You didn't rob him?" Dee burst out.

"No. There's other uses for a sword."

Dee's eyes widened further. "I didn't kill him, either. That blade was carbon steel, forged in the traditional style. I don't think there are more than a few dozen like it in the world today. He knew what it was worth."

Prophetess' mouth rounded into a silent exclamation. "You... you gave him your sword?"

"No, giving him my sword would have been stupid. I traded him my sword for furs, oilskins, rations, boots, and the rest of this." I gestured at the pile.

Prophetess jumped up and threw her arms around me. "Thank you, Minos!"

Did that make it worthwhile? Right at that moment, with her head on my shoulder and her soft hair against my cheek, it did. "Well, that sword wouldn't do us much good against Yoshana if we can't reach her. Besides, somehow I don't think I can beat her in a stand-up fight no matter what sword I'm carrying."

We ate and rested well that evening and Prophetess found a church that offered mass. We left early the next day. The sun had come out, and much of the water had evaporated or oozed into the soil. But what was left had turned into a hard crust of ice and frost, for the air had turned colder still. Our breath misted in front of us, and we were glad for our new winter gear. It still seemed a good trade for the sword, and I could put aside the twinge of having traded away my only valuable possession, my legacy from my parents. In any case, that's what I told myself.

"I'm going to miss that place," Loris said. "Best food I've had in a long time."

Which, unfortunately, was true. Supper had allegedly been a lamb stew, which had seemed more like fatty mutton than lamb. Breakfast had been a sort of runny oatmeal with pieces of very old apple in it. And yet, it had in fact been the best we'd eaten in weeks. And would almost certainly be the best we'd have for weeks to come.

I'd never expected to have such fond memories of Thassa's cooking back in the Hole.

"Well, will you look at that," Loris added, poking my shoulder. I'd never cared for being prodded, but I had to take the familiarity as a good sign. So far, the three friends had regarded me with an uncomfortable mixture of fear, disgust, and grudging respect. A willingness to touch me was a step forward.

I followed Loris' pointing finger. We were leaving through the town's northern gate, but over the walls to the south we could clearly see a great metal cross, two hundred feet high, rising into the air. The huge monument must have been hidden from us by the previous day's rain - or we had simply missed it, numbed as we were from the cold.

"That's got to be a good sign for the journey," Loris said.

I had never quite understood why a means of torturing people to death was supposed to be reassuring, but I kept my mouth shut and nodded my head.

Our host had assured us that if we'd gone east, we would have found towns, or at least inns, an easy day's walk apart. Heading north we would have none of that. But the wooden shelters continued. The next day it began to snow, scattered flakes at first, and then a heavy fall of the stuff. But it was far less penetrating than the rain, and our new clothes turned it well. It didn't last long, though the sky turned a gray so relentlessly dull that it seemed the sun must have vanished forever.

"Fimbulwinter," Dee muttered. When I looked at him he explained, "The twilight of the gods in Norse mythology. At the end of the world the sun dies and the earth is plunged into endless winter before the final armageddon."

"That's not a Christian belief."

He grinned so widely I could see his chapped lips crack. "The task of the scholar is to find the elements of truth in everything. The Norse gods were simple barbaric superstition, not at all like our Prophetess' doctrine." He chuckled, although I didn't see the humor in what he said next. "But it hardly seems implausible that the world will perish in cold and Darkness, now does it?"

Three days and another snowstorm later, the road led us past the edge of a deserted city of some size. It was surprisingly intact. There was no shortage of shelter, but as the gray light began to fade, Hadal pointed out a faint glow to the east.

"What's that?"

The light reflected from the smothering clouds, pale but white and steady, not like the flickering red glow of firelight.

"Let's find out," Dee said eagerly.

"Let's not," I retorted. "This place is dead. Whatever's making that light, I'm not sure it's anything we want to meet."

"Where's your sense of adventure, Minos?" Dee repeated.

"I'm pretty sure it froze and fell off in that rainstorm. Why don't you go back and look for it?"

Prophetess smiled tolerantly at our bickering. "Let's go see what it is. Carefully."

There's an unearthly, lifeless silence when the ground is covered in snow. There were no birds, no animals, no gentle rush of blowing leaves or grass. Sometimes the wind came whistling up, scattering icy crystals through the air, but otherwise a total stillness prevailed. Except the crunching of our boots, and Dee's insistence on trying to start a conversation every five minutes. Each time I poked him with my stick.

As part of the exchange for my blade, I had gotten a five foot hickory staff from the outfitter - good, tough wood, but if it came to a fight, it was no sword. Still, the stick was over a foot longer than my sword had been, which was an advantage for poking loudmouthed occultists.

As we neared the center of town, the buildings became grander and better preserved. It was strange that none of it had been stripped. There were only a handful of the great towers that formed the core of Acceptance or Oldtown, but there were many large structures of brick and stone, decorated with carving that as much as declared, "We built this for the ages."

Unfortunately, there had come a time when the ages didn't care anymore.

We had been following what must have been a street, although the carpet of snow made it impossible to be sure. Our path ended in a row of buildings. Giant, leafless trees filled the spaces between them. The light was brighter here, its source clearly nearby.

"You're sure about this?" I hissed to Prophetess. She considered a moment and nodded.

The bare trunks of the trees gave some cover as we made our way between buildings. Beyond it we peered out into an open rectangle, lightly wooded, and framed on all sides by more structures. It stretched perhaps a hundred yards across and a quarter mile long. The light rose from a point south of the rectangle, obscured by a large, domed building at its end.

"What do you suppose this place was?" Prophetess asked.

I shrugged. "Parade ground, maybe? This could have been some kind of military complex."

Dee favored me with a little smirk but, amazingly, held his peace.

We moved south in the shadow of the buildings, finding what cover we could behind trees and columned porticos. I glared nervously at the gaping windows whose glass had long ago been shattered. I saw no footprints of anything larger than a rabbit in the snow, but who knew what might lair in those abandoned places?

As we crept past the domed structure, Dee suddenly bounded forward and pointed. "Look!"

"You idiot," I growled, and stumbled after him, my feet breaking through crusts of ice and catching in the loose snow beneath.

Then I stopped and stared. A raised platform stood in front of us, dotted with posts. Each post held a single globe that shone the purest white. Some few were dead, the globes crushed or black, but most produced the steady glow we had seen reflected from miles away. Crystals swirled around them in the wind, gleaming in the misty light.

It was breathtakingly beautiful.

"I thought so," Dee cried triumphantly. "This was one of the ancients' great centers of learning. One of the world's greatest libraries lies below us, marked by the eternal light of truth."

"I don't know about eternal," Loris said. "Some of them lights have burned out."

Dee's face fell. "Yes they have."

We sheltered in the lee of the domed building for the night. Despite the cold and wind, no one was much inclined to go in. Dee complained bitterly that the wisdom of the ages was rotting away beneath our feet, but even he acknowledged the risks involved in exploring.

"We don't have time to do it carefully, John," I told him. My next remark was needlessly cruel - but I made it anyway. "Of course, you're welcome to stay behind and explore. Or try to find your way into it tonight."

The look he gave me was so reproachful that I added, "If we survive what's coming, we can return together. And if we don't, Prophetess says the world's going to end anyway."

Prophetess must not have approved of my tone, because she said waspishly, "The Lord told me I must confront Yoshana to save the world. He didn't tell me we have to survive."

There wasn't much to say to that, so I wrapped myself in my furs and went to sleep.

Dee assured us that not only did he know where we were but, if we walked due north, we would meet up with the main road again. To my great surprise, he was right.

"Strange that nothing got looted in the city," I said. "It should be worthwhile even for people from Opportunity to salvage here, if there's no town closer."

"They're afraid," Dee said. "They say the Darkness was created in this very place, centuries ago."

I had never seen anyone's mouth literally fall open in shock. I realized mine had. I glared at the occultist. "And you didn't think it might be a good idea to tell us before we spent the night here?"

"If I'd told you, you wouldn't have spent the night," he replied with a tranquil smile.

The next days passed in a white haze. The land was flat as a tabletop, and the wind howled across it. Every night there was a shelter, and then there was more snow. What fallen wood we could find was not dry enough to catch fire. We refilled our water skins with snow, and it melted next to our bodies. We were all well past tired of the tough, chewy pemmican that made up our rations, but there was no other food to be found. Once we spied a small pack of gaunt wolves that looked hungrier than we were. Our two parties traded suspicious glares and went our separate ways.

The road turned sharply east at a giant pit in the ground. Dee said it was a mine of some sort. If it was, the scale dwarfed the Flow - if we clawed at the Last Days' garbage for a hundred years, we would never dig so deep.

The occultist said the place had been abandoned because we were within miles of the ice sheets themselves. I was completely prepared to believe him. The wind from the north was biting. Our clothing continued to prove its worth, but every inch of exposed skin stung, and had to be covered periodically lest it become numb and frostbitten. I could feel ice forming on the hairs inside my nose when I breathed.

I had lost track of the days by the time we saw smoke. Once again, Hadal was the first to point it out. "What do you suppose it's from?"

"Who cares? It's going to be warm." If it turned out to be Yoshana's legions roasting their enemies, and they intended to use us as logs on the fire, at that moment I wouldn't have complained.

The smoke proved to be rising, not from the flames of war, but from the chimney of a small, stone farmhouse standing alone. I would have said nothing could keep us from stopping and knocking at that door, except that as we approached, gold winked in the distance beyond. By the time we reached the house, the light had resolved into a dome, flanked by spires, all rising above a vast curtain wall.

"Is that...?" Prophetess breathed.

"Our Lady," Dee nodded.

We lurched into a staggering trot that brought us, gasping and exhausted, to the foot of the stone wall. It reared thirty feet into the air, the road leading to a huge, ornately carved gate that seemed too massive to move. Around it spread houses and small shops, wisps of smoke rising from most. But we had eyes only for the portal in front of us.

"Umm..." said Loris, "How do we get in?"

"Knock?" I suggested.

No one moved. Even Prophetess seemed overawed.

"Oh, fine. I'll do it." Why shouldn't a manifestation of the Fall demand admittance to the Universal Church's citadel?

On closer inspection, a much smaller door was set into the great gate, with a simple, iron ring mounted on the dark, deeply carved wood. I rapped with it, then, unimpressed with the sound, rapped harder.

Nothing happened.

"Nobody home?" I suggested.

I took another look at the door. Next to it hung a chain, vanishing into the very top of the wall above the gate. Well… it probably wouldn't bring boiling oil down on my head if I pulled on it. So I tried.

A bell clanged, deep and loud, shocking in the winter stillness. I took a step back. "Well, that should get their attention," I muttered nervously.

Within a minute a small, wooden panel at the level of my face slid aside. The eyes staring out at us were protected by an iron grate set into the other side of the door.

"We open for trade at Sext," came a man's voice. "You can stay in the town until then."

Dee stepped smoothly in front of me. "We are not traders, but pilgrims."

The doorman seemed taken aback. "At this time of year? Are you mad?"

"He said we were pilgrims. He never said we were smart," I grumbled.

Somewhat to my surprise, the man laughed, and noisily shot a pair of massive bolts securing the door. We stepped inside in single file, Dee taking the lead. "Four men, a woman and a Select knocked at the gates of Our Lady one freezing day," the doorman said. "That's either a bad joke or one hell of a story."

I thought about pointing out that the Select was a man too, but I was inside the wall, and I preferred to stay that way. It seemed wiser to let the comment pass.

This side of the wall was worth staying on. A small patch of fields and orchards, snow-covered now, nestled inside the northwest corner of the wall. Straight ahead, a road wound between two small lakes. Beyond the town spread in a wondrous vista, all cream-colored brick and peaked roofs. It was smaller than the great cities like Acceptance or Oldtown, but infinitely more substantial than a village like Brambledge. The buildings most resembled the dead town where we had seen the eternal lights, but this place lived. Smoke rose from the chimneys, and even at a distance we could see fur-bundled figures shuffling between buildings. The road led directly to the golden-domed edifice we had seen from a distance, a steepled church rising next to it.

I was not the only one gawking, and the guard was enjoying it. He smiled broadly and said, "It's something, isn't it? Even living here my whole life I don't get tired of looking at it. Guess it must be even more impressive if you're coming from the back of beyond."

I bristled a bit - I had seen towers that overtopped these by hundreds of feet, passed through cities where all of Our Lady would have been swallowed up like a single stand of trees in a forest. But he wasn't wrong.

"It's something," I agreed.

Prophetess made the sign of the cross on her chest and bowed her head.

"Well, we don't get pilgrims this time of year, but guess I'd best take you to the rectory and let them get you squared away."

And with that he led us down the road past a squat building that had the look of a barracks. I heard a horse whinny from the far side - so a stable as well. No other guards appeared, though, and our escort carried no visible weapons at all.

Dee began to ask him this and that, all manner of questions about the town, and the man happily chattered away. Apparently we had just missed the turning of the fall leaves, which in his opinion was a sight unparalleled in the known world; as well as the fall apples, which were the finest food known to man. I began to wonder whether he was a guard or a tour guide.

A black iron fence ten feet high and topped with spikes encircled the inner compound, so perhaps the people of Our Lady were not so trusting after all. I wondered aloud why the outer wall extended so far beyond the buildings, which must make it harder to defend.

The guard's eyes narrowed a bit, then he smiled again. "You Select, always ready for a fight, eh? No secret to it, I suppose. Having the lakes, and some fields and orchards, all inside the wall gives us food and water if we're besieged. The greater part of the town's outside the wall to the south, but those folks can always take refuge inside if there's an attack. Hasn't happened in my time, though it did in my father's." He crossed himself. "God willing I won't see it, nor my children either."

Prophetess and I exchanged glances. Yoshana's legions would be passing a hundred miles south of here, seeking to conquer the whole of the Source. War might come to this beautiful place far too soon. I looked at the iron fence. Posts as thick as my wrist were spaced ideally for defenders to thrust spears between them. Attackers would face plunging fire from the buildings beyond. And the thirty foot stone outer wall would not yield easily. The Universal Church had given thought to war as well as peace. But I doubted they'd reckoned with Yoshana and the Darkness.

A small guardhouse stood inside the ornately wrought gate at the end of the road. A man emerged, wrapped in black furs. Only the plumed steel helm on his head identified him as a guard. A pike leaned against the guardhouse wall, but he made no move to take it.

"By God it's cold out here, Allem," he protested. "What have you got that's dragging me away from my fire?"

"Ah, quit your bellyaching, Tolf," retorted our guide good-humoredly. "I had to walk 'em in from the outer gate and you don't see me complaining."

"Yeah, but you kept yourself warm running your mouth the whole time, or I'm a Select." He ran his eyes over my face. "Oh, look, you've got a Select. Wherever did you find one of those?"

"Fished him out of the lake, didn't I? They're pilgrims, you silly bastard."

There followed some debate over who was a bastard, and by whom, and who had been sleeping with whose mother, sister, grandmother, and sheep. It seemed wildly inappropriate for the citadel of the Church. I turned to Prophetess, expecting to find her face burning, but she just wore a tolerant smile.

"Grew up on a farm with two brothers," she whispered.

"Well, best get 'em inside before they freeze," said Tolf. He produced a massive keychain and fumbled at the lock with gloved hands. "Suppose they'll need to go to the rectory to see Father Juniper. Heh. A Select. What a thing."

Our original escort left us at the gate after exchanging a few parting insults with Tolf. We climbed a little slope past a candle-filled grotto. Some sort of shrine, I supposed. The rectory proved to be the impressive, golden-domed building we had seen from a distance.

The place reeked of antiquity. The structure was in good repair, but age hung on it, from the weathering of the ivy-coated, cream-colored bricks to the oft-patched cracks in the pavement underfoot. We entered through a wooden door, large, but not of the scale I would have expected. Maybe it was the servants' entrance.

Inside, dark marble steps rose to a landing. I blinked, eyes adjusting to the dimness. Before us stood a high stool and a sort of lectern with a little bell on it. A set of double doors separated us from the rest of the building.

"Oh, sure," Tolf grumbled. "I can stand outside in the cold all day, but this lazy git can't be bothered to sit where he belongs in the nice, warm foyer." He rang the bell with alarming force, sending up a raucous clangor. "Probably off drinking."

Nothing happened, and Tolf's face darkened. This time I was amazed that the ringing didn't send the clapper flying off.

I heard the sound of running feet and a young man in a rough woolen tunic and pants burst through the doors.

Tolf surveyed him sourly. "Not even a novice?" He turned to me. "No robe," he whispered.

"Postulant," said the youth, bowing his head.

"Pustulant, more like it. Off dipping your beak while you were supposed to be watching the door, I'll wager. Who knows what all might have come through? Look, I've a Select here." Tolf pointed accusingly at me, clear evidence of the kind of abomination that might penetrate an unguarded door. He winked.

"I was just using the bathroom," the postulant stammered.

Tolf's accusing finger shifted from me to him. Dee and I exchanged glances. It was all too easy to guess the direction the guard's harassment of the boy might take next.

"Well, he's here now," Dee interrupted hastily. "Who was it you said we needed to see? Father Juniper, was it?"

Tolf shot Dee a disapproving look. The postulant seized the opportunity like a drowning man grasping a log. "I'll run fetch him!" And he was gone.

"Got to watch these kids," Tolf said severely, shaking his head. "This younger generation, heading straight to hell they are." He either hadn't noticed or had willfully ignored the fact that none of us except Dee was older than the postulant.

Only a short time passed before we heard the youth returning, his voice raised in excitement. The inner door opened, and the postulant anxiously followed a stout, bearded man. Even I could tell he was a priest by his robe and collar, although the pipe he was puffing didn't fit my image of a holy man.

His eyes widened a bit when he saw me. "So. We really do have a Select." He stuck out a thick-fingered hand. "I've never met a Select before. Welcome. I'm Father Juniper."

"Minos," I said, taking his hand a little warily. He had a strong grip.

"And I am Doctor John Dee, student of all matters physical and metaphysical," the occultist chimed in.

The priest looked at him through slightly narrowed eyes. "You, I've heard of."

Dee beamed, although I didn't get the feeling the comment had been meant in an entirely positive way.

Loris, Hadal, and Doral all introduced themselves. Prophetess looked down, then met the priest's eyes squarely.

"I'm very pleased to meet you, Father. I am called to be Prophetess of the Lord. Will you hear my confession before I speak to the Metropolitan?"

Father Juniper's eyes widened and he pinched the bridge of his nose, as if struck by a sudden, blinding headache. I recognized the feeling.

"And I thought the Select was going to be the strange one," he muttered with his teeth clenched on his pipestem.

We had been shown to hot showers, after which I was the only one whose skin still looked gray. And we had been fed. It was simple bread, cheese and stew, but it was warm and none of it was hard, stale, or tasted like it had spent two weeks inside a leather sack.

In a show of trust that amazed me, we had been given almost complete freedom within the huge compound. Dee had been shown to a library and had promptly vanished. Loris, Hadal, and Doral were resting in a guest room that was small and spartan, but clean and warm.

I was sitting in a public area of the huge rectory. Father Juniper had explained simply that places behind locked doors were off limits to us, but we could go anywhere else. Then he had taken Prophetess to hear her confession. I couldn't imagine what she might have to confess.

I had found a comfortable, padded bench in front of a large, elaborate clock. It was like no timepiece I had ever seen. The face was beautifully enameled blue, darker in the center, lighter toward the edges. But there seemed to be two hour tracks, eccentric circles one within the other and joined at the bottom. The outer track was gold, the inner silver. A golden sun reined over the outer circle at twelve o'clock, while below at the top of the inner circle an opening showed the phase of the moon. Hours were marked on both circles, and so were what I took to be times of prayer - sext, none, vespers, and so forth. The elaborately wrought hour hand appeared to float, not visibly joined to the dial. At the moment, it showed a bit after five in the afternoon, following the golden outer circle but nearing the point of convergence with the silver circle within.

Father Juniper joined me there. "I see you found the Ermel Clock."

I nodded.

"It's one of my favorite things," he continued. "From before the Fall. You see, the hour hand follows the inner track during the hours of the night, but extends to the outer track during the day. It helps remind me that even when we descend into darkness, we still emerge into a new dawn."

"And then fall into darkness again."

"Well. Yes. I prefer to think of it as showing man's perpetual passing through darkness into the light."

We sat in silence for a time. Every minute or so he blew smoke from his pipe.

"My friend... Prophetess..." I sputtered to a halt.

"Yes. Of course, one doesn't simply arrive at Our Lady and demand to see the Metropolitan. There are procedures. She's in the hands of the bureaucracy now."

"Of course. I suppose if someone really was a prophet... or thought they were..."

"Not for me to say what she is or isn't, my boy. She certainly thinks she is." He puffed several times. "There are at least two, maybe three people between her and the Metropolitan who think she's crazy."

I winced. "I don't suppose there's a lot of precedent for a farm girl saying she's a prophet and trying to round up an army to save the world."

"Oh, I wouldn't say that. There's Saint Joan of Arc. Pretty directly on point, there. That'll make sure she gets a hearing, at least. Still some guilt within the Church about burning a saint at the stake, even a thousand years later. But there are a lot of frauds and lunatics, too."

I bit my lip, then blurted out, "I saw her cast the Darkness out of a woman. I'm no Universalist, Father, but if there is such a thing as a prophet, she probably is one."

The priest gave me a long look, took a deep pull on his pipe, and blew out a huge cloud of smoke. "Why do I always get all the strange ones?"

I saw little of the others in the days that followed. Dee remained ensconced in the library, emerging only to eat and sleep. Loris, Hadal, and Doral seemed content to do nothing other than eat and sleep. They seemed to be convinced that Prophetess would now raise an army and march triumphant into Stephensburg. Until they joined that glorious host, they were going to rest up and fill their bellies.

I wandered around, exploring. The compound was beautiful, and while I got a few odd looks, no one threw anything at me, or even said anything rude. Still, soon enough I drifted down to the guard post where we had entered and found Tolf, who seemed happy to see me. Since I now had no weapon aside from my hickory stick, he arranged for me to practice fighting with staves with him and some other guards. I picked up plenty of bruises but soon enough was giving them back. The exercise in the crisp air felt good, and I no longer felt quite as unarmed as I had since giving up my sword.

At one point, Tolf commented, "So your friend the prophet is going to lead an army against Yoshana, eh?"

I blinked sweat out of my eyes and shook my head. "First off, I don't know if she's a prophet or not. Second, the only army she's got is the five of us you saw come in with her."

Tolf feinted at my head, then swept his staff into the back of my shin, dumping me on the ground. "Sure does look like she needs a better army."

Father Juniper found me after one of the practice sessions, slightly sweaty and absentmindedly rubbing at the new dents in my staff as I watched the Ermel Clock pass its noon apex and begin the daily slide back toward darkness.

He flicked the staff with a thick finger. "Hickory?"

I nodded.

"Tough wood, hickory. Hard to shape. But it holds like almost nothing else once you've turned it into what it's meant to be." He gave me a little smile that I didn't know how to read. "You're wanted at a hearing for your friend. Doctor Dee has already spoken about the incident at Brambledge, but by all accounts you were closer."

"What should I tell them?"

He sucked in smoke, then blew it out through his nose like some sort of bearded dragon. "I'd suggest the truth."

The Advocate for Justice sat in a little office with a high window, light streaming through it onto his desk of pale wood. He waved me to a seat across from him, then rose and shut the door behind me.

"The title sounds more impressive than the role really is," he said easily. He rested his chin on steepled hands, looking at me unblinkingly. His piercing eyes and slightly hooked nose reminded me of a bird of prey.

The title "Grand Inquisitor" would have been more intimidating, but not by much. He gave me a little smile that I found utterly unconvincing.

"The question at hand," he went on, "is whether your nameless friend, who rather maddeningly insists on calling herself only Prophetess, is one in fact, or just in her mind." He looked at me expectantly.

"And... if she isn't?" I asked.

He waved a hand airily. "Oh, no ill will befall her, young man. The Church hasn't burned heretics or witches for almost a thousand years."

"Unless they happen to be infected with the Darkness."

"Ah! As you must know, that is not a punishment, but a violent and lethal cure for a most terrible disease. And ultimately, that brings us to why you're here." The predatory eyes locked onto mine. If this man was intimidated by my blank, black gaze, it didn't show. "Your friend would generally be easy enough to dismiss. Certainly she's likable, and quite intelligent despite her rudimentary schooling. Charismatic, even. That trio you picked up near the river seem very taken with her, although I dare say they're intellectually... undemanding." The little smile widened, inviting me to join him in mocking the rubes. I could tell I was being manipulated - which didn't mean it wasn't working.

"Doctor John Dee is also rather taken with her, although I think somewhat in the sense of a man examining a new species of beetle. One way or another, there will be a story for him from that acquaintance."

I found myself staring at tiny nicks and scars in the Advocate's desk. Centuries worth, no doubt, old gouges worn smooth over time, new scratches added on top. A chronicle of tiny corruptions and imperfections. The sort of thing that, among humans, the Advocate would try to obliterate.

He was looking fixedly at me again. "So that brings us to you. A Select. A member of a race renowned for its rationality. Both this so-called Prophetess and the equally self-professed Doctor John Dee say you were in a jail cell when she cast the Darkness out of a peasant girl."

"A miller's daughter, actually," I said, meeting the priest's eyes. "And yes, I was there. And yes, she cast the Darkness out of the girl."

"Through the power of the Lord?"

I leaned back in my chair. This would be the crux of the question. *Be honest,* Father Juniper had said. "I don't know. It's pretty well understood that the Darkness finds it easier to possess the weak-minded than the strong-minded. And Prophetess is nothing if not strong-minded. I've never seen or heard of anyone persuading someone else to reject the Darkness - lending their mental strength to the struggle, I guess. But it seems possible."

"Ahh. Then you don't see a miracle."

"With all due respect, sir, I don't share your faith or Prophetess'. She persuaded. And she prayed. I couldn't begin to tell you if the prayers were even orthodox, much less if they followed your rite of exorcism. All I can tell you is it worked." I thought a moment more. "That, and though I don't share your faith, I've never seen anyone represent it better than that woman. She's fearless. Not that she's never afraid, but she'll always do what she thinks is right anyway. Forget Brambledge. I've seen her bury days-old corpses I would have left lying. I've seen her offer comfort to people I would have preferred to avoid. And I've seen her smack a drelb in the face with a stick when I'm sure she would rather have been running away."

The Advocate's eyes widened. So no one had mentioned the drelb before. "I don't know what a Universalist prophet looks like. But if there is such a thing, I hope it looks like her."

Two days later our whole group was called to an audience with the Metropolitan.

"The bishop of the western world, Minos," Dee enthused. "Quite an honor."

We entered the basilica through a small side door, its frame carved with images of saints. I read the words beneath and realized that one was Joan of Arc. That had to be a good sign. Didn't it? Prophetess crossed herself, Dee opened the door for her, and we went in.

We were clean, but our clothes were the same ones we had worn through the whole long trek. We approached the ragged edge of respectability, and I couldn't say from which direction. That is, until I took in the interior of the church. Less impressive than the rectory from the outside, within it was a marvel of gilded marble columns, ornate carvings, and stained glass. Flights of angels looked down on us from a deep blue ceiling dozens of yards above our heads. If a pack of mangy dogs had wandered in and relieved themselves on the floor, they wouldn't have looked much more out of place than we did.

I glanced around nervously. I had only occasionally entered a church, always just slightly afraid that I might burst into flames. The stern gazes of the saints surrounding us looked like they could easily ignite better men than me.

I wanted to slip into a pew at the back, or maybe hide behind a pillar, but Dee kept tugging at me. "We're up front," he hissed.

Most of that vast space was empty, but a cluster of robed priests congregated near the altar. And some rumor must have spread that excitement was forthcoming, because small knots of people were beginning to filter in, lurking in the wings. They didn't look threatening - except in the sense that a crowd gathering to watch a heretic burned at the stake might be threatening if you happened to be the heretic in question.

Atop the dais in front of us, a figure in purple stood alone before the altar. He was not a large man, but he stood straight and radiated authority. Dee went down on one knee and sketched the sign of the cross. I bowed my head.

"Kneeling might be wise," Dee whispered.

"I was taught it's rude to pretend a religious conviction you don't hold," I murmured back.

"I can see why the Select are unpopular."

Dee nudged me into the second pew next to Loris, Hadal and Doral. Prophetess sat in front of us, between two priests. One was Father Juniper.

Another priest stood at the foot of the dais, bowed to the man on it, turned to us, and announced, "His Eminence the Metropolitan of Our Lady, Bishop of the West." He could have added "leader of the Universal Church in the known world," but I suppose that would have been gilding the lily.

The Metropolitan glanced from side to side. He gave the impression of a serious man, thin and with close-cropped white hair. Still, I thought I detected just the hint of a smile as he said, "I would have preferred to keep this a more private matter, but the news that a prophet may be among us has aroused quite a lot of curiosity in our community."

I could see Prophetess' shoulders tense, and apparently the Metropolitan did as well. "I don't blame you, child. It's natural enough, I suppose." He surveyed the church with a long look, before his eyes settled on her again. "Some members of this community have suggested we are called to raise an army to march with you on Stephensburg. A number of others have suggested, rather more forcefully, that you should be tried as a fraud and a heretic."

I shot furtive glances toward the exits to either side. There were far too many people between us and the doors, and I was unarmed.

"The question, of course," the Metropolitan continued, "is whether you are in fact a prophet."

I could see Prophetess shift on the bench as she prepared to stand. And also Father Juniper's hand rest on her leg as he ever so gently shook his head.

"Fortunately, we are not required to answer that question. You have requested nothing more than shelter from the weather, and assistance in reaching Stephensburg. Those things may be provided out of charity, without the need to address the presence or absence of divine inspiration behind the request."

A low rumbling of conversation broke out.

"It has been argued," the Metropolitan said more loudly, in a voice that suddenly filled the basilica, "that it is in our interest to move now to oppose Yoshana, while she can still be opposed. It has been argued that we are a church militant. That does not, however, mean we are a church military. It has been a thousand years since the Universal Church launched crusades into the wider world. I don't propose to start today."

Some of the muttering died down.

"It has conversely been argued that we must not permit the preaching, much less give encouragement, to a false prophet who claims to speak in the name of the Lord. Certainly there have been a multiplicity of self-appointed prophets since the Fall, but none save Saint Arvan and Saint Siles were found by the Church to be worthy of the name."

Again Prophetess stirred, and again the bearded priest restrained her with the slightest pressure.

"I have also been reminded of the Gospel according to Mark." The Metropolitan's eyes shifted briefly to Dee. "Our Lord's disciples told him of a man who cast out demons in the Lord's name, but was not one of them. The disciples commanded the man to stop. But Jesus told them that no one who did God's work in his name could be our enemy, and that those who are not against us are with us."

He looked back to Prophetess. I realized his eyes were the same bright gray as hers. "Of course, the gospel continues that any who lead the innocent into sin would better have a mill wheel tied around their necks and be thrown into the sea."

The Ice Fields were frozen over, but a hole could no doubt be cut if needed. I wondered if the Church kept mill wheels handy. Could we make it to the exit after all?

"As I said, I am not prepared to reach a conclusion on this point. At this time, there is no need to do so. Your interests and ours coincide on the matter of Yoshana establishing herself in Stephensburg. You will be given mounts and provisions." He paused. "And any who choose to accompany you may be excused from their duties to do so. It is in the Church's interests to have witnesses in Stephensburg."

The rumbling increased into a babble of voices, which the Metropolitan permitted for a long moment before he held up his hand for silence. "Go with the blessings of God."

11. Face to Face

The horses were proving to be a mixed blessing. We made somewhat better time, but I had not ridden for years, and never for an extended period. I was sore in muscles I didn't know I had, and chafed in places best left unmentioned. Prophetess had laughed herself silly at me the first time I got down and lurched forward in a stiff, shuffling stumble. Until she got down herself. She was less of a horseman than I.

Despite the Metropolitan's grant of leave, our ranks had not swelled by much. Tolf, two more guardsmen, and a pair of postulants had joined our group. Loris had complained loudly, bitterly disappointed in the lack of an army. Prophetess had silenced him, saying the Church had been generous in what it had supplied us, and stating that the Lord had never said she would lead a great host - only that she must go herself. She counted every other hand joined with hers as a great blessing.

Still, she was tense and withdrawn. I agreed that we had done well enough by the Metropolitan. Some scruffy horses, a supply of food, and five new companions was a lot better than being burned at the stake or thrown into the sea. But I wouldn't have minded ten thousand spears ranked around us - and I sensed Prophetess wouldn't either.

"Force on force would never have worked," Dee said. "I hardly think the Church is in a position to instantly place at our disposal an army large enough to face the world's most dangerous Overlord and an army of veterans."

"No," I agreed. "But if Yoshana's planning to besiege Stephensburg, even a relatively small relief force hitting from behind could break the siege." I shrugged.

"Do you think she has a plan?" Dee asked, cocking his head toward Prophetess.

"I think she's winging it." I paused. "And I think she's scared."

Dee nodded, silent for once. That might have been the most frightening thing of all.

Villages were strung all along the road southeast to Stephensburg, proof of its trade with Our Lady. The Church had provided us with letters of credit that meant we slept at inns rather than out in the weather. Despite the cold and the saddle sores, it was the most physically pleasant week of travel I could recall.

But though my belly was well filled, the farther south we went the less comfortable I felt. We began to meet travelers heading north, a few at first, then a steady stream of wagons, mules, and families staggering under the weight of their possessions. Refugees.

"Yoshana's coming," was the common refrain.

"Why Stephensburg?" I asked Dee. "Isn't Yoshana picking a fight with the Universal Church by coming here?"

"That may be part of why she's doing it. If she takes the Source, the Church can't lead it against her. And I hardly think she'd be welcome in the capital of the Green Heart. What with having invaded it before her death and conversion."

"It's symbolic," said Prophetess, coming up next to us. "Saint Siles was driven out of Stephensburg. He's the last canonical prophet of the Universal Church. Yoshana calls herself a prophet - she's bringing the Word back to Siles' home."

"Why was Siles kicked out in the first place?"

"For being a pain in the neck." She managed a weak smile. "It's in the job description."

One evening as we plodded into the fenced yard of a large inn, a groom stared at us in disbelief.

"You're the only people I've seen heading south in three days."

Dee raised his eyebrows, surveying the shifting mass of horses, oxen and other beasts of burden that were churning the inn yard into mud. "It looks like all of Stephensburg is heading north."

The groom, no older than I, worked his mouth and spat. "Yoshana's legions slipped past Stephen's army. Folks are saying the troops he's got left are fortifying the inner city. Say he'll give up the Midwalls without a fight."

"That's madness," blurted Tolf. "Why would he trap himself like a rat in one square mile? If he's got even a tenth her strength he should be able to hold the outer walls for weeks at least. Pull back if he needs to, sure, but why start that way?"

"That's what they say," the lad replied truculently.

Tolf shook his head and addressed Prophetess. "Three layers of defenses at Stephensburg. There's a good stone wall around the whole city. A second around the administrative precinct. Everything between's called the Midwalls - where most folks live. In the very center is Stephen's Keep."

The soldier chewed his lower lip. "Stephen's no warrior, but he wouldn't just abandon the outer wall. No one would." He waved his arm at the yard. "This lot'll be the cowards that bolted before anyone even saw smoke from Yoshana's cookfires on the horizon, spreading tales to justify their own gutlessness."

He nodded firmly - but it struck me he was mostly trying to convince himself.

"Well, whatever's may be, may be," said the groom, "You can keep on south and find out. We've no more room here."

"Now see here," Tolf protested, "We have letters of credit from Our Lady."

"You can have a letter from the Metropolitan his own self -"

"As a matter of fact, we do."

The boy's eyes widened. "Well, I'm sorry, but we really are out of room. As you can see."

He considered a bit. "Reckon you could shelter up against the side of the barn, and we could come up with something hot from the kitchen for you."

It was the worst night of the journey, and not just because of a snow flurry that the side of the barn did little to deflect. The stew the groom brought smelled good, but with the churning in my guts I waved it away. Only Tolf and Dee seemed to have much appetite.

"Always worse the night before than the day of," the soldier said cheerfully.

"I thought Our Lady hadn't been attacked in your lifetime?" I asked.

"Well, that's what the old farts that lived through it say, and I'll take 'em at their word. They must have done something right to survive. Anyway, who wants to die on an empty stomach?"

Dee somehow put two bowls of stew into his gangly frame. But then, he would need energy to run away in the face of battle.

Prophetess had gone around the barn to pray. The rest of the group was huddled miserably in their blankets, trying to get to sleep. I was still awake when she came back and sank down in the space Dee and I had left between us.

I was bone weary, but I couldn't keep my eyes closed. Thoughts chased through my head like fever dreams, each more disturbing than the one it pursued. Finally I said, "I don't understand confession. It seems like the church says you're always sinning, even if all you've done is think about something bad. So you always have to confess something. Seems like you're supposed to be feeling guilty all the time. Wouldn't it make more sense to have a more realistic set of rules?"

"Are you perfect, Minos?" Prophetess said softly.

"Obviously not."

"Confession reminds us of that. It brings you closer to God. Not a bad thing at a time like this."

I thought about that. "I don't suppose it works if you're not a Universalist."

Dee spoke up sleepily. "Doctrine states that the sacrament of reconciliation is only effective if you're baptized."

"It also says that anyone can baptize," Prophetess said. "Do you want to be baptized, Minos?"

"Seems a little blasphemous to be baptized just because I'm afraid the antichrist is going to rip my skin off tomorrow."

After a moment, Dee mumbled, "It's too bad we don't have a fiddle. It's traditional to settle a fight with the devil with a fiddle."

"Can you play a fiddle?"

"No."

"Just as well," Prophetess said. "There was a traveling minstrel who used to come around our farm. Had the worst voice ever, though. Then he spent everything he had getting himself the fanciest fiddle you ever saw. Called it a violin. It was even worse. Sounded like he was torturing a cat."

"Your point being?"

"Violins never solve anything."

The next day dawned bright and clear. But I hadn't slept well. Nor did the grim faces around me suggest the others had. I couldn't recall my dreams, but I thought the fanged cloud had figured in them again.

I suppose bold deeds always seem more attractive from a safe distance.

The groom came out again with some porridge and apples for us. We ate a bit and mounted up. I got halfway through an apple over the first few miles, then gave up and tossed it into the weeds at the side of the road. My horse gave me a reproachful look. I mentally apologized to the beast and patted its neck. "All the apples you want if I live through this."

The animal tossed its head peevishly as if to say, "Sure, like that's going to happen."

Woods and brush gave way to the stubble of well-tended fields, enclosed within neat fences. A prosperous land. The Source took its name from the abundance of its agriculture.

The sun wasn't yet at its zenith when we saw the wall of Stephensburg rising up before us. Not long after that we began to see tents pitched in the fields on either side of the road. Banners flew among them, white with a gold symbol I had never seen before. It looked like some sort of odd double-headed halberd, a crescent moon shape on each side of an elongated diamond.

"My God, they're ahead of us," Tolf exclaimed.

"Is that Yoshana's standard?"

"It's not Stephen's. Or anyone else's I've seen. So who else?"

"What do we do?" I asked Prophetess.

"What can we do? Ride on."

"Are you insane?" I snapped. "Through the enemy's army?"

She set her jaw. "I must see Stephen. If the army's in the way, we go through the army."

She crossed herself and kicked her mount forward. I sputtered words that never made it past my lips. Some were unprintable. Some were pleas to reason.

Some were suggestions, like sneaking in under cover of darkness. Not a one found voice. I stopped talking to myself and followed.

We came abreast of the camp, which swarmed with armed men. We were noticed but not stopped.

"Not exactly alert," I muttered.

"We're too small a group to be a factor either way," Tolf replied.

I debated whether to be relieved or offended. Relief won easily. Of course, if we tried to run later, there was now an army between us and any possible safety. I had an idea how Pharaoh's troops must have felt following the Israelites into the sea with destruction poised on either side, wondering when the safe passage would collapse on them.

As we neared the wall, though, we could see the gates standing open. A river bounded the city's western edge, and the bridge across was fortified at both ends. Troops with the white and gold standard held it, but there was no sign of siege equipment. Or any great degree of activity.

Tolf cursed under his breath. "I didn't believe it, but damn me to hell if they weren't right. He gave up the outer wall without a fight."

At the foot of the bridge a soldier finally moved to block our path. He kept his spear at casual attention, however, and merely held up a hand. "Glory to God in the highest," he proclaimed.

Prophetess reined in her horse and replied, "Glory to God."

I pulled up next to Tolf and whispered, "Are you sure these are the enemy?"

Tolf shrugged. Dee urged his mount around to the other side of mine and murmured, "Remember, Yoshana calls herself a prophet as well." He nodded at the standard. "That symbol's clever."

I raised my eyebrows, but he just repeated, "Clever."

"What brings you to Stephensburg?" the soldier was asking.

Prophetess hesitated for a second, and my mouth ran ahead of me again. "We are emissaries from the Metropolitan at Our Lady, come to speak with Stephen."

Prophetess, Dee and Tolf all stared at me. The soldier dipped his head and cleared his throat. "I'm going to have to run this one up the tree," he said. "If you'll wait here?"

He jogged away across the bridge, leaving his spear propped against a wall.

I shrugged. "If Yoshana's claiming to be a prophet of God, can she obstruct ambassadors from the largest church in the known world?"

"My dear young friend, you really don't know much about religion, do you?" Dee said. "One thing a prophet can't stand is another prophet. If Yoshana's created some sort of syncretic, pan-Abrahamic religion as I suspect she has, the last thing she'll want is a representative of Universalist orthodoxy to question her."

I shrugged again. It wouldn't be the first time I'd put my foot in my mouth. But there was always a first time for it to be fatal.

My stomach was turning like a waterwheel by the time the soldier came back across the bridge. He was accompanied by only one other figure, but the way he hurried ahead, then periodically shot a nervous glance back over his shoulder, suggested he'd wound up going further up the chain of command than he'd expected.

I blinked, then stared as the two came up to us. The second person was a woman. She was armored like the first soldier in studded leather, covered with a cloak that failed to conceal the curves of her figure. Her shoulders were broad, but there was nothing masculine about her. Her skin was a deep tan, her hair and eyes a brown so dark as to be almost black. Her features were beautiful, her form perfect. I could feel my face heat and was glad Select did not visibly blush. Her effect on me was unlike anything I had ever experienced before.

"You can shut your mouth now before your tongue falls out," Prophetess hissed.

I considered a response but decided I was better off shutting my mouth instead.

"Come down, please," the woman said. She was speaking to me. It didn't occur to me to refuse.

"Interesting. A Select as an emissary of the Universal Church?" Her voice was soft and pleasant. She stepped forward, only a pace away from me. Only as her hand started toward my face did I notice the black haze forming around her fingertips.

I flinched back and my horse whinnied nervously.

"Shh, shh," she soothed. "I won't hurt you." Her eyes were locked on mine. Her hand came up slowly, fingertips softly brushing my temples. They lingered there for moments that seemed like a lifetime.

"Hmm. True, or nearly enough. Well. Yoshana is meeting with Stephen this afternoon. I'm sure after that he'll make himself available to the Universal Church."

"We'll see him now, please," Prophetess said, a slight tremor in her voice.

"And you are?"

"As my escort said, a representative of the Universal Church." She eyed the dark woman through narrowed eyes. "And you won't be touching me."

The other smiled. "Do you fear the Darkness?" She was still standing within arm's reach of me. I didn't feel a desire to step back.

"Fear it? No. But its corruption will not touch me."

The dark woman gave a low chuckle. "The Darkness Radiant is not your enemy, whatever you may believe. But you'd be wise to respect it." She laughed louder, amused at something in her own thoughts. "I think I'll let Yoshana deal with you."

She turned to the soldier. "Escort them to the inner wall on my authority. It will be up to them to get past Stephen's guards. Somehow I don't think they'll find that a challenge." Turning back to us, she added, "You'll leave your horses here. We'll look after them for you." She was still smiling, and she didn't say *assuming you survive*, but I heard it anyway.

She remained behind, moving away to converse with the encamped troops. Our new escort shook his head as we followed him, on foot, across the bridge.

"You're just lucky you're Select," he said.

"What does that mean?"

"You're just lucky, is all."

Tolf, unable to contain himself, blurted out, "Who was that?"

The soldier laughed. "That? That was just Commander Roshel, that's all."

"She's…"

"One of the top brass of the whole legion? An Overlord? Able to strip the flesh from your bones without moving a finger? All of the above, friend, all of the above. Not hard on the eyes, though. No she isn't. Wouldn't mind her running those fingers over my face. Except of course if she decided to make my brains dribble out my ears. Always the downside, that."

My pulse was finally getting back to normal. Stunning though she was, Roshel's impact on me had to be an effect of the Darkness.

Didn't it?

Another branch of the river was contained within the city walls, and we followed it back north toward the inner administrative district. The city was quiet, but not empty of inhabitants. Some shops were open and doing business, despite the presence of Yoshana's occupying force. I had to say, they were amazingly restrained for invaders. I wondered if they were paying for what they took. That would be unprecedented, and I hadn't heard that the army was flush with silver. The troops were certainly in evidence, some encamped in public areas, some patrolling the streets. None interfered with us, escorted as we were.

Tolf and Dee were trying to extract information from our guide, whose name was Carse. They learned little except that the men of the Darkness Radiant were fiercely loyal to Yoshana and her lieutenants, in this case Roshel.

The seductive Overlord's words echoed in my head. *I think I'll let Yoshana deal with you.* If Yoshana chose to destroy us - and how would she not - I couldn't begin to think how we could overcome her. The truth seemed like an awfully feeble weapon.

And even the righteousness of our cause was beginning to look questionable. Our enemy's forces professed a faith in God, showed impeccable behavior, and had no evident weaknesses.

The inner wall was at least five miles away, but we reached it all too soon.

Here, at last, we saw something that resembled a siege. A large contingent of Yoshana's men, banners flying, was camped outside a vast, arched gate. Above the gate on a parapet, a smaller group of soldiers in gray tabards looked down suspiciously on them - and us.

"Brought another damn Select?" one of them called down. "We already told you no more of your lot can go inside. And one Select is more than enough."

"Why don't you come down here and we'll have that conversation face to face?" snapped one of Yoshana's men.

"These are Grigg's troops," our guide said softly. "They don't take kindly to cracks about the Select." He looked at me and chuckled. "Lucky again. Maybe."

Prophetess stepped forward. "We do not serve the Darkness Radiant. We serve only God. We have come from Our Lady."

I didn't like the tone of the laughter that followed. I liked it less when one of the guards on the wall spat down near us.

"Our Lady sends a little girl, a Select, and a half dozen beggars in rags? Well, that's a relief. I thought we were on our own in here."

I shrugged and turned to Prophetess. "It looks like we're not welcome. Maybe we should go."

Carse favored me with a wide smirk. Prophetess gave me a withering look that promised a scolding later, if we lived. She turned back to the guards. "Perhaps you should be grateful for what help is sent. We will see Stephen now, if you please."

"That you will not. His Majesty Stephen holds audience after the hour of afternoon rest. So if he were inclined to see you, which I highly doubt, he would see you in two hours."

One of the invaders, who I took for some sort of junior officer, chimed in. "And not then either, because he's meeting with Yoshana herself." The tone of his voice when he spoke the name was almost worshipful.

"Really," retorted the local, "and why should our lord hear your lady and not whoever else pleases him in his own hall?"

"Because our lady has waited patiently despite arriving at the head of an army you couldn't hope to resist."

"I'm confused," said the other, and spat again. "Did you say you come in friendship or in force?"

Yoshana's man opened his mouth again, then was pulled aside by one of his fellows. A heated exchange of whispers followed. While that went on, the huge gate swung open. A squad of the gray-uniformed guards looked out at us. One beckoned.

"You can't be worse than what's already inside. Pass, and if you truly serve God, may he watch over you."

"Lucky," Carse repeated. His grin was wicked.

The architecture of the central district reminded me of Our Lady, though it seemed less pleasant and harmonious to me. But perhaps that was just the circumstances. Here the city was silent. Not the stillness of the dead places we had passed before, but the hush of indrawn breath. Here, within Stephen's stronghold, I felt the terrible, oppressive weight of fear.

Our new escort of a half dozen men in gray led us quickly on, unspeaking. Prophetess moved up to thank the leader for guiding us. He had a young, open face, and there was something like pity in it.

"We would have been kinder to turn you back, ma'am. I've seen Yoshana, and I hope never to do it again."

Then Stephen's palace itself was before us, a vast structure of red brick and white stone, rendered more impressive still by the expanse of manicured gardens stretching in front of it.

A semicircle of brick pavement fronted the building, decorated with statuary. Past Stephens, I imagined, all in some noble pose or other. Another group of Yoshana's troops, several dozen of them, stood around or sat on decoratively carved marble benches. A slightly smaller contingent of Stephen's guards was braced at attention against the facade of the palace. The tautness of their pose was a sharp contrast to the apparent unconcern shown by the besiegers. Here was their sovereign's last line of defense.

We marched through the Overlord's loitering troops, straight up to the double doors of wood and leaded glass.

"Representatives from Our Lady to see his Majesty," the leader of our escort announced. Out of the corner of my eye, I noticed a shift in the stance of the nearest soldiers in white and gold.

Stephen's guard turned to us. "We allowed only the Overlord herself and one bodyguard to pass into our lord's hall. I'm afraid we must apply the same restrictions to you."

Prophetess and I looked at each other. "I guess it's just you and me again," I said lightly, as my intestines tied themselves into knots.

Dee said, "Much as I would love to accompany you, I must bow to circumstances. And indeed, some deeds are best chronicled from the perspective of a certain distance."

The guard came closer and whispered, "These troops around you may not look like anything special, but they're Yoshana's personal guard, her Knights of Resurrection." His eyes swept Dee and Tolf, identifying them as the leaders of our group remaining outside. "If something happens, I suggest you run."

I summoned a weak smile. "Not to worry. In that particular matter we have one of the world's foremost experts."

And then the guards swung open the doors and Prophetess and I stepped inside.

We were in some sort of antechamber, more of Stephen's guards facing us. Light streamed in through huge windows above, reflecting from marble tiles.

"Representatives of Our Lady to see his Majesty," repeated one of the men holding the door, and then shut it behind us.

A small, balding man I hadn't noticed got up from a cushioned chair and looked at us with evident irritation. He was finely dressed, and plainly no soldier. Some sort of chamberlain, or whatever the appropriate word was to describe the doorman who kept the rabble away from royalty.

"This is very irregular. At least the Overlord sent an envoy to request an audience." His eyes traveled up and down our clothes, and his nose wrinkled. "And dressed appropriately."

"If you're determined to be impressed with the things of this world, you may not find the next to be congenial," Prophetess said coldly.

It took the man a second to process the statement, then he flinched as if slapped. I realized my mouth was open and shut it. I had never heard Prophetess use that tone before. Much less indirectly threaten someone with damnation.

I looked at her more closely and realized every muscle in her body was quivering, every sinew vibrating like a plucked harp string. She had walked in here so boldly I hadn't realized she was terrified.

More than anything I wanted to put my arm around her, but that would be out of place. So I just watched her stare at that man, her jaw clenched.

He looked away and cleared his throat. "I'll just announce you, then."

Prophetess nodded tightly, and I don't think the chamberlain noticed the suppressed tears reddening her eyes.

The inner doors of the antechamber matched those outside, and for the third time in as many minutes we were announced, "Representatives of Our Lady to see his Majesty."

It wasn't exactly a lie.

The hall beyond was long but not wide, paneled in dark wood and dimly lit with torches. It took my eyes a moment to adjust. Chairs were ranked on either side of a central aisle like pews in a church. And like a Universalist church, steps led up to a white marble dais, but with a huge golden chair where an altar would be.

Guards stood at attention against the walls. Two figures stood on the dais, one on the steps, the other at the level of the throne, though a distance from it. We were already walking forward before I realized neither was Stephen.

The nearer was Select. And massive. He stood several inches taller than I, and must have weighed at least fifty pounds more, none of it fat.

The other brought me to a dead stop.

Yoshana was not a large woman. She was shorter than Prophetess, and lean. But even had she not been at the top of the steps, she would have loomed over us. From a dozen paces away, I reeled in the presence of something more than human.

It wasn't her appearance, though that was striking. It must have been true that she was part Select, because her hair was as white as mine. Her skin was the reddish color of mahogany, her eyes a startling blue. She wore a simple, belted tunic as white as her hair, the golden symbol of the Darkness Radiant embroidered over her heart.

Her eyes narrowed just the tiniest bit as she looked at us, the faint distaste of someone spotting a large cockroach scuttling across the dining room floor. I thought a hint of black haze shimmered in the air around her, but that might have been my imagination.

I had never wanted so much to be somewhere else.

Prophetess had lurched to a halt when I did, but now continued forward. I let her go. There was none of Roshel's seduction about Yoshana. She was beautiful as a storm is beautiful. An awesome aura of power, barely contained.

To challenge that power meant death. Prophetess slowed, each step more hesitant than the last. I stayed where I was. This time, Prophetess had stepped into something she could not overcome. But I might just be far enough away that I would be allowed to live when the storm was unleashed.

The big Select - it must have been Grigg himself - was looking at me with something that might have been sympathy. Or pity. Or condescension.

Ah, dammit.

I forced my leaden feet to take a half dozen long strides to Prophetess' side.

Yoshana's lieutenant favored me with a tiny half smile. The Overlord herself was not amused.

"I don't remember asking for witnesses to my audience." Her voice was clear and fluid as a river. Somehow the words *my audience* suggested that Stephen had sought the audience with her, rather than vice versa.

"How could it ever be a bad time to shine God's light into darkness?" Prophetess asked.

The Darkness can kill in a hundred ways, as subtle as stopping the heart, as brutal as rending the flesh. I wondered which it would be for us.

A dozen heartbeats later, when the faint grimace of annoyance on Yoshana's face hadn't turned into anything worse, I let myself breathe again.

"Glory to God in the highest," said the most dangerous person in the world.

"Glory to God," repeated Prophetess, and bowed her head.

I couldn't imagine what Stephen's guards were making of this, but someone watching through a spy hole must have rushed off to tell the monarch his guests were about to make a mess on his floor. Moments later a door opened behind the throne and a herald announced in booming tones, "His august Majesty, lord of the Source, Stephen, twenty-seventh of his name."

The door was wide, and it needed to be. A quartet of bearers emerged carrying a gilded sedan chair. The herald followed, reverently cradling an ornate staff.

I stared.

Stephen was not so much fat as almost gelatinous. Liquid folds wobbled on his jowls and exposed arms. The sweating bearers set the chair on the floor a pace from the throne. The herald handed the staff to his lord. It was painful to watch Stephen laboriously lever himself up and take two tottering steps before slumping into his cushioned perch.

He peered out at us all with piercing gray eyes.

Yoshana, who had turned her back on us to face him, dipped her head. "My lord Stephen."

"Ah. A strange turn," the ruler of the Source said, voice throaty but strong. "A season ago we would have addressed each other monarch to monarch, but now here you stand, an exile at the head of a motley army with nowhere to call home."

Which seemed like a bold statement when that army was occupying his city.

The Overlord replied, "I prefer to think of myself as a prophet leading God's host to a new land."

Stephen grunted. "Well, I can see why you would prefer to think that." His eyes turned to us. "And you? Not leading another of God's hosts, I hope? I could hardly accommodate two of them."

"I am Prophetess. I come from Our Lady."

Again, a lie only by implication.

"This is remarkable. Two prophets, each with her own Select."

"The world tends to fill up with false prophets in such troubled times," Yoshana said smoothly.

"Yes it does," Prophetess agreed.

"Only one of whom has something to offer you," the Overlord added. "Specifically, an army."

"Go on," Stephen said.

"As you so astutely observed, my lord, I have an army without a home. Whereas you are the master of a home with, forgive me, not much of an army."

I shot a glance at the soldiers lining the walls. Some of them looked less than pleased to be described as "not much of an army." But none seemed inclined to forcibly disagree with Yoshana or her hulking bodyguard.

The Overlord continued, "This is a troubled age, my lord. The nations of the world war against each other while the demons rise in the east and the Darkness spreads untamed over the face of the earth. The land needs a strong hand to unite it. That hand should be yours - your hand, clasping the sword of God. The Lord says to my lord, sit at my right hand, until I make your enemies a footstool for your feet."

Prophetess stiffened at that last. "So it's true what they say - even the devil can quote scripture when it suits her."

Yoshana turned slowly toward her. "The very devil? That's quite an accusation, little girl."

"Can you doubt it?" Prophetess exclaimed. Her eyes implored Stephen. "Look at her, clothed in the Darkness!"

"Even the Darkness is radiant in his sight," the Overlord said easily. "The Lord can use any tool at hand. Even that one."

"It is sin!"

Yoshana waved her hand impatiently. "It's a tool. No different than fire." Her eyes locked on mine for a moment, and I struggled not to step back. "Unless like the paleos you believe all human artifice is an offense to God's order?"

She turned back to Stephen. "The Darkness is dangerous if not controlled, yes. Or in the hands of those who can't control it. You wouldn't set a flame raging in a dry field, or give a burning torch to an infant. But as a weapon in a strong hand like yours... Blind force must be managed by intellect and will."

A look almost like lust was spreading across Stephen's sagging face. I imagined my own face when Roshel had touched me, and was disgusted with myself. But I felt nothing like that for Yoshana - if anything, the fear, the urge to flee, had intensified.

Prophetess cried desperately, "He has shown you, O mortal, what is good. And what does the Lord require of you? To act justly and to love mercy and to walk humbly with your God. For you were once darkness, but now you are light in the Lord. Live as children of light."

"Enough," Yoshana snapped.

"Turn away from the Darkness, Lord Stephen," Prophetess begged, and took a step forward.

"I said *enough*!" The Overlord turned and the Darkness rose from her in a cloud, making her huge. It swirled above her, gathering like a snake about to strike.

I grabbed Prophetess' shoulder and pulled her behind me.

Yoshana laughed.

In three long strides, Grigg stepped between us, shielding both Prophetess and me. "No, Yosha."

The Overlord's mouth twisted with rage and the Darkness lashed out. An answering cloud billowed out of the Select and for a moment the swirling masses met, clawing at each other.

"You'll just make her a martyr," Grigg said.

The black cloud drew back toward Yoshana and her face eased into a puzzled frown. Her bodyguard drew a deep breath, and the Darkness around him faded to a haze.

"Well," said Stephen. "That was instructive."

I stole a look at Prophetess' face and for the first time allowed myself to hope. Yoshana had revealed herself, and we had lived. Could we have both stopped her and escaped unharmed?

The Overlord turned back to the lord of the Source.

"Instructive," he repeated. He licked his lips. "Such power."

"No," Prophetess murmured weakly.

"Would you see what it can do, my lord?" Yoshana asked in a voice of silk.

Prophetess made a soft sound in her throat and tried to step forward. I realized I was still holding her shoulder. Grigg turned to me and gave the smallest shake of his head.

"Yes," Stephen said.

The Darkness coiling around Yoshana oozed forward to the man on the throne, surrounded him. Entered him.

Liquid began to seep from his pores, drops, then rivulets. It congealed into a white, oily mass as it coated the gilded chair and dripped to the floor. I abruptly recognized it as liquified fat.

In two years mining garbage I had never seen anything that sickened me more. Behind me several of the guards gagged noisily.

Stephen stood. The skin of his arms and face didn't hang empty, but clung to his frame in the image of muscular health.

"I am strong," he breathed.

"You were always strong," Yoshana said. "Now your body matches your will."

"*Your* will," Prophetess said to the Overlord, but the words were so soft that only I, and perhaps Grigg, could hear them.

Stephen looked out at us, flexing his hands, a wide smile on his face. "We have seen the truth revealed," he said. "You may go, little girl, and tell them in Our Lady that God's strong sword has come to the Source."

Tears trickled down Prophetess' cheeks. She opened her mouth one more time but no sound came out. Then she turned on her heel and walked away.

Grigg gave me a sad little smile as I followed her.

12. Another Such Victory

"I didn't sign up for this!"

Four of Stephen's guards had said words to that effect as they threw down their spears and followed us out. With the sick taste of bile in my mouth, I couldn't help but agree.

More soldiers joined us as we made our way back to the Midwalls, accreting to the first group of deserters like raindrops flowing together. By the time we had collected the rest of our group and passed back through the gate into the territory controlled by Yoshana's troops, our ranks had swollen by over a dozen.

It didn't matter. The Darkness Radiant was flooding the administrative district. The siege was over.

"What happened?" Dee demanded, over and over. I didn't answer. Neither did Prophetess. But Stephen's men were quick enough to babble out what they had seen.

"Not even a damn stick," I muttered.

Prophetess turned to me. "What?"

"At least your God gave Moses a stick. He didn't even give you that."

And then, to my everlasting shock, her face cracked into a smile. "He gave me what I needed."

"How did he possibly do that?"

"He gave me you, to stand between me and death. And gave us Grigg's heart, when he stepped in front of us. What more could I ask for?"

"Maybe something that would have let us win? Let all of this not be for nothing?"

"But he did. I did what he asked of me, and we won."

I was dumbfounded. "How can you call that a victory?"

"How can you not? We faced Yoshana and lived. We proved there's a choice beyond bowing to her or being destroyed by her." She swept Stephen's guards with a gesture. "They saw that. They'll bear witness."

"Another such victory and I am undone," I grumbled.

"Pyrrhus," Dee said later. "Very good."

"This is ridiculous," I said. "We dragged ourselves halfway across the continent to stop Yoshana from taking over the Source. Yoshana took over the Source anyway. Now Prophetess is saying her prophecy is fulfilled. If we'd died, she'd have gasped out 'my prophecy is fulfilled' with her last breath. How do you argue with someone who can't be proved wrong?"

"That's faith for you," Dee said.

"That's a big, steaming pile of... if God is all-knowing and all-powerful, how do you square that with his prophet getting her butt kicked when she's doing his work?"

"Ah, the problem of evil." Dee rubbed his hands together.

"I'm going to regret asking this," I said.

Dee smiled wickedly. "Why does God allow evil? Why do bad things happen to good people? Why did God create mosquitoes? These are all questions that have vexed believers for centuries. The easiest answer is that his ways are not our ways, and we can't understand his plans. But I prefer quantum physics."

"What?"

"I am a philosopher, Minos. I told you that you know a bit too much, and understand a bit too little. Where God and nature come together is where truth is found. The Universal Church tells us that man has free will, not so?" He didn't wait for me to answer. "But how can that be if God knows all? Doesn't he know what we will do? Isn't the universe like a great clock, and he knows every movement that has been, and every movement that will be?"

I shrugged.

"But the ancients discovered that when you come to see the smallest building blocks of the universe, you can know where they are, or where they are going, but not both. The act of observing changes that which is observed. What a wonderful thing! God created the universe in a way that it is unknowable, and so - free will! And the freedom to choose right or wrong. Stephen chose wrong. But the chance to choose right remains."

The chance to choose right. Prophetess' gray eyes, dancing with light. Her smile as she offered gentle encouragement to the men who had joined us, to the refugees we passed on the road. Her tall, straight figure at the head of our column, brown hair streaming behind her in the breeze. Had I chosen right? I hoped so.

Snow was falling outside the rectory at Our Lady. Father Juniper found me sitting on a bench, watching the Ermel Clock. The hour hand stood at six, where the circles touched.

"Ah," he said, "Transition."

I nodded.

"The question is," I said, "whether we're passing out of darkness, or into it."

Book Two - Flight from Darkness

"Evil is the form which God's mercy takes in this world."
Simone Weil

1. Marking Time

"Ow! Son of a -!" I bit off the last word, remembering where I was.

Tolf laughed. He had rapped me solidly on the knuckles with his staff. It was bitterly cold outside, which made the blow hurt even more. The wind swept in off the Ice Fields to the north, scattering snowflakes and biting at my skin. I was younger, bigger, stronger, and faster. The guardsman still abused me when we sparred.

"Tomorrow I'm going to knock that pin right off you," I said.

"Why do you have to be like that about the pin, Minos?" he asked plaintively. "You were there with her too."

And that was the point. I had been there with Prophetess from the beginning, long before Tolf and the rest of the Order of Thorns got involved. When she had faced Yoshana, I had been beside her. Not the Order. I had stood between her and the Darkness. And I had done it without the promise of heaven or the threat of hell pushing me.

Now she was a hero. To at least some in Our Lady, she was a prophet not just in name. The Order of Thorns had sprung up within days of our return from Stephensburg. The pewter pin Tolf wore was its symbol, a circle of roses nestled within spines - the sharp edges defending the blossoms. It was a sign of their faith, and therein lay the problem - it was a faith I didn't share.

"Ah, I'm just getting a little stir-crazy," I said. "Tess may think we won a round against Yoshana because we lived and neither of us wet ourselves, but Yoshana's spent three months building her armies and we haven't done squat."

"We've got nearly a hundred in the Order and more every day."

I looked across the snow-covered field we called a drill yard, shimmering white under the perpetually gray sky of winter in Our Lady. From the elegant dome and spires of the rectory and basilica at the north end to the sprawl of buildings at the south, it measured nearly a quarter of a mile long and several hundred feet wide. The complex enclosed within the walls was huge, dozens of massive structures of cream-colored brick and stone, wrapped in ancient vines. It could house tens of thousands. The religious community numbered less than fifteen hundred, and few of them were under arms. Whole buildings stood empty. We had room for an army - but we didn't have one. Tolf's hundred men would be lost in this space. But not the enemy's legions.

"Yoshana's got thousands of veterans in the Darkness Radiant alone, not counting all of Stephen's troops. She's got Stephen convinced he's going to rule the world. You should have seen the look on his face. If she gets him to turn all of the Source's production toward war... imagine ten thousand men with repeating rifles all answering to her. They'd roll over us without even knowing they were in a fight."

"They wouldn't dare attack Our Lady..."

"Maybe. I'd bet that depends on how much of a pain Yoshana thinks we might be. And if there are no survivors, who's to say what happened?"

"You're a real ray of sunshine."

I picked up the staff I'd dropped, shaking off the snow that had stuck to it. "That's why you all love me so much."

There was a particular bench in the rectory, facing the Ermel Clock. Most days I would spend time sitting there, watching the hands trace their slow circuit. It was like no other clock I had seen - it showed the hours on two eccentric circles, joined at six o'clock, the hours of the night on the smaller circle inside the hours of the day on the larger. If I got up early enough, I could watch us pass out of darkness. Mostly I watched us pass into it.

Sometimes Father Juniper would join me, and the old, bearded priest would sit and puff on his pipe, and maybe say something profound.

This time I was joined by Father Roric instead. His title was Advocate for Justice, which suggested the medieval Inquisition. His bearing and temperament were less welcoming than that.

"You've been exercising," he observed. I was probably still sweaty. I tried to make sure I didn't drip on the bench.

"An unpleasant pastime. I try to avoid it." He smiled, which put me in mind of a wolf examining a particularly helpless sheep.

He was thin as a whip, and sharp as one. If he didn't exercise, he must not eat much. Maybe it was hard to find babies to devour.

"Quarterstaves with the guard?" he asked.

"I'm flattered you know me so well. I think." *Terrified* was a more accurate word.

"You're worth observing. Intelligent, honest, and the center of this whole matter of... the Prophetess." He rolled the word around in his mouth like a lump of phlegm he badly wanted to spit out, but whose appearance would revolt him if he let it emerge.

"And yet, no..." he twirled his finger at my chest. I followed his meaning well enough. No pin. I wasn't a member of the Order of Thorns.

"You know I'm not a Universalist, Father."

His predatory smile widened. "And yet, you were her closest companion. You traveled with her for what, three months?"

"More like two."

"Two. Still, in all that time she failed to convert you. That's a rather extraordinary thing for a prophet, wouldn't you say?"

"I couldn't tell you, Father. I've never known any other prophets. Unless you count Yoshana."

The grin vanished. "Very amusing. Well then, you've met them both. Which did you find the more impressive?"

"I certainly found Yoshana considerably more terrifying, but is that really the criterion we're looking for?"

If that was the standard, Roric had Prophetess beat hands down, although he was a poor second to the Overlord.

The smile spread slowly across his face again. "I enjoy our little chats, Minos. You're a stubborn creature, but I find you enlightening."

"I believe Father Juniper once compared me to a hickory stick." I nodded at my staff.

"Mm. He probably meant it in some sort of positive way. He's a kindly soul."

I had never imagined a priest could make *kindly* sound like a bad word.

There was no clearer sign of my malaise than the fact that I sought out Doctor John Dee. The pretentious occultist was a fountain of non-stop babble on every conceivable subject, a walking cure for insomnia.

He was also the only other person of my acquaintance not passionately dedicated to one side or the other of the Prophetess debate.

"I can't take it, Dee," I said. "We need to be preparing for a war with Yoshana, but all anyone cares about is whether God's speaking through Tess. I understand this is a religious community, but how is that the most urgent point?"

"Father Roric tracked you down, eh?"

"Are you following me around too? How did you know that?"

Dee grinned. "Well, he got done with me yesterday, so it was logical. And clearly something has you upset. He's a fascinating man, isn't he? But I can see how he might be disturbing to a sensitive temperament."

I narrowed my black eyes and glared at the gangly man, a cowardly assortment of loose limbs animated by an inexhaustible supply of hot air. "One thing Select are not is sensitive."

He laughed. "Fine. Not sensitive in the least. But you are upset."

"Tolf's acting like I should be burned at the stake for not treating Tess like some kind of messiah." That was a gross exaggeration, but I was venting. "Roric probably wants to burn her and me both at the stake. Again, how is this the most productive use of anyone's time when a megalomaniacal Overlord is building the army of darkness on our doorstep?"

Dee leaned back in his chair and sucked his teeth. "Let's go back to a conversation you and I had months ago, Minos. Why is Yoshana dangerous?"

"Because she's a homicidal maniac who can use the Darkness to flay the flesh off your bones."

"No!" Dee gave me an exasperated grimace.

"All right, but you weren't in the room with her when she got mad. You're saying she's dangerous because people follow her."

"Yes. And now people need to decide if they're going to follow Prophetess the same way. That's why this matters."

I sighed. "I guess I understand that. And I feel like if I can't jump on her bandwagon, I'm undermining her. But I came here following a person, not a symbol. I can't be part of the Order of Thorns if that means pretending to a faith I don't have. I thought I wanted to be part of a cause, but now that I am, I don't think I like it."

The occultist shrugged. "Maybe it isn't the right cause for you."

Weeks passed, and the weather improved. In a way. The training ground melted from hard-packed earth dusted with snow to a clinging mud. The first tentative green shoots began to appear on trees. The golden dome of the rectory shone like a beacon in the sun.

A beacon to what, that was the question. Campaigning season would be upon us soon. No one would besiege Our Lady in the winter. The surrounding townsfolk would just flee with their goods into the protection of the walls, and the attackers would starve, shivering in the abandoned buildings, their supply lines vulnerable to snowstorms and hypothermia.

Soon, though, it would be warm enough to see what Yoshana's intentions truly were.

That conversation was already making the rounds in the visitors' dining hall. Of course, "visitor" was an interesting term for the few dozen assorted refugees we had accumulated. It implied we were there temporarily, but our motley crew had been occupying the dormitory for months. There were more than a dozen former soldiers of Stephensburg who had been disgusted by their master's alliance with Yoshana and joined us instead. Another score of civilians had attached themselves to us as we made our way from Stephensburg back to Our Lady. And then there were the original six - Dee, Hadal, Doral, Loris, Prophetess, and me. All of the able-bodied men except Dee and I had joined the Order of Thorns. I wasn't a Universalist, and Dee was devoted only to knowledge and saving his own skin. I had never met a man so eager to poke his nose into dangerous places yet so quick to run away from physical confrontation.

The midday meal was served at long tables. A mix of nuns and lay sisters brought food around on trays. It was simple and decent and hadn't varied much over the winter. The women among the refugees helped in the kitchen, cooking and serving before sitting to eat. Prophetess came by with a tray of rolls. Some of her more fanatical devotees were scandalized whenever they saw her cooking, or serving, or cleaning. They spent quite a bit of time being scandalized because she did a lot of it. I was more perturbed that she didn't spend time in councils of war.

"I'm no soldier, Minos," she had said. "And God hasn't told me that I should make war. When the time comes, he'll guide me."

She was no pacifist. Sometimes she would exercise with a staff, though I was the only one who would really spar with her. She was quick and strong and had good reach. She was no match for me, much less someone with Tolf's skill, but she was by no means helpless. But her swinging a stick around wasn't going to defeat Yoshana.

I had read the classics of strategy and tactics, as almost every Select did. But no one asked for my opinion. Not that I had any brilliant ideas how we could face down a force that was larger, better trained, better equipped, and led by one of the most fearsome generals of our age.

Maybe I didn't like this cause because it was so obviously lost.

"Roll?" Prophetess repeated, prodding my shoulder with her tray.

I blinked and shook my head, trying to reclaim my wandering thoughts. Only after refusing did it occur to me that I would like a roll after all.

"Haven't seen you in a couple of days," I said lamely.

"I've been spending a lot of time with Father Juniper. And we were out most of yesterday hoeing the north field. And you've been busy staring at that clock all day."

"That's not fair," I protested. "Sometimes I let Tolf hit me with a stick."

She grinned. "I miss spending time with you. I got used to it after two months walking north together."

My heart sped up. I might not want to be involved with the Order of Thorns, but Prophetess herself... "We could always walk back down south together now the weather's clearing."

I like to think her smile was a little sad. "I don't know what I'm supposed to do next, but for now, I stay here."

"Can't fault a man for trying. Maybe after dinner you'd like to sit and look at my clock with me."

"Oh, so it's your clock now?"

"Wouldn't you say so?"

"Oh, I definitely would. I'm just a little surprised to hear you admit it. Now that it's getting warmer, how about if we sit outside and look at the stars instead?"

"The clock has stars on it…"

She hit me with a roll.

That night we sat on a freezing stone bench between the rectory and the cathedral and watched the clouds chase across the stars.

"Cold," I muttered. Which wasn't a completely bad thing, because it meant we sat very close together for warmth.

"We've been colder." And that was true. We'd nearly frozen to death on the way to Our Lady. We wouldn't have made it if I hadn't bartered my sword for better clothing.

That sword was another worm of resentment gnawing at my heart. It had been a carbon steel blade forged and folded in the traditional style, a gift from my parents. Prophetess had thanked me warmly for what I'd done - and then it had never been mentioned again. I knew it was petty, but in my mind it was a symbol of what I'd given up, for no purpose I could now see. We hadn't defeated Yoshana, and we were sitting around doing nothing. I was lodged like an irritating grain of sand inside the shell of the Universalist faith, treated politely enough but set apart because I didn't share their beliefs. I didn't think I was turning into a pearl, either.

As a Select, I had always been apart. Gray skin, white hair and solid black eyes marked our kind. Dee had once called it the mark of Cain, and it was close enough. But I had fit in better a thousand miles southwest of here, mining garbage on the Flow. I hadn't thought that would be something I'd miss.

"What are you thinking?" Prophetess asked.

"Nothing important." I searched for a better answer. "About family, I guess. Whether my parents were at the Paint… whether they survived if they were."

She nodded. "It's hard."

"What about you?" I asked awkwardly. "I don't suppose you've heard anything from your brothers?"

I hadn't even known she had siblings. Dee had told me. The older one had run off to join the army of Rockwall. Prophetess had worried that the younger one might follow him after she left home.

The fact that I'd known her longer than Dee and hadn't bothered to find out about her family didn't make me feel any better about myself. Maybe I really was best suited to a solitary life digging through garbage.

"No. Kafer never wrote after he left home. And Lito… I don't know. I used to take him with me when I preached around the Flow. I hope he learned something from it… that he isn't going to just run off to war and get himself killed."

"You do know the Order of Thorns is probably a bunch of people who will wind up running off to war and getting themselves killed," I said unkindly.

"Why do you assume it has to come to war with Yoshana, Minos?"

"What else is there? She made it pretty clear she means to rule the world. I don't think you're going to change her mind by appealing to her better nature. And you're the one who said if she succeeds, the whole world will be damned."

She gave me a reproachful look, but I kept going.

"The Order of Thorns is a military force, Tess. It's just not a very good one. From what I can see, it looks like you're meaning to get into a fight with Yoshana, but you've got no chance of winning it."

"There are more ways to resist than trying to stab her in the heart, Minos."

"I sure hope so, because someone did that, and it didn't stop her. And I don't think we're going to get nearly as good a shot at her as they did."

"Let's talk about something else."

So we did, but my heart wasn't in it. If I'd known what was coming, I would have tried harder.

2. Arrivals and Departures

"Minos! You'd better get out here!"

Tolf was sweating and out of breath. I looked up at him and back down at my plate. "Can't it wait? We haven't had bacon in months."

"No, it can't, Minos. Now."

I stuffed a last slice in my mouth and wiped the grease on my pants.

"All right, I'm coming." There was no graceful way to get off the long bench with people to either side. I did the best I could not to jostle Loris or Dee. "What's going on?"

"You've got a visitor." I tried to puzzle that one out as I joined Tolf and we hurried up the stairs from the dining hall. Who did I know that knew I was here?

"He's Select."

I nearly tripped. Could it be my father? How would he know where to find me? "Who?"

"Just move it. You'll see for yourself."

It was only a short jog from the residence hall to Our Lady's inner gate. Tolf must have sprinted before to be gasping so hard.

Just outside the gate, a squad of guards held spears leveled at a large, gray-skinned figure. For a moment I was about to protest. Then I realized who it was.

"Oh my God."

"Yeah," Tolf said. "He made it this far before one of the guys from Stephensburg recognized him." We had slowed to a walk, and Tolf put his hand on my shoulder, stopping me completely. "He said he was here to see you. What's that about, Minos?"

"How would I know? You think I invited him?"

The big Select looked remarkably at ease for someone with half a dozen spearpoints in his face. But then, I wouldn't expect Yoshana's lieutenant to be easily rattled.

"Ah, Minos," Grigg called as we neared. "Your friends aren't very welcoming."

"Did you really think bringing the Darkness into Our Lady was going to go over well?"

He shrugged. "I wasn't really thinking about that - I was just thinking in terms of bringing myself."

That seemed hard to believe. No matter how accustomed he was to the substance that the Universal Church called the physical embodiment of sin, I

153

found it incredible he wouldn't even think about how others might react to it. Unless, for all his supposed mastery, the infection controlled him more than he controlled it.

He looked around at the hedge of spears. "Be that as it may, not much of a greeting for someone who saved your life."

That was unarguably true. He had stepped between me and Yoshana when she had lashed out at Prophetess in Stephensburg. I had no doubt that without his intervention, the Darkness boiling out of the enraged Overlord would have torn me to shreds.

"So let's say I'm calling in the favor." He gave me an easy smile.

"And what exactly is the price of my life?"

"Just to listen to me." His grin widened. "Out of deference to your friends' nerves, how about if we talk outside the walls?"

"How about if you don't?" Tolf snapped. "Seems to me like you're ignoring the fact that it was your boss tried to kill Prophetess in the first place. Reminds me of that joke where you push your buddy in front of a wagon then pull him back and say, 'I saved you!' Never thought that one was especially funny."

Grigg's expression remained perfectly pleasant. "You seem to have accumulated a rude collection of friends, Minos. I'm not here to order you around. If you want to talk, I'll be waiting outside."

The big Select turned, apparently oblivious to the spears at his back, and strolled calmly back toward the outer wall.

"Hope he stays out there until he freezes," Tolf growled.

"I dunno. Would it hurt to hear what he has to say?"

The guard gaped at me. "You're not thinking of going out there?" It was more of a statement than a question. I found that it annoyed me.

"He's not the only one who isn't going to order me around." I poked the circle of roses and thorns on Tolf's chest. "I'm not part of the Order of Thorns, remember? I don't take orders from you."

"You think Prophetess would want you talking to Yoshana's dog?"

"Comes to that, I don't take orders from Tess, either."

I started down the path after my enemy's lieutenant. "Hey, Grigg. Wait up."

There was nowhere to sit outside the high, stone wall. I suppose we could have found a tavern in the town that sprawled around Our Lady, but two Select together would draw a lot of attention. And I wouldn't make any friends if the owner realized I was bringing in Yoshana's henchman, literally seething with the Darkness.

Well, not that I saw him seething with it now. But I'd seen it before. It was there.

So we leaned against the wall instead. I wondered if Tolf and half the Order of Thorns were on the other side eavesdropping. Grigg had to be considering the same possibility, but seemed completely at ease. He was one of the calmest men I'd met.

Not exactly what I'd expected from someone helping to enslave the world.

For a man who'd braved the heart of his enemies' stronghold to talk to me, he didn't seem to be in a hurry to say anything. He just lounged against the wall, looking at me with a little smile on his face.

"Long walk from Stephensburg for a conversation," I said. "Especially if you're not going to have it."

He grinned. "We already had the most important part of it when you came out here with me."

I thought that over for a second and shook my head. "You've lost me already."

"I needed to see if you'd have an open mind. If you'd be willing to talk at all. You are, so that's half the battle right there."

I stared into his eyes, black and unreadable as my own. There weren't any answers there. I looked up into the early spring sky instead, blue and cloudless, innocent of threat or evil. No answers there either.

I heaved a deep breath. "Depends what you want to talk about. I appreciate what you did back in Stephensburg, but unless you're here to defect, we're working for opposite sides."

"That's one of the things we need to talk about. You and Prophetess seem to think the sides are her and Yoshana. I can tell you they're not." He paused, looking for a reaction, but I could wait, too. "In the end, there's three ways the world ends up, Minos. Controlled by humanity, controlled by the demons, or controlled by the Darkness. Everything else is details."

"Just so I'm clear, which of those three scenarios is it with Yoshana in charge?"

The big man looked exasperated for the first time. "Come on, Minos. The Darkness is a tool, if you know how to use it. If you don't control it - it's like the difference between a lantern and a forest fire. If the Darkness isn't controlled, in time it'll scour the world clean. And the demons - well, we've seen they're not going to just sit in the Darklands."

"Unless I'm misremembering, it was your boss who helped them break out."

"She's learned, Minos. She's changed."

I gave a nervous half-chuckle that ended in a shiver. "If that was the kinder, gentler Yoshana at Stephensburg, I would have hated to meet her before."

"Yes, you would have." He seemed lost in thought for a moment. "You wouldn't have survived it."

Conversations with Prophetess came back to me. The Overlord struck down and reborn, claiming she was resurrected as God's tool. Yoshana had claimed to be a prophet herself at Stephensburg - and Prophetess had once said the Overlord might actually believe it.

"You're saying Yoshana is really doing God's work and not her own?"

"She's a sharp-edged sword, Minos. The sharpest. But she's the best weapon humanity has in this war. If we fight among ourselves, the demons and the Darkness are the winners."

"What exactly are you asking, Grigg? The Church won't follow Yoshana."

"No. Nobody's asking it to. But you're building an army here. Oh, don't look so surprised - you must know we've got eyes everywhere. Of one kind or another."

Not a pleasant thought.

"The Church isn't a military operation, Minos. I'm sure you see that. We're not asking for its troops or its blessing. But if we're going to take the fight to the enemies of humanity, we can't be worried about a knife in our back. No uprisings. No preaching anathema against us. That's all we ask."

"You know I'm not the one who makes that call."

"I know. But you talk to the people who do. The person, really. At a time like this, people need to rally around someone. If Prophetess rallies them against us, well…" He shrugged.

"Should've killed us when you had the chance," I said, half-joking.

His silence was the most disturbing thing I'd ever heard. The joke wasn't funny anymore.

The gap stretched uncomfortably. At last I said, "Those are pretty words, Grigg." The words he'd said, not the regrets left unspoken. "But I don't know that I believe them myself, much less that I could sell them to Prophetess."

"I'm not asking you to take it on faith, Minos. I know faith isn't your thing."

How much did his eyes see and his ears hear inside Our Lady? Obviously too much.

"We've got an offer for you. Yoshana's going to the Darklands. There's a threat we need to deal with now, or every argument you and I could ever have will be irrelevant. She wants you to see what we're fighting against. She wants you to come with us."

"Are you insane?" Tolf blurted. The candle flame in front of us danced wildly in that brief torrent of words.

Tolf, Prophetess, Dee and I sat around a little wooden table in the dormitory's common room. Night had fallen.

Grigg had given me twenty-four hours to come up with my answer. I had turned the idea over and over in my head all day, putting off questions from my friends. I hadn't made a decision. I wasn't sure it was entirely mine to make. So I had called together the ones whose opinions mattered most.

"To start with, you'll die," Tolf continued, waving his hands. "Plus, you're supporting the enemy. Did I mention you'll die?"

"If Grigg had wanted to kill Minos, Minos would be dead," Dee said gently. "No offense, my friend, but Grigg is bigger, stronger, much better trained... not to mention his command of the Darkness. Once they got outside the walls, Minos wouldn't have stood a chance."

"Thanks for the vote of confidence," I muttered. Although everything he'd said was perfectly true.

"I told you it was crazy to go with him in the first place," Tolf snapped at me.

"In case you didn't notice, he didn't actually kill me," I retorted. We glared at each other.

Dee drummed his fingers on the table and looked thoughtful. "If there's really an opportunity for peace here, we should explore it. If nothing else, Minos could learn things that might be useful to us."

"And they could learn things from him that might be useful to them," Tolf shot back.

"Such as?" Dee asked mildly. "Grigg has demonstrated that they either have spies in our midst, or are using the Darkness to observe us, or both."

Tolf hastily crossed himself and looked suspiciously around the room.

"There's no sense being shocked," Dee continued. "The Darkness was a surveillance tool before it was a weapon. Although if they're manipulating it from outside the walls, that would challenge what we know about its effective range..." He shook himself as if to clear his head. "In any case, there frankly isn't much useful information they can get from Minos. No offense - there just isn't much to know, is there? However, we could learn quite a lot about their intentions and capabilities. And, as I don't see what Yoshana has to gain from this besides what Grigg said, I suggest - despite her penchant for deception - we take her at her word. The possibility of peace should never be ignored."

"Peace?" Tolf spat. "A peace where we agree not to move or even speak against them, while they gather their strength? A peace for them to conquer the rest of the world and deal with us at their leisure? What sort of peace is that, exactly?"

"The usual kind," said Dee brightly. "The interlude between wars, in which rivals build their forces and look for each other's weaknesses."

He smiled apologetically to Prophetess. "Until the ultimate peace of Christ, of course."

She nodded but didn't say a word. She hadn't spoken yet.

Listening to Tolf and Dee argue, with interludes for Tolf to berate me and Dee to point out how useless I was, didn't really help me make up my mind. I stared at Prophetess.

"What do you think?" I asked.

She shrugged helplessly. "You should do what you think is right."

That wasn't what I wanted to hear. I found myself unaccountably angry. I suppose I had hoped to hear that despite it all, she still needed me. Obviously she didn't. "I think I should go, then. I'm not accomplishing anything here."

She looked sad and shrugged again.

"So I'll go." And that was how it was decided.

There was a commotion the next day, of course. I assumed that was thanks to Dee - the man had all the discretion of a cat in heat.

Mostly it was sidelong glances and whispers behind hands. No one was curious enough to actually talk to me, as if they thought I was contagious. It was pretty clear they thought I was betraying the cause, rather than doing my best to help. Or maybe they thought they smelled the stench of death on me, figuring the moment I left Our Lady, Yoshana would skin me alive and stick my severed head on a pike as an example.

That was possible.

I didn't have the stomach to sit at the breakfast table with everyone else. I grabbed a warm roll and ate it standing by the door of the dining hall, trying to decide whether to go around and say goodbye to everyone.

I decided against it. Hadal, Doral, and Loris looked at me like they'd always known I was unreliable and this just confirmed it. I had never socialized much with the other refugees.

Prophetess was serving scrambled eggs from a big bowl. I walked over to her.

"So. No point keeping Grigg waiting, I guess." My mouth ground to a halt. I couldn't find any other words.

"Take care of yourself," she said.

I nodded. I thought about asking her to pray for me, but it didn't seem right. I turned and left.

Dee caught up with me on the way out. "Take good notes, if you can," he said. "You'll be as close to the heart of the Darkness Radiant as anyone I know. It's a wonderful opportunity."

I tried to summon up a smile but didn't have much success.

"Also, try not to die," he added. He clapped me on the shoulder and went back to his meal.

By any rational measure, it had been stupid for me to offer to escort Prophetess north into Yoshana's teeth in the first place. Was it really that much more foolish to charge directly into the lion's den with the terror herself? I walked out into the bright morning sunlight and mentally directed my rhetorical question at the sky.

I couldn't be sure, but I got the strong feeling the sky told me I was an idiot.

"Minos."

The deep voice at my elbow nearly startled me out of my skin.

Father Juniper must have been waiting for me. The fact that I had missed the smell of his pipe showed how distracted I was.

"Father." My mouth, running ahead of my brain, added, "Here to bless me or curse me?"

He smiled broadly. "You have to do what you think is right."

"Prophetess said exactly that. Aren't you both supposed to be spiritual guides?"

"Are you asking me for spiritual guidance?"

I thought about that. If he told me to stay, would I?

I was still thinking when he said, "It's hard for her too, you know."

"Is it?" She was the center of an adoring cult, not an outcast at the margin of this society.

He nodded. "It is."

He grasped my arms and looked into my eyes. His hands were thick and strong. His bushy beard was white and gray, stained yellow around the mouth from the pipe. A weathered mass of wrinkled skin hid behind that hair, but his eyes sparkled with life.

"You'll be all right," he said. I had to smile.

"I think," he added. "I'll pray for you."

Something in his tone at the end was not entirely reassuring.

Grigg got easily to his feet as I passed through the little door in Our Lady's outer wall. He had been sitting cross-legged - meditating?

"I was hoping you'd come. Unless this is just a polite refusal? Your friends inside didn't seem like the politely refusing type. More like the 'boiling oil over the parapet' type. I have to admit, I wondered sometimes whether this was the best place to sit."

159

He smiled as he said it all, but I still felt compelled to defend the people whose home I'd shared all winter.

"They wouldn't murder you by surprise." And then, because I was feeling peevish, I added, "Isn't that more Yoshana's style?"

"Yes," he agreed, completely unfazed. "That's why you're much better off not fighting her."

"I might feel better about this expedition of yours if you'd at least deny any intention of sticking a knife in my back."

"And would you believe a denial like that? If you have to ask the question, does my answer make a difference?"

"I suppose not. You know, you can be as annoying to talk to as Prophetess."

The big Select chuckled. "I'm going to assume that was meant as some kind of back-handed compliment."

I shrugged. "That's one way to take it."

"You've been spending too much time with priests and prophets. You don't have to prove you can be ambiguous too. That can come across as rude, you know, and that can be unhealthy. Yoshana isn't known for her sense of humor."

It occurred to me that I had been freely sarcastic with a very dangerous man. A captain of Yoshana's legions, who had at least briefly battled her to a standstill in a contest of the Darkness. A man who, as Dee had pointed out, would find me no more troublesome to crush than an ant underfoot.

This suddenly seemed like a very bad idea. What would happen if I turned around and pounded on the door, demanding to be let back in? Embarrassing, surely, but no one had ever died of embarrassment. I suspected the list of people who had died of irritating Yoshana and Grigg might be very long indeed.

"So let's be direct," Grigg said, still smiling. "Are you joining us, or are you conveying your regrets?"

I wondered if I would live long enough to get back through the door if I rejected his offer.

"Let's go," I said. There didn't seem to be any other answer.

3. Renewing Acquaintances

"You're packed awfully light for the trip to Stephensburg," I remarked to Grigg's broad back. He wore a heavy fur cloak over leather, but aside from a sword, a water skin and a few small pouches, he was unburdened with equipment. I had my hickory staff, bedroll, cloak, and the same small bundle of possessions I'd brought north from Rockwall months ago.

He set a brisk pace, and I had taken advantage of that to study him before catching up. I was very conscious that I was looking directly at the back of his neck. He had at least three inches on me and probably fifty pounds, none of it fat. He could have been anywhere from twenty to forty years old. His close-cropped hair was bone white, like every Select's, and like all of us his eyes were jet black from sclera to pupil. His gray skin was unlined. He carried himself with total ease, but I could sense the energy of a coiled spring under that placid surface.

He looked back at me and grinned. "Oh, we're not going to Stephensburg."

I jogged three steps to come up next to him.

"You mean it's just the two of us going to the Darklands?"

"You're awfully thick today, Minos. No, it's not just us. But we're in a hurry. Everyone we need is here in town."

"Everyone... Yoshana is here?"

His smile widened. "That's right."

My stomach dropped. I'd expected to have a week to nerve myself for that meeting, to pry the Overlord's true intentions from her lieutenant - to make a run for it in the night while he was asleep, if it came to that.

"What's wrong, Minos? You look like you just swallowed a bug."

That would probably have left me feeling a lot less nauseated.

Grigg pushed open the door of the rundown inn at the edge of town and announced, "Success!"

I stepped in cautiously after him, eyes slowly adjusting to the dimness. There was only one group of people in the common room, all seated around a large table.

My breath caught at the first face I recognized. Roshel, Yoshana's beautiful Overlord lieutenant, stared back at me. Her eyes were dark, in a normal human way. Her skin had retained its tan color through the winter. Her long hair was as black as mine was white. There was nothing about her appearance to suggest she wasn't an ordinary human - except perhaps the effect she had on my breathing and heartbeat.

The impact wasn't as pronounced as it had been that first time at Stephensburg - maybe I was getting used to her? I managed a tight smile as I surveyed the rest of the group.

Four hard-eyed men sat to Roshel's left. Weather-beaten but far from elderly, they each had that same harnessed energy as Grigg. These would be veterans of Yoshana's wars. The oldest of them, a bearded man with a scar on his cheek, gave me a long, appraising look. I had the feeling he could chew Tolf up and spit out the pieces.

The sixth person's back was to me, shrouded even in the relative warmth inside by a hooded cloak. My stomach was completing its descent into my bowels even before she slowly turned and I recognized Yoshana herself. Unlike Roshel, this Overlord's inhuman heritage showed in her appearance - though her long, white hair came from her Select ancestry, not her demon blood. The mahogany tone of her skin might be from the Hellguard. Where she got the startling blue eyes I couldn't guess. Maybe she'd met someone who had those eyes, liked them, and decided to pluck them out for herself. I didn't really believe that, but I doubted neither her willingness nor her ability to do it.

Some terrors faded when you saw them up close. Yoshana wasn't one of those. She had frightened me at a distance, and then terrified me beyond measure at Stephensburg.

It wasn't that Yoshana's appearance was in any way horrifying. She looked more human than I did, and her sharp features were classically beautiful. The horror of Yoshana was knowing what she was.

Though maybe like Roshel, her effect faded just a bit on repeated exposure. I met the sapphire eyes without backing out the door.

"Kept us waiting long enough," growled the scarred man, continuing to stare at me with challenge all over his face. "You sure it was worth it for one more Select?" His glance flickered to Grigg. "No offense."

A slow smile spread across the Overlord general's face. "Absolutely. This one's special."

She turned that smile on the scowling, scarred man, who was now glaring at me even more intensely. "As Grigg explained, Minos is Prophetess' personal bodyguard."

The man's grunt showed what he thought of that honor. Which wasn't even true anymore.

"This is Erev," Yoshana continued, dipping her chin toward him. "And Rosc, Joav, and Talman. I believe you've met Roshel."

I nodded, not trusting what might come out of my mouth. The dark-haired Overlord stood up, smiling. "Good to see you again, Minos. I'm glad you lived."

She was wearing less armor than the last time I'd seen her. While her pants were studded leather similar to Grigg's, above the sword belt at her waist she wore only a white blouse. I had thought her leather armor did little to hide her curves. The blouse did less.

I swallowed, feeling like an idiot. Though Select don't visibly blush, I could feel my face heating. Desperately searching for something to say, I blurted, "Aren't these your top lieutenants? If they're both here, who's minding the store?"

As if it were sane to question her.

The horror smiled tolerantly.

"Maybe Grigg wasn't clear, Minos. If we don't deal with this threat, there's no store left to mind. The Darkness Radiant is garrisoned at Stephensburg. I have competent officers. If my army can't hold a friendly city without me, it's not much of an army. But this task requires my best."

"And what exactly is the task?"

She barked out an incredulous laugh. "He really wasn't clear! He didn't tell you?"

"He said there was a threat in the Darklands."

"Yes, that's quite true. Specifically, my sources tell me the second in command of the Hellguard is pressuring his commander to accelerate their invasion plans. We're not ready yet. So we need to kill him."

"Kill the second in command of the Hellguard," I repeated stupidly.

"Yes. His name is Yashuath."

"He's... a demon."

Again that slow smile. "Yes, one of the very strongest. By definition."

I swallowed. "Well. At least you're not doing anything difficult."

The smile widened. I was just a bit surprised to see that her teeth weren't sharp. "How's your geography, Minos?"

"What do you mean?"

"To reach the Darklands from here, we'll need to pass through the heart of the Sorrows. The Darkness there is so thick that the demons themselves can't control it. Relatively speaking, killing Yashuath may be the easy part."

I turned and glared at Grigg. "I don't think you're my favorite person anymore."

Roshel said, "Maybe I could be your new favorite person." My temperature must have shot up another five degrees.

Erev laughed nastily. "If you need a baby to care for, there you go," he said to Roshel. He stared at me. "Tell you what, just so we're clear. You're not going to be my favorite person."

There were horses. I supposed it beat walking, but I felt like I had just recovered from the saddle sores I'd accumulated going to Stephensburg and back. My mount was quiet enough, a dun gelding with the disposition of a pack horse, which was probably what it was. Just as well - a spirited warhorse like Yoshana's white would most likely have deposited me on the ground in minutes.

We spread in a short, irregular column down the road. The scarred man rode with Yoshana at the front, Roshel and the other three soldiers behind them. Grigg and I brought up the rear. Grigg had passed me a heavy pack, matching everyone else's. I had combined it with my own gear and loaded it onto one of the three remaining pack animals, each of which was led by one of the human soldiers.

Everyone but me wore a belted sword and carried a carbine in a saddle holster. Not that being unarmed in that company made me nervous. Hah. To be honest, it wasn't the main thing that made me nervous. It wasn't even in the top three.

"Erev doesn't seem to like me," I commented to Grigg.

"He doesn't like anyone very much, except Yoshana."

I nodded. "I noticed that. He, uh, doesn't seem as respectful to you and Roshel as he might."

"He's a senior sergeant of the Knights of Resurrection. He answers only to his direct superiors, and Yoshana."

"Wouldn't his superiors include you?"

The big Select shook his head. "We're Darkness Radiant. The Knights of Resurrection are Yoshana's personal guard. Like Prophetess' Order of Thorns." Again, demonstrating that he knew more than he should.

"I thought it was two names for the same thing."

"I guess a lot of people think that. But it's not true. Yoshana picks good officers, like she said. But the ones that are unconditionally loyal to her - they go into the Knights. Erev, Rosc, Joav, and Talman are all Knights. I don't think I have to tell you not to say anything bad about her where they can hear you. They'd probably cut your tongue out."

I started to ask if he was serious, then decided I'd rather not know.

I asked another dangerous question instead. "Did you... did Yoshana kill the innkeeper back there?"

Grigg laughed. "Do you really think we're that kind of monsters? Why'd you join us if you thought that? Yoshana's ruthless, but she's not cruel." A brief hesitation, something left unsaid. "We paid him not to go telling tales."

"You said it, she's ruthless. And she doesn't exactly blend in, even with a hood on. What made her think he'd stay bribed, not go running off and spreading the word?"

He chuckled, not in a pleasant way. "You really think she wouldn't know?"

I shook my head, my stomach churning more than when I thought she might have murdered someone to cover her tracks.

"Does she seem like someone who would sit with her back to the door, Minos?"

I shook my head again.

"So, why would she do that?"

I thought about the implications of everything he'd said, recalling my conversation with Dee before I'd left. "Because she doesn't need her eyes to see."

The other Select nodded. "You need to understand what she is, Minos. What she has to be. Why she's humanity's only hope."

"You really believe that."

He nodded emphatically. "Of course I do. What I said to you before... we can't defeat the demons or the Darkness if we're not united. Since the end of the Age of Fear, what progress has there been?"

The great civilization of the Last Days had ended with the Second Fall. Scripture said brother had turned against brother as the stain of the Darkness spread across the land. The ancients' pride and unnatural tampering had broken the world, subjecting it to the scourge of the Darkness, and the Hellguard... and the Select.

According to Prophetess, the Universal Church didn't hold the Select responsible for the Fall. We were a symptom, not a cause. So that was comforting.

The Darkness, though...

"Prophetess says the Darkness is the manifestation of original sin. I can't imagine she would ever accept Yoshana using it. Or you using it."

Grigg snorted dismissively. "Who do you think understands the Darkness better, Prophetess or Yoshana? With all due respect, Prophetess is a farm girl from the back end of nowhere who had never seen the Darkness until six months ago."

And how did he know that?

But he was continuing. "Yoshana's an Overlord. She learned to control the Darkness as a child. Can you imagine the discipline that takes, Minos? The willpower? Most Overlords don't survive childhood. When the Hellguard turned on her, when she fought them... she's as strong as a demon herself. Who could possibly understand it better than her?"

"And you?" I asked. "When were you -" I struggled for a word that wouldn't offend, then gave up. "When were you infected?"

"After I met her. After she showed me what it could do."

"You let it in you on purpose?"

He nodded fiercely. "There aren't many people who can control the Darkness. The Hellguard. The Overlords that survive it. A few other humans. And most of the Select. Most of us have the mental discipline for it. That's why it's hard for it to possess us, if we choose to keep it out." His eyebrows went up, and he laughed. "It's funny. Your Prophetess is probably one of the handful of ordinary humans who could master it, and she won't."

"You can't imagine how offensive she would find that suggestion."

"Sure I can. I grew up in the Monolith. I was a Josephite before I met Yoshana."

That seemed incredible. The Josephites were far more conservative than the Universalists or even the Reborn.

"I didn't think the Josephites liked the Select very much."

"You mean because they say we're damned? No, they don't like us. They're pragmatists, though. They'll hire Select mercenaries. That's what my parents were. When they died fighting against Rockwall, the church raised me. They're decent people, Minos. Generous, even. Still, it's tough living where you don't really fit in."

Wasn't that the truth.

We camped at the side of the road that night. The way was broad and straight, one the ancients' greater roadways, but now overgrown and little used. We were passing too close to the Ice Fields for anyone to want to live here. I pulled my cloak tighter. Even in early spring it was cold, especially once the sun was down.

"You going to teach your friend how to fight?" Erev asked Grigg. "Or is he just going to watch when we kill Yashuath?" He looked me up and down. "He's got nice, long legs - I guess he could run away."

Grigg looked just the slightest bit irritated, but merely said, "He stepped between Yoshana and Prophetess in Stephensburg. I don't think he's afraid of a fight."

"Not the wisest thing he ever did," said the white-haired Overlord mildly. Her eyes locked on mine from the other side of the fire, flames dancing in them.

"Eh, so not a coward. I just heard stupid, though. And nobody's said he can fight. I don't see him carrying a weapon. So I'm still thinking useless."

Grigg pulled two sticks from the edge of the fire, each an inch thick and around three feet long. "Close enough." He tossed one to me. "Swords."

The tip of my "blade" was smoldering, and I beat it out on the grass before I stood. I winced, stretching to work the stiffness out of my legs. Grigg waited until I took my stance, then lunged at me with a wild overhand blow.

I stepped in and brought up my stick in a Flowing Water cut that would take his hand off if I were using a real blade. He pivoted, allowed his strike to pass harmlessly outside my counter, and kicked me between the legs.

While I was doubled over gasping and trying not to throw up he smacked the back of my neck with his stick. Erev laughed.

"Let's try that again," I wheezed.

Grigg waited patiently until I caught my breath. But the instant I began to step forward he launched a ferocious backhand. I parried. The force of the blow almost tore the piece of wood from my hand. With my blade deflected out of line, he jabbed me in the side of the face with his left fist. I staggered under the force of the blow. He swept a forehand slash at me, and I just barely interposed my stick, but this time I did lose my grip on it and it flew wide. His third stroke caught me just under the ribs.

"Ow," I said.

"Took three blows that time, Grigg," Erev said. "He's getting better." He laughed again.

The Select doctrine of the sword said that most fights should be decided in three strikes. It didn't make me feel any better. I had expected Grigg to be stronger and more skilled than I was. I hadn't expected it to be by that much. He wasn't even breathing hard.

"That wasn't bad," Yoshana said. "Grigg, give him some real instruction tomorrow night. Don't just abuse him. We know he can take a beating."

I sat back down. Grigg threw both sticks on the fire and clapped me on the shoulder, then easily folded his legs and lowered himself to the ground next to me. If my eyes stung, it must have been from the smoke and the lingering effects of the punch to the head.

Roshel, who had been close to Yoshana, got up and moved to sit at my left.

Had I said her effect on me was weaker? It wasn't just the fire heating my face.

"Going to nurse him back to health?" Erev asked.

The dark-haired Overlord snapped, "You and me, then, Erev? You can have a sword. I'll go barehanded."

"Not exactly fair bringing the Darkness into it," he protested.

"What's fair got to do with fighting? That didn't look like a fair fight between Grigg and Minos. Yoshana never fights fair if she can help it. All that time following her around and you haven't learned much from it." Her tone was mockingly sweet.

Erev threw up his hands. "I yield."

Roshel put her arm around my shoulders. "I'd like to tell you his bark is worse than his bite, but it isn't. He'll stick a knife in your guts if you give him half a chance. He's a total bastard."

The scarred man laughed. "True, every word of it."

Even Yoshana grinned.

With that laughter, it felt like I had been accepted, if just a bit, into that deadly little group. Somewhat to my surprise, it felt good.

The days wore on. We set the fastest pace the horses could sustain, but the pass through the Sorrows wasn't close. It was just as well. In the nights, once our camp was set, Grigg would help me practice with the sword. He'd found two sticks he liked, and we kept those "blades" with us.

I knew all the basic elements he used, but he taught me to refine and combine them. I couldn't match his strength and probably never would, so he helped me learn to turn and deflect his strokes rather than blocking them. He was a good instructor, but as ruthless as Yoshana herself. No opportunity was lost to trip me, ram me with his shoulder, or knee me in the crotch. Between the daily pounding of the saddle and the nightly beating at Grigg's hands, my whole body was a solid, throbbing ache.

Roshel was another kind of ache. I felt flushed and nervous when she was with me, but had no desire to be away from her. She frequently rode with Grigg and me, sometimes chatting easily and sometimes in a comfortable silence. Comfortable for her, anyway.

I felt disloyal to Prophetess. To the person and to the cause. There had been nothing physical between Tess and me, though I certainly wouldn't have objected if there had been. Not that there was anything between Roshel and me either, yet - but there the attraction burned. Prophetess was someone I respected, admired, and cared for. I didn't want to examine my feelings toward Roshel too closely, because I was afraid of what I might find.

About a week after leaving Our Lady, we saw the castle in the distance. There was really nothing else to call it - a massive stone fortress, looking like it was torn from the pages of some medieval history book.

Grigg rode up to the front of the column. "Think that's it?" he asked Yoshana.

"What else could it be?"

"Want to just pass by? We're in a hurry."

She gave a little laugh. "Really? I wouldn't mind a roof over my head tonight."

The Select shrugged and rode back to me. "Guess we'll sample the local hospitality."

The castle stood half a mile from the road down a dirt lane. Tilled fields spread around it, and low outbuildings hugged the massive stone walls. The lane led straight to the fortress' open gate, a huge affair of iron and wood. We could have ridden the horses in two or three abreast.

One of the pair of guards leaning indolently on spears waved to a low hitching rail. "You can tie up here if you've come to see our lord." He jerked his thumb at a little shed next to it. "Weapons in there."

Yoshana's hood was up, hiding her features. "We are travelers from Stephensburg. It's a long road and we'd ask your lord for food and shelter."

It seemed like a good enough idea to me. At this point I would take a bed full of fleas over the ground, and I was already tired of pemmican and hard bread.

"Sure. Horses there, weapons there, in you go. I'm sure my lord will take care of you."

The guard seemed utterly unconcerned. Even without being able to see Yoshana's face, I would have found a company including two Select and four hard-eyed veterans a little intimidating. My eyes went to the arrow slits piercing the stone wall above the gate. Maybe the guard was so unconcerned because the odds were more favorable to him than they appeared.

I thought Yoshana - or at least Erev - might protest giving up their swords and guns, but they stacked them in the shed meekly enough. I had nothing much to give up, but set my staff in with the weaponry.

"Go on in, then," the guard said.

The hallway within was more like a tunnel. Torches were set in sconces, but none were lit. Some light leaked in from behind us, and I could see more ahead, but the corridor itself was nearly pitch black.

Yoshana marched along it readily enough. Maybe she figured there couldn't be anything in there worse than her. The rest of us followed.

The passage opened out into a large, vaulted hall, lit by leaded glass windows set high in the walls. Images of angels and saints were worked into them. The light filtered down through airborne dust motes onto three wooden tables, two lengthwise to us and the third at the far end of the hall, crosswise. At this last, three men lounged, hands casually on the hilts of weapons.

"Welcome," boomed the man on the far side of that farthest table. He was short, stocky and bald, with a wild beard. "Welcome to my hall. I'm Lord Brom of Icefall, and you'll find the price of lodging fair and reasonable. I'll take no more than you have."

The other two snickered, slouching relaxed on stools on the nearer side of the table. Their hands didn't leave their swords.

"We are emissaries from Stephensburg, on Stephen's business," Yoshana replied. She continued to walk toward them, in no hurry. "We regret to impose, but we brought little coin."

"You misunderstand," Brom said. "I'll take what I will of what you have. Your clothes seem very fine, for example. As does your friend there." He leered at Roshel. "And perhaps you too, under that hood."

"There are more of us than there are of you," Yoshana observed.

"But I have a bit of an advantage in position." He waved stubby fingers.

I looked up and around. A balcony ringed half the hall behind us and to the sides. Four men in leather armor with nocked bows grinned down.

It was a neat trap. I might have admired it if I hadn't been in it.

One of the bowmen screamed, "My eyes!"

Blood poured from his mouth and he fell, slamming with a dull thud to the floor behind us. The other three crumpled where they stood, writhing silently, red stains spreading around them. One of the men at the table staggered toward us, knocking over his stool, before he collapsed. The other simply slid to the ground, dead.

"There are more of us than there are of you," Yoshana repeated.

She kept walking, not breaking her stride even when she stepped on the man who had tried to charge us. Lord Brom gave an inarticulate cry and leapt onto the table, swinging a spiked mace.

The weapon flew from his hand before he reached Yoshana, shedding sparks as it skidded across the stone floor. Brom's arm kept moving without it and she caught his wrist. Despite his bulk and momentum, she gave no more ground than if she'd been forged from iron. Her other hand went around his throat.

That's what I thought at first. My gorge rose when I realized her hand was *in* his throat.

"Stephen doesn't appreciate you robbing his citizens," she said. "I don't especially care for it myself."

I think the point was lost on him, considering the amount of blood that came out of his neck when she removed her hand. None of it stuck to her.

She turned and smiled at me. "It's amazing how little force you have to apply when it's targeted. It's very easy for the Darkness to sever the optic nerves and the walls of the carotid artery, for example." She nodded at the dead bowmen, then glanced back at Brom's corpse. "I'll admit that part was a little messier than it needed to be."

Erev's grin would have given a demon nightmares.

My legs trembled like leaves in the wind. I staggered to a bench at the nearest table and sat heavily.

"I like that," said Erev. "Just sit right down like you own the place. And here I thought you wouldn't have the guts for this."

His men chuckled.

Grigg was heading back down the corridor the way we'd come. Roshel reported, "Only four household staff besides the dead and the two outside. Three women and one old man. They don't know what's happened yet." She hadn't moved since the brief battle - massacre, really. However she knew what she'd reported, it wasn't something she'd learned with a normal human's five senses.

Yoshana waved lazily. "Go round them up."

She walked around the lord's table and sat in his chair. High and carved, I suppose the word "throne" might have applied.

The Overlord put her booted feet up on the table. "More comfortable than a saddle, anyway."

She pushed back her hood and looked me straight in the eyes. Hers were no softer than the sapphire they resembled. "The Darkness was a reconnaissance tool before it was a weapon. I knew what was waiting for us before we crossed the threshold. Like I said, it doesn't take much to break apart cell walls. By the time we were in this room, there was enough of the Darkness in all of them that it was just a matter of willing them to die."

She apparently didn't need to blink. I wanted to look away, but didn't want to see the dead men or Erev's mocking smile.

"Are you frightened?" she asked.

I nodded. What point in lying?

"Good. This is what the Hellguard can do. The Darkness wraiths in the northern Sorrows - they're almost gods. If you're going to play this game, you need to understand the players." The sweep of her arm encompassed the room full of death. "And the rules."

Grigg came back, herding the two gate guards. They were both unarmed.

"God!" one burst out as he surveyed the carnage. The other clapped his hand to his mouth, then pivoted around the big Select, trying to bolt. Grigg caught him by the neck and held him in place. Whether it was his immense strength or the Darkness at work I didn't know or want to know.

Yoshana stood and walked toward them, in no hurry. Halfway there the Darkness began to pour out of her like a cloud of black smoke. Their eyes bulged and they cringed back.

I felt like I should say something, but what? Plead for the lives of these men who would have robbed and perhaps murdered us? And if I did, how long would I live?

And so I said nothing.

"Stephen is not pleased," the Overlord said. "Robbing travelers in his lands is..." she looked around. "Well, it's a capital offense, isn't it?"

The Darkness surged around her, then swept forward, covering the two men. They both screamed.

"Go to Stephensburg and report to Commander Stannick," she said. The black stain was disappearing - into them? "Tell him the Darkness Radiant is to take possession of this fortress and use it as an outpost. Take horses from your stable and go as fast as you can. If you don't... the Darkness in you will know. It will tear you apart from the inside out. Slowly. If that happens, your bodies will still reach Commander Stannick to report - though no one will recognize them as human."

She stepped a foot closer. "Go!"

The two stumbled over each other in their mad rush down the corridor.

"Didn't think it could hold a command at that kind of distance from you," Erev said as the sound of their running feet receded.

"It can't." Yoshana smiled. "They don't know that. By the time they're a hundred yards from here it will be out of their bodies. I can't control it much past that range, and God knows what it would do to them."

She turned back to me. "There are ways and ways."

Roshel brought in three women and an old man, just as she had said. One of the younger women broke into loud sobs, but the others stood silently. The old man dabbed at his eyes.

"Clean up this mess," Yoshana told them. "And then we'll eat. After that you can show us where to rest."

The Darkness still coiled around her. "Needless to say, if you try to poison us, or murder us in our sleep, we'll know, and then... well, it would be convenient if there were staff in this place when my troops arrive, but not essential."

Light still danced in the dust motes. Above us, angels and saints looked down from the leaded glass. Whatever they thought, they didn't say.

4. Where Angels Fear to Tread

I was glad to be on the road again. Had I wanted a bed under a roof? I hadn't counted on it being a dead man's bed, his corpse still cooling outside. I had tossed and turned all night in that dark room. I couldn't have said whether it was my conscience or fear that one of those four silent servants would murder me in my sleep.

Grigg had laughed at me when I mentioned it.

"None of them could have killed us even if they'd worked up the nerve to try. We're warded every night. You figured out that Yoshana doesn't need her eyes on you to see you - she doesn't need them open, either. Neither do I. That's just the most basic use of the Darkness."

So much for slipping away in the night.

Grigg had just confirmed it didn't take a visible amount of the Darkness to set a perimeter. Yoshana had said there was enough of it in Brom's guards to kill them by the time they drew their bows on us. "How much of that stuff is in me?" I asked.

"Weather's getting better," he replied.

That was true enough. We had begun to turn south, away from the Ice Fields. That, and the coming of spring, made the temperature far more pleasant. But icy fingers crawled up my spine. As terrifying as I'd thought this group before, I'd never truly seen them in action. Tolf had been right - I'd blundered into Grigg's mission like a man stepping into a pond and discovering there was no bottom. The reality was worse than my nightmares.

Had I thought they'd accepted me? Maybe the way a bloody-handed band of robbers might adopt a puppy. Until they got tired of it, or it became inconvenient.

Sometimes Erev would look at me and chuckle.

That night Grigg jerked his thumb at me, calling me to practice. I unbuckled the dead man's sword I now wore on my belt, a heavy, double-edged blade nothing like my old katana. But as I went to my pack for the practice sticks, Yoshana said to her lieutenant, "Give him a rest tonight. Let's you and me go."

What was the Overlord trying to prove? As deadly as she had showed herself to be, Grigg had half a foot of reach and a hundred pounds on her.

Out came Grigg's sword - steel, not stick. The firelight ran strangely on it, reflecting from the blade as if it were some kind of liquid glass rather than metal. The Overlord's weapon was just as odd, as dull as Grigg's was bright.

The two circled warily, and smoke from the fire swirled around them.

No, not smoke. The Darkness.

They were together and apart again in an instant. I had been utterly wrong. For all Grigg's strength and skill, Yoshana was inhumanly fast. I couldn't imagine how he might touch her.

The Darkness coiled, flowing and striking, like a poisonous tide or a black, shapeless serpent. The Overlord charged, dark blade a blur. Grigg pivoted and struck hard, but her blade eased his aside and she was past him, striking him in the thigh on the backswing. Even as the blood started out from his leg, a line of red opened on each of his cheeks as the Darkness lashed at him.

"Dammit!" he growled.

She grinned, and again I was surprised not to see fangs in that smile.

This time he was the one to attack, and then the Darkness was in his face, and she was under and inside his guard, and the hilt of her sword caught him in the pit of his stomach. Another bloody line opened on both sides of his face, making a pair of X's.

"Enough?" she asked lightly as she danced back, but the look on her face was wolfish.

The big Select spun his sword, scattering light and shadow. Then he took a deep, shuddering breath, and plunged it into the ground.

"Yeah, that'll just about do it."

Yoshana laughed. "One of these days you'll manage to hit me and you'll split me open like a melon."

He shook his head. "If it hasn't happened yet I don't think it's going to."

The Darkness faded. As I watched, the wounds on Grigg's face and leg closed.

He looked at me. "Safe enough if we're careful. Still hurts like a bastard, though." He circled the fire and sat next to Yoshana, who leaned against him.

I looked up just in time to catch the stick Erev tossed at me. "Let's see if he teaches better than he fights."

Grigg answered the sneer with a slow smile and put his arm around Yoshana.

I got to my feet and we squared off. Erev would be tough as old leather stretched over wood. I was sure he was strong - but he couldn't be as strong as Grigg. And he was a couple of inches shorter than me. I'd meet his first attack, and then I'd decide how to deal with him.

That's what my head told me. My guts were turning watery again.

The Knight of Resurrection came in fast with an overhead strike I turned easily enough. But unlike the technique Grigg and I practiced, this engagement wasn't strike, parry, riposte and disengage. Instead, another blow followed, and another, falling like hail.

Off balance, I gave ground. I stopped each swing and thrust but the next came instantly. The wood of my stick dug painfully into my palm with each strike.

Then my feet were out from under me and I was on my back, all the breath whooshing out of me. Erev had backed me into a fallen log and I'd tripped over it.

"Guess not," he said.

I clumsily regained my feet. My face was hot. Erev had already turned his back to me and was putting his stick in my saddlebag. For a second I wanted to demand a rematch. But even I knew it would sound petulant and childish, and I might easily be defeated again. I had already embarrassed Grigg and myself enough. So I sank down by the fire instead, staring into the flames.

Roshel settled next to me before I realized she had moved. She put a hand on my arm and leaned close.

"Don't worry about Erev. He's not a factor," she murmured softly.

I turned. This close, even in the firelight, I could see her dark eyes were brown rather than black. I swallowed. "What do you mean?"

She moved her shoulders in a little shrug. "Yoshana told you about understanding the players in this game. Of course she's one. Grigg and I are too. And your Prophetess, even though she may not know it. Erev isn't a player. He's just a piece on the board."

I thought about that. I looked down, realized where my glance was going and met her eyes again. She wore a little smile.

"And what am I?" I asked.

"That depends on what you want to be."

The order of march changed. Grigg spent most of his time at the front of the column with Yoshana, though at night he still trained with me. I wondered if he did it to annoy Erev - that certainly seemed to be one effect. I hadn't realized the Select was romantically attached to the Overlord, but now it was obvious.

Roshel had taken his place at the back, with me. I can't say I objected to the change. She still exerted a powerful attraction, but I was getting used to having her close. She was easy to talk to. And though she was an Overlord herself, sharing the same half-demon heritage as Yoshana, she in no way looked inhuman. She was far less intimidating than her leader, or even than Grigg. I knew she commanded the Darkness, and I didn't doubt she could handle a sword. But she didn't seem likely to spontaneously murder me.

As the countryside grew more hospitable, we began to encounter towns and villages where we could spend the night. Yoshana paid, and at least as far as I know, she didn't use the Darkness to slaughter the innkeepers after we left.

But then, why would she? We were firmly in Stephen's territory, and she was Stephen's hand now. Or maybe the hand behind Stephen.

Civilization began to thin, though, as we approached the Sorrows. By the time the mountains rose into a wall of forested slopes in front of us, all sign of human habitation had faded away. It wasn't like that in the Green Heart, where I had grown up. People had built into the very foothills of the range. But according to Yoshana, the Darkness was thicker here in the north - and I had no reason to doubt her when it came to the Darkness.

Our shadows were stretched out long in front of the horses when the road began to rise and the trees closed in around us. I asked Roshel, "Wouldn't it make sense to stop for the night? Before we get into… that?" I waved my hand at the tree-shrouded hills.

Yoshana was twenty yards in front of us and conversing with Grigg. She shouldn't have heard me. But I wasn't surprised when she turned in the saddle and said, "Don't worry, we've got a destination tonight."

Then she added, "You're right to be afraid of the Sorrows. But this is the last night we'll be safe. This would be the time to turn back."

Could I do that and live? It was very tempting to find out.

Erev smirked. "If you're scared, I'm sure Roshel will hold your hand."

I scowled at him and any chance I might have had to leave was gone.

The road grew steeper, the trees closer. The clopping of the horses' hooves echoed back at us. I stole a glance over my shoulder at the sun-dappled grasslands behind. Ahead there was only the encroaching shadow of the trees. And the Darkness.

The hills formed a solid barrier in front us, dark and forbidding. I abruptly realized the road went into them, not over them. A tunnel mouth gaped in our path, black as a demon's heart.

We're going in there? The words didn't quite make it out of my mouth. If they had, they would have squeaked.

The lightless passage was terrifying, but wide and mercifully short. No sooner did we emerge than Yoshana swung her horse off to the right side of the path and vanished into the trees. The rest of the column followed, and I found myself on a narrower, steeper track. At my right hand the land climbed up, a long outcrop of rock dotted with shrubs and trees, a hill taller than the one we'd just passed through. To the left it fell away back into the forest. The road was wide enough for a cart, but I nervously edged my mount to the right side of the trail.

We circled as we ascended, at last reaching an arch of coarse stone. Coal smoldered sullenly in iron braziers set into the rock. Beyond was a small, level space, and then the path turned into wide steps, roughly carved into a sheer cliff face. Yoshana had already dismounted and was leading her horse up. I noticed she was hooded.

How safe was this, really?

The horses didn't like the steps and didn't seem to care for the cliff walls rising to either side of us. They balked and jerked at their leads, their eyes rolling nervously. The Knights of Resurrection struggled with the pack animals. Roshel moved forward and laid a hand on each horse's head, and they quieted.

Mine didn't seem nervous. He just set his hooves and refused to move. I climbed a couple of steps ahead of him and jerked on the reins. "Come on, stupid," I growled. "Unless you want the Darkness crawling around inside your head."

The words couldn't have meant anything to his dim mind, but he took something from my tone. Reluctantly he followed me up. "I'm not too thrilled about this either," I muttered.

The stairs curved which, combined with the walls of stone rising to either side, made it impossible to see what was ahead. Brom of Icefall was a rank amateur compared to whoever had devised this approach. We had no visibility climbing up; all a defender had to do was roll a big rock down the stairway. I found myself fervently hoping Yoshana was probing ahead with the Darkness. It's a lot more comfortable to reflect on the morality of your allies' methods when you aren't being crushed by your enemies.

My gelding didn't like the steps any better now that he was partway up. He tossed his head, nearly pulling me backwards. "Cut it out," I snapped. "You're going to break both our fool necks if you try to back your way down now."

Which was true enough. The only way was forward. I yanked hard on the reins, wishing I'd asked Roshel to calm the animal with the Darkness. Part of me wished she'd done the same to me.

Did Yoshana control her troops that way? Did they march into battle incapable of feeling fear?

The cleft in the rock straightened, and even as it did, I practically walked into the back of Roshel's mount. We had halted on the stair.

I edged around the horse and looked up. Another stone arch stood above us, but this one was closed by a wrought iron gate. Braziers were set here as well, but there were more of them. On the other side of the gate stood three men.

Two held long poles topped with torches, each in the form of a brass crucifix. Flames licked up from a reservoir of oil to cover the metal, spreading over the limbs of the crucified Christ. I had seen these torches before at the other edge of the Source. I hadn't liked them then, and the people who had wielded them hadn't been friendly.

Standing between those two, the third man was huge, as large as Grigg. He was no Select, though, pale skinned with a shaggy mane of dirty blond hair. In one hand he held a curved knife, in the other a revolver, crude-looking but of a ridiculously large caliber.

"That all of you?" he asked when he saw me. "Welcome to World's End. I'm Hafnum Furat. Travelers are welcome." I could hear a "but" at the end. I wondered if those torches would keep the Darkness from infecting him and his men. I doubted it. His defenses might be better than Brom's, but I didn't think the outcome would be.

"I'll need your arms to test for the Darkness." He hefted the knife. The light from the torches played on the edge.

"You don't need to do that," Yoshana said.

"And why not?" Furat had the easy assurance of the man on the high ground, behind a gate, with a gun. A lot like Brom's assurance, in fact.

"Because I can tell you we're quite thoroughly infected." The Overlord threw back her hood.

"Oh. Oh!" The big man's hand went to a ring of keys at his belt. He realized that hand held his gun, looked at the other hand clutching the knife, and stared at both in embarrassment, as though wondering how the weapons could possibly have come into his possession. Unable to decide which to holster first, he dropped them both, then fumbled for the keys.

"Thank you," Yoshana said.

"I'm a loyal servant of Stephen," Furat said hastily. Then, more softly, "Besides, I'm allergic to being dead."

"I understand," Yoshana said. "I tried it once and it didn't agree with me. I had to give it up."

The expression on the man's face turned even more sickly. I was impressed he didn't drizzle down his leg. He obviously knew exactly who and what he was dealing with.

The gates swung open and Furat shoved his two associates out of the way.

"But, boss -" one began.

"Shut up," he snapped. "I'll tell you later."

He scrambled in the dirt to retrieve his knife and pistol, hastily shoving the gun through his belt and dropping the knife into a pocket. I hoped he didn't accidentally stab himself.

Past the gate, a sprawl of stone and timber buildings stood atop a small plateau. The view was breathtaking. An ocean of wooded hills spread before us in the dying light.

"Stable's to the left," Furat said. "Shilah, help them get their horses settled." He took the great brass torch from one of his men, handed it to the other, and then moved the first toward the stable with a little push.

"Guest rooms over on the right, no one here now but you, so take whatever you like the look of. I'll go see to supper, that's straight down these steps here." He jerked his head, pointing over his shoulder with his chin. "We can get you provisioned in the morning, for now just get your gear stowed and we'll get you fed."

I was the last one up the steps, and my horse was still nervous. By the time I finished with him and made my way into the dining hall, everyone else was seated. Everyone except Yoshana. She was nowhere to be seen.

This part of the complex was cut directly into the rock. Windows opened to the west, the last of the sunlight winking on the fields of grass below. The glass was thick and lightly rippled, set into diamond panes. I stood there looking out.

"Quite a view, isn't it?" Furat said. He handed me a bowl of hot stew.

"Quite a place. What is it?"

He grinned. "That's not a short answer. You want to sit?"

I surveyed the room. Erev and his men sat at one table, Grigg and Roshel at another. I joined the Select and Overlord. Furat produced two mugs of beer and sat with us. Grigg and Roshel were already eating.

"Best guess is the ancients built this around the start of the Age of Fear. Defensible. Obviously. It was abandoned when I got here."

"Why World's End?"

He shrugged. "Farthest east you can go before you get into the Sorrows. Darklands are on the other side. Far as most people are concerned, this is the end of the world."

"So, no offense, but why live here?"

"Prospectors. There's a fortune in ancient goods up in the Sorrows. I feed and equip the folks that go hunting for it. That's what brought me out here in the first place, but after I went in there... like I said, I'm allergic to dying."

"People do that? Go in there?"

"Oh, sure. There's good money in it." I had mined the ancients' garbage for two years. I nodded. "But a lot that go in don't come back out. Or they make it back here, but the Darkness is in 'em. That's why we test for it. Sorry about that."

Grigg waved away the apology and kept eating. Roshel winked. Furat's face turned bright red.

"How did you already know about Brom?" I asked, changing the subject.

"Who?"

"When you said you were allergic to dying, I thought you knew... uh..."

I looked at my companions. Was what happened meant to be secret?

"Brom of Icefall," Grigg said around a mouthful of stew. "He wasn't very hospitable."

"Oh. Icefall... is he that creep that took over a fort up by the Ice Fields and robbed travelers? I had a couple of people come through here that ran into him. They got here with their packs a lot lighter than when they started. I've heard worse than that about him. Probably deserved whatever Yoshana did to him."

"She stuck her hand into his throat and pulled out his windpipe. After she killed all his men in front of him," Grigg said, still eating.

"Oh," Furat said. "That's... pretty final."

"Yup," Grigg nodded.

"But if you didn't know about that...?" I continued.

"No offense, but Yoshana has a reputation. You don't make her mad and live to tell about it."

I barely suppressed a shudder as I thought about the Darkness boiling out of her in Stephensburg when Prophetess and I had confronted her.

"Nope," Grigg agreed. "Unless you can talk without your trachea."

Furat stood up. "Let me just go check on your friends." He hurried off to Erev's table.

I looked around. The Knights were twenty feet away, engrossed in their own conversation. They barely noticed when Furat joined them. Yoshana was still nowhere to be seen, though I suppose that didn't mean she wasn't somehow present.

Still, I looked into Grigg's eyes - black and empty as my own - and asked him, "How are you sure you're on the right side? A week ago Yoshana killed a fort full of men. This guy here is trying to be friendly, but he's obviously terrified of you. And you're not exactly going out of your way to put him at ease."

I swallowed, and added, "There's a reason Prophetess thinks you're in the service of hell."

"The just man is a light in the darkness to the upright. Psalm one hundred and twelve," Grigg said. Roshel shot him an exasperated look.

"Huh?" I said.

He grinned. "You have to believe in the truth of what you're doing. You have to trust your conscience, and the people around you." He sobered abruptly. "It isn't an easy calling. But if you believe the options are what Yoshana says they are, what choice is there? Sit back and watch the demons and the Darkness roll over the world, while mankind squabbles and suffers? Refuse to get your hands dirty because keeping them clean feels more comfortable? One of the ancients said there's nothing more irrelevant than a pacifist, and he was right."

"But the Darkness? Using that?"

"Like Yoshana says, it's a tool. It's a dangerous one, just like fire. But shoving it away because you're scared of it is no smarter than paleos being afraid to use matches."

I felt my jaw clench. "I don't think it's quite the same thing."

"No. The Darkness is more dangerous. That's where your conscience comes into it. Just like fire, the Darkness is going to rage out of control if you let it. So you can't let it. Sometimes you have to hold it back. Sometimes you have to do something that's hard, that isn't expedient. Like keep your boss from killing somebody annoying. Because if you don't do things like that sometimes, it'll take your soul."

Stephensburg. Grigg stepping into the path of Yoshana's wrath, protecting Prophetess and me.

I wasn't at all sure how wise my next question would be. The death I had avoided at Stephensburg still hovered around me like a clinging mist.

"And Yoshana? I don't see her sparing lives when it's inconvenient to her."

"Spared yours, didn't she? Anyway, Yoshana's different. She's so much stronger than any of us. Her will's as hard as a demon's. I don't think the Darkness could ever take her."

"Except what's in the Sorrows," Roshel said quietly. "Even Yoshana's afraid of that."

Grigg snorted. "Anyone who isn't an idiot is afraid of that."

Shockingly, I didn't sleep very well after that conversation. The bed was comfortable enough, and a sliver of pale moonlight in the window kept my dim room from being pitch black. It should have kept the nightmares at bay. But it was hard to get to sleep at all when I knew the next day I'd be leaping from the frying pan into the fire.

"Even Yoshana's afraid of that," Roshel had said. What business did I have with something that frightened the Overlords?

So I was up early the next day, somewhat rested physically but not at all mentally. A carved stone parapet ringed the site. I leaned on it and looked east, shielding my eyes from the rising sun. The land fell away below me in a rocky slope, then rose again, the green hills of the Sorrows marching like waves into the distance.

I ran my finger over delicate tracery carved in the stone - worn now by the elements, but still evidence of fine work. Whoever had built this place had given an attention to detail that spoke of more than just defense.

"Quite a view, isn't it?" Furat repeated, leaning his elbows on the wall.

"Doesn't look so bad in the daylight," I said.

"Yeah, you'd think that. Once you're down in there, though... I've seen clouds of the Darkness just drifting through the trees, wide enough you can't see either edge of them. The natives in there..."

"People still live in there?"

"Oh, sure. I mean, they walk on two legs and they talk like people. Likely as not to kill you outright, or sacrifice you, though. I think the Darkness is in most of them. But even that doesn't keep them safe. When it really comes together, condenses… they call those gods. They might be gods. One of the truly big masses, it might not even bother possessing you. Just rip you apart for raw materials so it can keep growing. Some of the bodies that people bring out… sure, a lot of folks die in there speared by the natives, or eaten by wolves or drelb, or even just falling down a hill and breaking their fool necks. But some of them… well." He looked at me out of the corner of his eye. "Not scaring you too much?"

"Oh hell yeah."

"Good." Furat nodded. "That's a good place to get killed."

"Yoshana said I should be afraid. So did Roshel."

"They're right. I'm no coward, but you wouldn't get me back in there."

So why was I going? It was hard to remember why I'd ever thought this might be a good idea. Was I really helping Prophetess… and if so, how exactly? Or was it because I wanted to be a "factor," as Roshel had called it?

I looked over at Furat. The big man was resting easily on his forearms, looking out over the sea of trees. His eyes were nearly as blue as Yoshana's.

I said, "Yoshana and Roshel both said this was a game, and you could either be a player or a piece."

Furat turned to me. "Maybe. But player or piece, that's a game where you're going to get hurt. Me, I'm going to be a spectator just as long as I can."

5. The Depths of Sorrow

I don't think I'd ever been sorrier to leave a place. The World's End was beautiful, and Furat was a good host - helped along, no doubt, by his well-founded terror of Yoshana. But my old plastic-sided hovel where I'd lived mining garbage on the Flow seemed like paradise on earth compared to where we were going.

We had traded our horses to Furat for rations, gallons of small beer, and trade goods that might - or might not - appeal to any natives we encountered. I think Furat got the best of the deal, although I didn't know what he could do with the horses up there. With what felt like a hundred pounds of gear on my back, I missed my stupid, skittish mount before I was all the way back down the hill. And I wasn't even carrying a carbine and two bandoliers of shells like the others.

Nor had I appreciated how relaxed Yoshana's force had been until suddenly they weren't. On the decayed remnant of a road, hemmed in by ancient trees, every one of them was twitchily alert in a way I'd never seen. Even in Brom's stronghold they'd been at their ease. Not now.

"You're as good as dead walking in here without being able to control the Darkness," Roshel murmured softly as her head swiveled and her eyes darted about. "But it's dangerous to use it here, too."

"How do you mean?"

"The Darkness responds to the will. The closer it is to you, the better you can control it. Out there, in the rest of world, I can cover a hundred yards all around me. Yoshana can control it farther than that. But in here, as it gets farther from you, there's a risk something else might take it away from you. And then turn it on you, or track it back."

She stopped and turned in a little circle before continuing. "A wraith like the one your Prophetess turned, I would have no trouble controlling. Yoshana could absorb it without even thinking. But the largest wraiths in here could pull the Darkness away even from Yoshana and turn it on her."

We walked a bit more, and she added, "So it's different. Out there, we're never surprised. In here, the Darkness could be blinded, or lying to us, or turned against us. But without it, we're defenseless." She smiled fiercely. "So, excitement. Yoshana lives for this kind of thing."

There was the same tone in her voice that Tolf used when he talked about Prophetess. Yoshana might motivate some people through fear, but others were driven by hero-worship.

"You agree with Grigg that the only choices are Yoshana, the Darkness or the demons?"

"Minos, who else? That wreck, Stephen? Another of the greedy little dictators fighting for territory while they can barely keep their own land protected? It's been three hundred years since the Fall and what's happened? The Darkness is farther west every day, the demons are on the border of the Green Heart, and civilization hasn't climbed up an inch from the depths it fell into during the Age of Fear. Someone with your potential - don't you want something better than to be digging for scraps in the ancients' rotting bones?"

I looked around. I hoped Roshel, Grigg and Yoshana had the Darkness firmly under their control, because I could barely see thirty feet through the shadows among the trees. "Right now I'd be happy if nothing winds up digging for scraps in my rotting bones."

The Overlord just laughed softly.

Five minutes later, I added, "That rustling off to our left isn't anything likely to kill us?"

"We're being paced by a drelb. I wouldn't worry about it."

A cold sweat started on my forehead. Prophetess and I had fought a drelb to a standstill and fled from it a thousand miles west of here. I hoped never to meet another. Dee said the creatures were bears twisted by the Darkness. They were huge, hideous, foul tempered, and hard to kill.

"Oh. Just a drelb."

"Yes, just a drelb." She saw the look on my face and put a hand on my arm. Even after weeks around her, that touch still sent an electric tingle through me. "I don't think it'll try to attack us, but I can deal with a drelb if it comes to that. That thing's the least of our worries in here."

That didn't make me feel better.

It was dark in the Sorrows. The trees overhung what was left of the road, and soon Yoshana led us into the underbrush. She said nothing in explanation, but Roshel leaned close and whispered, "Too many things that might stake out the path. The natives for sure, and maybe wraiths. The deeper we get, the stronger they'll be."

So we made our way through the woods. At least the ground underfoot was fairly clear - the trees choked out the light that lesser plants would need to live. I stayed very near to Roshel. It didn't do my ego any good to admit that she was far more likely to protect me than vice versa, but even here in this terrible place, I enjoyed being near her.

Maybe in some strange way I enjoyed it more here.

It was hard to judge time. The quality of the half light didn't seem to change. But it must have been hours later when the column froze. Roshel held my arm with her right hand and pointed with her left.

At first I didn't see anything. Just a hint of movement, the shifting shadows of leaves. What was I looking for? A drelb? A war party of degenerate humans?

Then I realized I wasn't seeing the wind moving the trees. The shadows themselves were drifting, like a black mist. It was what Furat had described - a cloud of Darkness so wide I couldn't see the edges of it.

I stood very still. Roshel's hand tightened on my arm. Ten paces ahead of us, Grigg and Yoshana were equally frozen in place. In the dim light I could just see Erev's eyes darting from side to side, liked a panicked animal's.

The mist billowed, eddying forward. Toward us. One of the Knights of Resurrection took a half step backward. Erev's hand clamped down on his shoulder.

The Darkness thickened, a solid mass of shadow coalescing no more than fifty feet from us. That cloud must have been over ten feet in diameter, denser and a dozen times larger than what Prophetess had driven out half a year before in Brambledge.

Then it spread again, melted back into the trees, and was gone.

I let out a breath I didn't realize I'd been holding.

"That could have been bad." Roshel's voice was shaky. She still held my arm. I realized she was very close, and that as formidable as she was, the top of her head barely reached past my chin.

She didn't let go, and I didn't want her to. The group still wasn't moving.

"What exactly was that?" I asked quietly.

"Probably the most dangerous thing in here. We can sense the big wraiths. When the Darkness comes together, it has a will of its own, and you can feel it. But this whole forest is permeated with the stuff. A sheet of it like that, before it comes together, doesn't have any consciousness. You can't detect it - it's no different from the background Darkness. But it's just dense enough that it can come together, and if it does, you've got a small god right in front of you, looking for something to control. Or consume. Yoshana must have been able to mask us."

"You can't do that?"

She turned big, dark eyes to me. "I can. I didn't. I've heard stories about the Sorrows, but I've never been here before. I've never dealt with anything like that before. I froze up completely."

She shuddered. "There's a reason why the demons don't come through here."

Grigg made his way back toward us, treading carefully and quietly. "We're going to make for higher ground," he murmured. "Yoshana thinks it might be thinner up there. Maybe."

The ground began to slope up, gradually at first, then more steeply. Accustomed as I was to walking on a flat surface - and I had walked a thousand miles from the Flow to Our Lady - my legs were aching by the time we emerged from the trees onto a rocky promontory.

The sun was past its zenith but still high in the west. I stood and let its light wash over my gray skin, warming my face. I wasn't the only one. A vast sigh seemed to go out of the whole group.

"It's clear up here," Yoshana announced. "We'll break for lunch."

She folded her legs and sank to the ground, shedding her pack as she did. She was graceful as a hunting cat. If the burden of her pack and the tension of the forest weighed on her there was no sign of it now.

"Don't get too comfortable," she added, though she now looked completely at ease herself. "Just because there's nothing here doesn't mean nothing will come. The Darkness prefers the shadows, but it's not afraid of sunlight. Especially in the quantities we're dealing with here."

"Then why does she look so relaxed?" I whispered to Roshel.

Yoshana shouldn't have been able to hear but shot me a little smirk anyway. I had to remember that my words were never secret from her - and possibly not even my thoughts.

"We can see it coming here," said Roshel. "Whatever may come up, we'll at least have some warning."

She shuddered. "That cloud was scary. I don't walk into traps. I haven't felt so blind since Yoshana first showed me the Darkness."

Something nagged at my mind as she said that. "Grigg told me Overlords are born with the Darkness in them." My train of thought ground to a halt. I thought back, realized I had only one soldier's word for it that Roshel actually was an Overlord. Could she be fully human?

"Are you...?" I couldn't get the question out. How do you ask a pretty girl if she's half demon?

She took pity on me. "I'm an Overlord, yes. Just as much as Yoshana. By birth, anyway. My father - that is, my mother's husband - was a powerful man in the Shield. After my mother... well, my father was able to have the Darkness drawn out of me. I don't know how. If your Prophetess can do it, I suppose it only makes sense that others can. Growing up I knew what I was, in a way."

She seemed to lose focus, looking off over the ocean of trees. "People whispered it behind my back. I think somehow it was the worst of all worlds. I was a monster, seed of a demon, but without a demon's powers. My father didn't want that for me."

Her eyes were shining. I didn't know what to say. Though I had been born not far from the Shield, I knew little about Overlords' parentage, beyond the common claim that they were half demon.

"And your mother?" I asked.

186

Her mouth opened in an "O" of surprise. Nearly as wide as mine must have opened for me to put my foot in it.

"She didn't live. No woman who gives birth to an Overlord ever does. The Darkness in the child, when it's expelled from the womb, it lashes out. You really don't know anything about us, do you?"

I shook my head. "I left the Green Heart when I was thirteen. I know what everyone knows."

She dropped her eyes. "The Shield sometimes provides women to the Hellguard for… companionship. Sometimes the women are prisoners of war, or sacrifices. Sometimes the demons just take what they want. If the woman conceives, and the Overlord child survives, the demons deliver it to the rulers of the Shield. That's the bargain. Although it turns out the demons have been breaking it and keeping some of the Overlords to use as shock troops."

She shuddered, took a deep breath, and continued. "My mother was captured in a Hellguard raid across the border. I don't think they realized she was part of the Shield's nobility. My father - her husband - got her back, but by that time it was too late. She was pregnant with me."

She met my eyes again. "It's a terrible thing to be an Overlord. We're conceived in violence and born in death. But Yoshana showed me how we can be the hope of the world."

She looked so human. Much more so than I did. But the mark of Cain she carried inside was far worse than the one the Select wore in our skin and eyes.

Deep inside, part of me gave a bitter, mocking laugh. Yoshana was forging the world's deadliest army around a core of broken souls, the cast-off rejects of society. I'd fit right in.

That wasn't the part of me that put my hand on Roshel's shoulder. She smiled softly at the contact.

"We're losing daylight," Yoshana snapped from the far side of the clearing. "Feed your faces and let's move."

"She didn't stay happy for long," I muttered.

"Can't you see why?" Roshel swept the trees stretching below us with her gaze. The ridge of stone we stood on was no more than an outcrop, an island surrounded by the forest. If we wanted to move forward, we would have to plunge back into the dark of the wood.

"Yeah. Now I'm not happy either."

We tried to follow the back of the ridge, but it wasn't easy among the trees. To add another little touch of misery, it began to drizzle. Mostly the water hit us as a fine mist, but fat drops sometimes accumulated in the leaves above us and spattered down onto our heads.

We squelched through the mud, grumpy and tense. With our sight lines reduced, we could blunder right into a cloud of the Darkness like the one we'd narrowly avoided before. At last, we trudged up a hill, slipping in wet grass and mud, and Yoshana decreed we'd had enough.

Trees still surrounded and loomed over us. This was not like the haven where we'd stopped earlier. "Closest thing to a defensible position I've seen," Yoshana muttered, "which isn't saying much."

I realized that while she looked as disgruntled as the rest of us, the Overlord wasn't wet. A huge raindrop fell from above and slithered down her arm, leaving no trace.

Next to me, Roshel's hair was lank and plastered against her, as were her clothes. I shook myself and turned my attention back to her hair and face.

"Why are you and Grigg wet and Yoshana isn't?" I asked.

"She's using the Darkness to turn the water. Grigg and I could do that out in the open. But even there we wouldn't. It's a question of control. When we first met her, she was using the Darkness to change her appearance. She can do things without even concentrating that no one else can do at all."

Dee had called Yoshana the most dangerous person in the world. He'd also said that was less because of what she could do with the Darkness than because of what she could do with the people around her. Listening to Roshel's tone as she described her leader, I could understand that.

It wasn't yet night, but we were all exhausted by the time we had made a cold, wet camp and half-heartedly swallowed a meal. The overcast sky conspired with the trees to bring on a premature twilight.

Our thin canvas tarps gave us a choice - place them under our bedrolls to keep the sodden grass from soaking our bedding, or stretch them above to keep off the drizzle. I opted for a dry floor and no roof, a bet that the rain would die down during the night.

"Set watches," Yoshana said to Erev. He nodded and gave crisp orders to the other Knights of Resurrection. Grigg, Roshel, Yoshana and I were assigned no turns.

"We'll need all the sleep we can get to handle the Darkness tomorrow," Roshel said. "And we'll still set wards. They just won't be as effective."

"I can take a watch," I said.

She smiled. "You can go tell Erev if you want."

I found I didn't want to.

I had bet right. By the time sunlight returned, the rain had faded to a fine mist. It had still been a cold, damp, miserable night.

Erev propped himself up on one elbow, then sat bolt upright. "Where the hell is Rosc?"

Talman sat up and yawned. "Probably just went to take a leak."

"He can do that when he's not on watch," the senior Knight snapped.

"Calm down," Talman said, yawning again. "I'm sure he'll be back in a minute."

"He's not within a hundred yards of us," Yoshana announced. "Alive or dead."

We never saw him again.

Nerves were taught as bowstrings after that.

"I don't know!" Roshel flared at me when I asked how a sentry could vanish without disturbing the wards Grigg and the two Overlords had set.

I'd never seen her angry before.

"I'm sorry," she said a moment later. "I don't know. It shouldn't happen. He could have wandered off..."

But none of us believed that. Whatever else I might think of Erev and the Knights, they were disciplined. And only a fool would desert in the middle of the night in that Darkness-infested forest.

The idea of a search was rejected almost instantly. We would have to split up to meaningfully extend the range of Roshel, Grigg, and Yoshana's senses - and that could mean death for any or all of us. We packed our camp in silence.

Talman ventured, "Maybe we'll find him on the way." But no one believed that.

There was a new quality to Roshel this morning. Yesterday I had seen vulnerability for the first time. Now she was frightened. She was becoming human. It made her even more attractive. Although my dominant emotion for the rest of that day was a nebulous, lurking terror. The dripping overcast didn't help, fine drops blurring vision and soaking our clothes into squelching, chafing misery.

Even Grigg was on edge. Only Yoshana seemed unperturbed - wary, but apparently immune to the fear that burdened us lesser mortals.

Near midday we halted again. The mist had slowly faded away, but the forest remained dark with shadow.

Around a mouthful of food, Yoshana said, "We're one day in and we've lost a man. It's at least a week across the Sorrows. At this rate there won't be anyone left by the time we reach the Darklands. We have to do something different."

Grigg raised his eyebrows. I wondered suddenly if they could read each others' thoughts.

"We're going to find a village," Yoshana said.

"What?" the big Select erupted, disbelief raising his deep voice to a squeak. Evidently they couldn't read each others' minds after all.

"Yosha, anyone that lives in here is controlled by the Darkness, a murderous cannibal, a raving lunatic, or all three."

"We need a guide. Anyone that lives here and reaches adulthood must know how to survive in this place. And since when can't we handle murderous, cannibal lunatics?"

The grin on her face made me briefly pity the natives.

Man plans; God laughs. Dee had said that to me once. It was one thing for the world's deadliest warlord to decide we would find a village. It was another thing to actually do it.

The sun was setting by the time we gave up. We hadn't seen a single trace of humanity.

Yoshana wasn't visibly frustrated. But no one made a comment. Even I was wise enough to keep my mouth shut.

We found a little clearing with some fallen wood dry enough to make a fire after Yoshana used her inhuman abilities to force the damp out of it. "Might keep the Darkness away," Yoshana muttered, almost to herself. "And it might attract the natives. Win-win."

I thought that would depend on how many natives it attracted.

We sat in a circle around the blaze, no sentries posted. Yoshana, Grigg and Roshel must have trusted enough in their mastery of the Darkness to risk the night-blindness of looking into the flames.

For the first time since I'd joined this group, conversation failed. It was as if Rosc's ghost haunted us. Assuming he was in fact dead.

Hah. Of course he was dead. Although I thought about Furat, telling me that sometimes people came out of the Sorrows possessed by the Darkness. Or Yoshana's bluff at Icefall, that the guards would be eaten up from within, living but no longer human.

If Rosc was lucky, he was dead.

More to distract myself from that line of thought than anything else, I turned to Grigg and asked, "What I still don't understand is how you met Yoshana in the first place. The Monolith's on the far side of the continent."

The white-haired Overlord grinned wickedly. "Ah. This is a good story."

Grigg looked pained, but he took a swallow from his water skin and cleared his throat. "I made some people unhappy."

"Oh, come on," Yoshana said. "The whole thing. Our new friend should know."

The big Select stared into the fire, his eyes losing their focus. Looking into the past. "There was a town called Riverside in the disputed territory between the Monolith and Rockwall. Not too far south of the Principalities. Their council declared for Rockwall, asked to be annexed. We couldn't allow that."

He sipped again from the water skin. "There was a Monolith captain named Everad. A Paladin of the Third Gray Shield, that was the official rank. He had this staff. Shiniest wood you ever saw, with a steel cap at each end, all decorated with scrollwork. He was good with it, too. You wouldn't have thought... anyway. I don't think I ever thought much of him as an officer, but he sure could knock the hell out of people with that staff.

"He had command of a battalion of auxiliaries from around Steel City, the southernmost Principality. I was the most junior officer there was, a First White Shield. I had a squad of Monolith regulars. We had rear guard. Mostly just to keep the auxiliaries from running away if things got tough.

"But that's not what happened. We thought Riverside might have brought in Rockwall troops, or mercenaries. At least a real militia. But they didn't. They shut the gates, but they barely put up a fight. By the time my squad got to the walls, everything was over. The auxiliaries were inside."

His hand clenched suddenly on the water skin, and liquid splashed on the ground. He carefully capped the skin and set it down.

"Everad's troops were running riot in the city. I tried to find him. I saw... horrible things. More than I can count. I've been at war for years since then, but sometimes, when I close my eyes, I still see Riverside."

His hand found the water skin again, and he took another drink, still staring at the fire.

"Everad was in the town hospital. He had two doctors, one sewing up a cut on his arm, the other working on a little scratch on his cheek. There were people dying in that hospital, his troops and the townspeople. Mostly the townspeople. But he had two doctors. Just as I was coming in, he was waggling that staff - he still had it in his hand. He was saying to the doctor working on his face that he'd use it on her if she left a scar."

"'Do you know what your men are doing out there, Everad?' I said. He just laughed. 'Ten blows with a cane,' I said."

"Ten blows with a cane is the Monolith's penalty for rape of an enemy civilian in wartime," Yoshana said quietly.

"Ten blows with a cane," Grigg repeated. "He said, 'That's for real soldiers, not Principalities rabble. Let the barbarians sort the barbarians. It's no affair of ours.' I said, 'They're your men. You answer for them.' He said, 'Answer to who? To you?' And I said, 'You'll answer to God, but before that yes, you'll answer to me.'

"He hit me twice with that staff before I took it away from him. I swear it hadn't occurred to me until it was in my hands, but it made a good cane. Afterwards, the doctors said I kept screaming at him, 'ten blows for rape, a hundred rapes.'"

"A thousand blows," Yoshana added, in case I couldn't do the math.

"I didn't hit him a thousand times. I'm sure of it. I didn't even hit him that hard. At least, not after he stopped trying to fight back. Stopped trying to get away. I didn't kill him. But he never could walk again. Or feed himself."

"No less than he deserved," Roshel said, softly but viciously.

Grigg turned to me. "No, no less than he deserved. I'm not sorry. But he had friends. I had some too, so when they put us both on trial they judged the matter settled. I had struck a superior officer, but he had violated the laws of war and hit me first without due cause. Everyone in the hospital testified for me."

He gave me a sickly grin. "But his friends were higher placed than mine. When rumor came of some mad Overlord's insurrection against Master Karst's rule of the Shield in the far east, I got sent out as an observer. I wasn't meant to come back."

The grin widened. "And you know, I never did."

He'd become part of Yoshana's army instead. Part of her crusade. For the first time, it truly sank in that Yoshana's troops didn't see themselves as villains. In their minds, they were heroes.

I'm not sorry. No less than he deserved. On the long trek north from Rockwall with Prophetess, we had been attacked by paleo savages. I had killed two and crippled one, crushing his knee so he couldn't follow us. Had I said those exact words to Prophetess? They had been close enough.

I didn't sleep well that night. In my dreams my boot came down on the paleo's knee over and over again as I counted… nine hundred and twenty three… nine hundred and twenty four…

In the morning Talman was gone.

Erev was beside himself. Yoshana just repeated, "At this rate, there won't be anyone left. We have to change the equation."

The land began to slope downward, the trees to thin.

"Are we coming out of it?" I asked, unable to keep the eager hope out of my voice.

Roshel shook her head. "Going deeper into it. This must be the High Valley. The center of the Sorrows."

"So at least we're halfway there," I said, still looking for a silver lining.

"No," said Yoshana from the head of our ever-shrinking column. "The valley's wide. We'll likely be days crossing it. But the maps say there's a river, and I'll bet we find someone living by it."

I wasn't as happy about that as she was.

The Overlord got her wish. Before midday we came upon a vast, meandering river, hundreds of yards across. Looking downstream we saw a bridge that spanned it, only half a mile away. There were ruins as we got closer. An ancient town, completely reclaimed by the forest. Moss and creepers, encouraged by the clinging mist rising from the water, had devoured wood and engulfed brick and stone.

"Think there's anyone here?" I whispered to Grigg.

He shrugged. "I'm not sensing anyone, but that doesn't prove anything. They could be out of range, or even hidden from me somehow - hey, watch out!"

I danced back, struggling clumsily with my sword, scanning wildly for danger. "What is it?"

"Poison ivy." He grinned. "Don't want to step in it."

I glared at him, and he laughed. "Seriously, though. Itches for days. Well, not for me. But for someone like you..."

Someone without the unnatural powers of the Darkness.

The crumbling concrete arches of the bridge were as thickly layered as the rest of the town with the creeping vines. They had penetrated the substance and carved out great chunks. Yoshana probed the structure and pronounced it sound, and we made it across without incident. I kept looking back over my shoulder for threats within the ruins, but saw nothing.

Not long after, though, we came across the strangest palisade I'd ever laid eyes on. The wall wasn't built of logs, and there was no cleared area around it from which timber had been taken. Instead, trees grew together into an impenetrable barrier. Branches interlocked, limbs jutting out into huge thorny growths.

"Could you do that?" Grigg asked Yoshana.

"I think so." The Overlord's voice was tentative, uncharacteristically unsure. "It would take a long time. At least, I hope it took a long time."

"What do they mean?" I asked Roshel. I was tired, and not at my quickest.

"Someone must have used the Darkness to make the trees grow like that. I've never seen that done. Looks like Yoshana hasn't either." There was a tension, almost a disbelief in those last words. As if Roshel refused to accept someone might use the Darkness in a way Yoshana couldn't.

"It's a strange thing to do," Roshel continued. "Plants grow slowly. It would take a lot longer to do this than just to make a regular wall... unless whoever did it is really, really strong. Stronger than anyone we've ever seen."

"So… whoever did this is either insane, or insanely powerful?"

"That's about right."

Great.

Yoshana was leading us around the wall to the north.

"Wouldn't it be better to just go straight back into the woods to get around this?" I asked Roshel.

Again, Yoshana answered, a lilt in her voice. "Around? Why would we want to go around? We're looking for the way in."

She and Prophetess might be the bitterest of enemies, but I was starting to see a certain resemblance. Both women would charge into situations I would much rather avoid.

Judging by its curvature, the wall was not long, and it was all too soon that we found an opening. Nothing so conventional as a gate - it was simply a place where the twined branches parted, leaving a space a dozen feet high and half as wide, the limbs meeting above to create a kind of arch.

Skulls hung suspended in the archway, some pierced by the branches, others hanging from vines. I saw pigs, something that might have been a bear or a drelb, and several that were obviously human.

I gasped and took a step back as a figure slid around the edge of the opening. The man was completely naked except for a kind of apron around his waist, secured by a rope belt with a blade stuck through it. His skin was a pattern of light and dark, wild geometric shapes and hideous, staring faces. Lank, dark hair hung past his shoulders. The look in his eyes was utterly mad.

"Yesss?" he hissed, smiling wide to reveal dark-stained teeth.

Yoshana made no move away from this creature, but matched his smile with her own. "We've been passing through your forest and found it inhospitable. We're looking for a guide to take us safely to the other side."

"Bargain, you want?" the apparition drawled.

"Just so."

"Two of yours," he said. "One for us, one for the gods. Then the rest live. You choose the two," he added magnanimously.

Yoshana's ruthlessness was the stuff of legend. She didn't spend her forces lightly, but she'd spend them all to achieve her goals. I shot a nervous glance at Joav, the last remaining Knight except for Erev. We were the two obvious sacrifices.

But the Overlord was shaking her head. "I've lost two already. No more. Go find those two if you want bodies."

"Little girl will lose all, alone in the woods. Bargain, or no bargain. Two, or all. You choose." He leaned against the tangled wall, a picture of violence at rest, like some sort of feline predator twisted into human form.

"Unacceptable," Yoshana said. "We have weapons, supplies, trade goods. We'll deal in something besides flesh."

"No." From his slouch, the man flowed back into poised readiness. "I will have what I want. Your weapons? Hah. Nothing to me."

He pulled the knife from his belt. I realized it was a single, curved bone, sharpened and etched with designs that mirrored his skin.

"The gods are in me, little white-haired girl. Nothing can harm me." He dug the point of the bone blade into his left forearm, tracing a deep gash toward his wrist. Darkness bubbled up and sealed the wound.

"Hmm. Really?"

Yoshana's sword had cleared its sheath and severed his head before I knew she was moving. For a frozen instant, the Darkness hovered over the two halves of the native's neck. Then it rose up in a cloud, abandoning the body, and the blood rushed out.

"Didn't think so."

The Overlord raised her left hand to the cloud, already beginning to dissipate. It swirled, hung suspended as if in thought, and then streamed into her body. She closed her eyes for a moment.

When she opened them they were, for only a second, as black as mine. Then their startling blue color returned. She examined her strange, dull sword, finding it entirely free of blood.

"Interesting," she said, and sheathed it. "Let's see if his shaman is more cooperative."

"Shaman?" Grigg asked.

"That's how he thought of the one that did this." She touched the wall, then pointed straight ahead. "This way."

The compound was small, no more than a hundred yards across. Primitive thatched huts ringed the periphery. Yoshana led us toward one of those.

The center of the area was not cleared. Trees and other plants grew riotously. Some were heavily laden with fruits or vegetables, far out of season. Every one of them was swollen beyond its normal size, colors unnaturally bright. I looked sidelong at an apple the size of a small melon, a red so vivid it seemed venomous.

"Bets on what you'd find if you cut it open?" Grigg murmured.

A man burst from the trees a dozen paces from us, an ax in his hand, face contorted in hate.

Yoshana brought her carbine around without unslinging it. The action of firing, working the bolt, and firing again was almost too fast to follow.

As the third round smashed through the attacker's heart, a rush of Darkness boiled out of him and spread into the air. This time the Overlord showed no interest in catching it.

Instead she said, "Active perimeter. Some of them might be able to project. If they can, that's next."

A smoky triangle formed around our group, with Yoshana, Grigg, and Roshel at the vertices. The Overlord looked over her shoulder at me. "Stay inside if you want to live."

Erev, Joav, and I crowded the center of the triangle. The two Knights had their guns drawn.

The hut we were approaching was no bigger than the others, perhaps twenty feet across. There was an opening with no door, and Yoshana clearly felt she needed no invitation to enter. Grigg and Roshel remained outside. Our shield of Darkness flowed around the doorway, half in, half out. I peered past our leader into the dimness beyond.

I wished I hadn't.

There was only one person inside with Yoshana. Where the other two natives had appeared outwardly healthy, this was only a withered husk. I couldn't tell if it was male or female. It sat on a pile of rotting animal carcasses, slowly drooling from a mouth empty of teeth.

At its shoulder pulsed the thickest cloud of Darkness I'd ever seen. It was as large as a man, too dense to see through. Thick tendrils of its substance flowed into the shaman like obscene umbilical cords.

"Well. You're more horrible than I expected," Yoshana said.

The entity didn't seem interested in banter. The cloud shifted and throbbed. Its human half drooled.

"As you know, we're interested in a guide across the Sorrows. We can make it worth your while…" But Yoshana's voice trailed off. Her eyes were locked on the ruined body squatting in filth. The Darkness could have filled the shaman with unnatural health. If it hadn't, that was because it simply didn't care. No human consideration would matter.

"There is only death here," sighed the living corpse in front of us.

Yoshana nodded. "Yes."

Her shot took the shaman between the eyes even as the cloud of Darkness rushed at her. The triangle of protection was gone, all the Darkness that Yoshana could command pulled into a barrier in front of her.

"Torches!" she screamed.

Any prudent traveler carried oil-soaked torches. Fire was one of the few things the Darkness feared. For all their mastery of it, Yoshana's company took the same precautions. Grigg flung down his pack and busied himself with flint and steel.

Of course, that's when the rest of the natives attacked.

Grigg was focused on his task. Yoshana had all she could handle battling the cloud. Roshel and I were watching her in horrified fascination. And the unnatural defenses that shielded us at all other times were gone, pulled into Yoshana's struggle.

I could see why Yoshana valued Erev, mean-tempered bastard that he was. The crack of his carbine behind me was the first warning I had that we were in no less danger outside the hut than the Overlord was inside.

Joav fired too, and both their shots were true. But they didn't have Yoshana's inhuman speed or aim, and our enemies were creatures of the Darkness. Two staggered but didn't drop. And there were a dozen more.

Roshel took the last available second to aim her gun while I dropped my staff and fumbled out my heavy, double-edged sword. Her bullet took a native in the face two strides before he reached her. The cloud of Darkness escaping showed that one was dead.

Roshel looked at the cloud, perhaps tempted for an instant to seize it and replenish what Yoshana had stripped from her. She snatched up my staff instead.

"Keep them at a distance," she shouted.

They were on us. One swung a sharpened iron pole at me. I brought my blade up to parry, and the force knocked me staggering back, loosening my grip on my weapon. I had fought paleos, and I had fought a drelb. This was far worse - the human intelligence of the former blended with the inhuman strength of the latter.

To my left, Erev's sword was a wall of steel, holding two attackers at bay. But Joav was falling, a native's fingers sunk deep into his right arm. Roshel smashed my staff into one's face, pivoted, and kicked a second.

Then the iron pole was swinging at me again and I gave ground. A weight hit my back, and an arm like a metal bar went around my throat. I stabbed blindly over my shoulder and felt the blade bite home. The savage with the pole thrust at me and I turned. The point slid by me and must have struck the creature on my back, because it released its grip. As it fell away, it kicked me in the knee, and I collapsed to the ground.

"Here!" Grigg bellowed. He held three lighted torches. Two he tossed at Yoshana. He drove the third into a native's eyes and followed up with a disembhoweling backhand with his blade. Two more jumped on him.

A ruined face crashed into mine, bloody mouth leering. The man who had been behind me, wounded rather than killed. I kneed him in the crotch and tried to kick him away. Over his shoulder I could see my other assailant looking for a place to stab me without skewering his comrade. Staring at his bloodthirsty grin, I wondered if he wouldn't just impale us both.

There was a roar like thunder as the shaman's hut exploded in flame. The native on top of me glanced over his shoulder, while the one with the pole turned to stare. That was the last thing he ever saw as Yoshana's sword took his head off.

The Overlord sucked in the Darkness, ripping it from the natives around her and hurling it back at them. Where it struck, it tore at their faces and they fell screaming. She moved through them like a reaper scything wheat. Grigg cut his way free of the two that had seized him and hewed down a third.

The man on top of me realized the tide had turned and leaped up to run. A bullet from Roshel's carbine caught him in the back of the head.

And it was over.

Erev was on his knees, exhausted but unhurt. He had held two of them off until Yoshana could finish them.

Joav rolled from under the body he had knifed a dozen times. He had been a quiet man as long as I'd known him, and all he said was "ouch" as he examined the deep holes the savage's fingers had gouged into his biceps.

As the Darkness settled, I realized smoke was rising from Yoshana's hair and clothes. For the first time since I'd met her, the Overlord looked like she'd been in a fight.

"We need a new plan," she said.

6. All the Colors of Darkness

We camped several miles from the compound. Yoshana was fairly sure we'd killed everything in it, but there could have been hunting parties out. None of us wanted to chance it. And there was nothing in that lair of twisted life and putrid death that any of us wanted to see again.

The Overlord herself was tending to Joav's arm. Eventually she shook her head, cut off a strip of her cloak, and wrapped it around the wound.

"It should heal. It's cleaned, and I got the flesh started knitting itself back together. It'll take time, though. Even under ideal conditions, the Darkness just won't heal someone else the way it heals its master. I never understood why."

She glanced over at Grigg. "Nearly killed me, that time I brought you back."

"Pretty sure it did kill you," the Select replied.

"No, that was the spear afterwards. Anyway, that was on a battlefield, but nothing like this cesspit where God knows what could happen if I let my guard down."

She actually sounded apologetic, as if she truly regretted she couldn't do more for the Knight.

"Thank you, mistress," Joav said. He produced a tight little grin. "I'll take it from here."

"Get some rest," the Overlord told him. "Erev, Minos, you too. Grigg, Roshel, and I will take the watches tonight. We're not going anywhere tomorrow."

"Don't you want to put some distance between us and that place?" Roshel asked.

Yoshana shook her head. "Like I said, we need a new plan."

I woke in the morning to the sun and the sound of birds. Roshel sat on a rock a few feet from the ashes of our fire. I quickly counted heads - no one had vanished in the night. Despite the horror of the day before, the forest seemed peaceful.

I sat up, and Roshel gave me a tired smile.

"Rough night?" I asked.

"Uneventful," she replied. "But after we lost a sentry two nights in a row, I kept the perimeter on a lot higher alert than usual. I've killed five squirrels, two foxes, and an owl that got too close."

She stood up and stretched. "Guess I'll go collect them. We shouldn't let the meat go to waste."

"I'll go with you."

She shook her head, though her smile widened. "Better keep an eye on things here." She nodded at the four sleeping figures around us.

"That's a surprise," I said. "I didn't figure any of this crew for heavy sleepers."

"Grigg and Yoshana kept the same kind of watch I did. There's probably a bunch more dead animals that they took out on the perimeter. And everybody's worn out after the last couple of days. Soldiers learn to sleep when we can."

She moved off into the trees. I was disappointed I couldn't go with her, but rather than examine that emotion too closely I looked at our slumbering companions instead.

In repose, only Grigg looked dangerous. He was huge, tall and solid as a rock. His white hair was cut close to his gray scalp, though I'd never seen him trim it.

Erev and Joav looked peaceful in sleep, the hard lines relaxed out of their faces. Neither was a large man - Erev was average height, lean and tough rather than bulky. Joav was smaller still. The younger Knight twitched and grimaced briefly in his sleep. His arm must have pained him. The wound was horrifying - crippling and perhaps fatal from infection without Yoshana's intervention.

The terror herself had the smooth, unlined face of a young girl. It meant nothing - even a normal Select aged slowly, and the half of her that wasn't Select was demon, and immortal. Between that and her mastery of the Darkness, I had no doubt she could look unchanged for centuries. But from what was known of her, she really was young, likely no more than thirty. And she was no taller than Roshel - for all her presence, she didn't reach past my chin. Curled up in her bedroll, her long, white hair puddled around her face, there was nothing but her unusual coloring to suggest she was the most dangerous human being on the continent.

Grass rustled behind me, and I spun to see Roshel emerging from the trees with her arms full of small furred and feathered bodies, a fox dangling by its tail in each of her hands.

She dumped the collection of squirrels, rabbits, weasels, and birds near the remains of the fire. She looked down at the foxes regretfully.

"It's a shame. I like foxes. But what's done is done, and at least we can use the fur and the meat."

She pointed back the way she had come. "Oh, and someone killed a boar about thirty yards that way. Can you go get it?"

"You sure it's dead?" Wild boar weren't something you messed with.

She laughed. "It's not breathing, and it's in the kill zone."

"Not infected with the Darkness, is it?"

She sobered. "I've heard of the Darkness taking pigs, but it looked normal enough. Anyhow, infected or not, it's dead now. If it comes back to life, just yell."

Sure. Just yell. Help would definitely reach me in time if I was set upon by the living corpse of a boar animated by the malign power of the Darkness. Right.

You wouldn't think a dead pig would be hard to find, but there had been no struggle, no disturbance of the brush. It took me a few minutes of searching to come across the body, lying on its side in a stand of tall grass next to an oak tree. It had simply fallen where Yoshana or Grigg had killed it, rupturing who knew what blood vessels or vital organs.

I watched the body for a time. Roshel had been right - it wasn't breathing, and there was no indication it was anything other than a dead pig. A big, dead pig. I stepped up and grasped it by the hind legs. The beast must have weighed a hundred and fifty pounds.

It would have been impressive to sling the carcass onto my shoulder and carry it into camp like a conquering hero. I dragged it through the grass instead. That thing was heavy.

Everyone was awake by the time I got back. I hadn't thought I'd been out that long.

"How about a new rule," I gasped. "Whoever kills the big, heavy thing in the woods gets to bring it back?"

Grigg chuckled.

Yoshana said, "We need to talk."

I held up my hands. "Hey, if it was you, I'm happy to carry it."

She didn't smile. Not the fierce, wild grin she had when she fought, or her tight little smirk of superiority. My stomach dropped. This couldn't be good. For weeks I had played with fire. Now I was going to get burned. Maybe fatally.

I looked around the group. Grigg's good humor had vanished. Erev was looking at me with a hungry intensity. Roshel offered me a small smile, but it was a weak effort.

"So let's talk," I said. I couldn't run. There would be no escaping her, and no surviving in the Sorrows if somehow I got away.

Now the corner of her mouth quirked up. "It's not like that. I said we need a new plan. If we're going to make it through this, we need to be stronger. That was too close back there."

I nodded.

"We need you to master the Darkness."

Useless as it was, I backed away. I stumbled over the dead pig I had dragged into the camp, windmilled my arms, nearly went down. "What? I'm not letting that in me!"

Yoshana shook her head. "Don't be foolish, Minos. You've seen people who control the Darkness, and yesterday you saw what happens when the Darkness controls people. This is what we've been trying to explain to you. We need to control the Darkness, and there aren't many who can. You're one of them. Either you help us, or we fail here. And you die, or it takes you."

My heart raced. There was no denying I'd been almost useless in the fight. Even Joav and Erev, hardened veterans though they were, hadn't contributed much more. Grigg, Roshel, and of course Yoshana had been the ones that made the difference.

He's not a factor, Roshel had said about Erev. Was this what she'd meant?

And what am I? That depends on what you want to be.

I looked at Roshel. She nodded, just a little.

So, did I want it? Did I want to be a factor?

Did I have a choice?

Player or piece, that's a game where you're going to get hurt. I'm going to be a spectator just as long as I can. That's what Furat had said. But if anything was true, it was that I wasn't in a position to be a spectator.

"Not a lot of people can control it, Minos," Grigg spoke up. "But a lot of Select can. We're sure you're one of them."

Prophetess called the Darkness the physical manifestation of sin. The literal agent of hell on earth. I had never believed that, before I met her. Did I believe it now?

"If we live, Minos, you could build a bridge of peace between Our Lady and the Darkness Radiant," Roshel said softly. It was like she was reading my thoughts. Maybe she was. "You've lived with Prophetess and understood her. Now you can understand us."

The possibility of peace should never be ignored. You should do what you think is right.

Erev spat on the ground. "You're going to make this one a master of the Darkness?" he rasped. "What's your next trick, Roshel? Teaching a cow to juggle?"

He looked me in the eye. "No offense."

"None taken," I replied. I turned to Yoshana. "Let's do it. I've always wanted to see a cow juggle."

I sat on a fallen tree. Yoshana was next to me. After weeks of traveling together, this was the first time she had been close enough to touch. It was disconcerting.

A sphere of the Darkness pulsed in her open palm.

My heart raced as I watched that shifting mass. It was the key to the power that set Yoshana, Roshel, and Grigg apart. It fascinated me - and terrified me.

The Overlord set her left hand lightly on my leg. "Pay attention. This is critical. The Darkness responds to human will. That's how it was created. But your will doesn't mean your surface thoughts. The Darkness reacts most strongly to your strongest feelings. That's generally going to be fear, rage, and lust."

I remembered the possessed miller's daughter in the village of Brambledge. She had been a creature of wild, uncontrollable urges until Prophetess had driven the Darkness out of her. Yoshana's description seemed about right.

"So you have to still yourself. The way you're all keyed up now - that wouldn't end well."

I grimaced. "Grigg said sometimes you have to resist it."

"You have to master it. You've heard us use the fire analogy often enough. It's really pretty close. You have to keep it under control. For you, that's going to mean centering exercises."

"I can do that. I've had some training." I looked straight into those shockingly blue eyes. "You say for me. Not for you?"

"No. Not for me." I was surprised to see her face light up in a smile. "I'm special."

"Um. Now? The centering exercises, I mean?"

"Unless you have somewhere else to go."

I closed my eyes and breathed deep. And again. In my mind, I heard the long, slow tolling of a bell. I imagined myself a stone statue, and bit by bit my body lost its muscle tension, my jaw unclenched, my hands lay limp on my thighs.

With my body stilled, I returned my mind to the tolling of the bell. Slowly, slowly, my brain emptied of thoughts.

And then, in that emptiness, I wasn't alone.

My eyes snapped open. Yoshana's right hand was on my heart. The sphere of darkness was gone.

The exercise came undone in an instant. My pulse raced.

"Ssh," she soothed, her palm warm on my chest.

"It's -"

"In you. Yes. It's all right."

"When you said I needed to practice centering, I thought you meant for more than a few seconds." Inside me, something coiled and seethed.

"Calm down. Deep breath. Go back to your center."

I started to open my mouth, then obeyed instead. I closed my eyes, took deep breaths, let my muscles relax. The presence that now shared my body quieted.

Yoshana nodded. "Good. Normally we'd have practiced meditation for a few days before we let the Darkness in, but we don't have time. You're going to be my most accelerated student. Don't worry, the amount in you now is easily manageable. Less than what was in that peasant girl your Prophetess exorcised."

She paused, then added, "Under normal circumstances, if you couldn't handle this much, I'd just pull it out of you."

"But?"

"But here, with so much of it in the air around us, it would just find its way back in now that you've been opened to it. So if you can't control it, I'll have to kill you."

She gave me her wild grin, and patted my leg. "Calm down. Deep breath. Go back to your center." And she laughed.

Terrible and awesome as she was, Yoshana was a surprisingly good teacher. She was patient and methodical, and if at times she was shockingly blunt, by the same token she seemed to hold nothing back.

Of course, I might have expected her methods to be as brutal as they were effective.

"Let's test integration," she said, and in a single, smooth motion produced a blade from her boot and slashed it across the back of my hand.

"Ow!"

I grabbed my wounded right hand with the left, but where I had thought to see blood, black particles welled up instead. The cut had severed two large veins, but they didn't bleed.

"Good," Yoshana said. "Keep an image of your body integrity. If you think of yourself as whole, you'll heal. Don't let your mind form thoughts of yourself being crippled, or bad things will happen. Always stay focused on your goals."

Grigg walked up. "Focus and restraint must be the bastions of your will."

Yoshana glared at him. "Let's keep it to one instructor. We can't afford for him to get confused."

She gave me a long look. "Although I can't spend the next week doing nothing else but train you. I'll give you as much time as I can, but when we're moving or bunking down, Roshel will take over."

My pulse sped up for an entirely different reason. Yoshana laughed at me again. "Calm down. Deep breath. Go back to your center."

As distracting as Roshel had been before, it was ten times worse now. If I allowed my thoughts to turn to her at all, the presence inside me surged with violent desire. The miller's daughter in Brambledge had gouged deep wounds into a romantic rival's face. Now I could understand why. The feelings took all my willpower to control. And Roshel's knowing smile didn't help any.

We had remained in camp all morning, and when the sun was overhead, we made a meal of some of the small animals the group had killed in the night. The pig was slowly roasting on a spit - I supposed that would be dinner.

Yoshana summoned up another, larger cloud of the Darkness. "I'd like to give you more time, but we don't have it. We need to get moving tomorrow. What's in you now isn't enough to accomplish much. You've handled it acceptably so far. I'm going to take you up to your capacity."

"What does that mean?"

"There's a limit to how much of the Darkness someone can handle. It's not physical - there's a surprising amount of room for it in your body. It's a question of control. The more there is, the harder it is to master, and the more it will sweep you up and carry your mind away. What's in you now could only possesses someone with a very weak will, but like I said, it's not enough to help us much. Taking you to your capacity means you'll be much stronger and more useful, but it's risky. That concentration can control the vast majority of humans."

Rather than think about that, and what would happen if she was wrong about how much I could manage, I asked, "And what's your capacity?"

The grin again. "A lot more than yours."

"And that thing that was attached to the shaman?"

The smile vanished. "More still. More than I could control. The shaman was just a shell. It wanted a human body for some reason, but that wasn't a possession. That was a Darkness wraith controlling a living corpse. The wraiths get even bigger than that, but if we fight one, we aren't going to win."

"You said it responds to human will."

She nodded. "To a point. In your typical possession, the Darkness is still doing what the host wants. Not what he consciously wants, but what the deepest parts of the mind want. The id, the subconscious, was what they called it in the Last Days."

"Monsters from the id," Grigg chimed in.

"Would you stop that?" Yoshana snapped. The Select just grinned.

"Anyhow, when the concentration gets thick enough, it starts to think for itself. It develops its own will. If a cloud like that holds together, it's almost like a god."

I nodded. "We had those down in the Green Heart, in the foothills of the Sorrows. Way down at the southern end, I mean. Some people worshipped them. The folks on the edge of the Sorrows down there... they weren't quite right."

"Yes. And the wraiths up here get far bigger than that. There's a reason the demons won't move through these hills. Not even the Hellguard could cope with some of what's in here."

"But we're going to."

"No. We're going to avoid it. I made a mistake in that last village. I had expected a human leader, no stronger than me. Not as strong as me. The way it turned out, we're lucky we survived. We can't afford any more surprises. So far we've lost two men, and Joav's hurt. That's why I need you able to help with scouting."

I nodded again. This was the Overlord Yoshana, admitting error, taking me into her confidence, treating me almost like an equal. "Show me what I need to do."

The presence in me was stronger now. No - that's not quite right. It wasn't *in* me. It *was* me. The Darkness was as much a part of me as my eyes or my hands.

"That's right," Yoshana urged. "But keep yourself centered. What you feel, it feels. What you want, it wants. Control yourself, and control the Darkness. Then let it flow with you."

Each individual particle of the Darkness was tiny. It could ooze out through my pores and I didn't even feel it. And when it was outside my body, it was as if I was larger. I could feel the wind on parts of me beyond my skin. I could see all around myself without turning my head. It was amazing.

"Maximum control range for most people is about a hundred yards," the Overlord explained. "You run a trickle of it out - it can be a thin enough strand to be invisible, but you get enough sensory input for it to be useful."

I concentrated, trying to extend my focus.

"No! Not here. In this environment, something can latch onto that string and follow it back to you. And it may not be something we can deal with."

Chagrined, I pulled the whole cloud back inside my body.

Yoshana grinned and patted my shoulder. "You had the right idea, but we're going to have to train you a little differently than normal. I want you to learn how to sense concentrations of the Darkness, and avoid them. Let's play a game."

For the next hour, I practiced sending out probes of the Darkness. Soon, the Overlord began to parry them with her own. And then the "game" began in earnest. If the strand of Darkness under her control detected mine, it followed back to me and struck.

Just hard enough to draw blood.

"It's a two-for-one exercise," she laughed. "You're getting practice healing yourself, too."

I growled. She had slashed me open a dozen times. The Darkness within me sealed my wounds, but it still hurt.

By the time the sun was low in the west, I was exhausted. I understood now why Yoshana, Grigg, and Roshel hadn't taken watches when we'd been marching. The total concentration required to keep my extra senses alert and under control was more draining than any physical exercise. And there were worse things out there than Yoshana, that would hurt me far more.

"You've done well," the Overlord said. "Excellent progress for the first day. Let's eat."

The fire was warm and bright, and the roast pig was delicious. Grigg and Roshel sat on either side of me. The Select punched my arm and said, "Now you know what it feels like to be on the receiving end of Yoshana's lessons. Worse than mine, aren't they?"

We all chuckled. With the power of the Darkness in me, I was truly one of them now.

"Let's bunk down early and make some progress tomorrow," Yoshana declared. "Same watches as last night."

I was asleep the instant my head touched the ground.

We were in a deep cavern or a vast, stone-sided well. There was no sky I could see above, or floor I could touch with my feet. We all bobbed and floated in thick, viscous blood. There were dozens of us, human and not, demons and drelb, men in armor and paleos in ragged hides. Whenever one of us came near another, we would rush together, grappling in a frenzy each to submerge the other, drowning our foes in the thick, choking liquid.

And as we thrashed and fought and died we all laughed in the glory of it.

A woman was near me, and I knotted my hands in her hair and held her under until the struggling stopped and only afterwards I realized that it had been Prophetess.

I was just beginning to wonder if I should feel something when Yoshana leapt onto my back and plunged my face beneath the surface.

I woke up screaming.

"Calm down. Deep breath. Find your center," said Yoshana. The Overlord sat by the fire ten feet away, a little smile on her face. I felt a hand on my shoulder and flinched violently, sat bolt upright, realized it was Roshel. My heart was pounding like it was trying to burst out of my chest.

"Deep breath," Yoshana repeated, more forcefully.

I inhaled through my mouth, held it, and let the air out in a ragged gasp. And again. After the third breath I realized a cloud of Darkness was surrounding me. I flailed my arms at it, then realized it was my own.

"Object lesson," the Overlord said, her white hair stained as red as her skin by the firelight. It reminded me of my dream, and I looked away.

"You absolutely must still your mind before you go to sleep," she continued. "I put Roshel next to you because she can take care of herself. If Erev or Joav had been near you, you might have killed them."

I looked again at the cloud around me. It shifted and seethed, as perturbed as I was.

"You knew this would happen?" I accused her.

"Sure. It always does."

"Don't you think you could have warned me?"

"I find this gets the point across more effectively." Her smile broadened.

"Told you her lessons were harder than mine," Grigg said.

I spent half an hour meditating before I dared go to sleep again. But I had no more dreams - or at least none that I remembered, or that made me wake screaming.

"Your Prophetess is right about one thing," Yoshana said the next morning. "The Darkness is dangerous. Control it, or it controls you."

I nodded shakily. She had driven that point home with a hammer.

We moved slowly that day, but we moved. After a breakfast of smoked pork and dried fruit, I felt well enough to let the Darkness out and put Yoshana's lessons into practice.

Questing out with my new senses, I could feel the edges of the probes emanating from Grigg, Roshel, and Yoshana. Yoshana's I recognized instantly, and I found I could distinguish the others' as well. There was a kind of intention radiating from each strand of Darkness, imbued with the character of its master.

Yoshana had been right, of course - the Sorrows were saturated with the stuff. Tiny particles of it were almost everywhere, most so dispersed they were barely perceptible. Any time I sensed any concentration at all, I reported it to Yoshana. After a while she got sick of it.

"If it's smaller than what we first put in you, just ignore it," she said. "That's no threat. Unless it's a thread leading back somewhere."

"How do I know if it's a thread? Do you want me to follow it?"

She sighed, and Grigg laughed. "You wanted to train him. It's a fair question."

"Exercise your judgment," the Overlord said.

"His whole day's worth of it?" Erev snapped. "He just fell off the turnip wagon and we're supposed to trust his judgment?"

I had seen lots of expressions on Yoshana's face. I didn't ever want to see that one again, even directed at somebody else. Erev obviously felt the same way. He mumbled an apology and moved out of her line of sight - although of course nothing was really out of Yoshana's line of sight.

Yoshana was many things. But I shivered at the reminder that one of those things would always be a ruthless killer with a short temper.

There was a brief round of drizzle in the afternoon, which didn't improve anyone's mood. None of us had slept well, and progress was slow enough without the rain. Yoshana called a halt well before sundown, in a little clearing with a fire pit in its center.

"Think it's safe to camp where the natives do?" Erev asked tentatively.

"Not really. I don't think anywhere else in here is safe either. At least we can make a fire."

We set out to gather wood, searching for downed branches that weren't too wet. We paired off as a precaution, and I was not at all displeased to go with Roshel.

"You're doing well," she said. "I think you're picking it up faster than I did."

I grinned. "So am I a factor now?"

"Oh, I should certainly think so." And she grinned back.

We were still smiling at each other as we reentered the camp, loads of slightly damp wood in our arms. The fire was already roaring - Yoshana must have again used the Darkness to drive water out of the logs.

The white-haired Overlord sat on the far side of the fire pit, next to Erev. She leaned over and whispered in his ear. Even by the firelight, I could see his face go pale.

He looked at me and rasped, "Gray skin paying off for you, huh?"

I set down my sticks at the edge of the pit and asked, "What do you mean?"

He jerked his chin at Roshel. "She had a thing for Grigg, you know. Couldn't have him, so… guess you're the next best option."

Roshel put her hand on my shoulder. I shrugged her off. *Fear, lust, and rage,* Yoshana had said. That was clearly just about right.

"Why don't you come on around to this side of the fire, Erev? I think it's just about time we had a rematch." I picked up two of the sticks I'd dropped.

The soldier got to his feet, shot Yoshana a glance, and headed my way. I tossed a stick at him. Yoshana bared her teeth like a wolf.

Erev snatched the branch out of the air, but there was no swagger in his stance. The look on his face was pure resignation.

He came fast and sudden, just like before, but the blood pounding through my veins was black and no creature of flesh alone could be a match for me. I shifted outside his stroke, smacked his wrist with my stick. Something cracked, wood or bone I wasn't sure. He lost his grip on his "blade" and I dropped mine, grabbed him by throat and crotch, and threw him. He landed in a heap ten feet away.

No one around the fire moved.

Erev slowly climbed to his feet. "I'm all right," he announced, though he picked his way as stiffly as an old man. And he made no move to reclaim his stick. With a sudden flash of insight, I recognized the look on his face. It was the realization that Yoshana was willing to sacrifice him to make me into whatever I was becoming.

The Overlord was grinning from ear to ear.

Whatever I was becoming, I liked it.

7. The Bones of Yesterday

We developed a cadence, efficient but punishing. A day's march through the forest, alertness stretched taught as a bowstring. I found I was good at it. Perhaps because my studies of the Darkness began in the toxic stew of the Sorrows, my touch was lighter than the others'… maybe even than Yoshana's. On one occasion I guided us around a mass that clung to a tree like some giant, black hornet's nest. I probed close enough to find strangely dissolved bodies of animals surrounding it.

"The Darkness reproduces itself," Yoshana explained. "There's thousands of times more of it in the world now than there was at the Fall. It needs certain minerals to do that. It can find some of those in the bodies of animals. And of course humans."

After dinner there was training. The first night I learned to set a ward.

"Most times we just use a circle on the ground. With a little practice, you can maintain it in your sleep. Anything crosses it, you wake up."

The white-haired Overlord sighed. The color of her hair didn't make her unlined face look old, any more than it did mine. Most of the time she radiated an energy that made me think she must live forever, as elemental as the sky. And perhaps she would. A Select could live well over a hundred years. The Hellguard, as I understood it, were older than the Fall. With her mastery of the Darkness, there was no reason to think wounds or disease or age itself would ever overcome Yoshana.

But now she seemed tired. "In here, you have to make a cage. Surround the whole camp, in the air too. You can't keep that going in your sleep. It's not that easy awake, either."

She let out another long sigh. "It wasn't this thick in the Sorrows before. It's always been bad, but it's getting worse. Nothing I read suggested the concentrations we've been seeing."

"You're worried about some kind of giant wraith?"

"A little. I'm more worried about it getting out. The pressure's building in here. There have been leaks forever, sure. A cloud drifts out. Someone comes in, gets possessed, spreads it. The paleos that got infected scattered it all over the place in the Age of Fear. But if it comes roaring out of here in a flood? I can barely operate in this environment, Minos. How do you think everyone else is going to do?"

It was a terrifying thought. "Is preventing that really the reason for this crusade? For the Darkness Radiant?"

She gave me a thin smile. "We've been saying so, haven't we? Look, Minos, I like being in charge. And I'm good at it. But the Darkness Radiant isn't my quest for personal power. It's the only hope I see for a world where humanity controls its own destiny."

There was such sincerity in her tone. I quirked a corner of my mouth and dared, "Your mission from God, then?"

Her smile broadened. "Let's teach you to build a cage."

Yoshana was right, of course. The cage was not easy to construct or maintain. My first step was simply to examine the one she had erected, using the Darkness as my eyes, because the strands that made up the cage were far too thin to be seen by any normal means.

Then I had to try to imitate it. As she'd said, the original warding circle on the ground was easy enough. The Darkness might tend to ooze around a bit, but it took little effort to keep it a constant distance from me. The vertical dimension was much harder.

"If you could literally make a smooth dome out of it, that wouldn't be so bad," Yoshana said. "But it would get much too thin at any kind of useful diameter. With the kind of distance you'd have between particles, they'd lose cohesion and start drifting off. You can't maintain a solid sheet that big. And if you cut the diameter down to where you can hold it together, it'll be so small that it gives you no warning at all."

So instead the cage was made of strands of the Darkness, vertical lines of it meeting at the top of the dome, horizontal circles at intervals - like the latitude and longitude lines on a globe.

Now imagine trying to make those lines out of hot wax. Or live cats. The lines would try to flow together into clumps, leaving huge holes. Or a section would float away following an air current, or a speck of dust. It was infuriating. And tiring.

"How do you get any rest at all while you're holding this thing?" I gasped an hour into the lesson. The dome of Darkness took advantage of my distraction to collapse on me like a melting igloo.

"You don't. That's why we used regular wards the first two nights. You saw how well that worked."

I nodded and set about rebuilding the dome.

That night I took a turn on watch. There was no risk of falling asleep; any lapse in concentration immediately set the defenses crumbling and jerked me back to alertness. And small creatures were constantly brushing the edges. I hadn't yet learned to kill with the Darkness, so I simply flinched and endured their presence. It was such an irritation to my heightened senses that I could understand why the others reflexively murdered anything that touched the ward.

I suspected I could strike something - or someone - dead with a furious rush of the Darkness, but I didn't have the knowledge or control to cleanly sever nerves and blood vessels. So I endured the scrabbling of mice and shrews and owls until Roshel relieved me two hours later.

I was exhausted, but I was careful to meditate at length before I fell asleep.

As tiring as my daily and nightly vigilance was, at least it kept my mind off Roshel. Whenever I had a moment to relax, my thoughts turned instantly to her. I looked for whatever opportunities I could for us to be alone, and she didn't seem to be avoiding me. There had been that one time she'd sent me off to fetch the boar by myself, but now she seemed nearly as eager as I was to spend time together. Because the Darkness was in me now? Because I was a "factor," more nearly her equal?

How true was it that she had been attracted first to Grigg, and now wanted to be with me only because I was also Select? I found I didn't care very much.

I was gnawed by a vague sense of disloyalty to Prophetess. But disloyalty to what, exactly? To a physical relationship that had never existed? To a cause I had never really embraced? Yes, Prophetess was my friend, and I admired her, but she was the one who had sent me away to do what I thought was best.

And would she approve of what I'd done? Of course not. Set aside my attraction to Roshel - which for some reason had seemed to annoy Prophetess when she'd first noticed it. She would never accept my use of the Darkness. We'd never even agreed on what it was. To any rational student of history and science, it was no more or less than a dangerous tool that had gotten catastrophically out of control. In Yoshana's words, like an open flame mishandled in a dry forest.

To Prophetess and the Universal Church it was sin itself. But that was ridiculous. It hadn't crawled up from hell; it had been created by humans in a laboratory.

Although Yoshana herself had admitted that the Darkness responded most strongly to fear, rage, and lust. At least two of those made the list of deadly sins.

Most of the time I was too busy to be tempted.

The second night I was on watch, I felt something that wasn't an animal approach the edge of the dome. It was a tendril of Darkness, thin, but not like the random particles that filled the air. I sensed an intention in it, but it didn't feel like Yoshana, or Roshel, or Grigg. It didn't feel human. It felt - hungry.

I didn't want to touch it. Even more, I didn't want it to touch me. The Darkness of the dome was part of my body, and the touch of this probe would be as alien and disgusting as a spider crawling up my leg. And if I could sense its nature, maybe it could sense mine - and maybe it was something that thought of humans as prey.

I had no idea what was on the other end of that tendril, and I didn't want to find out the hard way. I pulled the dome back tight around us and ran over to shake Yoshana.

She was awake before I touched her, her hand catching my wrist in the air. "What?"

"Something out there. Maybe a wraith."

I sensed her probes a moment later, passing through the lattice of the dome.

"Good idea to pull back," she said. Her brow furrowed as she concentrated. "You're right, it's a wraith. Not a large one."

Another handful of seconds passed, and she sat back and exhaled roughly. The flow of Darkness back in through the dome was thicker than the probe that had gone out. It was big enough to see.

"What did you do?" I asked.

"I absorbed some of it. The rest fled. It's probably too small to maintain coherence now. Not a threat."

"Sorry to wake you, then."

She shook her head. "No. You did well. Very well. You sensed it before it sensed you. It didn't know we were here. I caught it completely by surprise."

She stood and slapped me on the shoulder. "Get some sleep. I'll take it from here."

I lay down near Roshel and began to ease into my meditation. Tension and adrenaline leached out of my body, leaving me as limp as a rag.

Roshel rolled over, cracked an eye, and said, "That was good. She was impressed. I think she's starting to like you." She paused. "She doesn't like very many people, you know."

That thought turned over and over in my head as I tried to meditate... more distracting in that moment even than Roshel herself.

The light drizzle returned the next morning, not enough to soak us through, but uncomfortable.

"You want to teach me to keep the rain off?" I asked Yoshana. For all the concentration she might need here in the depths of the Sorrows, she was still waterproof.

"Not going to be your next lesson, no."

I was tempted to stick out my tongue at her, but decided I would prefer to live. The Overlord might be starting to like me, but there was no point pushing my luck.

"You should try running a layer over yourself every day or so, though. Kills the lice and fleas and any other passengers you've picked up."

That thought was very appealing. But, "I don't know how to kill things yet."

She grinned. "*That's* going to be your next lesson."

The enthusiasm in her voice made my stomach tighten.

We were making slightly faster progress, the land remaining essentially flat here in the High Valley, and my skill gradually increasing. But it was of course Yoshana, with her greater range of control, who next called us to a halt.

"Something ahead," she said. "Ruins. Big."

"Should we go around?" Roshel asked.

That seemed like a good idea to me. Our last encounter with human habitation in the Sorrows had almost ended very badly.

But of course I wasn't the one who made those decisions.

"Through," Yoshana decided. "I don't know how wide it is, but it's not small. Who knows how far out of our way it would take us. Besides, I've never seen anything quite like this."

That didn't sound like much of a recommendation.

I saw what she meant as the trees began to give way to buildings. In the south and the west, the tide of civilization had receded gradually. Usually a town's outlying buildings would be stripped to their foundations, materials going into a wall around a smaller, defensible core. Sometimes that core had died as well, like the city of Acceptance in Rockwall. Other cities that had fallen at the beginning of the Age of Fear had been looted over the centuries, stripped of everything of value. A few, like the one on the river, had been overtaken completely by nature.

But here, the remains of the Last Days seemed to have been abandoned in place. Trees, grasses, and vines ran riot over crumbling walls, but nothing had been pulled down or salvaged. Constructions large and small stretched among the forest as far as the eye could see, some structures clustered together, some so isolated as to be clearly indefensible. The ancients had felt so secure, they had built with no concept of threat or defense.

Pavement was long since cracked and overrun with vegetation, but the crumbling iron hulks of vehicles lay decomposing in those roadways, a fortune in scrap metal. Even the shunned city of eternal lights where the Darkness had originated had not been left so intact. Now I understood why scavengers would brave the Sorrows. Who knew what treasures might lie in the dead buildings? I could mine the Flow my entire life and find less than a single week's haul from this place.

Of course, the problem was getting the goods - and yourself - back out alive.

Yoshana had her strange, matte gray sword out. "This sword came from a place like this," she said. "No one even knows what it is anymore, much less how to make it. It's harder than steel, won't rust, won't dull. This is what we've lost."

Grigg was looking at his own weapon. "Same kind of story." Weak sunlight played on the shining blade. "It's steel, but nothing anyone can make now. Almost more like a piece of glass than something forged, but it'll take the hardest impact without even chipping. God knows how I'd sharpen it if I did notch it somehow. It's a totally different material than Yosha's, but both of them make anything we can craft now look like a paleo's pointed stick. And until we take the world back, there's no way to make another."

Each of their blades had the shape of a katana, painfully reminding me of my own lost sword. The one I'd traded away for Prophetess' mission.

"Don't suppose there's likely to be any lying around in here," I mused wistfully.

To my surprise, Yoshana said, "Doesn't hurt to look."

We began a ghoulish inspection, probing first with the Darkness, then venturing into buildings ourselves. Wooden doors had often fallen to rot and termites, and sometimes the structures themselves had collapsed. But sometimes we would find a house or shop nearly intact, glass still in the windows. Many of the things I saw puzzled me, machines whose use I couldn't guess. Almost everywhere there were free-standing sheets of glass enclosed in metal or plastic frames, like mirrors that didn't reflect.

Some buildings were clearly homes, others places of business. Some were so strange, none of us had any idea what their purpose might have been. Everywhere in our fallen world we lived among the bones of the Last Days, but this town was more like a mummified corpse, enough flesh left to guess at but not truly know the appearance of what had gone before.

In one house I found a family of raccoons. When I went in, they snarled at me, more angry than afraid. Small as they were, their teeth were long and sharp. I wondered if they might be rabid, or infected with worse things. Yoshana launched a cloud of Darkness that left one dead and the others fleeing in panic.

"Will you teach me to do that?" I asked. In the face of danger, my squeamishness about her methods vanished.

She grinned. "Like I said. That, I'll teach you."

In a room of white tile and gray stone, I found knives stuck into a moldering wooden block. Most of the blades had gone to rust, but I saw one that gleamed almost wetly under its dusty coat. Eagerly I seized it and wiped it clean on my pants. The metal had the same glassy appearance as Grigg's sword.

"Look at this," I announced to Yoshana.

I tested the edge on my thumb and was shocked when I cut myself. Droplets of the Darkness welled up.

The Overlord laughed. "Good find, as long as you don't kill yourself with it."

The knife was one solid piece of steel, the blade itself almost a foot long. The hilt was dimpled to give a better grip on the glassy metal. I couldn't just stick it through my belt - it would stab me in the thigh or slice through the leather. I rooted through the sagging remains of wooden shelves and drawers until I found what must have been its sheath, made of a black, woven fabric that was lighter than canvas or hide but had completely resisted decay. The sheath had a loop, and I hung the knife from my belt.

I searched the rest of the house. The ground floor yielded nothing more interesting than pots, plates, decaying furniture, and a huge amount of technology with no obvious use. Nothing worth carrying away.

The stairs to the upper story protested when I put my weight on them, but they held. A corridor led to several bedrooms, the largest of them big enough to be a separate dwelling in its own right. A heavy, wooden case held rows on rows of books. I picked one out and it came apart in my hands. Another glass-fronted cabinet held a dozen wristwatches. I pulled one out and gave the crown a few turns, then shook it. To my surprise, it started up. Mechanical, then, and the intricate mechanism had survived the centuries. Remembering the Flow and how Luco and Fenn had coveted working timepieces, I was seized with a sudden nostalgia for the simple days when avoiding the pockets of fetid gas in the landfill had been my greatest worry.

I put two of the wristwatches in my pack, one for Luco and one for Fenn. Ridiculously unlikely though it was that I would ever see them again.

Below the watches, another drawer revealed a woman's jewelry, gems glittering in gold rings and necklaces. All abandoned here when the inhabitants had - fled? Died?

Who had these people been? Wealthy, it seemed. Frames hung on the walls, but the pictures within were long faded. Might they have been Select, like me? The histories said the Select had numbered among the rich and powerful of the Last Days. The genetic manipulation that created the Select had been the province of the elite. For all I knew, this was the house of my ancestors.

I sneezed, and a cloud of dust rose up. I blinked to clear my watering eyes. The jewels in front of me were worth a small fortune in our world, but this grave robbery had suddenly lost its appeal.

I didn't put the watches back, though.

My loss of enthusiasm seemed to be catching, and soon we stopped searching the buildings. Besides, the dead town turned oppressive as the shadows grew longer. I had passed through dozens of ruins in my travels, but somehow here it was more disturbing to witness the ancients' civilization losing its slow battle against the forest.

Erev and Joav both became twitchy, and Roshel moved closer to me as we made our way forward. Not that I minded.

"Creepy, isn't it?" I asked.

She nodded, but Yoshana spoke up from a dozen paces ahead. "It's not the place, or not just that. We're not alone here."

Grigg asked, "You find something?"

The Overlord shook her head. "Nothing I can detect directly, but there's a current in the Darkness here. It's not natural."

"By definition," I said.

She gave me a nasty look. "Not the natural flow of the Darkness out in the forest, I mean. It's almost like…" She stopped and looked around. "Like a spider web, and we've stepped on a strand."

My stomach sank. She was right. I could feel it now - a kind of *alertness* in the Darkness around us.

"We're walking into a trap, then."

"In it already, I'd say," Yoshana confirmed.

Roshel was very close, practically touching me. She had her carbine out.

"Back the way we came?" Grigg asked.

Yoshana shook her head again. "Whatever this is, it's aware of us already. It could hit us on the way back just as easily as on the way through. And even if we made it out, we'd have to find a way around the town. We'll keep going."

"Have you noticed her approach to ambushes is always to charge into them?" I whispered to Roshel.

Of course, Yoshana heard me. "I haven't gone up against anything yet that was worse than me." She grinned.

"Except the time the Hellguard double-crossed you," Grigg pointed out. "And that time you got stabbed through the heart."

Her expression soured. "I'm starting to see what Minos meant. I don't think you're my favorite Select anymore. I don't think you're even my favorite Select in this group."

Somewhere in the banter they had both drawn their rifles.

"Watch it!" Joav called, pointing. He spoke so rarely that the warning distracted me, trying to guess what horror would squeeze words out of him. Yoshana, of course, reacted with the speed and efficiency of a rattlesnake striking. Her gun came up and a bullet caught a man in mid-air as he leapt down at us from the low roof of a house. She chambered another round but didn't fire.

The wounded man writhed on the ground ten feet from me. A wicked hatchet that didn't look at all primitive had fallen from his hand. Yoshana strode over and peered down at him like a scientist examining an unusual insect. He was tan with lank, dark hair, similar in appearance to the natives we had fought earlier, though without the strange markings. Instead of skins, he wore what might have been the tattered remains of ancient clothing.

Sudden as a spring uncoiling he surged up and lunged at the Overlord. Her left fist met his face, shattering teeth. He staggered but didn't go down. Yoshana swung her carbine like a club, catching him in the neck. I heard bones crunch.

Still he stood.

"This is going to be annoying," the Overlord said, and discharged the weapon into his face at point blank range. A cloud of Darkness poured out of the hole in his skull as he fell.

"They're surrounding us," Grigg commented calmly.

Yoshana nodded. "Feels like some sort of collective. Pack hunters."

"Into the house?" the Select asked.

"Yep."

Grigg kicked open the door to the little building from which our attacker had jumped. I wondered if this might be their lair, and hastily flooded the place with tendrils of Darkness. I sensed nothing but similar probes from the others. The native must have climbed the building hoping to surprise us.

The house was small by the standards of the town, a rough square perhaps thirty feet on a side. There were only four rooms.

"Roshel, you've got the bathroom," Yoshana ordered. "Erev and Joav, take the bedroom. Minos, you're up front here with me. Everyone watch your ammo. There are a lot of these guys."

The front room had one door and three windows. "Take that window on the east side," Yoshana told me. "Grigg can give you some cover fire from the kitchen if he doesn't get too busy."

I was the only one without a carbine. The Overlord gave me her wolfish grin. "This is probably a good time to show you how to kill with the Darkness."

She cocked her head, as if listening. "Maybe after this first rush."

I peered through the dirty glass into the gathering dimness. Across the street, among the trees, shapes were in motion. They closed with unnatural speed in a loping gait that didn't look human. Grigg's gun went off ten feet to my left, the crack far louder than the shattering window as he fired through it. One went down. More came on. And now gunshots from behind me.

The whole house shuddered as a wave of bodies struck it at once. One barreled through the open front entrance, another slammed into the back door and knocked it out of its frame. Windows burst as more leapt through.

The first one in was already dead, split from crotch to throat by a blow from Yoshana's blade that even the Darkness could never close. Grigg severed the head of the one at the back a heartbeat later.

Coming through the window rather than the door slowed the one attacking me hardly at all. It sprang, agile as a cat, oblivious to the shards of glass. My heavy sword met its chest as it came into the room. Adrenaline pounded through my body, fear and rage blasting a cloud of Darkness out of me. It swirled wildly and I hacked again at the creature's back as it fell, and then the native shuddered and went limp as life and the unnatural vitality of the Darkness abandoned it.

"Your left!" Yoshana called. Even as she spoke she was cutting down another that had broken the window to my right. The moment it spent stumbling over a rotting couch was all it took for her to slash its legs. It flailed at her with something like a scythe, and she stabbed at it again and again.

To my left, in the kitchen, Grigg was engaged with one, while another was closing on him from behind. Madly I willed the Darkness in a wave at the creature about to strike at his back. The cloud washed over it and the attacker screamed in rage and pain, turning on me. Wounds on its face were healing as it bared its teeth in a snarl that was far more animal than human.

The sword it spun was the work of man, though. Where had this beast gotten a katana? Debased and feral as it was, the native handled the weapon like it knew how to use a blade. I had little confidence in my ability to match its strokes with my clumsy broadsword.

I didn't find out. Grigg had finished his opponent and with an almost casual swing struck off the head of mine from behind.

"Watch the front door, Minos," said Yoshana. "The others aren't doing so well."

And with that she dashed down the little hallway toward the bedroom and bathroom.

The others weren't doing well? Roshel was there. I started after Yoshana.

"Stay. She'll handle it. We need you here," Grigg said over his shoulder, as he returned to the back door.

I stopped, then took another step toward the hall.

"Stay."

I don't know if the weight of the Darkness was somehow behind that command, but I stayed put and peered around the door frame into the darkening night. Nothing moved outside. To my right, down the hall, metal rang on metal, and a body thudded against a wall.

"They'll be all right," Grigg said, before I could begin to move again. How could he know that? Roshel would not fall easily, but she'd been isolated in a room.

Yoshana returned, followed by Erev and Joav. Joav was bleeding from his shoulder, and walked with a limp. Roshel wasn't with them.

I rushed past them into the hall.

Roshel backed out of the bathroom and turned to face me, her tunic covered in blood.

She must have seen the horror on my face. "Not mine," she said.

I wanted to rush to her and fold her into my arms, but was suddenly embarrassed. Instead I just nodded awkwardly, and said, "Good."

She crossed the few yards that separated us, leaned against me, and gave me a quick hug. She probably got blood all over me, but I didn't care. Then she was past and moving to join the others.

"Too many access points with them jumping through the windows like that," Yoshana declared. "We'll hold in this room instead."

"Think they're coming again?" Grigg asked.

"I don't sense another wave," the Overlord replied. "Good thing. If they'd followed up right away, we would have been in trouble. But they know they lost their whole force, and that they didn't get any of us. They're cautious now."

She cocked her head as if listening again. "But I don't think they're done yet."

I opened my senses to the flow of the Darkness, allowing my perception to extend beyond the walls of the house. I could still feel the pressure we had sensed before, and nodded. "Seems like there's still something out there. What's next?"

With the six of us in one room, we had only the front door, three windows, and the passages into the hall and the kitchen to protect. But I didn't relish the idea of the rest of the house filling up with those mad creatures.

Abruptly I sensed Yoshana forging the links of a dome around the house, and pulled my tendrils in hastily. I didn't want her reflexively lashing out at me. "I think they'll take another poke at us. But cautiously next time. The first one that jumped us was a probe. I should have killed it faster. Maybe that would have scared them off."

She grinned at me. "You're getting pretty good at sensing them, Minos. Let's you and me see if we can't convince them to move on."

Grigg kicked one of the corpses. "What should we do with these?"

"Eat 'em?" Yoshana suggested. "That's what they were going to do with us. Seems only fair."

At my look of horror, she chuckled and said, "Just kidding."

But I wondered. Obviously these possessed were cannibals. The paleos considered it a waste not to eat a slain enemy. Ruthless as Yoshana was, would she scruple to eat the dead?

"Let's dump them out the front door," Grigg suggested. "There's enough we can use them as a barricade."

"Good thought," Yoshana replied, "but let's use them to block the hall and the kitchen instead. The door's narrow enough as it is. Better to create obstacles here inside."

"That's a little icky, having them all oozing and rotting in here with us."

She shrugged. "We'll be gone before they start to stink too much."

They stank already. The natives didn't seem to wash, and some of their intestines had been opened, or their bowels had voided. But I breathed through my mouth as we hauled corpses out of the other rooms and heaped up our macabre barriers. It was no worse than hitting a gas pocket on the Flow.

Although the possessed wore clothes and looked human enough in death, I found that I couldn't regard them as people. The ones we had fought before, in the shaman's camp, had at least spoken. These leaping, snapping things reminded me of nothing so much as man-shaped wolves.

Yoshana seemed to sense my thoughts. "This is the evolution of the Darkness. It's what will happen to us all if we don't take back the world."

"But these are different from the others."

"The Darkness is experimenting. Not consciously. But you've seen normal possessed, like the one your Prophetess exorcised. Do you think something like that could cooperate with others?"

I thought about it, then slowly shook my head.

"So the Darkness forms new societies. The one before, governed by a powerful wraith, speaking through the shaman. This one is some kind of hunting collective. Their minds are linked. I think they all must share one consciousness, to some extent."

"How do we beat something like that?"

The grin again. "Convince it that we can kill the whole thing."

It was nearly an hour later when the possessed tried again.

"I've got something to our left," Yoshana whispered to me. The others were resting, not quite asleep, not quite awake. The two of us were sitting cross-legged on the floor.

Carefully, I eased a tendril of Darkness between the bars of her warding dome. She didn't seem to notice. Outside, my probe brushed the edge of a consciousness, feral, hungry. Inhuman in its essence.

"I'm going to drop the cage so you can sense it."

So she hadn't noticed my probe. I felt a rush of pride that I could sneak my consciousness past the mistress of the Darkness herself, but I kept quiet and merely nodded.

"When you feel it, strike. But these things are thoroughly infected, so you'll need to hit hard. What I did back at Icefall won't work. The Darkness was a surveillance tool before it was a weapon, but it was a medical tool before that. The problem is they'll fix precise, surgical cuts without even noticing them.

And just lashing out at them like you did earlier won't do much more than annoy them."

"So? What do I do?"

"Focus your attack. Hit a vulnerable organ that's hard to repair. Go for the eyes."

I summoned up the Darkness within me, the tendril becoming a rope of blackness. It coiled outside. As it thickened, my impression of the stalker sharpened. It was human enough in shape, but crept on the ground on all fours. I realized that a cloud of Darkness radiated around it, and pulled back. It halted and sniffed at the window. I felt all of its senses bearing on us, looking for weaknesses.

"Now," Yoshana hissed.

The debased creature disgusted me, and I gathered up my will to strike. But where in the heat of battle I had instinctively flung the Darkness to wound the native attacking Grigg, I now found it hard to focus my loathing into action.

"Do you know what it would do to us?" the Overlord whispered. "Do you know what they would have done to Roshel? What they'll do now if they have the chance to tear and rip and chew tender flesh like that?"

A wave of hate washed over me, and the Darkness struck the possessed in the face, clawing at its eyes. The creature wailed, a long howl like a wolf.

And then Yoshana was there, the weight of her presence as thick as tar around the native, flowing into every pore and opening in its body, seizing control of the Darkness within it. And then - the creature simply came apart. The Darkness ruptured every organ at once, shattering cell walls, not a surgical cut but a crushing tsunami of devastation set loose from the inside.

The body slumped in a liquid mass, bones surrounded by a soup of pulped tissues.

"Let's see if that gets the point across," Yoshana said.

I pulled my senses back into my own body and turned away, fighting down a rising tide of bile.

"That was good," the Overlord said, coming easily to her feet and patting me on the shoulder.

I swallowed, trying to think of something to say. In the end, I managed a weak smile. Like it or not, I was part of this dark fraternity now.

"It'll come easier with time," Yoshana murmured. "The Darkness flows naturally down the channels of emotion, but you'll learn to direct it with your will."

She paused a moment, then added, "Oh, and you really didn't need to worry so much about Roshel. I taught her to go for the eyes years ago. The two that made it into the bathroom with her were blind and dying long before I got there. Still, it was sweet of you to be concerned. I'm sure she appreciates it."

The Overlord stretched like a cat. "They're pulling back. I think we've convinced them we're more trouble than we're worth. Get some sleep. I'll take first watch."

I was ancient and strong, my body honed by experience yet flushed with the vigor of youth. My comrades and I loped through the empty streets, on two legs or four, as it suited us. There was a scent of blood in the air, and soon we would feed.

My eyes snapped open. Yoshana reclined on the moldering remains of an overstuffed chair, one leg draped over the crumbling arm. She gave me a little half smile and winked at me.

I had forgotten to still my thoughts before allowing sleep to take me. You'd think one object lesson would be enough. I didn't know if the dream had been a product of my imagination, or the touch of the possessed pack's collective consciousness.

I shuddered. Whichever it was, I didn't want to feel it again.

Meditation came easier this time than after the nightmare in the bloody cavern, and within minutes I was ready to sleep again. Yoshana's breathing was deep and regular, as if she were asleep herself. Someone was snoring.

I let a fine tendril of Darkness quest out. The dome was in place - Yoshana was alert. Not that I'd really doubted it. I could still question many things about the leader of the Darkness Radiant, but her competence wasn't one of them.

On a whim, I eased the tendril between the bars of Yoshana's cage. Once again, it slipped through unnoticed. I scented the air outside. It was true, the pressure had eased. We were alone in the night. I pulled the thread back inside, and began another round of meditation. But I allowed a tiny, self-satisfied smile to creep onto my lips. Yoshana's power was orders of magnitude beyond mine, but in this one, small matter, the delicacy of my senses, I was fully her equal.

8. The Serpent

I woke to the gray light of dawn and Joav moaning softly in his sleep. As I rolled over to look at the wounded soldier, Erev nudged him, and Joav blinked and came awake. He tried to sit up, groaned a kind of drawn out sigh, then turned on his side and laboriously pushed himself to his feet.

Yoshana eyed him critically. "Right shoulder, right arm, right leg. Too bad you're not left-handed. Not going to be much use in a fight. And you'll be slow on the march."

Joav watched her in silence. The look in his eyes might have been pleading, but it might just have been resignation.

Erev opened his mouth, but his mistress held up a finger and no words came out.

It would be no kindness to leave Joav here. He would never make it out of the Sorrows alone, and the natives would come snuffling around long before he could heal.

I could think of nothing to say, so like a coward I turned away instead.

"Grigg, go find something he can use as a crutch. Minos, you'd better take his carbine, one-handed he'll be even clumsier with it than you. Everyone hurry up and get some food in yourselves. If we're going to be moving slower, we'd better get started early."

She favored me with that grin again. "What kind of monster do you think I am, Minos?"

I didn't look back at the house of death, with its heaped corpses and the puddle of bones outside the window. We didn't feel the pressure of the possessed collective as we made our way out of town, although once or twice I seemed to catch the edge of a presence that fled before us. I wasn't sorry to see the back of that place, and I didn't think its inhabitants were sorry to see the back of us.

I fingered the knife at my hip. I had gained two weapons, because at the last minute I'd wrapped the native's rusty katana in a cloth and stuffed it in my pack. Three weapons, if you counted my new mastery of the Darkness as a killing tool. They had cost Joav two more wounds, though thankfully not his life.

I wondered if Prophetess would think they had cost me my soul.

"Yoshana always surprises me," I whispered to Roshel, though I was sure the white-haired Overlord could hear us anyway.

Roshel smiled, but there was a sadness in it. "After all this, you're still thinking of us as evil."

I shook my head ruefully. "I spent a lot of time with Prophetess."

"Dammit, Minos!" Erev turned to stare briefly at the vehemence in Roshel's tone, then put his eyes forward and continued trudging along. "Can't you understand that this is a crusade? We're the only hope there is for the world. What has Prophetess done to make anything better for anyone? Cling to some moldy dogma that says we're damned for using the tools we have to try to make a difference? Do I look like the enemy of humanity?"

I couldn't help it. I let my eyes move up and down her body. "You look pretty good to me."

She punched my arm. "That's not what I mean!"

She did look good, though. She looked warm, and human. What I felt for her was more than just physical attraction - although I had to admit there was a lot of that. I wanted to hold her, to protect her - much as I did with Prophetess. But Prophetess was far away and had no need for me, while Roshel was right here.

"I know," I said. "It's not really what I meant either."

She was very close, and it was all I could do not to suggest maybe the two of us should go scouting along a trail in a different direction. I thought I caught a hint of amusement from Yoshana, but that might have been my imagination.

By the end of the day, the ground was definitely sloping up.

"I think we're coming out of the High Valley," Yoshana said. "So we're only a few days from the Darklands. Hellguard territory."

We were making our camp among the trees. We had no roof and only a tiny fire, but we were all happy to be free of the ruins.

"So the Darklands are going to be the easy part compared to this, right?" I said brightly. "That's what you said."

"I lied," the Overlord replied flatly. "This was bad. Trying to kill a demon in his own stronghold will be worse."

I hadn't really expected it to be simple, but my guts still knotted. I suppose I had thought that an enemy Yoshana could face head on would be easy prey for her.

She did her mind reading trick again. "I may be able to control the Darkness as well as some of the Hellguard. But not as well as the strongest. They were bred specifically for it. And they've had centuries to master that skill. Plus, physically they're... big. And tough. Yashuath more than most."

"Bred for it? By who?" The origins of the demons were obscure in the Books of the Fall, and I'd never learned much more about them from any other sources. The traditions of the Select didn't say much other than that the Hellguard were immortal, and didn't like us.

Yoshana raised an eyebrow. "Education really doesn't amount to much outside of the Shield, does it? They're soldiers. Created by the ancients in the Last Days."

"Soldiers?"

She frowned. I'm sure she wasn't used to repeating herself. I stammered, "It's just - I mean, I didn't think they had literally crawled up out of hell, but you're saying they were made the way they are on purpose?"

"The Darkness was a deliberate creation, and so were the Hellguard. They were made to be complementary to each other. The ancients lost control of both. Now we're living with the consequences."

Grigg interjected, "They can be fought. And beaten. But Yoshana's right, they're incredibly tough."

"And these creations have been around since the Fall?"

"Since before it. They've got all the physical and mental enhancements of a Select, and then some. Plus complete mastery of the Darkness. For all practical purposes, they're immortal."

My stomach turned over again. "But we're going to kill one."

The smile on Yoshana's face was as wild as any I'd seen. "Not just any one - one of their leaders. But if we can catch him alone, there's four of us that can use the Darkness, and only one of him. You've learned an incredible amount in a very short time. You've got a lifetime to practice and perfect your skills, but there are really only two big things left for you to learn."

A lifetime to practice... that might not be very long at all.

But she was continuing. "First, and you have to be ready for this, the Darkness can be used in much more subtle ways than you know. You've already figured out it can effectively read thoughts. It can also influence them."

My skin crawled. "What do you mean?"

"Call it an aura. What do you feel toward Roshel?"

I reddened.

"No need to be embarrassed. Her aura creates attraction. It's a very basic response." She locked eyes with me. "Me, I prefer something even more visceral."

"Fear," I murmured.

She nodded. I looked from one Overlord to the other, and then at Grigg. "What about him?"

Yoshana's grin, which had faded, widened again. "It's more complex than ours, but I'm surprised you haven't figured it out."

I shook my head. She chuckled. "Trustworthiness. How do you think we got you here?"

Grigg looked into the fire, not meeting my eyes. How much of my feelings were the product of their manipulation?

Yoshana laughed out loud. "It's not mind control, Minos. Like I said, it's subtle, and it has to build on something real. Roshel really is attractive. Grigg really is trustworthy. And of course, I really am terrifying."

Her face hardened. "But the demons can use it too. They deceived me. And I'm not easily deceived. So you need to watch for that."

Then her tone lightened again. "And speaking of deception, here's the second thing I wanted to show you."

Her skin began to change color. "When Grigg first met me, I looked as human as Roshel. You perhaps noticed that my natural appearance stands out a bit. Sometimes it's better to be less conspicuous. But since I'm traveling with two Select, let's try something different."

The mahogany tone of her flesh leached away, leaving gray behind. Her hair remained white, but her eyes darkened - iris and sclera fading to black.

She was obviously Select.

"I suppose my mother must have looked like this," she mused. "Seems appropriate for killing a demon."

It was harder than usual to still my mind that night. Disturbing thoughts spun around my head like a pack of dogs chasing each others' tails. My most basic emotions had been manipulated by Yoshana, and Roshel, and Grigg. I shouldn't have been surprised at that, but it was still somehow disappointing. How much of what I felt toward any of them was real? Of course, we all showed the face we wanted to the world, but this was different. Wasn't it?

And whatever I thought about my allies, what about my enemies? Yoshana had as much as said her terrible rush to make me into a weapon had been not just to survive the Sorrows, but to defeat Yashuath.

But then, that had been her stated goal from the beginning. And Grigg had said as much - as dangerous and deceitful as Yoshana might be, she was humanity's best hope against the demons. Immortal soldiers, bred to use the Darkness, physically and mentally stronger than Yoshana herself... maybe I should be glad the Overlord was as subtle and ruthless as a snake. Nothing less would let us survive this confrontation.

Again I allowed the Darkness to spread beyond my body before preparing myself for sleep. Roshel was on watch, and the bars of the cage tasted of her - warmer, softer than Yoshana's aura. If that was an illusion, it was convincing.

I played the same game with Roshel that I had with the more senior Overlord, easing a tendril of Darkness through the gaps in the dome to explore the night beyond. Roshel didn't detect me either, and a quick reconnaissance of the surrounding area revealed no threats.

I pulled my senses back in to myself. I had come too far to turn back. I breathed deeply, quieted my thoughts, and let myself fall from meditation into sleep.

The going was slow the next day. We continued uphill, and the woods were thick. Joav's bad leg was on the same side as his bad arm. Yoshana had closed his shoulder and leg just as she had done with his arm after the first battle with the natives, but they still clearly pained him. Twice before midday he fell and had to be helped up. He never complained, but the tightness around his mouth and eyes spoke volumes.

At times I was impatient, eager to be free of this forest of the damned - because if any place deserved that superstitious epithet, the Sorrows did. Then I remembered where we were going, and wasn't sorry to be delayed.

After lunch, Grigg took me aside.

"You know how to use that thing?" he asked, pointing at the carbine slung across my back.

"Point it at someone you don't like and pull the trigger?"

"Heh. Good start. Maybe more than you know. For instance, don't ever point it at anyone or anything you're not willing to kill. Even if you don't think you've got a round chambered. Which you don't, by the way."

I hadn't known that, and must have looked surprised.

"A little safer that way. You won't shoot yourself or me if you fall and somehow jostle the trigger. Slower in a fight, of course, 'cause you have to work the bolt."

"Do you keep a round chambered?"

"Of course I do."

I was a little offended, but the truth was I had almost no experience with firearms. Grigg probably wasn't wrong that I was as much of a threat to myself as to our enemies.

"Go ahead and unsling it," he said. "Now work the bolt. Good. Now it's ready to fire. Butt against your shoulder, and line up the sights. It's heavy enough it won't kick much, and at the kind of range you're going to be dealing with, you won't need to worry about wind or drop. Sight on the big knot on that birch tree. Squeeze the trigger, don't jerk it."

The sound of the blast made my ears ring, but Grigg had been right - the weapon thudded back against my shoulder, but not enough to hurt. Wood chips flew a few inches below and to the right of the knot.

"Not bad. Remember, if you're going to fire again, you need to work the bolt again. Now reload. You've got a seven-shot internal magazine in the stock. Unscrew the ring and load another shell point first."

"I can't help but notice that I've got one bandolier and everyone else has two."

He laughed. "That's because we stripped your second one to reload everyone else's. Not that we don't think you're any good with a rifle..."

"...But you don't think I'm any good with a rifle."

Grigg nodded.

"Okay, fair enough. Can I take a few more shots?"

"Normally I'd say of course, but there's nowhere we can resupply until this is over, and we've got no way of knowing how many rounds we're going to need. Sorry."

I could only nod. *No way of knowing how many rounds we're going to need.* One more unwelcome reminder of what lay ahead.

The sun wasn't yet low when we crested a ridge and saw the land beyond falling away before us. Miles and miles lay ahead, but it was literally all downhill from here.

Literally, yes. Figuratively, not so much.

"We can camp here," Yoshana said. "The sight lines are good. We can't make the river by nightfall, but this should be our last night in the Sorrows."

"And then?" Grigg asked.

And then? Were they making this up as they went along?

"Then we go into the Darklands, interrogate some natives, find Yashuath, kill him, and go home. It's not complicated."

The big Select shook his head. "I figured you'd have a little more of a plan by now."

"We've got the necessary force, now we just find the right point to apply it. Boldness in war has its own prerogative. It is a genuinely creative force."

Grigg groaned. "Oh, God. Not Clausewitz again."

"You Select really need to read someone besides Sun Tzu."

"Oh, come on. You of all people should value Sun Tzu's appreciation of intelligence and deception. The only reason you like Clausewitz with his 'hey diddle diddle, straight up the middle' is because it gives you an excuse to be reckless when you want to."

"As the great man said, genius amounts to admitting that rules are not only made for idiots, but are idiotic in themselves. You of all people should appreciate the concept of friction in war, and that no battle plan survives contact with the enemy. I like treachery and deceit as much as the next person -"

Grigg snorted rudely, and Yoshana glared at him and continued, "But sometimes the simplest way is best."

"Even when you have a force of six people attacking an enemy superior in every way?"

"Men - always obsessed with size. It's not about the size of your force. It's about what you do with it."

Roshel whispered to me, "This is always entertaining to watch. You notice how they just completely switched sides? Clausewitz always emphasized massing an overwhelming force, and now Yoshana's arguing against that."

"I heard that," the white-haired Overlord snapped. "It's about the force you bring to bear *at the critical point.* Any idiot can read Clausewitz and say you just need the biggest army you can get. That's not what he meant at all."

"I'm pretty sure it is," Grigg retorted.

Erev and Joav were both lying down, heads on their bedrolls, eyes closed.

"Heard this argument too many times before," Roshel whispered.

"I heard that too," Yoshana said.

It really was entertaining to watch the banter, but something gnawed at me. "You said we interrogate some natives. Are there humans in the Darklands? I can't imagine we're going to interrogate the demons."

"Of course there are humans," Yoshana replied. "In a sense. The Hellguard aren't going to grow crops, feed pigs, clean up garbage, all that. They have slaves."

"Human slaves."

"Yes... and no. The name notwithstanding, the Darklands aren't as infested with the Darkness as the Sorrows. But there's a fair amount of it loose in the air. Enough to be a real possession risk for the weak-minded. So the Hellguard... protect... their slaves from it. They call it circumcising the mind. They use the Darkness to remove the slaves' will. With no fears or desires, there's nothing for the Darkness to manipulate. And of course, it makes the slaves far more docile. They're as intelligent as anyone else, but have no more self will than your rifle."

I swallowed. "That's obscene."

"That's what we're fighting against. It's why they kidnap women from outside, or take them as tribute. Apparently they like their concubines to have some fight left in them. Until they eventually die giving birth to an Overlord, of course."

My throat was thick. "Are you sure we only need to kill one of them?"

231

Her smile was a terrible thing.

Yoshana's mother had been a Select, like me. Like my mother. The Hellguard truly were devils, stripping the very humanity from their slaves, subjecting captive women to torture and death. Yoshana was right - the demons were more than some abstract terror. They were a foulness that had to be burned from the earth.

For the first time, Yoshana practiced kata before we slept. It was amazing to watch, a flowing symphony of movement with the grace of a dancer and the speed of a viper. The Darkness flowed like water on her blade, coiling around her, shifting in a perfect counterpoint to her steps and cuts. Her pace quickened as she went on, until by the end she was moving faster than my eye could follow. All I could see was a lethal blur. It was as beautiful and terrifying as a storm.

And then she was done, the blade sheathed, the Darkness gathered into her, and she folded effortlessly into a lazy, cross-legged seat on the ground.

I was glad she was on my side.

Once more I tested our cage before settling into my meditation that night. Grigg had first watch, and I could feel his calm strength. He didn't notice me as I eased my senses beyond the dome, quickly scanned the night, and pulled them back. I smiled to myself. I was no match for Grigg or Roshel - much less their mistress - in most ways, but I would find a way to make myself useful.

As I withdrew my probes, I brushed against a strand that felt like Yoshana. I flinched away reflexively. No surprise, I suppose, that she might deploy a layer of her own protection even within the dome, especially this close to the Darklands. Or was she perhaps spying on me, testing my feelings, trying to understand my resolve as we entered the critical phase of the mission?

Let her test. I was committed.

With a goal fixed in my mind, it was easy to quiet my thoughts and sink into sleep.

The next morning Joav was dead.

His eyes were closed, and there was a small, peaceful smile on his face. That was telling because Erev was kicking him, trying to wake him up.

Yoshana gently pushed Erev aside and knelt over Joav. A cloud of Darkness crawled over the body.

"No infection. It looks like his heart just stopped in the night." She heaved a ragged sigh. "We pushed him too hard."

"What choice did we have?" asked Roshel. "He would have died if we'd left him behind. At least he saw the mission through to the edge of the Sorrows. I think he would have wanted that."

We had no shovels, so we heaped stones over Joav as a cairn instead. The sunrise painted the underside of the clouds pink as we looked down from his grave to the east. He couldn't see it, but it was a beautiful place to rest.

"Lucky bastard," Erev muttered thickly. "We'll wind up strewn around in pieces in some godawful ruin down there while he's up here in the sunlight laughing at us."

I awkwardly clapped the soldier on the shoulder. It was like hitting leather wrapped around wood. "He was a good man."

Erev nodded, weathered face looking not just hard but old for the first time. "Yeah. He was."

The sun was directly overhead when we saw the river, and not long after that we made out the town off to the right. We angled toward it.

Even from a distance it was a strange place, the buildings crawling up the riverbanks as if they had spawned in the water and clawed their way up onto the land. Some had crumbled and been swept away by the current, but most remained, clinging like barnacles in a position I would have thought too precarious to last decades, much less centuries. Equally oddly, the town spread no more than a few hundred yards from either side of the river; a strange, aquatic creature that didn't dare stray too far from its origin.

Across the river stretched a bridge. And on the far side of it burned a pair of fires.

So it wasn't abandoned after all.

"Hellguard outpost protecting the crossing," Grigg murmured.

"But couldn't the Darkness or the natives cross anywhere?" I asked. "I thought it was a myth it couldn't cross water."

Yoshana answered. "The Darkness can cross water. So can anyone infected with it. But the Darkness and the natives will tend to follow the path of least resistance. That's going to be across the bridge."

"Easy enough for us to ford it upstream," Grigg said.

"I hate getting wet. Besides, this will give us our first chance to question the Darklanders. And put a roof over our heads tonight."

Because that had worked out so well the last couple of times.

"Those aren't demons down there, are they?" I found that I was profoundly unready to meet an enemy stronger than Yoshana.

"I wouldn't think so. There's not so many of them that they'd waste their time guarding some border crossing in the middle of nowhere. Those are almost certainly slaves."

"How do we get close enough to find out for sure?" We were at the edge of the tree line now. The land fell away in a grassy slope for half a mile before it reached the near edge of the town. There was no cover on that approach.

Yoshana showed me her wicked grin. "Maybe there are a few more things I haven't showed you yet. You and Erev stay here. Grigg, Roshel, you're with me."

The Darkness oozed out of the three of them, spreading into a diffuse cloud, blurring their outlines. They stepped out of the woods shrouded in a kind of mist. By the time they were a hundred yards away, I could barely focus on them, even knowing where they were.

"That's a neat trick," I muttered.

"She's full of them," Erev grunted.

It was easy to see why the Overlord favored deception. It was still disconcerting enough to see her as a Select. Now she had nearly vanished altogether. She could approach in concealment or disguise, and by the time you knew what was coming, the Darkness would finish you off. If the demons truly were more dangerous, I really wasn't looking forward to meeting them. Much less trying to kill one.

I could just barely catch glimpses of the three of them as they made their way into the town. Only the tiniest hint of movement betrayed them. Soon they were at the edge of the bridge, which stretched a couple of hundred yards across the river. The Muddy was wider even at its narrowest point, but this was no little stream. The riverbanks fell dozens of feet to the water below.

"Not even she can kill at that range," Erev said. His voice was tense. "They'll have to go out onto the bridge before she can take out the guards."

"I still don't see anyone. Just the fires."

But even as I said it, the faintest shimmer revealed one of our three companions moving out onto the bridge. And in an instant, a figure stepped away from the left-most blaze and sent a flaming arrow arcing across the span. The guard had stood so still that I hadn't seen him until he moved to loose the shaft.

The cracks of rifle shots floated up on the air. The guard and another like him fell. Three figures charged across the bridge, the camouflage of the Darkness gone. More fire arrows looped down from a building on the other side.

"We'd better get down there!" Erev barked, and took off in a lurching sprint down the slope. I followed, then passed him, longer legs and younger lungs pulling me ahead. But by the time we got there, it was all over.

Two men in dark leather armor lay dead at the feet of massive braziers, bows and unused arrows fallen around them.

Grigg and Yoshana emerged from the building that had been the source of the additional arrows. The Select manhandled another soldier in similar armor. The man's wrists were bound behind his back, and Grigg's big hand was at the base of his neck. The captive's face was completely impassive.

The bridge turned into a road that disappeared around a bend to the east, and Roshel came trotting back toward us. She carried her carbine propped on her shoulder.

"Two of them were making a break for it on horses," she announced. "I got them both."

If Grigg's prisoner was dismayed, his face gave no sign of it.

Yoshana nodded. "Let's see what this one can tell us."

Grigg gripped the man firmly by the shoulders, though he still offered no resistance. The senior Overlord's hand went to his face, Darkness oozing from her palm into his flesh. After less than a minute, she stepped back.

"There were only six." She jerked her chin toward the building. "With the other one we killed in there, that's all of them. I can't get an exact feeling for how long until they're relieved, but it's weeks at least. And no more troops for miles. We're in."

She smiled, letting out a long sigh. I was beginning to feel the tension draining from my own body when her sword whipped out and pierced the soldier's heart.

He looked down for a moment, then crumpled to the ground as Grigg released him.

Yoshana met my eyes. "They're not really human. Not after what the demons have done to them. Remember that."

I looked at the corpse, blood puddling beneath it. Not really human.

Were we?

The building the bridge guards had occupied was sparsely furnished, but comfortable enough. They seemed to have shared one common room for sleeping and cooking, but the rest of the structure was sound and reasonably clean.

A sizable cache of bread, jerky, and dried fruit reinforced the idea that the squad had been provisioned for a long stay. There were also barrels of mildly alcoholic cider, which I preferred to small beer. A smaller brazier near the windows had served to light the fire arrows, and there were enough full quivers to hold off an army.

"No rifles?" I asked. "If the demons were soldiers from the Last Days, I'd expect better equipment."

"Oh, they have them," Yoshana replied. "But fire arrows are more effective against Darkness clouds, and the possessed are afraid of them. Plus the Hellguard don't like to issue guns to their slaves unless they have to. Their will may have been cut away, but the demons don't like to take chances."

"They haven't lived three hundred years by being reckless," Grigg said waspishly.

"Clausewitz says you're wrong."

"Clausewitz is dead."

I left them bickering and explored the other rooms.

"Wouldn't mind a little privacy for once," Roshel said at my shoulder. "Not having to listen to Grigg snore."

My heart sped up. "When you say privacy…"

She smiled and shook her head. "Not now. Not here."

I tried to keep my tone light. "You're right, of course."

She smiled again, and I don't think it was just the aura of the Darkness that suggested "not now" didn't mean "not ever."

We had eaten, then dragged the soldiers' straw-stuffed pallets into different rooms. Except for Yoshana and Grigg, who had taken a room together.

I sat and went through my pack. I had taken as much of the dead guards' provender as I could carry, and filled my water skin with cider. My new knife was still secure in its strange, black sheath. Carefully, I withdrew the ancient katana the possessed had carried back in the ruined town.

The blade was spotted with rust, and the original fittings of the hilt had long since decayed and been replaced with a wrapping of uncured hide strips, clumsily secured with sinews passed through the peg holes. But it had once been a fine weapon, perhaps as fine as the one I'd sacrificed for Prophetess months ago. A lifetime ago. If I lived, I would restore this one.

I spent an hour working at the rust with my whetstone before I lay down to compose my mind for sleep. Finally free of the Sorrows, we would not need the cage to protect ourselves here. We would lay down warding circles, but those we could maintain in our sleep. For the first time since leaving Furat's outpost, we would rest.

And so, of course, peace eluded me. Though I knew I shouldn't, I sent a tendril of Darkness to Roshel's room. Her presence was there, soft and warm, relaxed in sleep. The circle of Darkness on the floor was no barrier at all. My senses hovered over her.

I shook my head and pulled away. I had spent nights with my arm around Prophetess and remained a gentleman. Despite her aura and the Darkness surging in me, I would do the same with Roshel. I told myself that, but my consciousness didn't return to my body.

Some sound or movement tugged at my attention from Grigg and Yoshana's room.

Even more wrong to pry there than to invade Roshel's privacy. But still my consciousness reached out.

Yoshana had created a cage around the room. I was deterred, but not defeated. I had insinuated my senses through that protection before. I did it again.

They had shoved their two pallets together and were lying on them, talking softly.

"...but even if we do, I don't see how we've solved the problem of Our Lady," Grigg was saying.

"Don't you?" Yoshana laughed musically.

The Select snorted in exasperation. "I understand we needed to teach him to use the Darkness, but Roshel's totally wrong. He can never bridge the two sides now. You should have seen the looks on their faces when they realized who I was. They'll never believe anything he says now that the Darkness is in him."

"Maybe, maybe not. But you're probably right. Still, that was never the idea."

"What do you mean?"

"Give yourself some credit for persuasiveness. And Roshel should have his blood boiling quite nicely. Nothing as easy to stir up as young lust. He's ours now. He'll convince Prophetess, or not. And if he doesn't, he'll kill her."

The Select snorted incredulously. "You don't believe that."

"After all we've been through together? All we'll go through together? Once the word 'abomination' passes that girl's lips, there'll be no containing his rage. He's more than strong enough now. And Roshel has him well hooked."

Grigg sighed. "I suppose I should have known. But be careful there. I think Roshel really cares for him. If he kills Prophetess and it breaks him, we might lose Roshel too."

"If we have to, we have to. There's not much hope left for the world. I'll sacrifice whatever I need to so we can keep what little we have. I can't have that self-important farm girl building an army to oppose me."

"The cost -"

"I sacrificed Jylen. Don't talk to me about cost."

"That was before. Haven't you changed at all?"

"What I'm fighting for has changed. How I fight - there's only one way I know how to do that, and that's with everything I have." She heaved a deep breath. "I don't want to hear about it from you, Grigg. If you hadn't stopped me from killing her in Stephensburg, we wouldn't be having this discussion now."

"She would have been a martyr then. She still will be."

"Less impressive when she's murdered by her own lieutenant. That's the point of the exercise. You think I make convoluted plans just for the sake of complexity?"

"Sometimes, yes."

She chuckled. "Shut up and come to bed."

I fled back to my body, which I found shaking and drenched in sweat and tears.

9. The Road Not Taken

I didn't sleep at all.

I was Yoshana's weapon, not against the demons, but against Prophetess.

I had known Yoshana was ruthless. And she'd never made a secret of her goals, or the threat she thought Prophetess posed to them. I had watched her use Erev, a man totally loyal to her, to sharpen my edge. The night I'd called Erev out, in that exchange of glances between the two of them by the firelight, I'd seen them both accept that I might kill the old soldier.

So why should I be surprised that she'd use me?

I had to laugh at myself through the pain. Roshel had said I'd elevated myself from being a piece in Yoshana's game to being a player. I'd let myself believe it. I'd been proud to believe it. But all I'd really become was a more valuable piece.

I'd just seen more of the board. Did that make me a player, for the first time? Whether it did or not, Furat had been so very right. Player or piece, this was a game where I'd get hurt.

Or not survive. Even with the Darkness in me, there was no chance at all I could confront Yoshana and live. I didn't even know if I wanted to confront her. Her methods were cold, heartless, calculating… but more and more, I believed her goal was right.

I'd seen the possessed in the Sorrows. Now I'd seen the demons' slaves, emotion and will stripped from them. And I'd seen the bickering of the weak princelings who ruled the lands under human control. Would the petty tyrants in Rockwall and the Monolith who set mercenaries to burning and raping be able to stop the Darkness or the Hellguard? Would that wreck Stephen, who couldn't stop a thief like Brom of Icefall from robbing his own citizens?

I wasn't quite sure what Yoshana was - if she was a monster, or a fanatic whose flame burned so bright it singed everything around her. Maybe she had been one, and was becoming the other. Or maybe she was one and was pretending to be the other.

But, monster or fanatic, what if she was right?

I realized I still thought she was right.

So, what then? Could I allow myself to continue, swept along in her wake like a leaf in a stream? What happened when that stream flowed back to Our Lady?

Grigg wasn't wrong, of course. Roshel had lied to me, or perhaps simply not understood. If I returned to Our Lady as Yoshana's creature, I wouldn't even make it past the gate. Dee might be intrigued. But to Tolf and the others, I was an outsider already, not fully trusted. They'd never accept me now. And neither would Prophetess.

And if she wouldn't listen, what then?

I wouldn't kill Prophetess. I couldn't. Not for Yoshana's plans. Not to save the world.

So what exactly was my path forward?

Light was beginning to leak in through the dirty windows, and I had found only one option. I wouldn't support Yoshana against Prophetess. So I had to support Prophetess against Yoshana. The Overlord had turned me into a weapon. It was one that could be turned back on her.

The Church, and Prophetess herself, would hardly embrace someone infected with the Darkness. It wasn't a tool to them, but the physical manifestation of sin. But I had seen pragmatism from Prophetess before. Even the Metropolitan at Our Lady had been subtle enough to use our expedition to Stephensburg for his own ends. It would take some convincing - but they'd have to understand that no army without the Darkness could stand against one with it. Without my protection, Prophetess could be silently assassinated as she slept. Yoshana feared Our Lady was a force that could stand against her, and I'd help turn it into just that. And if to Prophetess' way of thinking the cost was one Select's soul, surely that would be a price she'd be more than willing to pay.

The betrayal of an Overlord with the ability to read your mind is not a project undertaken lightly.

Erev was rattling around in the common room, making breakfast. He gave me a long look as I walked in. "You look like hell."

"Yeah." I had my story prepared. "After Yoshana talked up how nasty the Hellguard are, for some reason I didn't sleep so well in their outpost."

The soldier shrugged. "Those guards went down easy enough. If one of the demons shows, that's on Yoshana to take care of. Grigg and Roshel, too. You and me, not so much."

He kept staring at me, as if doing some kind of mental calculus. "You've come up a long way, kid, and I guess you think you're something now, with the Darkness in you. Comes to that, I guess you are something. A factor, or whatever Roshel calls it."

He must have read my face, because he barked out a little laugh. "I may not be able to use the Darkness, but I'm not deaf or stupid. Maybe even more than the other two, Roshel acts like you all, you with the Darkness, you're better than the rest of us. I guess maybe you are. And I guess she needs to think so, too. It's a hard thing that happened to her mother. Yoshana doesn't have that kind of chip on her shoulder, but I guess all of us are just tools to her."

Maybe my mouth was hanging open, because he laughed again. "Didn't think I had that many words in me? I've been tough on you, 'cause you needed toughening. And 'cause she wanted me to be. And, hell, 'cause I didn't like you very much. But you've come through it okay. You've done what you needed to do. And now what you need to do is rest. You want to be a soldier, you gotta learn to sleep whenever you can, wherever you can. That corner's good."

He jerked his thumb at an unused pallet.

I'd heard much the same thing from Tolf. Would the two of them have gotten along? Probably not. They were each too devoted to their respective causes. To their respective prophets.

Somehow, though, Erev's words let me quiet my mind, and I began to drift off on the pallet.

His voice interrupted me. "And I guess with Joav gone, the chances don't look so good for me. I've been through a lot with Yoshana. But maybe not this one. Guess I want somebody to remember me when it's all done. Even if it's just you."

"I love you too."

When you thought about it, the odds weren't great that I was going to outlive Erev. He would have killed me himself, if he'd known what I planned. But still I fell asleep to the sound of him cooking.

There had been a horse for each of the dead guards. The two whose riders Roshel had killed had escaped but had returned soon enough, looking for food. We left one behind and took five, one for each of us. A big part of me wasn't looking forward to rediscovering the joys of saddle sores, but on the whole it beat walking.

"I've never been this far north in the Darklands before," Yoshana admitted. "I crossed the border with the Shield a couple of times when we were allies, but I didn't get past their southernmost city. Still, it's a big place, and the Hellguard are thin on the ground. I'm betting Yashuath is farther north, at Imperium, but we could spend a lot of time just looking for him."

"As long as we find him before the rest of the Hellguard find us," Grigg said.

I don't know what I'd imagined the Darklands would be like, but it hadn't been this. Once we left the abandoned town on the river, the country turned to rolling green hills, lushly carpeted with trees. As I extended my senses, I found no trace of the Darkness. In the Sorrows, it had always been a lurking presence, thin wisps of the stuff everywhere. This was nothing like those haunted woods. In the budding warmth of spring it was a gentle, pleasant country.

Or it would have been, if I hadn't been plotting to break faith with my comrades while hunting a demon lord in his own territory.

We ambled northeast on the remnants of a highway, a crumbling stretch of asphalt that wouldn't have looked out of place in the Source or Rockwall. Just as in the west, we sometimes passed weed-choked ruins at the sides of the road. Unlike in any of my previous travels, I was able to probe them with the Darkness and find them empty of anything but rats, raccoons, and once a small den of wolves. The wolves were no more of a threat to me now than the rats.

I had seen the assurance of this group before we entered the Sorrows. Now I truly understood it. In the Sorrows, with the Darkness wild and unchecked everywhere, I had been prey. Here, I was an apex predator. I liked it.

Did I really want to give it up?

But I wouldn't give it up. The only chance for Prophetess and Our Lady was if I didn't give it up. In the end, Roshel had been right after all that I would be a factor. Just not the way she had planned.

I regretted it, in a way. I liked Roshel, even though her attention toward me might be no more than a part of Yoshana's plan. I liked Grigg, too. Shockingly, I'd even grown fond of the great terror herself. Even if, as Erev said, we were all just tools to her.

"Enjoying yourself?" Roshel pulled up next to me.

I suppressed a guilty start. "I guess I am. Beats that sewer in the Sorrows. I hadn't realized what it was like to just let my senses roam."

She nodded. "It's amazing, isn't it? Like you were blind and now you can see. Don't get too cocky, though. The demons have range on us. If we get too close to one, he'll spot us before we spot him."

That was a bucket of cold water. "And how do we avoid that?"

From ahead, Yoshana said, "Cross your fingers and hope for the best."

Grigg shuddered dramatically. "Sun Tzu is rolling in his grave."

We camped in a copse of trees at the side of the road. It was warm enough that we had no need of shelter. Yoshana decided against a fire.

"I've got no idea what kind of patrols the demons maintain here. There's only a couple hundred Hellguards - almost no chance we'll stumble across one of them. But their soldiers could be anywhere. Better not to send up smoke for them to investigate."

So we sat facing each other across the space where a fire would have been and ate cold rations.

"What's going on?" Roshel asked.

I nearly jumped out of my skin. "What do you mean?"

I applied all my discipline to keeping my heart rate at a normal level. If she probed my mind, I wouldn't even have time to stand up before they killed me.

"You've been quiet all day. Figured you'd be a little more talkative now that we're out of the Sorrows." She elbowed me playfully.

"Sorry. I've been thinking about the demons. I really believed what Yoshana had said about this being the easy part." I shot a glance at the white-haired Overlord, now disguised as a white-haired Select. "The Sorrows were awful. And like you said, it seems so much better here. But, if the demons are that strong, how do we kill one?"

"Same way you kill anyone else," Yoshana said. "Enough bullets, in the right places, and he'll go down. Then you burn the body to make sure he doesn't come back."

She met my eyes squarely. It was all I could do not to flinch away. "The hard part is making sure he doesn't kill you first."

And she laughed.

Everyone was asleep, and had been for hours. I had waited, to be sure. It was time to make my move. I would have to escape back through the Sorrows. It seemed ludicrous to think of that corrupted sea of trees as a refuge, but there I was. If I was going turn against Yoshana and live, the only cover I could possibly find would be in that place where the Darkness was so thick and unpredictable that demons feared to tread. I might not survive the wraiths and possessed even with my new mastery of the Darkness, but it was my only hope of losing Grigg and the Overlords.

The longer we traveled in the Darklands, the farther we would get from the border, and the longer I would be at risk when I fled. I was confident that not even Yoshana could track me once I got back into those haunted woods. Here, where she could sweep a radius of hundreds of yards with the Darkness, scanning for every footprint? The only thing I could do was be faster.

No one was on watch. We trusted in our warding circles. And it was only then, as I silently climbed to my feet, that I realized I was trapped.

I had learned to thread my tendrils of Darkness through the bars of the sophisticated protective cages we had used in the Sorrows. But while I could sense the ward with no difficulty, and extend my senses beyond it with only the most trivial effort, I couldn't cross it physically. Not without being detected. I could simply walk over it and explain I was going to relieve myself. But if someone stayed awake? It wouldn't be long until I was missed. I could use the Darkness to spook the horses and flee in the confusion, but again, how much of a lead would I have? Minutes? Not enough.

I cursed under my breath. For all my new abilities, I was no more able to slip Yoshana and live than I had been weeks ago.

Would I have to see this mission through? Help kill the demon and only then be able to free myself? Would I escape even then? I swore continuously, silently, fighting back tears of frustration. Tired as I was, and despite my meditation, sleep eluded me for the second night in a row.

I was bleary-eyed and thick-headed the next day.

"What's eating you?" Grigg asked. So now they had all noticed. Only Yoshana had failed to comment, and I had no illusions that she wasn't aware. She probably kept track of how often we all breathed.

"Still worried about the demons?" There was a scornful tone in Erev's voice, as if he regretted sharing confidences with me the day before.

"He's not wrong to worry," Yoshana said. "Nothing you can do about it, though, so no sense losing sleep over it."

Her black eyes bored into mine. She was harder to read as a Select than in her true form. I thought I would know if she probed me with the Darkness, but would I really? I certainly couldn't stop her.

"That's what I said," Erev agreed.

"Do you sense something?" the Overlord asked, still holding my gaze. "I think you may be more sensitive than the rest of us, from learning in the Sorrows."

I fleetingly considered a lie, then decided on a version of the truth instead. "No, I don't feel a thing. Maybe that's the problem. I'm used to touching the currents in the Darkness. Back there I could sense a threat coming... remember that pressure we felt in the ruins? Here, I know the demons are out there, but I can't sense anything."

Yoshana nodded, finally breaking eye contact. "Makes sense. We've never trained someone in such a Darkness-saturated environment before. It stands to reason you'd actually feel uncomfortable away from it."

I summoned up a feeble smile of agreement. "So why do they call this the Darklands, if the Darkness is so thin here?"

"Because this is where it started. Where the Hellguard staked out their territory, where the paleos let the Darkness loose into the world. And don't misunderstand - it's thicker here than anywhere but the Sorrows. There's a good chance we'll run into some small clouds of it. I don't expect anything we can't handle, but there's a reason the Hellguard circumcise their slaves' minds, and it's not just about controlling them. A normal person wouldn't last long here. It won't get you within hours or days like in the worst of the Sorrows, but over the course of a lifetime... it's thicker here than in the Shield, and there's plenty of it there."

"For you - for us - that's an advantage, isn't it? If you use up some of it, it's easier to replace?"

She gave me a calculating look. "That's right. It's not often you lose what you control, but it happens. I lost most of mine in the fight with that shaman - but then I took it back from his followers. And of course I left quite a bit embedded in Stephen. That took longer to replace. So yes, I'm a bit stronger here, I can be a bit less careful. But don't get overconfident. We all have limits. If you try to control too much, it *will* control you instead."

We ate, broke camp, and resumed our ride northeast. I turned her words over in my head, wondering if they gave me any more options. Could I somehow flood our camp with the Darkness and escape in the chaos? Could I seize control of the others' wards? I didn't know how. Yoshana had wrested the Darkness from the shaman's servants, but she was much stronger. Was there any hope of doing the same to her while she slept?

I was so wrapped up in my thoughts that my mount bumped into Grigg's when he halted in front of me. I gave the horse a dirty look. "You had one job," I muttered under my breath.

It was only when I had stopped that I heard the faint ringing of a hammer on metal.

"Still quite a ways off," Yoshana said softly.

"Go around?" Grigg asked.

"No. Let's see what we can learn here. Off the road into the woods."

We dismounted and led the horses into the forest flanking the northwestern edge of the road. As the clanging grew louder, we tied our mounts to trees and left them behind.

The overgrown remnants of a town dotted the other side of the highway. Choked with grass and weeds, it showed no signs of life but for the sound and faint wisps of smoke farther ahead.

As we made our way north, the nature of the ruins changed abruptly. Structures that had been ravaged by time gave way to wreckage that had been far more actively devastated.

"Who's attacking a town in Hellguard territory?" Grigg murmured.

I had to smile as I shook my head. "Not attacking. Mining. They're stripping the buildings. Harvesting whatever they can reuse."

"How are you so sure?" asked the other Select.

"I spent two years mining garbage. I know what a salvage operation looks like."

Yoshana nodded. "Makes sense. This is a big place, and thinly settled. The demons will have been at it for centuries. Jackals gnawing away at the bones of human civilization."

I shrugged. We did the same thing on the Flow. Furat supplied pioneers who risked their lives doing it in the Sorrows. Somebody would make use of what had been abandoned, or it would be only so much junk decaying to rust and mold.

Soon enough we saw the signs of the demons' miners. A line of flat, open carts stood on a side street leading eastward into the rubble. Stolid, thick-bodied horses were yoked to the vehicles, placidly cropping what grass they could reach. One sentry watched the animals. He held a metal-shod staff, but I thought his role was less defense and more to make sure none of the beasts got loose and wandered off. Long torches were set into the ground, burning in the bright sunlight. In case someone unearthed a nest of the Darkness, I supposed.

"Easy enough to go around," Grigg hissed. "But we're not going to, are we?"

"There's some danger in having them behind us. And they might know something useful." Yoshana turned and faced me directly. "The key is not to let any of them escape. We absolutely cannot risk them alerting their masters, or we're done for. No misplaced pity, Minos. You'll be doing them a favor to end the half-lives they're living. We'll circle, and close in from four directions. Prisoners are good, but do *not* let any of them out alive."

I bobbed my head once.

"I'll work my way to the far side of where they're salvaging and hit them from the east. Grigg, you come in from the north, Roshel from the south. Minos, Erev, you head straight in when the rest of us are in position. Extend the Darkness as far as you can toward Grigg and Roshel. They'll reach out to you and to me. We'll be able to maintain contact over a square two hundred yards or so on a side. That should be big enough. As we move in, the links will make sure nothing sneaks by between us."

The plan was simple enough - with the aid of the Darkness. Without it, a dozen things could go wrong. With it? As long as we each knew where the others were, it was easy.

As long as we each knew where the others were...

Yoshana, Roshel, and Grigg moved silently into the ruins. I could feel them as I stretched my senses. Soon, Roshel and Grigg began to trail their own tendrils of Darkness behind, maintaining contact with mine. But my strands could be cut free, and then...

I had planned to escape in the night, quietly. Not to abandon my companions in the middle of a fight. It would be the ultimate betrayal.

Not that it would make a difference to Yoshana. However I left her, the penalty if she caught me would be death.

"Can you take the guard?" Erev whispered. With the Darkness, he meant.

I nodded. "Does it bother you, at all? That Yoshana uses everyone?" Grigg and Roshel were beyond my range. The edges of my probes were touching the edges of theirs.

"Nah. Everyone gets used. Soldiers especially. At least she doesn't just waste her troops. She'll throw you away, but it's for a reason."

"Yeah." I severed my connection to my probes, leaving them to hang in the air. They would float, dissipate - but for a time, they would feel like me. "I'm sorry."

I already had the Darkness in Erev. It slashed his Achilles tendons, his vocal cords, the ligaments in his wrists. He fell, grunting out a rush of air. The wounds were small, and I had no doubt Yoshana could heal him. If she didn't kill him for letting me escape.

I was disgusted with what I had done, but I couldn't have him following me, or calling out... or shooting me in the back.

I turned and ran, leaving the soldier flopping on the ground behind me.

I had minutes at best before Grigg and Roshel realized something was wrong. I dodged through the trees, leaping over roots, branches whipping at my face. What would happen if the demons' slaves fled through the hole I had left in our perimeter? If they escaped and alerted the Hellguard, Yoshana's whole mission might fail.

I put it from my mind and rushed on. If Yoshana captured me, I'd never find out whether she succeeded or failed. Although she might carry my head around as a reminder of what happened if you crossed her.

The horses shied as I burst into the little clearing where they were tethered. I fumbled at the reins, freeing the animals. Grigg had pulled his knot so tight that I gave up and cut through the leather with the strange knife I'd found in the Sorrows. The tough material parted easily under that razor edge.

I untied my own mount last and swung up onto its back. Nearly a minute lost - I could only hope this would be worth it. My store of the Darkness was depleted from the tendrils I had abandoned, but I marshaled what was left and shrieked *Fear!* into the feeble minds of the horses.

The four riderless beasts wheeled, snorted, and galloped away in a mad panic, each in a different direction. Unfortunately, mine was affected as well. It plunged north, deeper into the woods. A small branch cut my face, drawing a stream of blood or Darkness - I couldn't tell, and didn't dare take a hand from the reins to touch my face.

I wanted to go west, and I hauled roughly at the animal's mouth. It staggered and slewed around in an ungainly slide. I think it nearly went down. I know I nearly fell off. I lurched one way, then the other, and if I hadn't been so terrified of pursuit I would have simply let go and allowed myself to drop.

As it was I lost the reins and found myself leaning far to the left of my seat, desperately holding on by the saddle horn and the horse's mane. Another tree limb struck me in the head and for a moment all I saw was a flash of red.

I realized my unbalanced weight was pulling the horse around, and it was now charging south. I was very nearly going in a circle. I flung myself forward, wrapped my arms around the long neck, and leaned right. The horse launched itself even faster and shifted direction again, coming back around to the west but now moving so fast it was bound to break a leg on a root, if it didn't rush headlong into a tree.

Sitting a maddened, galloping steed was nothing like rolling along at a walk. I was a poor rider at the best of times, and this was very far from the best of times.

From my rudimentary riding lessons I knew I should lean back to slow the animal, but that went against every instinct as well as the force of gravity. And I realized that my own panic was feeding the horse's, augmented no doubt by the Darkness. Clinging like some deranged monkey to my mount's neck, I did my best to quiet my mind.

And then the shots began behind me.

My heart went into my throat, and the horse surged into even more desperate motion. But the blasts were distant, and repeated. Not the sounds of pursuit, but of Yoshana executing the demons' slaves.

"Still, that's us if they catch us," I muttered. But by now we must be at least half a mile away, beyond the range of even Yoshana's senses. I fumbled for the dangling reins and caught them, then slowly checked the horse's wild flight.

If they were pursuing now, it would be on foot. They could take the pack horses from the demons' salvage train, but those hadn't been saddled. With any luck they wouldn't know exactly which way I'd gone, with five trails crashing in different directions through the forest.

I brought my mount to an uncomfortable trot. Any one of Yoshana, Grigg, or Roshel would be more than a match for me, but even if they split up, the chances of any of them catching up to me should be low. The farther I went, the more the arc of unknown direction should work in my favor. I hoped they'd assume I'd returned southwest, to the bridge we had crossed. But I realized that due west would also look like an attractive option. I turned northwest instead.

How long could a horse run? Not long at a full gallop, I thought. But mine should be able to sustain this trot for some time.

Of course, now that the terror had worn off, it didn't want to. As if realizing it had been lucky not to break a leg, or its neck, the beast slowed to a careful walk. I kicked at its sides, but earned nothing more than a reproachful look.

Perhaps I was far enough away to be safe.

Yoshana's Darkness flowed into the native, into every pore and opening of its body, and then - the creature simply came apart in a tsunami of devastation set loose from the inside.

"Let's see if that gets the point across," Yoshana said.

It would be like that, but slower - so I would fully appreciate what was happening.

I laid my hand on the horse's neck. "Fear," I whispered. And we were off again.

A few minutes later we burst from the trees onto a muddy track that had once been a road. I saw no signs that anything else had traveled it recently. My mount shuddered to a walk, blowing great, ragged breaths. I looked back down the path. It stretched out behind us, disappearing around a bend in the trees. If someone came around that curve, we would be clearly visible. I set my palm on the horse's heaving side. It needed another jolt of terror to get moving again, and here we didn't need to worry about slamming into a tree.

But I could feel the animal's mind and body as I touched it. The beast's heart was hammering, its lungs gasping for air. It was nearly exhausted. There was another sprint left in that body. With the Darkness infiltrating its organs, that sprint could be a long one. But then the horse would die.

Of course, if Yoshana came around that bend in the road, I would die.

I sighed. "All right, you miserable creature. Let's walk a bit."

The horse plodded forward. I hoped it was grateful.

The ground to either side gradually gave way to a swampy muck. Ancient trees rose from it, trunks so thick I couldn't have put my arms around them. Though I was on a path, the canopy of leaves overhead blotted out the sun.

Branches rustled, and something huge launched itself into the air and erupted from the trees with a beating of wings. Some kind of eagle, larger than any I had seen before. I took deep breaths to still the pounding of my heart and swallowed several times, trying to get my stomach back down into my abdomen.

I looked back over my shoulder again. The bend in the road was far behind, but the line of sight was clear. To the left and right, the bog would be virtually impassable on horseback. If someone came up behind us, there was nowhere to go but straight ahead.

"Let's get a move on, horse," I said. I kicked it sharply. It stopped dead in its tracks and turned its head, glaring balefully at me and baring its teeth.

"You asked for it."

Fear.

Only after we had galloped a mile and passed two turnings in the road did I ease the animal back to a trot. I kept that pace as the swamp turned slowly back to solid ground, and the road took a determined northerly direction. I guided the horse back into the trees, letting it settle into a shambling walk. I occasionally encouraged it with my heels, but didn't use the Darkness again.

Truth be told, I was as exhausted as my mount. I had hardly slept for two nights, and the adrenaline was leaching away. More than once I swayed in the saddle, my eyelids growing heavy.

Once my eyes snapped open, my heart pounding. I thought I heard hoofbeats behind us, gaining fast. But as I pulled the horse to a halt and sat stock still, I could hear nothing. It must have been my imagination as I drifted in and out of sleep.

I didn't dare extend the Darkness behind me. If I'd been fully alert I might have chanced it, trusting to my Sorrows-born training that I could sense my pursuers before they sensed me. But not now. Not as tired as I was.

I wasn't probing in front of me either. Careless.

So I was surprised when the trees ended and a short, grassy plain led down to a river. The same one we had crossed before? Its banks were nowhere near as steep, but it was almost as wide. I guided my mount toward it.

A few yards from the bank, the tall grass turned to huge, smooth rocks. The horse was reluctant to step on them, and I kicked at it impatiently until it grudgingly moved forward, one tentative step at a time. When it was on the stone, where I would leave no footprints, I slid off its back and untied my pack from the saddle.

"You can go now," I said. It looked at me stupidly.

"Beat it." It bent its head to eat instead.

Exasperated, I pulled the bundled-up katana from my pack and smacked the horse across the rump. It whinnied in shock and annoyance, gave a kick back at me, missed, and charged off to the north. A hundred yards away it stopped, gave me one last disgusted backwards glance, and returned to cropping grass.

I sighed. I'd hoped the beast would move farther off, in case I'd been followed. But I was done with it. Shrugging the pack onto my back, I picked my way down the rocks into the river.

The water was cold and the current, while not torrential, was swift. The shock of it chased away my drowsiness. I could still see the bottom several yards in, but no farther. I had no idea how deep it was. There was nothing for it but to find out the hard way.

It was deeper than I was tall. By the time I had gone ten paces, I was swimming, or trying. I was completely soaked, and so was everything I was carrying. Twenty paces in and the current had me. I was being swept downstream, doing my best to make forward progress. My head went under, and only the direction of the current kept me oriented when I struggled back to the surface.

Twice more I went under, sodden clothes and pack pulling me down. I fought for breath. It would be ironic to drown after all that I'd been through, but with water filling my nose and mouth, I didn't really appreciate the humor.

And then my boot touched gravel, and I was dragging myself out onto the other bank, a mirror of the one I had left. Trees loomed in front of me. Cautiously, I extended the Darkness into those woods, and found the answering eddy of the Sorrows' malignant currents.

I was back to hell on earth. And it felt like home.

I crawled at first, then picked myself up and staggered into the trees. I cast one last look back over my shoulder as I slipped between the trunks. I didn't see anyone behind me, but lurched another hundred yards or so deeper into the forest anyway. I selected an ancient oak tree and with the last of my strength pulled myself up into the branches, ten feet off the ground, and wedged myself into the crotch of two heavy limbs.

In the most dangerous place in the world, I felt safe for the first time in two days. And fell asleep.

10. The Devil You Don't Know

I woke a few hours later, the sun still in the sky. I had set no wards, hadn't meditated. And I had lived. I extended my senses and found nothing unusual, beyond the normal, brooding presence of the Darkness in the Sorrows.

The tree was as safe a place as any, and likely safer than most. But I felt refreshed, and it made sense to get farther from the river and make what westward progress I could while it was still light.

But I sat in the tree for a while instead. There was no one telling me to move on. There was no one for me to protect. For the first time in half a year, I answered to nobody. I was in a place of great danger, but I had become pretty dangerous myself. The sense of freedom was intoxicating.

I sighed. Free or not, it was time to go. It was hard to imagine Yoshana swimming across the river and beating the bushes for me when I was outside the range of her senses and she had no trail to follow, but the deeper I got in the Sorrows, the safer I would be from her. Another half mile into the forest would make me completely impossible to find.

Reluctantly I climbed down from my perch. The warm air and the sun filtering through the leaves had been enough to dry me. My gear was another story. But I would move farther from the river before I checked it. I shouldered my pack and headed generally toward the setting sun, following no particular path, just letting the terrain guide me. I was alert now, and the Darkness ranged out around me.

Once I felt a slight thickening in the currents and adjusted my course to avoid whatever it was. Half an hour later I found a small clearing I liked. I pulled the Darkness fully into myself. An ordinary warding circle would endanger me more than it would protect me - something might feel it, and be drawn to me, and a cloud of Darkness could float right over it undetected. A full cage would give me more warning, but would take too much of my attention and create the same risk of something sensing it from the outside. I opted for nothing instead.

I dumped the contents of my pack on the ground. A trickle of water spattered out. My jerky and dried fruit went on a rock in the sun. They should dry before they rotted. The soggy bread I flung into the woods to be food for whatever might choose to eat grain rather than people.

Most of the other gear would recover from its wetting. I shook water off my cooking pan, flint, and other durables. The oil-soaked torches we all carried were now water-soaked as well. They would probably still light, although they wouldn't burn well until they dried. There wasn't much to do about that.

The strange, glistening blade of my knife shed drops as if it were oiled, although it wasn't. So did the black material that sheathed it. The katana was another story. I unwrapped it from its waterlogged rags and threw them away. I wiped down the blade on my pants, then oiled it. The uncured leather hilt was sodden and would likely rot. I'd carry the sword in my hand - the pack was too wet, and I had nothing left to wrap it. It wasn't a bad idea to have a blade out, in any case.

The two wristwatches I had looted lay forlorn in the mud. I cleaned them off on my tunic. Neither seemed to have taken on water. I gave the crown of each one a few turns, and was relieved to see the tiny second hands begin to move. It would have been a shame if the delicate mechanisms had survived the centuries only to be spoiled in the river.

I didn't know what to do about the carbine. The cartridges were sealed metal, and should be all right. But I should strip the gun's mechanism to dry it before rust set in. Unfortunately, Grigg hadn't taught me how to do that, and I had no confidence that I could put the weapon back together if I took it apart. I'd just have to hope for the best. If I needed to fire it, it would either shoot or it wouldn't. If my life depended on it - and it probably would if I needed to use the carbine - I would be rolling the dice. But some chance that it would work was better than none.

This was as good a place to stop as any, and my things could dry further overnight. The second wind my nap had given me was fading. I considered going up another tree, but couldn't summon up the energy. I lay down on my back in the center of the clearing, katana in my hand, knife at my belt. In the end, I extended a simple ward in a circle a dozen feet across. If something entered the clearing it would see me anyway, and the ward would give me a second or two of warning.

Meditation brought questions. Had I done the right thing? I'd abandoned my companions in the middle of a fight. I'd crippled Erev, and it was no stretch of the imagination to see Yoshana leaving him to die, or tearing him apart in a fit of rage. Was he dead now? Dragging himself to shelter on hands and knees, abandoned? Or healed, and bent on vengeance?

Maybe I should have killed him. As I thought about it, it was hard to see any upside to leaving him alive.

Prophetess wouldn't have approved of killing him. But Prophetess wouldn't approve of anything I had done since I'd let the Darkness into my body. Let it into my soul, she'd say.

Didn't leaving Yoshana prove it hadn't corrupted me? Didn't sparing Erev?

If I'd spared him.

I closed my eyes, but rest didn't come easily.

Nothing molested me during the night. Maybe the monsters of the darkness had sensed my mood, and thought it best to leave me alone.

More likely nothing of any size had stumbled across me.

The risk of an encounter with something large was very real. In that first rush of freedom from Yoshana I'd put that out of my mind. But something had taken Rosc and Talman while we'd slept. One native I could handle - but not a hunting pack. And a large cloud would be far more than I could deal with.

Yoshana had said it - there were reasons why even the demons didn't come in here.

There was nothing for it but to move on, be careful, and hope for the best. I found that the clumsily wrapped hilt of the katana was comforting in my hand as I moved deeper into the forest. I followed a ridgeline that tended southwest, staying above the deepest shadow without highlighting myself against the sky.

It should have been safe enough... or as safe as I could be in the Sorrows. And the currents seemed thin. Almost surprisingly so. Perhaps the route we'd taken before had been more heavily infested. Or I was just getting used to it.

I was at the point of resting under a huge tree when I saw the bones.

A dozen partially dissolved skeletons littered the forest floor around the trunk. Most were smaller animals, birds or rodents, but I saw one that was likely a boar, and another that might have been a wolf. I pulled my senses back in, then carefully extended the most delicate of probes toward the tree.

Once I felt it, it was easy enough to see with my own eyes. Twenty feet up, a thick mass of Darkness pulsed, shadowed by the leaves, like a monstrous wasps' nest. It was at least as large and dense as the cloud that had possessed the native shaman. As I scanned more carefully, I could sense tendrils reaching out from it across the ground and through the air.

I recalled the similar trap I'd come across before with Yoshana and the others. The Darkness reproduced and spread. Yoshana had said it consumed nutrients from living things. Things whose bones lay scattered here.

When we'd all been traveling together, we'd found the lurking mass in time and avoided it. This one was far larger, and I was standing inside the nest's sensory network. From where the bodies had fallen, it looked like the Darkness usually let them get closer before it attacked. Maybe I could back away and live.

Or maybe it would rush me if it felt me trying to escape. I'd seen how quickly the Darkness could move. I had no illusions that I could outrun it, or fight off such a thick concentration.

It feared fire. Lighting a torch might provoke it, but it might also be my only chance. Slowly, trying not to move abruptly, I sank the point of my sword into the earth, shifted my pack, and withdrew a torch, flint, and steel.

"God, I know I'm probably not too high up on your list right now, but I'm trying to do the right thing for your church," I muttered. "So I'd really appreciate it if this torch would light and you didn't let this cloud eat me."

The flint sparked, the oil-soaked rag caught, and the torch sputtered fitfully to life.

"Thank you," I whispered. "I owe you one."

The mass in the tree quivered, disturbed. Its tendrils writhed in the air, circling around me but keeping a wary distance. I backed slowly away.

"Let's you and me make a deal too," I said. "I don't burn you, you don't tear me apart."

There was nothing as human as anger in the cloud - just a bottomless hunger. But I could sense its frustration held barely in check by fear as I moved away.

I stopped feeling its presence less than a hundred feet from the tree. I went ten times that far before I ground out the torch in a pile of damp leaves. The smoke would be marking me for any roving bands of natives in the area, but that was by far the lesser evil until the nest was out of range.

I sat on a rock and took deep, shaky breaths. I had very nearly blundered into something far beyond my ability to defeat. It would take me at least a week to cross the Sorrows. I had almost died on the second day.

I scanned the sky. I should move away from the remnants of the smoke I had trailed behind me.

So why was there smoke in front of me?

It was a thin column, like a cooking fire. Probably several miles to the northwest, but clearly visible against the blue sky. It could be anything, spanning the full range from salvation to doom. I was deep in the Sorrows, but scavengers from the Source might conceivably have gotten this far. The natives we had seen hadn't used fire, nor did it seem likely they would if they were possessed. But I didn't fool myself into believing I had encountered every form of awfulness these woods held.

Or it might be as simple as a natural blaze, smoldering from some past lightning strike I hadn't seen. A forest fire might clear a path for me through the terrors of the Sorrows, unless it turned back and consumed me. Yoshana had repeatedly compared the Darkness to fire, and they were both unpredictable and dangerous.

The encounter with the nest had shaken me. If there was a chance for help, I would take it. I set out to the northwest.

The column of smoke served as a guidepost, continuing unabated. It seemed it must be manmade - if it were natural, it would certainly have sputtered out or grown into an inferno.

I crested a low hill and found it rising from the center of a depression in a circle of trees. I couldn't quite make out the fire from my vantage point, but it was clear that this was some sort of camp.

The question was whose?

I crept down through the foliage, keeping low, sword out, Darkness questing in front of me. Well before I reached the clearing, my probes had reconnoitered it.

There was a small, thatch-roofed cabin, a fire pit, and - oddly - a stone statue between me and the center of the circle. Some ancient site, then, with new inhabitants. Again, the question was who those inhabitants were. I sensed no one there. Not in the clearing, not in the hut, not in the woods immediately around us. As quietly as I could, I approached the statue, and peered out from behind it. The scene was just what the Darkness had told me - a rustic encampment, but a permanent one.

The edge of the sculpture's plinth was sharp under my knee. Too sharp. A woman was carved into the pale rock as if emerging from cloud. But there was no weathering of the stone. It might have been hewn yesterday, but the quality of the work matched anything I'd seen in ancient ruins. Where had it come from, how had it survived unscathed in the middle of nowhere, and what did it have to do with this campsite, abandoned now, but obviously tenanted?

"Looking for someone?"

I spun around, slamming my back into the statue, bringing my sword up. Darkness rushed in around me like a shield. In front of me - two steps behind me, before I had turned - was a figure called up from hell itself.

The man was as huge as the booming voice would suggest. Bigger. He stood inches taller than Grigg, inches broader across the shoulders. He must have outweighed the big Select by fifty pounds or more of solid, bulging muscle. His skin was a deeper red than Yoshana's, the color of a ripe cherry, almost black. Eyes and hair were dark as the Overlord's heart.

He leaned easily on a pointed metal staff etched all along its seven-foot length with symbols and patterns. The shaft was at least an inch thick. If it was the solid steel I suspected it was, the weapon must have weighed thirty pounds. Seeing me eying the staff, the giant grinned and spun it lazily in one hand. Teeth gleamed white in that awful smile.

I didn't doubt for a second I was facing a demon.

"Don't get a lot of Select through here," he rumbled. "Don't think I've seen one for two hundred years."

I edged sideways. Maybe I could put the statue between us. Although I didn't know how much of an obstacle even solid stone would be to that staff. Much less the Darkness. Speaking of the Darkness, how had he gotten behind me without my sensing him? I didn't think even Yoshana could do that.

My mouth was open, and some sort of squeak came out. A sensation like a spider skittered across the surface of my mind.

"You're not totally clumsy with the prant, but not nearly good enough to make it out of here alive," the demon declared.

I shied away from the thought of not making it out alive and tried to keep the creature talking while I considered my options. "Prant?"

"Psycho-Reactive Autonomous Nano Technology. PRANT. Don't they teach you people anything anymore? Last thing I thought I'd meet today was an ignorant Select. Y'all are supposed to be smart." The monster chuckled. "What you call the Darkness, boy. You think that was its name back in the day?"

The demon shifted his grip on the staff, and I tensed. I might possibly be able to deflect the first blow and run as fast I could into the woods.

He stabbed the weapon deep into the ground and stepped forward, thrusting out a massive hand. "My bad. Haven't been very welcoming. Don't get much company. I'm Seven."

I sat on a stump near the fire, three feet from a demon. I was still having trouble processing that fact.

"Ages since I've been this close to anyone but the possessed, and they're lousy conversationalists," the creature that called itself Seven was saying. "How'd you come to be here anyway? Hadn't thought to see a Select so near the Darklands."

"Um." I wondered what to say. Not the truth, certainly. "Well, no... I, uh, didn't think the, uh, that is, the Hellguard cared much for the Select."

"Oh, hell no. Why would we?"

"Um, why wouldn't you? I never understood that."

The giant's mouth hung open for a moment. "They really don't teach you anything, do they? Do you even know what you are?"

"Of course," I snapped, then instantly regretted being peevish to something that could snap me like a twig. "We were designed to be... superior. After the Fall, something went wrong. We're still stronger, smarter, tougher than other people, but now we're marked."

Our gray skin, solid black eyes, and white hair had been called the mark of Cain. Considering how popular we were in human society, it wasn't far off.

"Rich kids," the demon growled. "Parents wanted their kids perfect. Perfect hair, perfect teeth, perfect everything. Designer babies. You could even pick the skin color, eye color, hair color. Problem turned out to be, the base coat of paint was gray. You don't insert any genes for appearance, you get -" the demon waved his hand at me, "you."

"I knew that."

"Right. You know what I am?"

"No."

"I'm you. But better. Bigger, stronger, faster, tougher. And a lot more willpower. Did you know there's a gene for self-control? Turns out there is. And you need a lot of self-control if you want to use the prant."

"Yo - that is, I heard you were soldiers."

"That's right. Special forces. Army created us to be physically perfect, plus able to master the prant. Recon, field medicine, assassination, ops in toxic environments, you name it, we could do it."

Yoshana had told me before, but I still struggled with the idea that the monster had actually been created this way on purpose. "So what happened?"

The demon leaned back on his wooden bench and sighed. "Seems like it's always the Germans that screw things up. When the civil war in the Islamic Republic spilled into the northern Med, all hell really broke loose. We were on the ground bumping off radical cell leaders. Nasty work. Dangerous. You know something about the prant. You can't control it past maybe two hundred yards - not you, not me, not anyone. That puts you pretty close to the action."

He sighed again. "The Northern Concordance got in on the fight. Afraid if southern Europe fell, they'd be next. So they deployed their own specialists. But they'd been casualty averse for a century. Thought they could extend the range of the prant through sarns."

I must have looked blank.

"Semi Autonomous Relay Nodes. The idea is you float a drone with a basic AI and a heavy nucleus of the prant about a hundred, hundred and fifty yards out."

I didn't understand half of what he'd said, but I nodded anyway. He went on.

"That gives you a link in a chain. Then another, and another. With the sarns, the Concordance operators could sit back a mile away from the action. Great idea. Except the links weren't strong enough. Got too far out, they lost control of the prant. Some of it went rogue. Some got taken over. What went rogue started to spread, reproduce. About the same time terror cells set off the nukes here on the eastern seaboard. Little ones, tac nukes really, but somebody'd wrapped some nasty isotopes around them. The fallout was bad. The bigwigs pulled us out of the theater, put us on reclamation duty at home instead. Went from dodging bullets to hip-deep in radioactive waste."

The dark eyes lost focus, staring into an unhappy past.

"That wasn't much fun. ID'ing bodies from pieces and DNA kits. Folks that survived but were too sick or hurt to make their way out, and we'd find 'em. Mostly dying from radiation sickness. Lots we found too late - survived the blasts, but coughed their lungs out. Or too weak to get to water and just dehydrated. The kids were the worst."

I didn't remember much of the Books of the Fall, but that part I remembered. *"Then came the great fires that burned the capitals, and the air itself was set aflame. And sons could not find their fathers, nor could mothers find their daughters. The great cities were cast down, and those that lived were covered in sores like leprosy, and died soon after. The leaders of the people perished too in the fire. Those that remained said, Let the Hellguard go forth! Let the demons and the Darkness reclaim what we have lost. For are we not masters of every power?"*

"Heh. Yeah. It wasn't that poetic being there in it, but that's the gist of it. Book of Arvan, right? You know the part that comes next?"

I didn't recall it as well, certainly not to quote it. "Something about the Darkness being unleashed across the western sea?"

"Yup. I remember I got interviewed once by some general in the Central Republican Army, years before it all went down the toilet. Our guys were trying to explain why you needed the genetic engineering and training to control the prant. He wasn't buying it. They were always in a hurry, and they got spooked when the nukes went off. The Central Republic was closer to the action in the Middle East than we were, and I guess they thought it was only a matter of time before someone lit them up. Idiots. Four thousand year old civilization, you'd think they'd have learned some patience. They figured if a few hundred of our guys with the prant was good, a few thousand of their guys was better."

The demon shook his head. "That did not go well."

He turned to me. "You've seen the possessed." I nodded. "It went quick over there. They thought their psych screening and a few months of training were enough to control the prant. They were wrong. Really wrong. We never did know how many lost control. It was a lot. There were mutinies. And then it got out into the population, and then it was all over the country there, faster than you can imagine. And that's when it all went wrong."

"Sounds like it went wrong long before that."

He gave a little snorting chuckle, almost like a bull. "From our perspective, I mean. The Hellguard's. I guess living three centuries don't make you any less self-centered. Probably more, if anything."

There was a little smile on his face, but his eyes were locked on mine, and there was no humor in them. I had been growing more comfortable with the giant as he talked. I was reminded suddenly of what sort of ancient, deadly thing he was.

"You asked why we don't like the Select. See, after what went down in Europe and Asia, no one trusted us anymore. They figured if the prant could get loose there, it could get loose here. The public started calling for the Hellguard to be shut down. For our kind of people, 'shut down' don't mean a retirement villa in Tuscany."

I swallowed. "And the Select?"

"You might have thought... we thought... the Select would defend us. We were the same, but what was done to you for your damn vanity was done to us for our country. You might have thought that... but you'd have been wrong. There were politicians everyone knew were Select. They could have spoken up for us. But they were the loudest saying we were dangerous."

Of course they were dangerous. This one was looking very dangerous right now.

He heaved a deep breath. "Looking out for number one, I guess. Must have figured they didn't want to be associated with us. Tarred with the same brush. Decided the only way to protect themselves was to be more Catholic than the Pope."

The demon laughed. "Guess that didn't work out so well for you in the end."

There was a brief thrashing in the woods. I twitched, almost reaching for my sword, almost extending the Darkness. I did neither.

My host stood up. "'Scuse me. That's lunch." He stalked off into the trees, completely silent for all his bulk.

I waited in place for a moment, but found I couldn't sit still. I walked over to the statue. The craftsmanship continued to impress me. From the front, I could see the woman's face was beautiful, but anguished. On the base were carved the words, "I Told The Priest, Don't Count On Any Second Coming. God Got His Ass Kicked The First Time He Came Down Here Slumming."

The Hellguard chuckled behind me. I hadn't heard him return. He carried a dead boar slung casually over his shoulder.

"That's Wendy," he said. "My concrete blonde."

He grinned, as if expecting the words to mean something to me. When I didn't react, he sighed. "Never mind. It isn't funny if you have to explain it."

"You made this?"

He nodded. "It's amazing what you can do with the prant and a little patience."

"You carved this with the Darkness?"

"Yep. No finer tool."

I was side by side with one of the world's most ancient horrors. The kind of creature that seared the will from the minds of its human slaves. A terror greater even than Yoshana. I took a breath and plunged in. "Can you teach me to use it that way?"

The demon's smile widened. "Let's eat first."

He roasted the boar on a spit, seasoning it as it turned. The meat may have been the best I'd ever had.

"Where did you get salt?" I asked.

"I'm pretty near immortal, kid." Darkness crawled over his outstretched hand, forming a mesmerizing pattern before it dissipated. "I've got a tool that can filter chemicals pretty close to the atomic level, and nothing but time. There's not a lot I can't do."

He nodded at the statue.

Powerful as he was, the demon didn't terrify me the way Yoshana did. Not that I thought he was any less deadly - but he seemed somehow less likely to kill me on a whim.

It wasn't a safe question, but I asked anyway. "So why are you out here?"

He cocked his head at me.

"I mean, we, that is, I didn't think demons lived in the Sorrows."

"First off, let's you and me make a deal, kid. I don't rip your arms off and beat you to death with them, and you stop calling me a demon."

I swallowed. "Sorry. I didn't mean - I didn't think you minded. I heard you call yourself a Hellguard."

"Not the same word at all."

"But -"

"Hellguard's just a name. Like Devil Dogs."

I blinked at him.

"Ignorant. Just plain ignorant," he muttered, shaking his head. "They called the Marines Devil Dogs. Story is it was 'cause they fought so hard in the first world war. Apparently the Marines made that story up, but that's par for the course for those jarheads. Anyway, that's what the Army called us. The Hellguard. 'Cause we're scary. Doesn't mean we actually come from hell, or that we're demons, or something."

"Sorry," I repeated.

"I mean, just 'cause a guy's six and a half feet tall and red, and commands the powers of Darkness..." It began to coil around his arms, and the demon - the Hellguard - flashed me another grin.

"But still - I thought the Hellguard stayed out of the Sorrows."

The smile vanished like a torch blowing out. There was something like pain on his face. "We do. Well, the rest of 'em do."

"What happened?"

"I guess I didn't finish the story. When the recall order came, we didn't answer. Not a big deal, at first. Not much anyone could do about it. Sure, it was mutiny, and the idea didn't sit so good with some of us, but we weren't going to let ourselves get put down like dogs. And with everything else going on, the Army wasn't going to mount up a brigade in environment suits to hunt us down. Couldn't bomb us out either - so much of the sensory grid was fried out here, they really had no idea where we were once we stopped transmitting. So that was okay. Everything north of DC and east of the Appalachians had been evacuated. We had eight whole states to ourselves. Not a bad deal."

"But?"

"But. There's always some nut job that can make any bad situation worse. This set of nut jobs called themselves paleos."

"I know them."

"Yeah. I hear they're still around, which is amazing and shows there ain't no justice in the world. Big group of 'em decided to move in and squat in what looked like open territory. Which would have been fine. There was plenty of room. But these guys were fanatics. Hated anything to do with technology. Which included us. It's pretty funny when some morons start throwing spears until one of 'em actually hits you."

"They threw a lot of spears at the Select after we started to look like this. They hit a lot of us."

The Hellguard winced. "Yeah, like I said, you guys didn't wind up doing so good out of the deal. Obviously they couldn't kill any of us, but they pissed us off bad enough that some of the younger guys hit 'em with the prant. Which would have been fine if we'd killed all of 'em. But we didn't."

"And the survivors spread the Darkness."

"Yep. Well, there was sure as hell no going back after that. We'd pretty much destroyed civilization on this continent because some of the guys couldn't keep their prant in their pants."

His mouth twisted sourly. "Thought that would sound funnier."

It was hard to make a good joke about the Fall of human civilization.

"I assume you know what happened next," he said.

"To the rest of us. Not to you. Not to the Hellguard. We don't really know anything about you. At least - no one outside the Shield and the Darklands does."

"Just demons, huh? That's sad. But I guess it's no surprise. See, when the prant started to get out of control, everybody pulled back into towns, built walls around them, stripped or abandoned whatever was outside. Afraid of infection."

I nodded.

He went on, "No trade, no gas, no electricity, no water purification… everything fell apart real fast."

"The Age of Fear."

"Yeah, good name for it. But you got even more of the nuts that didn't want to be cooped up in some town. We got another wave of paleos moving in on us. And that's when most of my guys… turned."

"What do you mean?"

262

The huge man took a deep, shuddering breath. "You've got to understand. The world had turned on us first. Our own government was going to kill us, for God's sake. And those people... some of those paleos weren't much better than animals."

I didn't disagree. I liked pigs better than paleos - and I didn't like pigs.

"There were only ten of us, in the beginning." I didn't understand, but didn't interrupt. The Hellguard seemed lost inside his own mind. "Primus, Secundus, up through Decimus. The first ten created. I was Septimus. Seemed kinda pretentious, so now I just go by Seven. We'd been around longer than the others. We knew more... regular humans. And most folks had treated us decent enough. But the newer guys, they'd never known anything but growing up in the lab, and training, and war. I don't think they saw the paleos as people at all. The paleos weren't like us. They were just animals. Just things. Time went by, some of our crew started to think about everybody that wasn't us that way."

His eyes were on the fire, not focused on anything in this world. "And once a person's just a thing... it doesn't matter what you do to him anymore. Or her."

The dark, red face turned back to me. "I couldn't take it. I don't think the other originals liked it either, but there were three hundred of the new guys, and only six of us left. And the new guys were stronger - hooray for progress. The other five went along, but I wouldn't. So I left."

"How long have you been here? Alone?"

"Three hundred years, give or take."

I tried to fathom the loneliness of it.

"It's not so bad," he said, reading my mind - perhaps literally. "Sometimes I go farther west where the prospectors come in, and I get close enough to scan 'em. Learn a little about what's going on outside. Over the centuries I've even had a couple of visitors that weren't so crazy I had to kill them. And of course I've got Wendy."

"You don't think about going out? Not back to the Darklands, but west? With... people?"

"Yeah, that would go over like a lead balloon. Can you imagine? They don't like you. They'd really love me. No one even knows what we really are anymore. I guess after the Fall, people made a point of forgetting, and I guess I can maybe see why. Renamed every town, stopped using any name that reminded them of the past. At best, I'm a reminder of things they don't want to remember. At worst... you said it. People think we're actually demons."

"But you could..." I trailed off.

"Yeah? I could do what, kid?"

What, indeed?

Seven had never trained anyone to use the Darkness. He was less skilled as a teacher than Yoshana, and often couldn't explain exactly what he wanted me to do. "You just do it, that's all," he'd growl.

But he knew things I was pretty sure she didn't.

"You're all brute force," he complained. "No fine control at all."

Offended, I explained that I'd been able to pierce the others' wards without being detected.

"Then whoever trained you really is about as subtle as a bull in rut."

I had to laugh. "Yoshana wouldn't be very pleased to hear you say that."

"Yoshana?"

Oops. Somehow I'd neglected to mention where I'd spent the last couple of months.

"I guess I'd better explain."

The Hellguard nodded. "I guess you'd better."

I didn't leave anything out. When I had finished, I waited for his reaction. He was silent for a time.

"Well, she's got guts, I'll say that for her. Going to need more than guts to take down Ypsilon, though."

"Who?"

"Yashuath. Used to be Ypsilon. Decided he wanted something that sounded more biblical. Some of them started to take the demon stuff pretty seriously." He leaned back, thinking. "Dunno. You said you're more sensitive than the others 'cause you were trained in here. Makes sense. Guess I've probably learned some tricks over the last few centuries that the rest of the guys may not know. Still, comes to a stand-up fight, subtle's only worth so much. And Yashuath is as strong as they come."

"You don't think she'll manage it?"

"Didn't say that. She hasn't been around long, but she's picked up a hell of a reputation. Even I know who she is, and I'm stuck here. Gurath and the guys have faced down a lot of Overlords over the years, but word is she's different."

"Gurath?"

"Gamma. He's in charge. Yashuath's his number two. And the more aggressive of them. Your Yoshana must be figuring that if she takes down Yashuath, Gurath will regroup and give her time to build her new army. It's not a terrible idea."

I said, "She's not my Yoshana."

"Guess not anymore."

I thought that, perhaps more than anyone, Seven would understand my next question. "Did I do the right thing? When I left her?"

"You sure I'm the right guy to ask? I've been living in the woods for three hundred years with nowhere to go 'cause I bailed out on my buddies."

"I've got somewhere to go," I said defensively.

"Yeah, you picked your side."

I had, of course. I just wasn't completely sure I'd picked the right one. Or for the right reasons.

"I don't think Yoshana's wrong about everything," I said. "We do need humanity to pull together, and we don't have that now. She's right that our leaders aren't good for anything but squabbling with each other."

"Those who consider the history of similar divisions and confederacies will understand that they would neither love nor trust one another, but on the contrary would be prey to discord, jealousy, and mutual injuries. In short, they would be formidable only to each other," Seven recited.

"Who said that?"

"The guys who founded the country that used to be here. Explaining why it had to be under one government, and not a bunch of different ones. They weren't wrong. This place had a good run, while it lasted."

"So you agree with her."

The Hellguard shrugged.

Could I change my mind? Could I go back to Yoshana and help in her mission? Would she let me? Would Seven? For all that the Hellguard had abandoned his own companions, I wasn't sure he would let me join in an attack on them.

I wouldn't help the Darkness Radiant kill Prophetess. But Yoshana might not be wrong that Prophetess stood in the way of unification. If I rejoined the Overlord - and she didn't kill me - I might be able to protect Prophetess, while getting her out of the way.

But even if Yoshana was right, she was also ruthless, even brutal. Though we might need only one government, I wasn't sure I wanted Yoshana to be the one to govern.

I gave Seven an anguished look.

"Only the dead have seen the end of war," he said. From his tone, I was sure he was quoting again.

"So what does that mean?"

"It means there's always conflict. It means there's no easy answer whether what you're doing is right or wrong." The Hellguard shook his head. "It means I don't know."

"Just get the feeling of the blade. Understand its shape," Seven said, exasperated. We had set philosophy aside, and he was trying again to refine my use of the Darkness. My clumsiness was becoming a recurring theme with him.

"It's a curved sword. I understand its shape."

"No! You need to get the exact imprint of it in your mind. When you know every bit of the sword, all you have to do is use the prant to take that out of the wood."

I was holding a gently curved tree limb some three feet long. The Hellguard was convinced I could make it into both a sheath and a hilt for the katana. Two shattered branches at my feet suggested he was wrong.

"I've been doing that."

"No. You've got to be patient. The prant's all about applying just as much force as you need, no more. Little by little. Don't just fling a pile of it like some kind of grenade."

I chuckled. "Yoshana would quote Clausewitz at you. About how you have to apply all the force you can."

"No! You have to apply all the force you *need*."

It was strange to hear someone that looked like the Hellguard counseling delicacy. But he had carved that statue, and had sneaked up on me undetected.

"Don't rush it," he was saying. "Let it flow, let it do its work."

I tried. I eased a little current of the Darkness into the branch. It seemed to nibble a bit at the wood, producing a tiny clump of sawdust. "I've got the image in my mind," I snapped. "If I try to put that image into the branch, it just rips apart. If I go slow, I get an eighth of an inch of carving I could have done faster with a knife."

Seven shook his head in disgust. "You're not patient. You can't keep anything in your head."

He thought for a moment, while I regarded the tree branch with open hatred. "Did you happen to run into that big nest of the prant up in a tree, a few miles southeast?"

"Yeah. It almost ate me."

The Hellguard nodded emphatically. "Why?"

"Because I didn't even feel it until it was almost too late."

"Exactly. That nest is patient. It's subtle. It doesn't go flinging around big globs of itself. Just enough to sense its prey. It waits. That thing's been there a hundred years, getting bigger and bigger, bit by bit. Who knows what it'll be in another hundred years."

"That's not really the same thing…"

"It's exactly the same thing. That's the problem with you, the problem with Ypsilon, the problem with Yoshana. No patience."

"Kind of hard to be patient when the world's going to hell."

"Maybe that's exactly when you need to be patient. The problem with revolution is then you get revolutionaries in charge. Historically that hasn't worked out so well."

His words mirrored my own fears of Yoshana so closely I wondered again if he was in my head. "So the answer is to hide out in the woods instead?"

I hadn't intended the words to be as nasty as they'd come out, but Seven just shook his head and said mildly, "God will get things sorted in his time, not yours."

I was surprised. "I hadn't expected..." I trailed off.

"Hadn't expected a demon to talk about God?"

I pointed to the mocking inscription on the statue.

"Well, yeah. I hope he's got a sense of humor. But what do you think I believe in, a pig's head on a stick?"

"I guess I thought you believed in yourself." In the end, that seemed to be what Yoshana believed in.

"There's been entirely too much of that going around for the last few hundred years. Come on, let's get back to your saya. You ain't gonna get out of work by changing the subject."

Seven gave me a thick blanket and let me sleep by the remains of the fire. He didn't invite me to see the inside of his hut, and I wasn't sorry. He had been perfectly hospitable, but the fact remained that he was what he was. I didn't expect to find his dwelling decorated with human skulls and flayed skins, but I also really didn't want to find out for sure.

"Not much left around here stupid enough to mess with me," he said, "and I'm pretty sure nothing followed you here. Still..."

He spent nearly an hour teaching me a new ward, a network of fine tendrils; broader yet more subtle than Yoshana's basic circle, easier to maintain than the cage.

"She did teach you to meditate before you sleep?" he asked.

"Yeah, I learned that the hard way."

"Didn't kill anyone, did you?"

I shook my head violently.

"Good. Wasn't really the hard way, then." And he left me to think about that as I tried to rest.

The next morning we breakfasted on berries and warmed over pork. With the Hellguard's continuous prodding, I was able to finish the sheath and hilt for the katana.

"Kinda disgraceful the way you've got the blade," he said, glaring at the rust.

"This wasn't mine, you know. I've been trying to clean it up."

His expression couldn't have been more contemptuous if I'd told him I was licking it clean with my tongue. "With a rock?" he asked sarcastically. "Didn't occur to you that you've got better tools?"

"I've been using the Darkness for two weeks, not three hundred years. It doesn't come quite as naturally to me."

The huge man shrugged. "Fair enough. But now you know. Use it."

Stripping rust was far easier than carving a saya. Within fifteen minutes, the blade was gleaming.

"Good. You're learning." The Hellguard shot me a look that seemed almost shy, then said gruffly, "There's still a lot more I could teach you. You could stay. If you want."

Apprenticed to a demon.

Why not? I'd been infected with the Darkness by an Overlord. The progression seemed only logical. I hadn't fit in at Our Lady. I'd felt more at home among Yoshana's bloody-handed gang. Maybe the best place for me was here in these haunted woods, with an outcast Hellguard.

The just man is a light in darkness to the upright, Grigg had said. But what was I now? Was I a just man? What was I meant to do?

I missed Grigg. Whatever his involvement in Yoshana's schemes - and I couldn't deny he was involved - he had always seemed a steady, dependable figure, like an older brother I'd never had. Missing Roshel was like a physical ache. From the way Grigg and Yoshana had talked, the younger Overlord might not have known their plans for me. Grigg had said Roshel truly cared for me.

I even missed the horror herself. There was something strangely pure in her ruthlessness.

"I don't have your patience," I told Seven. "I can't sit here and wait it out. I'm not a three hundred year old immortal."

"You could be. With your blood and the prant, I could teach you to live forever."

"Not to sit here while my friends fight and die."

The Hellguard gave me a sad smile. "So you decided which direction you're going?"

Darkness flowed from Seven's fingers, playing over my face, penetrating my skull. A path formed in my mind.

"It's been a while, but it's not like the place should have moved," he said. "Keep your probes thin like I showed you. You don't see as much, but it's harder for anyone or anything else to see you."

I nodded.

"If you stay longer, I could teach you to deflect. No one would see you coming."

"And how long would that take? Somehow I don't think that's quick."

"No. That's not quick."

"I don't have that much time. If I wait, it'll all be over before I'm done here."

The Hellguard nodded. "I get it. Sometimes I regret sitting it all out. Too late for me now. If you change your mind... if you get sick of it..." he chuckled ruefully. "It's a good bet I'll still be here."

"Thanks."

Awkwardly, I held out my hand. The demon's huge, reddish paw engulfed it, and we shook. I turned and walked away, and didn't look back.

11. Going Home Again

After a week of walking, you wouldn't have thought the stone steps at the end would tire me so much. But I was gasping for breath by the time I reached the second gate at the top.

"Oh, it's you," Furat said. "Glad you made it back."

"Don't want to talk about it," I wheezed. The last week had been hellish. Even with the techniques Seven had taught me, I had almost been killed twice. Not counting the time I'd been running away and tumbled a hundred feet down an embankment. If not for my unnatural healing, infection from all the dirt-filled scrapes and cuts I'd picked up might have finished me off. I shuddered, recalling things I'd rather forget. For the record, pigs could be infected with the Darkness.

Seeing that Furat recognized me, his torch-bearing companions backed off. He still held out his knife, though.

"Rules are rules," he said. Even if those rules didn't apply to grumpy Overlords.

"Don't bother," I replied. I summoned up a ball of the Darkness in my palm.

"Oh. So it's like that, huh? I guess I shouldn't be surprised. So where are the others?" He sheathed the blade. Apparently the rules didn't apply to Select either, if they controlled the Darkness and were known to travel with grumpy Overlords.

"Hopefully a long way behind me still." I'd scanned Furat's stronghold very thoroughly before going up, to make sure they hadn't gotten in front of me. "We didn't part on the best of terms."

The big man's eyes widened. He had been turning the key in the iron gate's heavy lock. He stopped.

"I won't stay long. If they do catch up with me, that's not a fight I can win. But I could really use some hot food and a place to lie down for a little while. And if you happen to still have that stupid horse of mine, I've got some things you might like in trade."

I didn't really want to give up either the ancient knife or the newly refurbished katana, but I'd need the horse if I wanted to be sure of reaching Our Lady before Yoshana caught up with me. Furat eyed me dubiously, then finished unlocking the gate.

"I guess you'd better come in and tell me about it." He wrinkled his nose and looked me over again. "Although come to think of it, there's a bathtub in the second building on the right. I'll send some water down. The story can wait."

I was clean, wearing fresh, loose-fitting clothes that might have been my host's. There was a bowl of stew in front of me, which I'd been eating as I talked. The story lasted longer than the stew.

"Wow," Furat said when I'd finished. "You have really stepped in it. You did the exact opposite of listening when I told you people got hurt playing this game."

"What should I have done?" I snapped.

He shrugged. "I don't know. Staying in the Sorrows with the demon might have been a good option."

I'd had that same thought quite a few times over the past week. Seven was deadly enough to protect himself - and me - but had not seemed to be a homicidal maniac, unlike a certain Overlord I could mention. Yoshana would most likely never have found me there, and if somehow she had, even she would have thought twice about taking me on in the Hellguard's home. Instead I had fought my way through the Darkness and its creatures so I could rejoin the weaker side in what might turn into the greatest war since the Fall.

"They're going to kill Prophetess. With me or without me, if they take down Yashuath, Prophetess is next. I couldn't hide out in the woods and let that happen."

"And you think you can stop Yoshana?"

I conjured the Darkness in my palm again. Serpentine, it twined around my fingers. "I think I'm the only chance Prophetess has."

Furat stared at my hand, then murmured, "I don't think you answered the question."

I withdrew the Darkness. "I didn't say it was a good chance."

He sighed and stood up. He really was massive - that he looked like an ordinary man to me now was only by contrast to the Hellguard. "I make my living off people that come through here with more guts than brains. I don't know why I should care whether you get your dumb self killed or not."

"Everybody loves me. It's my winning personality. Does that mean you'll sell me my horse back?"

"Oh, just take the miserable animal. It eats too much and I can't do anything with it here."

"Thanks, Furat. I really appreciate it. Is there anything I can do for you?"

"Yeah. Get out of here in the morning."

The outpost was wonderfully defensible against most enemies, but against Yoshana it was just a deathtrap with no back door. When I said, "No problem," I meant it.

The dun gelding didn't seem especially pleased to see me.

"I didn't miss you either," I muttered. I certainly wasn't looking forward to leading the balky animal down the stairs. I had the tools now to calm his mind with the Darkness as Roshel had done, but I wasn't sure I could do it without harming the beast.

"Good luck," Furat said. He hadn't exactly been hurrying me, but I had no doubt he'd be glad to see me go.

"Thanks again," I replied. "Yoshana may come here, if she manages to kill Yashuath. Tell her I went west."

"Got it. You're going south?"

"No, I'm going west. She'll get it out of you one way or the other. It'll go easier if you just tell her the truth."

"If she catches you…"

"That would be bad."

Maybe the Darkness transmitted some of my urgency to my mount. We reached ground level uneventfully, and trotted through the tunnel that took us from the dark forests of the Sorrows back into the wide, green fields of the Source. The flowers of spring dotted the landscape. I breathed deep, inhaling their scent and the clean smell of the grass. Out of the Darklands, out of the Sorrows, in the bright, warm sunlight, I could almost forget that hell might be riding behind me. Almost.

I made good time. I slept in the open most nights, stretching the thin webs of Darkness that Seven had showed me. Sometimes I killed a rabbit or squirrel, and ate the meat raw. I didn't like it, but I didn't dare take the time to cook them, or send up the resulting column of smoke. I had no idea how far behind me Yoshana might be, but I wasn't going to take chances. I didn't even boil water, trusting instead that the Darkness could scour away any contaminants. It must have worked, because I didn't get sick.

On the third day I rode into a walled town. My horse was tiring from the pace, and I felt something in his stride that hinted at the beginning of lameness. I traded him for another mount, sweetening the deal with silver earned from selling the carbine. The hostler still tried to cheat me. I could sense the abscess in the first animal he offered, and the deception in his mind.

I thickened my probes, allowing them to become visible. "Yoshana wouldn't be pleased," I said mildly.

The man blanched whiter than my hair and babbled apologies. The second horse he produced was finer than the one I was giving up. He waved away the payment I had offered.

"If I'd known you were on the general's business…" he stammered.

"No harm done," I said, and rode on. I had to smile. If she ever found out, would Yoshana be angry I had taken her name in vain, or amused at its power - even when it was being used against her interests?

"I am going to miss those guys," I commented to the horse, a massive black gelding. Of course, if they caught me, they wouldn't miss me - I was pretty sure Yoshana's first shot would hit me right between the eyes. Or not - she might cripple me so she could tear me apart at her leisure.

"Let's see how fast you can go," I suggested to my new steed.

I passed within half a mile of Icefall. A heavy garrison of Darkness Radiant troops inhabited the place, their odd double crescent banner flying from its towers. Soldiers drilled in the courtyard. I went no closer, and they didn't challenge me.

I was less than a week from Our Lady, if I kept my current pace. Logic suggested that no pursuit was breathing down my neck. I was making good time, and even if Yoshana, Grigg, and Roshel knew exactly where I was going, they wouldn't find it easy to overtake me. Still, it was all I could do not to urge my mount to a gallop - which would just wear out the horse and slow me down in the end.

One night I forgot to meditate. I watched myself as if from above as my blade sank into a paleo's filthy throat, into another's chest. I stamped on the knee of a third as he lay prone, and ground my heel until the bones were pulped. Darkness poured out of me, and I charged into a mass of humanoid shapes, sword tearing, Darkness rending. My enemies fell before me, wounded, dying. Until only a dark cloud remained before me.

Red, flaming eyes blinked open in the seething mass. A white-fanged mouth leered. "Good," hissed Yoshana. "But it's all mine. *You're* mine."

The Darkness abandoned me, flooding back to its mistress. And then it reached for me.

Shivering, sweat-soaked, I saddled my horse by the moonlight and climbed onto his back. "Come on, you lazy beast. Let's get moving."

I never fully recovered from that dream. I didn't dare sleep long enough, and mental stillness eluded me. I cleared my mind well enough at night to avoid a recurrence of the nightmare, but I still woke before dawn every day, uneasy at the best of times, seized with a vague terror at the worst.

"Patience," Seven had said. Easy enough for an immortal demon safe in his haunted clearing. Harder when three of my former friends, each stronger than I, might be hours behind me, coming for my head.

Or they might be dead in the Darklands, their mission failed because I'd abandoned them. That thought troubled me almost as much as the idea of them catching me.

Fear and guilt made wonderful distractions. I had lost all track of time when the edges of the town around Our Lady rose in front of me.

Unlike the citadel itself, and most of what was left of human civilization, the town wasn't walled. My horse plodded along unchallenged down its cobbled streets. We drew a few stares, but no one commented aloud at the sight of an exhausted Select on a weary, black horse.

Our Lady's massive wood and iron gate stood open. With winter past, pilgrims and trade flowed freely. A guard I vaguely recognized was controlling the traffic.

"My God! Minos?" he exclaimed.

I slid out of the saddle, landing unsteadily on my feet. "Can someone feed and stable him?" I asked, patting the horse's nose. "He's come a long way."

"Tolf!" the guard was shouting. "Somebody get Tolf!"

I stepped into the walled enclosure and leaned against a fence rail. The lakes that provided a source of water inside the walls shimmered in the sunlight. Some kind of crop was just beginning to sprout in the big northwest field. Past the lakes, the golden dome of the rectory gleamed like a beacon.

I began to drift off.

The sky darkened, black clouds roiling and swirling, drawn to the light of Our Lady's dome like moths to a flame. The darkness swept down from the sky and through the gates, unopposed, and where it passed, every living thing died.

"Minos! I thought for sure you were dead!"

My eyes snapped open. Tolf clapped me on the shoulders, then grabbed me in a fierce embrace.

"Oh ye of little faith," I muttered, shivering despite the warmth of the day.

"Tell me all about it! Come on, let's go find Prophetess." He tugged me down the path toward the heart of the Universal Church's citadel.

I looked around as we went. "Where are the troops?" I asked. Nothing seemed changed. The cream-colored brick of the buildings gleamed where the vines hadn't taken over. The first shoots of crops poked up in the fields. It was the image of peace, of a world free from the shadow of war. I had been expecting to see legions of the Order of Thorns marching around the walls. My brief vision, that half-waking nightmare, tainted the bright sunlight with danger.

"What do you mean? There are guards in the barracks, same as ever."

"But the Order? It's been months."

"Well, sure, Minos, but nothing's happened. It's not like we're under attack."

"Nothing's happened because Yoshana's been with me, you idiot. And now if she's still alive, she's going to be coming here. Killing Yashuath was first on her list. Prophetess is next."

Tolf went white. "I'll call up the Ministry of Defense."

The Ministry seemed to be no more than a fancy name for the usual suspects. Dee was there, of course. So was the captain of the guard, a man named Marek. Father Juniper was there. And so was Father Roric.

Tolf caught my expression. He whispered, "If we're going to be launching a crusade, we need to be on solid ground. Theologically speaking. The Metropolitan insisted."

The Advocate for Justice peered at me like I was an oddly-shaped beetle. Like Tolf, he seemed surprised to see me alive. Unlike Tolf, he didn't look especially pleased.

Dee was effusive, though. "The stories you must have for us! I can't wait to hear it all. I have so -"

Prophetess walked in behind me. "Sorry I'm late. I was just -"

The way her face lit up made the pain of the past few weeks worthwhile. She charged and flung her arms around me. Tolf chuckled.

Father Roric cleared his throat, injecting more disapproval into that small sound than most people could manage with a flung brick. "If this is just a reunion, I don't believe we need the entire Ministry present."

"I imagine Minos is going to brief us on what he's learned about the leadership of the Darkness Radiant," Father Juniper said mildly.

"Then perhaps he could proceed to do so?"

I patted Prophetess awkwardly on the back. She hadn't let go. She stepped away and blinked at me with a teary smile.

Everyone's eyes were on me. And somehow during the long ride from the Sorrows, I had failed to prepare for this moment. I should have had a narrative, a rousing speech, a stirring appeal. A plea for understanding. Instead, exhausted and anxious, I let the words pour out.

"Yoshana is in the Darklands. Or she was when I left her. She took her top lieutenants to assassinate the second in command of the Hellguard."

Marek nodded. "She's looking for revenge on them, for when they betrayed her in the Green Heart."

"No. She's looking for time. She wants to unify humanity under her banner. She believes... or at least she says, and I think she believes it... she believes she's the only one who can bring mankind together to stop the demons and the Darkness."

Roric gave a disgusted snort. "She's a creature of the demons and the Darkness."

I met his eyes. "Yes. I've spent two months closer to her than I am to you. I know what she is. And I know what she can do."

Dee's enthusiasm bubbled over. "You were actually with Yoshana herself this whole time?"

"Yes, Dee, and I'm guessing you'll see her soon enough. She wants Prophetess dead. I heard that from her own lips. And this -" I waved my hand. "This Ministry isn't going to stop her."

"Hold on -" Tolf began.

"She can change her appearance, Tolf. I've seen it. She could walk right through that front gate and no one would even know it. Or she can make herself practically invisible. And if she were in this room right now, you'd all be dead before you could lift a finger. I've *seen her*. You don't know what we're fighting."

"So what are you saying, Minos?" Tolf growled. "We give up? Because I'll tell you I'm not going to do that."

"No, we fight. But one thing Yoshana's right about. It takes the Darkness to fight the Darkness."

"What are you saying?"

"This." A sphere formed in my hand, pulsing, twining through my fingers.

The response could have been no more extreme if I'd grown into a demon on the spot, complete with horns and tail. Tolf, Marek, Juniper, and Roric all scrambled away, stopping only when they hit the wall. Even Dee took three long steps back, though he then craned forward to peer at the Darkness in my palm.

Only Prophetess stayed where she was. "Minos," she whispered.

"It's the only way," I said.

Marek had a knife at his belt. It was suddenly in his hand. The sphere of Darkness swelled.

"No," I said. He froze.

"You brought that here?" Roric demanded. "What are you now?"

"I'm the one who's going to keep Prophetess alive."

Now she backed away. "Not like this."

"Dammit, Tess! You don't understand what I've seen. It's a tool, and we have to use it."

"No."

"Tess, listen to reason. You have to let me explain."

"Take no part in the fruitless works of darkness," Roric intoned. "Rather expose them... For it is shameful even to mention the things done by them in secret..."

But everything by the light becomes visible… For everything that becomes visible is light…"

I whirled on him. "Do you think you can exorcise *me*?"

The sphere was a cloud. It loomed huge, filling the room. I hadn't realized there was so much of it in me. I was far too strong to be stopped.

"Minos, get out!" Prophetess screamed.

"What?" I turned on her. The cloud seethed, boiling with my rage. After all I had been through. I had abandoned Yoshana and Grigg. I had abandoned Roshel. I had crossed the Sorrows alone to help this woman, risking my life, betraying my friends. And now she was rejecting me?

"Get out!"

The Darkness coiled to strike.

There'll be no containing his rage, Yoshana had said.

I'd come all this way just to do her will.

The Darkness slammed back into me so hard it hurt and I fled, nearly blinded by angry tears.

12. The Outsider

I was more than half asleep, head down on the table. My back was to the door, but tendrils of Darkness ranged around me. The tavern wasn't far from the citadel, and I hadn't gone to any trouble to hide my trail. I wasn't afraid of anyone in Our Lady. They couldn't get close enough to hurt me.

If Yoshana caught up with me… well, she could have a good laugh before she finished me off.

"Hello, Father," I said, not lifting my head. I sensed the priest stop in the doorway. I sensed his hesitation. The urge to back away and not return radiated from him like a stench.

He came in anyway.

I sat up and turned to face him. "You said I'd be all right."

Father Juniper sighed. The bearded face seemed older than it had just hours earlier. "I've been wrong before. I'll be wrong again. That's part of being human. What happened out there? With Yoshana?"

I shrugged. "The Darkness? We were in the Sorrows. She and her lieutenants control the Darkness. She had four soldiers. Ordinary men but veterans, tough as they come. By the time we got out of that forest, three of them were dead. She said I needed to master the Darkness if I wanted to live. I believed her."

He nodded. "That's it?"

"It made me strong. You have no idea what I can do."

He nodded again.

"I met a demon, you know. He didn't seem…" I laughed bitterly. "He didn't seem like a bad person."

"But you left Yoshana."

"Like I said. I overheard her say she needed Prophetess out of the way. That she would either convince her or kill her. That *I* would convince her or kill her."

"You nearly did."

"But I didn't!" I took a deep, steadying breath. Around me the tendrils were thickening, coiling. I pulled them in. They were dangerous… and I didn't like feeling the priest's fear. "I left Yoshana and came here instead. But you're all too stubborn to listen."

Father Juniper gestured to a chair. "May I?"

"Sure."

He sat. "You can't have imagined we could embrace the Darkness. You may not think of it as the incarnation of sin, but you know the Church does."

"I'm not asking anyone to use it but me. Your precious consciences would be clear."

"Really? When we allowed a man to be corrupted in our service? Set aside the moral issue for a moment. Think of the benefit that would bring to Yoshana's cause. How could we claim to be any better than her when we used the Darkness ourselves? By adopting her methods, we would become nothing more than a pale imitation of the Darkness Radiant."

"Then what was I supposed to do?"

The priest sighed. "Once you embraced the Darkness, every path led to Yoshana's victory. Consider. If you had somehow convinced Prophetess not to oppose the Darkness Radiant, Yoshana wins. If you had killed Prophetess, Yoshana wins. If you had convinced Prophetess to use the Darkness as a tool, Yoshana wins."

"So the best option is what we have now. Me leaving."

"Yoshana still wins. Prophetess is deprived of a friend and protector."

I glared. "Then there's no option at all."

"The serpent is ancient and cunning. Perhaps we were wrong to let you go. But free will is also part of God's plan." He hesitated, then said, "You asked me before if I would give you spiritual guidance. I'll do it now, even though you haven't asked for it. If the Darkness can be cast out of the possessed, it must be possible to cast it out of one who claims to control it."

"You think Prophetess can exorcise me?"

"If anyone can."

"And then? When Yoshana comes she cuts us apart? With all due respect, Father, she'll probably kill the rest of you quickly. Whatever she does to me, it won't be quick."

"If she gave you the choice of killing Prophetess with your own hand, or being cut down, which would you choose?"

I scowled. "I like to think I'd die first."

"Just so. Some things are worth dying for."

"And some things are worth fighting for. A man once said the almighty gave us our lives, and I suppose he meant us to defend them."

"So what will you do?" he asked.

"I'll think of something."

Father Juniper nodded and stood. He said, "Ever since man rejected the Light that was meant to show him the way, everything has become for us an obstacle and a danger; we live in the shadow of death."

He paused in the doorway. "I brought you a friend. I thought you might need one."

If you'd told me six months before that Doctor John Dee would be my last friend in the world, I'd have laughed in your face.

For a wonder, he just sat and listened, quiet as a tomb, while the story came out in every vicious detail, every treacherous thought. At the end, he said, "You'll write it all down, I hope?"

"I suppose."

"What will you do now?"

"Leave here. I'm not doing anyone any good. You'll have to protect Prophetess as best you can. Maybe Yoshana won't want to do the dirty work herself as long as she thinks I might still do it for her."

"Where will you go?"

I shrugged. "We'll see. I have to think. The only two paths can't be this self-righteous refusal to see reality at Our Lady or Yoshana's ruthless murder of everyone who stands in her way. There has to be a third path between them. I just need to find it."

The occultist nodded. "I'd... that is..."

And if you'd told me I'd be sad to leave that loudmouth behind, I'd probably have coughed up a lung. I could feel his fear even without the Darkness.

"It might not be safe to be with me, Dee. You stay here. Take care of Tess."

"I'll do that, Minos." He reached into his pack and pulled out a heavy, leather-bound book. "As you explore both without and within, you might find this useful. Howard Phillips Lovecraft was the greatest occultist of his day."

During the long hours of dusk, I would rest under trees and read as I cooked. The book was entertaining, if a bit of an acquired taste... like Dee himself. He had helpfully dog-eared one chapter titled "The Case of Charles Dexter Ward." In case I missed the point, he had underlined the phrase, "Do not call up any that you can not put down."

Dee meant the Darkness, no doubt. But I returned again and again to a passage from a different chapter:

Now I ride with the mocking and friendly ghouls on the night-wind, and play by day amongst the catacombs... yet in my new wildness and freedom I almost welcome the bitterness of alienage. I know always that I am an outsider; a stranger in this century and among those who are still men. This I have known ever since I stretched out my fingers to the abomination within that great gilded frame; stretched out my fingers and touched a cold and unyielding surface of polished glass.

Book Three - Called to Darkness

"But what is liberty without wisdom and without virtue?
It is the greatest of all possible evils;
For it is folly, vice, and madness, without tuition or restraint."
Edmund Burke

1. Curiosity

I was free.

Free of Prophetess, free of Yoshana. I was living off the land, and untraceable. Even the world's most dangerous Overlord couldn't quarter the earth to find me. And with the Darkness in me, I was deadlier than anything but the Darkness Radiant, the Hellguard, or the great wraiths of the Sorrows.

None of which were to be found in the middle of nowhere in the Source.

I had drifted aimlessly for weeks. The weather was good, and I slept on the ground, tendrils of Darkness warding me. I woke to find food waiting for me, animals I'd killed in my sleep as they drew too near.

I was slowly working my way west, away from Yoshana and Prophetess. I no longer had anything to do with the war between the Darkness Radiant and Our Lady. I had rejected one side, and the other had rejected me.

I spent weeks more in the great underground library buried beneath the dead city of eternal lights. It was built on multiple floors, descending into the earth. Perhaps it had been made that way to survive disaster. I had explored, the Darkness questing before me, but found nothing more dangerous than mice and several families of raccoons. The second level down opened into a square courtyard exposed to the sky, with a huge tree growing in its center. Concrete benches made a pleasant place to read once I cleared aside the brush that had overrun them.

Many of the books set out in rack upon rack of shelves had crumbled to dust, but those that survived showed the self-styled Doctor John Dee had been right. The Darkness had indeed been created in this place. Ironically, none remained. I had probed carefully, even venturing into the abandoned laboratory where the scourge had been born. There was no trace of it now.

I had always known something of the Darkness, of course. I had learned more from Yoshana, and more still from the Hellguard who called himself Seven. What I read in the library confirmed it. The Psycho-Reactive Autonomous Nano Technology had been created as a medical tool, designed to fight cancers and perform surgery at a microscopic level. Its value had quickly been seen by the military, who put it to other uses. But as new versions became more independent to be effective at greater range, they became harder to control. The military bred a race of soldiers able to master it. The library's records ceased not long after the Hellguard rebelled, leaving the demons and the Darkness as a curse on the world that had created them.

I read extensively. Yoshana and Grigg had bickered endlessly about military strategy, and I found a volume of Clausewitz. His prose was nearly impenetrable, and I gave up. Another author, Mao Zedong, yielded deep insights on the effective use of an inferior force. That would have been invaluable to Our Lady in the coming war. It was a shame I couldn't take it to them.

I didn't just study war. The library had volumes of geography, science, philosophy. I couldn't have absorbed it all in a hundred lifetimes. One day as I sat on my bench, I read, "He who fights with monsters should look to it that he himself does not become a monster. And when you gaze long into an abyss, the abyss also gazes into you."

I shivered a bit in the bright afternoon light, and it seemed as if a shadow passed over the sun. I let the Darkness come out and play on my skin. I had no interest in fighting monsters anymore. And I had already become one.

Most days I could honestly say I wished Prophetess and her forces well. Not that my wishes mattered. Without me, they stood no chance. I wasn't a match for Yoshana, or even her lieutenants, Grigg and Roshel. But with no command at all of the Darkness, Our Lady's cause was lost from the outset.

Eventually I moved on. I avoided the trading town of Opportunity. I had toyed with the idea of trying to buy back my old katana, exchanging it for either the one I had taken from a native in the Sorrows or the strange, glassy knife I had found in the same place. But they would test me for the Darkness, and while perhaps I could prevent my body from betraying my nature, it was more trouble than it was worth. The blade that had been my inheritance was probably gone, traded away in the months past. With war on the horizon, it would have been a great prize to someone.

I briefly considered terrorizing the inhospitable fortress of Coalville out of sheer spite. They had slammed the door in my face almost a year before, claiming my companions and I might belong to the Darkness Radiant. Now that Yoshana had trained me and made me over into one of her tools, all their spears and fire could never hope to keep me out. But although the Darkness boiled in me when I remembered the humiliation, I wouldn't kill or maim just to avenge a slight.

Yoshana would. It was important to remind myself that I wasn't her. Sometimes, when the Darkness coiled in me, it could be hard to remember.

I lay on a sandbank on the shore of the Big Muddy, basking in the warmth of early summer. Above me, a strange bridge of two parallel metal pipes stretched over the water. I had studied geography as well as science and war during my time in the library. I knew now that structure had been a natural gas pipeline, providing the ancients with fuel. When I had first encountered it, I had feared it carried the Darkness. If at any point in its history it ever had, it didn't now.

The bridge marked a decision point for me. I could continue on my path southwest, cross the disputed territory on the other side of the Muddy, and return to Rockwall. I could follow the river south, and then turn east again into the Green Heart, where my parents had lived and perhaps still did. Or I could go upriver to the northeast, taking the route Prophetess and I had originally intended to reach Stephensburg. The northeast fork would eventually take me back to the Sorrows.

Seven lived deep in the Sorrows. In many ways, that was the logical place to go. The Hellguard had been kind to me, and had taught me a tremendous amount in the single day I'd spent with him. If anyone would understand me, it was that lonely warrior in his self-imposed exile. He had invited me to rejoin him, if I grew as sick of the world as he had.

My parents had said the opposite. For my own safety, and to keep the Select race alive, they'd told me to leave the Green Heart and never return. But Yoshana and the Hellguard were gone from my old home. And I was now strong enough to face anything else. I didn't even know if my parents were alive or dead. I could at least learn the truth of that - although I dreaded to know it.

There was nothing for me in Rockwall except the garbage mine on the Flow, in the shadow of the dead city of Acceptance. Yet somehow, I had felt at home there. It made no sense, but something in me felt that I needed to return, to erase the failure of my journey with Prophetess. To start over, even though I was changed irrevocably.

And besides, I had two wristwatches in my pack I had taken for Luco and Fenn, friends I had left on the Flow. It seemed silly to have hauled them out of the Sorrows for nothing.

It was sillier to make my way back to the garbage mine for no better reason than that. But there was no one now to tell me I was wrong. And so I climbed the rusting iron ladder to the pipeline bridge and made my way southwest.

Summer had been ending when last I had passed through this land. The battles between Rockwall's peasant levies and the Monolith's proxies would have ground to a halt during the winter. Neither side cared enough about that war to risk their troops freezing to death when the snow came. Of course, towns or farmsteads looted and burned by the combatants wouldn't be so lucky.

It was possible that peace had broken out - the warring states might have reached a settlement, or simply gotten tired of wasting their resources. The state of hostilities would determine how safe the roads were. The Hawk's Nest was close, and their mercenaries were notorious for robbing anyone they encountered. They called it "living off the land" or "field requisitions." It sounded more respectable that way.

I wasn't terribly concerned. I could avoid the Hawks easily enough in the woods. If it came to a fight, they would be a threat to me only in large numbers, or at a range where their rifles could hit me but the Darkness couldn't kill them. I wasn't likely to be facing them on those terms. Still, I'd rather not take the risk, or stain my conscience with more deaths - even the deaths of bloody-handed pirates who gave mercenaries a bad name.

I set out cross country from the bridge. I would come to a road eventually, and follow it cautiously until I learned more one way or the other. But that first night west of the Muddy, I slept in the woods.

Farther southwest of here, Prophetess, Dee, and I had encountered a drelb. Dee had told us the monsters were bears, twisted by the Darkness. Whatever Dee's faults - consisting mostly of abject cowardice and the non-stop running of his mouth - he had proved well-informed about the Darkness. I had no reason to doubt him where the drelb were concerned. The one Prophetess and I had fought before had nearly killed us. But that was before I commanded the Darkness myself. While I didn't relish the idea of encountering another, the sad, violent creatures no longer terrified me. I was far more dangerous than they.

Still, I started awake that night when the tendrils of my extended senses touched something large. It was no drelb, but rather a wolf, snuffling its way toward me and now about fifty feet away. It hadn't reached the range where the Darkness would have simply killed it without waking me.

The Darkness was sentient, after a fashion. It followed my will, but had a certain initiative of its own. It had seen fit to alert me when it first brushed up against the predator's consciousness. That flexibility made the Darkness a better tool - and also riskier to its master. By its nature, the construct took its cues from the depths of my mind - which could be dark places. "Monsters from the id," as Grigg had said.

Now I used it to touch the wolf's thoughts. The big canine was curious, hungry, cautious - in almost equal parts.

What would it be like to have a pet wolf? I had little doubt I could turn the animal's mind and bring it under my control.

I shook my head in disgust. The wolf would be little better than a drelb, a monster bent out of its natural shape. There was an elemental beauty to the creature now, a beauty I would only destroy. I prodded it with the lightest mental touch.

"*Fear*," I sent.

Instantly it turned tail and fled into the woods. I hoped that in whatever way wolves communicated, this one would tell its brothers to leave the strange, gray-skinned biped alone. I didn't want to have to kill any of them.

Two days later I found a road, and not long after that a tiny, fortified village by its side.

Most towns made do with a wooden palisade. This one was surrounded by a massive wall of cinderblocks, complete with crenellations and arrow slits. I would have avoided it entirely except for the brightly painted sign on its heavy gate that read, "Paying Travelers Welcome."

I still thought twice about it. It was hard to forget the "hospitality" of Brom of Icefall, the bandit lord in the northeastern Source who had robbed travelers unfortunate enough to visit his keep. Or he had until Yoshana slaughtered his men in front of him and tore out his throat.

I had a meaningful fraction of Yoshana's power now. I could probe the intentions of those inside, infiltrate their bodies with the Darkness. If they moved against me, I could destroy them from the inside out.

But I didn't want to. Grigg, Yoshana's Select lieutenant, had told me that to give in completely to the power of the Darkness was to let it consume you. Whatever lies Grigg and Yoshana and Roshel had told me, that I believed.

"You gonna come in, or you just gonna stand there?"

A face peered out at me between the crenellations. I couldn't see it well enough to judge the features, but the nasal, querulous voice sounded female.

For some reason I found a woman less threatening - even though Yoshana was both a woman and the most terrifying being I had ever met, making no exception for the Hellguard.

"I don't have much or need much," I called up. "But I'll swap you stories for stories."

"Fair," said the voice as the face disappeared. The last words floated up faintly over the wall. "We'll kick you out when you get boring."

A massive bar was set aside with a thud and the gate creaked open. I stepped into a dirt courtyard, with room for dozens of wagons and teams. It was empty. At one side of the gate stood a short, stout woman in early middle age. A gangly youth who might have been her son manhandled the other leaf of the door back into place behind me. Both wore knives long enough to serve as short swords, but neither looked like they knew how to use them.

This pair would pose no threat to me even if I were armed with no more than my hickory walking stick... and I had a finely made katana and a broad knife of ancient, unnaturally sharp steel. Not to mention the Darkness.

Still, I cast a calculating eye around the courtyard. Outbuildings stood around the walls, and a squat keep of the same cinderblocks as the wall faced me fifty feet away. Arrows or enemies could come from any of them. The absence of anyone else - anyone visible - made me nervous. I began to extend probes.

"No travelers worth speaking of in I don't know how long," the woman said. "Damn Hawks rampaging all over the countryside seen to that."

And that answered my main question. The roads were still not safe.

"Surprised you haven't run into them," she continued, looking me up and down.

"Who says I haven't?" I gave her a slow smile.

"Not known for their tolerance, the Hawks."

Not many people cared for the Select. Masses of armed men had a way of letting their prejudices show.

Some of Yoshana must have rubbed off on me. My grin widened. "There are three possibilities. First, the Hawks are mercenaries. The Select are often mercenaries. Perhaps I'm in their service."

She took a small step back. I pressed on. "Second, the Hawks are mercenaries. The Select are better mercenaries. Perhaps I met some and they didn't survive the encounter."

The step back was longer now. "Or third, perhaps I'm new to the area and just haven't run into them yet."

And then I was ashamed of myself. The sort of games that amused the mistress of the Darkness Radiant were not kind. "It's the third, by the way. My name's Minos. I just crossed the Muddy three days ago."

"Well. I'm Delet, this is Scon. Pleased to meet you." She didn't sound entirely sincere, and it was hard to blame her. I had not been a model guest so far. But then, I hadn't interacted with humans since I'd left Our Lady months ago. And that interaction hadn't gone at all well.

A Select's black eyes, sclera and iris as dark as the pupil, were supposed to be unreadable. But Delet must have seen something in my face, because again she stepped away.

"I'm sorry," I said. "Let's start again. I'm Minos. I've crossed over from the Source because I want no part of the Darkness Radiant. I've seen it much too close."

And that was certainly true.

"Well, come on in and have some lunch." She turned and led me into the keep, the boy trailing behind. "Scon, why don't you go bring us all some stew and cider?"

There was a vast room inside, wooden tables and benches that could seat a small army. It was as empty as the courtyard. Light filtered in through arrow slits high in the walls, reached by stone stairs leading up to a narrow firing platform that ringed half the building. Scon continued deeper inside, vanishing through a wooden door at the far end.

"Sit wherever you like," Delet said. "Plenty of room."

"There's no one at all on the road?" I eased myself onto a bench. It was hard, but more comfortable than the ground.

"Nah. There's been others like you. A few families traveling together came through about a week, ten days ago. Doing the same thing you're doing. Didn't want to live in the Source with Yoshana in charge."

The Overlord had taken Stephensburg in early winter, six months past. "Took them a while to make up their minds," I said.

"Guess they thought maybe she'd get herself killed out east. But when she came back and started recruiting more soldiers…"

"She's back?"

"That's what I said, isn't it? What they said, anyway. Thought you'd seen 'em up close."

I'd seen Yoshana far too close. I'd traveled with her for months. She'd taught me to use the Darkness. She was making me her tool against Prophetess and Our Lady when I'd abandoned her in the Darklands.

I'd assumed she'd survived, but I hadn't been sure. Hearing she was back in Stephensburg was like a punch in the gut.

"Did they say if she'd succeeded? If she did what she set out to do?"

"Nope. Don't even know what that was." She cocked her head and stared at me.

I'd said I would trade stories for stories. "She was going to kill a demon. If she's back, I suppose she did." I had been meant to help her do that, too.

Delet shook her head. "Demons and Overlords can kill each other 'til the world ends for all I care. Don't like it so much when they come this way, though."

Yoshana would make war on the darkness of the Hellguard and the uncompromising light of Our Lady. Her legions, the Darkness Radiant, stood between the two, opposed to both. It seemed like an awful position, but I for one wouldn't bet against her.

"Where'd those refugees go?" I asked. In case they had any ideas worth copying. There wasn't much I feared anymore, but Yoshana was at the top of the list.

"West. Making for the Monolith, they said. Figured no one's army was going to get up into those mountains if the Josephites didn't want 'em to."

There was something to that idea. But the land between here and the borders of the Monolith was unsettled at the best of times. "Think they'll make it?"

"No," she said flatly. "I told 'em it was mad. Hawks on the road, paleos in the woods. Both of 'em crazy and mean. Hawks'll rob you. Paleos'll eat you."

"They went anyway?"

She shrugged. "Not much choice. Couldn't stay here forever. We haven't the food for it. With no trade we've got only what we can grow."

Scon returned at that moment carrying a tray with bowls of stew and mugs of cider.

"If you're running short of food…" I began.

Delet waved my objection away. "One bowl isn't the difference between living and dying. Not yet, anyway."

I wasn't proud of it, but I probed the edges of her thoughts. I'd run across more places than Icefall that would rob travelers. Poison would be a good way of doing it.

Roshel could read a man's mind if she touched him. I suspected Yoshana could do it from farther away, though she hadn't detected my betrayal. I wasn't as strong or as skilled as those two. All I could pick up were faint surface impressions.

I perceived no malice. And I suspected that the Darkness could neutralize most poisons in any case. I spooned up chunks of potato and some kind of tough, stringy meat, feeling a bit guilty about my suspicions. But it was the way of our fallen world.

"So where are you headed?" Delet asked.

I considered. There was a part of me that wondered if I shouldn't try to catch the refugee caravan. I could protect them, and they'd need protecting. And it was true that the Monolith was strong, and far from Yoshana's legions. The Josephites had a reputation as religious fanatics who despised my race, but Grigg had served them. They were pragmatic enough to accept the Select when we were useful to them. And I could make myself very useful.

It seemed like the right thing to do.

So had returning to Our Lady to put the Darkness into their service against Yoshana. Things that seemed like a good idea at the time hadn't worked out well for me.

In a world where I suspected the worst of everyone and they returned the favor, a life of mining garbage with the rough crew on the Flow held an aching appeal.

"Southwest," I said. "Toward Rockwall."

"Lots of bad things between here and there," Delet said.

"I'm pretty sure none of them are worse than me."

Without telling all of it, I described some of the horrors of the Sorrows. I'm not sure she believed it. She seemed openly skeptical that I'd truly entered the Darklands and seen the demons' slaves. I didn't even mention the strangest parts of the story... that I had been as close to Yoshana as her chief lieutenants... that I had perhaps believed myself in love with one of them... that I had been trained by one of the Hellguard.

In fact, I didn't mention Seven at all. The immortal soldier was doing no harm to anyone. Better that he be allowed to stay undisturbed in the depths of the forest.

Delet believed enough of what I said - or found it sufficiently entertaining - to provide me a bed for the night. It was hard and lumpy, but like the bench, it was better than the ground. It was also full of fleas. The Darkness made short work of them. Of all the benefits I had gained from that grim power, being free of nasty little parasites crawling in my clothes and hair was one of the most trivial and yet most satisfying.

I set wards on general principles, not because I feared any treachery from my hosts. I had sensed more people than I had seen, but the vague impression I had of their thoughts tasted of indifference rather than malice. I made sure the tendrils wouldn't kill anything that blundered into them. And I was even more careful than usual to meditate before I fell asleep. The nightmares that the Darkness could bring were bad enough when I was alone - I didn't want a murder on my conscience if it lashed out while I slept.

The night passed uneventfully, but in the morning it was clear that the credit from my tales had run out. While Delet was cordial enough, breakfast consisted of a soft, wrinkled apple that might have been kept in a cellar since last fall. I didn't mind. Our conversation had fixed my mind on the decision to return to the Flow. It was time to be going.

I would stick to the forest. The Hawks on the road were a greater danger than the paleos in the woods - the Hawks would travel in greater numbers, and their weapons would have greater range. I wasn't really afraid of either group, but I wasn't sure exactly how many enemies I could strike down at once with the Darkness, or at what range. A platoon of mercenaries with bows or rifles might pose a real threat. A handful of savages with sharpened sticks worried me far less.

So I found myself again among the trees. The air was cool under their branches, and I enjoyed the sharp scent of the pines. With the Darkness ranged around me, the rustling of leaves and cracking of twigs resolved into rabbits, squirrels, foxes, pheasants, deer. There were no terrors hiding in the shadows. Once, days after leaving the walled village, I encountered a small cloud of the Darkness drifting aimlessly. It was just barely large enough to possess a child or perhaps an unusually weak-willed adult. I allowed it to sense what I was, and it fled.

What did it say about me that I felt a brief, bizarre pang of nostalgia for the Sorrows? Nothing good, I'm sure.

I was in a stretch of forest that I thought was west of the place where Prophetess and I had fought the drelb. There was a nice clearing, a circle of stones in its center long overtaken by moss, yet clearly the site of an ancient fire pit. I found some wild blackberries that were close to ripe, skinned and cooked a hare that the Darkness killed, and settled down to sleep.

I woke in the thin light of the moon. There was something coming toward me. It wasn't an animal.

The invader moved stealthily, slowly, not a twig snapping or a leaf crackling under its feet. If not for the Darkness I would never have known it was coming.

The tendrils of my senses thickened around my unwelcome guest, invisible in the night. Particles penetrated the pores of its body, unseen and unfelt. A knife in its hand left little doubt of its intentions.

I sat up. "Looking for something? Or just lost?"

The paleo jumped a foot in the air and let out a squawk. I let the Darkness pour from my body, circling the attacker in thick, rotating bands, visible even in the dim moonlight. "Don't go anywhere."

The paleos were filthy, murderous savages. They hated all civilized people, but despised the Select most of all. The feeling was mutual. I'd killed two of them and crippled another when they'd attacked Prophetess, Dee, and me on our way to Our Lady.

This one wore rags that had perhaps been looted from the corpse of a victim. The knife in its hand was nothing more than a length of bone sharpened to a point. It would have been perfectly effective for murdering me in my sleep, though.

The Darkness circled.

The paleo dropped to its knees. "Shadow warrior," it murmured.

The voice was high. The figure was slight. I realized my attacker was a woman.

I stood up and took a dozen steps closer. Under the dirt, she was young - younger than I was. She looked up at me with wide eyes. Her face was full of terror, but mixed with the same resignation I'd seen a year ago when I'd faced another of her race who'd expected me to kill him.

"Not polite, creeping up on people in the night," I said. I pointed to the bone knife. "What were you going to do with that?"

"Kill," she said softly. "Eat."

She certainly wasn't trying very hard to win me over. Not that I would have believed any other answer.

"Not know what you were," she added.

"Oh? Would that have made a difference?"

She barked out a laugh. "Not stupid, me." She paused and thought, as if considering her position. "Not so, so stupid. Can't kill what doesn't die."

What exactly did she think I was? A demon? Myths of the paleos' disastrous war with the Hellguard must have been passed down among her kind.

The paleos rejected all civilization. The more artificial it seemed to them, the more they hated it. The Select and the Hellguard were creations of genetic manipulation, abominations in their minds. Over the centuries, many Select had died at the hands of the paleos. They'd attacked the Hellguard as well, but that fight had been one-sided. Genetically engineered soldiers who controlled the Darkness had nothing to fear from savages with wooden spears.

Her statement wasn't so far wrong. Compared to Seven or Yoshana, I was a weakling, an amateur warrior at best. Compared to a paleo girl with a sharpened bone, I was Death itself.

I could have killed her with a thought when I first woke up. I nearly had. Now it seemed cruel, like crushing a beetle that crossed my path.

I pulled the Darkness back into myself. "Go."

The paleo stayed on her knees, staring. After a time she shook her head. "No."

"What? You want me to kill you?"

She shrugged. "You kill. Wolves kill. Drelb kills. Hunger kills. Dead is dead. Shadows kill quick. So kill." She shut her eyes, squared her shoulders, and jutted out her chin at me.

This was ridiculous. "I'm letting you go, you idiot."

"Go where? Alone. Nowhere to go. Good place to die, here."

"Go back to the rest of your flea-bitten people." I considered. If she had nowhere to go... "Did the Hawks kill them?"

She shook her head. "No. Cast out, me. Exile."

What kind of awful thing did you have to do to get exiled by the paleos? "What did you do?"

"Curious, me. Cat, me."

Was that her name? "It's good to be curious."

She laughed again, a single explosion of sound. "For trolls. Not for people."

The paleos called civilized humanity trolls because we tried to control everything. *Control, controlling, controlled, slaver and slave*, one had said to me. Right before I crushed his kneecap and left him lying crippled in the road.

"Go starve somewhere else, curious cat," I said. "I'm not killing you here."

"No," she repeated. She stayed put.

"Suit yourself. I'm going to sleep." I went back to my blanket, lay down on it, and turned my back to the paleo. I didn't need to be looking at her to watch her.

"Sleep, shadow warrior. Cat stays. Cat watches."

Apparently boneless, she shifted effortlessly into sitting cross-legged.

I rolled onto my back and glared up at the sky. "You've got a lousy sense of humor," I muttered.

2. Where It All Began

Cat was still there in the morning, sleeping curled up on the ground like her namesake. In the daylight the paleo was a little thing, even shorter and thinner than she'd appeared at night. Her skin seemed surprisingly pallid for someone who spent all her time outdoors, although it was hard to be sure through the layers of grime. Black hair combined with the pale skin to create a striking appearance - almost the opposite of my own gray skin and white hair.

Her bone knife lay a foot away from her. Aside from the rags she wore and a flat water skin, it seemed to be her only possession.

I stared down at her for a time, making sure she was still breathing and I hadn't accidentally killed her in the night. It was hard to say why that would have bothered me, since she had fully intended to kill me on purpose.

I gathered my things silently. "Goodbye, nasty little cat," I whispered under my breath.

She was awake and on her feet so fast I recoiled.

"Cat stays," she announced.

"Fine. Cat stays. I'm moving along." I looked at the blanket in my hand and considered the shreds of her clothing. It was warm now, but it wouldn't be in the fall - if she lived that long. I tossed the blanket to her. "Here. You need it more than I do."

She caught it with a snakelike swipe of her arm and took three long steps toward me. "Cat stays with you."

"No you absolutely do not! I'm Select, for God's sake. I've been trained by the Hellguard. You're a paleo. There is no one I would like less to be with than you, and there can't be many people you'd like less to be with than me."

"Cast out, me. Not of the people. Cat needs new people. Strong people. Shadow warrior is strong."

"I follow that logic, but you missed a part. I don't need you. And I don't want you."

She showed a little smile. "Cat knows woods. Where people are. Where Hawks are. Where drelb are. Where safety is."

"What makes you think I care about any of that? Do you think any of those are a threat to me?" They were, of course, at least to a degree. But she didn't need to know that.

Her face fell. She looked down, and when her eyes came back to me, a tear was trickling from one of them. "Please?"

Oh, for... I looked up into the sky again. "You're really not funny. You know that."

I killed a couple of rabbits with the Darkness. Cat watched wide-eyed as I walked back into the clearing with the little bodies. Fast and quiet as she was, it would still be no easy thing to hunt with only a sharpened bone. It was easy to forget how different life had been before Yoshana had taught me to use the Darkness.

Before I had been damned in Prophetess' eyes.

The paleo backed away from something in my face. I forced a smile. "It's nothing. Last time I came through here I was with a friend. We're not friends anymore."

The girl nodded solemnly. "Cat knows."

And of course an exile from a shunned race would know more than anyone about losing friends. *Exile from a shunned race...* that could describe either of us. I felt a sudden rush of sympathy for my new companion. Maybe we were more alike than I could have imagined.

I started a fire, then began to skin the first rabbit with the knife of glassy metal I'd found in the Sorrows. Cat's eyes were fixed on the meat, unblinking as - well, as a cat's.

"What?" I said.

"Can -" her eyes flicked to the second rabbit on the ground. "Can?"

I nodded, and like lightning she was on the furry body. A savage twist and the head was off and she was drinking the blood. She hooked her fingers into the loose skin at the neck and tore a section of the pelt free, then sank her teeth into the flesh.

My skin crawled. That would have been me if I hadn't been shielded by the Darkness. This wild thing wasn't much like me at all.

She met my eyes, her mouth smeared with blood.

"Hungry," she said. It sounded just a bit defensive, even apologetic. Maybe my horror had showed on my face. She seemed to read me easily enough. Perhaps the paleos made up in animal intuition what they lacked in civilized patterns of thought.

"So, just to be clear, you were only going to kill me and eat me last night because you were hungry?"

She nodded emphatically. "Trolls kill to kill. Not people. Kill for food. For land. For quarrels." She shrugged. "No land, me. No quarrels, me. Kill for food, only."

I couldn't let that pass. "Your people killed a lot of my people over the years. That sounds like a quarrel to me."

She tore loose another piece of the rabbit and wolfed it down. "Not Cat's quarrel."

"So you don't mind the Select?"

"Cat needs new people. Shadow warrior is strong. Teach me. Make Cat shadow warrior. New people, us. Strong."

"You think I can make you Select?"

She spat a small bone in my direction. "Not grayskin. Shadow warrior. Use shadows, like you. Shadows see, shadows hunt, shadows kill."

"You want me to teach you to use the Darkness."

She grinned, showing red-stained teeth. "Curious, me. Learn."

Teaching a paleo to use the Darkness. I probably couldn't think of a worse idea if I spent a year trying. "Almost no one can control the Darkness. The Hellguard can. The Overlords can. Some Select. Very few normal humans. One of your people? I don't think so."

Not that I'd have any idea how to teach her even if I wanted to. I said as much. "The ones who taught me were very strong. Stronger than me. Older than me." In Seven's case hundreds of years older. "I wouldn't know how to teach you."

She looked up from worrying at the rabbit again and met my eyes. "Stronger. Older. Time needs, only. Time, me." And then, with a frown of concentration, "I have all the time in the world."

"Wait! You can talk like that?"

"Can, me. Want to, why?" She flashed another blood-soaked grin and went back to the little corpse she was devouring.

Somehow I had acquired a paleo sidekick and would-be apprentice. Yoshana would have laughed herself silly. I couldn't imagine what Prophetess would have said.

As we continued southwest, Cat would spend most of the day at my side, chattering at me, asking questions. If I ignored her she'd shut up - she was clearly still afraid of angering me. Whatever she thought a shadow warrior was, and however much she wanted to be one, it was something that also frightened her. And rightly so. If I'd had Dee's unceasing blather to contend with, the Darkness might have stopped his mouth permanently.

But most of the time, I found I didn't mind talking with Cat. I even learned things about the paleos. She insisted their speech patterns weren't because they were stupid or ignorant - though I couldn't imagine she had a meaningful standard of comparison - but because they prized simplicity in all things. It was true that I could understand her well enough, and she was able to convey complex concepts in a handful of words.

When I asked how she'd learn to speak like a "troll," she revealed - reluctantly - that she'd taught herself to read books in the ruined town where her clan laired.

Reading was apparently a grave sin among the paleos, and she'd never been caught at it.

"Skin still on, me."

"You mean they'd have skinned you if they'd caught you reading?"

She'd nodded seriously. I didn't think she was joking, though it turned out she had a playful sense of humor.

Often when I didn't want to talk to her, she'd range away from me, scouting or scavenging. I had at first hoped she might not come back, but she always did. She was a skilled tracker, and could catch up with me easily even if I changed my route. Of course, I could evade her forever, dodging behind trees, using the Darkness to see which way she was coming and doubling back.

"Not fair!" she announced after I'd led her in a circle only to wait sitting on a stump she'd already passed. She threw a pinecone at me, which she'd obviously collected for just that purpose.

I grinned. "Shadow warriors don't fight fair. By definition."

She didn't bother me again about teaching her to use the Darkness. Our worst disagreement came when we found a broad, shallow stream.

"Take a bath," I said.

She shook her head. I was none too clean myself, but she was far dirtier. There were even small twigs and leaves matted in her long, black hair.

"Not like water, people. Or cats," she said firmly.

"Shadow warriors do. And you stink." She still looked mutinous.

"If you don't go wash yourself, I'll pick you up and throw you in."

"Picked wrong new people, me," she grumbled. But she waded into the stream. For a moment I was afraid that she was going to strip her clothes off in front of me - I didn't imagine modesty was especially important to the paleos. But she went in clothes and all, which was for the best in a number of ways. The clothes needed washing as much as she did, and there was nothing clean for her to change into.

I did the same. My pack, weapons, and boots stayed on the shore, but the rest went into the water with me. Afterwards I lay on the bank, drying out in the warm sun.

"Not like water, cats," my companion repeated. She stood next to me, dripping and looking miserable. She shook her long hair, scattering drops of cold water on my face.

She hadn't put much effort into scrubbing off the dirt, and the stream could only do so much on its own. Still, her pallor was even more obvious. I wondered if that pointed to disease or some unusual mix in her ancestry. The debris had mostly come out of her hair, but it remained matted and tangled.

"Better," I said. "But there's a little more we can do."

"Enough, that," she protested.

I extended a thin cloud of the Darkness toward her. She squeaked and took a step back, but it enveloped her, settling onto her body. She stared at it, eyes wide. Half a minute later it returned to me.

"That should get rid of any passengers you've picked up." She looked blank. "Fleas, lice…"

She nodded firmly. "Good. Picked right new people, me."

So I had finally found a use for myself in society, as a paleo delousing service. My parents would have been so proud.

I steered our course farther west, trying to avoid civilization. I could have easily concealed my use of the Darkness, and the Select, while not popular, were generally accepted. It would be much harder to hide Cat's origins, and the paleos aroused far more hatred than my race. Better to avoid people altogether.

I judged we were due north of Acceptance when we saw the dead town. Well, dead in one sense. It crawled with activity, but that was the life of ants and maggots on a day-old carcass. A small army was camped in and around the place - perhaps Hawks, or some other local band pledged by coin or other ties to the Monolith, or even Monolith troops themselves. I didn't want to get close enough to find out.

This site was not like the ruins of the Last Days that we found strewn across the continent. It had fallen within the past generation. The gutted structures had been built to modern standards, with modern tools - that is to say, they were less decayed but of far lower quality than anything built hundreds of years ago.

It didn't seem that this army had sacked the place, however. There were bonfires, but no buildings were aflame. I saw no signs of prisoners. These soldiers hadn't killed the town - they were merely resting in its corpse.

Cat's eyes were big. "Patrols," she said.

Not that we saw any, but she was right. If these men were at all professional, they would have scouts posted.

I shrugged. "Probably sense them first. Kill them, if they see us."

Despite her ability to speak in civilized patterns, Cat had no interest in doing so. Instead, to my alarm, I sometimes found myself talking more like her.

"Good," was all she said.

We were in tall grass, crouching at the top of a low ridge - more like the lip of a gully. The land here was flat, the lines of sight almost infinite. The soldiers were camped to our west, the setting sun in our eyes as we watched. The palco launched into a crouching lope, following the depression southeast. I sighed and followed more slowly. But I sent a particularly long tendril after her, to watch for danger.

If there were patrols, they didn't come anywhere near us. We crossed a crumbling, ancient bridge over what I thought was the Whitewater and lay down when the sun set, concealed in the grass. I didn't dare make a fire. There was a bit of pheasant left that I'd killed and cooked in the morning, and we ate that cold.

"We should be at the Flow in a week or so," I said. "They'll take you in there, I think. They'll take anybody. They took me."

"Stay with you," Cat insisted.

"I'll stay there too," I said. "I've got nowhere else to go."

"Good."

Some time later, she asked, "The Flow, what?"

"It's a garbage dump from the Last Days. We mine it, find things to sell. Metal, mostly. Sometimes we find things that can't be made anymore. Some of those still work. They're worth a lot."

"Old death. Vultures eat old death. Not cats. Not people."

"Yeah, not shadow warriors either, generally. But I spent two years on the Flow and never had to kill anybody, and never had anybody try to kill me. Can't say that for the year since I left."

Cat snorted. "Shadow warrior, you. Not vulture."

We approached the Flow from the north six days later, skirting the edge of the ruined city of Acceptance. Cat shot nervous glances at the walls and shattered towers of the city until we had left them behind.

"Not right," she repeated periodically.

I didn't disagree. Rumor on the Flow peopled the dead city with strange animals, humans degraded below the level of the paleos, and the Darkness itself. No one had ventured inside in living memory. Even with what I'd seen and what I'd become, the place filled me with a superstitious dread.

There were farms just to the west, but we avoided those, even though it put us uncomfortably close to the walls. And then, faintly at first, I began to hear the sound of a hammer on iron.

Cat stared at the stupid grin spreading across my face. "What?"

It felt as if a band around my chest had been loosened. A tension I hadn't known I felt dropped away.

"It's the forge. I'm... I'm home."

"Minos?" Dodd and Fenn stared at me open-mouthed. The smith set his hammer down and enfolded me in a bear hug that made my ribs creak. His apprentice grinned.

"You've gotten bigger," Dodd said. He took a step back, then shook my hand just as he had when I'd left - hard enough to hurt. I squeezed back. "And tougher," he added approvingly.

Cat poked her head in through the plastic flap.

"And you've brought a friend. That's not the same girl you left with, boy."

Cat stepped inside cautiously, eyes darting from side to side.

"God, Minos," Dodd burst out, hand twitching toward his hammer, "Is that a paleo? What have you been up to?"

"I can honestly say you wouldn't believe me if I told you."

We sat in the Hole, a cave carved into the western wall of the giant landfill. The Hole was crowded, which made it hot. I had forgotten how bad the Flow smelled. Even Cat had wrinkled her nose, and the paleo's standards of cleanliness set the bar pretty low.

Everyone was there, but Cat had a space to herself. The miners were tolerant, in their own rude way, but no one wanted to sit next to a murderous savage. They didn't know that on any objective scale, I was now far more dangerous than she was. As I told the story of the last year, I didn't fully enlighten them on that point.

Not to suggest that my tale was received as enlightenment in any case. Every time I mentioned a woman, the question, "How was she in the sack?" would float up from somewhere in the dark room. That applied to Prophetess, the possessed miller's daughter, Roshel, and even Yoshana. It's a good thing Select don't blush.

Yoshana didn't mean much to the miners on the Flow. She was a nebulous evil, poorly understood - not the terror that she represented to those closer to her. To these people, my encounters with the Darkness were far more exciting. The Darkness was a real threat in their minds. Even Cat represented more of a danger than some distant Overlord.

In glossing over my new relationship with the Darkness, I had left out the reason for some key decisions I'd made - and that had been made for me.

"What I don't get," Luco asked, "is why you bailed out on Prophetess *after* you went into the Sorrows. Wouldn't it have been smarter to make that decision *before* you went into that hellhole?"

It was an excellent question. The truest answer, of course, was that Prophetess had thrown me out of Our Lady after I'd revealed that I carried the Darkness in me.

"Because I'm not very smart?" I suggested instead. "I guess it's because I realized I didn't agree with either side. I think Yoshana's right that we have to unite against the demons and the Darkness, but I can't stomach her methods. Prophetess is more honest, but she's too rigid. The truth must be somewhere between them, but that's not a healthy place to be standing."

There was a brief silence, then Luco continued, "So you came back here to dig garbage instead?"

There were snorts of laughter. If I'd really done everything I said - crossed the continent, fought drelb and the possessed, confronted and then traveled with and then betrayed Yoshana herself - then coming back to the Flow seemed like a ludicrous step backwards.

"I know what I'm doing here," I said. And that was true. "Besides, Cat needs somewhere to live. I didn't figure there were a lot of places that would take in an exiled paleo, but this might be one."

"Depends what she eats," Joran snapped. He'd never been shy with his opinions. And it was widely - and accurately - believed that the paleos were cannibals.

"What is there, hmm?" Cat asked, staring fixedly at him.

He must have been nearly twice her weight, but he backed away.

"Thassa's a good cook," I said quickly, hoping to defuse the tension. I wasn't ready to get kicked out of another community. "Where is she, anyway?"

"Gone," Dorren rumbled from the back of the Hole. The headman of the miners emerged from the darkness, stopping a few feet from me. He was half a head shorter than I, but he had a certain presence. He'd intimidated me when I'd first lived on the Flow, but his aura of command was nothing compared to Yoshana's. Now he was just a man in charge of a couple dozen garbage pickers.

"She went to the army. They always need cooks that can make something out of not very much. Kala too."

If Kala had gone to the army, it hadn't been to cook.

Dorren stared up into my black eyes. "You're different now, Minos. It's not just the miles. You're not the same person that left. But you're welcome to stay. Your friend, too, as long as you keep her under control."

"Thanks. I appreciate it."

"Yeah. Stay as long as you want."

By the time we were all done catching up, the shadows were getting long outside.

"I, uh, don't suppose my place is still there?" I asked. "Place" was about the best you could have said for it - a spot against the vertical bank of the dried-up riverbed that formed the Flow. Its other walls and roof were sheets of

300

corrugated tin, with a flap of plastic for the door. I had slept in much better places since I'd left; although I'd also slept in much worse, including the fork of a tree in a Darkness-haunted forest.

"All yours," Luco said. "No one new has come to take it."

Which was a polite way of saying none of the other miners liked it enough to move in. That was no surprise. The most coveted spots were either natural caves like the Hole, or better reinforced with cinder blocks or sturdier metal. The only question had really been whether someone had scavenged the materials.

"Uh, torches might be gone," Luco admitted.

Ah. Well, that was to be expected. The oil-soaked wood was valuable.

"No problem. We're used to doing without." The paleos didn't make fire. And I didn't need it to protect myself against the Darkness - at least, not in the quantities we might see here. I had torches in my pack - even Yoshana carried them, just in case - but I wouldn't need them tonight.

"Come on, Cat."

The girl stretched like her namesake and followed me out. The shelter was only a few hundred yards from the Hole, and we covered the distance in easy silence. Cat cocked her head skeptically when we reached the tiny structure, little more than six feet on a side.

"Out here, me," she announced.

That was a relief. We had traveled together for a week, but always slept a distance apart. I had been careful to meditate every night so I wouldn't hurt her in my sleep - but it didn't pay to take chances with the Darkness.

"Cat, not dog," the paleo complained the next morning. "Too much digging."

We had bought shovels on credit and were gouging away at the surface of the Flow in search of the buried treasures of the ancients. The first hour had yielded nothing except the protest from Cat. She was a tough little thing, but had no practice at this sort of work. Even I was finding that the calluses I had from my sword practice weren't up to the rigors of constant digging, and my muscles were no longer used to it. Dodd was no doubt right that I was a much harder man than I'd been a year ago, but not in all the same places.

"Shadow warrior, you. Cat, me. Not vulture, either," Cat continued in a peevish tone.

"You want to eat? Then dig, you."

The paleo gave me a rebellious look, but jabbed the shovel viciously into the ground.

There was a loud crack.

"Aww... move it, Cat." I shouldered her aside and gingerly probed around the edge of the hole she'd made, first with my shovel, then with my hands. I quickly unearthed a large, square, ceramic vessel, which looked like it had been intact before Cat had cracked it in two.

"You broke it," I said. "That's the kind of thing we're looking for."

"Dig hard. Don't dig hard. Decide, you." With a snort of disgust, she moved away and attacked the ground in another spot.

It had been the kind of bad luck that could happen to anyone, but there was a certain skill required to unearth our prizes without damaging them. If Cat didn't have any interest in learning, she could still successfully dig up scrap metal, but other pieces would be spoiled.

I stuck my shovel in the ground and went over to her. "Let me show you. You have to dig firmly, but carefully. You can't just jab the shovel in."

"Old death," Cat snarled. She spat and made some kind of sign with her right hand. "Trolls chewing bones of trolls." She swept her arm in an arc, encompassing the Flow and the City beyond. "Dead, rotting. Wrong."

"Dammit, Cat!" I flared. Anger welled up in me. I'd let this savage travel with me, protected her, brought her to the only place a barbarian cannibal with no useful skills might be accepted. And now this?

She was on her knees, eyes wide. I realized the Darkness surrounded me, swirling like smoke.

I took a deep, steadying breath. Then another. "Sorry, Cat."

"Shadow warrior, you," she said in a small voice. "Not vulture."

I sat with Luco in the darkness at the back of the Hole. Cat was off exploring the Flow. And giving me some space.

"I don't know," I said. "I didn't want to be in the middle of a war. I thought I wanted to be back somewhere quiet. But, y'know... it's a garbage mine, man. We're picking over stuff that people two hundred years ago thought was junk."

We sometimes found items of great value in the Flow. Things no one could make anymore. But Cat hadn't been far wrong with "dead, rotting."

I grimaced. "And I guess I thought even if I didn't stay, at least I could leave Cat here, but she doesn't like it at all."

"Minos... not to pry, but why do you care? What do you owe her? You said she would have killed you if you hadn't woken up."

"She's just a kid. A kid that's been raised by wolves. And I guess... I saw a lot of bad things this last year. I did a lot of things I'm not real proud of. I killed two of her people and crippled another one. In the Sorrows I killed things that may not have been people anymore, but they still looked a lot like people."

I hadn't told Luco or the others how I'd left Yoshana's soldier Erev lying on the ground, unable to move or speak. I didn't mention it now. "I guess I need to watch out for her so I know I'm not one of the bad things myself."

The kind of thing Yoshana was. Grigg had said that once the Darkness was in you, your conscience had to keep it in check or it would consume you. The way it had boiled out at Cat was just the way it had boiled out in Our Lady, when Prophetess sent me away. I was afraid of it sometimes. Sometimes I was a little bit afraid of myself.

Luco was watching me but didn't say anything. I felt compelled to fill the silence. "I don't know where I belong anymore."

He grinned. "I've got an idea."

3. Servants of Mars

"This is not a good idea."

"You don't want to mine garbage anymore," Luco retorted. "You've been trained to fight by Our Lady and the Darkness Radiant both. And Rockwall's army is paying really good recruiting bonuses. What part of it isn't a good idea?"

"The part where I said I didn't want to be between two groups of people trying to kill each other - did you miss that? If Rockwall is paying recruiting bonuses, it's because they're bulking up to throw their army against the Monolith. They don't pay you extra to sit around warming a bench in the barracks."

For as long as I could remember, the armies of Rockwall and the Monolith had skirmished over the rich farmland bordered on the west by the Barrier Range, on the north by the Ice Fields, on the east by the Muddy, and on the south by the Whitewater. The war was eternally inconclusive. The Monolith had allies among the city-states in the disputed territory, and spent its men in battle and its silver in hiring mercenaries. Rockwall put less effort into the struggle. But the people of the area were mostly Reborn, and preferred Rockwall's easy mix of Reborn and Universalist beliefs to the zealous Josephites of the Monolith.

It was hard to think of a bigger waste of human effort than stepping into that conflict.

"Well, yeah, people say there's going to be real fighting this time," Luco said. "They say with the Hawks harassing traffic on the Whitewater this past year, even those lazy bastards in Panther City finally decided they have to do something about it."

"Coming to terms would be an idea. Rockwall's never going to control that territory." They had never really tried.

"And you want those Josephite freaks on our border?" Luco snapped. "The way I hear it, they don't care for your kind."

I was startled by his vehemence. He wasn't the sort of person to refer to "my kind" like that. He must have been more of a patriot than I'd thought. And it was true enough that the Josephites despised the Select even more than the Reborn and the Universalists did.

Still... "You'd rather have the Darkness flooding around unchecked up there? That's what happens when no one's in control. Remember, I've been there, and I ran into the Darkness, a drelb, and paleos, all in one trip."

Whatever you might think of the Council in Panther City, Rockwall's seat of government, they maintained a semblance of order. At least, fire wardens patrolled the roads and cities to beat back the Darkness.

"That's why we have to kick out the Monolith once and for all. If the Principalities and the Hawks like those Josephites so much, they can convert and go live with them up in the mountains. But you know almost everyone there would rather be part of Rockwall."

I had the feeling that almost everyone there would rather be left alone... although they'd probably be willing to pay taxes to a government that drove out the Darkness, and the drelb, and the paleos.

"I didn't know you felt so strongly about it." I'd known Luco for two years. I hadn't known he had any opinion at all on the subject.

The rigid lines of his face cracked into a sudden grin. "Well, maybe more of it's I want to get out of here too. Been thinking about it since you left. Then you came back, and you've been everywhere and seen everything... I can't believe you'd just settle back in here and dig through broken pots and old diapers for the rest of your life."

Shadow warrior, you. Not vulture.

Something dark and powerful rolled over inside me. I was probably the deadliest thing in this backwater - Rockwall had no masters of the Darkness, or even Select mercenaries that I knew of. I could make a mark here.

"I've still got Cat to think about," I said weakly.

"The army needs scouts. You don't think a paleo would be good at that?"

She was stealthy, a practiced tracker and woodsman. And it occurred to me that the skills of a paleo scout might explain things I learned through other means, without me having to reveal my nature.

"I guess she'd probably like that better than digging."

Luco slapped me on the shoulder and smiled broadly. "Come on. We're joining the army!"

Cat was thrilled. "Hunt, kill, eat?"

I tried for the third or fourth time to explain the reconnaissance functions of a military scout. She flapped her hands at me impatiently. "Noise, talk, yes, understand. Hunt, kill, eat!"

I had the feeling that the paleo's encounter with military discipline would be the infamous meeting of the immovable object and the irresistible force. Still, sufficient unto the day is the evil thereof. For the moment, she was happy.

Dorren just laughed at me when I sheepishly told him we were leaving.

"Didn't think you'd stick," he said. "Thought you'd last longer than a day, though."

I remembered what he'd said - *Stay as long as you want.* It seemed he might know me better than I knew myself. He didn't even seem annoyed when Luco revealed he'd be going with me. As if Dorren had seen that coming too. I was tempted to tell him everything, including the Darkness and the real reason I'd left Our Lady. Tempted to ask his advice.

But I didn't.

I found a chance to take Fenn aside privately and give him the wristwatch I'd looted from the dead, ancient town in the Sorrows. He was so absurdly grateful that I was embarrassed.

I said a few more awkward goodbyes, and then the three of us - Luco, Cat, and I - were on our way.

"There's a recruiting camp at the south end of the Flow," Luco explained. "Or at least there was last I heard."

"Might as well start there," I said. I fished the other watch out of my pack. "Brought this for you."

His eyes lit up. "My God, Minos. It's beautiful. That's amazing. Where'd you get it?"

"You'd probably rather not know."

He laughed and shook the watch, then gave the crown a few turns. He grinned like a maniac when the delicate second hand started up. "Now it almost seems like a shame to go running off to get myself killed."

"Want to go back?"

He didn't hesitate for an instant. "No."

We hiked south along the western bank of the Flow. It would be slow - and foolhardy - to walk on the landfill itself. Sure, we spent all day on it mining, but then you moved carefully, testing each step. The garbage had mostly compressed to a stable surface, but there were occasional crusts that formed over empty pockets. What festered inside those pockets was usually foul and potentially dangerous if you fell onto something sharp.

Not that the land west of the dried riverbed was exceptionally pleasant. Early summer in this part of Rockwall was hot. From here the land rose slowly into the Low Furnace, a vast expanse of desert that stretched to the foothills of the Barrier Range. The ground was an orange clay I had never seen anywhere else, and in the dry air it turned into a clinging dust.

Cat worked her mouth and spat, and I could see she instantly regretted it. It didn't pay to waste moisture. We each had a skin of small beer, just enough alcohol in it to kill whatever was in the water and keep it from going off. But that would have to last us until we found either the recruiting post or another water source. Cat was leaner and hungrier even than a garbage miner - she knew all about starvation and thirst.

"Fight for this, why?"

"Not for this, Cat. Rockwall controls this land. They're fighting - we're going to be fighting - for the land back where we met." Land that was far more fertile and better watered.

She nodded emphatically. "Fight for that, yes." Her brow furrowed. "Fight people?"

I realized she meant other paleos. It made perfect sense that killing "trolls" wouldn't upset her in the least - after all, she'd fully intended to kill me.

"That's not the idea. We'll fight the Monolith. They're like us. Civilized."

We killed each other in an organized manner and didn't eat the corpses. I suppose that counted as civilization.

"Kill trolls. Good."

Luco shot her a nervous look. "I'm not sure your new friend is completely domesticated, Minos."

"Domesticated, me?" She bared her teeth in a snarl. "Domesticate this, troll."

"We don't kill and eat our friends, Cat," I said mildly.

"Your friend."

"My friends are your friends, Cat." My tone changed. It was not a suggestion, or even a statement. It was an order. She knew it.

"Shadow warrior says. Cat does." She gave Luco a disdainful sniff. "Not eat."

"Why does she call you that?"

"I guess because I'm gray. And she knows what I can do." Which was not exactly a lie, but was certainly a deliberate evasion. Cat knew that too. She snorted but kept her peace. I hadn't told her not to discuss my mastery of the Darkness - it really hadn't occurred to me that she might hold a conversation with anyone. But I thought she understood that I didn't want my abilities to be known. For all her savage barbarism, I had the strong feeling the paleo girl was nobody's fool.

I wondered whether her untrained intellect would realize that if Rockwall truly came to control the disputed land north of the Whitewater, its soldiers would eradicate the paleos there. I wondered how the exile would feel about that if she figured it out.

Sufficient unto the day is the evil thereof was quickly becoming my motto. Maybe I'd ask to have it etched on my tombstone.

"Is that it?"

A log palisade stretched in front of us, a wall a couple of hundred yards long and twenty feet high. Wooden observation towers rose another thirty feet above the wall. The troops must have been logging the forests to the east and hauling the wood from there - the trees around us were scrub oaks whose twisted trunks and limbs wouldn't have yielded enough straight lumber for a chair, much less a wall.

"Can't think what else," Luco replied. "And this is about where it was supposed to be. I wonder why they need the defenses, though? We're deep in Rockwall land here."

"Building it gives the troops something to do. And if you're sleeping inside, it's a lot harder to decide you've gotten sick of military life and wander back to your farm." Most of my reading had focused on strategy and tactics. But sometimes the great thinkers had taken a moment to comment on routine matters of discipline. It seemed like the phrase *idle hands are the Devil's playground* might well have originated in the army.

Luco grimaced. "I've been digging stuff out of holes in the ground pretty much my whole life. I didn't plan on digging more holes to put stakes into the ground."

I chuckled. I had done just that my first night off the Flow with Prophetess. Maybe history was repeating itself.

"From my experience with adventure, digging holes is right about the best part." As compared to, say, fighting monsters, nearly freezing to death, or fleeing from allies you'd betrayed. All of those things seemed like more fun when they weren't actually happening to you.

Luco shot me a look. "You can go back if you want. You might still make it before nightfall… if the things that come out at night still worry you."

They didn't, of course. And I wasn't going to go back. "No. The Flow's not for me anymore. It surely isn't for Cat. Shadow warriors don't dig for garbage, right?"

The paleo nodded emphatically.

"Come on," I continued. "It's getting hot out here."

It had been hot all day and was getting hotter still. But now Luco was the one hanging back.

"Ah, c'mon," I said. "What could go wrong? A paleo, a Select, and some guy dumb enough to be walking with them go up to an army camp. There's got to be a good punchline to that joke, right?"

"'And the soldiers shot them with arrows until the bodies stopped twitching.' Yeah, that's hilarious."

"Fight here?" Cat asked.

"Nah. It'll be fine. Come on," I urged. Prophetess and Yoshana had each walked blithely into situations far more potentially dangerous. Of course, Prophetess believed she was on a mission from God. And Yoshana operated on the theory - so far correct - that no enemy springing a trap could be as dangerous as she was. Well, that was probably true for me too, in this part of the world.

Although it would be a real irony if after surviving drelb, paleos, possessed, Overlords, demons, and the Darkness itself, I was now killed by the army I was trying to join.

"Oh, come on, you two," I insisted. "It's not getting any cooler out here and I'm not walking back." I started off toward the palisade. Thanks to the Darkness, I didn't need to turn my head to know that Luco and Cat were following.

I also began to get a sense of the camp once we were within a hundred yards of the open gate. There were sentries inside resting under awnings. They weren't aware of us yet. Lookouts posted in the watchtowers were likewise oblivious. There was a table and benches outside where perhaps the recruiters were meant to sit, but no one was there. A wind kicked up and swirled orange dust through the air, stinging my eyes and clogging my throat. Maybe that explained why nobody was outside.

"Make for the wall to the right of the gate," I said quietly over my shoulder. "Let's make an entrance."

"Is that a good idea?"

"Only if you want a better assignment than digging holes for stakes."

"Point taken."

The readiness level was pathetic. Yoshana would have cut down everyone inside like a wind out of hell, just on general principles. It was hard to believe the same military produced Rockwall's fire wardens, hard-bitten soldiers who strapped naphtha-throwers on their backs to fight the Darkness. They weren't pleasant company, but at least they were professionals.

We made it to the palisade unnoticed. The men in the watchtowers couldn't see us from this angle even if they were looking, which they weren't. There was a rudimentary firing platform being built around the inside of the palisade, but no one was on it.

I whispered to Cat, "When the dust starts blowing, slip around behind the guards on the right-hand side of the gate. Don't touch them or make a sound."

She grinned fiercely and nodded.

I could have waited for the wind, but that would have been time wasted. Spraying dust through the air was a trivial task for the Darkness. I tapped Cat's shoulder. "Now."

I could hear the two sentries coughing and cursing on the other side of the wall as I blew dust in their faces. I waited a few seconds, let it subside, and stepped around the corner. Luco followed hesitantly.

"Better hope the Monolith isn't hiring paleo scouts," I said.

One of the guards lurched to his feet, right hand falling to the hilt of his sheathed sword. He brushed orange grit from his face with his left hand.

"Who the hell are you?" he demanded.

"Your better question is who is she?" I smiled and pointed behind them. They both glanced over their shoulders. Cat laughed silently at them, mouth wide and teeth bared like a wolf.

The standing man's sword began to clear its sheath. It stopped when he realized the blade of my katana was touching his wrist.

"No shame in letting someone as stealthy as my friend Cat get the drop on you," I said, lying through my teeth. Their incompetence was revolting. "But let's not compound the error by picking a fight you're not going to win."

Even without the Darkness, months of training with Grigg made these two no more than an inconvenience to me. And I did have the Darkness. It was inside them already. If it came to blows, they would both be dead in the blink of an eye.

They couldn't know that, but hopefully a Select with a drawn sword would make them see that discretion was the better part of valor.

Cat had been right, in her simplistic way. My time with Yoshana's forces had done nothing to make me a better garbage miner, but it had turned me into an exceptional killer.

The man with his hand on the sword looked me up and down, his eyes lingering on my blade - and not just because it was a hairs-breadth away from taking his hand off, or at least severing critical veins and tendons. If he knew steel, he would recognize the pattern in the metal. There were few weapons forged and folded in the traditional style left in the world - I'd been privileged to own two of them. He couldn't see the glassy sheen of the ancient knife at my belt, but he could see its size, and perhaps notice the unusual material of the sheath.

He met my eyes. His were light brown, and they blinked when they stared into the unrelieved black of my pupil, iris, and sclera. The Select often served as mercenaries, and from my eyes to my gray skin to the white hair I now wore long and tied back, there was no doubting my race.

"Right," the soldier muttered quietly. He moved his hand away from the hilt of his weapon. His companion looked from me to Cat and stayed seated.

"Something we can help you with?" the standing man asked carefully.

"I'm hoping there's something we can help you with," I answered with a broad smile. "We hear you're recruiting."

"Right," he repeated. His eyes darted from me to Cat and back again. "We're set up here for processing and the first couple weeks of basic training. How to keep step and dig a latrine and which end of the spear you stick into the other guy. I'm guessing you're a little past that."

My grin widened. I was definitely an expert at digging, and fighting wouldn't be a problem for me either. If I'd never learned how to march, I didn't figure that would be a difficult skill to master.

"I think we can handle the basics, yes. Although Cat here is more of a recon type than a marching type." As of course was I.

"Yeah, I can see that. Where'd you train?"

I scowled. He took a step back and raised his hands. "Hey, I'm not saying I don't believe you, buddy. But I'm going to have to explain why I'm passing you straight through here. The lieutenant's going to ask."

"Fair enough. I was with the Darkness Radiant. I found Cat on my way down here. She says she trained by killing people in their sleep to drink their blood. Seeing as that's what she was trying to do to me when we met, I've been taking her word for it."

The paleo barked out a laugh.

"Jesus," the seated guard murmured.

"Better with us than against us, I guess," said the other, giving me an insincere smile.

"The Darkness Radiant and a goddamn paleo," his companion continued. "What's next, Yoshana?"

"Last time I talked to her, she was busy," I said.

"Jesus." He looked at Luco. "What's your story?"

"Me? I'm just along for the ride."

"You look smarter than that."

"Yeah. I guess looks really can be deceiving."

I might have laid it on too thick. We found ourselves in the lieutenant's office, a structure of rough-hewn planks at the center of the compound. Lieutenant Tir sat on the edge of his wooden desk, hands toying with a double-edged dagger as he stared at me. The room was not small, but the two gate guards and some other curious soldiers had shoved themselves in with us. No one was hostile, but I felt like the main attraction at the freak show.

That many people in a small space made Cat nervous, and Luco was uncomfortable with the whole situation. I could feel it in their breathing, their stance, even the smell of their sweat. It was starting to make me jumpy. That, and the Darkness, and a bunch of people with weapons all crammed together wasn't a good combination. I inhaled deeply and steadied my breathing.

"The Darkness Radiant," the lieutenant said. "You've come a long way."

Tir was a short, dark man with a mop of black hair and piercing, dark eyes. His words were polite enough. The tone conveyed mild disbelief with a hint of a sneer. There were clumsily made bookcases lining the walls, filled with volumes of military theory, treatises on leadership, even classical literature. Sun Tzu and Clausewitz, Machiavelli and Kissinger, Homer and Shakespeare.

Dozens of others, some I recognized, some I didn't. It was an impressive collection to haul into the middle of nowhere.

I didn't need to probe Tir's mind to read his thoughts. His uniform was unkempt but boasted a number of decorations. He regarded himself as a superior man, wasted in a backwoods recruiting post. Unimpressed with everything around him, he'd let discipline grow lax.

He wasn't impressed with us either.

"What legion did you serve in?" he asked.

I had no idea what the unit designations were in Yoshana's army.

"I was part of a reconnaissance force attached to the Knights of Resurrection."

The lieutenant looked at me through slitted eyes while digging under a fingernail with the point of his knife. "A very long way for one of Yoshana's personal corps."

I shrugged. "We've had a parting of the ways."

"You deserted from the Darkness Radiant? And you lived?"

The disbelief was open now. So was the sneer. I wasn't going to tell this self-important little slug how close I had really been to the supreme horror herself. I wasn't going to tell him about leaving the last of her human bodyguards twitching on the ground with his tendons and vocal cords severed, about fleeing blindly through the swampy forests of the demons' country until I reached the Darkness-haunted Sorrows that only a madman would call safety…

I drew in a deep, shuddering breath and willed the Darkness in me to subside. It had almost begun to boil out of my pores, and there would have been only one outcome then. It rolled over in my gut like an angry serpent, but slowly began to recede.

I shot a quick glance at Cat. She had sensed what was about to happen - her sharpened bone dagger was in her hand, and she was tensed like a coiled spring. If the room had erupted in chaos, the soldier nearest to her wouldn't have lived long enough for the Darkness to kill him.

But the room hadn't erupted, and none of the fools in it had any idea how close it had come. There was a calculating look in Tir's eye, but nothing like the fear there would have been if he'd known what I was.

Prophetess had understood that, at least. She'd cast me out after I'd risked my life to offer my abilities to her - but at least she'd known what she was rejecting.

"I was not going to be a part of Yoshana's attack on Our Lady. I'm no Universalist, Lieutenant, but there are some things I won't do."

That had been about Prophetess herself, not Our Lady. But that was something else I had no intention of explaining to this man.

"There's been no attack by the Darkness Radiant on Our Lady," Tir snapped.

"Yoshana was occupied in the Darklands. Our Lady is her next target. I don't know when that stroke's going to fall, but it will."

Tir waved a hand as if clearing away a bad smell. "Even if that's true, it doesn't explain what a Select mercenary, a paleo girl, and a garbage miner are doing in my camp."

"Lieutenant, I'm trained for war. I won't be a part of the fight between Yoshana and Our Lady. I heard Rockwall was recruiting. If you don't want me, I'll find another employer."

The Monolith employed Select mercenaries despite their religious prejudices against my race. Tir would know that. There was no point in making the threat explicit.

"Fine," the lieutenant grated. "Sergeant Tumner, process these three as front-line ready immediately. Send them on to Captain Almet's company. Lieutenant Pious' platoon."

The burly soldier to my left frowned. "Pious, sir? He's..." the man's voice trailed off.

"Yes, and if our friend here was really with the Darkness Radiant, I'm sure he'll fit right in." Tir's voice dripped sweet venom.

"Seems like that could have gone better," Luco said. "Why didn't you tell him you knew Yoshana?"

"He didn't even believe I'd been with her forces. How was I supposed to convince him I'd actually met her? Tell him about the strawberry-shaped birthmark on her butt?"

"She has a birthmark on her butt?"

"How would I know? I traveled with her, I didn't watch her taking a bath. And even if I did know, the real point is how would Tir know? Anything I could tell him that he'd know himself would, by definition, be common knowledge. So if he did know it, it wouldn't prove anything. And if he didn't know it, he'd have no way of knowing I was telling the truth."

He grinned. "So you're saying you didn't really think it through before you started shooting off your mouth about being part of the Darkness Radiant."

"Wouldn't be the first thing I didn't think through."

I didn't think it through would probably make an even better epitaph than *sufficient unto the day...* one probably being the logical corollary to the other.

"At least we're not digging latrines."

Instead we had been fed a quick and unappetizing meal and sent straight north to the front. A pair of troopers accompanied us, marching stolidly and silently before us. Behind came a half dozen other recruits. They had been in the camp for ten days; Tir had declared their training complete and sent them along with us.

He hadn't wanted to waste escorts on just the three of us. But he hadn't wanted us spending any more time in his camp either.

We'd set out in early afternoon in the heat of the day. A ridiculous time to start. We trudged right back up the track Luco, Cat, and I had come down. As we passed the trading post on the banks of the Flow where Dorren's miners hawked their wares, I saw a man named Sart leaning on the table, half-asleep. Apparently the biweekly convoy from the recruiting camp wasn't enough excitement to wake him up.

"The soldiers stop to talk and sometimes buy stuff on their way back down south," Luco explained quietly. "Never when they're going north with the newbies."

Sart and I hadn't exchanged ten words in the two years I'd been on the Flow. He was a taciturn fellow even by the standards of garbage miners, and I suppose I wasn't much of a conversationalist either. Luco lifted a hand in greeting, and Sart waved back.

The cactus patch seemed to have grown a little in the time I'd been away with Prophetess and Yoshana. Any life was a blessing in this dusty, orange waste, even the nasty prickly pears.

Cat looked at the salvaged goods arrayed on the table and scanned the expanse of the Flow beyond. "Old death," she muttered.

One of the soldiers heard her. "Aye, old death indeed. Up there more than here."

He pointed to the towers of Acceptance on the horizon. "We'll be stopping soon. Don't want to spend the night near the City. The monsters in it'll crack your bones for the marrow and swallow your soul down with your flesh."

He leered at us, trying to frighten the new recruits, but he flinched away when he met my eyes. There might be any number of things infesting the corpse of the City. Paleos or even monsters, if by monsters you meant wild dogs and giant rats. Possibly even the Darkness. But there would be nothing worse than what I'd fought before. As I'd said to Delet hundreds of miles north of here… nothing worse than me.

We camped at dusk in the lee of a low ridge. It wasn't much, but it broke the dusty wind sweeping in from the west.

"Don't normally stop south of the City," said the soldier who'd spoken before. "But it don't pay to take chances with the Darkness."

We had hard bread and pemmican that couldn't have been drier if it had baked under the sun for a year. We didn't dare use enough water to wash down much of either.

I assumed the water we'd been given had been boiled. If it hadn't, the Darkness would take care of any contaminants for me. Cat must be used to eating and drinking all kinds of awful things. I imagined paleos with weak immune systems didn't last very long. And as for Luco, a lifetime mining garbage had to be good for strengthening the stomach if nothing else.

We settled into a sort of straggling line on the ground, a soldier at each end. I was second behind the less talkative trooper, then Cat, then Luco. The other recruits stretched out past him. It might have been coincidence that they were as far from me as possible, but it probably wasn't.

"Is your friend really Select?" whispered the recruit closest to Luco. I had to grin. That was the least of the bad things I was.

The miner nodded. He was a tall, lean man, very like me in height and build. His skin was bronzed from the sun. Though he wasn't much older than I, tiny lines were already forming around his eyes and mouth.

As far as appearance went, there was nothing beyond the color of my eyes, skin, and hair to mark me apart from him, to suggest that I was a stranger, more frightening kind of being.

Prejudice against the Select ran deep.

"Shadow warrior, him," said Cat. She sniffed scornfully and turned her back on the others.

Always helpful, was my Cat.

"She really a paleo?" asked the soldier next to me, unconsciously mimicking the recruit.

Cat drew her lips back in something between a sneer and a snarl.

"That answer your question?" I replied.

"You really catch her trying to kill you?"

"Yep."

"And bringing her along with you seemed like the best possible idea?"

"How well do you know the territory where we're going to be fighting the Monolith? The hills, and forests, and swamps?"

"Not that well."

"Me either. She does. I figure someone who knows the lay of the land and has practice sneaking up and killing people bigger than she is might come in handy. You think?"

He shook his head in wonder. "Okay, point taken. But how did you catch her? And how do you know she's not gonna slit your throat tonight?"

I turned to the paleo. "Cat?"

"Shadow warrior, him. Shadow warrior me, soon."

"God. A Select with a paleo apprentice?"

"Yep."

"You have either the biggest balls or the smallest brain of anyone I've ever met." He leaned over and stuck out his hand. "I'm Talot."

"Minos."

A smile crept onto my lips as I drifted off to sleep. "Biggest balls" definitely wasn't true - at least two women, Yoshana and Prophetess, would take that title from me hands down. "Smallest brain" might be right, though.

Erev flopped on the ground like a landed fish, his mouth opening and closing. As I backed away he threw his crippled body toward me in convulsing heaves, now less like a fish than a snake with its back broken. Each time he flung himself up and crashed down, a cloud of Darkness puffed out at the impact, growing, spreading, until blazing eyes and a fanged mouth opened in the seething mass and laughed at me.

I jolted upright. A black cloud hung in front of my face. As I gasped in a ragged breath, I inhaled it back into my body.

To my right, Cat sat on her haunches, watching me with unblinking eyes. To my left, Talot snored, peacefully oblivious.

I had forgotten my meditation. That couldn't happen again. It was more important than ever now that I was among people again. I could have been seen by someone other than Cat. I remembered what Yoshana had said, when she'd set Roshel to watch over my sleep. I could have killed someone.

Thinking of Roshel caused the Darkness in me to roil again. I'd tried to put her out of my mind since I'd turned on the Darkness Radiant. Grigg had thought she really cared for me. It was hard to categorize my feelings for her, beyond lust. I thought that whatever the effects of her Darkness-spawned glamor, I had cared for her as a person too.

I pushed myself to my feet and made my way over the ridge. On the other side I stood, raised my arms, and opened my senses to the night. My awareness reached out, touching the others in our group, spreading past them. There was nothing larger than a lone coyote within a hundred yards of us. One exceptionally alert owl must have felt my consciousness brush past it, because it hooted and launched itself into the air just as I touched it.

I opened my human eyes and looked up at the sky. The stars shone down, obscured only a bit by racing shreds of cloud. The moon was a thin, waxing crescent.

I breathed in and out, drawing the Darkness back in, finding my center. What was past was past. Prophetess, Yoshana, Roshel were all behind me. I would be created anew in whatever lay ahead.

I was nearly as quiet as Cat making my way back over the ridge, but Talot woke and stared at me.

"Couldn't sleep," I whispered.

"Don't go wandering off," he murmured in reply. "There could be bad stuff out there."

He didn't know how right he was.

4. Pious

It took us four more days to reach the army. Though the land was flat, we heard the encampment before we saw it.

We had crossed a bridge over the Whitewater, a clumsy thing of heaped stones and sawn trunks lashed together. A trail led through the woods on the other side, less a road than a rutted path crushed through weeds and saplings. Larger trees bore the scars of torn bark and broken branches where wagons had scraped past them.

But we were still in the forest when the noise reached us. The muted roar of a thousand conversations, the clang of hammers on anvils, the braying of donkeys and lowing of oxen.

If there were pickets, they were so far apart that my senses couldn't reach them, and none were on this path. While presumably we were coming from the safest quarter, it still would have been only prudent to post sentries.

Then we were clear of the woods, and the fortified camp stretched out on the plain in front of us.

"Trolls," muttered Cat. "Trolls and trolls and trolls."

We stood on a slight rise. The land fell away, then gently sloped upward again. The army had built a palisade at the low point, but because of the angles we had a good view of everything inside. It was a sprawling collection of everything from wooden barracks to tents to shelter halves. Thousands of people milled about - many soldiers, but some obviously not. There were mule drivers, traders, women in gaudy clothes and hard-faced men who watched over them.

The smell hit us next. A mix of smoke from cook fires and forges, the waste of humans and animals, an ad hoc city full of sweaty, unwashed bodies. The stench was nowhere near as foul as a gas pocket on the Flow, but it had a density you could cut with a knife.

The more talkative soldier with us was named Bren. He spread his arms wide and declared, "Welcome to paradise!"

We made our way to an open gate. Here at last we were intercepted by a pair of guards wearing studded leather jerkins and slung swords. Each held a spear in a careless grip.

"Pretty thin pickings," said one, casting his eye over our small group. "Take 'em on in to Lieutenant Lang for processing."

"Nah," Bren said. "This lot's already assigned to Captain Almet. Lieutenant Pious' platoon."

"Jesus!" the guard blurted. "Who'd the poor stupid bastards piss off?"

"Lieutenant Tir hisself."

"What, one of 'em suggested he get his face out of his book and actually drag his worthless ass around the camp for a change?"

"Mind your mouth, son, that's my commanding officer you're talking about."

At which point both men doubled over in raucous laughter.

The other guard rolled his eyes. "Pious is off to the left, maybe two hundred yards over and halfway up to the ridge line. Get 'em delivered and bring something to drink on your way back, would you? It's hot out here."

It was hot. Of course, we'd been walking in it, not just standing around. I didn't point that out. Apparently we were in enough trouble already.

As I walked by, the second guard exclaimed, "Hey, that one's Select!"

Bren stopped and stared at me with wide eyes. "No! My God, you're right! There was so much dust on him when he got to us I didn't notice." He guffawed again.

"What's Pious going to do with a Select?" the guard mused. "I'd pay to see that, and no mistake."

"Come on, then. Think they're going to miss you here? Ain't like the Monolith's going to be coming in from this side."

The man shook his head sadly. "Nah, I'd pay to see it, but not with stripes on my back. You can tell me about it when you bring the cider."

"Deal."

Luco leaned close and whispered, "Joining the army was one of the dumbest ideas you've ever had, Minos."

"Yeah. Sorry. I don't know what I was thinking."

Lieutenant Pious reminded me of nothing so much as a picture I'd seen of a gorilla. His legs were short, his arms were long, and his chest was massive. Though he was no taller than me, he probably outweighed me by fifty pounds, most of it muscle. He squinted at us through piggy little eyes deeply set beneath a sloping forehead.

"A bunch of hog farmers and garbage miners," he snarled. "I can still smell the dung on all of you."

His eyes locked on me. They were pale blue, almost a silver gray. "What's a Select doing here? We're God-fearing soldiers."

Someone snickered behind him. He ignored it. "There's no place for mercenaries in the army of the righteous."

I met his glare. "I'm enlisting like everyone else."

He looked me up and down as if inspecting an old side of beef beginning to rot. "Fine. The sword and the knife you're carrying aren't standard issue. Turn them in to the quartermaster and draw regular gear."

I'd been expecting his hostility after all the comments we'd heard, but the demand still caught me off guard. I could feel the blood heating my face. My gray skin wouldn't show it, but the Darkness churned in my belly as well. I willed it down.

"No thank you, sir," I replied. I tried to keep my voice even.

"Thought you were enlisting like everyone else, blackeye. Or isn't regular army gear good enough for a Select?"

Of course it wasn't. The troops behind him were armed with wooden spears fitted with roughly forged iron heads that were probably cast in lots of a hundred. Their short swords had probably been horseshoes not long ago.

"Sir, my companion and I are trained scouts. With all due respect, we'll be more effective without standard issue equipment."

Pious took a long step forward and put his face inches from mine. "How about I just take it from you?"

"I wish you wouldn't, sir."

The lieutenant was an intimidating man, big, bad-tempered, and brutal. But he was far from the most frightening person I'd met. He wasn't even in the top five.

He stepped back, and the Darkness settled. It had been beginning to seep out of my palms.

"Fine, keep your toys, blackeye." His unnaturally long arm shot out like a snake and shoved me in the chest. I stumbled back two steps.

"Now get on to the quartermaster and draw gear. All of you worthless maggots. And you two -" he glared at Talot and Bren - "beat it and don't come back with a worthless pile of puke like this again."

He turned on his heel and stalked away.

"Minos?"

"Minos?" Luco repeated.

My face swung toward him and he backed away.

"Next time that paw touches me, he's not getting it back," I gritted. There was a haze around me that I hoped no one else noticed - I couldn't pull it in.

"Come on, Minos, it's okay," Luco cajoled.

I glanced at Cat. She had a wide grin splitting her face. "Not serve, shadow warrior. Leads pack, shadow warrior."

"That's not how it works in the army, Cat," Luco snapped. "We're men, not wolves."

The paleo blew a raspberry at him, still grinning. "Wolves, people, trolls. No different. Will see, you."

"No!" Cat's opinion of military gear was no higher than her opinion of military hierarchy. "Cat is Cat! Cat is not -" she flailed her arms, searching for an analogy - "cow!"

The standard uniform was a linen shirt and breeches, heavy leather boots, and a boiled leather breastplate that felt tough as iron and quite possibly heavier. A leather-lined iron cap, a wooden shield, and the low-grade spear and sword I'd seen before completed the load.

I had taken the armor, the shield, and the miserable spear. I'd told the quartermaster he could keep his pot-metal sword.

Cat was having none of it.

"At least take the spear, Cat," I wheedled. "I'll show you how to use it."

"Oh, yes," she snapped. "Stand in line, me. Hold spear, me. Horseman comes, in goes spear, up goes Cat, Cat goes for ride. Cat insults rider while she hangs on?"

I had to laugh at the image of the skinny paleo being carried away after plunging her weapon into a cavalry mount but not having enough weight to slow it down.

"Fine. Then take this." I handed her the ancient knife of glassy metal. "You're not going to stab through armor with a sharpened bone."

She snorted. "Not stab through armor, me. Stab *around* armor, me."

But she took the long knife. Pulling the weapon clear of its black sheath, she turned it, admiring the play of light along the blade. She tested the edge with her thumb, then jerked it away and sucked at a drop of blood.

"Good," she announced. She thrust the sheath through her rawhide belt, pulled out the bone that had been her only possession, and threw it away.

"You don't want to keep it?"

"Why?" She patted the new blade. "Better."

The paleos cultivated a detachment from material things. In that, at least, my exiled apprentice was a model of her people.

"I wouldn't mind you teaching me to use this spear," Luco interjected. "Since we missed the first two weeks of basic training after you were in such a rush to reach this heaven on earth."

"Sure. But let's get back to our platoon first. Pious hates us enough already."

We were still the last of the recruits to return.

Pious' camp was a rough circle of tents and bedrolls around a fire pit. As we approached, a man with his hair long on the left side of his head and shaved on the right leered at us.

"Scouts got lost finding their way back?"

The ear was missing on the shaven side. He'd tattooed a skull on his face, offset forty-five degrees. The skull's left eye was his right. The skull's right eye was the hole where his ear should have been. In addition to the unit blazes we had on our armor, his had a sergeant's studs.

"We got turned around, but Cat was able to find it by the smell," I replied.

He barked a laugh. "The lieutenant's gonna love that sense of humor. If he doesn't kill you first. Pretty sure he'll kill you first."

"Everybody dies sometime." Although in a fight between me and the lieutenant, I wouldn't be the one to be killed.

"Ain't that the truth. You're a little late for chow, but grab your bowl and have at what's left of the stew. Then we'll get you squared away. You got your pick of places to sleep." He swept the camp with his arm. "As long as you like the ground."

Along with the armor and weapons, we had each been issued a bedroll, a tin bowl, a spoon, a leather water skin, and a short, broad-bladed knife. It was all of mediocre quality at best; Luco and I already carried better examples of each piece of gear and had politely refused. Cat had accepted hers with ill grace, but was now the first to dip her bowl in the lukewarm stew. As always, she bolted the food as if it were the first she'd seen in weeks.

I wasn't as enthusiastic, but it wasn't awful. There was a stringy meat that I suspected was an army mule that had reached the end of its service. Still, it made a nice change from hard bread and pemmican.

"Fall in!"

Luco and I jumped to our feet. The tattooed sergeant stood behind us with a villainous grin. Cat looked at me quizzically.

"It means we line up with the other soldiers," I explained.

"Why?"

"Because he told us to."

"Leader, him?" Cat made a scoffing sound.

"Just line up, Cat."

"Shadow warrior, you. Cat, me. Not ants, us," she muttered. But she got in line with us and the other troopers forming up.

There were about two dozen in the platoon, not counting the nine in our recruit group. The veterans snapped to position with a speed and precision that spoke of practice - and perhaps fear. The rest of us shuffled awkwardly into place.

The tattooed man and another squat, bulky sergeant paced the length of the formation, prodding recruits into position with the butts of their spears. Then Pious appeared, stalking down the line like a hunting cat. He carried a military pick in his right hand, a massive, iron-headed hammer with a wicked spike projecting from it.

His veterans tensed to quivering attention, but Pious' focus wasn't on them. He headed straight for Cat. She didn't flinch from his glare.

The hulking lieutenant turned to me. "Your pet isn't in uniform, blackeye."

"A scout's not very stealthy in white linen and armor. Sir." The shirt and breeches were more the color of pine wood, and not much lighter than Cat's pale skin. But the principle was valid.

"I'm pretty sure I ordered you all to draw gear," Pious drawled. "And I'm pretty sure none of my soldiers would think of disobeying me. But maybe..." his eyes locked on mine, "maybe this here is your dog. And we couldn't expect a dog to wear a uniform, could we?"

There was snickering in the ranks.

"Cat, me. Not dog," the paleo growled.

"Well. Some kind of pet animal." Pious shrugged, then his left arm lashed out. Cat was quick enough to roll with the blow, though not avoid it. A shove that had sent me staggering flung her into the air, but she landed lightly and rolled to her feet. Her teeth were bared.

"Watch your beast, blackeye. It looks vicious. If it bites, I'll have to put it down."

"We'll be careful. Sir."

He stepped in close. "I don't know why that lazy bastard Tir sent you to me," he growled. "I don't know if he thought I could use you. If he did, he's not just lazy but stupid besides. Or maybe he thought I'd grind you down. That I can do. I can tell you've seen fights, boy, but believe me, I'm something completely different."

"I don't doubt it, sir." For a wonder, I managed to keep the contemptuous sneer off my face.

We settled into a kind of rhythm. Morning inspection, followed by breakfast - stew. Then calisthenics, formation drills, and combat drills. None of the troops were close to my equal with sword or spear. Pious noticed but made no comment. Then lunch - stew. A rest period, and more drills. Then dinner - stew. Inspection again, and we were dismissed. Most of the troops were in their bedrolls by the time the sun went down.

The stew declined in quality as the days went by. The mule seemed to have been a high point. I found myself hoping another one would expire.

323

Pious' opinion of me didn't improve either. He was always ready to send a snarl, a shove, or an insult my way. Luco and Cat suffered by association. He was cruel to all his men, but to us especially.

At least I was able to spend time teaching Luco the basics of the sword and spear. He turned out to have a natural talent for them, and quickly became as proficient as most of the other soldiers. Even Cat began to practice with the weapons, though she refused to learn to march or be part of a formation.

"Cat, me," was her disdainful response whenever I prodded her.

Pious promoted a new sergeant to supervise the recruits, a big man named Groff. He was, if not friendly, at least not hostile to us. Which seemed only fair - we had, after all, gotten him promoted.

"What's the story with Pious?" I asked one night. "He talks about the armies of the righteous sometimes, but I've never seen him pray."

That thought sent my mind painfully back to Prophetess, who'd prayed every night. "Or was he born with that name?"

Groff leaned in close. "Nah. He picked up that handle when he was a sergeant. He came up through the ranks, y'know, like you and me."

"Natural leader, huh?" I tried to keep the sarcasm out of my tone.

"Big, mean, and tough as hell. Comes back to the name. The Monolith officers, them Paladins? He likes crucifying 'em. Says if they're such fanatics, he wants to do his bit to bring 'em closer to God."

I might have underestimated the lieutenant. "Those Paladins are tough. How many has he killed?"

"Half a dozen, maybe. Thing is, first thing a Paladin does in a fight, he brings up that big shield they use. So Pious, *wham!*, he sweeps in with the pick, digs it into the shield, just rips it right out of the fellow's hand. Then, *bam!*, hits him with the backswing. Long as his arms are, he's faster than he looks, and that pick hits like God himself was swinging it."

I thought about that, then smiled. "Does he crucify everyone he doesn't like, or just Paladins?"

"Everyone else dies the regular way, but they still get wherever they're going with his mark on 'em. You looked at the point of that pick? It's shaped like a cross. If he sticks it in your skull, you'll have your very own personal blessing from the Father and the Son and the Holy Spirit while your brains leak out."

I winced.

"I've seen you fight, Minos. I know you can handle yourself - better'n me, I don't doubt. But you keep pissing off Pious, some day he's gonna lose it, and you're gonna end up dead. He's not an officer 'cause he's a great leader, though he's not the worst I've seen in this army. He got where he is 'cause he's a one-man wrecking crew, and you don't want to be in his way. I know they say you used to be with the Darkness Radiant, but I don't know if even there they had anyone quite like him."

Quite like him? Not that I'd met. Would Yoshana or Grigg or even Roshel have been afraid of him? Of course not.

But maybe I was, now, just a little bit.

"All right, you worthless sacks of skin!" Pious was bellowing at us louder than usual at morning inspection. "Pack your gear and tighten your boots! We're moving out. Got us some Pallies to kill."

Unlike some of the veterans, I had no tent to break down. I was ready to march in minutes. I caught up with Groff as he was chivying some of the recruits.

"We know where we're going?"

"There's a Monolith force camped about four days northwest of here at an abandoned town. Riverside, I think it's called. They've been using it as a base for attacks on the Whitewater. We thought they might come to us here, but since they haven't, we're going to them."

"I think I know the place. Cat and I passed something that fits the description on our way south."

"Huh. How do you like our chances?"

I considered. "I think there's more of us than them, unless they've reinforced it. Not much of a wall, and what there was of it wasn't in good shape. I couldn't say about relative readiness."

"I'll pass it on to Pious. You really might be useful if you live."

So of course the lieutenant posted us at the back of the column.

"We're trained scouts!" Technically a lie, but the substance was true enough. "Wouldn't it make sense to have us out front? Sir?"

His eyes narrowed so much they practically disappeared. "I'd heard you blackeyes were smart. You still don't seem to have chain of command figured out. You go where I tell you. And your little dog, too."

The Darkness swirled behind my eyes, but I nodded tightly. "Yes, sir."

As I turned, Pious said, "Blackeye. This platoon is on point. We're the tip of the spear. You and your pet will be plenty close enough to the fighting."

His laughter rang nastily behind me as I walked away.

The lieutenant himself walked point. Whatever I thought of his intelligence or leadership - which was very little - I had no doubt of his physical courage. Of course, you could say the same of the paleos, or the mad, Darkness-infested natives of the Sorrows... or for that matter the drelb. I wouldn't have wanted any of them for my commanding officer either.

First squad was led by the tattooed sergeant, Railes, and followed behind Pious. Third squad - our unit - was in the rear. Groff posted Cat and me to the very back of the formation.

"If you can't be up front, at least you can make sure nothing's sneaking up behind us," he explained.

Two roads led north from the huge field where the army was marshaled. We took the western-most of the two. The theory was that we would converge on Riverside in a pincer movement. I had little confidence this force could coordinate or communicate well enough to pull that off, but I wasn't in charge.

Within a mile of the camp, the woods had closed in around us, reducing the road to a narrow track. It was so little used that leaves and other debris had composted down into soil over the centuries, creating a weed-clogged surface. The forest had encroached far beyond where the original margins of the asphalt must have been. We marched two abreast - there would have barely been room for more. The supply wagons behind us would have tough going.

Cat ghosted into the trees, pacing us. I tracked her with a thin tendril of the Darkness; she was silent and invisible to normal senses. I stretched more threads into the woods in front of me. From the back of the column, I could only extend myself some fifty yards beyond Pious.

A bear - the regular kind, not a drelb - followed us curiously for a time, thirty yards to our left. Cat noticed it too, but it approached no closer, and then abruptly took fright and loped off into the deep woods. Nothing more eventful happened that day. Compared to trekking through the Sorrows with the Darkness Radiant, this was almost literally a walk in the park.

Pious originally ordered us to make camp among the trees as the sun sank in the west. He changed his mind when we realized the ground was pierced everywhere with outcroppings of limestone, as if the bones of the world were protruding from its flesh. There wasn't a flat surface to be found. I was amazed Cat had navigated it without stumbling. We camped on the road instead.

Groff jogged back to inform the next unit in line that we were stopping. He was gone for over an hour. The second platoon was several miles behind. I had less faith than ever in our ability to converge on a target three more days away.

I found myself missing the stew. The supply train was far behind us, and we were living out of our packs. It was hard bread and pemmican again.

"Stay close," I said to Luco and Cat as we spread our bedrolls. I picked a spot well back from the others, though not so far it would appear that I was deliberately separating us. I wanted my warding circle wide enough to give me some warning. Not that I thought we were likely to be ambushed, or set upon by wolves… or that Pious would smash my head in while I slept. But it didn't pay to be careless.

The second day was an almost perfect copy of the first. Except that when Groff trotted back to the platoon behind us, he didn't return for three hours.

"They must be at least six miles back," he panted as he trudged past me to report to Pious.

I exchanged glances with Luco.

"Don't do it," he said.

"Somebody has to."

"Yeah, but not you. Especially not you."

I got up anyway. Cat grinned. I passed Groff coming back as I made my way forward. "Don't do it," he said.

"Yeah, I've heard that. Did he listen to you?"

Groff barked out a scoffing laugh. "Me? I don't tell him what to do. I aim to survive my enlistment."

"When a commander's subordinates are afraid to give him advice, he becomes a bad commander."

"You're gonna die, you know."

"Yeah, that happens to people."

Pious, Railes, and a handful of soldiers were sitting around a small fire. I braced to attention and saluted.

"Something you want, blackeye?" A couple of the men chuckled. The tattooed sergeant grinned broadly. It twisted the skull's expression into a grimace.

"Sir. We're getting too far ahead of the following elements to provide an adequate screen. And they can't support us if we're ambushed. I recommend tomorrow we hold position until they catch up."

He pushed himself slowly to his feet.

"You recommend, do you? Still a little unclear on the chain of command, blackeye?" He took a step closer.

Railes met my eye. He mouthed the words, "Take it."

I knew what was coming this time. As Pious' arm whipped around in an open-handed slap, the Darkness flooded my veins, and I pivoted away, my left hand coming up and the Darkness lancing into his wrist and searing the bones as my fist closed and crushed - in my mind.

Back in the real world, his palm slammed into the side of my face and sent me spinning to the ground.

"Recommendation noted," he said. "If you're too much of a coward to move forward unsupported, you have my permission to fall back to where it's safer."

I picked myself up. "Not necessary, sir. Thank you."

He grinned at me as he sat. "Dismissed."

Railes nodded to me, just a little, as the others chortled.

Luco stared at the livid mark on my cheek. "Thought you were going to take his hand off the next time he hit you."

"Changed my mind." I willed the swollen tissues under my skin to heal, the pooled blood to reabsorb.

Luco goggled at me. "How did you do that?"

"The same way I take somebody's hand off."

Cat laughed. I smiled, lay down in my bedroll, and closed my eyes to begin the meditation that would control the murderous rage still flowing in me, so it wouldn't manifest in a killing cloud in my sleep. The Darkness showed Luco staring at me wide-eyed.

It was close to noon on the third day when I sensed the first ambusher ahead of our column in the forest to our left. The next was only two paces away, then another. Each was armed with a bow and a sword.

I stabbed the single word, *Come!* into Cat's consciousness. We had never communicated that way before, but she was at my side in seconds.

"Enemies ahead," I hissed. "Get behind them. Don't attack until we do."

"Kill, now." She grinned and vanished into the trees.

I had to hope she understood "now" meant "soon," not "immediately." Trying to act nonchalant, I quickened my pace toward the head of our column. As I advanced, I sensed more and more attackers ahead of us. There were dozens, thickly lining the road. Where the path curved ahead, a blocking force waited with pikes and shields. The archers would feather us when we bottled up against the pikemen.

By the time I reached Pious, he and a dozen others were already in the killing zone. I leaned in and whispered, "Sir, we're in an ambush. There's bowmen in the woods and a blocking force around that bend."

He shrugged his arm at me like a horse twitching a fly off its hide. "Your dog tell you that? She's got a hell of a nose if she can smell all that from the ass end of the line." And he laughed.

"Dammit, Lieutenant!"

He turned on me with fury in his eyes, and then there were no options left.

I leapt into the trees. They were not tightly spaced, but leafy branches grew between them, screening the ambushers. I flung Darkness into the eyes of the nearest and rammed my spear through his chest as he screamed. He wore a cloth jerkin of striped green and brown that helped him blend into the foliage but provided no protection at all.

I left the spear where it was and pulled my katana clear. The Darkness swirled around me and I turned on the man to my right, slashing with my blade and the black cloud both. The bowman shrieked, fell over backwards, and loosed his arrow into the air. My sword missed him entirely but the Darkness scored bloody furrows across his face. I sensed the man behind me turning to shoot, and spun to fling the katana at him. The blade fouled his shot and struck him a glancing blow to the shoulder. I leapt at him and punched him in the face, raining blow after blow with the inhuman strength of hell coursing through my blood. I stopped when he went limp.

Half our group had already entered the trap. When I sprang it, the archers began to loose. The cry of "Ambush!" erupted from a dozen throats.

I reclaimed my katana and continued down the enemy line as Pious blundered into the underbrush, swinging his hammer in a wild arc. An enemy stumbled away from him and I cut the man down from behind. Railes was following me, and I shouted "North!" over my shoulder. To the south, our men were moving into the woods to engage the attackers.

I spun back the way I had come. The bowman whose face I had slashed with the Darkness was crashing away through the woods. I let him go. Past him, Pious had taken an arrow in the thigh but had smashed his assailant's face to a bloody ruin. Another fired wildly at the lieutenant, hitting nothing. Pious roared and charged, but the vicious swing of his pick caught on a sapling. He roared louder still in frustrated rage.

"Retreat!" his attacker screamed as he threw down his bow and ran. I reached past Pious and wrapped the Darkness around the next man's throat, squeezing and tearing. The lieutenant hammered him as he fell, crushing his chest.

"Retreat! Demons! Retreat!" Panic spread like a fever among the ambushers. They blundered away into the woods in a clumsy, desperate rush utterly at odds with the carefully laid trap.

Pious turned and glowered at me. "I'm having you brought up on charges, blackeye."

Pious and I were still sitting across from each other, glaring like angry dogs, when Captain Almet came up three hours later. Four of our men were laid out dead in the road, killed in the initial hail of arrows. Three more besides Pious were wounded - two shot, one slashed with a sword, I suspected possibly his own as he charged into the woods.

Sergeant Erlston, the leader of second squad, was a passable field medic. He had pulled the arrow from the lieutenant's thigh and bandaged the wound. The shaft had penetrated into the meat but not struck any major blood vessels. The man who had taken the sword cut had a shallow, clean gash in his leg which had been easily bandaged. Our other wounded weren't so lucky. One was pierced through the shoulder, the other in the upper thigh near the groin. The latter was white-faced and breathing in rapid, shallow gasps. Erlston had tied off the leg, and he would lose it. Even so I didn't think he'd live. I had tried to insinuate the Darkness into the wound to stop the bleeding, but beyond that I didn't know how to help.

Nine enemies lay dead. Cat had stabbed three from behind, killing more than anyone else. And the man I had beaten with my fists was still unconscious, our only prisoner.

Almet was a trim man of middle height. He stamped angrily up to us, trailed by a coterie of aides and Sergeant Groff, who had once again been sent back to report.

"What the hell happened here?" he demanded.

Pious was on his feet with amazing agility for a wounded man. I was a second slower. We both braced and saluted.

"Sir, the enemy set a trap," Pious declared. "The blackeye here sprung it, and four of my men were killed and three more injured. His loyalty and judgment are both wanting. With your permission I'll have him whipped, stripped of his weapons, and dishonorably discharged."

I breathed very slowly, struggling to settle what was boiling behind my eyes.

The captain turned to Railes. "Sergeant, your assessment?"

"Sir, Minos, that's the Select, detected the ambush. He charged into it and took them by surprise, disrupting it. Half our platoon was already inside their kill zone. As the lieutenant said, we took casualties accordingly."

"Captain -" Pious interjected.

"Pious, you're an idiot," Almost snapped. "Shut your stupid mouth. You're already reduced in rank to sergeant. If I hear another word from you, you're a line trooper. You took your platoon too far forward to screen the main body of our force or be supported by it. Then you blundered into an ambush. By a miracle, there's twice as many of them dead as there are of ours, which I'm guessing is due entirely to the Select here."

Pious' mouth opened like a carp's. The captain looked at me. "Minos, is it? Report."

"Sir. The enemy deployed a variant of an L-shaped ambush, with bowmen lining the road and a blocking force around the bend ahead. As Sergeant Railes said, I judged the only option was attack… as Lieutenant Pious did not believe my report of the threat."

Pious glared daggers at me. If looks could kill, that one would have taken my head off.

Almet looked thoughtfully at the terrain. "And how exactly did you determine the shape of the ambush, trooper?"

This was the moment of truth. "Like this, sir." A sphere of Darkness formed over my upturned palm.

"God!" Almet exclaimed, and stepped back. So did most of the men around me, including Pious, Groff, and Luco. Cat just grinned. To my surprise, so did Sergeant Railes.

"Sergeant Groff mentioned you had been with the Darkness Radiant," Almet said carefully. "He didn't, ah…"

"No one asked," I replied. "I was *very* close to Yoshana, though not for long. She trained me personally for a particular set of missions."

"Those being?"

"Crossing the Sorrows, killing a demon, and assassinating Prophetess at Our Lady."

The captain's eyes were wide as saucers. He considered silently for a time, then said, "And did you?"

"In order, sir? Yes, no, and no. I had escorted Prophetess north from Rockwall to Our Lady. She's a friend of mine. Yoshana is very persuasive - and infinitely terrifying - but I wasn't going to kill my friend."

"And so how do you come to be here?"

"I returned to Our Lady and offered them my services and my abilities. As you might imagine -" though I hadn't at the time - "they weren't interested in using what they believe to be the powers of hell."

Almet nodded tightly. "Then their loss is our gain. I don't intend to give up the advantage of having a master of the Darkness on this campaign. Lieutenant Minos, it's obvious we need a recon platoon. You can choose whatever elements you want from Sergeant Pious' former unit. The rest will be reassigned. We'll find other recruits for you as you see the need."

"Thank you, sir. I'd like Troopers Cat and Luco, as well as Sergeants Railes and Groff. Also Troopers Ascon, Taba…" I considered and named another half-dozen soldiers I thought showed promise and would work with me.

It was petty, but the Darkness was still thick in my veins. I turned to Pious and said, "Sergeant? It should go without saying that if you ever touch me again, I'll kill you."

Almet's eyebrows went up, but he didn't say a word. Cat threw back her head and laughed. And I felt a fierce surge of joy as a veil of fear drew across the naked hatred in Pious' eyes.

"What are we up against?" Almet asked. We were sitting under a tarp stretched across poles. Each of us had a mug of cider. It was lukewarm, but better than the mildly questionable water I'd been drinking. It was good to be an officer.

"Sir, there were at least three dozen of them. The ambush was well-sited. They had appropriate weapons and camouflage. They knew what they were doing."

"That many? And you still drove them off?"

"Sir, they panicked. Say what you want about Pious," and I didn't have much good to say about him, "but he's scary in a fight. If they'd held, I don't think it would have gone our way."

"Pious is a moron. Or maybe to be a little fairer, he only knows how to do one thing. I promoted him past where he was useful." The captain sighed. "Speaking of leadership, did they have a Paladin in charge?"

"Sir, I don't know. Almost all of them were out of my line of sight, and at that kind of range the Darkness doesn't give me a lot of details."

He rubbed his hand across his eyes. "I don't suppose it matters. What I'm not quite sure of is why they did it. If the ambush had worked, it would have taken out one platoon in an entire battalion. It's annoying and demoralizing, but they've forfeited the element of surprise. Now we know they've scouted us."

"To delay us, sir. Don't you think? It was going to be hard enough coordinating the pincers. If they harass and delay our column, and let the other walk into a trap unsupported…"

"Damn! That feels right. I'll send a courier back to Colonel Royce and another through the woods to warn First Battalion."

"If I'm right, they'll have pickets in the woods to prevent that. I'll take my unit. That's what you created us for."

"And if you're right, you'll be walking into a trap."

I grinned. "Yessir. Looking forward to it, sir."

5. The Shadowed Hand

Logistics were easy enough. We rubbed dirt on our linen clothes to darken them. Armor, shields, and spears were left behind - we were a reconnaissance force, not a heavy combat force. We drew extra water skins from the quartermaster. They weighed us down, but would save time stopping to boil water for refills. Cat and I could probably drink anything without purifying it, but a bout of dysentery for the rest of the platoon would be somewhere between embarrassing and fatal.

The larger issue was that, for all my bravado, we weren't well suited to the task at hand. Cat was as stealthy as her namesake and just as lethal if she could strike by surprise, but her recent training in weapons couldn't make up for the fact that she weighed half as much as most soldiers. The rest of the platoon had the opposite problem - they were all competent fighters but I had no reason to believe any of them could move quietly through the woods.

But we would make do. If the Monolith forces were truly stringing pickets to intercept couriers, I assumed they would have to be spread fairly far apart - otherwise the manpower commitment would be unmanageable. I had to hope our force of a baker's dozen would be enough to overcome whatever we encountered.

We deployed in an arrowhead formation. I was in front, Cat and Railes behind on my left and right flanks. The others spread behind them. I extended a screen of the Darkness in a semicircle sixty yards in front of me, sacrificing range for width of coverage.

"Kill, now," Cat said smugly. "Not ant, not dog, not vulture, now. Shadow warriors."

The forest floor was thickly carpeted with pine needles. The paleo was silent as a shadow. I like to think I made no more noise than the chipmunks and squirrels that rustled through the underbrush. The rest of my team - let's just say we weren't likely to pass undetected.

The forest thinned and thickened, following no pattern I could discern. Where the sight lines were shorter, I was confident I could sense any pickets before they saw us, even if they heard us coming. Where the trees opened up, it was very likely a concealed enemy would see us long before we saw him. I just had to hope no one would try a sixty-yard shot.

Captain Almet thought the road the First Battalion was traveling was between five and ten miles away. Hopefully we would reach it before nightfall.

We had hopped over a small gully and were climbing the slope on the other side when I sensed the enemy almost directly in front of us. There were two of them, and they were alert.

I held up my hand, and the platoon halted behind me. I winced at the sounds of leaves and twigs crunching as the men went to ground.

Pulling the Darkness in, I sent concentrated tendrils forward. I didn't have Yoshana's fine control, especially at this distance, but time was on my side. When a sufficiently thick mass had oozed into each ambusher's throat, I set it into a ravening fury, tearing at blood vessels.

One of them somehow choked out a cry for help.

"Dammit! Get them!" I bellowed.

We charged up the slope. Both men were in plain view, flailing at the air and clutching their necks.

Railes already had his sword out and bulled ahead of me. Without breaking stride, he thrust the blade hilt-deep up under one man's ribcage.

Three paces behind, it took me a handful of seconds longer to unsheathe the katana and dispatch the other.

Odem, the only one of the new recruits I'd brought into the tiny platoon, was noisily sick.

"Puke later," Railes snarled. He seized a dead man's bow and fitted an arrow. "Incoming."

Two more of the Monolith soldiers were coming in from our left. The sergeant sent a shaft looping toward them. It missed, but they slowed and ducked into a stand of bushes. Railes cursed and fumbled for another arrow.

The rest of the platoon had reached our position. The Monolith troops, reassessing the odds, popped up to run. Cat appeared behind one and plunged her shining knife into his kidneys over and over again. As the other turned, Railes sighted more carefully and shot him through the shoulder. He gasped in pain, and the paleo leapt on him and slashed his throat.

"Two more hightailing it that way," Luco said, pointing to the right.

"Looks like there's a pair of them every hundred yards or so. Those two'll keep going until they've got enough friends to deal with us. We need to be gone by then. Take anything you can use from the corpses and let's go."

Odem came up to me, eyes downcast. "Sorry, Lieutenant."

I clapped him on the shoulder. "A wise woman once told me every life, even our enemies', belongs to God. I don't know that I agree with her, but there's nothing wrong with the sentiment. It's hard the first time you see a man killed."

"Was that Prophetess, sir?" he asked, his eyes lighting up.

"Yes it was."

I had killed three men today and contributed to the deaths of more. They had all been trying to kill me... but I was a bit surprised to find I felt no remorse at all.

Yoshana would be proud.

The pickets didn't organize fast enough to catch us. And there wasn't a second line of them. We reached First Battalion shortly before sundown without further incident - other than almost being shot by our own sentries. For once, though, my race worked in my favor. When I emerged from the woods loudly announcing, "Couriers from Second Battalion," I was actually recognized.

"It's that Select from Captain Almet's company," a grizzled sergeant declared. "Let him through."

"Thank you, Sergeant. We have an urgent message for Colonel Hake. Could you have someone escort us?"

The man peered at the bronze lieutenant's rank tabs pinned to my shoulders. "Pretty sure you were a line trooper three days ago. That's gotta be the fastest promotion in history. Uh, sir."

"Needs must when the devil drives, or however that phrase goes, Sergeant. We sort of stepped in it over there."

He goggled. "You lost so many officers they're promoting new recruits?"

I had to laugh. "No, nothing like that. But we needed a recon platoon, and Captain Almet wanted me running it. Now if we could see the colonel."

"Oh. Yessir. Sorry, sir."

The Darkness thrived on rage, lust, and fear. But I discovered that it didn't mind the taste of self-satisfaction.

Heads turned and whispers started up as we made our way north - we had met up with one of the last units in the column. I supposed that a Select, a paleo, and a man with a skull tattooed over half his face were worthy of comment.

Colonel Hake was surrounded by a headquarters company of clerks, adjutants, and assorted hangers-on. Sergeant Herin, who was guiding us himself, cut through them like a knife through butter. It was amazing the way, "begging your pardon, sir" could sound so much like "get the hell out of the way."

This roadway was considerably wider than the one our battalion had been using. Still, the colonel's command tent took up most of it.

"Courier from Second Battalion for Colonel Hake," our guide announced to the sentry.

"He's eating," the soldier drawled, utterly unconcerned.

"You're going to be eating my fist if you don't let us in, you twit. Second Battalion's had heavy contact with the enemy. You really think the colonel's gonna want to wait to hear that?"

The sentry paled and vanished through the tent flap. Herin winked at me.

The soldier reappeared moments later. "He'll see you."

I went in alone. Cat and Railes were my most trusted subordinates. Both were savage in appearance, spattered with blood, and didn't seem fit for polite company. Of course, I probably didn't look much better.

Hake was an older man, slightly below average height but well above average weight, reclining in a camp chair with a folding table in front of him. I had to guess he rode rather than marching. I felt sorry for the horse.

I braced to attention and saluted.

Hake returned it with a lazy wave. He peered at my rank tabs. "Huh. I knew Colonel Royce had a Select recruit in his battalion. I didn't know he had a Select lieutenant."

"Same one, sir. Battlefield promotion."

Hake made a harrumphing sound. "That's one hell of a fast promotion, boy. What the devil's going on over there? Bline said you'd engaged the enemy."

"It might be more accurate to say they engaged us, sir. Our lead platoon was ambushed around noon today."

"Lieutenant Pious' platoon, that would be? How'd they come through?"

It struck me that Hake might be fat, but he was no fool. To know who was commanding the other column's point platoon showed a fine knowledge of tactical detail.

"We did all right, sir. Four dead, four wounded, including Lieutenant Pious. Er. Sergeant Pious, now."

"Got his dumb ass demoted for blundering into it?"

"Something like that, sir."

The colonel leaned back farther in his chair and looked me in the eyes. "Pious is a bloodthirsty jackass. He can kill like a demon from hell, though. Royce and Almet wanted to reward him. Thought the troops would appreciate seeing one of their own made an officer. Stupid idea."

His eyes didn't leave mine. "You said 'we did all right.' You were there, were you?"

I nodded.

"And now you have Pious' platoon?"

"Not exactly, sir. Captain Almet wanted a recon platoon after what happened. I took some of Pious' men."

"A word of advice, boy. Lots of people aren't going to be too pleased about a Select getting jumped up from new recruit to lieutenant. I know your people have a military tradition, but still… don't get ahead of yourself. Don't be the next Pious."

I suppose he meant well. Still, the comparison raised my hackles. Whether it was wise or not, a demonstration was in order. "Sir, with all due respect, I'm considerably more than the next Pious."

Before he could retort, the Darkness was forming over my hand, first as a sphere, then as a gently winding helix. Hake nearly fell over backwards in his chair. I suppressed a grin.

"Sir, I was personally trained by Yoshana in the command of the Darkness."

The colonel had righted himself and was watching my display with a raised eyebrow. "And I suppose Almet thought that was too good an opportunity to waste."

"Yes, sir."

"Yeah. He would. Let's hope he's right. I think we'd better have the rest of your report, Lieutenant."

"Sir, after the ambush, I - that is, Captain Almet concluded that the enemy may be seeking to delay Second Battalion so that First Battalion walks into a larger enemy force unsupported, preventing the pincer from closing and defeating us in detail."

"Captain Almet concluded that, did he?"

"Yes, sir."

"Seems plausible." Hake took a deep breath and exhaled noisily. "And he sent his new recon platoon to report this conclusion?"

"Sir, we - that is, Captain Almet believed there might be enemy pickets posted between our forces to intercept couriers, so he felt it would be prudent to send a stronger group rather than a single man."

"I see. And were there pickets?"

"Yes, sir. Posted in pairs, about a hundred yards between each pair. We killed four. Another pair approached but disengaged."

"I imagine they did." He steepled his fingers and stared at me. "Your hypothesis - that is, your captain's hypothesis - seems reasonable enough. If it's true, we'll need regular courier contact between the battalions to maintain coordination."

"Yes, sir. My unit can continue to provide that."

"Yes. Was that Sergeant Herin who brought you here?"

"Yes, sir."

"Thought I recognized his voice. He can get your unit set up with carbines. Tell him it's on my orders. He'll make it happen. You can cross back over tomorrow."

I hesitated, then said, "Sir, I appreciate the offer, but the noise from the carbines will pinpoint us for the enemy. We scavenged four bows, and could use a few others."

He chuckled. "Your men are all trained archers, then?"

"Well, er, not that I know, sir."

"A bow's an excellent weapon for a scout who knows how to use it. But the skill's not trivial to learn. With the gun, you point it and shoot."

"Understood, sir. But we didn't have any trouble coming through this way. I doubt it will be any harder going back."

Hake levered himself out of his chair and took a step closer to me. "Maybe. Maybe not. Your enemy may well be too stupid to adapt to past failure. They may get dispirited and run off. Or they might try something new. Your opponent may well be an idiot, Lieutenant, but it's best not to count on it."

"Yes, sir."

He came a step closer still. Short and fat as he was, there was something about him that reminded me of a bulldog. "I said don't be the next Pious, son. You're smarter than he is, and I suppose you're even more dangerous. But that doesn't mean you can't step in it good by not thinking or not listening."

"Understood, sir." And I did understand. It was a fair point from a senior officer to a very junior one.

"Dismissed, then. Get those carbines, and have Herin fix you up with some food and bedrolls."

"Yes, sir. Thank you, sir." I snapped to attention, then turned to go. But because I was me, I added over my shoulder, "Sir? You said Pious fought like a demon. I've met a demon. Pious wouldn't last a second."

Hake grunted. "Overlords, demons, and Darkness. You are going to be a monumental pain in my ass, Lieutenant. Get going before you tell me something else that'll damn me to hell just for listening."

"Yes, sir. Sorry, sir." My back was to him, so I didn't bother keeping the grin off my face. He muttered something under his breath that I'm pretty sure was, "No, you're not."

Herin proved as ruthlessly effective at organizing gear for us as he'd been at securing an audience with the colonel. He slid around officers with vague allusions to orders from Colonel Hake. Enlisted men he simply bullied. We made our way to the front of the column, collecting weapons, bedrolls, and food as we went.

"I imagine you'll need to be up here first thing, sir? I figured it was easier to get you in place before you settle in." He had cleared a spot for us near the point platoon, then chivied troops to make us a fire.

"Yes, Sergeant. Perfect." In fact, he was a step ahead of me. Herin was a weathered stump of a man, but like Hake, he was not someone to underestimate.

The next morning, better fed and better equipped, we were heading back through the woods to Second Battalion.

"Lift feet *up*, you," Cat was chiding Luco in a hissing whisper. "Not scrape, scrape, scrape. *Look* where feet go down. Not on sticks. Not on dry leaves." Luco clumsily tried to copy her, and it did seem to cut down on the noise a bit.

"Alert! Sector thirteen! Alert! Sector thirteen!"

The shouting was ahead of us and to the right. The stationary pickets had seen us moving before we'd seen them. And this time they were calling for help before they engaged. Hake had been right - it didn't pay to assume the enemy was stupid.

"Alert! Sector thirteen!" sounded to the left, and then further to the right.

"Damn. Charge!" I bellowed. No chance for finesse here. We crashed through the trees toward the source of the first calls.

An arrow whistled past my ear, maybe a yard away.

"Groff, Ascon, Taba, Storr, suppressing fire!" I yelled. "Everyone else with me!"

Carbines opened up behind me. I doubted they came close to hitting anyone, but they kept the enemies' heads down. No more arrows came at us.

The Darkness was in its sixty-yard semicircle, and it pinpointed three bowmen crouched behind a boulder. I waved Cat and Railes around the flanks and went straight over the top. The Darkness preceded me and clawed at the men's eyes. It was over in seconds.

"Form up here," I called, cleaning and sheathing my katana and unslinging my carbine. "They'll flank from the left and right."

But they didn't. My troops formed a defensive circle around the huge rock, but no one came at us.

"They run off?" Luco asked. "Guns maybe scared 'em away?"

I shook my head. "I don't think so. I'm betting they've got some kind of mobile reserve headed for us. They learned from last time - they're not going to throw two or three-man squads at us again."

"So what do we do?" demanded Railes.

That was the question. If the enemy had a sense of the size of our unit - and the two men who'd gotten away last time had probably gotten a good look - they'd have made the reserve force big enough to stop us. That might also mean it was far enough away for us to escape it... if we didn't mind having it behind us the whole way back to Second Battalion.

These Monolith troops were better in the woods than most of my platoon. I didn't like the idea of their kill team breathing down our necks while we blundered through the forest.

"We take it to them," I decided. "I don't hear them, so they're coming slow. They'll be positioned ahead of us, to block. Off to the right or left - no way to know which. Cat, you go left. I'll go right. Everyone else stay here. Cat, don't engage. If you find them, report back."

The paleo nodded, grinned her hunter's grin, and disappeared into the trees.

"Here goes," I muttered, and went the other way with the Darkness extended before me.

"I don't like this," I heard Odem whisper as I moved away.

"Don't nobody like it, kid," Railes murmured back. "Just trust the lieutenant, is all."

Easy for him to say. I had no doubt I could keep myself alive. I wasn't nearly so sure I could keep them alive.

Just as our platoon moving through the woods was easier to see than stationary pickets, so the enemy force was louder than one man. They were good, though. They advanced in a kind of leapfrog movement, one soldier moving forward, then going to ground and another moving past. They were spread over a small front, three advancing at once. They were a team of about thirty. I caught up with them not much more than a hundred yards from our position.

My first instinct was to buy us a breathing space. There was no time for subtlety. I sent a thick strand of the Darkness along the forest floor to one of the three soldiers on point. It poured into his mouth and nose and he fell, choking. One of his companions, coming up past him, bent down.

"What the hell?"

I had no coherent plan. My only hope was to panic them. I pushed all the Darkness into a thick cloud that rose above the gagging man's body, then flung it at the soldier who had gone to his aid. He cried out and fell back, slashing at the air with a short sword.

"Demons!" They were a superstitious bunch. They seemed to yell that anytime they encountered something unexpected.

"Set a perimeter!" a voice ordered. Damn. Someone with sense was taking control.

I was on the ground behind a fallen tree. The wraith I was controlling would be nearly invulnerable unless they used fire against it. I had to drive them off before that occurred to them, or a skirmisher found me.

Only vaguely mastered by my own surging thoughts, the Darkness lashed wildly at the man it was enveloping, tearing countless tiny wounds into his skin. He fell to the ground sobbing, curling into a fetal ball. I took deep breaths, steadying my mind, and the cloud exploded from its victim and launched itself at the next soldier.

Only when the noise was almost on top of me did I realize there was shouting not just in front of me, but behind.

Led by Railes, my troops were charging the enemy with swords drawn. A pair of carbines fired, then more.

I stumbled to my feet. "No no no -" I didn't need them in this melee. I didn't want them.

No more than ten yards from me, Odem leapt like a mad thing at the Monolith soldiers. I think the man whose short sword came up reflexively and plunged into the recruit's belly was as surprised as Odem himself.

"No, goddammit!"

The wraith was shattered along with my concentration, but the Darkness flooded back into me as I rushed in and my katana split the Monolith ranger's head open before he could even pull his weapon free of Odem's body. I roared my rage, and the enemy troops broke and ran, leaving weapons behind in their mad flight. A few more gunshots followed the fleeing men, but brought none of them down that I could see.

"Sir?"

I whirled, and my skull-tattooed sergeant took two long steps back and raised his hands. "Sir?"

I drew a deep, shuddering breath and let the katana fall. I couldn't pull the Darkness fully back inside me, but it settled onto my skin, shimmering like a haze of angry smoke.

I knelt next to Odem, but he was already dead. The blade had gone up under his ribcage and pierced his heart. The look on his face was one of total confusion.

Groff came up behind me, but not too close.

"He's our only casualty, sir. I'll carry him," the big sergeant offered.

I shook my head. "No. I will."

Rage and pain and the Darkness in my veins got me back to Second Battalion with Odem still in my arms - or more accurately, slung over my shoulder. He was not a light man, and a corpse is not a balanced load to carry over stone- and root-choked terrain.

Even though the return through the woods had taken us hours, we still reached the road just as the point platoon was approaching. I left the dead recruit and my living troops with them and made my way down the column to find Captain Almet.

"You made it across?" were his first words.

I nodded tightly. "Lost one on the way back. There's a blocking force. They were better organized today than yesterday."

Almet pursed his lips, trying to read my face. I went on, "First Battalion must be fifteen miles ahead of us by now."

He grimaced. "They hit us in the night. Shot up the supply train with fire arrows. Then when we finally got moving this morning they hit the point platoon again. Nothing as sophisticated as what they did to you yesterday - just plinked with a few bowmen and then took off. It slowed us down a lot, though. They're doing what you thought they were."

"Learn anything from the prisoner? Sir?"

"What you'd have guessed already. There's a ranger company out there. Several different platoons harassing us. I spoke to Colonel Royce, but we're not sure what to do about it. We don't have forces that can match them in the woods."

"We halt both columns, sir, until we can deal with the issue. With your permission, I'll cross back over and suggest to Colonel Hake that he hold position until we do."

"We can't just camp in the road for a week," Almet snapped. "How exactly do you suggest we deal with the issue?"

"That's simple, sir," I threw over my shoulder as I turned and stalked back up toward the head of the column. "I'm going to kill them."

"Cat, I want you to spend the next three hours training the platoon in stealth. Then you'd better get some rest, because we're going out again tonight."

She raised her eyebrows. "You?"

"Me? I'm going back across."

"Alone?"

"Yeah. I don't think they'll catch me, and I'll be faster on my own. I should be back before dark. Railes, you're in charge while I'm gone." And with that I was off the road and in among the trees.

Odem's death gnawed at me. I'd lost companions before, in the ambush yesterday and on Yoshana's expedition to the Darklands. I'd exchanged more words with Joav, the tight-lipped Knight of Resurrection who'd died on the edge of the Sorrows, than I had with Odem. But Odem was the first man to die under my command. When it was my fault.

I hadn't left clear orders with the platoon. They'd rushed to help me when they'd thought I was in danger. As indeed I had been, but the mad charge that had gotten Odem killed hadn't been necessary. A frightened boy who'd been trying to prove himself and save his commander had died because I hadn't communicated properly. That ate at my guts as if the Darkness itself had turned on me.

I would have welcomed a patrol of Monolith rangers. What was churning in me needed release. So of course my path through the forest was completely clear of enemies.

Even so, First Battalion was well past when I reached the other roadway. Even the droppings the horses and oxen had left were cold.

Some of my anger had worked itself out in the woods. More leached away into fatigue as I jogged to catch up with the column. "There's such a thing as too much exercise," I muttered.

I was pleased but not surprised to see Sergeant Herin had attached himself to Colonel Hake's headquarters unit.

"Thought you might need me again," he remarked as I trotted up.

"You looking for a job, sergeant?"

"In your platoon, sir? With all due respect, it seems like way too much work and a real good chance of getting killed. But I'm happy to help with logistics."

"That's what I need, sergeant. I've got other guys to die for me," I added bitterly.

"Rough day, sir?"

"Lost one of my men today. He was a newbie. Didn't even have a chance to figure out what he was doing."

Herin nodded. "It happens, sir. Old farts like me get old by being lucky at first. Then we get enough experience to be careful. I'll take you to the colonel."

Once again the sergeant parted the humanity teeming around the colonel like an ice-breaker clearing a frozen river. The column was still in motion, so we found Hake astride a warhorse sturdy enough to handle his bulk.

He looked down at me with a little smile. "Good to see you made it through, Lieutenant."

"Yessir. Thank you for the carbines, sir. And the advice. You were absolutely right. They had adjusted their tactics. They hit us with a full platoon this time."

"Then I'm very glad to see you made it unscathed."

"Not unscathed, sir. I lost a man."

"One man? Against a superior force? You are a terror, aren't you?"

I shook my head. "I don't think my previous commander would have been impressed."

Hake pulled up his horse. "When we spoke yesterday, I told you not to get above yourself. That includes being harder on yourself than strictly necessary. You're not Yoshana. If what they say is true, then no one is except Yoshana.

You had command of your unit for a day. If it didn't perform perfectly, that's no reflection on you or them. If you made a mistake, learn from it. If a man died because you made a mistake, that's a damn shame, but it happens in war every day. Now report, Lieutenant."

I braced to attention. "Sir. Second Battalion is even farther behind - probably fifteen miles by now. They took additional harassing attacks last night and today. I recommend both columns halt until the Monolith rangers responsible are eliminated."

"And let me guess, Lieutenant. You're going to eliminate them."

"Yessir."

"And you really think you can."

"Yessir."

Hake nodded once, sharply. "Then do it."

It was pitch dark, but Cat could still follow the trail from the spot where Second Battalion's point platoon had been attacked. The enemy rangers' woodcraft was good - I doubted anyone but a paleo could have tracked them at night.

My whole unit was going - what was left of us. I'd considered taking just Cat and Railes for greater stealth, but if we were going to exterminate a whole platoon, it would take more than three of us. This time, though, I'd made the team's instructions explicit.

"Cat and I are in the lead. They'll have sentries. We should be able to take them silently, and then we'll get to work on the rest. I only need the rest of you involved if they wake up. If they do, hit them hard and fast with everything we have."

Was it dishonorable and bloodthirsty to ambush the Monolith troops while they slept? Probably. I didn't care. They'd ambushed us. And they'd killed Odem. Maybe if they came to fear the night, the rangers would leave the forest. That was an acceptable alternative. So was the one where they all died.

I winced every time a twig cracked behind me. Ahead of me was only Cat, and she was silent as the shadow of death. But the rest of the team wasn't so noisy, considering. Our hands, faces, and clothes were blackened with soot from cook fires. And we went slowly, giving the paleo time to puzzle out the track. We had all night.

The Darkness ranged in front of us, searching for our foes. An hour or so after we set out, I sensed a small wolf pack pacing us. One animal sniffed at the shifting tendrils, growled deep in its throat, and fled. The others followed. I ignored them and we continued to advance.

We heard the sneeze before Cat or I made contact. Voices followed.

"Jesus! I nearly shat myself. You just woke up the entire Rockwall army."

"Sorry. This pollen is killing me."

I slowly moved up past the paleo. The Darkness showed me a large clearing with three sentries on guard, one rubbing at his nose. Slumbering men turned and grunted in their bedrolls, their sleep disturbed by the noise.

I scowled. It was harder to murder the enemy when they acted human. I crawled backwards past Cat, motioning her to follow, until we rejoined the rest of our platoon.

"Change of plans," I hissed. "The point of the exercise is fear. I'm going in there alone. Don't engage them unless they try to attack me."

Railes shook his head. "The first plan was fine. We can take 'em all."

"We don't need to. This is better."

Even by the wan moonlight filtering through the trees I could tell the sergeant didn't agree, but he said nothing further. We moved up.

I had all the time in the world. Slowly, carefully, I eased the Darkness into the three sentries. Little by little, it flowed into their carotid arteries and blocked the blood flow. One sat down, then the others. Soon, all were unconscious.

I wrapped myself in the Darkness and entered the clearing. Silently I made my way to the center. And there, a dark mass in the thin moonlight, I bellowed, "Paladin!"

I had been right - he was sleeping in the center of the camp. The big man lurching to his feet in front of me, blade coming clear even as he stood, had to be the leader.

Of course, everyone else woke up as well. Most were stunned or sleep-fuddled, but one behind me stumbled up and reached for a bow.

"Sit!" I commanded. He ignored me.

A carbine cracked, then two more. The bowman fell and lay still.

"What are you?" hissed the Paladin, his blade angled toward me. He was a brave man - confronted with a humanoid cloud of blackness I would have run, at least before I became what I now was.

But a fair fight with a brave man didn't suit my purpose. My katana was made to slash, not stab, but it could do the latter when needed. The blade plunged into his heart, his parry failing as his sword fell from a hand rendered nerveless when the Darkness severed his tendons.

I set my left palm on his face as he hung impaled on my steel. The Darkness etched my handprint into his flesh, corruption blackening and dissolving the skin and the bone beneath.

"The Shadowed Hand is upon you," I said. I let the corpse fall and stalked back into the trees. No one moved to stop me. The nearer soldiers scuttled away in terror.

We spent the next day sweeping the forest. We found no one.

6. A Darker War

Captain Almet and I reclined on camp chairs under a canvas awning half a mile from the siege lines at Riverside. Both battalions had made their way north without further interference. But we had failed in our plan to encircle the Monolith army in the field. Alerted by the retreating rangers, they had pulled their forces back into the ruined town and fortified it as best they could. We didn't have the numbers to assault it, they didn't have the numbers to sally. For the moment, we glared at each other across their improvised defenses and called each other nasty names.

"What are you doing here, Minos?" Almet asked. The cider we were drinking had more alcohol than most, and he'd put away a lot of it. His speech was ever so slightly slurred.

I shrugged. "The Select are often warriors."

"The Select are often mercenaries." He jabbed an accusing finger at me. "But you, you enlisted like any common soldier. The Select demand far more pay than that. And Panther City's too cheap to cough up that much. So you are, as far as I know, the only Select in this entire army. So, again, why?"

It was a good question. Following the chain of events that had led me here, it was hard to see much logic guiding my decisions.

"I suppose these days I'm very good at only one thing."

"Still doesn't tell me why here. The Monolith will pay for Select mercenaries, you know. They've got 'em."

I breathed out a long sigh. "People in Rockwall always treated me decently. The Monolith - sure, they're pragmatic enough to hire us, but the Josephites think we're damned. I don't need much money, but with this in me -" I let a tendril of the Darkness coil around my hand, "I don't need anyone telling me I'm damned. I'm worried enough about that as it is."

I stared at the ground. Prophetess and the Universal Church called the Darkness the physical manifestation of sin. I didn't believe that. I told myself I'd done a merciful thing by frightening the Monolith rangers away instead of killing them all. But I couldn't erase from my mind the look of horror on the Paladin's face as I'd killed him in a fight where he'd stood no chance at all. And I couldn't forget the fierce rush of joy I'd felt as his men cowered, or how close I'd come to striking them down like the shadow of death as I'd passed by.

Almet didn't say a word. He was looking at me with an expression I couldn't read.

"How about you, sir?" I asked, changing the subject. "How did you decide on the military life?"

He cracked a lopsided smile, but it didn't seem to me there was much humor in it.

"Rockwall has no military academies or hereditary nobility, so it has two sources of commissioned officers. One is the field commission - that would be you. Any officer of the rank of captain or above can raise an enlisted man to the rank of lieutenant. No further, I'm afraid."

He locked eyes with me. "It isn't encouraged, because it can interfere with the army's revenues from regular commissions. Regular commissions are purchased, you see. Generally by younger sons of wealthy families with nothing better to do."

He spread his hands and the sad smile widened. "For example, I am the third son of Tessel Almet of Almet's Brewing, maker of fine lagers, ales, stouts, and ciders. This is ours, by the way. Good, isn't it?"

He raised his mug, and some of the cider sloshed over the rim.

"I must say, the ladies find an officer much more impressive than a third son who won't inherit much beyond an income... although I'm sure the income helps, too."

And so he felt guilty, and promoted men from the ranks who might or might not have the talent to be officers.

"You're a good leader, Captain," I said. He was, too. He was reasonably smart, fair, and bold. Decisive but willing to listen.

I stood up. "I need to go check on my troops. The Shadowed Hand should be just about ready to end the siege."

Almet peered at me in bleary confusion. "How do you think you're going to do that?"

"Fear. It's all about fear."

The platoon was conducting exercises in the woods. Word had spread that we'd driven off the Monolith rangers. Actually, word had mostly spread that we'd killed them all. In some versions, we'd scattered pieces of the bodies so widely they couldn't be found. I did nothing to discourage the rumors. They'd eventually be helpful.

They'd already gained us new volunteers for the platoon. Some were killers - or would-be killers - so vicious and bloodthirsty that even Railes had turned them away. But a few were very useful. One was a hunter named Sesk, a short, dark man nearly as at home in the woods as Cat. He was teaching the rest the basics of snares and traps, and helping the paleo instruct them in stealth and tracking.

I found Herin sitting on a fallen tree at the edge of the forest. He'd been formally attached to my unit. The grizzled sergeant was whittling a stake when I came up.

"This is as close to playing in the woods as I get, Lieutenant," he said.

"That's fine, sergeant. I don't need you sneaking around in the bushes. I've got Cat for that."

"That one's scary, sir. You'll want to be careful she don't slit your throat in your sleep."

"She tried once. It didn't work. How do you think I found her?"

He shook his head. "Sometimes I wonder if you're overdoing the spooky, sir."

I grinned. "You've been doing this stuff longer than I have, sergeant. You know perception is reality. If the other side thinks we're a terror they can't defeat, they've lost."

"You aiming to terrify them again soon, sir?"

My grin widened. "Yes I am."

I stepped in among the trees. The raucous caw of a crow sounded from my right, and then the woods fell silent. I froze in place and sent tendrils of the Darkness questing outwards.

There was nothing human within forty yards of me. My range was short, because I was covering a full circle around me. Even in the late morning sunlight, the trees shrouded everything in shadow. I could see no movement.

I could be a shadow myself. I had shaved my head so the white hair wouldn't stand out. Someone in the quartermaster's unit had found us brown and gray dyes to stripe our uniforms. And I had been experimenting with Yoshana's technique of using the Darkness to blur my outline. I wasn't going to be detected easily as I slid like a ghost among the trunks.

And crashed to the ground as I stumbled over a tripwire. I cursed and rolled to my feet. I could hear rustling somewhere beyond the range of the Darkness.

An arrow flew out of the woods to my right, barely missing me. With a direction to target, I focused my senses and located the archer. The thread of Darkness thickened into a rope that blocked his windpipe. I loped in that direction, a sixty degree wedge of smoky particles going in front of me.

It was luck or perhaps some movement of the air that made me twist and avoid the body hurtling from above. Rather than reach for my sword, I grabbed my attacker where arm met shoulder and heaved. My assailant flew into the underbrush with a squawk.

I was just bringing up the sheathed katana when an arrow from behind caught me in the shoulder blade.

"Ow! Dammit!"

The Darkness boiled in my blood and I forced it down with difficulty. Even blunted, those things hurt.

Cat popped up from the bushes where I'd thrown her, grinning like a fiend.

"That was good," I had to admit. "It didn't occur to me to check up in the trees."

Which was stupid, since I'd used the same trick to hide when I fled into the Sorrows to escape Yoshana.

Sesk came trotting up behind me. "You okay, sir?"

"Yeah. I thought that was you I'd choked."

"Pretty sure that was Taba, sir. I'll go check."

"He's gotten a lot better with a bow, then. He didn't miss by much."

"He has a good eye and a steady hand. Or did, if you killed him," Sesk continued as he made his way past me deeper into the woods.

I wasn't worried. I knew how to throttle a man unconscious with the Darkness. Still, it was a relief when the hunter announced, "He's fine."

More of my troops were emerging from behind trees. All wore our new camouflage uniforms. A few carried bows. Most wielded tree branches they would have used as clubs if they'd gotten close enough. Railes had found one with a particularly wicked cluster of knots at the end.

"You look way too eager to use that, sergeant."

"Not me, sir." But he whacked his palm suggestively.

Cat had a stick sharpened to a sort of notional point. If she'd jabbed my throat or under my ribs, it would have counted as a kill.

"That was good," I repeated when most of the platoon was around me. "Very good. If you can take me, you can take anyone you're going to meet this side of the Muddy."

It had been good. They'd only had the few minutes I'd spent talking to Herin to ready the ambush, though some elements, like the tripwire, they'd obviously arranged far earlier.

"How many of those ropes are stretched across this forest, anyway?" I asked.

"Only a couple, sir," Sesk replied. "You took the most obvious path from where Sergeant Herin was sitting, like we'd hoped."

I winced. I'd been careless, too confident in the advantages the Darkness gave me.

"Let's hope the enemy tonight's no smarter than I was this morning."

"We're going in?" Railes asked.

"We're going in."

The cheer that rose up reminded me of the throaty growl of a wolf pack.

I lurked in a pool of deep shadow along Riverside's western wall, blurred into virtual invisibility by the Darkness. The wall was the patched ruin of a palisade in places, courses of stones in others, and a fill of garbage and debris in still more. The defenders had torches up at night, but not many. They hadn't taken time to harvest the forest before retreating into the town, and they were conserving wood.

Our forces hadn't encircled Riverside. The cordon would have been too thin to prevent a sally, and a concentrated attack by the Monolith troops could have rolled up our lines. Instead we were drawn up facing what passed for the main gate, which wouldn't have been impressive even before the place was sacked years ago. Because this must be the same Riverside that Grigg had helped capture on the ill-fated mission that ultimately made him Yoshana's lieutenant.

The opposing army wasn't large. We estimated perhaps a thousand men, about half our size. It wasn't enough to thoroughly man the walls. Sentries were posted every hundred feet or so, with supplemental two-man patrols making a regular circuit.

I was crouched at a spot on the west side of the town, a quarter of the way around from our position to the south. An opening in a stone section of wall had been blocked with a wagon bed lashed to spears with rawhide cords. A guard was stationed just on the other side, but the angle of the wall put him out of sight of his fellows if he stepped down from the stack of boxes he used to gain a higher vantage point. The Darkness had eaten most of the way through the rawhide lashings the night before. Finishing the job would be easy.

Now the Darkness simultaneously tore at the bindings and clogged the sentry's arteries. I'd developed a touch for asphyxiation. He lurched drowsily down from the crates, yawned hugely, and collapsed into unconsciousness.

The only thing I hadn't taken into account was that he'd slump over onto just the section of wall I was weakening. The rawhide snapped under the added weight, and the wagon bed came crashing down. I ducked under it and took the weight on my shoulders.

"Get this guy off of here," I hissed.

Cat loomed up next to me, her pale face blackened with charcoal. Moments later, the burden on my back eased. I straightened and saw the paleo dragging the sentry outside.

"No, inside," I began. Then I saw she'd cut his throat. "You shouldn't have done that. If we'd left him unconscious inside, a patrol could walk right by and just think he was asleep at his post."

She shrugged. "Less to kill later."

I started to say the point of the exercise was fear, not death. To force the enemy to retreat, not to heap the ruins with their corpses. But it would be a waste of breath. And the Darkness was pulsing in my temples. It was time for actions, not words. There would be more death tonight.

The two of us slipped inside. Then the rest of my squad, who had crept up in the dark behind us. I would lead this group of ten myself. Railes and Groff would follow with their own units. I pointed southeast, deeper into the town, in the direction of the main gate. I assumed the enemy commanders would be there. The other squads would disperse and do some damage while we struck for the throat.

We each carried a bundle of oil-soaked torches. I lit one from the fire burning at the dead sentry's post. My men did the same. As we trotted down an alley, I lit a second brand and flung the first into the fallen remains of a wooden building. Flames immediately began to lick at the rotten beams. Arson was one of the easiest tricks in a guerilla's arsenal.

More torches flew and we left the alley ablaze behind us. We weren't going to be able to retreat this way. On the other hand, we weren't going to get hit from behind, either.

The Darkness didn't like this much fire. It swirled and eddied, skittish. Still, I sensed the patrol coming around the corner before it abruptly met us face to face.

It was only four men. My katana finished one before he understood what was happening. I engaged the second, while the squad made short work of the last two. Five to one simply wasn't winnable odds.

I caught the survivor's blade on mine, then seized his wrist with my left hand. The Darkness in me ruptured bones and sinews, and he dropped his weapon with a wordless cry.

"Where are your masters? Where are the Paladins?" I demanded.

"There," he stuttered, jerking his head to the southeast. I had guessed right.

"Run to them, little thing," I hissed. "And tell them the Shadowed Hand has fallen on them."

I passed my sword to Cat and put my right hand on his face. The Darkness marked him as it had the Paladin in the woods. As soon as I released him, he fled, sobbing in terror.

Every man - and the sole woman - in the platoon carried at their belts a sack full of charcoal dust. Three of my troopers used it to mark their handprints on the dead men's faces. Another gave the same treatment to a stone doorpost.

"Let's keep moving."

But the first Paladin found us before we found his friends.

He was at the head of a group of a dozen men with torches and spears. The Monolith officer was easy enough to recognize. He wore a shirt of fine chainmail and carried a broadsword and a huge shield. He looked like some sort of medieval knight.

Less primitive was the revolver one of his men pulled. Two of my troopers threw away swords and torches to bring up slung carbines.

I took a step forward. I didn't want a gunfight.

"You think you can face me?" I spat contemptuously at the man in armor.

He slapped his blade against his shield and charged.

I had never fought a skilled swordsman with a shield. The metal rectangle was massive, and he used it both to block and push at me. The heavy broadsword darted out like lightning from behind it, stabbing or slashing.

The Darkness seethed restlessly, upset by the torches, frustrated and angered by the obstacle in front of me. I had lost all fine control over it. Instead it boiled and raged, lashing at the shield, scattering from it like a wave on a rock.

"Monster! Demon!" the Paladin cried, but he didn't back down - he came in harder and faster.

"Yes," I said. I threw the katana at his face and when he interposed the shield, I grabbed it with both hands and used it to fling him. His blade came out and scored a line of fire down my side, but he flew through the air like a toy.

There was only rage. I leapt at him as he lay prone on his back. He batted me away with the shield, but I seized it again and held on, tearing it from his hands. He stumbled to his feet and I smashed the heavy sheet of metal into him. When he dropped his sword I launched myself at him again and bore him to the ground, raining blows into his face with all the mad strength of the Darkness in me. Bones cracked in his skull and my hands, but the Darkness healed me even as it tore at him.

When I stood over his still body and roared, his men threw down their weapons and ran.

We scattered caltrops behind us to cover our retreat, but no one pursued.

I was only dimly aware of the rest of the platoon joining us back at the Rockwall camp, only vaguely conscious of the reports that we had taken minor wounds but no losses. With adrenaline and the Darkness still pulsing through my body, I dragged my blanket to the edge of the woods and fell asleep a hundred feet from the camp.

A black fog oozed out from between the trees, fat tendrils of it questing like snakes. Roshel stepped out wrapped in layers of clinging mist and little else.

"I've been waiting for you." Her voice was as soft and seductive as I remembered. "For you to finish becoming what you are."

I stood as she closed the distance between us, and we embraced. The Darkness was all around us, hers, mine. As my lips found hers, the mist closed in, caressing, enfolding, smothering, clawing.

As her Darkness tore at me and mine tore at her, she whispered, "This is how we become one."

I jerked awake with icy sweat soaking my body and the Darkness whirling around me. Two dozen yards away, Cat crouched in the grass, watching me with wide eyes. It took nearly an hour for meditation to ease me to a sleep untroubled by nightmares.

"I want Pious."

"You're insane," Almet said. "I bet he wants you dead as much as the enemy does."

I let out a ragged breath. "Probably. But I need him. Those Paladins are hard to kill."

I wasn't sure I could win a fight like the last one against more than one of the Monolith officers. I was even less sure I could make it through another night like that and keep my sanity.

Almet shook his head. "If you want him, you can have him. I still think you're crazy. Then again, everything you do is crazy. You're lucky that didn't hit you."

He pointed to my torn tunic, slashed by the Paladin's blade.

"What makes you think it didn't?" I grinned, and the Darkness swirled into visibility around me.

The captain shook his head again, more violently this time. "Yeah, take Pious. The only person scarier and crazier than him in this army is you."

Some of Pious' squad was made up of his former platoon, but others had been reassigned from other elements of Almet's company. The captain seemed to have given him the most vicious and brutal men in the battalion. Two were among those I'd previously rejected for the Shadowed Hand. They were what I needed for tonight, though.

To say that Pious wasn't pleased with his new assignment would have been a bit of an understatement. His face was set like stone, but anger blazed in his eyes. I didn't need the Darkness to sense how he felt.

"You understand the mission, Sergeant?" I put a little extra emphasis on the last word. Making the point. If you thought badly of me, you might say twisting the knife. You wouldn't necessarily be wrong. I needed Pious, but seeing him face to face brought back a rush of loathing that twisted my guts and heated my face.

"I understand. Sir." That last with as much contempt as anyone could possibly put into a single syllable.

"You might want to at least pretend to show some respect for a superior officer, Pious."

He barked out a laugh. "Superior? You? You're not even human. You're a black-eyed, gray-skinned demon that walks like a man and maybe thinks it is one. But you're not. But now - now you want me to kill Paladins. And that I'll do. So that better be enough. Sir."

Pious was a bully, and a thug, and a fool. But he was no coward. I nodded. "That's enough. For now."

As I turned my back on him, I threw over my shoulder, "You're wrong, you know. I'm no demon. I've met one. He'd break you like a twig."

"Bad," Cat muttered at me. "Not trust."

"A little late for that now," I said, and loped on through the torchlit town, Cat and Railes to either side of me. Pious and his squad pounded along just behind. The rest of my men were spreading into other parts of Riverside, burning, killing, leaving the mark of the Shadowed Hand in their wake.

We'd come in from the east this time, and our main force was heading straight for the Paladins' compound. At least, where we thought it was.

We weren't wrong. Snipers on top of a three story brick building opened up on us from fifty yards away.

Within seconds they were screaming and clawing at their faces as the Darkness swarmed them. That made them easy targets for return fire from Pious' troops. I didn't really like having that man and his killers behind me with guns, but there are no perfect solutions in war.

"Don't fight fair, do you?" Pious gasped out as he broke into a sprint.

"Not really the point, is it?" I matched his pace.

"Nope."

A dozen men with swords and shields swarmed out of the building and charged us. Here was the core of the Monolith army's officers - its leaders and deadliest warriors.

Pious pushed past me and met the first with a monstrous sweep of his pick. It caught the Paladin's shield and flung him into the air. The sergeant's backswing hammered another enemy to his knees.

I could deal with the Paladins in front of me or sweep the rooftops for more snipers. Yoshana might have been able to do both - I couldn't. I concentrated on the more immediate problem.

More gunfire opened up from above. Pious' men answered, but were in an inferior tactical position.

There was a reason I hadn't brought my own troops to this battle.

The Darkness was a storm around me. It clawed at eyes, throat, wrists, wherever it found exposed flesh. This time it didn't batter at shields - it whipped around them like a malevolent whirlwind. Enemies fell back, even these hardened soldiers frightened by Pious' savagery and the onslaught of the Darkness.

A scarred, white-haired veteran stepped forward. "Stand and fight if you are a man, hellspawn!"

From within the cloud of Darkness, Cat leapt on him and plunged her gleaming knife into his throat. He flung her away, but it was too late. She rolled to her feet, grinning as he fell.

"Not man, me." She laughed.

The other Paladins stared in horror. For a tense moment the four of us held them - Pious, Railes, Cat, and I staring down three times as many of the Monolith's finest, as our troops exchanged gunfire with their snipers.

Pious was a fool, but he knew how to seize a moment. "Fire and charge," he bellowed.

His men turned their guns on the Paladins. Most of their shots missed, or ricocheted off the heavy shields. But one of the enemy officers went down. When Pious' squad roared and rushed forward, it was too much. The Paladins turned and ran.

Pious and Railes each hacked one down from behind. Cat leapt at another, grappling and slashing with the ancient knife. At the same time, the enemy gunmen turned their weapons on us.

Something stabbed at my right leg, hot and sharp and agonizing. My knee buckled and I went down.

The Darkness roared back into me then shot up in a fountain of black rage. I wasn't going to be used for target practice with victory in my grasp. Screaming in fury, I tore and bit at the snipers on the roof, the Darkness an extension of my clawed hands.

In my blind fury, I didn't know whether they died or fled. But no more shots came from the rooftop. I staggered to my feet and called my power back into myself, repairing broken blood vessels, forcing the invading bullet to the surface.

More enemy troops were pouring out of nearby buildings, confused and leaderless.

"Kill them all!" Pious shouted. His men skidded to a halt and unloaded another volley of gunfire.

I clutched the bloody bullet and raised my fist in the air. "The Shadowed Hand is upon you!"

Three days later I was sitting with Captain Almet, Colonel Royce, and Colonel Hake, watching the last fires in Riverside guttering out into lazy columns of smoke. A collection of adjutants milled around, chattering.

Pious had lost two men, and another three were badly injured. My squads had suffered no casualties, taking only minor wounds. The enemy had abandoned the town at first light, limping away to the north. We had done some damage to the column as they retreated, but had not seriously attempted to reengage.

"Still seems like a shame to burn the town," I remarked. "I wouldn't have minded a roof over my head for a change."

One of the staff officers glared at me, offended that a lieutenant had voiced an opinion in such august company.

Royce harrumphed and replied, "If headquarters says to destroy it, we destroy it. Don't want the enemy moving back in after we clear out, you know."

Colonel Royce struck me as a pompous idiot. He was a small man whose brain seemed empty of any original thought.

"Just so, sir," I agreed. "It just seems like a waste."

"War is always a waste," Hake growled. "In any case, we're moving on. The same courier that ordered us to fire the town had instructions that we're to move north and continue to engage any Monolith forces we encounter."

"Any forces, sir?" asked a captain whose name I didn't know. He was one of those that orbited the colonels, not a line commander. "What if the enemy forces are superior?"

Hake gave him a wry smile. "We're getting two additional battalions for reinforcements. And apparently we've now got a reputation back home."

He unfolded a sheet of paper and quoted from it. "'Based on your spectacular successes to date, we are confident you can overcome any resistance you encounter.'"

The colonel put the paper away. "We're taking the fight to the Monolith this time."

7. Meeting Interesting People

The Shadowed Hand had become strange. Even I could feel it. There was an almost mystical sense of invincibility in the platoon, which now included the survivors of Pious' squad. The sergeant still detested me, but no longer let it show.

We'd added a few more recruits, and there were almost forty of us now. We kept to ourselves. In theory we still reported to Captain Almet; in practice we were an independent reconnaissance company. Railes, Groff, Pious, and Sesk commanded my squads. When we were in the field, I used the finest threads of the Darkness to link them together. My senses were attenuated, but I could manage a radius of a hundred yards, and could relay simple messages to the squad leaders. If any of them objected to the Darkness touching their minds - and I'm sure at least Pious did - none of them complained.

Other soldiers edged away from us. The attitude was a mix of awe and fear, especially from the new battalions, who had been fed completely exaggerated stories of the fall of Riverside. Whispers buzzed whenever I approached, faded away lest I hear, then started up again in my wake. I didn't use Yoshana's trick of enhancing my hearing with the Darkness. I didn't really want to know what they were saying. It didn't matter.

So I was surprised when Luco approached me in camp accompanied by a solider I hadn't seen before. The man was tall, but visibly nervous. Not the kind of killer who normally came looking to join the Shadowed Hand.

"Got someone I thought you might like to meet, Minos. Anyway, he wanted to meet you."

The other soldier looked at the ground, not meeting my eyes. "Is it true you're the one who took Genia north?" he asked softly.

"Who?"

"Genia. Genia Carter. Umm... calls herself Prophetess?"

It was all I could do not to stagger back, struck by a wave of loss. Until that moment I hadn't realized how much I missed the stubborn farm girl who'd decided she was on a mission from God. "Her name's Genia? She wouldn't tell me."

"She always was stubborn." The man echoed my thoughts, then gave a nervous laugh. "She's my little sister, you know."

"You're... um..."

"Kafer."

"Kafer. Right. She... she missed you."

He stared at his feet. "She didn't like me going into the army. I didn't want to write to her. I guess I was mad at first. Then I guess I didn't want her convincing me to go home."

Was I still angry because she'd thrown me out of Our Lady? I didn't think so. Did I want her convincing me to give up all that I'd become to go back? No. I understood Kafer well enough. "Like you said, she's stubborn. And persuasive."

"Is she all right?"

"As far as I know she is. She's got her own army." I spread my fingers and let the Darkness coil around them. "Not as good as ours, though."

"No one's as good as you, sir."

It felt good to hear him say it. Almost as if Prophetess herself had. As if she had seen the value in what I'd become for her, instead of casting me aside.

I shrugged. "There are fighters better than me. None on this side of the Muddy, though."

"I want to be part of that."

I hesitated. Prophetess would hunt me down and skin me if I got her brother killed.

"Please," Kafer said.

And after all, why shouldn't he? He was a grown man, older than Prophetess, older than me. His decision was his own. And I - I owed Prophetess no duties anymore.

"Welcome to the Shadowed Hand."

"I don't think they like us," Kafer whispered, two weeks and hundreds of miles to the northwest.

"Our reputation precedes us."

I didn't even know the name of the town. Some insignificant village that had grown up around the main road into the Principalities. Most of the construction was recent, with almost none of the older and more advanced architecture from before the Fall. The place had probably developed after the Age of Fear, when commerce and travel began to slowly grow back from nothing to its current fitful trickle. They'd built a high, wooden palisade around the village, which not coincidentally blocked the road. They were used to collecting taxes from travelers.

The negotiations with the Rockwall army had not gone to the villagers' liking. We were compensating them for provisions, but rather than silver we paid in Rockwall scrip, which would be virtually useless here. They had initially demanded that the Shadowed Hand, and particularly its inhuman commander, remain outside the walls. I'd retorted that because I could sense an ambush or other treachery, not only would I be going in, I'd be going in first. That hadn't made them feel any better about it - but with nearly four thousand men now in our force, we'd been in a position to insist.

My senses ranged around me, but I wasn't concerned. These people weren't idiots. Our army was bigger than their entire population, and their gates were open. There was no chance they could resist us, unless they had a Monolith regiment stuffed into their primitive, dilapidated houses. And they didn't.

Still, I was the one leading the column, just in case. Most people peered out at us from behind shutters, but a few bolder citizens, children and adults alike, lined the narrow streets to stare. I gave them a show - a cloud of the Darkness around me thickened just enough to be visible. Luco, Kafer, and Cat were with me. The rest of the Shadowed Hand followed, each squad led by its sergeant, Railes, Groff, Sesk, and now Pious. The overall effect was intimidating.

Luco was with me because he was my friend, and had a good head on his shoulders. He could help if we needed to talk rather than kill. Cat... Cat was there in case we needed to kill rather than talk. And Kafer was there because I couldn't think of anywhere safer to put him than next to me.

A bald man with a long white beard, wearing a coarse robe cinched with a cord, stepped into our path and struck the ground with his staff.

"Brothers!" he cried. "For are we not all brothers? Do not make war on your brothers, for it is an abomination in the sight of God."

I reached back and put a hand on Cat's shoulder. I had felt her tensing to spring. That would be a bad approach here - although slitting the old man's throat would certainly be the fastest way to shut him up.

The village would likely be under the control of Steel City, southernmost of the three city-states that made up the Principalities. That would make them allies of the Monolith.

"Did you give the same speech to the Paladins when they came down to attack merchant ships on the Whitewater? You're old enough to have been here when their army passed through and laid waste to Riverside. I heard from someone who was there that the murder and rape were enough to turn the most hardened soldier's stomach. So did you lecture them too?"

He met my eyes. His were a piercing gray, like Prophetess'. If he was perturbed by my black scleras - or the Darkness pulsing around me - he gave no sign.

"I did."

"Didn't work very well, did it?"

"Their damnation is on their own heads. Just as your damnation will be on yours. It is not too late to repent."

The Darkness thickened. "Oh, I think it probably is."

"It is never too late."

Irritating old coot. It would have been easier if he'd just called me a hellspawn or a demon and gotten on with it.

"How about you move before I have another death on my conscience?"

I thought I saw the barest hint of a smile tug at the corner of his mouth. "Far be it from me to lead a man to sin."

He stepped aside with an expression of absolute serenity.

I glared at him and we resumed our march. But no sooner was I past him than he called out to the troops, "Repent! Lay down your weapons of war and return to the Lord. Though but one should turn aside from the path of destruction, there will be great celebration of all the choirs of angels. For did not the Lord say there will be more rejoicing in heaven over one sinner who repents than over ninety-nine righteous persons who do not need to repent?"

"Stupid old…" I snarled.

"Make quiet, me," the paleo suggested.

"Cat keeps her claws in her paws this time," I said. Behind us, I could hear the preacher continuing to harangue our soldiers. I wondered if one of my legion of killers - maybe Pious himself - would shut him up by force. But from the sound of his voice continuing to echo behind, I could tell no one did.

Luco came up to the fire where Cat and I sat late that night. I took a bite of hard bread and a sip of warm cider as he sank to the ground next to me.

"Bothered me a little." I knew he was talking about the old man.

Most of the soldiers were hard men but some, like Luco, were new to this. I imagined being threatened with hell was uncomfortable even for a veteran. As a Select, I'd been called damned so many times it felt like part of my name.

"It was meant to," I said. "The Monolith's not stupid. They can do their own psychological operations, just like we can. They know our men are decent people. They want to plant doubt. Easy enough when we're far from home… and not everyone's comfortable using the Darkness."

Luco's mouth dropped open. "You mean he was a Monolith spy?"

"Sure."

"Those…" he sputtered to an outraged halt, then sprang to his feet and hurried off to tell the others.

"Spy?" Cat asked. "Not kill, why?"

"He was no spy. He was a preacher trying to get people to stop killing each other. But the troops will feel better if they think he was a Monolith agent."

The paleo grinned, tapped her temple, and pointed at me. "Shadow warrior."

Yoshana would have been proud.

Somewhere on the long march through the plains, another band of enemy rangers decided to take a run at us. There weren't a lot of trees for cover, so they employed a tactic made famous centuries before by the land's original inhabitants… and, centuries before that, by the Mongols on another continent entirely.

They had two problems. First, the guys on the ground have an accuracy advantage over the guys jouncing along trying to fire their rifles from horseback. A good cavalry rush could have overcome that by letting them concentrate fire on us, except for the second problem - horses are easily spooked, and the Darkness is especially good at spooking them. The attackers left three dead comrades and four crippled mounts behind as they retreated. I felt bad for the horses. Cat butchered them with ruthless efficiency.

That night my platoon bedded down a few hundred yards ahead of the main column, circled around a roaring campfire. The enemy charge hit my wards well after midnight. There were far too many to kill, but their mounts panicked even more readily in the dark than during the daylight - even with the Darkness extended in a radius too wide to efficiently kill, it could induce fear. My men picked off half a dozen of them before they escaped.

I found one with his leg broken, his treacherous horse sidling nervously ten feet from where it had thrown him. I wrapped myself in the Darkness and picked him up.

"The Shadowed Hand owns the night. Fear the darkness," I told him. I marked his face to make the point, then I calmed his mount and slung him across its back.

"They'll wise up and hit somewhere further down the column behind us tomorrow," Railes said as we watched the horse gallop away, its rider flopping like a grain sack in the saddle.

"They might," I agreed. But they didn't.

It had been raining for almost a week when the city loomed up in front of us out of the curtains of water. The men were all soaked, but didn't seem to mind. The summer's heat had faded as we climbed up the long, gradual slope to the Barrier Range, but it was still uncomfortably warm in our gear.

I had figured out Yoshana's technique of using the Darkness to turn water from my body and clothes. It was hot and I wouldn't have objected to a good soaking, but the trick impressed the troops, so it seemed worth doing.

I didn't know how Steel City came by its name - Stone City would have been more appropriate. It was shielded by a massive wall of limestone, rising thirty feet to crenellations. Tall buildings within looked down on the wall, giving the

362

inhabitants further lines of fire. The builders had taken defense seriously. The Shadowed Hand wouldn't be getting in here the way we'd walked into Riverside.

Of course, some cretins had built outside the wall. Most had fled. Apparently one had remained.

General Hake - a promotion had accompanied his new orders - invited me to his tent and introduced me to a fat man with a thin weasel's face that contrasted grotesquely with his bulk.

"This is Roddib. He operates... let's call it an inn... built up against the wall. Food, drink, accommodations, female companionship. Just the things an army far from home might want. Isn't that right, Master Roddib?"

There was an edge to Hake's tone. An officer who cared as much about his troops as Hake did might not have much use for a brothel owner who exposed his employees to the mercy of an invading army. Or maybe he just didn't care for pimps in general.

Roddib's eyes darted between us. He reminded me of an obscene cross between a rat and a swine. The Darkness stirred in me in response.

Hake smiled a little, not pleasantly. "Master Roddib is willing to sell information, as well as food and flesh. So he's a traitor, in addition to his other charming pursuits. Now it occurred to me that a man eager to sell out his own people might not be entirely trustworthy, which is why I asked you to join us, Lieutenant."

The general's smile widened. "I assume word of the Shadowed Hand has reached you, Master Roddib. Lieutenant Minos commands it. In addition to his many other skills, the lieutenant can use the Darkness to sense the truth of any information given to us. Or pull that information directly from an uncooperative source's mind. I understand the latter is quite excruciatingly painful."

Hake was making the last part up. I could read Roddib's surface thoughts without hurting him at all. I didn't know how to go deeper - although I could always torture him. The Darkness would be good at that. And would probably enjoy it. The problem would be stopping while Roddib was still alive.

I grinned. And didn't need the Darkness to see the fear running down the fat man's narrow face in rivulets of sweat.

Roddib was staring at me in horror. Hake added mildly, "Why don't you tell Lieutenant Minos the secrets you were offering to retail to me? You'll be paid if they're true. If not... well..."

I stretched my hand toward the weaselly face. The Darkness flowed out, moving over his skin. He gave a little squeak just like a rat and flinched away.

I said, "There's no reason this has to hurt. If you're honest. And very, very forthcoming."

Roddib blinked back tears. I could almost feel sorry for him. Almost.

"You'll never take the city, sirs," he choked out. It wasn't defiance - he had none of that left in him, if there had ever been any. He was stating a fact. "The river brings in water, and there's more than enough food stored from the early harvest."

"Rivers can be poisoned," I said easily. "Give me facts. I'll form the military judgments."

I swallowed, my throat suddenly dry. Hake would be forming the military judgments, or at least he should be allowed to think so. I'd been careless in my words - and in my thoughts. The general let it pass without comment. There might or might not be an accounting later.

Roddib was far too terrified to notice. Words spilled out of him in a torrent. "The defenses, sir, I mean, there's the rangers, but you know that. That is, you've met them. Fought them. Killed them, that is. Mounted, all of them. Well armed, the Monolith gives them weapons. But only a few hundred, sir. Then mostly there's the militia, that must be nearly five thousand men, but they're catch as catch can when it comes to weapons. Not so much for training either, truth be told. No match for men like you, sir," he whined, offering me a tentative, ingratiating smile.

Hake and I exchanged glances. We had no siege engines. However poorly trained and equipped the militia might be, there was no way we would overrun five thousand armed men behind those high, stone walls.

There might be other options.

"How loyal is your prince to the Monolith?" I asked. We hadn't been ordered to reduce the city. We had been ordered to penetrate Monolith territory, making ourselves obnoxious as we went. Steel City was a gateway into the Barrier Mountains, and thus the Monolith itself. We couldn't leave it as a hostile presence behind us. But turning it was an option - as long as it stayed turned.

"Loyal is as loyal does, sir," the fat man offered, showing for the first time a hint of the brazen guile that led a man to operate a brothel in territory occupied by an enemy army. "There's favors done for Prince Jeral, weapons and the like, but his rangers do say he doesn't care to take orders from the Paladins. A proud man, is our prince, and no proud man likes to be told what to do and where to send his troops, isn't that so, sir?"

"I go where Rockwall tells me," I said coldly. "But I'm not a prince."

I hoped the general wouldn't feel the need to court-martial me for the direction I was going. "Rockwall isn't interested in vassals. My masters are interested in free trade, and an end to the Monolith's unprovoked harassment. How do we get an audience with your prince to explain our peaceful intentions?"

Calculation flashed behind Roddib's eyes as he tried to decide how he could profit, but it was abruptly washed away by fear. "It can't be done, sir. The

Monolith, they've got... they've got advisors, sir. They're... well, they're soldiers, sir, and they wouldn't let the prince be swayed..."

There was something about the way he said "soldiers" that made my gut clench. "What do you mean? What kind of advisors?"

The weaselly eyes darted furtively to the side, avoiding my gaze. "Well, that is..."

"Tell me!" The tendrils of Darkness eddying around his face thickened. Roddib gave a little cry and slumped to the ground.

"What the hell?" Hake bent over the fallen fat man. "Did you kill him, Minos?"

"No," I stammered. "I didn't even touch him."

The general shook his head. "Looks like the cowardly bastard just fainted. He's still breathing."

Hake opened the tent flap, addressing his guard. "Get a detail in here and clear this fat filth out. Dump it back in its... establishment. Doesn't have to be inside - out on the doorstep in the rain will do fine."

I tentatively offered, "We might want to keep him around, sir. There may be more he can tell us. And I don't know that we need to make any more of an enemy of him."

Hake snorted. "That kind has no more loyalty than a snake. Treat him well, treat him badly, he'll stab you in the back first time he thinks he can profit by it. I don't think there was much more to be gotten out of him. And honestly I couldn't take the stench of him anymore."

"Sir."

Still, for some reason what he'd stammered about the Monolith advisors gave me a chill that had nothing to do with the rain.

"It would be ideal if we can turn this Prince Jeral," General Hake told the group gathered in his tent. Colonel Royce was there, of course, as were the commanders of the two reinforcement battalions, Colonels Raji and Thonn. Hake's adjutant, Captain Selles, was there. So was Captain Almet. And so was I.

"Our supply lines are too long," Hake continued. "It's getting too arid up here to live off the land, and we can't reliably keep ourselves supplied this far from Rockwall. If we're going up into the Barrier Range, we need a friendly base here."

Raji scoffed. "And what makes you think this prince will come over to our side, General? Something a pimp babbled right before your tame monster scared him so badly he passed out?"

The colonel, a tall man with a tan complexion and dark hair, turned to me. "No offense."

"None taken, sir. And it's a fair question, with all due respect, General. Jeral's got all the time in the world behind that wall. We're not going to take them by storm, and we'll starve before they do." The fields around Steel City had been stripped bare. The harvest might not have been ready yet, but whatever there was to eat, they had it, and we didn't.

"If that fat heap Roddib's to be believed, we don't need to win, Lieutenant." Hake seemed completely oblivious to the irony of him commenting on Roddib's weight. Although to be fair, the general did somehow carry his bulk with more dignity. He continued, "We just need to be able to give Jeral an excuse. Are you telling me you can't give him that excuse?"

I felt my face heating. Was this his rebuke for my assumption of his authority when I'd interrogated Roddib? Or was he really challenging my effectiveness?

"No, sir," I answered. "I can give him an excuse."

Most of Roddib's "employees" huddled together in the evening mist shared haunted, furtive expressions that suggested more than just the fear of the moment. A few had the hollow-eyed stares of the hopeless. One redhead had a face hardened into lines of permanent anger, and she was arguing with the fat man.

"Dammit, I know you said we need to be out here in the dark. You still haven't said why, Roddib."

I paused as I walked past. The innkeeper flinched away from me. "I'm telling you, Moya, don't question."

I looked from one to the other. "Because you wouldn't want to be inside that building in about half an hour. Trust me."

I moved on, ignoring the irate glare the woman sent my way. I addressed Groff, who had temporary command of the platoon. "I said it before, but I'm going to say it again. As soon as you see anything moving up on the wall, get off that roof. They're ready for this."

Roddib's establishment was two stories high and built directly against Steel City's wall. A trap door opened onto the flat roof. From there, it was only ten feet to the battlements, and it had been easy enough to put together a half dozen scaling ladders. Those were waiting on the roof.

Waiting ten feet above on the other side of the wall, hidden behind the crenellations, was a cauldron of oil and a supply of torches. The militia had obviously assessed the potential threat the brothel posed long ago. Rather than demolish it, they'd left it as a trap for besiegers who thought they were clever.

That particular trap was easily detected by the Darkness. But I was still vaguely nervous about the Monolith advisors in the city. I wanted a distraction to see if I could provoke a response.

I also needed to be busy elsewhere.

"Give us thirty minutes," I continued. "Then get started."

I put a hand on Cat's shoulder. "Remember, you keep out of it. I need you watching for any surprises they have up their sleeves."

The paleo nodded.

"Good." I addressed my strike team. "Let's go."

Sesk, Railes, and Pious were with me. We walked briskly south around the wall, hopefully a small and routine patrol to the eyes of any defenders watching.

"Mile and a half by my pace count," Sesk announced later.

I surveyed the wall. This section looked a lot like all the rest of it - white, high, and sheer, with torches at wide intervals.

"Guess it's as good a place as any. They should be getting distracted right around now. You're sure you can get a grapple up there?"

The hunter gave me a reproachful look.

"Just checking. I'll clear a space." Choking the nearest guard into unconsciousness was easy. I even managed to keep him from falling off the walkway he patrolled.

"Remember, we're not killing people," I said. This was a dangerous team for the purpose. I'd chosen them because they could climb a thirty foot rope and watch my back on the other side. But it would be against Railes' nature to fight to stun rather than to kill. I suspected it might be nearly impossible for Pious. I wouldn't have brought him... if I hadn't been nagged by the question of what exactly the Monolith advisors might be.

Even with the Darkness enhancing my Select strength, hauling myself up to the battlements was an effort. I paused to gasp in three deep breaths when I reached the top, then cast my senses wide. I felt nothing more sinister than the other soldiers to either side, perhaps fifty feet away, visible enough in the torchlight. With five thousand men in the militia, the sentries were posted close to each other.

Of course, as luck would have it one of them turned and saw me. As he opened his mouth to shout, I triggered the Darkness I had already slipped into his body. This was no subtle easing into sleep. A mass filled his windpipe, stopping both his words and his breath. He staggered and clutched at his throat.

There was no time now for stealth. It was all about speed. A stone stairway led down to a courtyard, and I pounded down the steps.

The guard lost his balance and toppled over the walkway's low railing. He hit the ground with a sickening thud. I hoped he had survived, but wasn't optimistic.

"Hey!" Now the cry went up, and I wasn't in a position to stop it. I concentrated instead on the task at hand - an ancient wall of polished marble, timeworn but still smooth and bright. As the Darkness ate at the rock, I heard the sounds of a struggle above.

"Alarm!" Another voice bellowed. "Call the patrols! We're breached!"

I had done what I came to do. It wasn't fine work, but the message was clear. I set my palm to the stone and burned a black imprint into the marble. Then I rushed back up the steps, taking them two at a time.

I arrived, puffing and blowing, to find Railes and Pious engaged with three guards and more enemies rushing toward them. One sentry already lay crumpled at Pious' feet. My sergeants wielded clubs rather than swords, but the downed man looked very still. I had no doubt Pious' unnatural strength could kill with a length of wood almost as effectively as with his pick.

I bulled into one of the guards as he rushed past me to engage Railes. I slammed him into the battlements, punched him in the gut and in the face. He folded up in a heap. Pious hammered another man's sword arm so hard I heard the bone crack. He wailed and fell back, dropping his blade.

There were two between me and Railes. The sergeant took a step forward, feinting toward the nearer opponent's face as if his stick were a rapier. When the man blocked high, Railes jabbed him in the gut, knocking the wind out of him. I jumped the other from behind and he pitched forward, off balance. I rapped his head on the flagstones.

"Back down!" I bellowed.

"That's it?" Pious complained.

"That's it. Get moving."

More enemy soldiers were approaching, more cautiously now. Pious flung his stick at the nearest and went over the side like a monkey.

"You too," I said to Railes.

"What about you, sir?"

I grinned. "I can take care of myself."

As the other sergeant disappeared over the edge, I lashed out to either side with waves of Darkness. I wasn't trying to harm, but merely to frighten and confuse. I must have accomplished that goal, because the defenders came to a stumbling halt.

"Torches!" someone called.

That wasn't good. It was time for me to make a retreat myself.

I got down without incident, though I misjudged the distance and fell the last six feet. "Come on, let's get out of range before they bring up bows or guns. Good job covering me. I did what I needed to do."

"What exactly was that, sir?" Railes asked.

"I carved 'Isn't it better to talk than to fight?' into a building. Hopefully Prince Jeral will get the point that we can breach his defenses whenever we want to."

We were a couple of hundred yards from the city wall, and had slowed to a walk. Railes said tentatively, "Sir? Obviously you'd know better than me, but couldn't you have done that from out here without actually going inside?"

I managed to process the question without breaking stride. Just barely. "I needed to go in to prove we were actually inside and could take out his guards. I didn't want them killed, but it needs to be clear we could have killed them if we'd chosen."

I thought that sounded pretty convincing. The truth was, Railes had a point, and it hadn't even occurred to me. A number of people had told me over the past year that the Select weren't as smart as we thought we were. I was starting to wonder if maybe they were right.

"Lieutenant."

I blinked against the morning sunlight. For the first time in a week it wasn't overcast.

"Lieutenant."

The silhouette standing over me resolved into Captain Selles, Hake's adjutant. I pulled myself to my feet and produced a half-hearted salute.

"Jeral's negotiators showed up this early?" I asked. We weren't under attack. The logical conclusion was that last night's raid had produced the desired effect.

"Not exactly, I don't think. But two... persons... are here, and they asked to speak to you. They're in the officers' mess tent."

When we'd turned into a full-fledged brigade, a lot of logistics had come with it, including a full quartermaster's company. I usually ate with the Shadowed Hand, but I knew where the officers' mess was set up.

"You're being mysterious about our visitors, Captain."

"I'll let you form your own views, Lieutenant."

The remains of Roddib's place were still smoldering fitfully. The diversion had gone as planned. None of my men were hurt, but the burning oil had reduced the building to a pile of charred timbers.

Then we were at the mess tent, and I found myself unexpectedly reluctant to go in, even with two of our guards at the door. As if there were two people in Steel City I couldn't handle in a fight.

"These wouldn't be those Monolith advisors Roddib didn't want to talk about?" I asked.

"That would be my guess," Selles replied, and held the tent flap open for me. He didn't follow me in.

It was dim inside, light filtering through the canvas rather than being admitted by any windows. Two gray figures stood a few paces away, looking at me.

They weren't gray only because of the lack of light. They were Select.

"I'm Lalos. This is Tarc." They were almost indistinguishable in the gloom. Both were a bit taller and bulkier than me. Their white hair was cut short. It was hard to tell the age of Select, especially in the dark, but I guessed they might be around forty.

I ventured a little smile. "Haven't seen another Select in a while."

"No," Tarc said. "I'd think not. And that's the point. This absurdity of yours with the Shadowed Hand. It has to stop. You're endangering us all."

My eyebrows went up. "I'm sorry. Did you just walk into my camp to tell me to call off my operations? I thought mercenaries would be a little more... professional."

Lalos held up his hand. "This goes beyond today's dispute between the Monolith and Rockwall, Minos. This is about the survival of the Select, which must always be our highest calling. Minos, there's enough prejudice against our race as it is. But to use the Darkness - it makes our employers wonder whether the Select are allies of hell."

Blood rose to my face. "Really? Or does it make your employers wonder why I can rout an entire battalion with one platoon, and you can't? Are they questioning your morality, or your competence?"

Tarc snarled, "You egotistical little puppy!"

Lalos touched his arm. "Minos, you have to understand it's the interests of all the Select we're defending."

"Again, really? The way you defended Grigg so well he was sent halfway across the continent on a suicide mission?" That surprised them. Their black eyes widened. "You idiots. Who do you think made me what I am? I was trained by Grigg. And by the one who trained him."

Tarc took a step toward me, raising an accusing finger. "Corruption! Embracing the Darkness, consorting with paleos! You're a disgrace to our race."

"And here I thought a couple of sell-swords who would whore themselves out to a nation that calls us soulless and damned might be a disgrace," I growled.

"I'll teach you to address your betters -"

"You?" I burst out laughing. "My betters?"

The Darkness formed around me.

"Your Darkness has no power over the Select," Tarc spat. But he took a step back.

"You think so? Shall we test it?" The black mass seethed, pulsing to the furious beat of my heart. "You think because some thin cloud might not possess you, you can face someone taught by Yoshana?"

They were both scrambling away, and I realized my voice had risen to a roar. I throttled the Darkness back before it tore them apart. It clawed at my control.

"Because you're Select, I'll let you go," I ground out. "Don't presume on my goodwill again."

The two edged around me and bolted from the tent. I stayed inside until I could pull the roiling cloud back into my body. By the time I stepped out, they were long gone.

"Negotiations didn't go well?" Selles asked.

I nodded tightly. "Let's say no and leave it at that."

General Hake approached me some time later. Something in my face must have warned him, because he said very carefully, "So I suppose they weren't looking to surrender, eh?"

"They thought because I was Select they could convince me to withdraw the Shadowed Hand."

"Ah. And you told them...?"

"That if I saw them again I'd kill them."

"Ah." He turned to go, then glanced back. "I imagine that was hard for you, Lieutenant. Thank you."

I said tightly, "I'm loyal to people who are loyal to me, General. You've treated me fairly. I don't owe those two anything."

I was still seething that evening when Hake returned. There were three times as many torches on the walls as the night before.

"Are you going in again, Lieutenant?" he asked.

"I'd prefer to let them stew for a night, sir." I took a deep breath, and added, "I'm not sure I could limit casualties this time. It might do more harm than good."

The general could choose to believe I was afraid of facing stiffer resistance. I was more worried about holding back the Darkness in my present frame of mind. In any case, he nodded and let it go. I went to bed early, and spent nearly an hour meditating to settle my mind.

371

The next morning a messenger emerged from the postern gate under a white flag of truce. It wasn't either of the Select, and he asked to speak to General Hake, not me.

Hake went forward with a small bodyguard. If snipers on the wall or the buildings behind tried to pick him off, the soldiers would try to shield his body with their own. I went along to sniff for treachery. I could feel none in the messenger, or on the walls immediately behind. If the defenders were setting a trap, they had a good enough idea of my capabilities to hide it from me.

"Am I addressing the commander of the Rockwall forces?" the man asked politely. He was of medium height and build, handsome, and unarmed.

Hake nodded. "I'm General Hake, commanding the First Expeditionary Brigade of the Army of Rockwall."

The messenger bowed slightly. "I am Jyrus Brend, personal secretary to Prince Jeral. The prince has considered your invitation to talk." His eyes darted briefly to me.

"I'm pleased to hear that, Master Brend. Rockwall would be delighted to extend the hand of friendship and allegiance to Steel City."

Brend gave a little smile. "Friendship and allegiance are fine things, General. But the sad fact is, we've had quite enough friendship and allegiance from the Monolith. As I'm sure you'll understand. Prince Jeral therefore has another suggestion, which is that we settle for the mutual benefits of neutral commerce."

Hake frowned. "Neutral commerce is a fine thing too, but it might be a little difficult for your prince to maintain neutrality with Monolith troops in his city."

"Just so, General. And so my prince has asked his Monolith guests to depart, with the understanding merely that you will not harass or impede their passage. As it might seem inhospitable of him to ask them to leave if doing so were to put them in danger."

"I see. And after they left, unimpeded...?"

"After that we would be able to freely pursue that mutually beneficial commerce that neutrality permits. With your troops lodged comfortably outside our walls."

Hake's frown had never quite vanished, but he nodded. "I'll take some time to discuss your offer with my staff, Master Brend. I appreciate the offer, but as you can imagine, I do have to consider what's best for my four thousand troops. Camped outside your walls."

Brend's smile didn't falter. "Of course."

"Selles," Hake said, "Have our guest escorted to the officers' mess and see to some refreshments for him. Then get the battalion commanders to my tent. Minos, you're with me."

"It's not all I could have hoped for," Hake said five minutes later when we were assembled, "but it's not bad."

His eyes fixed on me.

"I don't think he was lying," I said carefully. "But that one's slippery. I could barely get a sense of his mind. He doesn't give much away."

Hake snorted. "I could have told you that without the Darkness." He surveyed the other men in the tent. "Gentlemen, how do you suggest we play this?"

"I'm with you, sir," Colonel Raji said. "It's better than I'd expected. Assuming he's telling the truth."

"But what do we do with it?" Hake asked. "I'm happy enough not to have to lay siege to the place, but I don't know that I trust them as a point of supply."

Raji shook his head emphatically. "Five minutes after we've marched up into those mountains, the Monolith will be back to plug us in like a cork in a bottle. You look up the word 'screwed' in the dictionary and they'll have a picture of us."

"You're saying Jeral will turn on us? Didn't our Select say this Brend fellow wasn't lying?" Thonn demanded.

I started to open my mouth to explain that wasn't exactly what I'd said, but Raji shot back, "It doesn't matter if he turns on us. He's got a couple hundred cavalrymen and a half-competent militia. That's plenty to hold the city, but he's not going to put them in the field. If the Monolith comes back with a brigade, why would he even think of opposing them?"

"So you're saying we can't march on the Monolith," Hake said.

"I'm saying we can't on these terms. And to be honest, I wouldn't trust any better terms Jeral offered us voluntarily. If we want to head into that pass, we need to take and garrison the city. Your Select's gotten in once. You say he drove the Monolith out of Riverside single-handed. So I say we tell this Brend cockroach that his little prince can surrender the city, or we'll take it. But either way, we're in charge."

"Minos?"

"General, I scared one Monolith battalion into giving up a ruined town with no defenses. I scratched some graffiti into a wall and scared Prince Jeral enough to consider talking instead of fighting. But for him to give up his crown while he's sitting in a fortified city with five thousand troops? I'm pretty sure that's not going to happen easily. I can get back inside. I can probably get a door open and let the army in. But a lot of people are going to die."

8. And Killing Them

Two dozen Monolith soldiers, led by two angry Select, trotted out through Steel City's postern on rangy little horses barely larger than ponies. The Select, in particular, looked ridiculous. We let them go, as we'd agreed. They headed north.

"Not into the mountains," Captain Almet observed.

Most of the command staff was assembled to watch the enemy retreat. A captain whose name I didn't know said, "They'll be heading up to Capitol or Queensboro. Probably looking to join up to a bigger force so they can come back and stomp us."

And that was the problem. Our brigade was too big to be stealthy, too big to live off the land. But too small to face the kind of armies the Monolith could field as we got closer to its territory.

General Hake had written off the idea of striking into the Monolith as lunacy. We would feint north ourselves, giving the impression we intended to extend our campaign into the other Principalities. Then we would swing east, back into the disputed breadbasket of the continent. Foraging would be easier, and the enemies more easily defeated. Hake's plan was to strike a blow at the Hawk's Nest, then return to Rockwall along the Muddy and Whitewater, cleaning the rivers of any opposing forces.

The Hawks' mercenary army was nearly twice our size, but it was deployed in the field. The general hoped an attack on their vulnerable homeland would disrupt their operations and pull the far-flung troops back - by which time we would be long gone.

I liked the plan. I'd contributed to it.

With the Monolith's soldiers now fleeing north, our quartermaster's company was resupplying the brigade from the city's stores. The company captain, a massive wall of flesh named Agga, was waving his hands and shouting. From what I overhead of the heated negotiations, Steel City's merchants wanted to be paid in silver rather than Rockwall scrip. I didn't blame them. I doubted our masters in Panther City would follow through and annex this territory - in which case the scrip was worth just about its value as tinder when the winter came.

Another loud dispute had broken out in the ruins of Roddib's establishment. We had put up tents for the women. One, the hard-faced redhead, stood outside shrieking curses at her employer.

"You can take my contract and shove it where the sun don't shine, you disgusting pig!"

"You'll keep a civil tongue in your head if you know what's good for you," the fat man growled. He employed two enforcers, heavyset men with wooden clubs. One moved toward the woman.

I strolled in that direction as the shouting continued. If the redhead was intimidated by Roddib's thug, she didn't show it. His hand had closed on her arm and she was slapping furiously at him when I arrived.

"Let go," I said quietly.

Roddib let out a bleat when he saw me and stumbled away. The bodyguard released the woman as if she'd caught fire.

"You have somewhere to go?" I asked her. "Moya, isn't it?"

She glared at me. "Anywhere's better than here with this swine."

I nodded. "Go ask for Sergeant Herin. Tell him I want you attached to Captain Agga. I assume you can cook or clean or sew?"

"I can make myself useful," she snapped.

"You don't want that ungrateful wench, master," Roddib burbled. "She's nothing but trouble, and her soul's stained black as a yard up a demon's bunghole."

I produced what I intended to be a smile. It probably wasn't, since the fat man took three more steps backward. "A preacher we met on the way here said it's never too late for anyone to repent. Personally I'm pretty sure he's wrong, but it doesn't hurt to try, now does it?"

"Only, she's got a contract with me, and that needs paying off..."

The expression on my face was now a smile only by Yoshana's standards. "Of course. Would you say it's worth more or less than your life?"

The Darkness surrounded me. Roddib bleated again and fled into a tent. The two bodyguards exchanged looks and followed. I glanced around and discovered that Moya had already marched off, perhaps in search of Herin, perhaps not.

I shrugged. I didn't doubt she had a vicious temper and a list of sins as long as my arm. But I really wasn't in a position to be casting stones.

War involved a lot of walking. We had completed our eastward pivot and been hiking for a week. General Hake's maps claimed the wide, flat road we were on would take us straight to the Hawk's Nest. I saw no reason to doubt them. Still, it would take weeks.

At least it had stopped raining.

The region's farmers had planted rows of trees and set up low stone walls to protect the wheat fields near the road. Those barriers were no more effective against the brigade than they would have been against a biblical plague of locusts. The grain was nearly ready for harvest, and the troops spread out and hacked down the stalks, passing the spikelets and chaff together to the quartermaster.

Some of the locals we plundered were brave enough to come out and complain. They got scrip as compensation. The ones that kept complaining got kicks or the flat of a sword for their troubles. It wasn't fair, but an army has to eat.

There were probably paleos and bandits in this country. None of them were stupid enough to get within sight of our column. The Shadowed Hand took point anyway, scouting ahead for Hawks, Monolith regulars, or anything else that might be a threat.

The enemy knew better than to try my force again. Instead, they hit the middle of the column in the dark of night. Their cavalry had ripped through Agga's cooks and launderers and vanished by the time my platoon got to the scene of the attack.

Medics were already at work. We had few dead, but many injured, some from the attackers' guns and swords, others trampled by panicked horses and mules. Moans, screams, and sobs rose up into the night.

Moya lay on a blanket, her remaining eye fixed on the clouded sky.

"She'll live, I think," said a nurse who saw me staring. A bullet had taken the redhead in the face, shattering her right cheek and driving shards of bone into the eye socket.

"I can -" I began, but her head turned toward me.

"Stay away from me," she hissed.

I took a step back. The Darkness, summoned to heal, began to boil instead.

Luco laid a hand on my shoulder, then recoiled at my expression. "Minos, should... I mean..."

"You and Kafer stay here," I said flatly.

"Why?"

"Because I don't want the two of you for what comes next."

"Minos, you can't blame yourself for this. For any of this."

I locked black eyes on his. "Do you really want to tell me what I can or can't feel?"

He shook his head.

"Good. Stay here. Kafer too."

Luco and Kafer were competent enough soldiers, but they weren't killers in their hearts. I had no use for them now. I was done minimizing casualties. Whether this attack was a betrayal by Steel City's rangers, or an assault by some other Monolith force, it was time to deliver a different message, written in blood.

"They're a good hour ahead," Sesk murmured.

"They'll stop to rest at some point. And then we'll kill them. Let's go."

The hunter and the paleo would have no trouble following the hoof prints even at night. But they were irrelevant. For the Darkness, this trail might as well have been blazoned with torches. I took off at a lope, my senses stretched out and scanning the ground before me, and the platoon jolted into motion behind. Luco and Kafer remained in the ruined camp, still as statues.

I slowed my pace so Sesk and Cat could keep up. I trusted the rest would follow as they could. But no more than twenty minutes had passed when Groff called out from the back of the straggling group. "Lieutenant!"

I angrily slowed to a walk, then turned back. "What is it, Sergeant?"

"Sir. We can't all keep up. This kind of pace," he gasped. Even in the dark, I could see his face was red and sweat-soaked. "You know every man. In the platoon. Can march forever. We'd all follow you. Into hell. But not all of us. Can run there as fast as you."

"I don't need all of you," I snapped. "Whoever can keep up, keeps up. The rest of you follow as you can. Or go back."

And with that I left him behind. With the Darkness in me, I could run until I died of dehydration - and probably after. There was no horseman who would outlast me.

It came to me as I ran that Yoshana had let me go when I'd fled her in the Darklands. Sesk could tell the difference between a horse with and without a rider by the depth of the hoof prints. That was beyond my skill, but Yoshana could surely do the same with her far greater mastery of the Darkness. And if I could run until I died, she could run until the sun went dark and the earth froze. If she hadn't caught me, it was because she hadn't wanted to.

Because she'd wanted me to return to Our Lady and kill Prophetess? In my rage, I had come close. I had turned aside from that, but I was made over as Yoshana's creation now.

The Monolith would learn what Yoshana's creation could do.

They'd made a cold camp, but I could hear the occasional whinny of a horse long before the Darkness sensed them. I supposed we'd been running for about an hour. Only Cat and Sesk were still with me, though when I stopped I could hear the grunting and panting of other soldiers behind. I guessed about half my force had kept up.

"What do we do?" Sesk whispered as he came up next to me, taking deep, controlled breaths.

"Get close enough to shoot. You'll know when."

The Darkness blurred my outline, turning me into a black cloud against the blackness of the night. It deadened the sound of my footfalls as I ran. There was a sentry looking almost directly at me, but he didn't know I was there until my sword cut his throat.

I raced through the camp, slashing at sleeping men as I went. Three more sentries guarded the other points of the compass. One turned to face me, and I moved toward him. He squinted into the night, seeing something, not knowing what. My blade tore him open before he knew how to react. He screamed as he fell.

The other two snatched at their carbines. A volley of gunfire cut them down.

Horses whinnied and stamped in panic. The camp came awake in a chaos of fear. More bullets found the first to take their feet.

There were nearly a hundred men in the enemy force. Plenty left to kill. I threw the Darkness wide in a stinging, clawing wave, and made my way back into their midst, hacking as I went.

My troops were beginning to join the melee. Pious was flinging bodies aside with great, sweeping swings of his pick, pausing only to hammer down the wounded and sleep-fuddled on the ground. I didn't want the Darkness to destroy my own men, but distinguishing friend from foe was beyond me now. We had struck from the north, so I made my way deeper into the south side of the camp.

I was the Darkness. We were one. It was not a tool, subordinate to me. We were a single creature of rage and death. Enemies rose up behind me, and I sensed them and killed them. A bullet pierced my left arm and the wound closed behind it, and then the gunman's eyes were gone and he was drowning in his own blood. Around me a hundred weak, feeble things hated and feared me. I hated them back with all my soul, but there was nothing in these pitiful husks to fear. I killed them because I could.

A gray figure in front of me fired a pistol as I closed on it. The first shot missed. The second pierced my leather jerkin and shattered a rib. The creature threw the gun away and raised its hands in surrender as I reached it. My first stroke took off its right hand. The second took its head.

Lalos fell dead at my feet. Tarc screamed wordlessly as he fired at me, all while scrambling onto his horse to flee. Others mounted and galloped into the night. I let them go. Gunfire from my platoon brought down a few more.

I kicked the Select's corpse. "I told you I wouldn't let you go again," I shouted. "Didn't you believe me?"

There weren't many Select left in the world. We tried not to fight each other. We tried harder not to kill each other. When Grigg had shielded me from Yoshana in Stephensburg, it had likely been in part because of our shared race.

I spat on the ground. I had given Lalos and Tarc one chance, as much as Grigg had given me. They'd ignored my warning and continued to serve a power that held the Select in contempt. Like cowards they'd attacked cooks and tailors in our supply train instead of facing our soldiers. Lalos deserved what he'd gotten.

"Salvage their guns and round up the horses that are left," I ordered. "Mount our wounded."

"What about theirs?" Railes asked.

"Leave them. If the survivors come back, the wounded will slow them down. If not," I shrugged. "The wolves and paleos can have them."

"Soldiers kill people," Cat grinned. "People's turn now."

I nodded. "Everybody's got to eat something."

Railes made a face. "Probably kinder to kill them."

I nodded again. "Probably would be. We're not going to."

The sergeant pointed to the two bloodstained holes in my jerkin. "You all right, boss?"

"I got lucky. First one went straight through the muscle. Second glanced off a rib. I'll be fine."

"You need me to bandage 'em up..." his voice trailed off.

I patted his shoulder. "Even after this you still think I'm human. I'm touched. Now let's get moving."

We gathered Groff and the stragglers who hadn't made it to the fight on our way back to the brigade. General Hake was overseeing the cleanup of the quartermaster's company. He made a beeline for me. Luco and Kafer trailed in his wake wearing expressions of stark terror.

"You want to explain what just happened?" the general demanded.

"A Monolith cavalry company hit us where we were weakest," I growled.

"That part I know. I'm wondering where my recon platoon's been for the past three hours. You know, in case this was a diversion and they hit us again."

My blood went cold. "Did they?"

"As it happens, no. But not because my scouts were scouting. Where the hell have you been?"

My face warmed with blood, though Select didn't visibly blush. "We tracked them and hit them back while they were sleeping. About half of them are dead or wounded. The other half got away, but I don't think we'll be seeing them again soon."

Hake spoke more quietly. "And on whose authority did you decide to leave the brigade to go chasing off after revenge?"

Luco and Kafer must have gotten the first taste of the general's wrath. I could sense the fear in the rest of the platoon. It made me angry.

"If my service isn't acceptable, general, you're of course within your authority to strip me of my commission."

"Are you looking for a fight, son?"

"No, sir. I was just in one." As usual. Doing all the work while four thousand other men in the brigade did nothing much.

There was a cold, hard calculation going on behind Hake's eyes. What he said was, "Next time, Lieutenant, get authorization before you detach yourself like that. We need you."

"Yes, sir."

We made our way back to our bedrolls at the front of the column. My pulse was pounding faster than it had during the battle. Someone muttered, "That's a pretty lousy thank you for taking down a whole cavalry company." Railes told him to shut up.

Roshel came again that night. I had forgotten to meditate. She coalesced out of a cloud of Darkness and her touch burned me like fire. I was throbbing with violent desire when I woke and found Cat next to me.

"Come here," I told her, voice deep and rasping in my throat. "I'll teach you what the Darkness is."

She flinched back.

"You wanted to be a shadow warrior," I said. "Come here and I'll show you how."

She shook her head. "Not like this."

She thought she had the right to refuse me? Her life was mine. She recoiled, fast, but I was faster. I grabbed her arm and dragged her close. She lashed out and scored my face with her fingernails. Furious, I struck her with the full force of my backhand. There was a crack, and her head lolled loose on her neck.

"Cat?" I shook her gently.

I probed with the Darkness. There was no life in her.

I looked around the camp. No one else was awake. There was time to conceal what I'd done. I'd seen Yoshana reduce a savage to a liquescent pile of ooze. I could do the same. The Darkness swirled as the little body broke down, dirt and grass rising up to open a rough pit. It was shocking how little space the crumbled bones and filthy liquid took up.

I screamed as I came truly awake. The Darkness really was swirling around me, and in a panic I looked for Cat. The paleo was twenty paces away, crouched and watching me with wide eyes.

I gulped in breath after shuddering breath, slowly bringing the hammering of my heart back to a normal rate. When I was finally steady, I pulled the Darkness back into myself.

Cat slowly, cautiously made her way over to me. I blinked back tears. She couldn't know what I'd dreamed, but she'd seen the Darkness loose. Very carefully, very slowly, she said, "I'm not sure I want to be a shadow warrior anymore."

I tried to smile and failed. "You and me both."

9. Regrets

I was in a little stand of trees a hundred yards from the column. The Darkness floated in front of me. The cloud was of impressive size.

"It's not you, it's me," I said. "I think you should infect other people."

How did you get rid of the Darkness when you didn't want it anymore?

"Go on," I said. "Beat it."

The cloud hovered. I could send it away, but I knew it would return. It was part of me. Or maybe I was part of it. If there was a difference. I told myself the Darkness had been in control the night before, when I'd cut down Lalos as he tried to surrender. Certainly it was the Darkness that had murdered Cat in my dream. Wasn't it?

I remembered the living corpse of a possessed shaman in the Sorrows, controlled by a cloud that still had a vaguely sensed need for a human host. I wondered if the native had begun his relationship with the Darkness believing he was in control.

Certainly Yoshana controlled the Darkness. And Seven. And Grigg and Roshel. So why couldn't I?

I thought back to what Grigg had said at the edge of the Sorrows. *The Darkness is going to rage out of control if you let it. So you can't let it. Sometimes you have to hold it back. Sometimes you have to do something that's hard, that isn't expedient. Because if you don't do things like that sometimes, it'll take your soul.*

Yoshana gave it free rein, but her power was of another order. I couldn't allow that. I'd let myself go too far.

If I couldn't get it out of me, I'd have to try harder to control it.

The sun was barely over the horizon, and we wouldn't be moving for a while yet. I walked down the column to General Hake's tent.

I thought the sentries looked at me a bit more suspiciously than usual, but one went inside to announce me. He emerged with the general.

Hake peered at me from under a furrowed brow. I didn't need to scan him to know he was wondering whether he wanted to be alone with me.

"Come in," he said gruffly. He gave the guard a little shove to move him out of the tent.

When the flap shut behind me, I braced and saluted. "I wanted to apologize, sir. I was rude and insubordinate last night."

Hake relaxed and returned the salute. "I imagine what's riding you isn't the easiest passenger."

I swallowed. He read me at least as easily as I read him. "No sir. They say it feeds on the darkest emotions, and that's right. There's a lot for it to eat on a battlefield. Last night... it was getting away from me."

I shook my head. "That's not quite right. It was starting to control me, instead of me controlling it. I've seen where that ends, and it isn't pretty."

An emaciated half-human thing, squatting in a pile of rotting animal carcasses.

"Can you still handle it?" Hake asked sharply.

"I think so, sir. Yes." I looked at my feet, then met his eyes. "We'd better hope so, because the amount that's in me would be a real danger if it got loose. Killing me wouldn't be a good solution. I'm not trying to make a threat, sir. Just explaining our options. If we had fire wardens handy..."

Not that I relished the idea of being burned alive in waves of naphtha. Neither did the Darkness. It seethed rebelliously in my guts.

"If you can control it, then you're far too useful to even consider getting rid of it. If you can't, I suppose we need to start looking for an exorcist."

That brought on a different kind of pang. "The only person I've ever known to cast out the Darkness is a thousand miles away. I'll handle it, sir."

The general nodded. "Good. I'd hate to lose you."

"Thank you, sir. I'd hate to be lost."

After that I kept to the head of the column. I wanted to be alone with my thoughts, and no one else seemed inclined to share them with me. Except for Cat. Cat didn't care what I was. Or if she did, she forgave me for it.

Sesk had been ranging off to the right, checking for tracks. After a while he came and walked next to me. It was nearly another hour before he spoke. He was a quiet man.

"The people who were here before the ancients had a story. An old man told his grandson there were two wolves inside everyone. One wolf was dark, and bitter, and proud, and resentful, and violent. The other was light, and gentle, and humble, and forgiving, and peaceful. The wolves are always fighting to control you. The boy asked which wolf wins."

"And?" I asked.

"The one you feed," Sesk answered.

"Huh."

We walked on for a while longer in silence. "There was a lot for the dark wolf to eat last night," Sesk said.

I'd said much the same to Hake. I just nodded.

I'd never spoken much to the taciturn hunter. After a while, I asked, "Why are you in the army anyway, Sesk? You're good at it, but you don't enjoy killing. You've got other skills. What are you doing here?"

He didn't answer at first, then shrugged. "The pay's regular. I figured if they were going to be paying people to kill other people, they might as well pay me."

"You're full of it," I replied.

He shrugged again. "You really want to know? It's stupid. You know how the old folks are always going on, everything was so much harder in the old days and how we've got it easy now? Or how much better everything was in the old days and how it's all going to hell now?"

I wondered how old the "old folks" were. Sesk was lined and weathered. He must have been nearly forty. But I nodded.

He continued, "I mean, they could feed you both lines of crap at the same time. But when I was growing up, it was mostly how much harder it was back when. How these days, there was trade again, people weren't afraid so much, the paleos were mostly gone. No offense." He glanced at Cat. She snorted.

"But for maybe the last ten years, it's been the other way. How the Darkness is moving west. Drelb moving south. Everything getting worse."

I nodded again. I'd seen the Darkness and drelb in the territory we were passing through now.

"I guess I thought, maybe the army could make it better. Clean the place up. And the pay really is good. The recruiting sergeant offered me double 'cause I can track and hunt. Course, then they stuck me in the regular infantry. I didn't do any scouting at all until I joined up with you."

I had to smile. "So you signed up to fight the Darkness and wound up working for the one guy in the army that uses the Darkness."

"Yeah. Go figure. At least you know what to do with me. Speaking of, I'm going to go check out those trees over there."

As he moved away again, he looked back over his shoulder. "Lieutenant."

"What?"

"Don't feed the dark wolf."

"They're behind us now," I said to General Hake a few days later. I had split the Shadowed Hand after my talk with Sesk. He was a skilled hunter, and he was wasted in the vanguard with me where his abilities and mine overlapped. So I'd carved out a rear guard squad for him. It hadn't taken him long to discover that Tarc and his cavalry unit were following us, replenished with more men.

"I guess I wasn't enough of a murderous bastard after all," I added apologetically.

"You killed one of those Select advisors," the general said. "Are your people vengeful at all?"

Only if, say, you killed one of the new recruits in our squad. Or maimed some camp follower that we felt responsible for. Tarc didn't have the Darkness in him, but I'd cut down his partner, a fellow Select. "A little bit, sometimes," I admitted.

"Think he'll do something stupid?"

"No. I don't know exactly how old he is, but he's seasoned. He'll wait for an opportunity. If we take on the Hawk's Nest, he'll hit us from behind."

"Recommendations?"

I let out a long breath. "Hard to say, sir. We could try setting an ambush, but he's going to be cautious now. And of course they're a lot more mobile than we are."

"And so?"

"Keep on, sir. Double the guards all along the column. They'll need carbines."

"We don't have that many. The Shadowed Hand has most of them." It wasn't an accusation, just a fact.

"I'll round them up, sir. You'd better get them distributed. Arrows aren't going to work well if they're hitting us at night on horseback."

Hake shook his head. "I don't know. You're the most effective company we've got. By a long shot."

I laughed. "You think we're only effective because we've got guns? We'll be all right. And, uh, did you say company?"

Hake grinned. "I did. Wouldn't be appropriate for a captain to be commanding a platoon, now would it?"

I was speechless. The general's grin widened. "Authorization came through from headquarters a few days ago. Congratulations, Captain Minos."

I stood dumbfounded as he pinned the rank tabs to the shoulders of my filthy uniform. "Captain Almet said a field commission couldn't go higher than lieutenant."

"Captain Almet doesn't know everything. There are always exceptions."

"Thank you, sir. I don't know what to say."

"Just keep winning for us."

Just keep winning for us. Easy for the general to say. *Don't feed the dark wolf.* Easy for Sesk to say. Doing both at the same time - not so easy for me. If there was a third way between Yoshana and Prophetess, I was having trouble finding it.

While I tried to figure it out, the column made camp early each day to fortify our position and set guards. That gave the Shadowed Hand time to train with the bow and arrow. Sesk was a master bowman, and the company improved rapidly. It was a more difficult weapon to use than the carbines, but within a week, most of the troops could reliably hit a man-sized target at twenty paces. Some were much better. No one was going to be winning archery contests, but we could make ourselves obnoxious at range without the carbines I had given to the sentries.

"Not being real subtle, are they?" Railes commented one morning, jerking a thumb over his shoulder. I had split the company into two platoons and gotten my former sergeant a field promotion to lieutenant. He was in charge of the rear guard now. Sesk had many useful skills, but leadership wasn't one of them.

I looked where Railes was pointing. We could actually see the enemy cavalry now. More accurately, we could see the dust they were kicking up on the road. They weren't being subtle, but then again, the land was flat as a tabletop. To conceal themselves, they would have needed to keep to the scattered trees on the side of the road, or stay much farther behind us. As it was, they must have been nearly ten miles away.

"No point, I guess. We know they're there. I suppose they know we know. Now we know that they know that we know."

"I think you're overthinking it, Captain."

"I know." I grinned and moved out of range. Railes was maybe the one man in the company who would dare to take a swing at me for being a pain in the neck. He made me feel human.

"What are we going to do about them, Captain?"

I shrugged. The road was broad and flat. There weren't even many places where the trees encroached on it. "Not much we can do. It's not like there's anywhere we could ambush them."

The next day I was proved wrong. A few hours before sundown we came to the abandoned ruins of a town. At its outskirts, just beyond an overpass we had to cross, a single building of rusted steel and broken glass rose ten stories above the featureless plain.

The overpass made me nervous. Was a concrete span hundreds of years old up to the challenge of four thousand men tramping over it?

Apparently it was. But that gave me an idea. I went to see the general.

"Do we have any dynamite?"

His eyebrows lifted. "Agga's got all kinds of stuff squirreled away. What do you want to blow up?"

"That bridge we just passed."

Hake frowned. "They'll just ride around, Minos. It won't slow them more than two minutes. Seems like a waste to destroy a bridge that's stood three hundred years just for that."

"I was thinking more while they were on it. While we're shooting arrows at them from that building next to it."

The frown slowly turned to a grin. "Now that idea I like better."

We put Sesk in charge of the demolition. Cat was even stealthier, but I didn't trust her as much with the dynamite. The rest of us took up positions in the ruined tower.

I scanned it first. Anything could lair in a place like that. Darkness, paleos, or who knew what sort of monstrosity. Nothing worse than me, of course.

The Darkness went before me, probing, and what it found, it killed. There was nothing larger than a rat. But if there had been paleos, I think I would have killed them too. I wasn't the same person who had spared Cat months ago. I was something darker now.

We took up positions on several of the higher floors. We had reclaimed the carbines for this ambush. Railes and I, and some of the better shots, were on the top level. The lieutenant tapped my arm.

"Captain? I think we've got a problem."

I followed the line of his pointing finger. "Oh crap."

From our vantage point, we could see the Monolith cavalry company and beyond. Beyond were infantry troops. Thousands of them, filling the wide road, stretching out for a mile at least. Tarc wasn't pursuing us with a detached company. It was a screening unit for an army.

"Let's get out of here."

"They didn't hit us that night just to mess with us," I told General Hake. "They wanted to slow us down, and we did exactly what they hoped we would. We stopped and dug in every night, and their main force got closer and closer."

"How many do you figure?"

"I couldn't get a good count, but it was a lot. At least as many as us."

"A Monolith brigade is five thousand men," said Colonel Raji. Hake had gathered his commanders together.

I nodded. "That would be about right."

"We're screwed," Raji declared. That seemed to be his favorite word. Not that he was necessarily wrong. He went on, "Monolith regulars are better trained than our troops. There's five thousand of them to four thousand of us. We'd be lucky to take them one on one, much less more of them supported by cavalry."

"All right," Hake said. "So what are our options?"

"They must have been hoping we wouldn't realize what was behind us until we hit the Hawk's Nest. Then they'd crush us from behind like a hammer on an anvil," Almet said.

"Yeah, doing that obviously isn't the right move," Hake snapped. "Let's try coming up with a good option, not just discarding the clearly stupid one."

Almet visibly cringed.

"We can take up defensive positions," Royce offered. "Take advantage of the terrain…"

"The terrain?" Raji shouted. "What terrain? We're marching across the flattest plane on the face of God's earth, you idiot."

Hake held up a hand. "There are basically two options. We fight or we run. We could turn south and make for Rockwall. The problem is the cavalry. If they get around us, coordinate with another Monolith force, we could get caught in a pincer. Or they could catch us while we're trying to ford a river."

Raji looked at me. "What if our scout company laid a false trail? Kept on toward the Hawk's Nest while the rest of the brigade went south?"

"Are you really that gutless?" Almet demanded. "You'd sacrifice our best unit - the unit responsible for every victory we've achieved - so you can get away?"

"So the rest of the brigade can get away. Captain." Colonel Raji glared at him. "If you can't understand the military necessity of sacrificing one company to preserve an entire brigade, you'll never become more than the company commander you are."

Hake said, "I doubt even Captain Minos can make a company look like a brigade, or cover the signs of a brigade's passage. Can you?"

I shook my head. "I don't see how. But Colonel Royce raised a valid point about making a defensive stand."

"There's no damned terrain, Captain," Raji growled. "Look at the maps. Hell, just look around."

"Exactly, sir," I replied. "Look around. There's no topography. But there's what's left of a city just north of us. We should be able to take up good enough defensive positions to gain an advantage."

"You're talking about a pitched battle."

"Yes, sir."

"One we can win?" Hake asked.

"I think so, sir. I hope so."

The brigade spent the night digging into the dead town. Not all of it had been as abandoned as the tower. In some of the buildings I found signs of recent human occupation. Which meant waste, and animal bones, and scraps of clothing that still stank of their owners.

"People," Cat confirmed. Meaning paleos. "Gone today."

They'd fled the army. The paleos were many loathsome things, but they weren't complete idiots.

This place must have fallen at the very beginning of the Age of Fear. There had been no attempt to build defenses. The ruins hadn't been completely stripped, but they were crumbling, choked with weeds and vines. Any valuables were long gone, but more salvageable metal remained than I'd thought to find outside the Sorrows. If the land were ever cleansed of paleos and bandits, it might be a more fruitful mining site than the Flow.

There was no wall of any kind. The buildings were clustered on the north side of the road. If we held there, the enemy would have no cover but the sparse trees to the south. The problem was we had no way to keep them from flanking us. So instead of a line, we deployed in a square. Only a quarter of our strength could bear on them at a time, but there were no undefended gaps in our position.

Needless to say, the Shadowed Hand took the point where we expected the heaviest combat, at the southwest corner of the square. I'd considered whether we should find an ambush site away from the main body of the brigade, but every plan I came up with resulted in certain death. Even our position on the front line of the square didn't look so good.

We'd heaped up furniture and the remains of vehicles to build barricades, and boarded up the windows of buildings leaving firing slits for gunmen and bowmen. I guessed it was around midnight by the time we finished. It wasn't a bad thing for the troops to be tired. They'd find it hard to sleep. Even I was nervous. It was one thing to storm the enemy's citadel; it was different to wait for them to come to us.

I spent an hour talking to my men. They all put on a brave face. Some I think really weren't bothered. Railes was as calm as ever. Pious honestly seemed thrilled.

Others were visibly nervous. I sat with Luco for a while.

"Any regrets?" I asked.

"What, you mean like only having one life to give for my country?"

"I meant more like having enlisted in the first place. It's been pretty exciting these last couple of months."

"I think I said something about not wanting to dig through broken pots and old diapers the rest of my life. I haven't been doing that. That's got to count for something."

I patted him on the shoulder. "You know the rest of our lives may not be very long."

He grimaced. "I don't think that's how you're supposed to reassure your troops."

"You and I go too far back. You get stuck with the truth."

"Lucky me. So what's the truth?"

I considered. "It's tough to say. We've got a good position. They may not even engage. If they were smart, they'd pin us down and wait for reinforcements."

"That's not encouraging."

"I don't think they're going to be smart. Tarc's angry. I think they'll hit us tomorrow."

"So that's good?"

"If they hit us tomorrow, I think we'll get the better of it. And it's definitely going to be more exciting than digging for broken pots and dirty diapers."

I moved on. Kafer was on the roof of a two story building, behind a parapet of overturned tables. He was one of our better archers.

"I wonder what your sister would think of all this."

He let out a thin chuckle and made a face. "She'd say it's a waste. She'd say we're idiots fighting other men for land we won't even hold while Yoshana schemes to enslave the world and claim our souls. She'd say we're doing the devil's work."

His words hit me like a physical blow. I tried to come up with a retort, failed.

Kafer gave me a twisted smile. "That's why I don't write to her."

10. Sacrifice

Tired as I'd been, I'd meditated for an hour before giving in to sleep. Part of me was tempted to let the Darkness build into the kind of murderous wave I'd experienced the night I'd killed Lalos. But I would have been a danger to my own troops. Even if there was no possibility of salvation left to me, I didn't want the deaths of my friends and allies on my conscience when I fell.

When I finished falling. If there was any farther to go. I was still alive, but from Prophetess' perspective - from Genia Carter's perspective - I must already be far beyond redemption.

What had that irritating old man said? *There will be more rejoicing in heaven over one sinner who repents...* He probably wasn't thinking about a member of a cursed race who'd willingly taken on the powers of hell and used them to carve a trail of death across the continent. In any case, at the moment I needed the powers of hell. I could think about repentance later. If I lived.

The brigade's square was about half a mile long on each side, with the quartermaster's company, medics, the headquarters company, and a reserve in the center. Adapting Colonel Raji's idea of a feint, one company was continuing to drive the wagons down the road toward the Hawk's Nest, hopefully kicking up enough dust to make the Monolith believe the entire brigade was still in motion. They'd swing back around when the fighting started. The rest of us were hunkered down inside buildings and behind barricades.

The idea was to let as much of the enemy army as possible draw abreast of us before we opened fire in a massive broadside. If we'd had carbines for the entire brigade, a successful execution of that plan might have ended the matter right there. As it was, we didn't even have enough bows to arm every soldier. It would come down to hand-to-hand combat unless they broke and ran.

Captain Almet's company was just to the east of mine. He stopped by in the early morning.

"We've been lucky so far," he said hopefully. "You've broken them three times with almost no losses. Think we can do it again?"

Part of me was flattered. A part of me very close to the Darkness thought his praise was no more than my due. But a different part said, "I think you're giving me too much credit."

I had almost added "sir." It was hard to remember we now held the same rank. I might have one of the shortest-lived captaincies in history.

I continued, "We've had other big advantages each time. Those rangers in the woods were out there all by themselves between two battalions of our troops. It wouldn't take much to panic even the bravest man in a situation like that. At Riverside we had them outnumbered, and they still didn't really understand what they were dealing with. And at Steel City, Prince Jeral didn't want the Monolith advisors in the first place. We just gave him an excuse to kick them out."

"We've got position, cover, and surprise here," Almet said hopefully.

"Yep. That's why I think we can win. But they're pissed off. This is the first time we've faced a unit that actually wants to engage us. We'll bloody them, but I don't think they're going to run just because they take a hit."

"You'll still…" he waved his hand vaguely in the air.

"Summon the Darkness up from hell to scare them as much as I possibly can? Of course. I want to live too."

The waiting really was the worst of it. The feeling reminded me of our mad venture with Prophetess to Stephensburg, not knowing exactly the form our confrontation with Yoshana would take, but dreading whatever it would be.

By comparison, the confrontation with the Monolith shouldn't have seemed so terrible. Prophetess would surely have pointed out that at most the Monolith could destroy my body, whereas Yoshana could annihilate my soul.

Prophetess had never sat on a roof watching five thousand enemy troops march by.

The cavalry was first, of course. They came just after noon at an easy walk, no faster than the infantry behind them. I briefly spotted Tarc as I peered through the gap between tables, then he passed out of sight. The main body followed close on their heels, tightly packed on the wide road. The column was perhaps a mile long. We could take half of them under fire at once.

They say no battle plan ever survives contact with the enemy. This one certainly didn't.

At least it wasn't any of my troops who opened fire early. Or Almet's. But someone panicked before the Monolith troops were even halfway down the length of our front. A single arrow arced out. Then, uncertainly, a couple more followed.

Cries of "ambush!" went up from the enemy force.

"Dammit! Fire at will! Fire at will!" I bellowed.

Guns cracked. Arrows plunged. In the road, men fell.

But I had been right. Paladins screamed, "engage!" In the face of our fire, the Monolith troops charged rather than retreat. Just as I had bulled ahead into the ambush in the woods south of Riverside, seeing no other option, the enemy did the same.

We were at the corner of the square, so I had a clear view of the Monolith soldiers moving around to flank us. We had anticipated that with our formation, but my position was right at the focal point of the enemy attack. I'd picked it that way. As had been pointed out to me multiple times, sometimes Select don't seem to have a lot of common sense.

There were archers somewhere in the mass of Monolith troops. Arrows began to answer ours. But where I was, the enemy's weapons of choice were spear and shield. We got in two more ragged volleys before they reached us.

Pious kicked open a door and waded into them. He truly was a terror with that pick. Yoshana was more lethal with her sword, and I had no doubt the demon Seven would be far deadlier with his sharpened staff. But Pious was as close to the Grim Reaper as any ordinary mortal had a right to be.

His men followed behind, wading into the breach in the charging line of spearmen. The enemy advance halted, then collapsed on that section of the front.

Elsewhere things didn't go as well. Isolated by the buildings and barricades, we had no coherent line. Some of our men attacked, like Pious. Others stayed under cover and took the shock of the Monolith charge. Those who stayed on the defensive generally did better. Archers and gunmen on upper stories and rooftops savaged the attackers. When our side tried to advance, we found the enemy shield wall almost impenetrable. Pious could break it open - others could not.

A hundred feet to my left, a group of attackers led by a Paladin breached our defenses and flooded into the building beyond. I sent the Darkness down in a stinging cloud to claw at their eyes. Blinded and disoriented, they fell back.

I sent a thread of Darkness to Cat, showing her where our line had failed. She raced to the reserves and called for reinforcements. I had agreed with Hake the night before that the paleo would act as our spotter and courier. If the soldiers disliked taking instructions from her - and I'm sure some of them did - they set it aside in the interest of survival.

Pious' men were in the middle of a struggling knot of troops. We continued to rain death from above, but it was hard to target the enemies closest to our men without hitting our own. Railes had repelled the Monolith's first assault on his position, and was leading his squad in a counterattack. As fierce as the tattooed lieutenant was, he couldn't match Pious' hurricane of violence. The enemy's line hardened and shoved him back.

We had exhausted the ammunition for our carbines. We were reduced to arrows now. Railes was down. So were at least half a dozen of Pious' men. The enemy dead lay heaped in front of us. I lashed the survivors with a wave of the Darkness.

The Monolith cavalry came thundering past in a frenzied retreat. "Pull back! Pull back!" someone was calling, maybe Tarc. The enemy withdrew, stumbling, their lines ragged, but with raised shields protecting them from our continued arrow rain.

Some took up positions across the road from us, in the shelter of the trees. Others moved into the ruins to the west. It was not an orderly maneuver, but within ten minutes, they had drawn up battle lines on two sides of our square.

I surveyed the carnage from my rooftop. Between the dead and crippled who still lay on the battlefield, the Monolith had lost four or five hundred men. Two dozen cavalry mounts lay still or thrashing feebly on the ground. Of perhaps a thousand men who had entered the ambush, nearly half hadn't made it out. Our losses were far less - perhaps fifty dead or badly wounded. The advantage of surprise and position had told heavily in our favor. But the enemy still outnumbered us, and our best bolt was spent.

I went downstairs to the battlefield. The men were dragging our casualties inside. Railes was ashen under his tattoo.

"Dunno where that damn spear came from," he gasped. Blood bubbled out of his mouth as he spoke. His left side was soaked red.

I probed with the Darkness. A blade had gone between his lower ribs and opened his lung. I put my hands on his bloody tunic and concentrated.

Yoshana was right. What the Darkness would do without thought for my own body was almost impossible to do for another's. Cell by cell, I slowly stitched the wound shut, drained the fluid from the lung. I was exhausted when I turned to Groff. "Get him to the medics. He should live if infection doesn't get him."

"Thanks, Captain," the lieutenant murmured weakly.

"If you survive, you might reconsider charging an enemy force six times your size. I kinda look like an idiot for giving you a commission," I growled.

He produced a strained smile. "Sorry, Captain. I'll keep that in mind for next time."

Pious had five dead in his squad, and another with deep wounds to shoulder and thigh who had already been sent back to the medics. Railes had three dead and another two wounded besides himself. One of our archers was out of action with an arrow to the shoulder. The Shadowed Hand had dealt a vicious blow to the Monolith, but suffered disproportionately ourselves.

I turned to Pious, now standing in the building with me, his pick dripping gore. "That goes for you too, Sergeant. We don't have the men for a war of attrition."

The hulking soldier scowled but dipped his head in a curt nod.

Cat appeared behind me. "General wants you."

"Yeah. I figured."

"Gentlemen," Hake rumbled. "It went... decently. That's about the best I can say."

"Now sir," Colonel Royce interjected. "My staff make the casualty count nearly ten to one in our favor. A bit better than 'decent,' I'd say."

The general glared at him. "We ambushed them from cover in a heavily fortified position. Ten to one is the least we should have hoped for. And unfortunately, we hit only a fraction of their column."

Royce blushed. "Er. Yes. Captain Tollert is investigating which of his men opened fire prematurely. He'll be disciplined, General."

Hake waved his hand like a man shooing a gnat. "No point, Colonel. Error is the one constant in war. It's unfortunate. Now we are where we are. We won the first engagement, but we're still outnumbered and outclassed."

"It's not too late to press our advantage," Colonel Raji declared. "We may still have momentum on our side. It would have been better if Royce's battalion had counterattacked immediately, but we can still take the battle to them."

Raji's forces made up the eastern side of the square. They hadn't engaged the enemy. Nor would they be the obvious candidates to lead his proposed assault.

The Darkness bubbled angrily in my gut. "Two of my squads counterattacked, Colonel. They both lost half their strength, despite heavy supporting fire from the rest of my men."

Raji turned to me with a little smirk. "Then I suppose the famous Shadowed Hand isn't quite what we had been led to believe, is it, Captain?"

Almet physically interposed himself between me and the colonel, which might have saved Raji's life. He snapped, "Are you really that much of a fool? We've all just got done saying how tough we had it when we had surprise and were dug in. You think we have a snowball's chance in hell in a charge against a prepared Monolith line?"

Raji purpled. "General, I demand a reprimand for that insubordination."

"Raji, you're being an idiot. Is that enough of a reprimand?" Hake growled. "Keep your mouth shut if you've got nothing useful to say, or you'll be leading your counterassault from the front."

The tall colonel's mouth compressed into a tight line. He kept whatever he was thinking to himself. I didn't like him, but he wasn't a stupid man.

Hake looked at me. "Any thoughts, Captain?"

"I don't think the situation has changed much, sir. From the Monolith's perspective, they just took a beating, but they're still liking the odds. And they're madder than ever."

"You think they're going to hit us again."

"I hope so, sir."

The enemy spent hours digging in. Our position was better, but they built up defenses in the ruins and woods with frightening speed and efficiency. Shortly before sundown they began to probe our square, feeling out the edges. Seeing whether we had a flank that could be turned. The remaining cavalrymen raced around us, taking our measure. We obligingly shot arrows at them when they got close enough. They lost two men before they learned to keep a more respectful distance. Then one of our better snipers took another in the head with a carbine. After that they stopped riding around for a while.

Their infantry didn't try to completely encircle us. They were content with their positions on our southern and western fronts. But they did extend their lines past our own. That would make it hard for us to launch a flanking attack, and easier for them to swing around and press the eastern and northern sides of the square.

We shifted a couple of companies to the west and south, but we were still outnumbered by more than two to one on each of those fronts. Ammunition for the carbines had been redistributed and was now critically low everywhere. If the Monolith did come, we would not have an easy time of it.

I spent another evening reassuring my troops. I tried to be a bit more upbeat with Luco. "We smacked them around before. We'll do it again."

"They didn't know what was coming last time. This time they will."

"I'm supposed to be the brutally honest one here."

He managed a weak smile. "Spent too much time with you."

I'd assigned what was left of Railes' squad to Pious. Groff's squad had moved from the second floor to ground level.

"You okay?" I asked the big sergeant.

"What's not to be okay about? We've been through worse." I couldn't tell if he was serious, sarcastic, or trying to cheer himself up.

I settled for clapping him on the arm and saying, "Exactly." Even though I was pretty sure we hadn't.

Sesk was repairing arrows the other side had fired at us. For a while I just watched the short, dark man reset arrowheads and adjust fletching. His squad was up on the roof, the only one left providing cover fire for our infantry on the ground. At least they would have plenty of arrows.

After a while he said, "Plenty for the dark wolf to eat today."

The sun was going down. Campfires and torches sprang up to mark the enemy lines. There were a lot of them.

"Still think I shouldn't feed it?" I asked.

He met my eyes and slowly shook his head. "Dunno."

Kafer was in Sesk's squad, and I settled down on the roof next to him. I pulled out my katana, inspected it, and allowed the Darkness to play over the blade, touching up tiny spots of corrosion. The weapon was carbon steel, and it rusted if you looked at it wrong.

"I think I miss your sister," I said. "Even if she would tell me I was damned."

He nodded. "I miss her all the time. I mean, she's a colossal pain in the ass, but still."

"Yeah. She's the best person I ever met, you know." I closed my eyes and let myself remember. "I was really angry at her. I risked my life for her, more than once. And then she just threw me out. Because of this."

I looked at the Darkness flowing over the sword. "But now I'm thinking she wasn't wrong."

"Just because she's a good person doesn't mean she's always right, Captain."

"No. But it's a better starting place than most. If we live, you should write to her. She worries about you."

"Have you been writing to her, Captain?"

"I'm not the kind of thing people worry about."

That wasn't fair. Sesk treated me like a person. So did Luco, and Groff, and Railes, and Almet. I was feeding the dark wolf again. It liked the taste of self-pity.

I summoned up a smile. "Don't die tomorrow. That would be the one thing she'd never be able to forgive."

"Same to you, Captain."

I was just finishing my meditation when something touched my face. My eyes snapped open to find Cat crouching over me.

She pulled her hand back, but said in a voice of great determination, "Not die, you."

I had to grin. "Is that a prediction, or an order?"

"Yes."

The Monolith infantry advanced in ranks two deep, shields locked and raised, spears poking over the edges. Most of our arrows clattered off harmlessly. Their archers returned fire in massive volleys, keeping our men under cover where we couldn't aim as well.

The day before, our guns and bows had slaughtered scores of the enemy before their wild charge even reached our positions. This time we brought down a few handfuls.

None of us rushed out to meet them this time, not even Pious. Instead we let them hack at doors and climb awkwardly through broken windows. A round of arrows met the first of them to clamber into the buildings. With their shields out of position, more fell. Then it descended into a chaotic melee, cutting and thrusting and smashing.

The weight of their numbers was telling. They got the worst of the initial assault, but more kept coming. I abandoned the roof, stumbled down the stairs, and hurled myself into the thick of it.

Bodies milled in the shadows, shattered windows blocked by more Monolith troops forcing their way in. All semblance of order was gone. To my left, Pious had opened a circle with vicious swings of his pick, but he was bleeding freely from his left arm. To my right, a crush of flailing limbs stabbed and beat at each other.

I launched the Darkness in a wave. It scored bloody rivulets in exposed skin and clawed at eyes. I flung myself into a gap and swung my katana in a wide, high arc. It sliced above a soldier's shield, laid open his cheek, deflected off the nose guard of his helmet, and cut a vicious chunk from his lip. I'm not sure he even noticed.

I stepped past him inside the guard of another spearman and rammed the blade to its hilt into his guts. That one noticed. Briefly.

I called the Darkness back. It spun around me in a cloud, fouling enemies' strokes, getting into their faces so they couldn't focus on me. Now I was behind the ones inside, cutting them down even as they turned in confusion. Pious exploited their disarray and smashed his way toward me.

Someone drove a spear through my leather jerkin just above my hip bone. I cut the shaft of the weapon in half and pulled the point free. My attacker gabbled in terror and flung himself out a window. I stuck the remains of the spear into a Monolith soldier's thigh, then set about me with the katana in both hands. The strength the Darkness gave me battered shields aside, hacked through armor.

A Paladin standing in the doorway screamed, "He is one man! Even if hell itself -"

He didn't manage to finish his thought because Pious' pick thudded into his helmeted skull so hard the point emerged from the other side.

"Mirt is dead! Fall back! Fall back!"

They retreated in good order, not a panicked rout. A few of my quicker thinkers picked up their bows and sped shafts after them, but brought no one down.

I sent a probe of the Darkness to our left. Pious and I were perhaps the fiercest melee fighters in the brigade. If we had barely repelled the enemy, I doubted things were going well elsewhere.

And they weren't. The third building in the line was overrun. Platoons of reserves were holding back breaches in almost every street, though our archers were inflicting crippling casualties when the enemy fought in the open.

I sent to Cat, "Raji and Thonn have to take them in the flanks! Attack now! Now!"

Cat passed the message to Hake. I scrambled back to the roof where I could see.

I stood at the edge, gasping. My side hurt where the spear had pierced me. The Darkness was at work on that wound and a half dozen lesser cuts and bruises.

"You might want to move back from there," Kafer said mildly. I had wedged myself out between two tables to get a better view. Prophetess' brother popped up, sighted carefully, and fired an arrow into the swirling mass in the street below. He was back behind cover before answering fire came from the woods and the second story of a house across the way.

I twitched out of the path of two arrows. "Let them waste their shots."

"Can you dodge bullets too?" Kafer asked.

I got back behind the tables. The Monolith forces didn't seem well-provisioned with firearms, but that didn't mean they didn't have any at all.

"There we go," I breathed. Either the enemy's plan or their discipline was less than perfect. Their projecting wings had swept in to strike our square. Raji and Thonn's troops were unfolding from cover like a flower opening, swinging around to hit the attackers from behind.

The Monolith cavalry had split into two groups. They came out of nowhere at a full charge to hit each of our flanking forces. They were less than a tenth the size of Raji and Thonn's battalions, but their mobility and the weight of their mounts let them do damage out of all proportion to their numbers.

Our archers engaged them to good effect, but our envelopment had lost momentum and devolved into yet another bloody melee.

Somebody on the other side had had enough. Horns sounded. Slowly, painfully, in struggling knots, the Monolith troops disengaged and pulled back to their defenses.

"How do you make their losses?" Hake asked.

Captain Selles, his adjutant, had been going from roof to roof, counting. He looked just a little bit ill. "Hard to tell for sure. They pulled their wounded in last night but not all of the dead. I'd say today there's somewhere between five hundred and a thousand of them lying out there."

The dead "out there" included heaps of enemy corpses we had pitched out of our defensive positions. We had taken a few prisoners. But not many. Bodies from both sides lay where they had fallen. It was amazing how quickly living men became masses of inert tissue with red things exposed that should have been decently hidden by skin.

The general nodded grimly. "Say a quarter of their force over two days. How did we do?"

"Better than they did. Not as well as we did yesterday. Nearly four hundred casualties. About half of those are wounded, but a lot of them won't make it."

The Shadowed Hand had taken another brutal beating. We had only three more dead, but another five in the infirmary. My company, always undersized, was down to little more than half its strength.

"You've called it pretty well so far, Minos. Think they'll try again?"

"I don't know, sir. We'll see."

"Last night you said 'I hope so.' Not looking forward to it this time?"

I tried to smile but couldn't quite pull it off. "It just isn't as much fun anymore, sir."

They didn't come again that day. Or the next. They didn't move, either. By noon of our fourth day in the ruins, the brigade's mood had soured even further. While the respite had been welcome for twenty-four hours, now we were back to waiting. Would they attack or wouldn't they, and when?

Both sides buried their dead, men sweating as they dug into cracked earth. The summer heat didn't fade even at night. The living smelled bad enough - the stench of the corpses was intolerable.

I spent time in the infirmary, doing my best to help. I didn't accomplish much. I could do things the medics couldn't, but I was slow, and the effort tired me. I like to think I saved a few lives in that little slice of hell on earth. Many of the wounded died anyway. It was hot, and humid, and stank of sweat and infection. We were running low on provisions. It was hard even to get enough water to keep the men hydrated.

Every few hours I would flood the place with the Darkness and kill all the flies that swarmed around the still or softly moaning bodies. I was good for that, at least. ▪

I could also talk to Railes. The only question around the camp had become, "You think they're going to hit us today?" Mostly people asked me that. I asked him instead.

"Why should they?" my lieutenant wheezed. "All they got to do is pin us down until reinforcements come up."

It wasn't that the tattooed soldier was a strategic genius. The situation was obvious. Outside the infirmary, the men were tense, and if anything the officers were worse.

"I sent couriers down to Rockwall yesterday," Hake said, "But who knows how long it'll take them to get through."

"If they do get through," Raji snapped. "Or if headquarters deigns to send us any support. The maps put us less than a week from the Hawks' Nest, and the enemy has an open road behind them. What are the chances we get reinforced before either another Monolith brigade or a couple of Hawk battalions come up? I'd say pretty damn close to none."

The general shrugged, suddenly weary. "We did the best we could with the hand we were dealt."

Raji glared at me. "It's maybe a shame we relied on a sorcerer for our tactics. When you sold your soul to hell, you might have asked for military genius as part of the exchange."

The Darkness pounded in my chest, a caged beast trying to claw its way free. I choked out, "I've still got one more trick up my sleeve, Colonel. But no one's going to like it."

"So…" I muttered to the cloud in front of me. "Let's see if we can do this without killing our own team, shall we?"

The cloud seethed and coiled, but said nothing in return.

In the end it was just Cat, Sesk, and Pious with me in the tangled, night-shrouded woods north of the enemy's position. The rest of the Shadowed Hand - what was left of it - was fifty paces behind with carbines and all the ammunition left in the brigade.

I trusted Cat and Sesk to stay out of my way. To be honest I didn't care if I killed Pious by mistake.

I pulled the eager Darkness back inside me, felt it bubbling behind my eyes. I heard it in my voice.

"Stay clear," I repeated. "This isn't like any other time. Sometimes you have to feed the dark wolf if you want to live."

The night was moonless. I didn't see as much as sense the hunter's frown. "There are worse things than dying," he muttered.

"I'm pretty sure I'm damned already, Sergeant. But I've made a habit of surviving over this past year. I don't care to give it up. And besides, it doesn't seem fair to sacrifice the whole brigade for what's left of my soul."

Sesk grunted. He disapproved, but he would follow me.

Even in the dark I could see Cat's white teeth in her wild grin. Without the Darkness I wouldn't have known she was frightened. Now I felt everything around me, the movement of every branch in the wind, the heartbeat of every field mouse. The Darkness and I were one.

This must have been what it felt like to be Yoshana, to let slip every constraint on the Darkness. It coiled and hissed, feeding on Cat and Sesk's fear, feeding on Pious' hate. It was growing maddened, a pressure building that would need the release of fight or flight. It fed on itself, a dark wolf chasing its own tail of rage and pain.

I wasn't Yoshana. I couldn't master that wild flow the way she could. But for one night, there would be no greater terror than me on this side of the Muddy.

Once I was moving, I couldn't say where my body ended and the Darkness began. The concept ceased to have meaning. Did I cut down the Monolith sentries with my blade or a million devouring mouths? It made no difference. They fell.

There was a sea of fear before me, and screams. I moved into it, drinking deeply from the well of its suffering. Behind me there were other, lesser things. They followed me, and I was angry. Did they want to steal my food? I nearly turned back to strike them down, but there was so much to kill in front of me. I would destroy the small creatures behind in due time.

Metal pierced the solid parts of me. I roared my rage and washed over the things that had hurt me. My solid core was vulnerable but strong enough, and I could repair the damage done to it. At least enough to keep killing. The things that fought me couldn't repair the damage I did to them. I laughed. I was predator. They were prey.

There were nodes in the sea of fear, almost solid. Some of the prey had a will of its own. I didn't like that.

Then there was fire. My limbs burned. I recoiled in pain. The prey should not use fire. There was a wall of it between me and the prey. I seethed, hurt and angry. I must flee, but that would mean abandoning my food. Rage and hunger and fear warred in me.

One of the nodes penetrated me, gripping my solid core. I lashed at it wildly. Wet and cold splashed my face.

"What?" I gasped.

Gunfire cracked behind me.

"We've got to go!" Sesk barked. I let him pull me stumbling back through the covering line of my troops. As the light of the enemy's torches played over him I could see there was something wrong with his face, but I wasn't sure what.

"Odd thing is it didn't bleed at all," Sesk said. "Can't say it don't hurt, though."

I couldn't take my eyes off the furrows gouged into his left cheek. "I'm sorry," I repeated, for perhaps the fourth time.

The hunter shrugged. "You warned us. Cat figured throwing water in your face might wake you up, but we needed to turn you around first. I got off pretty easy compared to all the Monolith troops you killed."

The attack had been chaos, but Sesk figured we'd killed several dozen and started a huge panic before the Paladins blocked me with torches. Consumed by the Darkness as I was, I hadn't been able to reason a way past the obstacle, and the assault had stalled.

It had been a distraction anyway, designed to sow confusion while we concentrated troops on our western flank and punched into their lines.

Unfortunately the Monolith's superior discipline had told. I'd hoped they would break, but they hadn't. Our best guess was that once again we'd gotten the better of the casualty ratio, but their lines had held. My last bolt was shot. I'd sacrificed what was left of my self-control and nearly killed a friend, and we were still just as trapped.

The Shadowed Hand was sitting in a wide ring around me on our rooftop. Other than Cat, Sesk, and Luco, none dared get too close, even though I looked sane now. But they were morbidly curious. My tunic was a mass of holes, my skin a moonscape of scars where the Darkness had done enough to keep me alive but hadn't worried about appearances. I had no sense for how many times I'd been stabbed, slashed, or shot. I didn't want to know.

I lay on my back, a bedroll pillowed under my head. I was exhausted. If I asked it to, the Darkness could sustain me until my body tore itself apart, and then it could put me back together. I preferred it the way it was now, quiet. If I let it out again, I wasn't sure a canteen full of water to the face would bring me back to myself.

"Any other ideas, boss?" Sesk asked.

"Just one. If by some chance we live, I know a girl named Quilla Farr in a village south of here called Brambledge who'd probably like to meet you."

Over the next days the Darkness was a throbbing ache rather than a boiling rage. I had no illusions, though. The time would come in one of Hake's staff meetings when Raji would push me a little too far, and I would kill him. I didn't want to - it would be the final loss of my humanity. But then again, it wasn't like any of us had much longer to live anyway.

There were no more assaults by either side. The Monolith cavalry would ride around our square occasionally, making sure we weren't breaking out to the north or east. We'd shoot arrows at them, but they had figured out our range and the only loss they took was a horse putting its foot wrong and coming up lame. Every now and then the opposing lines would fire a volley at each other, just because it seemed appropriate.

Mostly we waited. Our sharpest-eyed scouts stood on the rooftops and watched to the west, the east, and the south. We hoped against all reasonable expectation that the first troops we saw would be Rockwall reinforcements. A lot of the men and some of the officers found a new devotion to prayer. I'd never had that habit, and certainly wasn't in a position to start now.

It was the fifth day after our unsuccessful attack that one of our lookouts shouted, "Force approaching!"

The man was looking east.

"Coming in from the Hawks' Nest," Raji observed. "We're screwed."

As sick as I was of hearing that phrase from him, it was hard to disagree.

Oblivious to how undignified it might look, the whole command group crammed itself onto the roof of a four story building to watch the newcomers coming toward us.

"Only good news is there's not very many of them," Thonn said. "Doesn't look like more than a hundred men."

"Cavalry, though," Raji noted sourly.

Thonn shook his head. "Mounted infantry, I think."

"How can you tell the difference?"

"There's a way a cavalry trooper sits a horse, and a way some ground pounder with a sore butt does. These guys aren't comfortable in the saddle."

Hake shook his head. "Makes no sense. Why would the Hawks send one infantry company? That's not going to change the situation here."

"The Hawks aren't famous for being that bright, sir," Captain Selles remarked.

The oncoming column drew to a halt a mile away, as if they could hear us discussing them. After a time, a single horseman detached himself from the main group and came closer.

"Is that what I think it is?" Hake demanded.

"Looks like a white flag, sir."

"What the hell is this?" The general considered. "Whatever's going on, let's figure it out before the Monolith does. Get a patrol out there to see what these people want."

"I'll go, sir," I volunteered.

"You will not," Hake snapped. "We want to talk to them, not kill them. At least for now."

That hurt. I had engineered the negotiations with Prince Jeral without a death on either side. But then, that was perhaps not the same version of me that had entered into full communion with the Darkness. I nodded, silent.

Which made it all the more ironic when half an hour later a scout came puffing up the stairs and declared, "Captain Minos? They want to talk to you."

11. Together Again

The lanky figure that followed the soldier through the door might have been the last person I had ever expected to see on a battlefield.

"What on earth are you doing here?" I burst out.

"What a welcome. I am the herald of the Order of Thorns," Doctor John Dee declared.

"That's - what, that's Tolf out there?"

"Do you know these people, Captain?" Hake demanded.

"Commander Tolf, yes," Dee said, with a self-satisfied grin. "And Prophetess herself."

As I tried to digest that, Hake asked again, "Captain, what is the situation? What is the nature of this force?"

I held up one hand to forestall more questions, pinching the bridge of my nose with the other. I suddenly had the beginnings of the kind of headache I only associated with Prophetess. After a moment, I was able to say, "Sir, the Order of Thorns is a military force attached to the Universal Church at Our Lady. Specifically, it's the personal guard of a woman named Genia Carter, who calls herself Prophetess."

It was Dee's turn to goggle. Apparently he hadn't figured out her name yet. One point to me. I was briefly able to match his smirk and said, "I can find out things too, you know."

"Informative and yet unhelpful," General Hake snapped. "What are they doing here? Are they allies or enemies?"

"That's a very fair question, General, which takes us back to where we started. Dee, what are you doing here?"

"Depends on exactly what you choose to believe, *Captain* Minos." Dee put a great deal of emphasis on my title. His grin was back. "Either looking for allies, or looking for you."

"What?"

"Minos, I'm not giving anything away when I say in front of your friends here that we have sources inside Stephensburg. They tell us Yoshana will march on Our Lady next spring."

My headache was getting worse. "If Yoshana's allowed you to know that, you should be seriously considering the possibility that she's either marching on you already or intends to wait until hell freezes over. No one knows better than me how deceptive she is, but you should have gotten a pretty good idea yourself. Weren't you the one who told me she'd always be two steps ahead? Before you decided it would be a good idea for me to go off on a false peace mission where you couldn't conceive of any possible downside?"

Hake and the rest of the command staff had taken several steps away from me. I realized the Darkness had risen into a thin, smoky sheen over my body. I hadn't thought I would be angry at Dee - but I was.

I went on, not really able to stop. Or not wanting to. "And of course she's going to attack, you idiot. Didn't I tell you that? Didn't I tell you before I ever went off with her that the Order of Thorns needed to be an army, not a few dozen half-trained soldiers who'd never seen a fight, all worshipping Prophetess like a bunch of damn puppies? Didn't I tell you the same thing again when I came back from that seething hell in the Sorrows, after I turned on the whole damn world's most dangerous military leader for you? And if I remember correctly, you told me to get out."

The cloud was all around me now.

"So I got out. And I found someone who had a use for my talents. So yes, I'm a captain now. And in case you hadn't noticed, I'm busy being in the middle of a war here. And this -" I made a fist, and the Darkness thickened around it - "is what I am. And maybe Prophetess was right, and it's taken my soul. And as it turns out, the trade wasn't that great, because it's looking like we're all going to die here."

Everyone except Dee was up against the edge of the roof trying to get as far from me as possible. To my very great surprise, the occultist held his ground.

"She wants to talk to you, Minos. She told us we were coming west to find allies, but she's been on your trail the whole time."

Tears of frustration trickled down my face. The Darkness clawed them away. "It's a little late, Dee."

Hake spoke up, in as tentative a voice as I'd ever heard from him. "Late or not, a hundred men who might be on our side can't hurt. Let's have them join us here before the Monolith gets to them."

"Just so, General," Dee said brightly. I shook my head. I might have killed the prattling fool, yet the terror of my rage washed off him like water off a duck's back. He lifted his eyebrows at me. "I think she might tell you it's never too late. You remind me of one of my favorite Canticles of Holy Mary, about a knight who tried to sell his wife to the devil. In the end, Holy Mary herself takes the lady's form and goes to meet the devil, whose plot is of course foiled. The knight repents and becomes a devoted servant of Mary, just as his wife was."

I tried to wrap my mind around a point in his babble. The Darkness had subsided, but the headache was back. "What's that supposed to mean, Dee? I'm the knight, and the Darkness is the devil? Then who's Prophetess? Is she Mary? Or my wife?"

The occultist just smiled. "I'll leave that to you to decide."

The man was ridiculous. It was hard to stay angry at him, and I felt myself begin to relax. Then abruptly the dark wolf came roaring back, wounded and angry. The Darkness poured from my eyes, and my nose, and my mouth, and I heard myself snap, "I'll think about that. But while you're being biblical, how about you and Prophetess think about Psalm Eighty-eight?"

Dee's eyebrows went up again. "I'm not sure that off the top of my head..."

"'You have turned my friends and neighbors against me. Now Darkness is my one companion left.'"

My treacherous guts churned like an angry sea as I waited alone on the first floor to see Genia Carter, the farm girl who called herself Prophetess. I'd been less nervous going to war. I thought even Yoshana wouldn't disturb me as much. At least my feelings toward the Overlord were clear.

The person who stepped through the door was silhouetted by the light outside, but I knew the figure. I'd spent months as close to her as to my own shadow. She moved inside, blinking in the dim light. She found me standing in the center of the room.

I didn't know what to say.

She spoke first, but I didn't expect the words. "Minos, I'm sorry."

My mouth opened, but no sound came out.

"I was wrong to send you away when you needed me the most. But I was afraid for you."

When my voice came, it was little more than a whisper. "I think you mean you were afraid of me."

"No. Never that. I was afraid you might do something and you wouldn't be able to forgive yourself for it."

Hardened warriors had backed away from the grin I showed her. "Well, I've done those things now. But not in your service. So I suppose that's for the best. I guess you were right about what I'd become."

The Darkness began to leak out. It was visible even in the shadowed room. She held her ground.

"And what you've become, what you've done... are you proud of that?" she asked.

The flow of the Darkness became a roaring in my ears. I wanted to scream, *I've done what I had to do. I've become what you and Yoshana turned me into.*

But all I said was, "No."

And I was shocked to see tension ease out of her shoulders and a smile appear on her face. "Good. That's so good. Pride isn't just the worst sin because it's the one that all others flow from. It's also the one that's hardest to repent. If you're proud of what you've done, you can't ask God's forgiveness for it."

I raised my hands, and the Darkness swirled around them. "I don't think your God's going to forgive this."

To my continuing surprise, her smile broadened. "Now *that's* pride. God's mercy is infinite. Your sin is only human. You don't have the capacity to sin beyond God's ability to forgive, as long as you repent."

I stared at her, dumbfounded.

She asked, "Do you want that stuff out of you?"

The cloud coiled around me, angry. It was almost limitless strength at almost limitless cost. I had already learned it was not something to be easily set aside.

"Yes," I whispered.

"Good," she repeated happily. "Then we'll get rid of it."

I choked out a disbelieving laugh. "Tess, this isn't like the little cloud that possessed the miller's daughter in Brambledge. What's in me is a whole different order."

"And by the grace of God I've faced Yoshana and lived. You don't think you've become more terrible than her, do you?"

I recalled that Grigg and I had stepped in front of Prophetess to keep Yoshana from killing her, and Grigg had fought the Overlord, Darkness against Darkness. I wasn't sure it was entirely accurate for Prophetess to claim she'd faced Yoshana. What I said was, "It's maybe not the best time. I've got a battle to fight here."

"And the Darkness has been winning it for you?"

I had to concede her a rueful smile. "It's more that we're waiting to die."

Prophetess said, "It seems like a shame for two armies to destroy each other in front of me just when I need one."

"Dee said that. You weren't trying to recruit the Hawks, were you? They're the most incompetent band of cutthroats on the face of the earth."

"We were trying to decide between heading south to propose an alliance with Rockwall or west to propose an alliance with the Monolith."

I snorted. "The Monolith are Josephites. I don't think they'd welcome an alliance with the Universal Church."

"Dee says the Monolith are also pragmatists. He thought they might prefer to fight Yoshana in the Source rather than on their own borders once she gets done with us."

I nodded slowly. "There's something to be said for that. Well, there is conveniently a Monolith army here, likely with another one on the way. They just have to eliminate an annoying Rockwall brigade with a Select sorcerer in it."

She looked me in the eyes. "That is why I'm here, you know. We were sitting outside the Hawk's Nest arguing about which way to go when we heard about a terrifying army commanded by a Select wielding the powers of hell."

"'Commanded by' is overstating the case a little. I am kind of glad we got to be called terrifying, though."

She snorted, again the girl who'd never been quite as impressed with me as I might have wanted. "Really, Minos. The Shadowed Hand? A little dramatic for you."

"Says the woman who leads the Order of Thorns." I hadn't failed to notice the circle of roses and thorns stitched on her tunic.

She blushed. "Dee and Tolf think the symbol is important for morale."

"They're not wrong. A lot of war is in your mind, and your enemy's." An idea surfaced in my head. I turned it over in my brain, examining it from different angles. "Are you sure you can get this stuff out of me?"

"If you want to be free of it, I can cast it out."

I didn't need the Darkness to sense the doubt under the assurance she projected. I knew her too well. But she might be the only chance for the brigade. And for me.

12. Clothed in the Sun

"You're sure you can do this?" I repeated as we approached the meeting place.

"I told you I can do it if you want me to," Prophetess said. "I'm not worthy that the Lord should enter under my roof, but at a word of his my soul shall be healed. Yours too. All you have to do is reach up and grasp the hand he holds out to you."

"I'm just saying it's probably going to be briefly embarrassing and permanently fatal if it doesn't work."

"How about you shut up, Minos," General Hake growled. "You're not making me feel any better about staking my entire command on this scheme of yours."

"To be fair, General, I don't think the brigade is going to be any worse off than it was before if this goes badly. Except for you and me both being dead."

"Well, I don't suppose our tactics were winning for us anyway, so no great loss there. Other than personally."

"That's how I figured it."

It was somehow liberating to put my fate in someone else's hands. The Monolith had demanded to set the meeting place. Since we were both the party requesting the parley and in the weaker tactical position, we had accepted that condition, along with the limitation on our numbers.

Dee preceded our group with a huge white flag, which seemed entirely appropriate. He still embodied the strangest combination of foolhardy courage and abject cowardice I had ever encountered. Prophetess, Hake, and I followed. Tolf was there too as Prophetess' protector. The guardsman from Our Lady had done no more than nod at me when I'd greeted him. He looked like he expected me to eat Prophetess at any moment. That hurt. He'd been a friend.

We crossed the no man's land between the Rockwall and Monolith lines and approached the four story building the enemy had selected for the negotiations. I could see apprehensive faces and drawn bows in the windows. Thin tendrils of the Darkness showed me more soldiers behind and above. As we neared the door, a grizzled veteran with the shield and rank marks of a Paladin threw it open.

"Get in, then," he growled.

Dee struggled awkwardly to navigate the doorway with the flag of truce.

"Just leave that," snapped the Paladin. "We get the point. And it is not as if we trust your hellspawn any more because you have a bedsheet on a stick."

The Darkness growled within me, and I silenced it with an effort of will.

They had set torches in the stairwell inside, and the Darkness didn't like that either. Nor did it care for the soldiers aiming pistols at us on each landing. I can't say I liked that much myself.

It's funny how suspicious some people get when you come in the night and murder their friends.

We emerged onto the roof, returning to daylight. I relaxed fractionally. Our archers and gunmen couldn't really support us adequately here, at this range, but the ideal place for an ambush would have been inside. Maybe the Monolith intended to play this straight. Or maybe they'd been afraid of what I could do to them inside a dark, enclosed space. They hadn't been wrong on that score. I wouldn't have survived if they'd attacked, but their losses would have been the stuff of horrific legend.

I swallowed and throttled back the Darkness as it tried to rise up, buoyed by a rush of adrenaline. That was not something we could afford.

On the roof we found ourselves in a wide circle of gunmen, all aiming at us. Inside the circle stood Tarc and a half dozen Paladins.

Dee pointed to the one in the center, a big man with gray hair and beard. His tabard was black with a white cross, and he leaned on a huge metal shield with the same colors.

"A BlackShield," Dee said enthusiastically. "There aren't more than a dozen of them in the Monolith. They must really not like you, Minos."

The Paladin cleared his throat. His voice was deep and husky. The eyes that met mine were as gray as his hair. "I am aware that I will not make it off this roof alive if you decide to kill me, Select. Maybe no one will. But I have men on every rooftop around us, and trust me, they have your in their sights. If I do not walk away from this, neither will you."

"I wouldn't have it any other way... General? What do I call you?"

"I am BlackShield Jarl Lago. If you must address me, you may call me that."

"Seems a little unwieldy." I smiled as I said it. He did not return the gesture.

"A Monolith soldier would refer to him as 'Black,'" Dee added helpfully.

"You will not call me that."

I sent tiny strands of Darkness crawling over him. He was harder to read than Prince Jeral's envoy back in Steel City. If he was afraid of me, he did an admirable job of concealing it.

"What's your proposal, Minos?" growled Tarc. The big Select was an open book. He was looking for an excuse to order the gunmen to open fire. "Say something worthwhile, or get the hell off my roof."

The BlackShield shot him a warning glance. Tarc was overstepping his authority. It wasn't his roof.

But I didn't need to further antagonize the other Select. "Let me introduce my companions, and they'll explain. General Hake you'll know, at least by reputation."

"I had heard you were a colonel," the BlackShield said.

"The campaign's been good for me." That was a bold move by Hake, but I admired him for it. He was reminding the other side that even though we were in a bad position now, we'd been chalking up victories against the Monolith for the last couple of months.

"Until now," Lago grated.

The general smiled. "Unless you count casualties differently than I do, I'm still liking it. Let's not play games here, BlackShield. You've got us pinned here, and the smart money says your reinforcements arrive before ours do. But we'll bleed you bad before you take us down. We've won every single engagement we've fought against you. Every one. Unless you count the time your Select friend here hit our unarmed supply train in the middle of the night to slaughter a bunch of cooks and laundresses, and I don't think you enjoyed the aftermath of that one either."

Tarc growled and took a step forward. The look the BlackShield fixed on him would have reduced a lesser man to tears.

"Very well, General. As you say, enough games. Let us come to a point. Continue with your introductions, abomination. I do not think we enjoy each other's company enough to prolong this more than necessary."

I couldn't have said why, but the word "abomination" didn't bother me from the BlackShield. Maybe it was because I actually found myself just a little bit impressed by him. I hoped I wouldn't have to kill him in the next few minutes.

I nodded. "So, continuing. Doctor John Dee, herald of the Order of Thorns."

A short man, robed and hooded, pushed between two Paladins. I hadn't even noticed him. A prominent nose and wisps of beard protruded from beneath the hood. "Doctor John Dee? *The* Doctor John Dee?"

Dee swelled up like a rooster. "Indeed, sir. And you are?"

"I am Aharon, son of Malak."

"Not the same Aharon son of Malak who wrote the treatise on paleo ritual sorcery?"

The hooded man gave a little bow. "The same."

"Oh, a pleasure, sir, a pleasure."

"Enough," the BlackShield snapped. "This is a war parley, not a convention of witch finders. Save your mutual admiration for later, if you both live."

"I didn't think your people held with the occult, BlackShield," Hake sneered. He was going to push the enemy commander too far, but couldn't seem to help himself.

Lago scowled. "A Josephite does not study such things. The son of Malak is a Descendant. They have their uses, as do the Select. I did not think your people embraced the Darkness, General, but you seem to have found a use for that thing." He glared at me.

Dee's intervention was, for a wonder, timely. "Ah, well, that brings us close to the subject at hand, BlackShield Jarl Lago. Allow me to present Prophetess, principal of the Order of Thorns, representative of Our Lady, upon whom rests the hand of the Lord God."

One of the Paladins spat at Dee's feet. "This is too much! Bad enough you bring your filthy murdering sorcerer - we will not hear your heathen witch called a prophet of God!"

Tolf took three long steps and stuck his finger in the man's face. "Call her a witch again and you'll be eating that shield, you ignorant, sheep-loving hill savage."

With a quarterstaff, I would give Tolf decent odds against most men. He was unarmed. The Paladin would have him for lunch and use his bones for toothpicks. Guns swung around to fix on Tolf. The Darkness boiled inside me. This was going to end in disaster, but we weren't going to die alone.

"Stop that!" Prophetess' voice cracked like a whip. "This is what we cannot do! We can't fight each other while Yoshana plans to enslave us all."

Tolf ducked his head and slunk back to her side like a whipped dog.

"And do you speak for all those with you, little girl?" Lago demanded. "Do you command the armies of Rockwall?"

"I command this one."

The BlackShield snorted in surprise.

Hake nodded. "She speaks for me and my brigade. We've pledged ourselves to her. Listen to what she has to say."

But instead the hooded man interrupted. "You say this is a prophet, John Dee. You know of these things, but I am a Descendant of the Prophets. Where are her mighty deeds? Is the Word of God in her mouth? I see only a girl."

"Deborah was a woman and a prophet, Aharon son of Malak," Dee said.

"Deborah led the armies of Israel and crushed the king of the Canaanites. What has this one done?"

"I've seen her cast out the Darkness."

"*You* have seen," sneered the Paladin who had spat before. "All I have seen her cast out are words, and those not very impressive."

"Would you like to see the Darkness cast out, then?" I asked. I tried to keep my voice from shaking, but I don't think I quite managed it.

The Paladin opened his mouth, but Lago silenced him with a gesture. "Enough, Stonn. What are you offering, Select?"

"Do you know what I am? I was trained by Grigg of the Monolith and Yoshana herself. I've crossed the Sorrows and spoken with demons. I've killed Paladins in single combat and breached every defense you could erect. I am the Shadowed Hand."

I glanced at Prophetess. "She will end that."

The BlackShield looked from me to Hake, incredulous. "You would give that up? You *can* give that up?"

The general shrugged. "You said it yourself. It's a bargain with the devil, and for what? So we can kill some more of you before you drag us down? I can't ask my captain to sell his soul for that."

"That kind has no soul," said Stonn. I'd already decided that if things went badly, he was dying first. Tarc cleared his throat noisily. The Paladin had the decency to look just a bit embarrassed. It's not really polite to say out loud that your allies are soulless monsters, even if everyone knows you think it.

"No exorcism of that order has ever been performed," the Descendant protested.

At least not by anyone who didn't command the Darkness themselves. I had no doubt that Yoshana or Seven could pull the Darkness out of me, quite possibly even against my will. I kept that to myself.

I was worried enough about whether Prophetess could do it. And although she didn't show it, I knew she was too.

"Prophetess can cast it out of him," Dee said confidently. It was hard to know whether he was as sure as he sounded. He was a facile liar.

"A trick," Stonn muttered. "Just because the cloud departs him, does not mean it is banished..."

I nodded. "So bring torches. Burn it when it leaves. It's not a bad idea. It's going to be pissed off when it comes out." I managed to say "when" rather than "if."

It was getting pretty riled up already. It was intelligent enough, in its own way, to understand what was coming. The only reason it wasn't angrier was because it didn't believe Prophetess could do it.

A couple of the gunmen had scrambled to the door to demand torches from below. The tension in the air had a different character now.

Tarc stepped up to me and hissed, "If somehow your pretend prophet does this, you and I will have a reckoning, boy. For Lalos."

I nodded. Prophetess said to him, "We ask the Lord to forgive us our trespasses, as we forgive those who trespass against us."

"You don't know what he's done," the older Select snapped.

"The one to whom little is forgiven, loves little," she replied. "Perhaps too little has been forgiven you."

Tarc backed away. There was a new authority in Prophetess that I hadn't seen before. Maybe she could do this after all. As she turned to me, she seemed taller.

"You know the time," she intoned. "It is the hour now for you to awake from sleep. For our salvation is nearer now than when we first believed; the night is advanced, the day is at hand. Let us then throw off the works of darkness and put on the armor of the light; let us conduct ourselves properly as in the day, not in orgies and drunkenness, not in promiscuity and lust, not in rivalry and jealousy. But put on the Lord Jesus Christ, and make no provision for the desires of the flesh."

The Darkness rose in my throat like bile. I swallowed, afraid at any moment I would vomit it up.

"For you were once darkness, but now you are light in the Lord. Live as a child of light. Take no part in the fruitless works of darkness."

Fruitless, were they? Were the victories upon victories of the Shadowed Hand fruitless? That weakling Tarc dared to threaten me only because he thought I would give up my strength. He would run like a rabbit from my true form.

"Minos," Prophetess' voice cut across my thoughts like a knife. "Minos, do you reject the Enemy, and all his works of darkness?"

I shook my head. What enemy? Whose works? Mine?

The creature in front of me set its hand on my physical core and spoke again. "Do you reject the Enemy? Do you believe in God the Father Almighty, maker of heaven and earth?"

I burst out into my full form and roared, "There is no god but me, and I am my own prophet!"

How the little things feared me! Except for the one, so close, touching me. I reached out to tear it apart -

A cloud that had shadowed the sky moved aside in the wind. I felt something flood from Prophetess in waves, cutting through me like a radiant tide of light. The Darkness parted around her, and her tunic shone white in the sunlight. I staggered as the Darkness recoiled from her.

"A woman clothed in the sun," Dee breathed.

"Do you reject the Enemy and all his works?"

The Darkness was stunned. I stared into Prophetess' eyes and with my own voice whispered, "I do."

"Do you believe in the Father Almighty, Our Lord Jesus Christ, the Holy Spirit, the Universal Eucharistic Church, and life everlasting?"

I wasn't sure, but I gasped out, "I do" before the Darkness could seize me again.

"Then the power of the Enemy has no hold on you. Cast it out!"

415

We are one! the Darkness shrieked in my head.

I closed my eyes and let peace wash over my body from the woman in front of me. A wolf, bright as the sun on snow, howled triumphantly, and a dark one fled. *No we're not.*

I opened my eyes to see a vast cloud streaming away into the sunlight. The edge of its thoughts tasted of fear and despair.

The Descendant was the first to his knees. "Prophetess," he breathed. His hood had fallen back, and his blue eyes were full of tears.

All around, the Paladins and other Monolith troops laid down their weapons and knelt. Lago was the last, lowering himself stiffly.

"What is it you want from us?" he asked.

"The Darkness Radiant is far stronger and darker than what God has cast out of Minos," Prophetess said. "Yoshana's legions will engulf the world if we don't stop them, and all that is good and decent will fall. Will you help me stand against them, BlackShield Jarl Lago?"

The old warrior drew himself up and brought his fist to his heart. "As God is my witness, I will."

Tarc, who had not knelt, stepped closer to me and sneered softly, "Parlor tricks. Effective, though. The Josephites are a superstitious lot in the end."

I shook my head, still trembling with reaction. Out of the corner of my eye, I watched the Darkness spread thin and vanish as it fled. "It didn't feel like a parlor trick from where I was standing."

I had feared peace might not be so easily made between the Monolith and Rockwall troops, but I needn't have worried. After a week of facing each other across our lines, no one was eager to keep fighting until we were all dead.

Lago and Hake had each sent couriers to their respective headquarters, announcing their armies were now under Tess' command and would be accompanying her back to Our Lady. They'd both claimed to be acting in their nations' best interests, preempting invasion by Yoshana.

Hake had said to me, "Anyway, without her, we'd have wiped each other out. She saved us from that, so I figure we're hers now."

Lago seemed to have decided much the same thing.

The news that both armies were now following a prophet spread like wildfire, and the troops crowded around to stare at Prophetess. At first Tolf and the Order of Thorns had tried to form a protective cordon around her, but they quickly gave up. Especially when she kept slipping through to shake hands and give blessings.

I trailed along in her wake, still a bit stunned. Tolf came up and slapped me on the shoulder. "Doing okay, buddy?"

I raised my eyebrows. "So we're back to being buddies now?"

He gave me a wounded look. "Hey. Come on. It's not like you were the same person when you had that thing in you."

I thought about it for a moment, then said, "The worst part is, I was the same person. Just all the darkest parts of me kept bubbling to the top. But I don't think the Darkness put anything in me that wasn't there before."

"Scary stuff, Minos."

"That we can agree on. Speaking of scary stuff, why don't I introduce you to the Shadowed Hand?"

Prophetess had found Kafer. I preferred to give them some privacy, so I took Tolf to meet Sesk. I found the hunter huddled up with Luco. They both gave me guilty looks when I approached.

"I only just gave up the powers of hell and you're already conspiring against me?" I smiled.

"It's not like that, Minos," Luco said. "But... after this past week... after this past month... I'm not cut out for this. I've seen things I never would have seen back on the Flow, and I don't regret any of it, but... I figure I'm lucky to be making it out alive. I'm going home."

"I'll make sure he gets there," Sesk added.

"You too? We've finally got a cause you could feel good about, and this is when you leave?"

The hunter nodded. "I reckon I can head out now and not feel like I'm abandoning anybody. But I've been thinking ever since you asked me what I was doing here. I don't figure I ever did have a good answer to that."

He touched the four gouges I had clawed in his face. "I guess I might stop in and see that girl you mentioned. What town did you say it was? Brambledge?"

"Yeah. Quilla Farr, that was her name." I turned the defections over in my mind, then clasped hands with Sesk and Luco. "Good luck. You were there for me when I really needed it. I hope you find what you're looking for."

I was heading to see Railes when Prophetess caught up with me. Cat was trailing behind her.

"You made interesting friends, Minos," announced the representative of Our Lady and, by her own confession, God's prophet on earth.

The paleo cocked her head and stared intently at me. "Not shadow warrior?"

"Not anymore," I told her.

"Good."

"Good?"

She nodded emphatically. "Good."

"This girl is special, Minos," Prophetess said. "We need to take better care of her. She's smart."

"Yeah, she's clever for a paleo."

"Not 'clever for a paleo.' Smart by anyone's standards, Minos. Do you know she taught herself to read? Do you know what that means growing up the way she did?"

I shrugged. "Fine. She can be your bodyguard. She's good at that."

Tolf protested. "Prophetess has a bodyguard."

Cat was on him faster than thought. The guardsman found himself on his back in the dirt, the paleo's knife at his throat, her face inches from his. "Big dog. Woof woof woof. Cat better," she declared.

"You made your point, Cat. Let him up." She stepped away, and I helped Tolf to his feet.

"I can have two bodyguards," Prophetess said quickly.

The paleo made a dismissive scoffing sound. "Cat better."

"Where did you find her?" Tolf whispered.

"She found me. She was going to kill me in my sleep and eat me."

"I'm surprised she didn't." Cat leered at him.

"The Darkness was good for something."

Prophetess had come west with a single company and was returning with an army of over six thousand veterans. The combined Rockwall and Monolith brigades wouldn't be enough on their own to stop Yoshana's legions - but they'd give the Overlord something to think about.

The only question was whose commander would be in charge.

"I don't think you'd go wrong with either of them," I whispered to her as she convened the senior officers. "Hake is a good leader. He's smart, and he's tough. From what I sensed of Lago, though, he's one hell of a soldier. And the Paladins are real professionals."

The combined command staffs had assembled in the center of Rockwall's defensive square, where our headquarters had been during the battle. Even after peace had broken out, the two groups of officers stood a bit apart, eying each other nervously. But the general and the BlackShield had their heads together, muttering quietly. Lago was almost a foot taller than Hake, and he straightened to address Prophetess.

"My lady, General Hake and I both pledged our armies to you. We are at your disposal. You may place whatever officer you wish at their head. However, we are united in our recommendation on the subject."

Prophetess dipped her head. "Then it would be foolish of me not to listen, BlackShield Jarl Lago. Who do you recommend?"

"A man known to you and to both armies assembled here, respected and feared for his knowledge of the arts of war. The man you personally redeemed from darkness. We recommend you give command of our combined forces to the Select, Minos."

She smiled. "I accept your recommendation."

My head spun. A few months ago I had been free, without responsibilities, a power unto myself. Now, with the Darkness stripped from me, I was supposed to lead an army woven together from two bands of enemies, taking it into battle against the world's greatest military commander.

"I'm... honored," I stammered.

What could possibly go wrong?

Book Four - Reckoning with Darkness

"Hence it comes about that all armed prophets have been successful, and all unarmed prophets have been destroyed."

Niccolo Machiavelli

1. Confessions

Nearly seven thousand men churned the cold, damp earth of the practice yard into a muddy swamp. They were split into mixed forces, companies from Rockwall and the Monolith blended into two armies, drilling against each other. It was an absolute, chaotic debacle.

"Raji, he's turned your flank!" General Hake bellowed. "Second and third company form square! Form square!" Colonel Raji couldn't hear the general from halfway across that field, ringing with the sounds of wooden practice swords smashing on shields and the shouts of the men. Blunted practice arrows whirred in the air like a swarm of angry bees. Trumpeters and flagmen relayed the orders, but they too were ignored. Raji's left flank was gradually enveloped in a seething, struggling melee.

Not that BlackShield Jarl Lago's opposing forces were doing any better. Their center had collapsed, virtually splitting his army in half. The Monolith ranger units that had managed to sneak around behind Hake's men hadn't been supported when they attacked, and were all lying on the field in simulated death. There was barely a hint of a formation remaining on either side.

Somewhere beyond my hearing, Colonel Raji would be uttering his favorite phrase - "We're screwed." He wasn't wrong. My blood pressure rose as I watched the disaster unfolding before my eyes and tried, unsuccessfully, to imagine what we could do to fix the problem next time.

Railes came up as I muttered a continuous string of profane curses that weren't suitable to the leader of a religious crusade. The tattooed captain's breath steamed in the cold air. Without preamble, he said, "Pious has defected."

I shrugged. "I've always known Pious was defective. Tell me something new."

"Dammit, Minos!" he swore. "He's taken off - gone to join the Darkness Radiant!"

I sucked in a deep breath, let it out in a ragged sigh, and turned to look at him. In his agitation, the skull tattoo on the right side of his face became even more grotesque. I could hear the faint whistling behind his breath. Railes always wheezed - the spear that had punctured his lung at the Battle of the Cleansing hadn't killed him, but he'd never fully recovered.

"It's supposed to be a joke. Can't you suck up to your commanding officer and pretend it's funny?" I complained. "I understood you fine. I figured Pious would bolt when the weather cleared."

The big killer had always hated me. When I'd commanded the Darkness, he'd feared me, and perhaps respected me just a bit. And I'd helped him kill Paladins. Now that I was cleansed of the Darkness and the Paladins were our allies, he had no reason to stay in a force I commanded. Yoshana's brand of murderous ruthlessness was bound to appeal more.

I waved my hand at the practice yard. "We've got bigger problems than that homicidal jackass making a break for it. How many did he take with him?" I asked.

"His whole squad. No one else."

"That's not bad. How'd you find out?"

"Groff told me. I think some of the guys in Groff's other squads knew a while ago he was planning to bolt. I'm hacked off they didn't let me know."

I shrugged again. "Hard to rat out your platoon mates. And Pious isn't a guy you cross lightly. Let it go."

"We going after him?" The captain's hand tightened reflexively on his sword hilt. Even short of breath, Railes was a fearsome warrior, ruthless as Pious though not as brutal.

Six months ago, with the Darkness in me, I would have personally led the force that hunted the defectors down and executed them. I was trying to be a different person now. I was also trying to keep my temper under control. Results on both fronts were mixed.

"Let 'em go," I said. "We've got bigger things to worry about."

"They've got intel -"

"That Yoshana doesn't already know? That the Rockwall and Monolith troops still won't work together? Trust me, she knows that already."

That came out a little more bitter than I'd intended, but Railes hadn't picked the best time to give me more bad news. I was nominally in command of all the forces gathered at Our Lady, but General Hake of Rockwall and BlackShield Jarl Lago of the Monolith had far more experience than I. It had seemed logical to leave each in charge of the army he had pledged to Our Lady's service.

That had been a mistake, but I'd realized it too late. The two forces were almost completely incapable of coordination, or even basic cooperation. They were reasonably formidable separately, but to stand a chance against the Darkness Radiant they'd have to work together. I'd let the situation drag on, hoping it would improve naturally over time. It hadn't. Now I was trying to fix the problem by mixing the units, but campaign season was almost upon us and it was too late.

The one thing that had become crystal clear was that I had a good head for tactics but not for operations or strategy. Which was fine for a captain but not for a general. Or, more accurately, a judge.

Even my title had been a subject of dispute. Hake, a colonel when we'd left Rockwall together, had been promoted to general in the field. I didn't want to reduce him in rank and take the position myself, and besides, it wasn't clear that a general outranked Jarl Lago's title of BlackShield. I'd jokingly suggested "emperor," "dictator," and "warlord," but Prophetess had vetoed those ideas. She'd eventually settled on "judge."

"The judges were sent by the Lord to lead the ancient Israelites, the Chosen People, into battle in times of great peril," she'd said. "What could be more appropriate?"

So that had become my rank. It was only after we'd announced it that Doctor John Dee gleefully informed me that Minos had been a judge of the dead in Greek mythology.

"Minos, Judge of the Dead?" I'd growled at him. "It didn't occur to you to mention that before? That it might just possibly have a morale impact when we're facing a superior enemy and our commander is Minos, Judge of the Dead?"

The occultist had just grinned and shrugged. It wasn't his problem. When battle was joined he would run away and chronicle the massacre from a safe distance.

"You all right, Minos?" Railes brought me back to the present, where the melee in the practice yard had devolved into something more like a gigantic barroom brawl.

Railes was someone who got the whole truth from me, whether he wanted it or not. I gave him a thin smile. "Crisis of faith."

"I think I'm having a crisis of faith," I told Father Juniper as we sat in the rectory watching the Ermel Clock. The hour hand was near twelve o'clock, following the golden outer track that marked the daylight hours. The eccentric circles that indicated day and night were at their greatest separation at noon and midnight. At six o'clock the circles joined, passing into or out of darkness at twilight and daybreak.

The bearded priest smiled and puffed on his pipe. "That sounds serious, but not entirely without precedent in the history of Christendom."

I glanced over at him. His blue eyes twinkled, gently mocking me.

"Sure. But not a great attribute in the guy who's supposed to be leading the armies of righteousness. Prophetess pulled off an honest-to-God miracle when she cast the Darkness out of me. It made sense for me to lead the army she won for herself. But I think she may have picked the wrong man for the job. I don't feel very holy, and I'm not that great of a general. Can a prophet choose wrong?"

The priest smoked for a while, then said slowly, "God chooses his prophets, and his prophets choose their champions. The prophet and the champion are human, so neither is perfect."

"It's just - I feel like I should sense the Lord's hand on me or something. And I don't."

"Thus the crisis of faith."

I nodded. Sesk, a now-retired sergeant in the Shadowed Hand, had told me not to feed the dark wolf. By which he meant any tendency to be selfish, self-pitying, hateful, or generally cranky. I had the feeling the dark wolf had been eating pretty well lately, but I didn't know how to make it stop. There was a lot of food around.

"It's normal to have doubts," Father Juniper said. "You've come a long way in a short time, by a very hard road. But I think perhaps you should speak to my confessor."

"*Your* confessor? Who's that, the Metropolitan?"

"No, no. Just Father Roric." The priest's beatific smile barely concealed a yawning abyss of wicked amusement. Just Father Roric. The Advocate for Justice. Probably the most terrifying man in Our Lady.

"Couldn't I go tell Yoshana I'm sorry and see if we can all be friends instead? That sounds a lot less painful."

Father Juniper's expanding grin could have swallowed a melon.

Father Roric's study. The lion's den. We'd had a touchy relationship before I'd taken on the Darkness. It had gotten very much worse after that, when he'd tried to exorcise me and I'd come close to killing him. We hadn't spoken since I'd been cleansed.

He'd frightened me before I'd mastered the Darkness. He frightened me again now.

"Come in," I heard faintly as I knocked on his office door. I opened it and entered.

The priest didn't stand, but I knew he was nearly as tall as I, thin as a blade. His piercing gray eyes locked on me, and he motioned with his chin toward the seat on the other side of his desk. He wasn't going to make it easy for me, though. He simply sat and watched silently as I took the chair.

The room was small and unadorned. It was dominated by a worn desk of some pale wood, perhaps oak. Books and stacks of paper covered it. Bookcases of the same design lined the wall behind Roric. On my side of the desk there was nothing but the chair I was sitting in. Despite the small window with a view of the practice yard outside, the office gave the impression of an interrogation chamber. Though that was probably as much due to its inhabitant as anything else. Even after traveling with Yoshana, leading men in battle, and mastering and then being freed of the Darkness, somehow I still found the black-robed priest intimidating.

"Um. Father Juniper thinks I should speak to you. Confess."

He nodded. "Indeed. He mentioned it to me. There's a form for that, you know."

"Of course. Um. Bless me Father, for I have sinned. It's been... this is my first confession." I hesitated. "I suppose that's a lot of ground to cover."

"Technically," Roric said, "Your sins were wiped clean by Prophetess' rather unorthodox baptism. So you can start from there."

I thought, looked down at my lap, met his raptor's stare. "I think I'd like to start earlier, if I could."

"The sacrament is for your benefit. Start where you'd like."

I took a deep breath. "You know I've spent a lot of time with Prophetess. You said yourself that I spent two months with her and she didn't convert me. To be honest, I didn't feel a need to convert. I felt like I was already a pretty decent person. I didn't need your religion."

My eyes, black on black, stared into his. He just nodded, unflinching, utterly calm. If I'd offended him, he made no sign.

"But then, well. The Darkness. The Cleansing. I suppose I couldn't ask for more of a revelation on the road to Damascus."

The flow of words trickled to a halt. This time, he filled the void. "So you feel obligated? To Prophetess and the church?"

I shook my head. "It's not that. It's... once the Darkness was out of me, I suppose I thought I would become some sort of holy person. The man who'd been cleansed. But... I have to say it's been a disappointment. There was the moment when Prophetess cast the Darkness out and I really felt something - like God's light was shining through me."

It sounded like a foolish and presumptuous thing to say, even to a priest. Maybe especially to a priest. But I struggled on, trying to reach the festering core of the problem. "But I haven't felt it since then. All the thoughts I had when the Darkness was in me, they're still in me. I look at those idiots out there in the practice yard bickering instead of learning to work together, and sometimes I want to kill them - just one or two, by way of example. If I still had the Darkness in me, I might do it."

The nightmares of lust and violence had faded since the Cleansing. Roshel hadn't visited me in my dreams. But I still had plenty of wrath in me. As well as other things.

"And I still have thoughts about, you know... girls," I stammered, embarrassed. "So... where's the salvation? I know those urges are wrong, but I still have them. I still... sometimes I still wish I had the power to just smack those people around. Hurt them. Make them afraid. It doesn't seem like much of an improvement."

"It seems unfair?" said the priest. "You were saved, and yet, you're still tempted. You had a single transcendent moment, but it's not been repeated."

I nodded.

Roric steepled his fingers and regarded me levelly. "You've been baptized, so salvation is open to you. But you must understand that we have free will and thus, salvation is an ongoing battle. Even for great saints, those moments of transcendence are rare. Sometimes there is only one in a lifetime, and the rest of that life is spent struggling to reconnect, to live up to that instant of grace. As the pilot of a vessel is tried in the storm; as the wrestler is tried in the ring, the soldier in the battle, and the hero in adversity: so is the Christian tried in temptation."

"Prophetess seems immune," I remarked, maybe just a bit peevishly.

"No. Not her, not the Metropolitan, not me, not you. Not Saint Basil the Great, whom I was just quoting. No one who walks this earth today is free from temptation. Let me see." He thumbed through the stack of papers on his desk, selected one. "Dom Augustin Guillerand had some useful thoughts as well. The metaphor he uses might appeal to you, in your role."

If I'd wanted someone to quote the dead at me, I could have talked to Dee. But I didn't interrupt.

"'The life of prayer calls for continuous battles. It is the most important and the longest effort in a life dedicated to God. This effort has been given a beautiful name: it is called the guard of the heart. The human heart is a city; it was meant to be a stronghold. Sin surrendered it. Henceforth it is an open city, the walls of which have to be built up again. The enemy never ceases to do all he can to prevent this. He does this with his accustomed cleverness and strength, with stratagem and fury . . . he succeeds all along the line to distract us and entice us away from the divine presence. We must always be starting again. These continual recoveries, this endless beginning again, tires and disheartens us far more than the actual fighting. We would much prefer a real battle, fierce and decisive. But God, as a rule, thinks otherwise. He would rather we were in a constant state of war.'"

The priest continued, "There is no instant growth into holiness, and there is no final battle in this lifetime that offers a decisive victory. Because God gives us free will, at every moment we are free to choose right. Or wrong. Think of every frustration you feel as a tiny mortification, God's way of reminding you that you're mortal and the world isn't meant to go your way."

The piercing eyes bored into me. "Salvation can't be on our terms. It's on God's terms. You have to surrender to him. In the end, every action you take is either pleasing to God, or displeasing to God. To know which is which, all you need to do is pray."

I nodded as if in agreement, but then after a moment I asked, "Is that really going to help?" I couldn't keep the skepticism from my voice. Muttering to the divine seemed a little too much like talking to myself.

"True prayer is a conversation with God. If you let yourself have a sincere conversation, if you truly talk, and truly listen, perhaps sometimes he'll let you know whether you're pleasing him or not." The priest rubbed at the nicks in the wooden desk. "God gives us free will, and he won't make us perfect. Not you. Not me. But little by little, if we let him, he lets us see our imperfections. Not always to overcome them - sometimes we can't overcome them. But if we can make ourselves stop, and pray, sometimes we can manage to take hold of the hand he reaches down to us. Just for a little while. But personally, I like to think I'm able to grasp his hand longer each time."

He continued to hold my eyes. "That's your goal and mine. An aspiration to be better. Not achieving it, but aspiring to it, and making the effort every day to reach for it."

I had to admit I was taken aback. He was a figure of such terrible sternness - it was shocking to hear him not just speak with sympathy, but to admit his own weakness. It made me bolder still, no longer challenging him, but letting my doubts pour out. "And how does reaching for God's hand square with my role as a warlord? A big part of that job is killing people."

The priest leaned back and let out a long breath. "Ah. I think perhaps we're coming a bit closer to the heart of the matter."

"There's a lot of blood on my hands, Father. Whatever you say Prophetess may have done to wash it away. There's likely to be a lot more."

He nodded. "There are relevant doctrines. The theory of just war. *Jus ad bellum* and *jus in bello*. Whether a war is just, and whether it is conducted justly. You must examine the cause of the war, whether it is necessary and unavoidable, and whether it is conducted to minimize the suffering and injustice that always accompany it."

"Are we talking about what I've done, or what I'm going to do?"

"Again, this is your confession. That choice is yours."

I took a deep breath. "Let's start with when I decided to kill people for a living, Father. I didn't have to join Rockwall's army. I could have stayed on the Flow digging through garbage. I could have gone a hundred different places. I chose to enlist in wartime."

My throat tightened. I found it hard to continue, to meet the priest's eyes, but I did. "And once I did, I killed a lot of people. I… I honestly can't count. Twice, when I let the Darkness take me… I've tried to remember how many I killed, but I just can't. I killed a Select, though. We don't do that. I suppose it shouldn't be any different, a person's a person, but we don't kill our own."

No more words would come. Roric and I sat silently on opposite sides of his desk for a moment.

Then he said, "As it happens, I've made myself familiar with the story of the Shadowed Hand. Many soldiers seek confession. While I can't of course tell you the sins of others, I can give you my impression of your campaign."

The lean priest raised a finger. "First, Rockwall's war in the disputed area with the Monolith is clearly unjust. While the Monolith was responsible for recent provocations, an offensive for territorial expansion is never justified. I know that both sides portray it as an attempt to civilize the territory, but no meaningful diplomacy has been undertaken, and neither state has in practice shown any interest in the welfare of the inhabitants."

I nodded. There wasn't much I could say to that. I didn't disagree. He went on, "However, it is accepted that a citizen of a state enlisted in the lawful army of that state is not morally responsible for determining *jus ad bellum*. As I understand it, you did not enter Rockwall with the intention of taking up a position as a mercenary soldier, but rather enlisted after you had chosen to make that state your domicile for other purposes. I do not believe blame attaches to you for your decision to join the army. The political decisions were, as they say, above your pay grade."

I was a bit surprised that he was letting me off the hook so easily. I supposed the hook would be sunk deeper and then twisted when it came to my personal conduct.

He raised a second finger. "As far as your actions when you commanded the Shadowed Hand, a number of your fellow soldiers noted that you generally went to some lengths to minimize enemy casualties, and you never endangered noncombatants. With respect to your behavior when you were under the control of the Darkness, I believe we have to consider that you were not in control of yourself at that time."

I shook my head. "No. That's not true. The Darkness makes you follow your own worst impulses, but they're still your own impulses."

"I understand that. But the impulse toward sin is an unavoidable part of the human condition. Moral success or failure derives from resisting or succumbing to that impulse. To have a fleeting rush of anger is not sinful. To indulge that anger, whether through violence or even merely wishing evil to its object, is a sin. When you were infected with the Darkness, your ability to resist sin was suppressed. Your moral fault is thus mitigated. However, I should note that if you were ever to knowingly employ the Darkness again -" and here his tone sharpened, "that would be an entirely different question."

In my mind, I replayed Lalos raising his hands, dropping his pistol, my blade severing his hand and then his head.

"I killed a man after he surrendered."

"I don't believe I violate the confidence of the confessional when I say that more than one witness described that event to me. As I understand it, the Select shot at you, in fact hitting you, and surrendered only in the fraction of a second when it became clear you would kill him before he could kill you. I have a vivid memory of a statement by one of your men. 'The captain felt bad about it afterwards, but that treacherous Select bastard had it coming.' Frankly, I'm rather inclined to agree."

I had some trouble processing what I was hearing. "Are you saying I didn't do anything wrong when the Darkness was in me?"

"I'm saying that you were not the monster you seem to believe yourself to have been. Your concerns do you credit, but you should be confident in the power of your baptism to free you from the evil that possessed you."

"So I guess it's only trying to fight a just war against a totally superior enemy I have to worry about."

The priest leaned forward, hawk's nose pointing at me. "Indeed. The cause is just this time. But the conduct of the struggle is your responsibility, both professionally and morally. I can't say I envy you."

He turned and rummaged in the bookshelf behind his desk, finally pulling out a thick, black volume. "St. Thomas Aquinas. *Summa Theologica*. It includes a discussion of just war theory, as well as many other interesting matters." He handed me the book. It must have weighed five pounds.

I opened the massive tome. Each sheet was as thin as onion skin. It was over three thousand pages long. "Um, where exactly is the section on just war?"

Roric smiled wickedly. "The whole volume is profitable for you. I suggest you read it cover to cover." Then he took pity on my anguished look. "It has an index."

"I see you survived," John Dee said lightly. The lanky, loud-mouthed occultist who was now my army's unlikely herald had intercepted me at the foot of the rectory stairs. He'd probably been lurking in wait.

"Got off with an Our Father and a Hail Mary. And a ridiculously long book to read." I was still shocked. I'd more than half expected Father Roric to condemn me to eternal hellfire or douse me with holy water to see if I burst into flames. Part of the weight I'd been carrying was lifted... but I still didn't know how I was going to turn two brigades that couldn't work together into an army that could stand up to the Darkness Radiant.

"Why don't you make yourself useful and go round up the Ministry of Defense?" I said.

Dee drew himself up to his full, gangling height. "Make myself useful? I do believe power has gone to your head, my friend. I am a scholar, not an errand boy. Why, just before I came here I was conversing with Aharon son of Malak on -"

"Something completely irrelevant to anyone but the two of you," I snapped. "You may not be an errand boy, but you're supposed to be my herald. Go herald. Somehow you always seem to know where everyone is and what they're doing. So how about we put that to good purpose?"

"Knowledge is my purpose," Dee said with the wounded dignity of a cat that had fallen off a window ledge. "But if using it to your vulgar ends is the cost of scholarship, so be it."

"Thank you. Wouldn't it have been easier to just say, 'Sure, Minos, happy to help'?"

He looked down his nose at me. "No."

But he went.

The Ministry met regularly in an upper room of the rectory, windowless, paneled in dark wood, lit by a half dozen torches. It looked like the kind of place great conspiracies were born. The reality was less impressive.

These days our group consisted of General Hake and BlackShield Jarl Lago, Tolf as commander of Prophetess' personal guard, Prophetess herself, and me. Marek, captain of Our Lady's limited troops, was there because it would be impolite to exclude the commander of the Metropolitan's forces in his own citadel, even if those forces were militarily irrelevant. And of course Doctor John Dee, who couldn't be kept out of anything interesting.

At one point both Father Juniper and Father Roric had joined the council, but both had gotten bored as our military grew more professional and the discussions moved outside their field of expertise.

It was a smart, tough, experienced team, but we seemed to have trouble actually getting things done. Somehow an army that could make snap decisions in the field settled into a kind of bureaucratic inertia in garrison. Even with the nebulous threat of Yoshana hanging over us.

I caught a glimpse of Cat as Tolf shut the door behind Prophetess. The soldier let out a long sigh of relief.

"This is just about the only place Prophetess and I can go without that damn paleo shadowing us. The girl takes her bodyguarding a little too seriously. And I always see her sizing me up, like she's planning to replace me. If I don't show up for work some day, you'll know she's slit my throat in my sleep."

"Nah," I said. "That would be too obvious. She'd cut you open, pull out your guts, and wear you like a suit of armor. No one would ever know until she talked."

Tolf shivered theatrically. "Thanks for that. Now I'm never going to be able to sleep again."

"Cut it out, you two," Prophetess snapped. Lago looked stern and disapproving. Dee and Hake both chuckled nervously. The occultist was just a bit frightened of Cat. Hake knew her well enough to wonder how seriously to take my joke.

The slight paleo girl was a killer who could give Pious or Railes a run for their money, but she was smart and quick and had become devoted to Prophetess. In a war where the other side could send in a shape-shifting assassin or a murderous thread of Darkness, the paleo's preternatural senses and vicious instincts were the best defense we had.

At least since I'd given up the Darkness.

"Have we heard anything from Rockwall or the Monolith?" I asked even before everyone was seated. It was rude, but my mind was still churning with unhappy thoughts of strategy. I was starting to get the gnawing feeling that we didn't have a lot of time for pleasantries and formality.

Heads shook around the table. That was no surprise. We'd sent emissaries in the fall, before winter made travel a matter of life or death. Nearly six months later we'd heard nothing.

The good news was there had been no irate demands for the return of the troops that had pledged themselves to Our Lady. The bad news was no reinforcements had been offered either. My best guess was that Rockwall and the Monolith were each hedging their bets, willing to sacrifice a brigade to stop Yoshana from reaching their borders, but wanting plausible deniability if she did.

"So we have just under seven thousand men." We had nearly a thousand more who had been badly wounded in the Battle of the Cleansing, who'd lived but were crippled, who'd lost limbs or eyes, or just the will to fight. I forced myself to visit the infirmary sometimes, even though it always made me feel guilty. Because it always made me feel guilty. Some of those men I'd put there myself.

"Yoshana's got three thousand of her original veterans," I continued. "We know Stephen neglected his army, but she's had over a year to recruit, equip, and train them. So assume at least twenty thousand more from the Source, probably better armed and better trained than us by now."

Lago bowed his head formally and said, "Judge Minos, with respect, we have known this for months. What has changed that makes you convene this group so urgently?"

"Two things." I copied Father Roric and held up a finger. "First, I've just been reminded of my duty to minimize losses on both sides, not to mention among our civilians."

I took a deep breath and raised another finger. "Second, it's become obvious to me that the Rockwall and Monolith troops aren't cooperating effectively and won't be by the time the spring campaign season begins."

I was expecting an argument. I was half hoping for a loud assurance that I was wrong. Instead the two commanders exchanged sheepish looks and reluctantly nodded.

Great.

"I'm afraid you're right, Minos." Hake had been my commanding officer too long for my title to come easily to his lips. I didn't mind. "BlackShield Lago's forces have excellent discipline, and I suppose we'd expected that to make integration easy. But I'm afraid their very unit cohesion, combined with the religious differences, are in fact making it quite difficult for us to work together."

Lago looked like he'd bitten a lemon. Hake had managed to compliment the BlackShield's troops while suggesting the problems were all their fault. It was an obnoxious move, but I had to admire it.

The truth was, the issues were on both sides. The Monolith soldiers were pious Josephites. They revered Prophetess personally after many of them had witnessed her cast the Darkness out of me, but they weren't entirely comfortable serving the Universal Church.

On the other hand, the Rockwall troops lacked the discipline of their Monolith counterparts. They were veterans with generally decent officers and acceptable readiness, but, feeling more secure in Our Lady, they had been known to taunt and pick fights with Lago's men.

As I'd observed earlier, keeping the soldiers in their old units instead of mixing them had been a mistake, but one I'd seen too late.

"All right, Minos," Prophetess cut in. "What's the solution? I assume you didn't just call us here to complain."

I glared at her. In fact, I had no solution. I'd hoped someone would offer one, or at least commiserate.

Waspishly, I said, "You might try praying harder. We're going to need a miracle and that's your department, not mine."

Tolf interjected quickly, "C'mon, Minos. It can't be as bad as all that. Even if they've got us outnumbered three to one, that's not bad odds when we're behind these walls."

I sighed. "We could hold the walls with half as many. And we might be better off. Once the siege starts and the townspeople flood in here, it's going to start getting awfully hungry. Seven thousand troops eat a lot. We've gone through most of the winter reserve already. If she hits us before the crops come in - and I don't see why she wouldn't - she can just park her army outside and starve us out. We've got too many troops to garrison and too few to sally. And that's setting aside how miserable she can make us with the Darkness."

I looked at Lago. "What I did to you when we were enemies? She has at least three masters of the Darkness that are stronger than I was, and a lot less squeamish about how they use it."

Tolf and Lago both looked a little green. Hake seemed more composed, but he'd expected Lago's forces to kill us at the Battle of the Cleansing. He'd told me he considered every day after that to be a gift.

Dee said cheerfully, "Then we'd better start thinking outside the box, hadn't we?"

Easier said than done. When I had been fighting the Monolith, we'd been mobile, with momentum and surprise on our side. Now we were a sitting target, defending a fixed location against a superior enemy. The vast infrastructure of Our Lady could hold five times as many men, but we didn't have them and if we had, we couldn't feed them. Half an hour of discussion yielded no revelations. As it became increasingly obvious we were getting nowhere, the various members of the Ministry began to excuse themselves. In the end, only Prophetess and I remained.

She sat upright in her chair, ramrod straight. She stood that way too. She was tall, with piercing gray eyes and light brown hair. A stranger might think she was aloof. I knew she held herself at attention because if she once let herself bow down, the weight of her responsibilities would overwhelm her.

"I'm sorry about before," I said. "The bit about you praying harder."

She nodded, finally letting her shoulders slump and the mental exhaustion show. "It's hard."

"For you and me both. At least God's giving you a direction. All I know is I'm supposed to give you an army that can stop Yoshana, and I don't have one. It feels like I'm trying to make chicken salad out of chicken sh…" I trailed off. She was a prophet of the Lord, after all.

Tess gave me a strained smile. "Sometimes he shows me what he wants me to do, but usually he's a little vague on how. A year ago I wouldn't have guessed I'd have a Select who'd been infected with the Darkness leading God's army."

"A year ago I wouldn't have thought so either. Especially not this Select." I fingered the circle of roses and thorns embroidered on my jacket. I'd refused to join the Order of Thorns at first, not having been a Universalist at the time. I'd come a long, strange way in twelve months.

I pushed back from the table. "We'd better get moving. If we stay in here alone too much longer they're going to think we've been up to something besides working."

You don't hear what you don't expect. Prophetess spoke softly, and I didn't quite catch the words.

"What?" I asked.

She shook her head and stood. "Never mind."

It was only after we'd left the room that my mind processed what she'd said. I couldn't be completely sure, but I thought it was, "Do you want to give them a reason?"

2. First Move

I spent hours turning those words over in my head. Did I want to change the nature of my relationship with Prophetess to something more than her friend and champion? Of course I did. Was the run-up to Yoshana's campaign against us the right time for another complication? Not really. I found myself thinking life would be simpler if the Overlord just got on with attacking us.

Be careful what you wish for.

I was playing chess with Kafer, Prophetess' older brother. He had been promoted to sergeant and led a squad of Our Lady's militia under Captain Marek. He'd made it clear to me that he felt ready for commissioned rank, but I had no valid reason to elevate him further. Of course, once battle was joined, there would likely be plenty of openings for battlefield promotions. Although they were likely to be short-lived.

In any event, Kafer was one of the few people willing to play chess with me. Prophetess, Dee, Hake, Lago, and Father Juniper didn't play. Tolf was terrible. I'd heard Father Roric and the Metropolitan were excellent players, but I was still a little bit intimidated by both of them, as was the rest of Our Lady; they only played against each other. Everyone else was a little bit intimidated by me. Except for Tarc, the only other Select in the army. And he was still holding a grudge over my killing of his friend, Lalos. He would play, but he sneered when he beat me. And he always beat me.

"Mate in... two," I concluded, looking up from the board at Kafer. He considered the pieces, then tipped his king.

He looked at me narrowly. "So... what's up with you and my little sister, anyway?"

My face heated. That wasn't a conversation I was prepared to have with anyone just yet, much less Prophetess' brother. Had she said something to him?

"What do you mean?"

"By my count, you've risked your life for her three times. Bringing her here, ditching Yoshana for her, and now leading her army. In my experience, a guy doesn't do all that for a girl unless he's got something in mind."

I didn't know what to say and put myself to resetting the board, buying time. I was actually relieved - though only briefly - when Tolf came around the corner, puffing and blowing. I frowned up at him. "If I remember right, last time you came running up like that, I wound up infected with the Darkness."

"I told you. Not to go," he gasped.

And that was true.

"Okay, so you're smarter than I am, even if you are a lousy chess player. What is it this time?"

"Sedition," he wheezed.

"What? What are you talking about?"

Kafer suddenly remembered that Tolf was a superior officer and offered his chair. The older soldier sank into it gratefully and took several deep breaths before continuing.

"There's talk of surrender in the town. All over the marketplace. Going on about how we're all going to die if we fight. And all Yoshana wants is for us to shut up and leave her alone. How Prophetess and the Metropolitan are crazy not to agree to those terms. You too."

"I'm not sure that's sedition." I wasn't even sure it was wrong. I understood the moral imperative to oppose Yoshana, but we truly were picking a fight I didn't think we could win.

Tolf shook his head violently. "This isn't like a couple of people having second thoughts, or muttering behind closed doors that it's nuts to be dragged into war by some lunatic farm girl and an underage blackeye mercenary."

He looked apologetic, and I was pretty sure that was a direct quote from someone. Maybe several someones.

He went on, "This flamed up too fast. Folks aren't saying 'maybe' or 'we oughta think about it.' It's being told as fact, and it's everywhere, all of a sudden, all at once."

Information warfare. Sowing fear before the assault. Breaking the enemy's will before breaking our bodies. It was basic strategy. I'd done it myself. It stood to reason Yoshana would too, only better.

Mechanically, I finished resetting the pieces on the chessboard.

"She's just advanced her first pawn."

"Is he in?"

The chamberlain's secretary glared at me from her single eye. The other socket was empty, a puckered mass of badly healed scar tissue. Knowing her as well as I did, I assumed she left it uncovered mostly to intimidate people.

Moya didn't seem to like anybody. As best I could tell, she liked me less than most. Maybe she held me responsible for her injury, because I'd recruited her into the Rockwall quartermaster company where she'd been hurt. Maybe she held me responsible because I hadn't been there to defend that company, and the fact that I'd avenged her by hunting down and killing half the men who'd attacked it wasn't good enough. Maybe she didn't like the Select. Maybe she just didn't like me.

I'd sometimes wondered whether she'd make a good match for Railes, who had highlighted the loss of one ear by having a skull tattooed on his face. Railes was tough enough to deal with Moya. But I liked Railes, and I wouldn't wish the one-eyed redhead on anyone.

Father Doreden, the Metropolitan's chamberlain, employed Moya because she helped keep people away from him. And his job was to keep people away from the Metropolitan.

I found Doreden nearly as disagreeable as Moya, but I had come to understand the need for him. Everyone wanted to see the Metropolitan all the time.

Despite my exalted rank, I didn't need a chamberlain or a secretary to keep people away from me. My race and generally unpleasant personality were enough. The fact that I'd been infected with the Darkness might have helped too.

Another part of the reason Moya might dislike me was because Doreden couldn't refuse to see the commander of Our Lady's armies. She nodded curtly and said, "I'll let him know you're here."

She vanished through a door into the chamberlain's office. Moya ruled over an outer reception area, richly carpeted and paneled in dark wood. Beyond that was Doreden's office and beyond that, the Metropolitan's suite. He had his own bathroom in there, and I could see why - getting out past Doreden and Moya every time he needed to use the facilities would be emotionally exhausting.

I sat in a chair that was beautifully carved but had probably been deliberately selected because it was uncomfortable. And waited.

The redhead emerged. "He'll see you in a bit."

I nodded and stayed in my uncomfortable chair. Doreden would make me wait. I highly doubted that he was doing anything important, or indeed that he ever had anything important to do. But if he couldn't refuse to see me, he could make me cool my heels.

In the old days, before Prophetess had cleansed me, I might have manifested the Darkness in his room to hurry him along. If I'd been in a good mood. If I'd been cranky, I would have just swept secretary and chamberlain aside.

Sometimes I missed the power, but I didn't miss what it had done to my character. I was obnoxious enough without it.

"Minos, sorry to keep you waiting," Father Doreden said, with all the warmth and sincerity of a rattlesnake.

He was a man of average height but above average weight, none of it muscle. I didn't think it could all be fat, though - there had to be room for all the self-importance he was stuffed full of.

"Father. I need to see the Metropolitan."

"Mmm," he smiled. "Everyone does."

"Yeah. Not everyone is trying to stop us from being overrun by a homicidal Overlord leading the armies of darkness."

A panicked look slid across the fat face. "She's not here? Not now?"

I considered lying to see if that would get things moving faster, but settled for the truth. "Not yet. But she's got agents in the town, saying we should surrender."

"Something to be said for talking rather than fighting, isn't there, Minos?"

"Last time we decided that, I wound up infected with the Darkness." I was getting a lot of mileage out of that phrase. Constantly reminding people of what I'd been probably didn't make me any more popular, but it sometimes got things done.

The chamberlain's expression soured. "I'll see if the Metropolitan can see you."

The basilica at Our Lady never ceased to impress me. Gilded stone columns stretched up to a deep blue ceiling. Angels looked down beatifically from those heights.

The first time I'd been in this grand space, we'd been sent to Stephensburg with a handful of volunteers. I'd wished then for thousands of soldiers to march against Yoshana. Now I had thousands of soldiers and would much rather head in some other direction all by myself.

Be careful what you wish for.

In all that vast hall there were only the Metropolitan, Father Roric, Prophetess, and Fedil Arnage, the mayor of the surrounding town. And me. Every word spoken at a normal volume echoed. It was only natural that our voices sank to near whispers.

"Wouldn't meeting in the war room make more sense, Your Eminence?" I asked the Metropolitan. He was a trim man of slightly less than middle height, white hair receding on his scalp. There was nothing physically impressive about him, but some force of character always left me a bit awed in his presence.

"I'm more certain we won't be heard here. It seems to me that whatever response we formulate to the Overlord's first move, we'll want to keep it to ourselves until we're ready."

"Are you sure we wish to dignify these marketplace rumors with a response?" Roric asked.

I still wasn't sure exactly where Father Roric fell in the ecclesiastical hierarchy of Our Lady. His title, Advocate for Justice, was impressive, but I didn't think he was one of the senior members of the clergy. Interesting that he was the only one the Metropolitan had invited. But not surprising. He and I had not always seen eye to eye, but I'd be the first to admit he had a penetrating mind.

He was wrong this time, though. I said, "This won't blow over. Yoshana's undermining morale. Weakening support for the battle ahead. And it won't stay confined to the town. My troops go out there, and that talk will start to infect them. And if they don't think it's worth fighting, we've lost already."

"Are we sure it is worth fighting, though?" asked the mayor. On the continuum between Roric's razor intellect and Doreden's self-satisfied complacency, Arnage fell a lot closer to the chamberlain's end. He looked a bit like Doreden, too - big, fat, and soft. He wouldn't enjoy going on rations during a siege.

He continued, "If it's true that all Yoshana wants is for us to remain silent and neither act nor speak against her, why wouldn't we agree to it?"

"All that's required for evil to triumph is for good men to remain silent," Prophetess said.

I nodded. "That, and she'd come back for us when she was done with everyone else."

"You don't think she'll keep her word?" Arnage sounded shocked. I rolled my eyes.

"She's as much a politician as she is a warrior," I snapped. "Lying is second nature to her."

The Metropolitan shot me a disapproving look. I had been gratuitously rude to the mayor, although the implied insult seemed to have slid off him like water off a duck. Father Roric wore the tiniest smile. If thinking ill of your fellow man was truly a sin, I wondered how often the Advocate for Justice needed to go to confession. Probably almost as often as I should.

"We will not be staying silent," the Metropolitan said with great finality. I might be the military leader here, Arnage the civil authority, and Prophetess the voice of God... but the Metropolitan gave the orders in Our Lady. He looked at me. "You seem to understand Yoshana's strategy. How do we counter it?"

I shrugged. "This is a conventional opening. She undermines morale, we boost it. We'll make a demonstration."

It was really just logistics at that point, and the discussion was over soon enough. I found Cat lurking outside the door, waiting for Prophetess.

The paleo girl dipped her head to me. Even after six months of regular eating, she was still the pale, wiry creature she'd been when I first found her. Or technically, when she'd first found me, and tried to kill me.

"Minos," she said.

"Hey, Cat. You know, I have to admit I kind of liked it when you called me Shadow Warrior."

"Not shadow warrior now."

"No. No I'm not."

It was an impressive spectacle, if I did say so myself. My troops might not be able to coordinate on the field, but they could sure march in step.

Prophetess and the Metropolitan were at the very head of the column, with the Order of Thorns arrayed around and behind them. They both wore heavy robes, cream colored like the bricks of Our Lady's citadel, elaborately embroidered, and divided down the middle so they could ride. The two of them alone were mounted. The Order of Thorns, Prophetess' personal guard, wore white tabards embroidered with a circle of roses and thorns picked out in crimson and silver thread.

Behind came rank on rank of our infantry, alternating companies of Rockwall and Monolith troops in blocks five wide and twenty deep. They also bore the rose and thorn badge, but in a more sober gray on white. Fully armored and equipped with shield and spear, it was a formidable array. The rhythmic stamping of their boots as they marched echoed through the cold air. The soldiers' breath steamed, creating an effect like some sort of enormous, many-legged dragon with steel spears in place of fangs and claws.

It was impressive... and predictable. The remains of the Shadowed Hand and Lago's rangers were scouting outside the parade route. If Yoshana were to deploy the Darkness we had no direct counter to it, but my old company would be better prepared than anyone else in Our Lady. And the Monolith rangers were formidable, disciplined scouts with some experience of the Darkness - from having me use it on them back when we had been enemies.

The men at each corner of the infantry squares carried long poles with reservoirs of burning oil. It added to the spectacle and, more importantly, the Darkness didn't like fire.

The column was a mile long. Crowds lined the streets to watch as we made our way to the plaza fronting the town hall, where Arnage had assembled a reviewing stand for the local dignitaries to receive the host of the righteous. It was cold enough to give the mayor, councilmen, and wealthy citizens assembled there an opportunity to show off expensive cloaks and furs.

The march halted in the plaza. The mounts that the Metropolitan and Prophetess rode gave them an impressive height advantage that matched the mayor's elevation on the reviewing stand. The horses were large and powerful, although I knew Tess' at least had been chosen for an absolutely placid temperament. The beast would stand like a statue even in the face of gunfire, which suited her riding ability perfectly.

Nearly seven thousand soldiers grounded their spear butts with a resounding crash. The Metropolitan's steed took a quick sidestep, but he brought it under control with sure pressure on the reins and stirrups. He must have been fifty years older than Prophetess and I, but he was a much better horseman than either of us. As advertised, Prophetess' animal remained completely unperturbed.

A deacon with a chest like a bull bellowed into the echoing silence, "His Eminence the Metropolitan of Our Lady, Bishop of the West."

The Metropolitan stood in his stirrups, which I had never tried but didn't seem like something I could manage, and graciously inclined his head to the assembled dignitaries.

"Your Honor. Councilors. Citizens. The question has been asked, 'Why do we fight?'"

He paused and looked around. "It's a good question. War is never an option to be undertaken lightly. Wouldn't it be better to sit back, be quiet, and mind our own business?"

A few heads nodded, on the reviewing stand and in the crowd.

"I'll give you two thoughts. One is from the Psalms. 'The just man is a light in darkness to the upright.' And the other is from the Gospel according to Matthew. 'You are the light of the world. A city set on a mountain cannot be hidden.'"

He raised his voice. "There's a reason the scriptures refer so often to the symbol of light, shining in the darkness. We are the people of God, called to illuminate the nations with his truth. We will never abide the Darkness, and the Darkness will never abide a city of light that rebukes its very existence. This task is ours, but God has not set it to us unaided. We are in the presence of God's prophet on earth."

Which was the first time he had formally acknowledged Prophetess as such. It was a heck of an introduction. I hoped Tess didn't spoil it by falling off her horse.

She didn't try to stand in the stirrups, which was almost certainly for the best. Instead she merely said, "Thank you, Your Eminence. As you said, God gives us no cross we are unable to bear. A year ago our forces numbered in the hundreds. Now by the grace of our Lord they number in the thousands, and they are led by Judge Minos who knows the ways of the enemy like no other."

Which was a really slick spin to put on the fact that for a while I'd been working for the other side.

She continued, "We are truly the light of the world, a light that will never be overcome. But as the Metropolitan has said, the darkness will not accept the truth that challenges its lies. Yoshana may offer peace, but her promises are false, as evil's promises always are. She will always seek to extinguish our light."

Her voice rose. "But we will not be extinguished! The light of truth will not be dimmed. God has worked through me to stand against the Darkness and cast it out. As by his grace I cast it out of Judge Minos, by his grace we will all stand against it again, and cast it out of this nation. Be strong. Be faithful. And trust in the Lord!"

That was the signal, and the troops clashed their spears against their shields. We couldn't quite make it simultaneous, since only the men in the front could hear her, but the sound carried back in a wave all along the column.

"For God and Our Lady!"

That was spontaneous, and I couldn't tell who started it, but it was brilliant. I should have thought of it. The shout went up throughout the massed troops, spread to the surrounding civilians. Crash, crash, crash, went the spears on shields, and then, "For God and Our Lady," and it repeated. It went on for a full minute. It was amazing. It was a triumph.

And it worked like a charm to restore morale.

Until the next day when townspeople began to disappear.

3. Under Pressure

"In contests of strategy it is bad to be led about by the enemy. You must always be able to lead the enemy about."

"Sun Tzu again?" General Hake asked. He knew where most of my military quotes came from.

"Not this time. Musashi, from the Book of Five Rings. Although Sun Tzu said pretty much the same thing. I'm getting really sick of being a step behind, and I'm damned if I see how we get ahead."

I stopped myself. Under the circumstances I should be more careful with my swearing. It probably wasn't appropriate for the leader of the armies of God, and considering what I'd been, I should be careful what blasphemies I invoked. Although I really might be damned if I couldn't defend the civilians under my protection from Yoshana.

There had been nearly two dozen disappearances, mostly farmers vanishing from their fields, but also townspeople going to visit nearby villages who had never made it to their destinations.

We had a thousand men patrolling the roads and outlying farms in platoon strength. It was the only way we could reassure the population. But I figured it was only a matter of time before one of those platoons got ambushed and cut apart. The Darkness Radiant would get to pick the time and place of their attack, and would employ overwhelming force.

"You are afraid of Yoshana," BlackShield Jarl Lago said.

"Of course I'm afraid of her," I snapped. "Every sane person is afraid of her."

He shook his head. "You are allowing your fear of her to cloud your judgment. You assume she is always superior, always a step ahead. She has defeated you in your own mind. You were clever in manipulating my forces when we were at war. She is doing the same to you. You are letting her."

My face heated. "She's the greatest military leader of the modern age, and in case you hadn't noticed, I don't command the Darkness anymore. She does. So do her lieutenants. And they're all better at it than I ever was."

The bearded soldier scowled. "You had the Darkness when we engaged you at the battle of the Cleansing. We were still winning."

"There were more of you, you had better troops, and the casualty ratios were still in our favor. She outnumbers us three to one, and I'll bet you anything she has better equipment and probably better readiness."

"We are led by a prophet," Lago said stubbornly.

"So are they! The loyalty she commands is like nothing you've ever seen. Her men worship her like a god."

Tolf stood abruptly. "Minos, you're acting like we've got no chance at all."

I opened my mouth, shut it, and took a deep, shuddering breath. Railes had one eyebrow raised, which distorted the skull inked on his face. I didn't have a formal adjutant, but the tattooed captain was pretty close. Hake and Lago each had his executive officer present. Tolf represented the Order of Thorns and, in a strange way, Prophetess herself. They all stared at me, some more outwardly calm than others, but all at least mildly horrified.

I dipped my head to Lago. "I apologize, Black." I used the informal term a Monolith soldier would adopt in addressing an officer of the BlackShield's exalted rank.

"You're right, I'm letting her get into my head. I'm frustrated. The Metropolitan and Prophetess did a masterful job rallying the town and the troops, and then Yoshana threw it all over in a day. I'm afraid she'll do the same again. She's drawn a thousand of our men out of the citadel, where they can be defeated in detail. I can see what she'll do next, but I can't see the countermove."

Lago nodded back. "We know what we are facing. We know the battle will not be easy. But we must not let her defeat us before the first crossing of swords."

"You're right, of course."

"So. If we know where the stroke will fall, let us decide how to counter it, and perhaps how to strike a blow of our own."

It was absolutely sound strategy. We spent hours late into the night discussing how to react. We designated the Shadowed Hand and Monolith rangers as the core of a rapid reaction force. The rangers were able horsemen, and we decided on a crash course of riding for the Shadowed Hand. In turn, my former unit would train an ever-growing cadre in unconventional operations against the Darkness.

Of course, we were completely wrong about what Yoshana would do next.

"Minos!"

"Huh? Whuzzat?" I said. Or something to that effect.

My bedroom door shook again under the pounding of a fist. "Minos!" The voice was frantic.

I sat up. Aquinas' *Summa Theologica* slid off my bed onto the floor with a resounding thump. I tried to read a little of the massive book every night. If nothing else, it did tend to help me get to sleep.

"I'm coming." I staggered forward in darkness relieved only by faint moonlight leaking in through the window. My room was small, and in the army I'd developed the habit of getting my gear squared away. So I made it to the door without tripping over anything, even groggy as I was. I took a quick inventory of myself and verified I was wearing clothes, if only undershorts and a night shirt.

In the old days, inhuman senses would have alerted me before anyone got close enough to beat on my door. I was a lot less impressive now.

I peered through the peephole. Seeing Tolf outside, I shot the heavy brass bolt.

"It's Prophetess," he gasped.

I delayed only long enough to grab my katana.

Two floors down in the residence hall, half a dozen soldiers of the Order of Thorns stood nervously outside Prophetess' open door, blades in hand. Three of their fellows lay unmoving in the corridor. Another slumped against a wall, sobbing uncontrollably.

I pushed through them into her bedroom, sword drawn. If I'd allowed myself to think about going in there in my nightclothes, this wouldn't have been the way I'd have chosen to do it.

A pile of sheets burning on the floor shed the only light in the windowless chamber. I'd insisted on limiting access, over her objections. Obviously it hadn't been limited enough. In the flickering shadows I saw Cat crouched on the bed, one arm around Tess, the other clutching the glassy-bladed dagger I had given her. The knife dripped blood. The paleo's teeth were bared in a snarl, the skin of her face torn with dozens of tiny, bloodless gouges.

God's prophet on earth stared over Cat's shoulder with fear-widened eyes.

"What happened?" I demanded.

Cat growled wordlessly.

"Tess?"

Prophetess shook herself. "A maid came in with fresh sheets. She dropped them and she had a knife under them. She just looked at me and said, "Sorry," and then she came at me. Cat threw the oil lamp at her. While she was burning, Cat stabbed her in the chest."

"We're about one corpse short." When Cat stuck a knife in someone, they didn't live to tell about it.

Prophetess swallowed hard. "She just slapped Cat away. It made those marks on her face. The woman was on fire. She bolted. I screamed, and Keeley came." Keeley was a sergeant in the Order of Thorns. He wasn't the most brilliant of men or the best of soldiers, but like all the Order, he was devoted to Prophetess.

"She stabbed him. She didn't even slow down. She just kept going, and then she stabbed Torrel, and then… I don't know. Who else is dead out there, Minos? Who else did she kill?"

The hair on my arms rose. "What did this woman look like?"

"Short. Dark. Pretty. Beautiful, really, if you like them curvy…" her voice trailed off. "Oh my God."

"She was wearing armor the last time the two of you met."

Prophetess nodded. "I didn't even recognize her, but you're right."

Tolf grabbed my shoulder. "Who the hell are you talking about?"

I shook him off. I didn't want anyone binding up my arm. "Roshel. We got lucky. Incredibly lucky. She would have scanned the room before she went in, but didn't realize what Cat was. She thought Cat was just a maid. If it had been anyone but Cat in here, Tess would be dead."

I gently touched the paleo's wounded face. "Are you okay?"

"Hurts," she said, and shrugged. "Hurt before."

This would scar. Wounds inflicted by the Darkness didn't heal normally.

"Quick thinking to throw the lamp at her," I added. "It suppressed the Darkness. Otherwise she would have killed you both."

"Genius, me. Shadow killer, me." She barked out a little laugh. "Just lucky."

I shook my head and repeated myself. "If anyone else had been guarding Tess, she'd be dead. But Roshel isn't going to get caught off guard twice. Stay here."

In the corridor, I snapped at the nearest guard, "Go get four oil lamps, and then I want four of you in there with Prophetess until I tell you to leave. Move it." He hurried off.

Two soldiers were trying to comfort the one slumped against the wall. I knelt in front of him. "What happened?"

The man's face was wet with tears. He snuffled loudly. I didn't need the mind-reading powers of the Darkness to tell he was crippled with terror and humiliation. I stood, giving him a moment to collect himself while I quietly asked Tolf to remind me of his name.

"Mellar, what happened?" I repeated.

He briefly met my eyes, then looked down again.

"She just walked right past us," he said softly, addressing the ground. "I'd never seen her before in my life, but I didn't even think to question her. Going in, I mean, sir. It was just like she was supposed to be here. I swear, it didn't even occur to me she wasn't."

"No. It wouldn't have. It's not your fault." The brunette Overlord generally used the Darkness to project an aura of overwhelming physical desirability. She'd obviously tweaked it to create the impression she belonged, so no one would question the stranger in their midst. "Go on."

"She just went on in to Prophetess' room, sir. We didn't think anything of it, none of us did, I swear. Torrel was saying to Keeley that she was a fine-looking woman, and then we heard the scream, and Keeley was at the door, and she walked past him, and her clothes were on fire, and he pitched over on his face, and I didn't even realize she had a knife until she stuck it in Torrel, and then she threw it and took Jaren in the eye. And she bent over him then and took the knife back, and pulled off her blouse that was on fire, and just kept walking."

I was ashamed to admit that in the midst of the carnage, I was very distracted by the idea of Roshel being topless in our dormitory. It wasn't just her Darkness-spawned aura that inspired feelings of lust. She was an incredibly beautiful woman.

I dragged my treacherous mind out of the gutter as Mellar continued. "Sir, I was behind her the whole time, and, and she didn't see me, and... sir, and I didn't do anything. Sir, I was too scared."

His voice caught and his eyes filled with tears again.

I patted his shoulder. "You couldn't have touched her. She knew you were there. The only reason she didn't kill you too is because she was in a hurry and she didn't think you were a threat. If you'd taken a step toward her, you'd be another body on the ground."

Or if Roshel hadn't been on fire. If the Darkness had been operating freely, not suppressed by the burning oil Cat had flung at her, it would have snuffed Mellar out in passing.

"So all we need to do is look for a beautiful girl with no shirt. Shouldn't be hard to get a building full of soldiers organized around that," Tolf said.

I made a face at him. "She's long gone. She'll have found something to wear and gotten out. If we're lucky, she didn't kill anyone else on the way."

The soldier I'd sent off came trotting back, gingerly balancing four oil lamps.

"You and three more men get in there with Prophetess," I ordered. "If anyone comes in who isn't with me, throw the lamps at them and stab them until they stop moving. Then stab them some more."

"I thought she was long gone," Tolf said.

"I've been wrong a lot lately. And Roshel isn't the only person in the Darkness Radiant. Or the most dangerous."

If Grigg or, God help us, Yoshana herself came for Prophetess, not even four soldiers and Cat were going to keep her alive.

I went on, "Tolf, get General Hake, BlackShield Lago, Railes, and Tarc to the war room. Then wake up the rest of the Order and get them on guard. If they see any Select that isn't Tarc or me, they should kill him on sight."

He pursed his lips and said, "I'm not a hundred percent sure all the guys can tell Select apart that well, especially by torchlight..."

"That's why you're getting Tarc to the war room before you give that order."

He nodded. "What about Yoshana? Should I tell them to watch out for her?"

"Wouldn't do any good. She won't look like herself anyway. I've seen her change her appearance at will."

"So if she's here...?"

"If she's here then, to quote our dear friend Colonel Raji, we're screwed."

I took a perverse satisfaction in the looks of horror on every face in the room. At least everyone else finally understood what we were fighting. The torchlight was weak, but if anything my officers' fear was all the more obvious in the flickering shadow.

"That's what I've been talking about," I said.

"But... I don't understand," Hake muttered. "If they can just walk right past our defenses like that, why bother trying to turn the people against us? And why the hell do you look so happy, Minos?"

"Because now I do understand. Yoshana's been worried about making Tess into a martyr. So first she plants the idea that we're leading everyone into an unnecessary, unwinnable war. Then she shows we can't even defend our own population. When Tess goes down to an assassin's knife, everybody's quietly relieved. We make a big show of outrage, but the fight has gone out of us."

Hake glared. "And why are you happy about that?"

"Two reasons. First, she swung and she missed." I nodded to Lago. "You were right. In my head I've been making Yoshana ten feet tall and invincible, but she makes mistakes too. And second, she's trying to do this on the cheap."

"What do you mean?"

"She hasn't committed any forces at all. She's got us outnumbered and outclassed, but she's trying to avoid a stand-up fight to save resources."

"That does not sound like her," Lago rumbled.

"That's exactly like her. She'll send every man in the Darkness Radiant to his death if she needs to, but she won't sacrifice a single soldier she doesn't think she has to. If she's trying not to fight us, I've got an idea."

"Prophetess won't stand for surrender or Yoshana's terms," Tolf warned.

"Not what I was planning. I need two thousand soldiers all over this compound and the town, bellowing at the top of their lungs. The message is, 'Roshel, Minos wants to talk. Same place as before.'"

Tolf goggled at me. "You want to meet her?"

"Yup."

Lago said, "And if you are wrong? If this was a trick to draw you out?"

I shrugged. "Then after I'm dead you can find yourselves a smarter commanding officer."

The hours dragged by. She might have already left the town. She might ignore my invitation. She might fear a trap - though there was no trap I could set now that she couldn't detect.

It was late. The tavern where Grigg had taken me to meet Roshel, Yoshana, Erev, and the other Knights of Resurrection had been closed. They'd reluctantly opened up when I'd pounded on the door, offered quite a bit of silver, invoked the Metropolitan's name, and reminded the owner that his failure to report Yoshana's presence a year ago was likely treasonous.

I sat nursing a mug of hot but not particularly good cider, now gone lukewarm. The tavern keeper had been more than happy to return to his bed upstairs and leave me alone in darkness broken only by one small lamp.

The building was old, run down without being exactly dirty. Small gusts of cold air crept in under the door, stirring dust. The windows were thick, blurred by grime and the imperfection of the glass. Dim though the light was in the room, I could still see nothing of the street outside.

And then she was walking through the door, and it was the most natural thing in the world. She was still using her "I belong here" aura. The heart-stopping lust she normally aroused was absent.

She was still perhaps the most beautiful woman I'd ever seen. Tanned skin, dark hair and eyes, body fit but totally feminine.

"Have a seat," I offered. Even without the aura of attraction, my heart was pounding. I couldn't say exactly why, where the balance lay between fear and desire. I'd thought I was in love with her once. But now she might just kill me and walk away. She was an Overlord, a half-demon master of the Darkness, and there was nothing I could do to stop her.

Roshel sank gracefully into the chair across from me and stared into my eyes. Eventually she said, "I'm sorry."

"For what, exactly?"

"For what Yoshana did to you and wanted you to do. For trying to kill your friend. For the fact that we'll kill you."

"Not right now, I hope."

"No. Not right now."

"It's a shame. I like you, Roshel. I like Grigg. I've even got a weird fondness for the terror herself. While we're being sorry for things, I'm sorry I left you in the middle of a fight in the Darklands, although I guess you made it out all right." I sighed. "If somehow it had all been different..."

She gave me a sad smile. "I would have liked if it had all been different. But that's not why we're here."

"No. We're here because you picked the wrong side and tried to kill my friend." Her face clouded. I leaned forward and met her eyes squarely. "But I didn't come to talk about that. I don't blame you. I know you're following Yoshana's orders. And I know she hates waste. So I've got an offer for her. Trial by combat, her champion against ours. Two months from now."

The Darkness coalesced around me, caressing my face, ruffling my hair. It was cold outside, but the air in the tavern was thick and close. I tried hard not to flinch as a chill ran across my whole body.

"It's true," Roshel said. "It's not in you anymore. You'll stand no chance at all."

I smiled grimly. "That's why I need two months."

"I could put you out of your misery here, tonight. Why would Yoshana want me to wait?"

"You just said you weren't going to kill me now."

"A girl can change her mind."

She said it in a bantering tone. I didn't think she was serious. But I didn't like the turn the conversation was taking. "You know Yoshana wants to make a statement. Trial by combat will do that. Killing me now just means Prophetess gets a new general who knows better than to meet Overlords in taverns."

Roshel grinned, but then her expression turned serious. "I know. But if she takes your deal, you're just buying yourself two months. It might be better for you if I did it here. She won't let you die easily."

I swallowed. "I know."

4. Here We Go Again

"You are insane!" Tolf blurted.

I shrugged. "I don't see any other option."

"I can't begin to describe all the ways this is a bad idea." Someone had replaced the torches in the war room with oil lamps set on the table. The light cast harsh shadows on Tolf's face, carving sharp angles of frustration. I had just returned from meeting Roshel, it was well after midnight, and we were all running on fear and anger.

I'd had Railes, Dee, and Aharon join us in the planning session. Tarc was still there because I hadn't rescinded the "kill on sight" order for unknown Select, aimed at Grigg. Like a true soldier, he was dozing in a corner, catching up on his sleep while he had the chance. Marek was there because it was, after all, his boss' citadel that had just been infiltrated. He looked extremely upset, as if he were just beginning to understand how out of his depth he was. It was hard to blame him.

"You have to understand just how lucky we were," I replied. "If it had been anyone but Cat in that room with her, Prophetess would be dead. Yoshana and Roshel won't be caught by surprise again. We need to change the rules of engagement."

"Prophetess isn't going to like this," Tolf insisted.

"I'm betting she's liking the idea of being murdered in her sleep even less."

Lago wore a deeply unhappy frown. "What you are proposing, Judge Minos, seems of… questionable morality."

I turned to Aharon son of Malak, the BlackShield's occult advisor. "But necessary, no? Sometimes we have to fight fire with fire."

Lago and his Josephite troops despised the Darkness and the occult, but he had employed Aharon as a consultant on the subject. The Descendant steepled his fingers and rested his chin on them. His hands vanished entirely behind his long beard.

"A dangerous approach, Judge Minos. Recall that King Saul was destroyed after he consulted the Witch of Endor rather than heeding the prophet of the Lord."

Dee spoke up, "On the other hand, Solomon, wisest of the ancient kings, bound demons to his will."

Which was sort of funny, since Dee had once advised me not to call up anything that I could not put down. Did he now think I had somehow gained the wisdom of Solomon? Or was he just talking out of both sides of his mouth? It wasn't necessarily reassuring to have him taking my side.

The two occultists went off into some esoteric argument I couldn't begin to follow.

"Gentlemen!" I interrupted. "I promise I will discuss the moral aspects of this plan with Father Roric tomorrow."

I wasn't looking forward to that at all. I swallowed and went on. "I need your opinion from a military and technical perspective. Does anyone have any better ideas? Because I'll admit I'm not too thrilled with this one myself."

The commanders in the room exchanged glances. So did the scholars. Helpful alternatives were conspicuous by their absence. After a moment, Hake said, "Your judgment has been pretty good on this sort of thing, Minos. I don't like it either, but I don't suppose I see a better option."

I sighed. "Fine. Railes, while I'm gone, I want six of the Shadowed Hand with Prophetess at every single moment unless she's in the bathroom, and then I want Cat with her."

Tolf protested, "The Order of Thorns -"

"Isn't trained against the Darkness. The Shadowed Hand practiced with me. They're the best we've got." There were only two dozen of my old unit left, but it would be enough to keep a constant guard on Tess.

"Go now." Railes stood, saluted, and went to carry out his orders.

"Dee, get down to Stephensburg as fast as you can. Take as much of the Order for an escort as Tolf thinks you need. Get an audience with Yoshana, and repeat my terms. We meet sixty days from today. Tolf, I need you to set the location. I want a hill with a couple of trees on the crown. Make sure Yoshana is clear on the site - it would be embarrassing if we went to different places for the duel, and she might not take that well. Draw a map for her if you need to."

Tolf opened his mouth and shut it. He gave me a tight-lipped nod.

Dee opened his mouth and didn't shut it. "Minos, I believe perhaps you should reconsider your personnel assignments. I am a scholar, a chronicler, a -"

"You told me back at the Battle of the Cleansing you were Prophetess' herald. Now you're my herald. So herald."

"And I appreciate the honor. Deeply. But some events are best recorded from a more objective perspective, which requires a certain distance."

"She won't kill you, Dee. Probably. Unless you say something stupid. Or she's in a bad mood."

The occultist looked outraged and shot an appealing look at Aharon son of Malak. One pretend sorcerer to another, I supposed.

The Descendant had traveled with a military unit. He had been on that rooftop with me at the Cleansing when I was something of a terror myself, an unknown quantity to him except for the destruction I'd inflicted on his companions. He said, "If it pleases Judge Minos, I can deliver the message."

Dee harrumphed. "Certainly not. I appreciate the offer, of course, but this task has been entrusted to me and I will carry it out."

He might well have been the most exasperating human being on the planet. I waved him away. "Why don't you go prepare? You and Tolf can discuss logistics. And Tolf, cancel that kill order on the Select. I don't want Tarc or me getting skewered by someone who can't tell people with gray skin apart."

He saluted, and guided - or more accurately, pulled - Dee out of the room. I turned to Tarc. He was a seasoned officer and had been the military advisor to a prince. "Anything to add?"

He cracked an eyelid and gave me a slow smile. "Nope. Prophetess can have a smarter Select advisor after you're dead."

That line had seemed funnier when I'd said it.

I'd dreaded facing Father Roric more than facing Roshel. But the cleric hadn't bitten my head off. Yet. That didn't mean he liked my idea.

"You can't possibly expect me to approve, Minos."

"We've been over the military angles. None of my officers sees another solution. I don't like this option myself, but I don't see any other way to win."

Roric regarded me with narrowed eyes. "That suggests a certain lack of faith. The Gospel tells us to look at the birds in the sky - they do not sow or reap, they gather nothing into barns, yet our heavenly Father feeds them. So do not worry and say, 'what are we to eat' or 'what are we to drink' or 'what are we to wear?' Our heavenly Father knows we need them all. But seek first the kingdom of God and his righteousness, and all these things will be given to you besides."

I leaned back and took a deep breath. "Yeah. There's an old joke from before the Fall that still circulates among the Select. A pious man finds himself trapped in a flood and prays to the Lord for deliverance. As the water rises, he goes up to the second floor of his house. Two men come by in a boat. 'Get in,' they say. He says, 'No, the Lord will deliver me.' The water gets higher, and he goes up onto the roof. Another boat comes by, and the men in it call out, 'Get in.' 'No,' he says, 'the Lord will deliver me.' Finally, as the water is closing in around him, a helicopter comes by."

I paused, then added, "That was apparently some kind of airship."

The priest nodded. "I've seen pictures."

"The men in the helicopter say, 'Get in,' but the pious man says, 'No, the Lord will deliver me.' And then the water rises some more, and he drowns. When he gets to heaven and sees God he's furious, and he says, 'Why didn't you save me?'"

"And God says, 'I sent you two boats and a helicopter. What did you want?'" the priest concluded. "I've heard it."

"And?"

Roric sighed. "Saint Ignatius of Loyola tells us, 'Act as if everything depended on you; trust as if everything depended on God.' The point is perhaps somewhat similar."

"So isn't this a case of using all the tools God puts at our disposal?"

The Advocate for Justice looked down at his desktop, examining the accumulated centuries of nicks and scratches in the wood. He turned to a heavy, leather-bound Bible and began to leaf through it.

"A moment, please... it's not just a question of using any tool available to us. Some are legitimate, others are not. Because a thing can be done does not mean it should be done, even in a just cause. Ah, here!"

A bony finger stabbed at the page, and he read. "From the Book of Sirach. 'If you choose, you will keep the commandments and so be faithful to his will. He has set fire and water before you; put out your hand to whichever you prefer. A human being has life and death before him; whichever he prefers will be given him. For vast is the wisdom of the Lord; he is almighty and all-seeing. His eyes are on those who fear him, he notes every human action. He never commanded anyone to be godless, he has given no one permission to sin.'"

"But is this really sin, Father? A worse sin than doing nothing? You gave me Aquinas to read. He said nothing is evil in its essence, but only in its defective use. Doesn't that go for the Darkness too?"

Roric frowned. "I may come to regret giving you the *Summa*. Aquinas was the Church's greatest theologian, but even he was human, and fallible. Nor can we realistically expect him to have anticipated an abomination as far outside his experience as the Darkness."

I fought to keep my voice level. "You said our cause was just. You said we had a duty to minimize losses. Do you know how many will die if our armies meet in the field? Since we've got almost seven thousand men, I'd guess that's about seven thousand of us dead, plus however many of Yoshana's we take with us. If we allow her to put us under siege, how many innocents will starve? She won't wait until the harvest comes in."

Roric shook his head. "Then perhaps the answer is not to fight, but to bear witness against her. Our history is full of martyrs. It's not a calling I'd imagined for myself, but that may be the way."

"Do you think she'd let you bear witness? I've seen the withered husk of a human controlled by the Darkness. She saw that too. She killed it, but I'm sure she's thought of the implications. The last words that come from your mouth won't be yours, Father."

He grimaced. "You're entirely too skilled at painting a terrifying picture."

"I learned it from her."

The lean priest's eagle eyes softened. It made him seem old. His next words didn't come with their characteristic edge. "You've always been smart, Minos, as long as I've known you. Too smart for your own good, that's what people say about the Select, and it could have applied to you. But you've seen many things this last year. You've lived through things I never have and hope I never will. And you've begun to become wise."

I was surprised. I didn't know what to say.

He went on, "But even wisdom can be a trap. That jackass Dee brought up Solomon, didn't he?"

I nodded wordlessly, surprised again, on several levels. Roric's insight was as penetrating as his stare. I couldn't say I liked him, but I had to admire him. And he had not previously voiced an opinion of Dee. I was almost tempted to defend the occultist, but I didn't. I'd called him a jackass in my mind a dozen times at least.

"Solomon was wise, none wiser," the priest continued. "And one of the greatest kings of Israel. But he grew proud, and fell into temptation."

"I've got you and Prophetess to keep me from getting proud, Father."

That earned me a thin smile. Emboldened, I continued, "So... I know you don't approve of my proposal, but do you object?"

The eagle-eyed glare was back. "Do I formally object? No. Do I approve? No. You understand that you're morally responsible for the consequences of what you're bringing here... which could be quite grave."

"I understand, Father. I just don't see another path."

He grimaced. "Neither do I. However, we do appear to have a genuine prophet whom you were good enough to bring among us. Have you asked her?"

"She's next on my list to convince."

His smile returned, now mocking. "Good luck."

I winced and stood, but before I could turn he stretched out a thin, bony hand. "A moment. If you're determined to go forward, you should have this." In his palm was a silver disk, perhaps an inch across, attached to a thin chain.

I took the disk and examined it. The figure of a man was engraved on one side, a cross on the other. "What is it?"

"The medal of Saint Benedict. An ancient symbol within the Church. Among other things, it is effective against diabolical influences, temptation, delusion, and sin."

I couldn't keep the frown off my face. He raised an eyebrow. I said, "No disrespect, Father, but I'm not sure a magic amulet is going to help me against the Darkness."

It was his turn to scowl. "You misunderstand the use of sacramentals. The medal has no magical powers. But we humans are influenced by symbols.

When Christ healed the blind man by rubbing mud on his eyes, it was not a magic spell that required the use of mud. Christ could as easily have healed him by simply willing it to be so. But humans react to a physical manifestation. The medal is not some heathen idol, itself an object of faith. It is a reminder of faith. Where you're going, the reminder will do you good."

I turned that over in my head as I turned the disk over in my hands. I might have objected that I didn't need a little piece of metal to focus my mind, but then, I had nearly fallen under the control of the Darkness. It couldn't hurt.

The writing on the medal wasn't in English. "What does it say?"

"Most relevantly, the initials on and around the cross stand for *Crux sacra sit mihi lux; non draco sit mihi dux.* May the holy cross be my light; may the devil not be my prince. And *Vade retro satana; nunquam suade mihi vana; sunt mala quae libas; ipse venena bibas.* Get thee behind me Satan; never tempt me with your vanities; what you offer me is evil; drink the poison yourself."

A shiver went down my spine. "I suppose I see the relevance."

The priest took the medal back from me, said a short prayer over it, and returned it. I slipped the chain around my neck under my shirt.

As I turned to go, he added, "Oh. It also says *Eius in obitu nostro praesentia muniamur.* May we be strengthened by his presence in the hour of our death."

The shiver was stronger than before.

I knew that at any other time, I would have stood no chance at all of persuading Prophetess, but nearly being murdered in your bed by an Overlord changes your worldview.

That didn't mean convincing her was easy.

"No," was her opening response.

"You put me in charge of your military. This is a military matter."

Four of my Shadowed Hand troops stood in her room with us looking uncomfortable. I was sure the two outside the door were eavesdropping. Cat was as tense as a dog watching its owners fight. The paleo's lips were pulled back, baring her teeth. I wasn't completely sure she wouldn't bite me if the argument got too heated. Or stab me. I'd survive being bitten. No one but Roshel had ever survived being stabbed by Cat.

"This isn't an acceptable military solution, Minos," she snapped. "Do I really need to list all the things that could go wrong? You might not even make it there alive. He might not help you. Even if he helps you, we might not win. Not to mention I didn't cast the Darkness out of you just so you could go running right back to it!"

"Not exactly fair, Tess." I tried to keep my voice level. It was harder than with Roric. Cat's eyes were wide.

"As far as our chances, this is the best we've got," I continued. "Everyone agrees. Otherwise we're just sitting here, waiting for whatever Yoshana decides to do next. Take another shot at you, which won't miss next time. Kidnap some more townspeople. Start massacring our patrols. We can't just sit around. Saint Ignatius of Loyola said, 'Act as if everything depended on you, trust as if everything depended on God.' We have to act and trust."

She snarled, "Dee told you that one."

"Actually it was Father Roric."

She turned away from me, staring at the wall. After a moment, Cat hesitantly touched her back. Prophetess took the paleo's hand, but didn't face me.

"Tess?"

Still looking away, she spoke so quietly I had to strain to hear. "The First Book of the Fall says, 'In those days they called upon the Darkness to serve them and did not know that they instead would serve it.'"

"Tess, everyone agrees. If I don't do this, we're all going to die."

"Saint Siles said, 'In suffering, we open ourselves to salvation. Only when we fall do we look up.'"

I slapped my palm against the stone wall of the room. Cat spun at the noise, knife glistening in the lamplight. It wasn't quite pointed at me.

I ignored the blade. "Dammit, Tess! You said we needed to come here to stop Yoshana. You said we needed an army. I brought you here, I've got an army, but we're not going to stop Yoshana unless I do this!"

I stared at Cat, since Prophetess wouldn't meet my eyes. "I have to do it, Tess."

"I'm not stopping you," she said quietly.

She hadn't stopped me the last time I'd headed into the Sorrows either. That hadn't worked out so well. This time, though, I knew what I was getting into.

That just meant I knew exactly how lousy an idea it was.

I had two horses, gallons of small beer, weeks' worth of dried fruit and meat. It was a bad time of year to live off the land, and I couldn't use the Darkness anymore to hunt in my sleep, or kill the microbes in stagnant pools I might have to drink from.

"I'll go with you," Railes had said.

"You stay here. I think Yoshana will bite on this deal, but maybe she won't. You're the only one I trust to watch Tess. Besides Cat. And if I run into anything I have to fight with, I'll probably get the worst of it, whether there's one or two of us."

I still had my katana and a carbine, of course. I wasn't defenseless just because the Darkness wasn't in me. It only felt that way.

I left quietly, without fanfare. Other than the Ministry and a handful of others, no one was even informed. Not that I really thought I could keep my mission a secret, but why advertise?

For much the same reason I avoided settlements. A Select was conspicuous, and I had no way of knowing what instructions Yoshana might have left in the territory under her control. The days were chilly and the nights were frigid. It rained twice and soaked me thoroughly, with no dry wood available to make a fire. I was physically miserable in a way I hadn't been since my original journey north from Rockwall with Prophetess. It would have been ironic if I'd died of pneumonia before I reached the Sorrows.

My innate Select vitality was enough to see me through, cold and alone with my thoughts. I had plenty of time to think about what I was doing, and my relationship with Tess. My thoughts were not particularly good company.

I felt completely out of my depth, physically, intellectually, and morally. I'd been a competent leader of the Shadowed Hand. I'd flattered myself into believing I was some sort of minor military genius because I'd been clever at exploiting tactical advantages. But I'd nearly lost my soul in the process. I still remembered the dream where I'd killed Cat, dissolving her body to hide the evidence. It had felt very, very real. Months later I'd had a nightmare that it was true, and everything that had happened since had been in my imagination.

Tess had saved me. She'd cared enough to seek me out while she was searching for her army. She'd purged the Darkness from me and put me in charge of her crusade. She'd gone beyond any rational extreme to help me.

So why did I still feel like she didn't support me?

I suppose the demands felt unreasonable - that I was caught in a trap with no escape. I was fighting a monster with one hand tied behind my back. Success depended on untying that hand, but Tess was clearly disappointed in me. I didn't want her to be disappointed. But even more than that, I didn't want her head stuck on a pike on Our Lady's battlements with Yoshana's banner flying over it. So I was going to the Sorrows, and disappointing her.

One day shapes loomed out of the fine drizzle on the road ahead. A year earlier, in a foul temper I might not have given way. This time I pulled my hood further over my face and nudged my mount and packhorse to the side of the road, left hand on the reins, right near my sword hilt.

There were six men on horseback, tall, armored, white tabards blazoned with the strange golden double-crescent of the Darkness Radiant. Dee had called it the symbol of a syncretic, pan-Abrahamic religion, whatever that meant. These soldiers were dark-skinned and bearded, their long black hair pulled back and bound. Four carried lances couched vertically in stirrups. The other two carried the naphtha-throwers of fire wardens. So Yoshana was patrolling the roads now, clearing them of the Darkness and other vermin.

My horse squelched into a muddy, weed-choked ditch. The packhorse stopped, tossed its head, and stood there, stubbornly unwilling to venture into the treacherous surface. I considered jerking at its lead but decided that would only attract more attention. I shifted my hand farther from my weapon. This wouldn't go well if it came to a fight.

The patrol continued on without a word, their eyes passing over me without registering the least interest. Whatever I thought I was going to accomplish against Yoshana, to these troops I didn't merit a second glance.

I wondered if they were right.

Looking and feeling like a few hundred miles of bad road, a week later I hauled my weary body and two cranky horses up the carved stone steps of World's End and stopped in front of Hafnum Furat's iron gate. Just like the first time, he was flanked by two assistants, each with a massive bronze torch in the shape of a crucifix, flames licking up from an oil reservoir to play over the body of the crucified Christ.

The big, blond man stared at me. "Not a person I expected to see again."

"Why? Because you thought Yoshana would have killed me by now? Or because you thought I'd be smart enough to stay away?"

"Yes." Just as when I'd first met him, he held a large knife in one hand and a large pistol in the other.

"Just out of curiosity, which one?"

Furat shrugged. "Either. Both. I don't guess there's much point in testing you for the Darkness." He holstered both weapons and reached to his belt for the keys to the gate.

"Up to you. It's not in me anymore. You can test, or you can take my word for it."

He stopped with his hand halfway to the lock. "It's not in you?"

"No."

"So you can't make me let you in?"

I grimaced. "No, I can't. Although I really wish you would. I'm tired, and I'm hungry."

He turned the key and swung the gate open. "Hearing how you got rid of that stuff is worth the price of admission. Even though I've got the feeling I'll wind up regretting it."

Furat and I sat at a small table looking directly out toward the sunset. There had been stew for dinner the first time I'd come this way, with Yoshana and her company. There was stew again. It was good, though. The beer was better than what I was carrying, especially after mine had been in a leather sack for a week.

"Where do you get the meat and vegetables?" I asked. World's End stood at the top of a rocky outcrop, a natural fortress rising from the edge of the Sorrows' sea of trees, dropping away to the fields of the Source in the west. A tiny island wedged between the Darkness-haunted forest and Yoshana's domain.

"Trading down in the Source for the stuff the prospectors haul out of the Sorrows. In Waterblade, mostly. You probably would have gone by it on the way here. Little town on the south end of that lake." He pointed. I could make out sunlight winking off what might have been water.

"What prospectors? I've been here three times and there's never been anyone else."

He chuckled, though there wasn't much humor in it. "There's not many. But the ones who live find some impressive things in there."

I nodded. I'd seen it. The strange, glistening knife I'd given to Cat came from an abandoned town in the Sorrows. Of course, the natives who infested that place made the paleos look like the pinnacle of human civilization by comparison. They'd been a strange, terrifying hunting pack sharing a common bestial intelligence linked by the Darkness. Furat wasn't exaggerating when he said "the ones who live" to describe the prospectors. We'd lost three veterans of the Darkness Radiant in the Sorrows, despite the mastery of the Darkness of Yoshana, Grigg, and Roshel. And, at the end, me.

Furat shrugged and wiped foam from his beard. "There's some regulars. Guys who've lasted years in there, coming out to trade and resupply, and then going right back in again. They're rich enough to retire by now, but they just go back over and over. Crazy, but they keep me in business."

"Some people aren't made to retire. I know a woman who got herself a job as the general of the Source but now she's busy trying to take over the world. Did she and her crew come through here on their way back?"

"Most of them. The scariest ones. The big Select. The pretty one. The soldier with the beard and the scars. And her, of course."

The soldier with the beard and scars would be Erev. So he'd survived. I was glad of that.

"I guess the others didn't make it back," Furat continued.

"The others didn't even make it there. They died in the Sorrows. I guess they died. Two of them just vanished in the night." I ran my finger over the thick, rippled glass of the window. Heavy metal framing separated it into diamond-shaped panes. "Did she ask about me?"

He nodded. "Yeah. She seemed glad you'd lived. I figured she wanted to finish you off herself."

"She was hoping I'd kill Prophetess for her."

Furat's eyebrows went up. "But you didn't. Did you?"

"No," I said. He must have known I hadn't. He wasn't so isolated here that word wouldn't have reached him. Unless he thought perhaps I'd killed Tess and set up an impostor in her place. I frowned. It wasn't impossible. That was a risk worth considering in the future, if somehow we all survived what was to come.

I continued, "So now Yoshana does want me dead. Roshel told me so, right after she tried to stab Prophetess and got set on fire instead."

"Jesus. So what are you doing here? Hiding? I don't mean to be inhospitable, but can't you find somewhere else to die where you won't take me with you?"

I showed him my teeth. "I'm not hiding. I challenged Yoshana to a duel."

"Jesus," Furat repeated. "That's got to be the craziest thing I've ever heard, and I hang around people who go into the Sorrows for a living. So then what are you doing here?"

"I need you to help me find a demon."

Furat was more colorful than my colleagues back at Our Lady. Most of the words that came out of his mouth couldn't be repeated in polite company.

"You are insane," he sputtered when he ran out of obscenities.

"I've heard that one before."

"Okay, how about 'no'? Have you heard that one before?"

"Yep."

"Then what are you thinking?" Furat demanded, an exasperated scowl on his face. "Yeah, he didn't kill you last time you met him, but that doesn't mean he's going to love you now. And he's almost all the way across the Sorrows. Did you forget you almost died getting back from there, and that was when you were controlling the Darkness?"

"No, I remember that. That's why I need you to help me get through."

The big man stood up and glared down at me. "And why on earth would I want to do that? I told you before I'm allergic to being dead."

"How do you feel about being a slave? Because if Yoshana's running the show, you'll either be dead or under her thumb. You've got an Overlord on one side and the Sorrows on the other. Talk about being squeezed."

He raised an eyebrow. "Has it occurred to you that it's just a little bit ironic that you want to use the Darkness against the person who wants to use the Darkness against the Darkness?"

I opened my mouth and shut it, turning his words over in my head. The sun's dying light stained the rock walls of the dining hall red. It would be dark soon.

"I didn't turn against her because of the tools she used," I said slowly. "Or because I don't believe someone needs to make a stand against the demons and the Darkness. It was because she'll crush anyone who stands in her way with no more remorse than you'd feel stepping on a bug."

"She wants everyone under her thumb."

"Yes."

He sat down again and leaned toward me. It was a moment before he spoke.

"You sure that's a bad thing? I'm comfortable enough up here, but it's not so great down there." He waved his hand at the window, encompassing the Source with the sweep of his arm, then jerked his thumb over his shoulder toward the Sorrows. "Or in there. You think if the world was a decent place, people would risk their necks in that damn forest to scavenge three hundred year old garbage? And it's not getting any better. What's in there leaks out, more of it every year. The people in Waterblade are careful, but they still had three possessed last year. If Yoshana can push the Darkness back, create some order…"

"By stomping on everyone who crosses her."

"Conquerors don't play nice. The Romans didn't go around asking whether everyone wanted to join their empire, but they created the greatest civilization of their age. Peace given to the world, that's what they called it."

I closed my eyes. "They make a desert and call it peace. Decimations. Bodies hanging on crosses. Captives fed to lions for sport. A city leveled and the ground beneath sown with salt. Have we really fallen so far that we miss that?"

"Haven't we?"

"Yoshana Caesar. It has a certain ring to it." I puffed out air. "But I'm going to be one of the first to get fed to the lions. I guess I'll have to find Seven without you."

"You're really going to go in there alone?"

I shrugged. "I don't have much choice, do I?"

He showed big, white teeth. "I never said I wouldn't help you."

"What?"

"If she civilizes the world, it'll wreak havoc with my profits."

I went to sleep not understanding what had changed his mind.

The walls of my bedroom were rough timbers but they had been sanded, polished, and varnished. Like the rest of World's End, they conveyed a sense of great age. There was an impression of solidity and permanence to the place. If Furat was to be believed, it had been built as a fortress at the dawn of the Age of Fear and had endured ever since.

It was a refuge, a rock that stood above the mad tides engulfing the fallen world. Why would its master agree to leave it?

The next morning I found him looking out over the Sorrows and asked him. "I didn't think I was convincing you last night. Why'd you agree to go with me?"

Furat bent and picked up a pebble. He set it on the carved stone parapet and flicked it with a thick finger. We watched it vanish into the sea of trees below.

"I came out here because I didn't want to answer to anyone." He didn't turn to face me as he spoke. His gaze was lost somewhere in the endless miles of forest. "I've told you I'm no coward. I'm not a fool, and folks that are reckless don't survive the Sorrows. But I'm no coward. That woman, though, or whatever she is… twice she's been here, and twice my guts turned to water and I crawled for her like a damn whipped dog. I guess… I guess if it's a choice between taking my chances down there or living another fifty years under her boot, I'll take my chances down there."

"Not quite ready for the return of the empire after all?"

"I guess I'm not." He pushed away from the wall. "C'mon, let's get some breakfast and get ourselves organized. We'll want as much daylight as possible. It sucks all the time in there, but it sucks worse at night."

Breakfast was pancakes and bacon. I filled up. Furat barked instructions at his assistants.

"I'm only going to be gone for two weeks. Three tops. I'd better not find a mess here when I get back."

"What if it's more than three weeks?" I asked softly.

"Then we'll be dead, and it won't be my problem." He bellowed, "Morfah, go get Sam. We should make introductions, since we're going to be spending time together."

"We're taking someone else with us?"

His chair scraped on the stone floor as he belched and stood. "Oh yeah."

Morfah, the shorter of Furat's helpers, emerged from the stables as we stood in the yard. He was being dragged forward by a wolf straining at its leash, shaggy fur white as bleached bones.

"Let her go," Furat called.

The beast charged. It picked up speed like a bullet. I had left my sword and rifle in my room. My folding knife would be a feeble defense against the creature lunging for me. I put up my arms to shield my face. Its front paws hit my chest as it reared up. Its muzzle darted out, its jaws gaped open, and it licked my chin.

Furat laughed.

The beast's tail wagged maniacally.

"Why on earth do you have a tame wolf?" I demanded. It continued to enthusiastically lick my face.

"It's not a wolf. It's a dog," he chuckled.

"Looks like a wolf to me. Anyway, dogs don't like Select."

"Sam likes everybody, even gray-skinned pains in my ass."

I tentatively patted the creature's shoulder. It wasn't as massive as I'd thought. Much of the apparent bulk was fur, which was surprisingly soft. It showed no sign of getting bored with slobbering on me.

"Okay, so you've got a big, friendly dog that looks like a wolf. Why would we take the poor thing into the Sorrows? Did it eat your favorite boots or something?"

The dog finally dropped to all fours and trotted to Furat. He scratched it absentmindedly behind the ears. "Nah. The Waterbladers breed 'em to detect the Darkness. Pushes our chances of survival way up from 'none' to 'slim.'"

I processed that. "If you've got a Darkness-detecting dog, why do you cut people's hands open to check for it?"

"She's still young and she's not quite trained yet. I didn't even have her last time you came through. And when I let her out of the stable she barks too damn much."

As if on cue, the dog looked at me and let out a piercing yip. I backed up a step.

"She wants you to play with her," Furat said.

"I'm surprised you just got one of them now. Seems like they'd be really useful here."

The big man's face clouded. "It was a long time before I could bring myself to get another one. I lost a dog like this in the Sorrows years ago. He went running off... I don't know what got him. The way he was howling, it didn't finish him quick."

I didn't know what to say. Furat glared at me.

"Don't look at me like that, Minos. Whatever killed that dog would have killed me too."

"I didn't say you should have gone after him, Furat."

"Damn right. I tell myself that pretty much every night." He patted Sam on the head, a huge, shaggy man with a huge, shaggy hound, like some ancient northern god torn from long-lost myth. The dog leaned against his leg, tongue hanging out of a mouth opened in a big, stupid canine grin.

5. Sorrow Revisited

I had my carbine and my katana. Furat had his massive knife on one hip and the huge revolver on the other. The walking stick he carried was big enough to use as a quarterstaff. I wasn't quite sure what to make of the glass spheres slung on a bandolier across his chest.

"Oil grenades." Some kind of striker mechanism was attached to each one. He hefted one, flicked the striker, and a wick sputtered to smoldering life. He pinched it out between his thumb and forefinger. "Not the safest things in the world, but the Darkness doesn't like 'em at all."

"I should take some back to Cat. Better than throwing lamps at Overlords." And then of course I had to explain that story.

Furat shook his head. "You really are the craziest person I've ever met. A Select with a pet paleo. Who he has protecting a prophet from Yoshana, while he goes into the Sorrows to find a demon. If I live, no one's ever going to believe half of this story."

I would have happily stood around bantering all day, but my guide insisted we get moving early. He was right, of course. The dog pulled eagerly at her leather leash the whole way down the stone stairs into the forest.

"I'm not even going to last long enough to get killed by the Darkness," Furat grumbled. "This stupid mutt's going to break my neck on these steps."

And then we were in among the trees, and we fell silent. The leaves were just beginning to bud, but the branches themselves cast deep shadows that seemed somehow to stifle sound as well as light. Compared to the forests of the west, the Sorrows were unnaturally quiet. Even the dog was subdued, sniffing tentatively at shrubs but no longer trying to rush ahead.

"Due north for now," Furat whispered, moving off the road into the underbrush. "That's been pretty safe for a while. Of course, anywhere enough prospectors go, something's going to stake out eventually."

It had been bad traversing the Sorrows with Yoshana. It had been worse by myself, even with the Darkness in me. This was almost intolerable. There was no way of knowing what might be stalking us. Furat had the dog's leash in one hand and his walking stick in the other, but I could tell he was itching to draw his pistol. My katana was bared in my hand.

Not even an hour had passed when Sam came to an abrupt halt, backed two steps, and growled low in her throat. We froze.

"There." Furat gestured with his staff. A cloud drifted through the trees, perhaps twenty yards away. It was about man-sized, but thin. What I'd controlled before the Cleansing had been larger.

"Shouldn't be a threat," I murmured. But we waited until it had faded from sight before we moved on.

We continued for the rest of the day without incident. Twice more the dog had become skittish, and we'd avoided the areas that made her uncomfortable. There was no question she'd earned her keep. Each time she sensed something Furat gave her a piece of jerky, which she gobbled down like the wolf she resembled.

We found a small clearing and made camp well before sunset. My companion began gathering wood.

"Are you sure a fire's a good idea?" I asked.

He shrugged. "You have to balance the risks. The worst things in here are afraid of fire. Some of the others might be afraid of the dog. For the rest -" he jerked his chin at my carbine, "you better hope you're a good shot."

"I've gotten pretty good at killing people."

He nodded. "And if we're really lucky, what comes after us might be something you'd still call people."

I took the first shift. Furat was apparently able to fall asleep at will.

I had never cared for dogs, nor had they cared for me. But I sat next to Sam, leaned against a rock, and rested a hand on her soft coat. After a time she put her head on my leg. We were comfortable enough that I found myself struggling not to drift off.

And then the dog's muzzle lifted, her nostrils twitching. I grabbed the carbine next to me, straining all my senses. If the Darkness had still been in me, I would have risked sending a probe.

If the Darkness had still been in me, I wouldn't have been here.

I heard nothing. After a minute, Sam let out a soft *whuff* and her head sank back onto her paws. There was no more danger of me falling asleep on watch, though.

I nudged Furat awake when I thought the night was halfway past. He looked at me blearily.

"We're still alive, huh?"

"The dog must have heard or smelled something she didn't like, but it went away."

He got to his feet and stretched. "Stands to reason something would come take a look. Get some rest. If you hear me start shooting, we've got trouble. Otherwise I'll wake you up in the morning. If you don't wake up, it's 'cause whatever it was killed us in the night."

"You're a real bundle of joy, you know that?"

"Says the man who dragged me out of my nice, safe bed to go trudging through this hellhole."

I didn't have much to say to that.

We all survived the night, though my dreams had been haunted by something I couldn't quite recall. We ate hard bread and jerky, and Furat gave some more of the latter to Sam. Whatever had bothered her during the night, it didn't seem to have affected her appetite.

"That dog would weigh three hundred pounds if I let her eat as much as she wants," the big man grumbled, but his heart wasn't in it.

It seemed that just a day in, the trees were growing thicker with new leaves. The shadows deepened. If we'd been just a week or two earlier, the branches would have been bare. It was prettier this way, but far more threatening, and far harder to spot enemies coming.

We'd only been walking half an hour when a figure stepped out from between two trunks not a hundred feet away.

Furat dropped his walking stick and jerked his massive pistol out of its holster. I drove the point of my sword into the ground and unslung my carbine. Only the dog seemed unperturbed. She didn't growl, and her tail wagged tentatively.

The shape moved slowly toward us, human-like in size and general outline.

"If that's possessed..." I whispered.

"...Sam should sense it," Furat confirmed. But the dog still didn't growl. Instead, she let out a soft bark, but it didn't sound angry.

The figure was shorter than I, and much shorter than Furat. It was wearing a dark cloak with a hood that concealed its features.

"Stay where you are," Furat called.

It stopped and gently pushed back the hood. A girl looked out, nearly as pale as Cat and not much older. "Are you prospectors? Thank God. Come with me. I know a safe place."

Furat and I glanced at each other. I slung the carbine and retrieved my sword, but I didn't sheath it. Furat didn't put away the pistol.

"Who are you, and what are you doing out here?" he demanded.

She moved closer, slowly, hands in the air. "My name is Talith. I come from a village about a week north of here." Her voice was strangely accented and a bit hesitant, as if she were searching for words in a language that wasn't quite her own. "It is inside the forest, but we had always kept the Darkness out. Until a few months ago. The possessed always attacked, every year. But never so many..."

She looked down, then met our eyes again. "They were coming over the wall and we could not stop them. My parents told me to run, and I ran. I knew the forest, how to hide. I have found safe places to stay. But I hoped someone would find me and take me out of here."

Furat said, "We're going north, not south."

The girl nodded eagerly. "And I can help you get where you are going. As I said, I know safe places. But then, after you have found what you are looking for, you will take me back with you. Yes?"

The big man raised his eyebrows at me. I shrugged. "If she knows places we can stop for the night, we'll sleep a whole lot better. And the dog seems to like her."

She was close enough now that Sam could reach her. The shaggy animal licked Talith's hand, and the girl patted the dog's head.

"Stupid dog likes everyone," Furat complained. But he said to her, "Fine, you help us get where we're going, we'll take you out of the Sorrows and get you on your way to civilization."

She smiled. "You are very kind."

We made better time following Talith. She moved as easily through the trees as if she were a wraith herself, somehow guiding us down paths where no danger lurked. Yoshana had wanted a native guide when she'd led her commando team through the Sorrows - we had by sheer luck actually found one.

We must have covered several miles when we emerged into a clearing far larger than the one where Furat and I had spent the night. A fallen log lay at the center of it next to a stone-ringed fire pit.

"This place is safe," Talith announced. "Rest here."

And even as we sat on the log, she pulled up her hood and vanished into the trees.

"Hey, wait," Furat called.

I felt no inclination to follow her. "I don't know about you, but I can use a break."

He didn't disagree. So we rested, and soon enough Talith drifted back out of the trees and made her way toward us, graceful as a dancer, moving so softly her feet didn't even seem to touch the ground.

Bow-wow-wow-wow-wow-wow! Sam erupted into a frenzy of furious barking, and my vision cleared from the effects of the aura, and the cloaked figure wasn't touching the ground because it had no feet.

Furat plucked a grenade from his bandolier, flicked its wick to life, and hurled it backhand. It passed through the mass of Darkness filling the cloak and shattered on the fabric behind. The wraith was no larger than a man but it was incredibly dense, one of the thickest clouds I'd ever seen. It rose into the air inside the burning garment, and my mind resonated to its panicked psychic shriek.

The cloud was big but it was stupid. If it had just streamed out the front of the cloak, it could have escaped easily. Instead it flailed in the air, burning. Furat and I watched in fascinated horror as the substance of the Darkness itself caught fire. What escaped the conflagration wasn't enough to be a threat.

Talith raced back into the clearing before it was quite over, her hood thrown back again, shock and anger and fear mingled on her face.

"What's it you's done?" she screamed. And then her expression changed to something fawning. "Oh, heroes, what you have done! You have destroyed the monster -"

As she turned her smile on Furat, he shot her in the face.

I looked from the corpse to my companion. "She wasn't infected, you know." No cloud of Darkness emerged from the hole between her eyes or the shattered wreckage where the back of her head had been.

"I know." He spat on the ground near the body. "She was a collaborator. That's worse. I'd heard of it but hadn't ever seen it, and most people don't survive running into them. She was bait for that wraith."

"The wraith is gone. She wasn't a threat anymore."

He glared at me. "And what did you want me to do? She was going to kill us, and she probably did kill people I knew."

"Prophetess would be dead if I'd killed the last person who tried to assassinate me while I was sleeping."

Furat snorted. "So you think we should have turned her into a pet like your Cat?"

"Why not?"

Sam was sniffing at the body. Furat shoved the dog away with a foot. He let out a long sigh. "People say mercy is for the weak. That's bull. Mercy is for the strong. And in case you haven't noticed, we're not exactly in a position of strength here. When you decided not to kill that paleo, there was nothing within a thousand miles that stood a chance of hurting you - certainly not a little paleo girl. Us, here? That treacherous witch could have gotten us killed a hundred times a day."

And he wasn't wrong. I remembered a long-ago argument with Prophetess about the wisdom of killing a wounded paleo who'd attacked us. I'd crippled him instead, and he'd been less of a threat than Talith.

"Sorry," I said. "You made a call. I don't know if I would have made the same one, but I understand it."

And I understood it even better when we left the clearing and found the pile of skeletons heaped on the far side, where Talith must have dragged the bodies after the cloud had fed on them. Furat made a face and began to loot their equipment. When he saw me staring, he simply said, "What? A lot of this is good stuff. I sold it to them."

One man had a pair of oil grenades like Furat's. I took one, returned to the clearing, and detonated it on Talith's corpse. I couldn't have said whether it was out of consideration for the dead or to spite the Darkness so it couldn't profit from her body one last time. Maybe it was both.

"You think it's true about the town?" I asked. We were still headed due north, as best I could tell. Sam trotted at our side, sniffing.

Furat shrugged. "Could be. There's supposed to be a village up here that isn't infected. I was hoping we'd pick up a guide there. So it wouldn't be good if it's fallen. Some of what she said was a lie - she'd been working with that wraith for more than a couple of months."

"How do you know?" The skeletons had been picked very clean, but the Darkness could do that in minutes.

"Like I said, I recognize the gear. Some of those guys vanished years ago."

"Couldn't they have survived for years before the cloud got them?"

Furat shook his shaggy blond head. "You don't last for years at a time out here. No one does. Once someone's been in the Sorrows for a couple of months and you haven't heard from them, they're not coming back out again. Ever."

We continued in silence for some time. I asked, "If she wasn't from that village, where would she be from?"

He shrugged again. "No one knows what all's in here. Maybe some group of infected natives sometimes leaves someone clean as bait. Maybe she was from outside the Sorrows altogether… developed an unhealthy fascination with the place. Maybe in some town like Waterblade, a girl listened to the stories about the wraiths and liked what she heard. One day, she went to the edge of the Sorrows and met something, and somehow the two of them made a bargain. And then she started luring other people into the woods with tales of marvels she'd seen, and the cloud killed them. And she liked having the power of life and death, and pretty soon, every girl who'd teased her, and every boy who'd rejected her, had vanished into the woods. And when the townsfolk started getting suspicious, she vanished into the woods too. And she and her friend started looking for other prey. She seemed pretty well fed… maybe the wraith wasn't the only one with a taste for human flesh."

I suppressed a shudder. "You think that's true?"

"Probably not. But if it makes you feel better about me killing her, go with it."

I glanced over at him. He had a mocking little smile on his face. Fair enough. I'd encouraged people to believe comforting lies when I'd led the Shadowed Hand.

"What is truth?" I muttered.

Furat overheard me. "The guy who asked that question wound up with a pretty bad reputation, but he wasn't the one who got nailed to a cross."

"It was suggested to me that martyrdom was a better option than exposing myself to the Darkness again."

"And yet here you are."

I nodded. "And yet here I am."

We made it two more days without incident. Sam guided us away from clouds drifting through the trees or lairing in their branches. On the fourth morning, we heard a faint but continuous rustling far off to our right. The dog's lips pulled back from her teeth and she growled deep in her throat.

"Drelb?" Furat wondered quietly.

I shook my head. "Too many sounds. I mentioned the Darkness infects pigs, right?"

He nodded.

"Did I mention it had infected a lot of them?" In the biblical story, Christ had cast a legion of demons into a herd of swine. I had to guess the infected boars I'd encountered before were a pretty fair approximation.

"You didn't say what you did about them," Furat murmured.

"I ran like hell. And fell down an embankment." The creatures had not been impressed at all with my command of the Darkness. "They're probably scared of fire."

"Just how aggressive were these pigs?"

"You know how pigs are omnivores? And 'omni' means 'everything'? Let's just say humans are definitely part of 'everything.'"

I could see the underbrush moving now. I steadied the carbine on my shoulder. Sam quivered, snarling. A tusked, snouted head pushed through the weeds. Then another, and another, and more, a skirmish line of the beasts parallel to our path. They weren't much taller than Sam at the shoulder but the bodies were massive. Each one outweighed me. They approached slowly, mouths wide.

"Run like hell?" Furat asked.

"I should mention that falling down the embankment would probably have killed me if I hadn't had the Darkness healing me. Maybe up a tree..."

"You gonna carry the dog?"

"Good point." I fired at the nearest animal. The heavy slug took it just behind the head. It staggered and let out a piercing squeal, then charged. I cycled the bolt, fired again, and blasted a clump of grass in front of it.

The monster was forty feet away when Furat's bullet smashed its skull. It plowed face-first into the turf, then lurched unsteadily to its feet.

"You sure the dog can't climb?" I asked.

Furat fired again, destroying the pig's left eye. It stood for a moment, then the Darkness poured out of the wounds in its head and it fell. The cloud circled in the air, then settled on another of the boars that had continued their slow advance. That one roared a challenge that shook the trees.

"Uh oh."

Furat hurled a grenade. It burst inches from the boar's snout, sending up a sheet of flame. I fired, worked the bolt, and fired again. Both shots hit the beast and it staggered and went down.

To the north the pigs drew back a bit, but a half dozen to the south were working their way around behind us. Furat lobbed another grenade and they retreated.

We edged northwards, crab-walking to keep our weapons trained on the monsters to the east.

Another one charged. Furat and I both fired twice and it fell, leaking blood and Darkness. The pig closest to it began to chew on the corpse. As more Darkness flooded into the cannibal it raised its bloody muzzle and turned its evil little eyes back to us.

"Run?" I asked.

"Run," Furat agreed. He threw another grenade, cutting off the animals to the north, then flung one directly behind us.

"Two left," he gasped.

Sam raced along with us, far faster on four legs than we were on two. Once she darted too close to me and I almost tripped over her. I hurled curses at the dog but only in my mind - I saved my breath for running.

Fifteen minutes later we puffed to a halt. There were no immediate sounds of pursuit.

"Think we lost them?" I asked between gasps for breath.

"Lost 'em? No. Pigs track. By smell. But if we're lucky. They decided. To go chase something else."

A couple of hours before sundown we climbed a rocky outcrop on the back of a ridge. It fell away sharply to the northeast, a slope too extreme for the pigs to negotiate. We hoped. On the other sides we collected wood and heaped up a sort of low barricade. Thankfully it had been dry for the past week. As night came on, we set the barrier on fire.

"We might burn down the whole forest if we're not careful," I said.

"And that would break your heart, would it?"

"Not really, no."

471

Sam didn't like being encircled by flames, but seemed to understand the alternative was worse. She whined unhappily and bumped her head against Furat's leg.

"Good girl," he consoled her, scratching behind her ears. "Some of that pork would taste good now, huh?"

Even having harbored the Darkness in my own body, I felt a superstitious dread of eating something that had been infected with it. Not that the option was available. "You want to go back and get some?"

"Not really, no."

As night fell I noticed a glow to the northwest. It was hard to judge the distance without knowing the size of the light source, but I guessed it might be ten miles away. "Think that might be a town?" I asked Furat.

"I hope so. If they're using fire, they're probably not infected."

The issue became more urgent an hour later. Our first warning was when Sam started to growl, but not much later we could hear rustling and grunting in the trees beyond the edge of the firelight.

"Doesn't look like they decided to chase something else," I said.

"Nope."

The sounds continued, just beyond the edge of sight. We set watches again, but neither of us slept well. Once I woke to see Furat poking at the barrier with his staff, coaxing more flames from the charred wood. I sat up. "Is that going to last the night?"

He looked dubiously at the logs. "I wouldn't bet on it. I don't know how high the fire has to be to hold them back, but we might want to make a move."

I peered into the blackness behind us. "You mean over the ridge? In the dark? Down a rock slope?"

"Yeah."

"I can't imagine what could possibly go wrong with that plan."

"You like the alternative better?" He gestured beyond the ring of smoldering branches. The flames had subsided to the point we could just make out bulky shapes moving in the trees beyond. Occasionally piggy little eyes would reflect the firelight.

I shook my head. We could risk crippling injury on the slope, or face almost certain death torn apart by Darkness-maddened swine. It wasn't much of a choice, but the ridge was definitely more appealing.

Furat secured a length of rope around a projecting rock and tied the other end around his waist. "I'll chuck a grenade at them, then I'll head down. When I'm at the bottom, I'll throw the rope back up to you."

"How come you get to go down first?" I wasn't really complaining. My nerves just made my mouth move.

"You want to carry the dog instead?"

I didn't, so Furat threw another grenade into the trees just past the barricade, grabbed Sam, and launched himself backwards over the precipice. The dog put her front paws on his shoulders and gave a frightened yip as she plunged over the side into the darkness below.

Flames licked aggressively at the undergrowth and began to crawl up tree trunks. I wondered if we had in fact managed to set the woods on fire. Trapped on this outcrop of rock, that might prove even more definitively fatal than facing the pigs.

The end of the rope slapped onto the ground a few feet from me.

"Hurry up," Furat called from somewhere beyond sight. "Try not to land on us. There isn't a lot of room down here."

I looped the rope around my waist and tied a clumsy knot. Then I added another loop, just to be sure. I gathered my gear, grasped the rope, and readied myself at the edge of the cliff, my back to the abyss.

"Uh… how do I do this?" I called back to Furat.

"Just jump back. You'll swing back to the rock face, hit with your feet, and push off again. Two pushes should be enough to get you down. Hurry up. That grenade's not going to hold them forever."

It sounded easy enough. I swallowed, jumped out into space, swung back, and slammed into the rock face. The rope slipped through my hands, and I slid down in a bumping rush. I landed in a heap on something hard.

Sam licked my face.

"That wasn't quite as easy as you suggested," I croaked. It hadn't been as bad as my previous escape from pigs in the Sorrows because this time I hadn't ripped myself open on protruding roots and bushes while I tumbled down a cliff. On the other hand, the last time the Darkness had healed me.

"Let's get moving," Furat said. "Maybe they won't figure out how to follow us down here, but I don't want to bet on it."

We weren't close to the bottom of the ridge - we had just landed on a small level area twenty feet below the summit. By the dim light of a crescent moon I could faintly make out the outlines of low bushes and scraggly pines as the ground fell away before us. The angle wasn't nearly as steep as the bare rock face we'd just descended but it was uninviting in the dark.

"We want to chance this slope at night?" I asked. Not that I imagined it would look terribly friendly by day.

"No, but I really don't want those hogs to work their way around and catch us on the ledge while we wait for the sun to come up."

That was so self-evidently true there was really nothing else to say, so we began to pick our way down the slope, scuttling crablike on all fours. The dog, a natural quadruped, did better than we did.

Branches caught at my sleeves. Once I passed through a spiderweb and felt something crawling on my face. I flailed wildly until I was sure it was gone.

"You all right?" Furat asked.

"I hate spiders."

There could be far worse in the trees, of course. There was no way to see a cloud of the Darkness before we walked right into it. We had to trust that Sam would alert us.

It must have been an hour before we reached the bottom of the hill. Unfortunately, I had no doubt the pigs could cover the distance in a fraction of the time if they figured out a way past the outcrop. We paused only for a few moments, then I said, "Keep moving?"

I couldn't even tell whether Furat's big shadow nodded, but seconds later he was walking again, following a contour of the terrain in a direction I guessed was roughly northwest. The ground squelched underfoot, water accumulating in the low crease between the hills. I hoped it would confuse the pigs' scent tracking, but wasn't hugely optimistic.

We stumbled along for hours. The sky was just beginning to shift from black to gray when Sam stopped and growled.

"Damn," Furat muttered softly. "Figures something would have staked out anything like a natural path."

We backed half a dozen paces, then began to climb the slope to our right. We humans had no way of knowing if the threat we hadn't seen was following us. Because Sam was quiet, we assumed it wasn't. Still, the hair on the back of my neck stood up.

"Torches?" I asked.

It was light enough now that I could see him shake his head. "Walking up the face of the hill like this I'm afraid it would mark us for the pigs. Or something else."

That was the fatal dilemma in the Sorrows. Fire - or even the use of the Darkness by an adept like Grigg, Roshel, or Yoshana - might help detect or deter some dangers. But it might attract others. So we kept our torches in our packs and trusted in the dog. She'd steered us right so far.

We crested the hill and paused on the other side, far enough from the crown that we weren't silhouetted against the sky. By that time dawn had truly come. We sat in grass moist with dew and ate pemmican and hard bread, which it seemed were my constant companions on my treks across the continent. I'd come to heartily despise both. Sam seemed happy with them, though.

Furat watched her with a jaundiced eye. "That dog'll eat anything. I've seen her eat dirt and sticks. Wouldn't surprise me if she's related to those pigs."

If the dog was offended, she gave no sign.

For the next few hours we encountered neither pigs nor wraiths, but nothing in the Sorrows was easy. We blundered into a tangle of thorn bushes that snagged our clothing and tore at our skin. I realized how much of my woodcraft had depended on the Darkness. It would have detected the thorns and healed any scratches almost before I noticed them. I had learned useful skills in the past year, but many of them I needed to learn again without the powers of hell at my command.

After we had picked our way clear of the briars, which somehow the dog negotiated unscathed, Furat pointed north. I could make out thin wisps of smoke spreading on the wind.

"That the town we saw last night?"

"I hope so," he said. With no better option at hand, we headed toward it.

The trees ended abruptly in a vast cleared space. In its center rose a palisade of rough timbers, no more than trunks shorn of their branches. It was primitive, but far less disturbing than, say, an interlaced wall of living trees... like the one surrounding the infected village I'd encountered with Yoshana's war party. Just before I'd let her fill me with the Darkness.

There was a closed gate facing us, no more sophisticated than the rest of the construction. A couple of small columns of smoke emerged above the walls. On the far side of the enclosure, nearly a quarter of a mile away, a stream meandered through the clearing. It appeared to pass under the walls, supplying the settlement with water.

"Still looking good," Furat murmured. I tentatively agreed. Smoke meant fire, which probably meant no Darkness. Having a water source within the walls suggested the inhabitants might be nervous about venturing outside, which also suggested they weren't on friendly terms with the wraiths.

And as Yoshana had observed, sometimes there was no better option than walking into the possible trap and hoping for the best - and trusting in your ability to fight your way out of it. Easier when you were one of the world's foremost killers, of course.

We stepped out of the trees and made our way across the open area. It was not perfectly cleared, not the way farmland would have been. Trees had been cut down, but stumps remained. Grass reached to our knees. A lone trunk stood between us and the gate. It was dead, and a long rawhide strap had been secured to it with a heavy iron bolt.

"Should we be worried about that?"

"Oh, probably," Furat replied. But he called out, "Hello the town!"

Silence answered him. After half a minute he repeated himself.

A head appeared atop the palisade. "Ayuh?" it answered.

"We're travelers, seeking shelter and trade."

"Then t'll be walkin' t'gate an' leavin' t'guns at, an' backin' t'gain," the watcher stated bluntly. At least, I think that's what he said. The accent was barbarous and reminded me of Talith, though the man's diction was much less clear than the dead girl's. He was far harder to understand than Cat.

"He wants us to leave our guns at the gate and move away from them?" I whispered.

"I think so."

"You want to do that?"

"Got a better idea?"

The pigs were still out there somewhere, and no doubt worse things. We had only one oil grenade left, and perhaps half our ammunition. I didn't have a better idea. We did as we'd been asked.

The massive gate swung inward. "Swung" perhaps not being quite the right word. One leaf was dragged back, its lower edge following an old, deep gouge in the dirt and kicking up fresh dust. A man emerged dressed in ragged, uncured skins. While a second villager covered him with a primitive bow, the first darted out and seized our guns. He slung my carbine and pointed Furat's pistol at us like he knew how to use it.

"Come t'in then," said the gunman. The bowman slung his weapon and produced a very fine knife, of vastly better quality than anything we'd yet seen in the village.

"Testin'," he said with a grin. Half his teeth were missing.

Furat shrugged and walked forward. "We've come this far."

I didn't like the idea of these men taking a knife to my hand to test for the Darkness. It wasn't just that I didn't trust their intentions - and I didn't - but I didn't trust their hygiene either. Neither of them looked like they bathed much, if ever, and as we got closer the smell confirmed it. They used fire and tools, but they were as filthy as paleos. Without the Darkness in me, I was seriously worried about infection from the knife wound.

But Furat went up to them without hesitation, Sam trotting along beside him. She didn't seem put off by the smell. Reluctantly, I followed.

The villager was quick and efficient with the knife, and it was so sharp it barely hurt. Blood welled from small cuts in our left thumbs. No Darkness appeared to seal the wounds, and the dirty men nodded, satisfied. If they cared that I was Select, they gave no sign.

Up close, the offensive smell took on a new, multilayered character. It was a fetid mix of body odor, bad breath, and a hint of rotting flesh from the hides they wore. But in their ears and noses, each of the villagers wore multiple rings and bangles of exquisite workmanship, looted from the tombs of the ancients. The jewelry would have been worth a fortune in the Source or Rockwall.

Behind them was another gate. The villager with the knife shut and barred the outer door, then the man with Furat's gun yelled "Clear!" The inner barrier was hauled open.

Had I thought the villagers smelled bad? The stench of their home was overpowering. Added to the human odors were the reek of pig waste and rotting fish guts. Garbage and piles of offal lay scattered in heaps. I choked, fighting to keep my gorge down. Even the dog whined and backed away.

"Comin'," said the gunman, and he and his fellow entered the stockade, a place as squalid as any I could imagine. The garbage miners of the Flow wouldn't have lived in it. Furat had to jerk Sam's leash to get her to follow.

"And I've seen her eat a week-dead squirrel," he muttered. Thankfully our hosts didn't hear.

More villagers were visible, tending to their daily tasks. They didn't seem terribly interested in us, which I found a little odd. A third man, dressed like the other two, began to push the inner gate shut. But Furat stopped in its path.

"Thank you for your hospitality. Now that we're all safe inside, shall we make introductions and set the terms of trade? I'm Hafnum Furat, and my companion is Minos."

The villager with Furat's gun turned. He was a big-boned man of middle height, but gaunt. He looked small next to Furat. Maybe that's why he stepped closer to me instead. I wished he hadn't. Even amid the surrounding stench, his breath stood out as uniquely foul.

"T'm Jiddas. Soultree Post'n here. Lucky t'are'n here t'come'n, ayuh."

Furat smiled and nodded like he understood. Maybe he did. "I feared the post had fallen. We met a girl named Talith who said it had."

Jiddas spat in the dirt. "Hoor'd lie sooner'n tell t'truth. What's'n come'n 'er?"

Furat looked him straight in the eye. "I killed her."

The villager nodded, a single bob of his head. "No more'n deservin'. T'woulda turnt 'er out, but she's'n gone 'ersel'. Darkness in 'er, that'n. Loved it, 'er. Lived in't three year gone now."

"Not anymore."

"Inna soon enough."

"Well. I'm glad there's no hard feelings. Let's discuss terms of trade, shall we? We've got salt, cotton, twine…"

Furat had explained to me that trinkets and baubles would be of no value to the natives of the Sorrows - anything we could give them, they could find better in the ruins of the Last Days. The villagers' ornaments proved him right. But perishables, or cloth that would have rotted over the centuries, would be valuable.

My mind, however, was turning over the phrase "t'woulda turnt 'er out" in combination with the lone tree in the clearing.

Jiddas grinned, showing his handful of brown teeth. "Bide a bye. Trades 'n' salts 'n' this'n'thats, times 'n' times comin'. But first t'dog t'll have."

"No," Furat said flatly.

The villager grinned more broadly and waggled Furat's pistol. "Ayuh, t'dog t'll have, or one'n yous. Gods'n restless, needin' feedin'. Bad times t'pick fra visitin'." He shrugged. "Normals, one'n us'all turnt out. Fra satisfy gods, t'see. If'n visitors, one'n yous. Better. But spirit dog? Seein' gods? Best. Keepin' her, yous'n goes. One'n us'all turnt out 'stead. Trade, t'see? Fair. Dog, or one'n yous'n."

"I'm afraid those terms aren't acceptable," Furat said.

Jiddas shrugged again. "Shouldna be comin' bad times. Shouldna be turnin' over t'guns. Fair deal, t'think."

Blood was pounding in my temples, adrenaline flooding my veins. Sam didn't know what was being said, but she sensed Furat's tension. She growled.

Keeping my voice very level, trying not to let it crack, I said, "Because of who I represent, I can't be any less generous than the general of the Darkness Radiant under similar circumstances. Let us go, and no harm will come to you."

The other villagers had closed in as well. All three laughed. Jiddas turned the pistol on me and said, "Harm'n yous t'see -"

There is a technique called iaido. My katana didn't take his hand all the way off as it cleared its sheath, and the backswing caught in his vertebrae and didn't sever his head. With the Darkness in me it would have been different, as it had been with the Select Lalos. Yoshana could have cut him into four parts and sheathed her blade before his head hit the ground.

But dead was dead. Some things I needed to relearn without the Darkness in me. Killing wasn't one of them.

The man with the sharp knife lunged at me as I tried to pull my blade loose from Jiddas' spine. Sam leapt at him and her jaws snapped closed on his wrist. I heard bones crack even over his scream. Then my blade was free. The dog was in the way of the most obvious strokes, so I brought the sword straight down on his head. I'd have to sharpen it when this was over - splitting a skull was terrible for the edge - but that was a problem for later.

Furat had seized his pistol and my carbine from Jiddas' corpse. "Come on!" he shouted.

We raced into the entryway, Sam barking behind us. Furat tossed me my weapon, flung aside the heavy bar on the outer door, and dragged the heavy wooden barrier open. Without looking back we ran for the woods, past the tree where the villagers sometimes sacrificed visitors or each other to the Darkness wraiths they called gods.

We were thirty yards short of reaching cover when an arrow came looping down to land three feet in front of me. I turned, sighted on the face glaring at us above the palisade, and fired. The villager fell, and I ran on.

In the shelter of the trees, Furat panted, "Didn't want to see if you could convert them?"

"Oh, shut up."

We slogged east through the forest, and I turned Furat's sarcastic words over in my head. We weren't particularly afraid of pursuit - the villagers had seemed to fear leaving their compound, and we'd demonstrated we weren't easy prey. So I had as much chance to think as I ever got in the Sorrows.

I had literally killed more men than I could count when the Darkness was in me. In the two berserk furies it had brought, I could recall no precise number for the enemies I had cut down. It was a lot.

But these were the first I had killed since being freed from the Darkness. And I had felt no regret.

Jiddas and the villager with the knife I had struck down in the heat of combat. They could just as easily have killed me. The last one with the bow... He could have hit me. But after he missed, I could likely have reached the woods before he shot again. I had not, perhaps, needed to shoot him.

Had he deserved to die? Yoshana would certainly have said so. He and his kind were robbers and murderers, and he had been trying to kill me. But in Father Roric's formulation of just war, had I taken his life only as a last resort? Or had I been angry and wanted vengeance?

"Furat?" I asked.

"Hmm?"

"Why do those people live there? I mean, they aren't infected. Yeah, they get a few nice things from foraging or looting, like jewels or knives, but they live like savages walled up in a stinking compound. Why don't they just leave?"

He trudged on for a while before answering. "I dunno. History suggests people get used to living in the most godforsaken places you could imagine. Just inertia, I guess. Why do you ask?"

"It would help if I could convince myself they were malevolent fiends instead of people in a bad spot trying to get by."

"Huh. Well in that case, every single person in that village chose to move there because they're depraved, perverted monsters who enjoy human suffering."

"Not even close to true, is it?"

"Nope."

Sam started growling an hour or so later. Before, she had always stopped when she sensed something. This time, she danced nervously, straining at her leash.

"It's behind us," I murmured.

Furat nodded. "So much for them not following us."

I shook my head. "Not the villagers. They didn't bother her. They're not infected. How much you want to bet it's whatever they're afraid of?"

"No bet."

This wasn't good. I muttered, "We can't outrun it in here. Give me your grenade."

"I've only got the one left."

"I know. I'll make it count. You and Sam keep going. Make for that little rise over there, see with that big tree on it? Wait under the tree."

He frowned at me. "What are you doing?"

"Setting a trap. As it happens, I'm pretty good at ambushing things in the woods." I didn't mention that skill had depended heavily on my mastery of the Darkness. He didn't need to know.

I could tell he wasn't fully convinced, but neither did he see a lot of options. He continued toward the low hill, pulling the dog behind him. I went four paces into the undergrowth, climbed a tree, and waited.

Not a minute later I spotted a shape creeping along our trail, low to the ground. It was only when it passed directly below me that I realized it was a man, hunched over. And it was only after the first had passed that I realized there were two more. They were almost totally silent, as stealthy as Cat. They were even harder to spot, because they wore loose clothing mottled to resemble the foliage around us.

Maybe I was feeling bad about the man I'd shot. Maybe Prophetess was rubbing off on me. But instead of firing as the third man passed by, I called, "Hello down there."

The three spun, sinuous and catlike... I might even say Cat-like. Hah. Their eyes widened as they looked up and saw me.

They were cleaner than the villagers or paleos. But their faces were tattooed with strange patterns. My hair stood up as I saw the patterns were moving. But then, there was a reason Sam hadn't liked them.

"I hope you weren't planning on killing and eating us," I continued. "Because then I might have to shoot you all."

"Gray man," the one in the lead said softly. "You are enemies of Soultree Post? You and the big man, and the spirit dog?"

"They weren't very hospitable," I said. It was interesting that the infected native was far easier to understand than the villagers had been.

"We too are their enemies."

Furat had quietly approached from behind when they'd turned to face me. "The enemy of my enemy... is the enemy of my enemy," he said. "Doesn't make you our friends."

Sam growled, deep in her throat.

"We mean you no harm," said the man I was now thinking of as the leader.

"And yet here you are, sneaking after us." Furat's pistol was centered on the native's head. "Want to explain that? It needs to be some persuasive reason why I shouldn't shoot you."

The man straightened from his crouch. So did the other two. I could see that their clothes, while worn and patched, showed signs of careful upkeep. Each had a machete sheathed at the waist.

The leader spread his hands. "My clan is not strong. We take only as much of the Power as we can control. It is not so much. We look for what can help us."

"Like stealing weapons from travelers, for example?"

He shrugged. "Or finding allies. You are strong. More use as friends than prey."

Furat frowned, clearly unconvinced. "Not so strong as all that." I remembered what he had said before, that mercy was for the strong. If he felt threatened, I was sure he would open fire. I wasn't sure he was wrong.

The native looked back up at me. "You have a spirit dog. More, one of you is a gray man. The gray men are strong. It is known."

He took slow, careful steps toward my tree. "I am Midnight Owl. May I approach you, gray man?"

"How about you and your buddies back off and let me climb down from this tree, and then you can approach me. I don't have to tell you what happens if my friend thinks you're up to something." Midnight Owl nodded. If they had only a little of the Darkness in them, it would heal wounds but not save them from the heavy bullets of Furat's pistol or my carbine. I was reasonably confident they didn't control anywhere near as much as I had - if they did, they probably wouldn't have fallen for my ambush in the first place or would have tried to fight their way out.

Still, I was very careful descending the tree. There were only a handful of seconds when I couldn't bring the carbine to bear. They didn't try to take advantage of that vulnerability.

"These are River Mist and Blood Fang," the leader said, gesturing to the other natives. "May I approach you now, gray man?"

"Carefully." I held the carbine at waist height, pointed toward him. It was an awkward position and the recoil would hurt if I fired, but at this range I wouldn't miss.

His footfalls were as soft as Cat's. I had been right before - the patterns on his face shifted subtly, the Darkness visible on his skin. When he was two paces from me, he stretched out his hand. The marks on his face faded. What he extended toward me wasn't thick enough to see, but I knew it was there.

He drew back with a little whistling intake of breath. "It has been in you," he said, and then he bowed. The other two did the same.

"You are very strong, gray man. You have been a shadow warrior. Why no longer?"

"I did bad things when it was in me."

Midnight Owl nodded. "The Power is a fearsome thing. You know. You have held it and cast it out. You are strong. No one I know has done this."

I didn't feel a need to mention I hadn't done it myself, that I had tried and failed, that it had taken Prophetess to cleanse me. I was warming to the man. He understood what I had been, more than anyone else. Well - more than anyone who didn't currently want to kill me.

"Gray man, if you took up the Power again, you could lead our clan. Together we would be strong."

I turned that over in my head. Furat let out an exasperated grunt. "You are not seriously considering this."

"We still need guides. And I could use rangers that are as quiet as paleos and can heal themselves." I addressed Midnight Owl. "I have a mission. I need to find someone at the far side of the Sorrows. Then I have a war to fight. If you help me, when I've won I'll do what I can for your clan."

I was vague even in my own head on that last point. I wasn't going to come back and set myself up as some kind of bandit chieftain in the Sorrows. On the other hand, there was Yoshana to defeat before I even had to think about making good on the promise.

The native leader dipped his head. "We will help you. Blood Fang will go to gather our warriors. River Mist and I will lead you to the person you must find. Who is this person?"

"Have you heard of a demon who calls himself Seven?"

The native's face went so pale the Darkness tattooed on his skin stood out like ink on paper.

"This is not wise." That was the phrase of the day. Midnight Owl wasn't happy to seek out a Hellguard he knew only from terrifying legend. Furat wasn't happy to be guided by Darkness-infested natives. Each had pulled me aside and quietly explained their misgivings. We were going forward anyway.

Sam wasn't happy either. The normally friendly dog didn't like Midnight Owl or River Mist. She wouldn't go near them, and if they moved in her direction, her lips would pull back into a snarl that showed a lot of big teeth. We kept her and the natives separated. They seemed to respect the dog, but if the situation escalated, the Darkness could easily push them into doing something we would all regret.

They were excellent guides, though. They took the lead, and throughout the day seemed to know just where to go to avoid the Darkness and other terrors of the Sorrows. That night we camped near a stream, made a small fire, and shared most of the remaining rations Furat and I carried. We would need to find either food or Seven very quickly, or we'd start getting hungry. I didn't think we'd enjoy being with Owl and Mist if they got hungry.

They hadn't spoken at all during our march, communicating by hand signals. It was only when Mist finally addressed us that I realized from her voice that she was a woman. The loose clothes obscured her figure, and she and Midnight Owl both had long hair and hard, sharp-featured faces. I didn't assume her sex made her any less dangerous; Cat was one of the deadliest people I knew. Yoshana might be the deadliest of all.

We set watches. I didn't see evidence that the natives could extend wards as I'd learned to. They probably didn't have either enough Darkness at their command or the willpower to control it at range. So two of us stayed awake in shifts. I shared the watch with Owl. Not that Furat and I didn't fully trust our guides, but… we didn't fully trust our guides.

The hours crawled by uneventfully. I nudged Furat awake and Owl woke Mist. I wrapped myself in my cloak and, despite whatever misgivings I might have had, fell instantly asleep.

I sat up. The sky above was still pitch black and I couldn't say what had awakened me. Furat and Mist were slumped at their posts, dozing. I was about to poke Furat when something moved in the deeper darkness between the trees. As quietly as I could, I put my hand to my carbine.

"No need for that," came a soft voice. A figure stepped into the feeble glow of the dying fire. My breath caught as I recognized Roshel. She was wearing a sort of loose tunic, belted but slit up the sides. In the half light of the flames, her skin was as dark as her hair. Only her eyes shone brightly, reflecting red.

"Or maybe I should be more honest and say no use for that," she said. "Yoshana's not pleased with what you're up to."

"What does she plan to do about it?"

"This."

Thick, black tentacles burst from the openings in her clothes. Gaping mouths ringed with fangs drooled ooze at the end of some, clusters of barbed stingers emerged from others. Long tendrils writhed from her mouth and eyes. They all reached toward me, extending to impossible lengths as they clawed toward my face.

I jerked awake, bathed in cold sweat. River Mist turned and looked at me. "The Power calls you. It wants you back."

Sam opened one eye and growled softly.

Had the dream really been the Darkness touching me in my sleep? I'd experienced horrific dreams of Roshel while it had been in me. And Mist had sensed something - although maybe she was just guessing from my reaction as I'd jolted upright.

"Go to sleep," she said. "I will guard you."

Furat was staring at us curiously.

I shook my head. "I'll take care of it." I lay down again and closed my eyes. On impulse, I reached into my shirt and grasped the Saint Benedict medal Father Roric had given me, rubbing my thumb over the impressions in the disk. It helped a bit as I steadied my breathing and thoughts, beginning the meditation I'd used when I'd controlled the Darkness. If I could hold in check as much of it as had been in me, I would be able to shield myself from whatever little wisps of it were floating around loose in our camp.

At least I hoped so.

We survived the night, although the bugs that infested the Sorrows reminded me of my favorite use of the Darkness. Things had crawled on me and buzzed in my ears while I tried to sleep. I was pretty sure some were inside my clothes. Could just enough of the powers of hell to get rid of the fleas and ticks and mosquitoes really be so bad?

Insects aside, the next day proved amazingly uneventful. Once Owl and Mist stopped, listening to something off to our left that only they could hear. As they crouched silently, Sam interrupted with a loud bark. A chorus of howls came back. I was surprised to hear Sam howl in return.

"I told you she was a wolf," I told Furat.

"Dogs howl," he snapped. But he looked at the shaggy white canine just a little bit suspiciously.

The natives straightened up and continued. "Just wolves. Not dangerous to so many of us," Midnight Owl explained.

"What if they're infected?"

Owl shook his head. "The Power does not take wolves."

"It infects bears and pigs. Why not wolves?"

"The Power does not take wolves."

I hoped he was right. Whether he was or not, the wolves settled for howling twice more, then skulked away. I think Sam was disappointed.

It was near the end of the day when we saw a thin trail of smoke rising above the trees.

"This is it!" I exclaimed.

"Quietly, then," Owl scolded me. "We must go carefully."

I laughed. "No point."

And with that I pushed past Owl and Mist, trampling through the underbrush as if I were in a park at Our Lady. The natives followed me, nervously darting glances from side to side.

We had found the little dale where Seven made his home. There was still the fire pit with smoke rising from it, the thatched hut, the stone statue. The only thing I didn't see was the Hellguard himself.

"It is not here," Owl said quietly. "We can still escape."

"Just because you don't see him doesn't mean he's not here."

"We would sense a creature of that sort."

"No you wouldn't." The booming voice came from behind us. Sam let out a startled yelp from a dozen yards away. Owl and Mist spun, eyes wide with panic. The look of terror on Furat's face was priceless.

Furat was a big man, as massive as Grigg, Yoshana's hulking Select lieutenant. He looked puny next to the Hellguard. Seven stood at least six and a half feet tall, massively muscled, inhumanly broad shouldered. His close-cropped hair was as dark as his eyes, his skin a red so deep as to be almost black. He still carried the massive steel spear he'd used when I'd first met him, a seven-foot metal shaft an inch thick. It must have weighed thirty pounds, but it dangled in his massive fist like a twig.

"I said you were welcome to come back, Minos. I didn't say I was setting up a hotel. What's with the crowd?"

It only then occurred to me that a demon who'd lived in solitude for three hundred years might not take kindly to four uninvited guests and their dog. I swallowed hard and looked him in the eyes.

"I need your help."

Seven, Furat, and I sat on the fallen log by his fire. Owl and Mist squatted on the far side of the ring of stones, visibly terrified. I was between Seven and Furat, who was putting on a pretty brave face, all things considered. The Hellguard scratched Sam behind the ears. The dog seemed completely at ease with him, rubbing against his leg and wagging her tail enthusiastically.

"I've heard of these spirit dogs but never seen one," the demon said. "Looks like some kind of giant Samoyed."

"They breed them to detect the Darkness," Furat volunteered. "Cats are even better at it. But the first time a cat senses a wraith it takes off and you never see it again."

"How come she likes you so much?" I asked, then pointed to the natives. "She hates these two."

"I'm not using enough of it for her to sense. Usually I keep a shield right on my skin to deflect probes, but I pulled that in so I could pet her. 'Cause you're a pretty girl, aren't you?" He thumped the dog's shoulder. She put her head on his knee.

"Speaking of deflecting, Minos, either you got better at shielding than me over the last year, or it ain't in you anymore."

I stared at the ground, embarrassed. "Yeah, well, that's why I'm here. I couldn't control it, Seven. It was turning me into something I didn't like. Prophetess cast it out of me."

The Hellguard let out a low whistle. "That's pretty slick. I'd heard the Universal Church claimed it could exorcise the prant, but I didn't think it would work with as much as you had in you."

"Tess is pretty special. But now we have to face the Darkness Radiant, and I may possibly have challenged Yoshana to single combat without even having the Darkness in me anymore."

Seven stopped scratching behind Sam's ears. She butted him with her head, but he ignored her, staring at me instead. "And so that's why you thought it would be a good idea to haul your sorry ass across the Sorrows with a couple of possessed, some random dude, and your dog, and beg me for help. That about the size of it?"

I nodded and forced myself to meet his eyes. "Yep."

"I'll say this, kid. You are, without doubt, the craziest son of a bitch I've met in three hundred years."

6. On the Front

I'd forgotten the noise and stink of an army in the field. Back among the low, rolling hills of the Source, we saw my forces before we heard them or smelled them. But not by much. Oxen lowed, donkeys brayed, thousands of swords and pots and God knew what else clanged and rattled and thumped. Four thousand men shouted and laughed and cursed. And voided their bowels in shallow, hastily dug latrines. And didn't bathe. In a way completely different from the Sorrows, it was almost as overwhelming.

The complaints started the moment I arrived. To his credit, Railes had the unflappable Sergeant Herin square away my companions before he unloaded on me. But he started up as soon as they were out of earshot.

"Boss, the only reason you've still got a job is because no one else wants to be responsible for the cluster they see coming. The mayor's been spouting off ever since you left about how irresponsible it was for you to take off and leave your command. And our guys have been pretty good, but the Monolith folks keep whining about working with the Darkness. The hellfire and damnation stuff is getting old, and I can't get 'em to shut up, and Hake wasn't really trying, and Lago sure as hell isn't."

"'Our guys' have been pretty good?" I asked waspishly. "Isn't it supposed to be one army? Nice that even my own adjutant is playing 'us and them.'"

Railes spat in the grass, completely unabashed. "If we call a dog's tail a leg, how many legs does it have? Four, 'cause calling a tail a leg don't make it one. Pretending it's one army don't make it one, boss. Speaking of dogs, that was a good looking one you brought in. Or was it one of those wolves from up by the ice sheets?"

"Her owner keeps saying she's a dog. Looks more like a wolf to me. She's friendly, though, and she can sense the Darkness, which might very well come in handy." I noticed Railes had changed the subject. "Are you done griping at me, or is there more?"

"Oh, there's more. General Hake didn't like that his troops got left on garrison duty at Our Lady and Lago's guys are here at the front. The Shadowed Hand doesn't like that they're reporting to Lago 'cause they're the only Rockwall troops up here and Lago's in charge. Nobody likes the food. We've been set up here for two weeks and the guys are bored. Or nervous. Or nervous and bored. Nobody knew when you were showing up, or if you were showing up, and now that you've showed up, no one knows what's going to happen next. You want me to go on?"

I sighed. "Not really. I've got to go talk to Prophetess and get the other earful."

"You think this is going to work, boss?"

"Sure. I mean, it better."

I was hoping for one of Prophetess' spectacular hugs before she started on me. I didn't get it. "Minos, you've been gone too long. Everyone's in a panic."

Before I could either ask how long she had thought it was going to take or point out that I was back now, she was launching her second thrust. "I wasn't happy about one person infected with the Darkness. You brought dozens. What were you thinking?"

Twenty warriors from Midnight Owl's clan had joined us. It wasn't exactly dozens, but it was definitely more than one. "Um... the more the merrier?"

She didn't see the humor. "Also, your adjutant and Cat have gotten friendly while they've been guarding me."

"That's a good thing, isn't it?"

"Too friendly, Minos."

Light dawned. "Well, I guess she might stab him to death if they have a spat, but he's a big boy. He can take care of himself."

She actually stamped her foot in exasperation. "Minos, she can't be more than fifteen! He's at least ten years older than she is."

"Yeah, and I'm pretty sure she's past whatever the paleo age of consent is. She's killed more people than almost any veteran in this army. She can take care of herself too."

"Minos..."

"What do you want me to do, Tess? Tell Railes to leave her alone? Talk to him about the birds and the bees? Have you talked to Cat about that, by the way? Because I'm not having that conversation with her."

"Minos... never mind. I'm nervous. I don't think this is the right thing to do. I don't think BlackShield Lago does either. I know Mayor Arnage doesn't. There's been a lot of talk in the town and now in the camp."

"A little late now." I tried to keep my tone light, but I don't think I succeeded. The time to stop me, to come up with some better idea, would have been before I went into the Sorrows. Second-guessing at this point wasn't going to help.

Prophetess let out a long sigh and slumped, as if all the air were going out of her. "I know.... that... what you've brought...."

I was shocked to see tears welling up in her eyes. She continued in a small voice, frightened and angry. "Everybody's been looking at me while you've been gone, like I'm supposed to know how to run an army. Like I'm supposed to know how to comfort all these people. I don't know if we're doing the right thing, or if we're all going to die, or for that matter if we're all going to hell. Do you think this is going to work?"

I forced a smile.

"Sure. I mean, it better."

It had only taken a little over a month to make the trip to the Sorrows and back. I had more than three weeks before the duel. Plenty of time to prepare. And plenty of time for everyone to sit around getting even more nervous.

The Monolith troops had drawn up in an arc to the northwest of the hill Tolf had chosen. It had only one tree on its crown rather than several as I'd asked, but that one was big. It would do.

My next meeting was with BlackShield Jarl Lago. I'd left him in command of the Monolith forces, and put those forces in the field, for a reason. The Rockwall and Monolith brigades wouldn't work together effectively, so it was better to split them up. Except for my Shadowed Hand special forces, the Monolith troops were the better soldiers. Even if my old buddies from General Hake's Rockwall brigade felt like second-class citizens left behind to garrison Our Lady. They might thank me for it later.

"Judge Minos." Jarl Lago was old, tough, thick-bodied, and bearded. He had a deep, gruff voice and the calluses of an officer who still took part in close-combat drills. I wouldn't want to fight him hand to hand.

"BlackShield. The men seem to be in good order." Monolith discipline was famous. Man for man, his troops were better than Stephensburg's regulars as well as Rockwall's. Or they had been, until Stephen's men had fallen under the command and training regimen of the Darkness Radiant.

"Thank you. They are."

"You need to shift the anchor points of the formation, though. They can't be up against the forest."

Lago frowned. "Doctrine demands cover from flanking cavalry."

"Doctrine wasn't considering an enemy armed with the Darkness."

"Judge Minos, with all due respect, I have my rangers positioned in the woods. They will not be taken by surprise."

"BlackShield Lago, with all due respect, I personally routed a company of your rangers in the woods. By myself, before the Shadowed Hand was even trained. I don't know how many of Yoshana's army command the Darkness, but I know at least three of them are a lot stronger than I was. Move your men away from the trees, and set torches. Lots of torches. Set up barricades to protect against cavalry. I suggest cutting wood may be an excellent way to keep the troops busy."

Lago saluted. "It will be so."

"Also, I brought back some... irregular troops from the Sorrows."

The Paladin's eyes narrowed, virtually disappearing into a maze of wrinkles. "I have begun to hear rumors. Wild men touched by the Darkness. My soldiers will not like it."

"No, I don't expect they will. I'm putting the Shadowed Hand directly under my personal command and attaching the irregular troops to it."

"That is wise." If he was offended that I'd pulled my old unit out from under him, he gave no sign.

"And I need that hilltop under constant observation. Patrolled day and night. With torches. Yoshana's going to assume she can win a trial by combat, but she might try to cheat anyway. We need to make sure she doesn't sneak in and set any traps up there."

He repeated, "It will be so." The old soldier puffed out air, pursed his lips, and stared into my eyes. "This plan of yours, Judge Minos. It is clever, but I fear it may be too clever by half. You have said yourself that Yoshana is ruthless and cunning. Do you think this will work?"

"Sure. I mean, it better."

Doctor John Dee was, as always, an overflowing fountain of words.

"It's amazing, Minos. I'd heard of spirit dogs but I'd never seen one. And then those warriors of the Hidden Moon Clan, a whole tribe infected with the Darkness but retaining enough control to assert their human nature. Not to mention -"

"Dee. Rhapsodize later. Plan now. I need you to bring me up to date. What did Yoshana say?"

His face clouded. "Ah. Well. Evidently Roshel reached her with your proposal before I did."

"Yes, I assumed she would. Did you think you'd get there faster than an Overlord?"

"Yoshana asked whether you had sent me as a sacrifice, since you'd already sent a messenger."

"She was just kidding, Dee." That was a safe conclusion, since he was still alive.

"She was smiling when she said it. That did not give me a great deal of confidence that she was just kidding. She is a terrifying creature, Minos."

I didn't need to be reminded. I'd spent months in her company. The occasional nightmares about her had lasted far longer.

"She... er... she then went on at some length about what she was going to do to you. She was smiling when she said that as well, but I'm afraid I don't believe it was said in jest."

It wouldn't have been. I'd watched Yoshana pull out a man's trachea without changing expression, and reduce a native of the Sorrows to a shapeless mass of bones and fluids. And neither of them had annoyed her nearly as much as I had.

"I don't suppose any of it bears repeating?"

Dee looked like he might cry. "I'd rather not."

"Probably better." That bit of morbid curiosity would get satisfied the hard way if things didn't work out. I patted him on the shoulder. "She said she'd come, though?"

"Oh, yes. She seemed very enthusiastic."

For some reason it was those last words that really made my stomach sink.

"Minos... you've come very far and grown a great deal since we first met. But... do you really think this will work?"

"Sure. I mean, it better."

Sam and Furat quickly became favorites in the camp. The dog and her owner were both friendly and outgoing. I couldn't quite figure out what do with them, so I attached them to Tess' bodyguard. A big dog that could detect the Darkness would be helpful for protecting someone Roshel had already tried to kill once. And Furat was very quick with his huge pistol.

I'd been worried about how Cat would react to the giant animal, but after some cautious sniffing from both sides, they'd become fast friends.

I was surprised Furat had decided to join us and told him so, not for the first time.

"The food's got to be better back at your place." We were living on some kind of oatmeal gruel and thin beer. The days when Almet's Brewery was supplying the officers on the march with fine cider were long gone. I would have settled for some of the mule stew we'd gotten back in my Rockwall army days. I was going to have words with the quartermaster if I survived what was coming.

"Yep. So's the company." He grinned to take the sting out of the bantering insult. "But I figured if I was going to do the hard part of getting you through the Sorrows, I should stay around to watch the epic battle."

"I'm not going to tell you the same lie Yoshana told me. Getting through the Sorrows wasn't the hardest part."

He chuckled. "It was for me. I'm not fighting in the big duel."

"If everything goes according to plan. Which it very well may not. I've got four thousand soldiers here for a reason. This is not necessarily going to be a safe patch of land to be standing on."

"I thought you'd been telling everyone this plan of yours is going to work."

"Yeah. Like I keep saying, it better. Otherwise I'm dead and we're fighting an army that's almost certainly bigger than ours and almost certainly better armed and trained. The fact that we're screwed if the plan doesn't work doesn't actually mean it's going to."

Furat cracked a big grin. "So basically you've been feeding everyone a line of crap."

"I'm pretty sure that's what leaders do in a situation like this. Keeping up morale and all that."

Sam chose that moment to let out a piercing yip.

"Is that an editorial comment, dog?"

Her owner said, "She's probably hungry, as usual. Sometimes a bark is just a bark."

Tess didn't object to being guarded by Furat and his big, white hound. Somewhat to my surprise, she didn't even put up a fight over the Hidden Moon Clan. They had joined the Shadowed Hand in all its missions, including what I'd taken to calling the Prophetess Protection Program. They were strange and dangerous, even by the standards of my former command, but they fit in surprisingly well.

"They're not bad people," Prophetess said, "but we need to get the Darkness out of them."

"How about we at least wait until after this battle before we give up one of the few advantages we've got?"

"I'm not happy about your approach, Minos. How exactly are we different from Yoshana if we're using the Darkness too?"

"Tess, the Darkness was in Owl and his people long before I met them. It's not like we're infecting anyone else. And after this is over, you'll have an opportunity to help them give it up if they choose, an opportunity they wouldn't have had if they hadn't joined us. You're going to be doing good here."

She scowled at me. "'I will give you all these things if you will just bow down and worship me.' Satan was persuasive too."

I laughed. "Well, that's a promotion. I've gone from a mere symptom of the Fall to the devil himself."

"Not funny, Minos."

"Sorry. The waiting is always the worst for me. Aren't you nervous at all?" The woman radiated a calm I found unfathomable.

"Of course I am," she admitted. "But there's nothing I can do about it, is there? So why get myself worked up?"

Why indeed? There was something I could do, though, so I left her and went to check troop deployments and rehearse our plan for the tenth time.

As it turned out, we didn't have to wait nearly as long as I'd thought.

"They say the waiting's the worst part, but I don't think that's right," Furat said. I was coming to much the same conclusion. The experience of the Darkness Radiant was every bit as terrifying as the anticipation.

Rank on rank of spearmen and gunmen marched through the valley below us, a quarter mile away from the ridge line where we crouched under the cover of pine trees. They were flanked by cavalry, all ordered and resplendent in white tabards blazoned with Yoshana's strange double-headed halberd. Trumpets and drums sounded a martial tune that hammered the air around us even at that distance.

It wasn't that the enemy was a terrifying, barbaric horde. They were disciplined, clean, and - from my experience of them in Stephensburg - unusually polite. The problem was that disciplined troops trying to kill you under the command of a brilliant, murderous Overlord were far more dangerous than a wild, ravening mob.

"How ironic. That's another one of my favorite Canticles of Holy Mary they're playing," Dee remarked.

Before the Cleansing he had said I reminded him of one of the Canticles, specifically one where a knight tried to sell his wife to the devil. "How many of those things are there?" I asked.

"Oh, four hundred or so. Written or compiled by King Alphonse the Tenth of Spain, also known as Alphonse the Wise. I always wondered whether he had any time to govern between composing canticles. Perhaps he didn't and that's why he's remembered so fondly."

"And why would Yoshana use one of those as her marching song? She may be the world's greatest living general, but the Virgin Mary she's definitely not." It was hardly the most pressing question at hand, but a big part of me wanted a distraction from the very large array of troops passing by.

"This particular one promises salvation from sin and physical suffering for those who follow Mary. 'As for their sins men may be crippled, so through the Virgin they may return to health.' You can see the appeal of salvation through service to a divine power... and Yoshana does call herself a prophet."

It didn't take a lot of introspection to see his point. According to the Universal Church, Prophetess' exorcism and baptism had given me a chance at redemption after all I'd done. The veterans of the Darkness Radiant would have their own sins on their consciences. The appeal of following Yoshana on a path to heaven was obvious.

"Man, there's a lot of them," Furat muttered. He, Dee, and I had come to survey the enemy column when our scouts had reported it. Everyone else was busy checking weapons and defensive positions. Nothing like the approach of the armies of darkness to get you focused on your readiness state.

"Must be ten thousand of them," the big man continued.

I shook my head. "More like eight."

He glared at me. "You're an expert at counting enemy troops now, are you?"

"I've got more experience of it than I'd like. They still outnumber us two to one, and I'm seeing a lot of rifles. They're better equipped than us. Maybe better trained too, with a year serving under Yoshana."

"So if she decides to just turn this into a stand-up fight…"

"It's not going to go well for us."

Furat frowned. "You keep talking about how devious she is, and God knows that's her reputation. What are the chances she just accepted your challenge to pull your army out where she could rip it up?"

I met his eyes. "Definitely not zero. The thought had occurred to me. Way back when I came up with the idea. It's also possible even if she loses the duel, her men will attack anyway. That's why we've still got three thousand troops defending Our Lady, and the Shadowed Hand has orders to grab Prophetess and hightail it back there if things go south. This is not a sure thing. It's just the best chance I saw."

Furat shivered theatrically. "I feel like a goose just walked over my grave."

"No, more like an Overlord and her eight thousand soldiers."

Woof! Woof woof woof! Sam's whole chest shook as she barked her challenge at the passing army. The sound echoed in the valley.

"Dammit, dog," I growled. Although surely Yoshana's legions would have been barked at by plenty of farm dogs on their way here. I doubted they would pay much attention. I still crouched even lower behind the cover of the pine branches. "Furat, does that mean she senses something?"

He shrugged. "I don't think so. She's probably just excited to see so many people. That far away she couldn't sense anything anyway."

"Yeah, but some of them can make themselves almost invisible, and they might be scouting. Maybe somewhere a lot closer to us than the troops we can see."

Dee chimed in, "Perhaps this would be a good time to rejoin our forces, Minos. They'll be in need of your leadership."

The cowardly occultist wasn't wrong. We backed down off the ridge and headed back to camp, followed by the trumpets and drums of the Darkness Radiant and an uneasy prickling at the back of our necks that I hoped was just nerves.

Yoshana deployed her troops in a mirror image of ours, in a semicircle southeast of the hill. The formation was conventional, two wings and a center. Our scouts with telescopes reported the wings were commanded by Grigg and Roshel, the center by Yoshana herself. Those would be the Knights of Resurrection, her most loyal personal cadre, those who most fervently believed she was a messiah raised from the dead to deliver them.

Despite her numerical advantage, she made no attempt to flank us. If things went badly, I assumed the Knights of Resurrection would storm the hill and fall on our center, trying to get to Prophetess. I kept the Shadowed Hand around her, resisting the urge to put them in the woods to watch for infiltrators. Yoshana was devious, but she could also be very direct. I assumed with her advantages she'd opt for "hey diddle diddle, straight up the middle." Of course, there was the old saying that "assume" makes an "ass" out of "u" and "me." Especially if your enemy was a better general than you.

The Darkness Radiant made camp leisurely, in good order. Precise and efficient, but unhurried. If they thought we might make a desperate rush as they settled in, they gave no sign. The long afternoon turned to twilight, and there was no indication they intended to do anything more than set basic defensive positions, pitch their tents, and have their dinner.

I made the rounds of my troops, trying to reassure them. The fact that Yoshana had brought twice our numbers wouldn't be a coincidence. She'd have scouted our army while we were en route and made sure she had an overwhelming advantage, not least to intimidate us. Oddly, most of the concern I heard wasn't because of the size of the enemy force, but because they were two weeks early. It had taken the men off guard, even though we'd arrived long before.

"We should send them a thank you note," I joked. "Unless you wanted to keep eating that oatmeal for another two weeks."

Most of the men gave me a polite laugh. A few seemed to be thinking that at least two more weeks of eating nasty oatmeal was two more weeks of being alive. To them I said, "Prophetess has beaten the Darkness before. She'll beat it again."

I didn't mention the fact that I planned to use the Darkness to do it.

I went to Tess' tent as the sun was setting. It was surrounded by torches, my special forces with the black imprint of the Shadowed Hand on their sleeves, and Hidden Moon warriors in their loose-fitting camouflage. When I pulled the flap open, I was greeted by Cat pointing a knife at my face. I was pleased. Security was tight.

"I brought dinner," I announced.

Tess was sitting on her cot, eyes closed in prayer. A few moments later she opened them, smiled, and said, "What is it?"

"Oatmeal for Cat." The paleo made a face. "Oatmeal for me. And... oatmeal for you."

"Not much of a last meal."

"No, but room service from the army's commanding general has to count for something."

She smiled. "I've missed how we used to spend time together."

So had I, although that had mostly been on our long trek up to Our Lady, and it had largely been spent arguing, freezing, or running away from things.

"Mm. Me too. So, considering it might be our last chance, I thought I'd spend the night."

Her eyebrows went up and she blushed. "That seems wildly inappropriate."

"We've got Cat to chaperone and the Shadowed Hand outside. I thought it would be nice to sit and talk like in the old days." We'd traveled together alone before Dee and then others had joined us. Some nights we'd huddled together for warmth. It seemed strange, after what we'd been through together, to need supervision now. Maybe we'd waited too long and the moment had passed. Maybe I'd lost any chance of being more than friends and colleagues that night at Our Lady when I hadn't quite understood her suggestion in time.

"I'd like that," she said.

Or maybe not.

We sat and talked and ate bad oatmeal and reminisced about days when nobody, including me, believed she was a prophet and nobody, including her, thought I was any kind of warrior. We'd spent a lot of our first months together cold, hungry, and terrified, but it had been a simpler time.

We both sat on her cot. Cat was cross-legged on the ground, as relaxed and boneless as her namesake - and just as ready to launch herself in hissing fury if provoked. In my darkest hours, the paleo had kept me human. Now she kept Prophetess alive. In a strange way, the skinny, wild girl who had been my apprentice and was now Tess' bodyguard had become closer to me than family.

We talked for hours. Cat fell asleep. Tess was worried about her brother, Kafer, and what might happen to him if we failed here and Yoshana moved against Our Lady. She was even more concerned about Lito, the youngest of the three siblings. She assumed he was still back on their farm but feared he might have joined the army like Kafer. She didn't know if he was alive or dead. That stirred up bad memories. My parents had sent me away years before as the Hellguard legions neared our home, after they'd turned on Yoshana. The battle had turned into an ugly, multi-sided melee between the Hellguard, Yoshana's loyalists, Green Heart regulars, and a motley array of partisans. I didn't know if my parents had fought there. If they had, I didn't know if they'd survived. Yoshana herself had been struck down in the chaos, impaled with a spear. She had risen stronger. Others wouldn't have been so lucky.

It must have been near midnight. Cat was snoring.

I stood up and stretched. "You're right about it looking funny," I said regretfully. "We've got too many responsibilities to have people wondering why I'm leaving your tent in the morning. I'll go now."

She stood too. "Thank you for coming, Minos. Whatever happens tomorrow… I'm glad you chose this side."

"Whatever happens… so am I."

I hadn't even made it back to my tent before the Darkness Radiant started up with their drums and trumpets. They kept it up all night. Yoshana wanted us to know that as far as she was concerned, I had chosen the wrong side. And she wanted us to spend the night worrying about the consequences.

"Man, that's getting annoying," I groused to Railes as we sipped bad coffee outside my tent at first light.

"Just now getting annoying? You're more patient than I am, boss," my adjutant replied. The drummers and trumpeters must have been working in shifts. They were still at it. The Canticle of Holy Mary was catchy the first time you heard it. And the second. By the hundredth repetition it wore a little thin.

At one point in the night a single female voice had joined the music, high and clear and beautiful. It must have been either Roshel or Yoshana. I had no doubt one of the Overlords was using the Darkness to make herself heard. I couldn't understand the language of the song. Dee had said the words promised salvation, but to me they portended doom.

I pasted on a weak smile. "I just try to look on the bright side. It's got to be even louder in their own camp."

"Bet they slept through it better than our guys, though."

He was surely right. It wasn't intended as psychological warfare against their own. "You sleep okay?"

"Oh, sure. I can sleep through anything. You?"

"Same." And it was true. I might have fallen asleep in dread of what today would bring, but I still slept. Our experience in Rockwall's army had seen to that, at least. "This whole brigade was at the Battle of the Cleansing. They know how to rest when God only knows what crap is going to land on them later."

Which for the Monolith troops assembled here had meant nighttime attacks from me and the Shadowed Hand. Yoshana was a far greater terror than I'd ever been, but veterans of the campaign against me would not be easily intimidated. With that said, I hadn't slept quite as well as I might have without the trumpets and drums, or the knowledge of the upcoming confrontation. Thus the bad coffee in the morning.

When the music stopped, the silence was shocking.

"Suppose that's a good sign?" Railes asked.

"Suppose that's a flying pig?" I pointed up the hill at the sentry galloping down toward us, practically stumbling over his own feet.

The man skidded to a halt and snapped off a rough approximation of a salute. "Sir! Someone approaching under a white flag from the enemy camp. Looks like a Select, sir."

My adjutant and I exchanged glances. His raised eyebrow distorted the skull tattooed on his face. "That going to be Grigg, boss? The one you say is such a badass?"

I got to my feet. "Yep."

"You sure it's a good idea to go meet him yourself?"

"Best I've come up with." Which wasn't to say it was great. I'd anticipated Yoshana might send her Select lieutenant. I had toyed with the idea of sending BlackShield Jarl Lago to meet him, just to see how much that might disconcert the man who'd switched his allegiance from the Monolith to the Darkness Radiant. But in the end, going myself seemed like the least risky option.

Anyway, I was moving, and I'd look like an idiot if I stopped now. That combination of mindless inertia and fear of embarrassment seemed to explain a lot of human behavior. Or at least a lot of mine.

We had a whole platoon of thirty men guarding the top of the hill. I hiked up at the fastest march that would leave me some breath when I reached the summit, but Grigg was still there before me. My troops hadn't tried to stop him, which was definitely for the best. Not just because he was carrying a flag of truce - mostly because he could have killed them all if they'd put up a fight.

I walked around the single, large tree and went to meet him. "Grigg."

"Minos. It's been a while." He looked no different. Big, relaxed, supremely confident. A solid block of a man, as tall and broad as Furat and tougher, faster, stronger. The archetype of my race. Unfortunately sworn to the service of hell. He was radiating his usual "trust me" aura that almost made me forget who and what he represented.

"Yep. I already told Roshel, but I'll tell you too. I really do feel bad about ditching you guys in the Darklands. But killing Prophetess for you wasn't in the cards."

He shrugged. "I never wanted it to come to that."

"But it probably would have, if Yoshana had gotten her way."

"I guess it probably would."

We looked each other in the face for a moment, black eyes unblinking. He glanced away first. "Well, I don't suppose there's much point dragging this out, is there? She'll meet you here at noon, if that's all right by you."

"That works. Unless she wants to rest up first? It's been a long walk for you guys."

"You really think she's tired? No sense everyone sitting around here getting bored."

There wasn't really anything more to say, so I nodded. As he turned to go, I added, "By the way, my guys have a request. If your band is going to start up again, could they learn a different song? We're getting kind of sick of the one you played all night."

He looked back at me over his shoulder. His face was sad. "She's going to kill you, Minos. You chose wrong."

"Not from where I'm standing."

Prophetess and I got into an argument. The plan was for her to stay back in the camp. She insisted on accompanying me up the hill.

"I'm not letting you go up there by yourself. And don't even think of ordering your men to stop me. They won't obey that order, and if they do, Cat will hurt them."

The paleo grinned.

"The point of protecting you is not for you to go charging into the most dangerous spot on the battlefield," I grumbled. But I did it under my breath. I knew I'd lost. She pretended she didn't hear me.

We got to the top a little before noon. We held hands on the climb up. As her champion, it was appropriate for me to help her. Right. I probably got more support from the contact than she did. Although her face looked as pale and drawn as I'd ever seen it.

The trumpets and drums started up again a few minutes later. They hadn't changed their tune. Maybe they didn't know any others.

"They are moving," a sentry reported from the edge. "Thirty of them. The one in front... I think it is her."

I could hear the tension in his voice. It was no accident he didn't name Yoshana. At this distance, it was just her reputation causing the rising fear in our ranks. When she got closer, her aura of terror would precede her. The Monolith veterans were tough. They wouldn't run. But there was no need to make things harder than they needed to be.

"Pull back," I ordered. "Half circle, anchor on the tree." We'd rehearsed this, but it didn't hurt to remind them. I gave Prophetess a sharp look, and she retreated into the semicircle of our troops.

The Overlord and her men crested the hill. She led from the front, as she generally did. If I'd been inclined toward treachery, we could have riddled her with bullets. Which might or might not have killed her. And even if it had, we would have faced eight thousand soldiers hungry for vengeance, led by Grigg and Roshel.

She had new armor. It was tight red leather, the color of old blood, not so very different from the mahogany shade of her skin. A white cloak flowed around her, matching her hair, moving in ways that were not shaped by natural air currents. A heavy gold brooch in the shape of her double-crescent symbol closed it at her throat. Her blue eyes sparkled in the sunlight, hard and brilliant as sapphires.

She was stunning, beautiful, terrible. Relentless as a storm, regal as a queen. Her men spread to cover the half circle mine had abandoned. She strode to the middle of it, face to face with me. The tree was several paces behind my back. Knowing that there was a solid object there helped keep me from retreating.

She cocked her head and stared at me for a moment.

"From all that I hear, you were a force to be reckoned with in the west. Not that you could have faced me, but a force. Now, though… it's true. Grigg was right. The Darkness isn't in you. How did you think you could possibly fight me and live?" She sounded genuinely curious.

I forced a smile. "As it turns out, there are ways to conceal the Darkness, and conceal yourself from it."

She frowned, and I continued. "But just to be clear, I won't be fighting you."

Seven stepped from behind the tree and grinned. "Hello."

7. Trial

I'd seen the Overlord perturbed before but never dumbfounded.

"Where did you get a demon?"

In fact, it had been surprisingly easy to convince the Hellguard to leave his self-imposed exile. Apparently, three centuries of living alone in Darkness-haunted woods wasn't an idyllic existence. After only the briefest and almost perfunctory objections, he'd signed on to my attempt to make the world a better place. In other words, one without Yoshana in it. After all, he had been created to be a killer.

I'd gone over my next words carefully as I'd prepared for the duel. There were several audiences I was addressing.

"Scripture tells us that men can command demons. Tradition says King Solomon controlled them. Jesus and his disciples could compel them. Saint Arvan tells us our ancestors were their masters - or believed they were."

Yoshana's mouth opened for a retort. I held up my hand and continued. "But this is no demon. This is a man. A man bred to fight, a man bred to wield the Darkness, but a man. Like me. And like all men, he has the knowledge to tell good from evil. He knows evil when he sees it, Yoshana. That's why he's here to kill you."

She lifted an eyebrow and waited a heartbeat. "Are you done?"

Her poise was back. So was her little smile. "I'm impressed, Minos. I really am. This is the second time you've surprised me. If I fall here, I honestly think you might be able to take up humanity's war against the Darkness and the Hellguard and have a chance of winning."

Her eyes shifted to Seven. "But you've both miscalculated. I've killed demons before. Stronger ones than you."

The Hellguard matched her smile. He was huge, and for all her presence, Yoshana was not a large woman. The ancient warrior must have been twice her weight. His voice rumbled like an avalanche. "Yashuath, you mean? I'd heard that. But the question is, did you kill him all by yourself?"

"I didn't have to." Her smile broadened into the wolfish grin that turned men's guts to water. "I didn't say this wasn't going to be a new challenge. I like new challenges."

"Surrender now, Yoshana," I said. "Disband the Darkness Radiant. You don't have to die here."

I thought there was real amusement in the Overlord's face as she turned back to me. "Oh, Minos, you don't understand me at all, do you?"

She turned to her troops, and declared, "Hear, Israel. The Lord is our God. The Lord is one. There is no God but God. And he is with us!" Then she turned back to Seven, and winked. The Darkness rose off her in a cloud. It did the same from the Hellguard. I scrambled back into the circle of soldiers. The forces these two were about to unleash would tear me apart if I was in their path.

Seven began to spin his sharpened staff, thirty pounds of steel pointed at both ends, accelerating into a blur of silver light. Inhumanly tough as Yoshana was, a solid blow from that would rip her in half.

If the Overlord was intimidated she gave no sign of it. She drew her katana with her right hand and with her left uncoiled a whip from her belt. I hadn't seen her use that weapon before. Darkness played along its length.

The black clouds around them shifted as they began to edge toward each other, feet moving in tight, controlled steps. For all that both of them were still smiling, they each recognized their opponent as someone to take deadly seriously.

Yoshana's whip flicked out. For a moment I allowed myself to hope she was actually mad enough to entangle someone so much bigger and stronger, but the tip merely cracked at Seven's face. He batted it aside easily with the staff, but a rush of Darkness had flooded down the hissing leather and cut his cheek.

He nodded as the wound sealed. "That's a neat trick. I like that."

The Overlord was moving before he finished speaking, slashing low with the katana. Again the staff turned it harmlessly aside. The masses of Darkness surrounding the two merged, Yoshana spun and brought the whip around again and, quick as a striking viper, Seven pivoted and kicked her in the side, blocking the whip again with his staff. She flew through the air, rolled, and came up facing him. He hadn't moved to follow.

"Ouch," she said.

The force behind the Hellguard's booted foot would probably have crushed my ribs. If it had done as much to Yoshana, the Darkness had already made repairs. She went in for a third time, sword and whip and Darkness moving in a complex dance my eyes couldn't follow. Somehow in the process she unclasped her cloak and hurled it at his face.

But again Seven beat her back, and she danced away out of range. Sweat was beginning to trickle down from her hairline.

Then the Hellguard pressed the attack, darting forward catlike, staff blurring in high then sweeping back low. The Overlord twisted away and her whip curled around and tore open the back of Seven's shirt, drawing a spurt of what I first thought was blood but then realized was more of the Darkness. He stayed with her, not letting her disengage, the staff coming at her again and again. If no more than the sharpened point struck her squarely, the wound would be beyond even Yoshana's ability to close.

She was impossibly quick but the Hellguard was more than human in every way. Sparring with Grigg, Yoshana's speed and superior mastery of the Darkness had overmatched his greater strength and reach. But Seven was bigger, faster, and stronger than Grigg, and had spent three centuries perfecting his control of a weapon he had been bred to command. It was beyond my ability even to follow every move they made in that maelstrom of metal and leather and angry clouds of seething death, but at some point the Overlord must make a mistake and the Hellguard would finish her.

Yoshana dodged far more than she deflected, and even her inhuman strength wouldn't let her directly parry a blow from the staff. Once the huge steel spear caught the edge of her blade, and the sword pinged awfully as a sliver of its strange, gray material flew off.

Desperate, the Overlord lashed out with her whip. Seven caught it on the spinning staff and jerked it from her hands. But this time a bigger torrent of the Darkness followed, striking the Hellguard in the face. Somehow he deflected it to shield his eyes, but it tore his cheeks open and the flesh hung in unhealing shreds.

Yoshana leapt at him, face twisted into a hellish wide-mouthed snarl as the Darkness swirled around them. Her sword moved too fast to see. Seven batted it aside but now he was on the defensive, giving ground. The battle had shifted to a plane beyond the physical, the warriors' minds struggling for control of the Darkness while their bodies cut and thrust with mundane weapons.

The Overlord harried her larger opponent like a wolf snapping at a bull. Seven wasn't smiling anymore. He stepped back, and she didn't follow. But they had not disengaged. The black cloud seethed and ebbed and flowed between them. And then suddenly it rushed into Seven and vanished. He turned to me.

"Sorry," he said.

His body collapsed, every cell losing cohesion. Where a man had been a moment before, there was only a thick stew of tissues spread on the ground with bones floating in it.

I took a step forward, but there was nothing to do. He was gone.

Yoshana stabbed her blade into the ground and leaned on it, mouth hanging open, drawing great, panting gasps of air. The Darkness rose from Seven's remains and floated back into her.

The piercing sapphire eyes met mine. "That... was hard."

I didn't know what came next. I hadn't planned for a scenario where they fought and the ancient Hellguard lost.

The Overlord dragged herself upright. Exhaustion showed in every line of her body, but the mocking smile was back. "I don't know if you know, but in certain traditions of trial by combat, when your champion is defeated, your own life is forfeit. This is going to be one of those."

The tremendous cloud of Darkness lashed out, past me, straight into Prophetess.

And shattered as if it had struck a stone wall.

"What?" Yoshana gasped.

I stepped forward between them, drawing my sword. The Overlord snarled, slashed with her hand, and directed a stream of seething death at my face. I tried to spin aside, felt it tear at my flesh, and fell into blackness.

8. Judgment

There was a diffuse, gray light above me. I had no real consciousness of where I was, or sense of my body. The obvious conclusion was that I was dead.

Then there was pain. If I was dead, I was clearly in hell. In a panic, I flailed my arms. Ah, there they were.

"Easy," came a voice.

I realized I was on my back. I struggled to sit, and as my hands fought for balance, I oriented myself. I was on a cot, in a tent. My tent. The pain was localized in the left side of my face.

No, I realized, it was everywhere. It was just a lot worse on the left side of my face.

I managed to sit up, blinked, and the figure near me came into focus.

"Father Roric? I didn't even know you were in the camp." I turned that over in my head. "We are still in the camp? On the battlefield? What's happened?"

The tall, thin priest gave a tight little smile. "I've been here all along. A priest is a remarkably handy thing to have on a battlefield. Since we didn't agree on your methods, I didn't seek you out when you returned from the Sorrows, and you didn't seem terribly interested in looking for me either."

Was that a rebuke? The tone had been perfectly matter-of-fact. He continued, "However, it seemed prudent for someone to stay with you after your injury, and the troops are needed elsewhere. The situation has, so to speak, gone quite thoroughly to hell."

I shook my head to clear it, then immediately regretted that. The movement aggravated the stabbing pain in my face, and revealed a throbbing headache. "What's happened?" I repeated.

"To you personally? Or in general?"

Terror flooded back into me. "Tess? Is she all right?"

"Ah. Straight to the miracle. Prophetess resisted the full force of Yoshana's attack with the Darkness. After you attempted to intervene and were struck down, a general melee ensued as our soldiers counterattacked and Yoshana's supported her. Other troops then stormed the hill. Those Darkness-infected savages you brought from the Sorrows and Hafnum Furat's dog were the first to arrive on the scene and, I am forced to admit, were instrumental in saving Prophetess. They put themselves directly between her and Yoshana. Casualties among the savages were unfortunately quite high."

"Do you know who was hurt? And who died?"

He shook his head. "I'm afraid I don't know their names."

"What about the dog?"

Roric gave me a strange look.

"That dog saved my life more than once in the Sorrows," I explained.

"The dog is fine."

"You said everything has gone to hell. What happened next?"

"The Darkness Radiant ultimately retreated from the hill. But the outcome of your trial by combat is inconclusive. Clearly, Yoshana prevailed over your demon champion."

Angry, I pushed myself to my feet. Or tried. I didn't quite make it and sat down heavily on the cot. I glared at Roric. "He didn't like being called a demon. He was a man. He was born and raised to be a weapon, but he was a human being, and he was my friend, and I got him killed trying to help me."

The priest nodded. "I'm sorry. He could not help being made how he was, and he fell in the service of a just cause. So. Yoshana prevailed over your champion. But while her attempt to kill Prophetess might have been accepted as the spoils of victory, her failure to accomplish it has sown doubt through her ranks. Neither side has an uncontested claim of success in the duel. So both armies are now preparing to resolve the matter through battle. There have been no hostilities since the skirmish on the hilltop, but an engagement seems imminent."

"Okay. So that gets us up to the question of how long ago was all this, and why am I in this tent?"

"You have been unconscious a little over a day. When Yoshana struck you with the Darkness, you fell back and rolled down the hill. Apparently you hit your head, as well as pretty much everything else, on the way down."

"You mean I feel like this and I've been out of commission for a day because I fell down a hill?" That was embarrassing.

"Er... well. In large part." Roric produced a small mirror and handed it to me. There was a deep, wide gouge of disrupted flesh starting just above my lip and disappearing into the hair above my left ear. It had just missed my eye.

"Well, that's ironic."

"That you would be wounded by the dark power you once used?"

"No, that I once did the same thing to a friend of mine." Sesk had been a sergeant in the Shadowed Hand before he retired after the Battle of the Cleansing. Once, in a berserk state when I'd surrendered my will to the Darkness, I'd torn open his face. He'd been right - the wounds were bloodless, but they hurt like a son of a bitch. "I sort of miss being able to heal from this kind of thing."

"Do you really?"

I thought about it for a while before I answered. "I suppose not."

I reached into my shirt. The Saint Benedict medal was still there. I said to Roric, "I don't think this thing works."

The priest frowned. "I told you before, it's not a magic amulet. It reminds you of your promises to God, and his to you. It does not deflect attacks by the Darkness."

"I was kidding." I pushed myself to my feet again. This time I managed to stay there.

"I need to talk to Tess and check our deployments. If this really does turn into a pitched battle it's not going to go well for us. I have to get her an escort and see if I can convince her to get out of here. I don't suppose her bodyguards have already managed to get her out of here?" I asked hopefully.

"No, she is still in the camp. Don't underestimate her value in rallying the troops, Minos. She survived the full power of the Darkness, delivered by an enemy who had just killed a... a Hellguard."

"Yeah, but she's not going to survive a bullet to the face. Yoshana has plenty of other ways to kill people."

I took a couple of wobbling steps forward. I would have liked to sit down again or lean against some kind of support, but neither was an option. I concentrated on keeping my balance instead.

"I'm no doctor, Minos, but you need to rest. Leave this in others' hands for now."

I didn't dare shake my head, but I replied, "I'm in command here, Father. As long as I'm alive, I should be out commanding. Even if I've been doing a lousy job of it."

"I can't stop you?"

"Oh, you probably could, the shape I'm in. But I'd appreciate it if you could find Captain Railes for me instead. I'll be somewhere between here and Prophetess' tent. Hopefully upright."

My headache was clearing up and the assorted aches and pains in my body had largely faded by the time I reached the heart of the secure area where the Shadowed Hand guarded Prophetess. I was even pretty steady on my feet. The side of my face didn't hurt any less, but I imagined that would be true for a long time. Maybe as long as I lived, which might not be very long at all.

Sam greeted me with a chorus of high-pitched barks. They reawakened the throbbing in my skull.

"Could you maybe give me a break today, dog?" I muttered. She trotted up and butted me with her nose. "Okay, yeah, I'm glad to see you too."

Ten soldiers surrounded Tess' tent. Half of them held lit torches even though it was broad daylight, the other half held carbines. I approved. Prophetess had survived one assault from the Darkness and might even be somehow immune to it, but it was better not to take any chances.

Furat came up behind Sam. "How you feeling, Minos?"

"How do I look?"

"That bad?"

"Yeah, pretty much. How many did we lose on that hill?"

The big man sighed. "Midnight Owl didn't make it. River Mist is leading the clan now. They've got seven more dead and one who's gonna be called 'lefty' from now on. Those guys got right in between Prophetess and Yoshana when you went down. It wasn't a healthy place to be, but they kept her alive."

I hadn't exchanged many words with the clansmen from the Sorrows. They were quiet people. But Owl had been a good man. He would have died leading from the front. I sighed. "Who else didn't make it?"

"None of your Shadowed Hand guys bought the farm. They got Prophetess down off the hill. They made it up there fast, but not as fast as the Hidden Moon Clan. Fast enough to be useful, not fast enough to do any of the dying." He showed me a crooked smile. "You trained 'em right. And three dead from the soldiers on guard up there from the beginning. Another four that aren't going to be fighting any time soon, if ever."

"And on the front?"

"So far fire discipline's been good on both sides. Trading dirty looks but nothing else. At least as far as I know. I've been back here where you put me. That scary adjutant of yours could tell you more."

He meant Railes. Furat was by far the larger man, and plenty dangerous in a fight, but Railes was a killer through and through. The skull on the side of his face was a declaration of intention, not just a piece of deviant art.

"Thanks. That's about what I needed for now. I'm going to talk to Tess." I ruffled Sam's fur. "Good girl. I heard she went up with the Hidden Moon Clan. I guess she gets along with them now?"

Furat gave me a strange look. "Well now, sure. That's not a problem anymore."

I thought I was missing a piece of the conversation, but patted him on the shoulder and moved on.

"That Prophetess really is something," Furat said behind me. "I can see why you did it. Picking her side, I mean."

"Yep. I should have listened to her on this one." It seemed petty when lives had been lost, but the words came out anyway. "Now I'm never going to hear the end of it."

Entering the presence of the living saint. The undisputed prophet of the Lord. The woman who had faced Yoshana's wrath and lived. I should have been awed, humbled, reverent. I found myself mostly feeling cranky.

My head hurt.

Cat was with her, of course. The paleo glared at me. When Tess had pushed her way into the group going up the hill, I hadn't let Cat join us. She'd been angry about it at the time. She looked angrier now, even though she probably would have died up there. If she decided to make her displeasure known in a physical way, I was going to lose that fight.

I looked from one woman to the other. I couldn't read Tess' face. A series of emotions bubbled up in me. I couldn't catalog them, but none were pleasant. A half dozen waspish, defensive comments died before they reached my lips. In the end, exhaustion won out.

"I'm sorry," I said softly. "You were right. I was wrong."

The tall woman came forward and folded me into a hug. "Yes. You were."

She let that sit for a moment, then added, "Nobody had any better ideas."

Her arms were still around me. I said, "I didn't think she could beat a Hellguard one on one. I got Seven killed and nearly got you killed."

I took her shoulders and stared into her eyes. "How did you live?"

She shrugged. "Faith."

A miracle reduced to one word. A farm girl had resisted an attack that had ripped a three hundred year old genetically engineered warrior's cells apart. "That's it?"

"That's it. What do you want me to say? I believed that God wouldn't let her hurt me, and he didn't."

I shook my head and regretted it again. Aggravated by the pain, I snapped, "Faith doesn't win battles. Not against something like Yoshana."

Tess smiled sadly and stepped away from me. "Of course it does. Faith cast the Darkness out of you, but you still don't believe. Even Thomas believed when he stuck his hand into God's wounds. How much proof do you need? Put it in terms you'll understand, Minos. If the Darkness is controlled by the will, why wouldn't faith be able to turn it aside? You've said yourself the battle is won in your enemy's mind - but before that it has to be won in your own."

"That's -" I stopped. I was going to say that wasn't the way the Darkness worked. That control of psycho-reactive autonomous nano technology wasn't determined by mystical belief in a divine power, and neither was the outcome of a war. But Seven was dead, and Prophetess was alive. I wasn't in a strong position to argue.

I did anyway. "It's still a good thing we have the Hidden Moon Clan. The way I hear it, if it hadn't been for them - and the Darkness - you wouldn't have gotten out of there alive."

Prophetess looked down, and when she met my eyes again, there were tears in hers. "Eight of them died with that filth in them. I can only pray God's infinite mercy takes them to heaven anyway. And thank God the rest let me free them afterward."

"Let you free -" My headache came flooding back with crushing force. "You mean you cast the Darkness out of them?"

She nodded. "They were easier than you. There was less in them. And I think they wanted it gone more than you did."

"That - that was the only edge we had left! You saw how effective it made them, and you got rid of it?"

She flared back, "You'd ask them to give their souls for your military advantage? That's disgusting."

"I didn't put it in them! But with it there, we'd be idiots not to use it. So I guess we're idiots now. Dammit, Tess, you put me in charge of the military and that was a military decision. You couldn't have waited three days until the battle was over before you went and messed with my troops?"

Her voice was calmer than mine, but no less angry. "I put you in charge of the military, but God called me to save souls. You can't ask someone else to do what you wouldn't do yourself. If it was wrong for the Darkness to be in you, how could it be right to be in them? They're not things, or tools, or weapons, Minos. They're people. Like you said Seven was. I'm just sorry I didn't get it out of all of them before the fight. And out of him."

As if she could have exorcised a Hellguard. As if he would have let her. I said, "If you'd done that, you might have died up there."

"Maybe. One day I'll die. We all will. My life on this earth isn't worth anyone's eternal damnation."

I glanced at Cat. To Tess I said, "You're surrounded by people who'll kill for you. Who've killed before and will do it again. War isn't a game. If you fight, you fight to win."

She nodded. "Yes. God set me this task. But you don't win if you become what you're fighting."

I shuddered, remembering the words of a man long dead. *He who fights with monsters should look to it that he himself does not become a monster. And when you gaze long into an abyss, the abyss also gazes into you.*

We all danced on the edge of that abyss, Yoshana's troops and mine. There was a reason the Overlord used the Canticles of Holy Mary to motivate her troops. Faith was as important to her as it was to Prophetess. Her partisans truly believed they were the righteous.

Dee had seen it more clearly than I did. If we were going to have any hope of surviving the coming battle, I was going to need the occultist's help to appeal to faith more effectively than the Overlord did.

"I need to talk to Dee," I said. "I - I'm glad you're all right."

A half-formed plan ricocheted inside the walls of my aching head. I turned to go.

"You need to rest, Minos," Prophetess snapped. "You're hurt, and tired, and you look like hell."

"I wasn't that attractive to start with," I muttered, "unless you've got a thing for gray skin, black eyes, and white hair. The big scar just makes me look dashing. Doesn't it?"

"You look like hell, Minos," she repeated. "You're hardly in shape to think clearly, much less plan strategy. You need to go back to your tent and sleep for a day."

"If I go back to my tent and sleep for a day, I'm never going to wake up, and neither is anyone else. I know my record hasn't been great so far, but I'm the only supreme commander we've got. I need to get back to supreme commanding."

Railes was waiting for me outside. He was breathing hard, which was what happened any time he exerted himself. I'd spent the winter worried that he'd get pneumonia and die of the injury to his lung. I thought about that every time I heard him wheezing. Part of me wished he'd retire from the army, but there was no chance he would. And a bigger part of me needed him too much to want him to go.

"Boss, you look like hell," he said, unknowingly parroting Tess. A pretty damning statement coming from a guy with no right ear and a skull tattooed over half his face.

"Yeah, and you sound like hell," I retorted. "We make a great pair. I'm not going to look any better tomorrow, and you're not going to sound any better. So what's the front look like, and where's Dee?"

He grinned. "In that order? Yoshana's spread her wings to flank us. She's anchored on the woods to our left and right."

Where I hadn't let Lago position our troops. Now we were partially enveloped. I still thought we were better off not being infiltrated through the trees. "Did Lago dig in any more on the flanks?"

"Yeah, he's got the end companies in square, and barricades all around behind us. It'll slow them down if they come that way. Of course, it wreaks havoc with our line of retreat."

Retreat would be at the top of everyone's mind, facing an Overlord and outnumbered two to one. Making a break for Our Lady under the cover of darkness wasn't the worst idea out there. Getting Tess out was even more tempting. Between the Shadowed Hand, the Monolith rangers, and what was left of the Hidden Moon Clan - even without the Darkness - we had a company-sized escort with serious woodcraft. They should be able to escape.

"How's morale?" I asked.

"Surprisingly good, considering our general and his demon champion got their asses kicked. The troops like having a prophet who can face the Darkness and live. And to be honest, I'm not sure the Monolith guys were ever totally sold on you anyway."

"You're great for the self-esteem, you know that? Where's Dee?"

"Top of the hill, boss."

Of course he was.

For years I'd carried a katana shirasaya, without a hand guard and in a simple wooden scabbard so it resembled a walking stick. This was the first time I'd really needed to use it that way. I was wheezing worse than Railes by the time the two of us reached the hilltop.

"Don't you have troops to be watching?" I growled at the captain. I didn't need to be forcibly reminded that I now both looked and sounded worse than he did.

"I can see 'em just fine from up here."

Was he afraid I'd keel over, or that I'd go running off to do something stupid like challenge Yoshana to another duel? I supposed either worry was fair. I was tempted to snap something sarcastic at him, but I didn't have so many friends that I wanted to annoy one of the few I had.

The day was cloudy but still bright. The view from the height was impressive. In the distance, rolling grasslands stretched into infinity, interrupted by stretches of forest. This had probably been farm country in the Last Days, but with the Fall it had returned to nature.

Closer by the vista was dominated by the armies massed around us - my own behind, Yoshana's in front. It was disturbing how much larger hers was. Each was laid out in a semicircle centered on the hill. As Railes had said, the enemy flanks slightly overlapped ours, and battle would inevitably start on the wings. For the centers to meet, they would have to storm the hill, which for the moment Yoshana had left to us.

Both groups favored white tabards, ours emblazoned with the circle of roses and spines adopted from Prophetess' Order of Thorns, the Overlord's with the golden double halberd of the Darkness Radiant. It was going to be hard telling friend from foe if it came to a melee.

Doctor John Dee wore no uniform at all. The occultist still looked like an animated scarecrow, a tall, gangly man in loose clothes that looked like rags even when they were clean.

Not that I was in a position to talk. I was still wearing the traveling gear I'd taken into the Sorrows. It had been laundered in the two weeks we'd been waiting for Yoshana's arrival, but that could only accomplish so much. Falling down the hill hadn't helped. Dirty, wounded, ragged, and gasping, I must have looked like something that had crawled out of a shallow grave.

"Minos!" Dee cried happily. He was always happy to see me, whether I was in favor or a pariah. He was a loudmouthed braggart who could talk the ear off a deaf mule, and at the same time an unrepentant coward. There had been a time when he might have been my only friend in the world.

He clapped me on both shoulders and ran his eyes appraisingly up and down my body. "You look like hell."

"That's the consensus."

I looked past him. There was quite a bit of movement in Yoshana's camp, although it looked more like drills than preparation for an assault. "What are our friends up to down there?"

"They've been quite active since the duel yesterday. BlackShield Lago believes their officers are keeping them busy to get their minds off the fact that Yoshana was unable to kill Prophetess."

"Yeah. Prophetess surviving was about the only thing that went according to plan yesterday."

Dee said, "Yes. A defeat for utilitarianism, I must say."

I knew I was going to regret it, but I asked anyway. "What do you mean?"

His eyebrows went up, then he launched into full lecture. "Well, most simply, utilitarianism is the philosophy that the ends justify the means. Although more precisely that would simply be consequentialism, as utilitarianism also requires maximizing the good, however defined, for the greatest number -"

"I know what utilitarianism is. What do you mean that yesterday was a defeat for it?" I braced for another torrent of words. I should have just told him to shut up. Tess was right - I still wasn't thinking clearly.

He shrugged. "You believed that using an evil - the Darkness - to defeat another evil would be the most effective course. But in point of fact, your champion was defeated, and Yoshana was thwarted instead by Prophetess."

"That's idiotic. Seven didn't lose because I was morally wrong. He lost because Yoshana was stronger. If I'd had two Hellguards, she'd be a puddle of goo, and we wouldn't be having this conversation. And Prophetess didn't win, she survived, and only because she was saved by a bunch of other people who are infected with the Darkness. Or were until she decided it would be a good idea to exorcise them right before a battle."

The occultist smiled. "I believe you're missing the larger point. When your only measure of success is the military outcome, victory is decided only on the battlefield. When the righteousness of your cause and methods are also measures of success, victory can be achieved even in defeat. Two and a half millennia of Christian martyrs attest to that point."

Prophetess had said something similar when we'd first faced Yoshana at Stephensburg and lived to tell about it. It was a powerful argument, or at least it had gained us dozens of new adherents. I scowled at Dee. "If I were cynical, I'd say your argument's no less utilitarian than mine, you're just bringing in the second order consequences of the means being used. It's not that the means matter in themselves, it's that using good means is more likely to get you a good outcome because people perceive you as a good person."

Dee's smile widened. "Just so. Although that's not what Prophetess or Aquinas would say. They would say that right action is its own justification and reward. The more interesting question from your perspective is what Yoshana's troops think."

"Yeah, that's what I wanted to talk to you about."

He was beaming now. "Excellent! I knew you would eventually come to see the value of philosophy in all human endeavor, including war. Perhaps the blow to your head did you good."

I was tempted to see if a blow to the head would do him good, but I had come looking for the irritating windbag's advice. I laid out the problem. "Both sides are on their back foot now. We lost the duel, but Yoshana couldn't finish off an unarmed farm girl. I understand the morale impact on her troops, but I don't know what to do with it. They're well trained, and she's got a bunch of her veterans in the mix. They won't break if we attack, and I'm not sure our morale is much better than theirs - we did lose the duel. I see a head to head fight as a clear loss for us. We might pull off a retreat if we make a break for it tonight, but that puts us back in the box we were in before, waiting for Yoshana to march on Our Lady."

The occultist sucked his teeth, then smiled slyly and said, "I think you're focused on the wrong enemy. When you want to slay a serpent, you strike off its head."

"Dammit, Dee, that's what I just tried to do! The head bit me!"

For the first time, I let myself glance at the spot where Seven had fallen. Someone had cleaned up, buried or burned the remains. The grass was starting to turn brown. I supposed some part of the fallen Hellguard's fluids had been acidic, unless it was an effect of the Darkness itself.

Dee was still smiling. I really wanted to hit him.

"When you strike off a serpent's head, do you aim the blow at the head itself? Or just behind it?"

I growled, "You've lost me."

"You're something of a student of Yoshana. When she first moved against Prophetess, did she attack her directly?"

"You mean when she tried to turn me?"

"Exactly. The ideal pressure point may be neither the leader herself, nor the great mass of her followers. Yoshana attacked Prophetess through you. Similarly, her pressure point may be her key lieutenants. You told me you believed Roshel held some genuine affection for you. That could be exploited."

"Okay, first, which of us is a consequentialist now? That's pretty low. Second, Roshel worships Yoshana." I paused, forestalling Dee's response with a raised finger. "Third, that's maybe not the worst idea you've ever had."

I'd heard more than once that Roshel had wanted - and maybe had - a relationship with Grigg, only to be displaced by Yoshana. And if Roshel worshipped her leader with an almost religious fervor, how might that devotion have been shaken when Prophetess turned aside Yoshana's attack?

My head still hurt. I needed a new strategy, and I needed it fast, before Yoshana decided she was willing to suffer thousands of losses to crush us once and for all. I didn't even want to start cataloging the possible flaws in the occultist's reasoning, but I wanted to sit around waiting for the hammer to fall even less. "All right, Dee. My plan didn't work. Let's give yours a try."

Of course, the last idea Dee had advocated for was my mission to join Yoshana in the Sorrows. That hadn't gone well. And I found that I didn't want any more stains on my conscience. "But I'm not going to 'exploit' her affection for me, if there is any. I'm just going to talk to her."

"Just so."

9. Auld Lang Syne

I was lying on my cot again, watching the gray fabric of the tent above me darken as the sun went down. I wanted to sleep - preferably for several days - but I couldn't. Being flat on my back was restful, except when I was distracted by the pain in my face. Which was most of the time.

Railes hadn't liked Dee's plan. He'd berated me all the way down the hill. "What are you going to do, go sneaking off behind enemy lines to set up a date with that Overlord?"

"Yep."

"Do I even need to explain how stupid that is, boss? It would be stupid even if you were healthy. Which you aren't. You're going to get yourself killed."

"Remember what I said to General Hake right before the Cleansing?"

"Nope. I wasn't there. I was busy lying in the infirmary trying not to die. But I'm going to bet it was something stupid."

"I told him the army wouldn't be much worse off if we got killed, because our tactics weren't working. Same applies now."

The tattooed captain had scowled. "Like I said, something stupid."

"Railes, I can't come up with any better options. I'm going to get some rest, and then I'm going to go out when it's dark enough to give me some cover but before I start tripping over tree roots because I can't see."

He'd grabbed my shoulder, his face set in stubborn lines that reminded me of a particularly ill-tempered mule. "You don't have the Darkness in you anymore. You can barely walk. You're not going."

I'd smiled sadly. "I'm telling you, it's the best chance we've got, and you know it. Now let go of your superior officer so I can get some rest, or I'll court martial you."

"I'll tell Prophetess."

"She's not the military commander here, I am. And I really will court martial you if you tell her. Now go make sure everyone's got torches ready for tonight. I'll bet if Yoshana hits us, it'll be in the dark." Even with superior numbers, the Overlord would want to take advantage of the terror the Darkness would sow at night. She would be thinking in terms of morale too. She'd want to demonstrate that Prophetess' immunity to the Darkness didn't protect the rest of us.

Railes hadn't liked it, but he'd grumbled and left me on my cot. I smiled to myself in the dimness. He really did seem to care about me. Of course, it would be hard for him to find another commanding officer even uglier than he was.

When the light inside the tent had faded to the dull shades of twilight, I dragged myself to my feet, picked up my sword, and staggered out. Railes hadn't posted guards to stop me, which was good. I couldn't have put up much resistance if they'd forced me back into bed. Part of me was disappointed.

I had spent quite a bit of my time lying there considering my approach - both physical and emotional. The physical aspect was the more immediately troublesome. Roshel commanded Yoshana's left flank, which fronted on our right. It would be easy enough to just walk out into the no man's land between the lines. But the chances of getting shot were unpleasantly high. And if I carried a flag of truce, I might be taken to Yoshana rather than Roshel.

I preferred a more oblique route that would take me around the back of the opposing forces. I had no illusions that there wouldn't be sentries posted, but I liked my chances of bluffing my way past better.

Unfortunately that meant hobbling out through the back of our own lines, trudging up a forested rise, and using the cover of those trees to make my way around. While hoping Roshel didn't have sentries or Darkness wards posted in the woods.

I considered asking Furat to lend me Sam, but rejected the idea. The dog had been through enough, and this was one risk too many. It was ridiculous to jeopardize a mission of such importance because I was worried about a dog... but like I'd told Railes, I had enough on my conscience. At least Seven had known what he was getting into.

"Sir?"

And of course I had my own sentries to worry about. It was good to see this one at least was paying attention. As Railes had said, Lago had prepared for a flanking maneuver. I was exiting our lines far enough from the enemy that the barricades were perfunctory obstacles, designed more to slow an enemy attack than to stop it... and thus leave us the ability to get out if we needed to make a run for it. They had plenty of torches, though. I approved.

"Going to check out that forest. We don't want anything sneaking up through it, do we? I may be a while."

"Should I get some men to go with you, sir?"

"No. Thanks. Some things I can do better alone."

The soldier nodded. He wasn't one of my Shadowed Hand troops or a ranger, which meant he was a Monolith regular. I thought about what Railes had said, that they weren't totally sold on me. The captain had put it as a joke, but he was probably right. Prophetess was a hero to them, but I was a former enemy, dragged by her from the deepest darkness into the light. More or less into the light. My journey to the Sorrows and return with Seven and the Hidden Moon Clan wouldn't have helped their opinion of me. And the Josephite religion of the Monolith didn't have anything good to say about the Select, even when they hadn't been infected with the Darkness.

"What's your name?" I asked.

"Burha, sir."

"Right. Burha, if I'm not back in four hours, get a message to Prophetess. Tell her to talk to Captain Railes. He knows where I'm going."

"Yes, sir."

I stepped into the darkness behind our lines. Tall grass had been trampled flat in the camp. Here it brushed against my knees. It occurred to me that for all I was supposed to be the supreme commander of this army, and kept insisting I was supposed to be commanding it, I seemed to spend more time running off by myself. Which reinforced my suspicion that I probably wasn't a very good commander.

The bright side was the troops wouldn't miss me much if I got myself killed.

"Judge Minos?" the sentry called softly from behind me.

"Yes, Burha?"

"Are... are we going to be all right? Against Yoshana?"

"We've got God's own prophet on our side. Of course we will."

The setting sun was in my eyes, casting a long shadow behind me as I plodded along up to the wooded ridge. The good news was that anyone watching me would be staring into it too, and then I'd have it at my back once I reached the trees and swung around.

The woods weren't as thick as the Sorrows, and of course they were free of the constant, brooding presence of the Darkness. Still, I felt like I was being watched, and sometimes a loud rustling would sound in the distance. Over the past couple of years I'd learned that chipmunks and squirrels could make an amazing amount of noise scurrying through dry leaves, and I murmured a quick mantra to steady my nerves.

I moved slowly and kept my eyes and ears open. I was in no shape to go running through the trees, and I didn't want to.

The central hilltop where Seven and Yoshana had fought was an excellent vantage point, and I'd used it to pick the route I wanted. This long, low ridge extended southeast, past Roshel's position. Further on it split into two wooded wings with a grassy valley between. Roshel's troops were anchored on the nearer wing. I'd go into the valley, swing around the woods, and approach from open ground to the south, behind her lines, as if I were a messenger coming in from the southeast. I didn't want to come at her men straight out of the trees - like trying to approach from the front, it seemed like a good way to get shot.

The trick was staying oriented in the woods so I'd come out where I wanted.

Something moved in the shadows in front of me, far larger than any squirrel. I staggered back and jerked my blade clear. A deer stared at me wide-eyed, not ten feet away. It froze for a long moment, then turned and bounded off.

"Stupid animal," I muttered as the pounding of my heart gradually slowed. A beast that would stray so close to so many armed men was going to wind up getting eaten.

I wondered if I was any smarter than the deer.

The forest thinned in front of me, and I crouched in the cover of a bush and scanned the vista ahead. It looked like I'd caught my first break of the past forty-eight hours. I was exactly where I wanted to be, and the way was clear. The valley, shadowed by the trees behind, sloped gently down. The way I was feeling, I liked going down much better than up. I descended the gradual slope, starting to feel like this might actually work. Gently waving prairie grass brushed my thighs. It was like wading through a shallow, green sea. I rehearsed my conversation with Roshel in my mind.

They say you never hear the one that gets you. I definitely heard the crack of the gunshot, although I couldn't have honestly said whether that was before or after pain exploded in my knee.

Writhing where I collapsed on my back in the tall grass, I couldn't see my attacker. The katana had flown from my hand. I wanted to turn over and crawl in search of it, but my knee screamed in protest when I tried to move. Maybe if I lay very still, the gunman wouldn't be able to find me. It hardly seemed likely, but the fact was, I wasn't going anywhere.

I heard the rustling in the grass before I saw the figure silhouetted to the west. It moved with a strange, slow, shuffling gait, but it had a carbine and so it didn't need to be fast. Anyway, it was faster than me.

When it was twenty feet away I recognized Erev.

"Forgot about me, didn't you?"

His voice sounded like he'd inhaled fire. Or like someone had severed his vocal cords with the Darkness and they hadn't healed properly. His slow, painful walk was probably the result of me destroying the tendons in his ankles. Although evidently what I'd done to his wrists hadn't ruined his marksmanship. Unless he'd been aiming higher.

He was the only survivor of Yoshana's merely human bodyguards who'd crossed the Sorrows with us. I'd left him crippled when I fled back to Our Lady. I hadn't been sure it was a mercy not to finish him. Yoshana might easily have tortured him to death for letting me escape. It seemed instead she'd healed him. At least somewhat. Still, I could understand why he wasn't pleased to see me. Even in the half light, I could see that pain had carved new and deeper lines into his weathered face.

"Glad to see you made it out of the Sorrows alive," I said, trying to force a light tone through gritted teeth.

"Are you?" he croaked. "You always were stupid."

"I guess we're pretty close to even now," I grunted, "so I'll have to ask you not to come any closer. Or I'll be forced to kill you."

He barked out a rasping, coughing laugh. "It's not in you anymore, boy. Everyone knows that."

"Really? Same way everyone knew I had a Hellguard with me?"

"Only one way to find out." He took a shuffling step closer and leveled the carbine, sighting on my face. The bore of the muzzle looked much larger from that angle. I couldn't help staring at his finger on the trigger.

He laughed again and lowered the weapon, just a little. It was still pointing at me. "Didn't think so. Woulda been funny, though, me going to all this trouble to hunt you down and then you doing for me instead. Woulda been an end, so that's still good. But I like this end better."

I tried to sit, propping myself up on my elbows. The pain in my leg and the gun aimed at my belly convinced me otherwise and I fell back. I felt terribly vulnerable, which I suppose was the idea.

"I can't help but think killing me seems a little ungrateful."

"Why, because you let me live?" he rasped. "Live like this, half crippled? So I can stagger around behind Yoshana like some old dog that she can't even be bothered to put down? You would think that was doing me a favor, you stupid blackeyed freak."

"You'd rather I'd opened your throat?" I snapped. Which wasn't smart, but the pain and tension were getting to me.

"If you'd had any guts or any brains you would have. If you really stood for anything instead of blowing along like a leaf in the wind you would have. Your Prophetess would have."

He completely failed to understand her if he thought that, but he was continuing his hissing rant. "That was always your problem. No determination, no spine. You're too worried about hurting anyone's feelings to do the right thing. You're too *nice*." He sneered the last word.

"That's kind of ironic. You're the only person in the world who thinks so, and you want to kill me. So you're doing the right thing here?"

"I'm right the way the guy holding the gun is always right. Might makes right. By right or force. By right of force. Take your pick, the ancients had lots of ways of saying it. All of 'em true. You always wanted to do the decent thing. There's no room for decent men in war."

"Some people would argue that's exactly where you need decent men. Father Roric at Our Lady, for example, is very persuasive in his discussions of just war –"

"And you talk too damn much," Erev grated, raising the carbine.

His body jerked, then again and again, as Cat's shining knife plunged into his back over and over. He let out a sigh and the gun slid from his hands. He followed it to the ground and lay motionless in a widening pool of blood.

"Actually, I'd say I talked just about the right amount." I looked up at the paleo. "Took you long enough."

I'd managed a glimpse of her coming down the hill when I'd tried to sit. I hadn't been sure I could stall until she reached me.

"Railes above," she said, jerking her chin over her shoulder. The slight girl wiped her blade on Erev's pants and sheathed it, then reached down to help me stand. She was stronger than she looked, but couldn't support all my weight. I gritted my teeth to stifle a scream when I put pressure on the wounded knee.

My adjutant was coming down the slope, rifle in hand.

"You couldn't have just shot him?" I asked.

He shrugged. "Wasn't sure I'd get a clean kill without him squeezing off a round into you. You seemed to be keeping him busy. Friend of yours?"

"Let's say acquaintance. He was one of Yoshana's personal guard. He never did like me very much."

Railes showed me the twisted grin that made his skull tattoo even more hideous. "Seems like there's a lot of that going around, boss. You're not the most popular guy."

I grimaced. "Well, he maybe had more reason than most, since I crippled him with the Darkness and left him helpless in Hellguard territory. Still, he was a jerk before I did that. Speaking of which, thanks for saving me. I don't mean to complain."

"Second serious wound in two days can make anyone cranky, boss. Why don't you sit down and let me look at that before you bleed out?"

I was only too happy to sit again, or more accurately slump back to the ground. Railes used Cat's knife to cut my pants away above the knee, and peered at the injury in the fading light.

"Not that I mind, but what were the two of you doing out here?" I asked. Although it was pretty obvious.

"Figured you might get yourself killed out here all by yourself. Cat's the best tracker we've got, so we took off after you."

"I guess I'm lucky you two didn't stop to fool around in the woods."

To my amazement, Cat blushed. Railes said, "That would be unprofessional, boss. We were going to do that on the way back."

The paleo unleashed a punch to his shoulder that would have broken a lesser man's bones. The captain just grinned.

"Best I can tell, the slug hit the top of your kneecap and bounced off. You've lost barely any blood, but it's probably shattered the bone. Bet it hurts like a mother."

"Good guess."

"I'm not sure the two of us can carry you back. I'll stay here and Cat can go for help."

I shook my head. "The mission hasn't changed."

"Minos, you can't complete the mission."

"Sure I can. You two kept me alive, so the mission continues. Splint up my leg and find me a good stick I can use as a crutch."

"You try to walk on that leg, you're gonna make it worse. You'll cripple yourself for good."

"I don't go see Roshel, we're all going to die. The choice is actually pretty easy."

Railes snapped, "Cat, talk some sense into this idiot. Maybe he'll listen to you."

But the paleo just said, "Shadow warrior, him." For the first time in a long while, she was looking at me with something like the respect she'd first had for me.

"Thanks, Cat." It felt good through the pain to have earned that respect myself, instead of with the Darkness.

"Fine," Railes growled. "Stay here with him a minute. I'll go find the shadow warrior some branches."

The girl gathered up Erev's carbine and sank into the tall grass. After a moment I ventured tentatively, "Are you happy with Railes?"

She nodded and said quietly, "Good man, him."

Probably not by a lot of definitions. But her definition was what mattered.

"I'm glad," I said.

It was almost fully dark by the time Railes returned with an armful of branches. Cat held my leg with the knee slightly bent while he bound the wound with strips of cloth, then splinted it in place.

"Wouldn't it be better straight?" I asked.

"Yeah, until you put your weight on it and drive bone splinters into your leg. If you're gonna be an idiot and limp around on it, this might keep you from hurting yourself more."

It was hard to argue with that logic. Once he was satisfied with his work, he had Cat help me up again and trimmed a longer branch to the right length for a crutch. It had a bend that fit under my armpit, and was only moderately uncomfortable.

Supporting my own weight was another story, especially when I took my first clumsy step forward, nearly fell, and banged my makeshift crutch into my knee as I desperately tried to steady myself. I ground my teeth together and muttered, "Son of a -" under my breath.

"Still think this is a good idea?"

I am a shadow warrior. I could hardly back down now in front of Cat. "It's just going to take some practice." I took another step forward. This time I neither hurt myself nor almost landed on my face.

"Okay. If you're going to be that way about it, we'll take you to their lines." Railes didn't sound convinced.

"No, you won't. I'm going alone. I appreciate that you just saved my life, trust me, but if all three of us show up I'm just going to get shot again. Once was enough."

Even in the gloom I could see the mulish look on Railes' face. "Yeah, and if you show up all by yourself, you'll get shot again, all by yourself."

"Then somebody had better tell Tess I'm off doing something stupid and make some contingency plans. Thanks, Railes. I've got it from here."

My adjutant shook his head. "You really are the dumbest son of a bitch on God's green earth."

"So I've heard." I started limping toward the enemy position, and Railes and Cat made no move to follow me. I looked back over my shoulder at Erev's corpse cooling in the grass. "I feel like we should do something for him."

"That's what vultures are for, boss."

Like my own troops, Roshel's had set torches. It made sense. Between Seven and the Hidden Moon Clan, I'd shown myself willing and able to use the Darkness. She couldn't know I had no such capabilities left. And even without them, I could still have theoretically launched a surprise attack at night.

They knew what they were doing. The fires were bright and spaced at regular intervals, outside their picket lines. Inexperienced soldiers tended to set them too close, blinding themselves. The Darkness Radiant was not inexperienced in such matters.

Still, I could see the surprise on the nearest sentry's face as I limped into the firelight. The sun was long gone now - I'd moved so slowly I suspected a couple of snails and a tortoise had passed me. He raised a rifle, but didn't seem to regard me as much of a threat. It wasn't hard to see why.

"Glory to God," he declared. In a less friendly tone he demanded, "What's your business here?"

"Roshel sent for me."

He shook his head. "I didn't get orders to expect anyone." He stared me up and down again. I didn't look like anyone's idea of an emissary. "I'm going to have to call this in. You wait here while I get it figured out."

I tried to paste a friendly smile onto my face. I doubt I succeeded, but I wasn't trying that hard either. "Go ahead. I'm sure she's in a really good mood right now and won't mind the delay at all. As you might imagine," I glanced down at my leg, "I'm running a little late as it is."

The soldier thought about that, but not for very long. "All right. Come on with me while I find the sergeant of the guard."

"Yep. Don't mind me, I'll just be limping along behind. This won't take us out of our way at all, right?"

"Oh, for - fine. We'll go straight to her tent. The tribune can take care of herself." He called out to the nearest man to his right, some fifty feet away. "Gustas, I'm taking this guy back to see the tribune. Can you get my post covered?"

He set out at a brisk pace, only realizing after ten yards or so that I wasn't keeping up. He stopped to wait. "What the hell happened to you, anyway, buddy?" As rare as Select were, he didn't seem to have made the mental connection between me and the commander of the enemy forces. Maybe it was hard to imagine me as a general limping along in dirty, blood-stained rags with a tree branch as a crutch. I certainly didn't feel much like a general.

"You should see the other guy," I said.

"Rostan, you have got to be kidding me," snapped the guard outside Roshel's tent.

"He said he had to see the tribune," my escort whined. "I wasn't going to keep her waiting."

"And if I tell you Yoshana promoted me to centurion, are you going to start saluting me just 'cause I said so? I've been outside this tent for three hours, and the tribune's been inside, and she hasn't sent for anyone."

"Do you really think she has no means to summon me that you can't see? Who do you think you're serving under?" I asked.

The guard blanched.

"Look, this is easy enough," I said. "Open up the tent. If she wants to see me, she's going to be happy. If she doesn't want to see me, you've got a corpse to dispose of, but hey, this is war. Or you can send me away and find out the hard way if she wanted to see me or not when she starts wondering why I didn't show up. Totally up to you."

Before the soldier could decide what to make of that, the tent flap opened and a small, angry figure peered out. "What's going on out here?"

I'd seen Roshel seductive, commanding, frightened, exhilarated - but never peevish. I hadn't been wrong when I'd bluffed the sentry. The dark-haired Overlord was in a bad mood.

She did a double-take and stared at me open-mouthed. "Minos? What are you doing here? You look like hell."

The tent guard shot me a dirty look. "I knew - sorry, ma'am -"

"Get in here," Roshel said to me. To the soldiers, she said, "Get back to your posts. He is not here. If your tongues start wagging, they just might fall out."

The two braced to attention and saluted.

"Gentlemen," I said, and hobbled into the tent.

It was a lot like mine. There was a cot and a small table with a lamp on it. Apparently the tribunes of the Darkness Radiant didn't get any better accommodations than the judge of Our Lady. I wasn't surprised. Yoshana didn't strike me as the type to travel weighed down with luxuries, or permit it for her subordinates.

"What are you doing here, Minos?" Roshel repeated.

I really wanted to sit on her cot but kept myself upright. "I wanted to see if you were ready to surrender."

Her eyes went wide. She looked like she wanted to laugh, but couldn't quite get it out. "Did you hit your head when Yoshana did that to you?" She pointed at the livid wound on my face.

I had, actually. But I replied, "You know you're on the wrong side here, Roshel."

The Overlord scowled. "You don't believe that girl's stronger than Yoshana. Yoshana had just defeated a Hellguard in single combat, she was exhausted, trying to control the Darkness she'd taken from the demon. And yes, your little prophetess has a strong will. But that was a fluke, not a sign!"

She said it too loudly, too angrily. It struck me that while Roshel was less prone to violence than Yoshana, she was no less lethal if provoked. And the Darkness seethed inside her, as it once had in me. I kept my voice quiet and level. "Is that how she's explaining it? Maybe that's true. But I've seen Prophetess cast the Darkness out of me. A lot of it, Roshel. I was dark, and strong. And I've seen her resist a woman who killed a Hellguard. So maybe it was a fluke. Or maybe it's the hand of God. But that's not even what I mean, Roshel. You might or might not be on the stronger side. But you're not on the right one."

"Don't give me the hand of God," she spat. "Remember the Darkness was pulled out of me when I was a child. Unless you're going to claim the Overlords' surgeon sorcerers were holy men. God wasn't on that hill."

"Maybe." I shrugged. "Maybe Saul had an epileptic fit on the road to Damascus and Jesus' message got spread through the Roman Empire because he fell off his horse, bumped his head, and hallucinated. But right is right and wrong is wrong, and we know the difference."

"Yoshana doesn't think she's wrong."

"Yoshana makes her own truth, her own law. The question is whether you believe in an eternal truth, a real truth, God's truth - or Yoshana's truth. You're a good person. We both know that. But you're on the side of evil here. You shouldn't be."

"You said that before, at Our Lady. How dare you?" Her voice began to rise. "I'm on the side of evil because the Darkness is in me? Because we use it? Who are you to tell me that? Who are you to say you know God's truth? You used the Darkness too! You brought a demon to fight for you!"

There were angry tears in her eyes.

I nodded. "And I was wrong. I went against Prophetess' wishes - I went against God's wishes - and I was wrong. I'm no prophet and God knows I'm no saint. But look what happened, Roshel. Seven, the Hellguard who helped me, is dead. Prophetess is alive. If you keep using the Darkness to fight the Darkness, you'll lose, because there will always be an evil greater than you. Gurath, the huge wraiths in the sorrows, they'll win a battle of the Darkness. You need to use the light."

Roshel turned away from me. "You come limping in here half dead and tell me I'm losing and I should surrender? You really did hit your head."

"I'm here so tomorrow doesn't turn into good people killing each other while the Darkness watches and laughs. I'm here because I care about you. Prophetess was in tears because people died for her with the Darkness in them. She wouldn't want that for you either."

When the Overlord turned back, her face was composed. "You keep talking like we're going to lose, Minos. But that's not what's going to happen."

She stepped to me and touched my face. Heat rose through my body.

"We can heal you. She can make you stronger than you were before. You can be a commander, but on the winning side." Her hands ran over my chest. Her eyes were dark pools, beckoning me to dive in. "You are so much greater than the small people you serve. Taking orders from priests and prophets. Enduring injury that you could overcome with a thought. Enduring indignity you could end with a word."

And that was true, of course. From provocations like the disrespect of that useless bureaucrat Doreden to the humiliation of the wounds on my body, I could set all of that aside with the Darkness. But that wasn't the side I'd chosen.

"One of us chose the wrong side, but it wasn't me," Roshel continued, as if she could read my mind. This close to me, she could. This close to me... Her breath was warm on my face. I could feel the Darkness rise up around us.

"Deliver your army to Yoshana, Minos, and you can be her third tribune. You can see to it she lets Prophetess go. And then you and I together…"

Her hands brushed at my shirt, delicate, gently reaching to open buttons. My breath caught in my throat. And, just for a moment, her fingers pressed the Saint Benedict medal that hung around my neck into my skin.

I let my crutch fall and gasped as I took weight on the injured knee. A stabbing bolt of pain shot up my leg and settled into a throbbing ache in my gut. I set both hands on Roshel's shoulders and pushed her back.

"Stop that," I said. "It's beneath you. I'm being honest with you. I expect you to return the favor."

Her eyes widened again and she put her hand to her mouth, biting her knuckle. It was a gesture so vulnerable that I wondered if it was another part of her manipulation. But the overpowering aura of desirability was gone.

Not that Roshel wasn't desirable without it.

"Sit down before you fall down," she said quietly.

To hell with dignity. I didn't need to be told twice. My leg was killing me. I collapsed gracelessly onto her cot.

"I can heal it, you know," she said, but there was no seduction in her tone anymore. The Darkness had receded. "Yoshana said she'd marked you and then you fell down the hill. Did you break your leg rolling down?"

"No, that was Erev shooting me on the way here."

"Oh my God. What happened?"

"That. He tracked me down and shot me in the knee. I gather he's been holding a grudge."

"How did you get away?"

I put on a severe look. "Get away? I killed him. I'm a factor, remember?"

"Uh huh. How did you get away?"

"A couple of my soldiers tailed me. They figured I couldn't take care of myself and apparently they were right. They ambushed Erev after he ambushed me. He didn't survive."

"And then you limped over here to demand my surrender after being gunned down by one half-crippled Knight of the Resurrection?"

"I said I was right. I didn't say I was smart."

Roshel sighed. "I should just kill you now. Or give you to Yoshana so she can torture you to death." The Overlord looked at the ground, then back at me. "How about I heal your face and your leg and you go back to your camp?"

I shook my head. "No. No more of the Darkness. My face will remind me that I got Seven killed. My leg will remind me of what I did to Erev in the Darklands. I deserve both and more."

"If you deserve that then there's not much hope for me, is there?"

"They tell me that Christ forgives. I know Prophetess does. You know the liturgy. Lord, I'm not worthy that you should enter under my roof, but only say the word and my soul shall be healed. It's never too late to pick the right side."

She turned away. "You've changed again. You're... more than you were before. But I won't fight Yoshana."

"Then don't. Take your army and sit this one out. Help Yoshana against the Darkness and the Hellguard. But not against Prophetess."

"She'd never accept that. You're with her or you're against her."

"If she won't let you follow your conscience, that might be another sign that you're on the wrong side."

Roshel dropped into a crouch face to face with me. "Your timing sucks, Minos."

"Why? Planning a big surprise attack tonight? Then I'd say it's just about perfect."

"God damn you," she hissed. She handed me my crutch. "I'll arrange an escort to get you back to your lines."

"Does that mean you're going to do the right thing?"

"That means you're not my favorite person anymore," the Overlord growled.

10. The Serpent's Tooth

Roshel bundled me into a hooded cloak that concealed my face and assigned two soldiers to pass me through the front lines. Every step was its own little torture. Physically, because my knee jabbed a lance of pain up my thigh and into my gut every time it took the slightest bit of weight. And mentally as I dreaded Yoshana's attack beginning before I rejoined my troops.

If Roshel's men on the front thought it was odd to see a limping, cowled figure escorted past them, they didn't say so. They were probably used to strange things in the service of an Overlord, and it might be unhealthy to comment on them. If the men guarding me had an opinion, they kept it to themselves as well. They didn't say a word.

A hundred yards of no man's land between the lines was sunk into deep shadow, the flickering light of hundreds of torches on either side doing nothing to illuminate the middle. My escorts each carried a burning brand, partly so we wouldn't look like infiltrators and partly so I wouldn't trip in a gully or gopher hole and break my other leg. I suppose it worked - we reached Our Lady's defenses without falling or being shot.

Not without challenge, thankfully. Wounded and exhausted as I was, I still would have been outraged if we'd been able to simply pass through. At least, that's what I told myself as I hopped unsteadily in place with my crutch digging into my armpit.

"Who goes there?"

We were perhaps fifty feet from the sentry. The light of his torches didn't illuminate us, but our own did. One of my guards held his brand high while the other pulled my cloak back.

"We're returning this to you," he announced.

The sentry peered at me.

"It's Minos," I said. "I'm coming forward."

I began hobbling toward him. Roshel's men decided their work was done and turned back. I guess if my own guys shot me, that wasn't their problem.

"Judge Minos?" the sentry gasped. "What are you doing out there?"

Which was a fair question, if not one you addressed to your supreme commander.

"Get Captain Railes and BlackShield Jarl Lago," I demanded. "And sound the alarm - Yoshana's planning a surprise attack. And get me a chair."

That well and truly kicked over the anthill. The sentry rushed off. Horns sounded, a few at first, then throughout the camp. Men tumbled out of bedrolls, dragging on armor and sword belts. The tumult was deafening. If I was wrong, it was going to be a long night, and I was going to be really unpopular in the morning.

The sentry came rushing back with a whole squad. I suspect he didn't really recognize me and had realized there was at least one Select on the other side. I didn't mind - someone had brought a folding camp chair, and I collapsed into it.

A Paladin came stomping up soon after, a company captain whose name I didn't remember. He was a thickly built man, past middle age. He seemed to know me. At least, he saluted. "Judge Minos."

"Captain. Sorry, I'm not able to stand."

He looked me up and down. "What has happened, Judge Minos?"

"I'm pretty sure Yoshana's going to hit us tonight. Oh, and someone shot me in the leg."

"Where is the medic?" His tone was accusing.

"It's already splinted up. I'm not sure there's much else -"

"Where is the medic?" he roared at the squad of soldiers. Four of them bolted in different directions to find one.

"I apologize, Judge Minos. Perhaps the men forgot you no longer have the power of the Darkness at your command." He stared into my eyes. "Perhaps you forgot as well. Do we have no scouts, that you must reconnoiter enemy positions yourself?"

That drew a wry smile from me. "We certainly have scouts. But there are some things I do have to do myself."

"Ah." The Paladin squatted next to me, still holding my eyes. He stuck out a thick-fingered hand, clenched in a fist. "In my hand I have a talisman that will make a general win any battle against any foe."

I stretched out my palm, wondering what he held, and he opened his. It was empty.

"There's nothing there."

"Just so. Trust in God's will, Judge Minos. The outcome is in his hands, not yours."

"I'm trying to do that."

"Good." He brushed my cheek gently with rough fingers as he stood.

"Judge Minos!" BlackShield Jarl Lago thundered. "By God, where have you been? What have you done?"

Railes came puffing up behind the Monolith commander. He was half the BlackShield's age, but Lago hadn't been stabbed in the lung with a spear.

"Did you see Roshel, boss? Was she buying what you were selling?" he asked. I shrugged. I wished I knew.

Lago turned on my adjutant. "Roshel? He went to see that - that -" Words seemed to fail him. "And you let him?"

"He is our commanding officer. And in case you hadn't noticed, he's a little stubborn."

"Judge Minos, this is not wise. This meeting with the enemy. Combined with the use of the Darkness, it could create doubts…"

"For the men, BlackShield, or for you?" I was more snappish than I should have been. "I understand the morale issues as well as the moral issues, but there's only so much time I can spend managing people's feelings. I'm trying to keep us alive."

"At what cost, Judge Minos? At the cost of our souls?" Even by the torchlight I could tell his face was turning red.

"Leave the boy be, Black," said the other Paladin. "He is tired and wounded."

"He is no boy, Therac!"

"He is, Black."

"He cannot afford to be! We cannot afford for him to be! We all depend on him."

"Just so, Black. So he was explaining to me. And so he acts accordingly. I told him that it were better for him to depend on God. Must I explain the same to you? Ah, here is the medic." And with that, the Paladin gathered up the troops with a wave of his hand and marched off.

Lago blew out air and looked at me sidelong. "I sometimes wonder if Third GrayShield Tabra Therac is a saint. To be honest, he is not the cleverest soldier I know. But sometimes…"

I smiled. "If he is a saint, you might ask him to pray for us. We're getting to the point where that's looking like our best option."

The BlackShield nodded. "I will see to the deployment of the men. Captain Railes, will you inform the Shadowed Hand?"

And the two of them left me alone with the medic. He'd clearly been hoping to get some rest before casualties started coming in and was not pleased to be hauled out of bed to tend to my leg.

"Get up," he ordered, and shoved my crutch into my hands. With no further words he guided me, limping, into a tent, and helped me crawl up onto a wooden table. I was pretty sure he could have been gentler if he'd been in a better mood. When I let loose a cry as he probed the wound, he gave me a leather strip.

"Bite that," he said absently, then went back to poking at me. I wasn't sure how much he could see by the lamplight in the tent, and that might have accounted for some of the pain… but I still suspected a lot of it was bad temper.

"You are lucky, sir."

"Hmm?" I grunted around the gag.

"The kneecap is cracked, and there were some bone splinters stuck in the leg. I think I have removed them all. It could have been much worse."

It certainly didn't feel like it could have been much worse. But it sounded like I'd caught a break. "How long until it recovers?"

"Recovers? Do you mean fully? Oh, never. If you stay off it for two months or so, you will walk again. But you will be limping for the rest of your life."

That didn't sound like so much of a break after all. I felt a quick flash of regret that I hadn't let Roshel heal me.

"Two months off my feet isn't going to happen. There's a war out there."

I could see his sour expression clearly in the lamplight. "Yes, sir. I imagine we will be well supplied with wounded soon enough."

"Can you splint it back up like it was before? So I can at least get around on a crutch?"

"Yes, sir. But -"

"What were you thinking?" Prophetess demanded, bursting into the tent. "Sneaking off in the night to see that - woman?"

That woman? As if I'd gone out on a date? "Still trying to stop a war," I snapped. "It seemed like a better idea than waiting around for all of us to be massacred by a superior force."

"And it worked so well. You're wounded again, and the men are preparing for a fight."

"I wasn't going to be carving a great, glorious swath through the enemy with two good legs, and I found out there's probably an attack coming. How is discovering that a bad thing?"

We glared at each other. The medic bound up my knee again and began working on a better splint while pretending to be deaf. Since he was a Monolith soldier, he no doubt thought Tess was right and I was an idiot at best, a heretic at worst. I glared at him too.

"Minos, you've got to trust -"

"Yes, that was just explained to me. I can trust as if everything depends on God, but I still have to act as if everything depends on me."

"Don't go quoting saints at me."

"Said the prophet."

We glared at each other some more.

"Minos, you're going to get hurt." Her voice broke. "You're going to get killed. And I need you."

It seemed that my heart stopped for a moment. "You've got other generals. Some of them are probably smarter than I am."

"That's not what I meant."

The medic was trying even harder to pretend he was deaf. But whatever Prophetess might have added was interrupted by a soldier throwing wide the tent flap. I'd had more privacy out in the open.

"Judge Minos! Some kind of action in the enemy camp!"

My stomach did a slow somersault. I wasn't enjoying being right. I looked at the medic. He wasn't done with the splint. He shrugged and said, "I need several more minutes or your kneecap will split down the middle with the first step you take."

That must have been an exaggeration given I'd already taken quite a few steps, but I wasn't eager to press my luck. Or hobble on crutches to the top of the hill that would be the best vantage point. Maybe it really was time to sit back and let other people run around.

"I'm not going anywhere I can see the action any time soon," I told the man who'd reported the enemy activity. "Make sure BlackShield Jarl Lago is informed, and set up some relays to get information to me. But the BlackShield has operational command."

The soldier saluted. "Yes, sir."

After he'd left, Prophetess said, "You do realize they will have gone to Lago already? These are Monolith troops. You said it yourself, there are plenty of competent officers. You don't have to do everything."

"Not everything. But some things. Are you done with that?" I asked the medic.

He nodded.

"Thank you. Then how about you hand me my crutch and help me get back into that chair outside, and let's see what's going on."

Cat was outside with a half dozen of the Shadowed Hand.

"Where's the rest of her guards?" I demanded.

"Tent." Cat jerked her chin over her shoulder. Of course Tess would have stormed off as soon as she'd heard about my escapade, leaving confusion in her wake. Now her bodyguards were divided, and she was exposed.

"Get her back there. If this starts to go wrong, the whole Shadowed Hand makes a break for Our Lady with her. That includes the Hidden Moon Clan and Furat and his dog. Keep the dog as close to her as you can."

"Minos -" Tess protested.

"Shut up and for once in your life do what I say. The rest of us are expendable. You're not. Our Lady can hold, with you in it."

Tess swallowed hard. In the torchlight she looked young and vulnerable and not much like a powerful religious icon. She looked like I felt - like someone too young who'd bitten off more than they could chew.

"Is it going to go wrong?" she asked quietly.

I took a deep breath and held it a while before I answered. "If they hit us, it's not going to go well. They've got us outnumbered and outgunned. They'll hit us with the Darkness. Lago's troops are tough and they've got some experience dealing with this kind of thing…" Courtesy of me, when we'd been on opposite sides.

"There's a lot that can happen in a battle," I continued. "But yeah. If they're really coming, it's probably going to go wrong. So how about you go somewhere relatively safe and get ready to run."

Tess opened her mouth but didn't say anything.

Cat gently took her elbow and, to my amazement, Tess actually allowed herself to be led away. I let out a long sigh of relief and collapsed into my folding chair. She was as well defended as I could make her. It really was in God's hands now.

The bulk of the hill loomed dark in front of me and the reports dribbled in. It was agonizing to know that despite the line of couriers the troops set up between me and the hilltop, the news was a minute behind the action. And any questions I asked had a two minute turnaround time before they could be answered. Every few minutes, I considered struggling to my feet and limping to the top of that hill. Every time, pain convinced me otherwise. Instead I gritted my teeth and listened as bits of news and fragments of panicked speculation dribbled down from above. I had to hope not too much was distorted in the relay. More than that, I had to hope BlackShield Jarl Lago was directing the troops more effectively than I could.

I never even learned the name of the soldier at the end of the courier chain who reported to me, and in the dark I couldn't see his face. I wouldn't have recognized him in daylight. He was just a disembodied voice that brought the fragmentary news of our coming doom, and sometimes sent back my ineffectual questions.

"More fires alight in the enemy center."

"Movement. It looks like they are forming up."

"Yes, on the wings too. Not as fast as the center, though."

"Some confusion on the wings." I allowed myself to hope. Had Roshel refused to join the battle?

"No, now they are forming as well."

So I'd failed. The whole of the Darkness Radiant was massing. I sent orders to Railes, telling him to escape with Prophetess at the first sign our lines were buckling. I toyed with the idea of dispatching Furat and Sam to the right wing and the survivors of the Hidden Moon Clan to the left. They couldn't stop us from being flanked by the Darkness, but those forces would have the best chances of detecting and countering it. But in the end I decided against it. I needed them with Tess. Instead we would have to make do with the Monolith rangers. I gave commands that almost certainly duplicated Lago's and probably reinforced the view that I was a waste of flesh.

"Yes sir, we are dug in all along the line."

"Yes sir, the torches are set."

"Sir! Something strange in the enemy center. Fire, sir. Well, yes, sir, they have always had torches and bonfires, sir. I am not sure, sir. I will find out, sir."

"Almost like an explosion. That is what he said, sir."

"The wings! The wings are moving! They are coming!" I considered sending the retreat order to the Shadowed Hand immediately. We weren't likely to withstand the full force of the Darkness Radiant for long. But pulling Prophetess out would shatter morale and doom four thousand men. If we held against their first thrust, there was a small chance they wouldn't have the stomach for a full-scale battle in the dark. I held back.

"No incoming fire yet, sir. No, sir, no outgoing either. It cannot be long, sir." Even in the dark, I could see the courier's eyes wide with fear. These men had faced me and the Shadowed Hand at the Battle of the Cleansing, but Yoshana was something else altogether. I considered asking how our troops were holding up, but just asking the question would make things worse. I bit my tongue and waited.

And then, "They have pulled back, sir!"

What? Did we dare hope - a reprieve? Even - a victory?

"Yes, sir. Their wings have withdrawn. They have broken contact with us. Reformed a quarter of a mile back. They are not attacking, sir. They are not attacking!"

There was a kind of collective gasp of relief throughout the camp. The bulk of Yoshana's forces had pulled back, leaving only the center element facing us - two thousand of her eight thousand troops. They were Knights of Resurrection, her most fanatical corps, but only half our number, with the hill between them and us. They'd have to come over it, split to go around it, or expose their flank if they picked one side or the other. With Grigg and Roshel's men sitting out the battle, Yoshana didn't have the strength to face us.

Railes came running up fifteen minutes later, wheezing like an old tea kettle. "By God, you did it, Minos! Your idiot plan actually worked."

I had to smile. "Looks like it. Send Furat and the Hidden Moon Clan to help keep an eye on their wings, though. It would be just like Yoshana to let us think that and then swing around behind. Make sure they aren't sneaking forces off into the trees, and make sure the sentries stay alert."

The captain grinned. "Go teach your grandmother to suck eggs. Sir. But BlackShield Lago has released the bulk of the troops to rest."

There was a question in that last phrase, though it wasn't framed as one. I nodded. "Yes. Let the men get some sleep. We'll see what tomorrow brings... tomorrow."

Amazing! It seemed Roshel had listened, and not just that, but convinced Grigg as well. My body slumped, weak with relief. In some ways, we had achieved nothing beyond what Yoshana had first offered a year ago. Neutrality for Our Lady while she contended with the Hellguard and the Darkness. But on our terms now, the bulk of her troops refusing to meet us in the field. After she defeated her enemies to the east - if she defeated them - the Overlord wouldn't find it so easy to turn on us. Or so I hoped. So I needed to believe, if the deaths of Seven and Midnight Owl and dozens of others weren't to have been for nothing.

I fell asleep in my chair in the warm night, and wasn't troubled by dreams.

Someone was shaking me. There were trumpets and drums, and shouts, and gunshots. I blinked my eyes over and over in the gray light that came just before dawn. I wasn't sure where I was, or why I might be there.

"Judge Minos! Judge Minos!" A soldier had my shoulder, shaking it none too gently. I was still sitting in my chair. A low lying mist clung to the camp, blurring anything more than a hundred feet away into a haze. Awareness flooded in. The calm of the night before was shattered. We were in battle.

"Oh God, Judge Minos, they have unleashed hell itself! A demon serves them, a monster that cannot be killed, it is in our ranks, they have attacked, we cannot hold them!"

I struggled upright in the chair, trying to keep up with the flood of the man's babble. A demon? Were some of the Hellguard supporting Yoshana? Had Grigg and Roshel turned on us after all? The man's panic was in danger of infecting me. I could feel my pulse pounding in my temples. My knee and the wound on my face throbbed in sympathy.

"Pull yourself together and report properly," I snapped. "What's your name, soldier?"

"Wilm, sir."

"Wilm. All right, Wilm, are we engaged by the whole enemy army or just their center corps?"

"Just the center, sir, but we cannot stop them, the monster -"

"Hold up, Wilm. This monster. How big? What's it look like?"

"It is huge, sir. Arms longer than a man's body, and it cannot be stopped nor killed -"

"It's Pious," Railes said. I hadn't seen or heard him come up, even though he was gasping again. "He's got the Darkness in him. Must have. He's five times as strong as he was, and bullets don't stop him."

"God damn it." I grabbed my crutch and levered myself to my feet, then regretted both the phrase and the action. I stopped and sucked in a deep breath. "Yoshana had all the Darkness she took from Seven. She must have put it in Pious."

"But could he control that?" Railes asked.

"He isn't controlling it. She's made a berserker. Pointed him at us and told him to kill. Which is what he'd want to do anyway." I remembered the mindless bloodlust when I'd let the Darkness rule me, the boundless rage. That must be close to Pious' natural state. There would be no subtlety to the infected man, but he would be virtually unstoppable. "How are we doing?"

"Not good," Railes said. "They've come around the hill to our left and they're just rolling us up as they come. They're pretty much going through us like a knife through butter. What do we do?"

"Well, obviously we need to stop Pious. Keep shooting him. He can't survive that forever. Aim for the head. And get oil grenades or anything else that'll catch fire. We're going to have to burn him."

"Yessir. I'm on it." Railes lurched away.

"Hey, wait up!" I called. Which was stupid, because time was of the essence, and I was slow.

"Don't worry, boss," my adjutant called back. "You'll get a front row seat. He's heading this way."

I limped toward the front through a desolate landscape, a chaos of tents thrown down and cook pots kicked over as men scrambled to stop the unstoppable. Noise continued to build ahead, lost in the wall of fog.

And how exactly was I going to help? I had been more than a match for Pious with the Darkness in me and not in him. Now? He had been formidable when he was nothing more than a strong, brutal man. With all the Darkness of a Hellguard inside him, he would be one of the most dangerous creatures on the face of the earth.

Fire had stopped me when the Darkness had taken over my mind. I had to believe it could stop him too. In any case, I needed to be at the front to organize the defenses and try to turn Yoshana's tide. Pious was her one-man shock force, her battering ram, but the Overlord herself would be leading her troops to exploit the breach. We had the numbers, and the Monolith troops were disciplined veterans - as I'd learned to my cost fighting against them - but I also knew that fear would let a smaller force rout a far larger one.

My knee twinged with every clumsy step I took. The thought of facing Pious in my current state was ludicrous. I couldn't even run away from him.

A huge figure stepped around a tent in front of me. Its white tabard was soaked red with blood. A bare blade was in its hand.

I dropped my crutch, hopped on one foot, and jerked my katana clear of its sheath. I balanced precariously as it came on, features resolving into someone I recognized as the mist eddied away.

I felt as foolish as I looked when I realized it was Grigg. Not because I was so sure he was no threat to me, but because there was nothing I could do if he was.

"Roshel was right," the big man said. I realized gore was dripping from his sword. The blood on his clothes probably wasn't his. "You really do look like hell."

"People keep saying that." I tried to keep my voice steady. "You're going to give me a complex if you keep it up."

"What's got you limping your sorry butt to the front?"

I grounded my katana's point in the earth and leaned on it. "Yoshana's new monster needs killing."

"Ah. Yeah." He looked down at his blade. "That's taken care of already. It really doesn't matter how much of the Darkness is in you. Once your arms are cut off, your head's going to follow pretty close behind. Strong as a bull, that one, but just about as smart. Not real quick, either."

"I thought he was quick enough."

"Then I didn't teach you as much as I should have when we traveled together."

I pulled the katana's scabbard from my belt, sheathed the weapon, and leaned on that. It made a better crutch than the blade alone. I could still hear the sounds of combat through the mist. I didn't understand what was happening. "Why'd you do it, Grigg? Not that I'm not grateful. But killing Pious is different from standing aside."

He shrugged. "He was a jerk. Always going on about killing Paladins. I was a Paladin, you remember. I figure he did for a few of my friends and had it coming. The truth is, Minos, some things shouldn't exist. Pious with the Darkness in him was one of them."

"She's going to be furious."

Grigg shook his head. He looked sad. "I don't think so. It's over now anyway."

"What do you mean?" I pointed toward the front. "There's still fighting going on over there. I have to go help shut her down. We have the numbers, but now she's got momentum on her side."

He shook his head again. "She's not there. That assault's stalled. It was a feint anyway. You never were able to stay far enough ahead of her. But you shouldn't feel bad. No one ever could."

He looked at my blank stare and gave me a wan smile. "You play chess. You've heard of a back row mate?"

It was a particularly frustrating way of losing. After castling, the king could wind up undefended, trapped behind pawns that had never advanced. An enemy rook or queen in the back row could end the game instantly, regardless of what was happening elsewhere on the board.

"I think you've fallen for it."

My mind tried to catch up to what he was saying. For a year, Yoshana had been trying to discredit and kill Prophetess. Now, humiliated in a face to face confrontation and with her armies deserting her, the Overlord might be willing to settle for killing without discrediting. And our troops had been drawn away from Tess' position.

I hopped helplessly on my one good leg. "Run, Grigg. Please. Save her."

He pursed his lips, then nodded. "I'll go. But if I'm right, it's too late."

He jogged back the way I had come. I took two staggering hops forward, then drew the katana again and slashed the bindings that locked my knee in place. Using both legs and the sheathed sword as a cane, I made much better time, though a lance of agony stabbed me every time I put weight on the wounded joint.

But Grigg had been right. It was too late.

11. Darkness Falls

The big Select was standing helplessly a dozen paces from Prophetess' tent. Just outside, Tess stood with Yoshana's blade at her throat. Her Shadowed Hand bodyguards lay scattered on the ground. Cat's body was crumpled at Tess' feet.

I couldn't describe the feeling that came over me, if it was hot or cold, if it was rage or fear. It stopped me in my tracks. I could do nothing but stare.

My eyes went to the chip where Seven's staff had snapped a shard out of Yoshana's strange, dark sword. I was sure the rest of that matte gray blade was sharp enough to split a hair. Tess was very still, her mouth thinned to a tight line but her face composed. If I'd been in her place, I would have peed down my leg. I wasn't sure that I hadn't.

"A long-dead priest once wrote that prophets are fine, but their disciples are really hard to take," Yoshana said. "It seems to be true of you, Minos. You've certainly been a gigantic pain in my ass. You've defied me, you've betrayed me, you've even turned my own lieutenants against me."

Her glance swung balefully toward Grigg. He opened his mouth, then shut it again.

"But I have to say, I'm not liking your prophet very much either."

Prophetess swallowed, then flinched away as the movement brought her neck fractionally closer to the Overlord's blade. Yoshana smiled. It wasn't a nice expression. Her white cloak and hair swirled in a breeze of her own making as the Darkness stirred. Her crimson leather armor looked more like blood than ever, matching her mahogany skin. She was a thing of red and white, a goddess of blood and bone.

"Yosha, no," Grigg said.

"You shut up," she replied without heat. "If you hadn't interfered back in Stephensburg, we wouldn't be here now."

What could I say that would change what was about to happen? What could I do? There was nothing. Cat and the Shadowed Hand had tried to stop Yoshana, and done nothing but sacrifice themselves. I supposed I could at least do that.

"If I'm annoying you so much, maybe you should kill me instead." It was a stupid, reckless thing to say, and wasn't even much of a gambit - since nothing prevented her from killing us both.

The Overlord was ahead of me, as usual. She laughed. "'Instead?' Why not 'also?' Although it looks like you might keel over on your own. But you're not the point, Minos. She is. You can use the Darkness, but so can plenty of other people. She can turn it."

She touched the edge of Tess' throat with her blade. "Do you think you can turn my sword, too?"

"Do not be afraid of those who kill the body but cannot kill the soul; rather, be afraid of the one who can destroy both soul and body in Gehenna," Tess said softly.

Among the many things Tess did that were foolish and annoying, provoking Yoshana had to be the least helpful of all. I started to interject, to forestall the cut that would end Tess' life, but the Overlord just laughed. "What makes you think I can only do one and not the other?"

Even more quietly, Tess murmured, "Soul of Christ, sanctify me; body of Christ, save me; blood of Christ, inebriate me; water from Christ's side, wash me; passion of Christ, strengthen me; o good Jesus, hear me; within thy wounds hide me; suffer me not to be separated from thee; from the malicious enemy defend me; in the hour of my death call me."

"Huh. Anima Christi. I'd figured you'd go with Psalm Twenty Three. The valley of the shadow of death would be appropriate. But you see how annoying she is." Yoshana seemed to be addressing me. "Here she is, about to die, and she's mouthing pious nonsense like it's going to save her. When I can feel her fear. The thing is..."

The Overlord paused. Eerily, only her hair and cloak moved. "The thing is, at first I thought she was just an idiot with a big mouth. And then it turned out she was an idiot people followed. And then, well, then she was an idiot who could resist me."

The Overlord's eyes bored into mine. She didn't seem to blink. "That's a hell of a thing, Minos. To fear me - because she does fear me - and still resist me. And now... now she's even turning my own people. I was sure she wasn't a factor, not really. But now I'm not sure anymore."

Of course Prophetess was a factor. She was *the* factor. She was the king in the chess game between light and darkness. And our king had been checkmated.

"I can end it now." Again Yoshana seemed to read my mind. Even at this distance she probably could.

"Another will follow to stop you," Tess said softly.

"Maybe. I'm not sure." Again the hesitation.

"I'm not sure!" the Overlord repeated, snarling the words. "And that's the thing of it. I'm always sure. You wondered why I'm so much stronger than you, Minos? Why I control the Darkness so much better? Because I'm always sure. My will, my desires, my every thought, in perfect unity. That's why I'm the one to unite humanity, the one to stop the demons and the Darkness!"

Her face darkened with rage, and then stilled. "There can only be one of us to carry humanity's banner. I've engineered everything to be that one, and yet here I stand with my own armies deserting me. Clausewitz said war is the province of chance. In no other sphere of human activity must such a margin be left for this intruder. It increases the uncertainty of every circumstance and deranges the course of events."

She glared at Grigg, and moved her sword away from Tess' throat. With a fluid motion too fast to follow, she reversed the blade and stepped toward me, shoving Tess aside. "Who would have thought. There can only be one, and it isn't me."

I stood rooted as she came on. She stopped a foot away and extended the sword hilt. "Only one."

"Yosha, no!" Grigg exclaimed. "Why? Put the sword down and come away with me. We've fought enough, done enough. We can -"

"Go plant corn and raise children? You don't know me at all if you think I can just walk away. That would never have been, Grigg, even before you betrayed me."

"I -"

"Minos is inferior to you in every way except the one that matters. He stood up for his woman when it counted."

The big man looked like he'd been stabbed in the gut.

Yoshana thrust the sword hilt at me. "Better do it quickly. The Darkness has always obeyed me because it was aligned with my will. It's not liking this very much."

I grasped the sword. It was warm in my hand. I looked at Grigg's anguished face. "I can't."

The Overlord's mouth twisted. The sapphire eyes blazed into mine. "Do it, you worthless, gutless worm, or you and your girlfriend will end up like her useless bodyguards."

Cat's body accused me from the ground at Tess' feet. I brought the blade back.

"And now it's too late." Yoshana's hand locked around my wrist. I gasped as the bones ground together. Her eyes were as black as mine. The Darkness poured out of her skin, coiling around her arm, rising like serpents above her. The voice that came was nothing like hers. "Far too late, little - Ah!"

She staggered and loosed her grip. Behind her, Prophetess looked for another rock to throw.

The edge of the blade was sharper than thought. Yoshana's head fell cleanly away at my stroke.

For a moment, the Darkness held the blood in and her body remained standing. Then the cloud rushed out, huge and black, and she fell. The swirling mass gathered, hovered, floated toward Grigg. It almost reached him before it recoiled and streamed away into the sky.

The Select stood rooted for a moment that stretched on forever. I met his black eyes, not knowing what would come next. Then, slowly, he trudged up to me.

There were tears on his cheeks. Without a word he gathered up the body and head, cradling them in his arms. In death, Yoshana was a small woman.

"We have to burn the body," I choked out.

"No."

"Grigg, I'm sorry, but she's been dead before. We have to -"

"No." This time it was Tess that said it. I looked at her in surprise. "Let her rest, Minos. Let him take her."

She laid her hand on Grigg's shoulder. She was crying too. He gave her the barest of sad smiles, then turned and walked away.

12. Aftermath

Tess was in my arms, trembling and sobbing. I held her, stroked her hair, and wished there was a way to tell her that my leg really hurt and I wanted very badly to sit down.

"Headache, me," came a small voice from behind us. Tess spun out of my arms, and we both gawked to see Cat groggily sitting up. The other Shadowed Hand bodyguards were also beginning to stir.

"She must have just stunned them," I marveled. It was a technique I'd often used, throttling opponents into unconsciousness with the Darkness, but I hadn't imagined Yoshana would do anything other than kill. "She said - she implied -"

"She was making it easier for you." For the first time, there was respect and not just revulsion in Tess' voice when she spoke about Yoshana. "She was more complicated than I thought."

"Do you think she planned it this way when she first came for you?"

Tess shrugged and brushed at her tears. "I don't know. No? I was sure she was going to kill me. Maybe when she saw Grigg was with you...?"

"Happening, tell me," Cat demanded. So we did.

The battle was over by the time I hobbled to the front. Hundreds had died. We'd taken heavy losses at first, probably half from Pious himself. But when Grigg had cut him down, the offensive had stalled, and the weight of numbers had told against the Knights of Resurrection. They'd retreated in good order, but they'd suffered during the process.

Grigg had not returned to his troops. Two of Yoshana's three corps were left leaderless. I convened a parley with Roshel and explained the situation. At first she'd refused to believe, then she'd broken into tears. But she wasn't one of the deadliest warriors and most feared military leaders on the continent because she was weak-willed. In a moment she pulled herself together and took command of the entire host of the Darkness Radiant.

And then, on top of the hill where Seven and Yoshana had fought and Tess had resisted the Darkness, Roshel asked Tess to cast it out of her in front of everyone.

I had to admit my jaw fell open.

"Yoshana showed me a way to live with myself. To live with what I am," the dark-haired Overlord said. "But Prophetess showed me a better way."

The sun was high overhead, beating down on the hilltop. Tess' white robes shone in the light, and if I really tried, I could maybe feel something of what had washed over me when she'd freed me from the Darkness.

As they said the words together, Roshel bowed her head, and then raised it to the light and vomited up a black cloud that seemed too big to have fit in her body.

"Was there that much in me?" I asked Dee.

He shook his head. "I don't think so."

Soldiers with torches rushed in, but the Darkness was too quick for them. It shot straight up into the sky and vanished from sight.

Roshel slumped, shivering with reaction. Tess held her, then clasped her hand and lifted it into the air. The thunderous cheers and applause from our forces didn't surprise me. The cheers and applause from the Darkness Radiant did.

Roshel turned to face me. "Judge Minos, the Darkness Radiant is yours to command. Use it in the service of the light."

I sat on that hilltop with Railes, Lago, and - surprisingly and a little unnervingly - Father Roric. The warm sun beamed down out of a cloudless sky. Below, two armies were packing their gear, preparing to march for Stephensburg.

Roshel had kept almost all of the Darkness Radiant together. Yoshana's core loyalists, the Knights of Resurrection, had lost nearly two hundred men in Pious' charge. Another five companies had slunk away, unwilling to serve the man who'd killed their revered leader. But over twelve hundred of that group of hardened veterans remained, along with the six thousand who'd been under Grigg and Roshel's command.

Grigg still hadn't returned. It seemed that he might never come back. But a dozen of the Darkness Radiant's troopers with about as much of the Darkness in them as the Hidden Moon Clan had presented themselves for exorcism.

Seven, Yoshana, and Pious were dead. Grigg had left. The Darkness was driven out of Roshel and the other survivors. Sitting in the sun and looking out over the green fields and gentle rolling hills, it was easy to forget it still existed in the world.

But of course it did, and I now commanded almost fifteen thousand men and women dedicated to opposing it. Nearly twenty thousand more soldiers of the Source had answered to Yoshana and were now leaderless.

I turned Yoshana's blade over in my hands. Grigg hadn't claimed it, and I couldn't leave a weapon like that lying in the mud. It had the shape of a traditional katana, but the whole sword - blade, hilt, guard - seemed to be forged from a single piece of... what? It was a dull, matte gray. It was warmer to the touch than metal. The hilt was knurled for grip, rather than wrapped with cloth or leather. It was sharp enough to split a hair. The only flaw was the chip smashed out of its edge by Seven's spear. I had no idea how that could possibly be fixed.

The weapon was as unique and irreplaceable as its owner. The world wouldn't see the likes of either one again. After years of fearing her and fighting an impossible battle against her, I was free of Yoshana. I found I wanted to cry.

"What are you thinking, Judge Minos?" asked BlackShield Jarl Lago.

"I'm thinking I'm in pretty sorry shape to be commanding an army this big."

He rumbled a deep laugh. I'd deflected the question away from my true feelings, but I'd meant what I'd said. I had a real crutch now and my leg had been splinted again by the same medic, who hadn't said a word but who'd given me a very dirty look for making him repeat his efforts. My face still hurt from the gouge torn into it by the lash of Yoshana's Darkness. I hadn't asked any of the people I'd met who'd suffered similar wounds if it ever stopped hurting. I hoped it would. It was clear the scar would be with me forever. And now a swelling and livid bruise had risen on my wrist where Yoshana had seized me. She was gone, but she'd certainly left her mark on me - literally as well as figuratively.

"I guess… it's a shame. All those deaths, and then Yoshana just gave up in the end. There must have been a way forward to the same place that didn't waste so many lives."

Lago frowned. "How many died when you and I fought each other? Nearly ten times as many? And for what? So men in the Monolith or Rockwall could lay claim to land that was not theirs? All war is waste. Some wars more than others. We always wish there would be another way, unless we are monsters. Perhaps this time there was. But I did not see it. I was proud to serve with you. So were all those here."

I wasn't quite sure how true that was. The Monolith troops weren't necessarily my biggest fans. I looked over at Railes to check his reaction, but he was looking away.

"Uh oh," he said.

Painfully I craned my head around to follow his glance. Prophetess was stamping up the hill with a determined look on her face. She came to a stop two feet from me.

"Minos," she announced, "Some dead Overlord said I was your woman."

There were nervous chuckles from the three men around me. I sat motionless, transfixed with panic as she continued relentlessly.

"If I'm going to be your woman, I should get to know you better." She stuck out her hand. "My name's Genia Carter. I'm pleased to meet you."

Book Five - Covenant Against Darkness

"Our adherents never forgive us if we take sides against ourselves:
for in their eyes this means not only rejecting their love but also exposing their intelligence."

Friedrich Nietzsche

1. Stephen

"It's going to rain," I complained. "I can feel it."

Railes glared at me. The skull tattooed on the side of my adjutant's face contorted hideously. "Don't give me that. You're what, not even twenty, and you're already one of those old farts who feels the rain in his aching joints?"

I shrugged. "It's true."

And it was. Stephensburg was not far from the battleground where Yoshana had fallen and we'd seized control of the Darkness Radiant. But it had taken time for Roshel to reassign its officer corps under her leadership, rewarding talented veterans while purging the highest ranks of those most loyal to the previous Overlord commander. I'd given her as long as she wanted. My attempt to unify Rockwall and Monolith forces in the service of Our Lady had been an abysmal failure. I may not have been much of a general, but I wasn't going to make the same mistake twice.

It had taken time to bury the dead, too. Speaking of mistakes. Maybe BlackShield Jarl Lago had been right, and there hadn't been a better way. At least the death toll had been nowhere near as bad as the Battle of the Cleansing. Which meant our army had grown again. And big armies traveled slowly, at the pace of the most sluggish ox-drawn supply wagon. The fact that half those wagons had carried our wounded - including me - didn't make them any faster. None of us appreciated being jostled.

I'd enjoyed the time Tess and I spent sitting and holding hands in the wagon. Moments before she'd died, Yoshana had called Tess my woman. Somehow, the last words of an enemy had crystalized something between us that nothing else had. When I'd first met her, Tess had refused to even tell me her name, saying God had called her to be Prophetess and nothing more. I'd irreverently shortened the term to Tess. Now, with her mission achieved and Yoshana defeated, she was once again using her birth name of Genia Carter. But for me, she was still Tess. The nickname symbolized a bond formed through two years of struggle.

Anyway, all that time waiting and bouncing along in the wagon had given me plenty of opportunities to learn how my injured knee felt about changes in the weather. It was healing, thanks to my Select metabolism, but there was a special twinge when rain was coming.

Railes looked up at the sky, blue with scattered clouds. "Bull," he declared.

"Have it your way. Sleep outside tonight. You'll see."

"The way things are going, we might be sleeping outside this gate before they open up."

That was rapidly becoming a sore point. Our column was halted just outside Stephensburg's walled inner city. The troops holding the gate weren't in any hurry to let us in.

The situation was complicated. I was surprised to find myself thinking it, but we would have benefited from a professional politician. Yoshana had been Stephen's hand, commander of his armies. As well as the power behind his throne or, as Railes had so eloquently phrased it, "the arm stuck up his ass making his mouth move."

Yoshana was dead. Roshel was her most senior remaining officer and had taken command of her troops in the field, then pledged them to me. In one sense, that meant the Darkness Radiant answered to Our Lady. Except Stephen still thought it answered to Stephen, since they were mostly his men.

It had been nervous going when we'd first approached the city. Yoshana had split her forces into three legions commanded by herself, Roshel, and the Select Grigg. Portions of each legion had been in the battle against Our Lady's troops, what the men were now calling the Battle of Darkness Falling. It was a play on words, of course, because the Darkness - in the form of the demon Seven, the possessed berserker Pious, and Yoshana herself - had all fallen. With the Darkness cast out of Roshel and the rest of the infected on both sides, it had been a great victory for the light.

For Our Lady the words conveyed nothing but that victory. For the Darkness Radiant, I wasn't so sure. They'd lost their leader and surrendered to an inferior force. And so there was the question of what would happen with the remainder of each legion garrisoned at Stephensburg. It had been clear enough that Roshel's men in the city would follow us; the question of Yoshana and Grigg's troops had been more interesting.

"Interesting" in the way that a possible civil war in an urban environment was interesting.

We'd made the most triumphant approach to the city we could muster. Drums beat, trumpets sounded, the men marched in splendid order, tabards as white and shining as weeks in the field would allow. The wounded had followed behind, an unmentioned corollary to triumph. Like the dead. And Yoshana's Knights of Resurrection who'd deserted in disgust.

In the end it had proven to be a lot of worry over nothing. Even purged of the Darkness, Roshel was formidable enough to simply assert command and be accepted. True, we hadn't advertised the fact that she no longer had the power to melt flesh from bones at her slightest whim.

The only place we'd run into any difficulty was right here, at the gate to Stephensburg's inner administrative district. Obviously word of the change in command had gotten ahead of us, and Stephen was trying to decide what to make of it. He didn't seem to be in a hurry.

A soldier unfolded a camp chair behind me, and I gratefully sank into it. I wasn't going to trundle up to see Stephen sitting in a wagon, and riding a horse hurt more than walking. I could limp along and stand for a while using my katana as a cane - but not for very long. The question now would be whether I'd be able to get out of the chair again.

"What's taking so long?" Tess asked.

Prophetess Genia Carter, banisher of the Darkness, conqueror of Yoshana, spiritual leader to a combined army of nearly thirty thousand men. The closest thing there was to a living religious icon. Not, however, known for her patience.

"How would I know?" I said. Not the most insightful or respectful response from the general to his prophet, or perhaps the wisest way of speaking to my girlfriend. But it was true. I speculated, since I didn't have anything else to do. "I'd guess Stephen's trying to figure out if this is good or bad for him. He's out from under Yoshana's thumb, but his army just shifted allegiances without his permission. Kind of tough for a ruler to know what to make of that."

I let out a little grunt as my face twinged. Now that I was sitting, my knee didn't hurt as much. That meant the wound opening my cheek from lip to eyebrow got to take its turn demanding my attention.

In many ways I was lucky. Yoshana's burst of Darkness hadn't killed me or blinded me. The gouge it had ripped hadn't actually torn a hole all the way through my face, so I could eat without food falling out of the side of my mouth. There was no exposed bone.

But it wasn't the kind of dashing little scar that women admired. It was the kind of awful-looking thing people unconsciously backed away from, in case it was somehow contagious, or whatever had inflicted it was still following me around. I was lucky I already had a girl - to her credit and my relief, Tess never shied away from it.

The wound hadn't bled. That was the way of injuries dealt by the Darkness. They just hurt. It was healing, slowly. It would always be hideous, but I hoped that in time it would stop looking like raw meat. Railes was missing an ear on the tattooed side of his face and hissed like a teakettle when he exerted himself thanks to a spear he'd taken in the lung a year before. He was greatly amused that I was now both less mobile and uglier than he was.

"Open, me," Cat suggested, eyeing the gate. The paleo girl was Tess' bodyguard, Railes' lover, and one of my closest friends. She was also a vicious savage. When she suggested she could open the gate, she meant she could scale the wall and murder the guards.

"No, Cat."

She made a rude noise and went to play with Hafnum Furat's big, white dog, Sam. The dog - and Furat - were another critical part of Tess' protection. The dog could sense the Darkness, and Furat had a huge pistol and was good at shooting things with it. With Yoshana dead, Grigg vanished, Roshel on our side, and Tess perhaps immune to that sort of attack anyway, there shouldn't be much to worry about on that score - but it didn't pay to take chances with the Darkness.

We'd won a great victory, but the situation was still fluid. There were hundreds of Yoshana's veterans who hadn't accepted the outcome of the battle. I didn't know where they'd gone. Some might remain with our forces, a fifth column waiting to strike. I wasn't going to have our leader, who I happened to love, assassinated in our moment of triumph.

"Ah," boomed a voice from above. "The prophet of Our Lady and her Select."

I struggled to my feet. Stephen stood on the wall, gray-uniformed guards around him. He wasn't a tall man, but the silk shirt under his fur cloak was open to the waist, showing tanned, muscular flesh.

Or the appearance of it. When we'd first met, he had been so grotesquely fat he could barely walk. Yoshana had remade him with the Darkness. I suspected it remained in him, giving him an unnatural appearance of health. A woman, taller than he and regal in appearance, stood at his side.

"It's ironic, Minos," the lord of the Source continued. "Now you stand at the head of an army, but you seem so much the worse for wear."

"The price of war, Lord Stephen. Some paid a far higher price than I. But with peace restored, perhaps we could meet and discuss the disposition of this army?"

Stephen seemed to ignore my request. Instead he continued, "I'd heard you commanded the Darkness, but then gave it up. That seemed hard to credit, but by your condition, I suppose it must be true. How very strange."

Tess piped up, "Lord Stephen, both Minos and Roshel have rejected the Darkness. God has cast it out of them. I beg you, do the same."

He snorted. "Roshel, too? I'd heard it but didn't believe it. How can both of you be such fools?"

"Lord Stephen -"

"Be silent, peasant. I'm talking to your betters. Are all the rumors true, then, Minos? Yoshana dead, Grigg gone, the Darkness Radiant possessed of the Darkness no more?"

Tess nodded slowly, even though the question had been addressed to me. My blood had started to boil the moment "peasant" had passed the nasty little despot's lips, but she seemed unperturbed. Stephen was lucky I didn't have the Darkness in me anymore, or he wouldn't have enjoyed finding out which of us controlled it better.

A hellish smile spread across his face, almost as if he could read my thoughts. "Then I am truly the only power remaining. There is nothing to discuss. The Darkness Radiant is mine, Minos. You will return it to my direct command at once."

Tess shook her head. "Lord Stephen, the Darkness is the power of sin and corruption. It is evil given form. Reject it and return to the light."

"Insect! You dare make demands of me? I am the lawful ruler of the Source and master of its armies. My will is supreme!"

Cat was growling deep in her throat. I could tell she was trying to judge whether her knife, which wasn't balanced for throwing, could take him in the eye at that range. I was pretty sure it could. I was really tempted to let her find out but set a warning hand on her arm instead.

Sam either sensed the Darkness in Stephen or picked up on Cat's tension. The dog began barking furiously.

Stephen ranted on, oblivious. "My will is absolute! No one will deny me now, least some sniveling tool of an obsolete church. You will assemble my armies outside my walls at the first hour of the morning tomorrow, and then you may withdraw with the rabble you brought from Our Lady. Skulk back to your temples and mouth your prayers. Go preach repentance to the demons and see how it profits you. I don't care. But my men will be returned to me."

"We'll withdraw now and consider your proposal," I said, backing away, which seemed - just barely - like a better response than letting Cat try to kill him and start a civil war.

"Consider? You will obey! I will not tolerate defiance! At the first hour tomorrow, Select. You hear me?"

I nodded. "I hear."

"That could have gone better," I remarked when we'd returned to our headquarters outside the city.

Roshel, BlackShield Jarl Lago, and the other senior officers hadn't accompanied us and needed to be briefed. Afterward, Lago rumbled, "It is not very different from what I would expect, Judge Minos. Why would you have thought otherwise?"

"The Darkness has driven him mad," Tess said. "You should have seen his face."

The senior Paladin dipped his head respectfully to her. "That may be, Prophetess, but his behavior is like any ruler's. He claims what he believes to be his by right, and seizes any advantage he can."

"I'm with Lago," Roshel chimed in. "It's unfortunate you told him I'd been cleansed of the Darkness. He's going to be feeling pretty invincible now."

Tess glared at her. "So you think we should have lied?"

The beautiful, dark-haired Overlord who'd been one of the leaders of the Darkness Radiant shrugged. "Perfect honesty usually isn't the best policy in war. You don't have to be a creature of the Darkness to know that."

Her smile was perfectly sweet and perfectly calibrated to send Tess' blood pressure through the roof. I hurried to intervene.

"He'd heard the rumor already. He might not even have believed us if we'd denied it. The question is, what do we do now?"

I looked around at the assembly of officers and others, gathered under a broad awning stretched across poles. In addition to those with senior military roles like Roshel, Lago, and Railes, we had Tess and her most trusted guards - Cat, Furat, and his dog. And of course Doctor John Dee, the opinionated occultist who'd been at Tess' side for nearly two years and, with Cat, had become one of my closest and unlikeliest friends.

Dee was a windbag, a braggart, and a coward. His ideas had been sometimes brilliant and sometimes terrible, and had almost always nearly gotten me killed. I turned to him with a mixture of hope and trepidation.

"The questions are twofold," he said. "To how much of the army do we have a right? And how much of it can we control?"

Before anyone else could even try to answer, he plowed ahead. "As to the question of right, the greater part of what is now the Darkness Radiant was originally the army of Stephensburg, pledged to Stephen. For that matter, Yoshana pledged her own troops to Stephen as well. Even the forces of Our Lady are a bit questionable, as in civil matters Our Lady owes allegiance to the Source and Stephen as its ruler."

"I swore my troops to Prophetess, not to some Darkness-infested princeling," Lago growled.

"And I'm the commander of the Darkness Radiant now," Roshel added. "It goes where I tell it."

Dee smiled. "So let's simply say the issue of right is complex. Then as it so often does, it comes down to a question of might. How much of the army can we control?"

"My troops answer to me, to Judge Minos, to Prophetess, and to God," Lago declared. "Never to Stephen."

Dee raised a finger. "Very good. Four thousand in our column. Only, what, twenty five thousand yet to account for?"

Roshel said, "The ones that were in the field with me at Darkness Falling will be loyal. The others... I couldn't say yet. If it were a contest between Yoshana and Stephen, they'd almost all follow her. But I'm not Yoshana."

"So. Eleven thousand in total are ours. Some eighteen thousand of unknown allegiance. The easiest course would be to withdraw to Our Lady with our eleven thousand and let any others who choose follow us."

I shook my head. "Leaving eighteen thousand men under the control of a lunatic infected with the Darkness doesn't appeal much. Tess is right - he didn't look sane. I've had that stuff in me, and it works on your head. Not in good ways. God knows what he might do with that in him and without Yoshana controlling him."

Dee raised his eyebrows. "The alternative may be civil war. Inside a city, the bloodshed would be... considerable. I believe Father Roric specifically cautioned you on that point?"

Our Lady's Advocate for Justice had lectured me on the principles of just war. The cause had to be righteous, but the conduct of operations also had to minimize casualties.

Fortunately, Roric was with us in Stephensburg. Or perhaps unfortunately, since I still found the priest intimidating. "I can ask for his views," I said.

Roshel shook her head. "Let me take the temperature of the unit commanders in the city. I'll see which way they're going to jump, and see who I can influence. Just buy me some time tomorrow."

I didn't know exactly what Stephen expected. There wasn't room for twenty nine thousand men to assemble and pledge their allegiance to him outside the gate to the administrative district. And it would have looked like a prelude to invasion. I opted for a single battalion... consisting entirely of Lago's Monolith troops, who had no allegiance at all to Stephen. I was hoping that point would be lost on him.

There was a small chance that, with the night to sleep on it, he'd repented and decided to forego Yoshana's dubious "blessing." Tess could purge the Darkness from him. I didn't think it was likely, but I didn't have any brilliant ideas, so I prepared to stall for time while Roshel assessed divided loyalties. And we all hoped for the best.

The early morning was cool, even at the beginning of summer. A light rain had in fact fallen during the night, and mist rose off the puddles in the cobblestone streets. Nonetheless, the monarch appeared atop the wall as he had the day before, shirt open to reveal the appearance of tanned muscle. I had seen the Darkness melt the fat out of his body, liquid rivulets of it running like wax out of his pores. I fought down a wave of nausea at the memory.

Once again he was flanked by a small contingent of soldiers and the tall woman. Her angular face was composed and she regarded us with no more concern than she would have given an equal number of ants. Stephen smiled as he saw me watching her.

"This is Melaret, my consort. Another of the fine things one can have with the power you idiotically set aside. Have you come to deliver my troops to me, Select?"

I cleared my throat. My knee hurt. "Lord Stephen, you will appreciate that a transfer of power is not accomplished instantly. There is confusion among the men after the death of Yoshana. They were accustomed to answering to her."

"They answer to me!"

Even Stephen's guard recoiled fractionally at the shrill scream. Only Melaret remained unmoved.

He steadied his voice to a venomous hiss. "I am the lord of the Source. This city, these men, all the lands beyond, including your little prophet's church, they are all mine by right. And let's not play games, Select. They're mine by main force as well. Who will deny me that? You're no Yoshana. I don't share power with the likes of you, or peasant prophets, or Overlord whores who've set aside the source of their strength. Who else is fit to rule here but me? I didn't summon you to make excuses. I summoned you to deliver me my army."

I winced. "Lord Stephen, the issue is that your army may not be entirely ready to be delivered. A substantial part of it is pledged to the elimination of the Darkness. We need a bit more time -"

"Time?" Stephen roared. A black cloud began to form around him. "Time for treachery? Time for disloyalty? Bring the traitors to me and I will strike them down! I will purge the ranks until -"

His body went rigid as Melaret buried a knife in his back. When Cat stabbed someone from behind, the blade slid up under the ribs through the kidneys. Stephen's consort had driven her stiletto down from above in a clumsy overhand blow. It was amazing the knife hadn't caught on bone.

The Darkness seethed in the air. Face twisted into a mask of disgust, rage, and terror, the woman plunged the thin blade into him again and again.

It wouldn't have been possible to kill Yoshana that way. She would have healed as fast as the damage was done and swatted the attacker like a bug. Stephen wasn't Yoshana. The skin sagged on his bones as the Darkness left him. His body toppled from the wall and smashed onto the ground at our feet with a sickening crunch. I was pretty sure he was dead before he hit.

The Darkness continued to ooze out of the corpse, a pathetic mist that reminded me more of cockroaches fleeing the light than the gigantic, lethal mass that had streamed from Yoshana on her death.

The gray-uniformed guards on the wall were very still.

"Stephen is dead," Melaret announced. "Long live Stephen."

Tess and I sat at a huge table of elaborately carved mahogany and moved food around on our plates. Melaret picked daintily at an egg, exactly like a refined lady who hadn't just stabbed a man to death. Light streamed into the dining room through diamond-paned windows of exceptional clarity.

My plate was heaped with sausages, potatoes, eggs, and slices of a variety of fruit. It was the finest meal I'd ever been served. I had no appetite.

"Stephen was a monster," Melaret said calmly. "And a danger to the realm. It was obvious he was leading us to a senseless war."

Tess shot me a look I couldn't read. I met Melaret's eyes and nodded.

The tall woman continued. "I carry Stephen's child. Stephen, Twenty Eighth of His Name."

"If it's a boy," Tess said softly.

"Oh, he is."

I didn't ask how she could be so sure. I fought down a shudder. I didn't want to know.

"I will be regent until his majority. With the blessing of the Universal Church, the transition will be peaceful and free from any unpleasantness. And of course, the Church will have my full support in its holy crusade against the Darkness."

"That's very… civilized," I said.

"Just so." She smiled thinly. "You don't seem hungry. I apologize, I didn't ask if you'd already eaten. Please, don't let me detain you."

"Stay not on the order of your going, but go. So what do we do about Lady Macbeth?" Railes asked when we were safely back at our headquarters outside the city. The spot between my shoulder blades had finally stopped tingling in anticipation of an arrow.

"Not an entirely accurate epithet," Dee objected. "Lady Macbeth was quite loyal to her husband and didn't actually kill anyone."

I was impressed my adjutant knew ancient literature like Shakespeare at all. The tattooed killer didn't give the impression of being classically educated. Although the snarl he showed the occultist certainly looked medieval.

"Not really the point, Dee," I said. "The question's a good one. She's a murderer and I'd say slightly more cold-blooded than the average snake. She's looking to make a deal with us, but I don't trust her as far as I can throw her."

"She's looking for us to legitimize her," Tess corrected. "She needs the blessing of the Church."

"She is a regicide," Lago growled. "We cannot endorse that."

"Let's not be hasty," Dee interjected. "She would owe her legitimacy entirely to us, making her a more secure ally than any other we might imagine on the throne of the Source. And after all, she was acting against the Darkness."

"She was acting for her own ambition," Lago snarled. "It was her chance to seize power and rid herself of a man she hated."

Dee shrugged and smiled. "Different interests do coincide. Motives are rarely pure."

Lago snorted and looked away.

I sighed. "The fact is, this avoids a civil war. And there's going to be blood if we don't support her. Those guards of Stephen's didn't even flinch when she killed him. If she had them in her pocket, she'll have others. If we try to get rid of her, she won't go easily."

"Not overthrowing her doesn't mean we have to endorse her," Tess snapped.

"And then she's an enemy, and we're back to an army with divided loyalties."

"And you think she'll lead it against us?"

"No, but -"

"Then why exactly do you need thirty thousand men with undivided loyalties?"

I opened my mouth, then shut it. I felt like I'd been clobbered with a two-by-four from behind while focusing on the enemy in front of me. Probably a lot like Yoshana had felt when Tess beaned her in the back of the head with a rock.

"It's not my army," I said softly. "It's yours."

"Did I ask for it?"

"You went looking for an army to defeat Yoshana. I got you one. You put me in charge of it. What am I missing?"

"Apparently you're missing the fact that we defeated Yoshana. I'm very grateful, Minos. You did better than anyone could have expected. But the mission is over."

I looked around the pavilion for help. Railes shrugged. Lago wouldn't meet my eye. Cat and Furat decided it was a good time to look around everywhere else, in case an assassin was sneaking up on us in the midst of our own troops. Even Dee had nothing to offer. Sam wagged her tail at me, but that wasn't very helpful.

"You weren't in any hurry to turn our men over to Stephen," I objected.

"He was crazy. And infected with the Darkness."

"And Melaret is a murderer."

"Exactly. And you want us to give her the Universal Church's blessing?"

Backed into a rhetorical corner again. I loved the woman but, prophet or not, someone who'd grown up on a farm at the edge of a garbage dump had no business being able to argue circles around a Select.

"Tess, Yoshana may be dead, but there are still enemies out there. The Darkness is building in the Sorrows. Yoshana delayed the Hellguard's invasion when she killed Yashuath, but I doubt they've given up on the idea. This war isn't over. That's why we need an army with undivided loyalties. If our support for Melaret is the price of that, I think it's one we have to pay."

Her face set in lines of mulish stubbornness that weren't attractive at all. "I'm not giving the Church's blessing to that woman."

"You don't speak - huh." I held up a finger as I thought. "You're a prophet, but you're not the Church's envoy in the matter of coronations, now are you? So it really wouldn't be appropriate in the first place for you to formally recognize Melaret, would it?"

"You're splitting hairs."

"Damn right I am. Better hairs than heads. I had enough of that these past two years."

It was an ugly compromise that pleased no one, and we all plastered bright, false smiles over it and pretended to be thrilled.

There was a formal leave-taking at the bridge leading to Stephensburg's outer walls. Below, the river that defined the city's outer boundary rolled along sluggishly, unimpressed by coronations and machinations. Four thousand of Lago's men in white tabards blazoned with the roses and spines of the Order of Thorns stood at attention outside the city. Seven thousand of Roshel's troops in white tabards blazoned with the golden double crescent halberd of the Darkness Radiant stood with them.

A few hundred of Melaret's gray-clad household guard looked pretty lonely standing in the huge gateway on the other side of the bridge. The fact that there were thousands more troops behind them wearing the same white and gold as Roshel's men couldn't be lost on anybody.

Horns sounded, and Stephensburg's new ruler strode out onto the bridge with slow, measured steps. A herald with lungs like a bellows boomed out, "The Regent Melaret, Mother of Stephen Twenty Eighth of His Name, Liberator from Darkness, Servant of the Light."

The great and good of Stephensburg were gathered behind the gray troops. The wealthiest and most powerful of all had prime viewing positions on the wall, which was also conveniently removed from the line of fire if something went wrong. They cheered and applauded noisily. It would probably have been unwise and indeed unhealthy not to.

Trumpets sounded, drums rolled, and I stepped forward to the music of one of the Canticles of Holy Mary, which seemed to be the only piece that Roshel's military band knew. The song was beautiful but, having been subjected to it for an entire night when I was at war with the Darkness Radiant, I would have preferred just about anything else.

"Judge Minos, Supreme Commander of the Armies of Our Lady, Knight of the Order of Thorns," intoned my own herald. I wasn't sure he had quite the volume of Melaret's, but since he was shouting in my ear it was plenty loud enough. I also realized I had one less title than the new regent, but we hadn't come up with anything else that didn't sound ridiculous.

We stopped just short of each other, bowed slightly at the waist, and clasped hands. Each of us wore a smile of frightening insincerity.

"Judge Minos, you have driven the Darkness from the Source. We are grateful. Stephensburg is and remains at the disposal of the Holy Church."

More applause.

"Lady Melaret, you have driven the Darkness from Stephensburg." With a knife in its ruler's back. "The armies of Our Lady stand with the lawful ruler of the Source." Whose identity might be implied but was carefully unspecified.

And still more applause, and cheering, and another exchange of bows, and even bigger, falser smiles.

As Melaret and her men withdrew into the city, Roshel's troops followed in a magnificent procession. Lago's soldiers executed a precise about face and, in perfect unison, began the long march to Our Lady.

"You are so full of crap," Tess said.

2. The Mission

Word of the Battle of Darkness Falling had reached Our Lady long before we did, of course. The townspeople and the troops we'd left behind in garrison treated us to a heroes' welcome.

I couldn't say I minded. Being pelted with flowers was a nice change from being pelted with bullets and arrows. The contrast was that much greater because these were Rockwall troops cheering men from the Monolith - two groups that not long ago actually had been pelting each other with bullets and arrows.

"Get up and wave," Tess commanded. We were back to riding in a wagon. She stood and gave me a hand up. I waved, tentatively at first, then enthusiastically as the cheers grew louder.

"Don't get a swelled head," Tess muttered.

"But - you -" I glanced over and saw her grinning at me.

It was a long, slow ride through the winding streets of the surrounding town to the massive walls of Our Lady proper. I was tired and sweaty and my leg hurt by the time we got there.

Still. "Nice to be appreciated," I said.

We were met at the gate by an official delegation. The Metropolitan, the mayor, General Hake, and a swarm of functionaries waited for us. As the wagon rattled to a halt, Tolf burst from their ranks and ran to Prophetess in what must have been a huge breach of protocol.

"Thank God you're all right!"

Cat glared at him over the edge of the wagon. "With her, me."

"Like I said, thank God she's all right." Tolf had proclaimed himself head of Tess' personal guard long before the paleo had entered the picture. There was a fierce rivalry between them that was somewhat in good fun but mostly not. Tolf had half-jokingly suggested Cat might murder him to get him out of the way. It wasn't especially funny, considering I'd met her when she was sneaking up on me in the middle of the night to slit my throat and eat me. I'd only lived because at the time I'd been something far darker and more dangerous than her.

Mayor Arnage cleared his throat and interrupted, which was probably a good thing. I regarded him as a pompous windbag, but he might have been useful a week earlier dealing with Stephen and Melaret. Hopefully he'd be useful now keeping Tess' bodyguards from each other's throats.

"Judge Minos," he rumbled in full, rounded tones. "We are gratified at your victory. A sign of God's favor and the righteousness of our cause. Though there was never any doubt in the Lord's justice and mercy, still this is a time for celebration and thanksgiving."

Never any doubt. This from a man whose chief contribution to the undertaking had been the suggestion that we surrender.

The ability to squeeze a lie the size of a melon through a human throat without apparent discomfort was the main reason he would have been useful in Stephensburg. I plastered on the same false smile I'd worn with Melaret and said, "We are grateful for your unwavering support, Mayor Arnage."

He nodded happily and burbled on at length. I couldn't have recalled a syllable of what he said five seconds after it came out of his mouth. Eventually the flow of words dried up. My mind had wandered back to the battlefield, and I wasn't paying enough attention to know if I was supposed to say something. I smiled and nodded. It seemed to be enough.

The Metropolitan's quiet voice cut through the silence. "We need to talk."

There was an intimidating air of command about the Metropolitan, Bishop of Our Lady, the Universal Church's supreme ecclesiastical authority in the known world. He wasn't a large man or a loud man, but he was a man I took very seriously. He also liked to hold meetings in the basilica, where flights of angels stared down from the high, vaulted ceiling. Even now, I still glanced nervously up at them, worried that they might disapprove of me. The overall impression took me back to when I was a small boy and had broken something old and valuable.

If the Select were paranoid, it was just because everyone was out to get us.

Much like the last time the Metropolitan had convened a discussion in the basilica, there was only a bare handful of people present. Father Roric and Father Juniper had joined us, along with General Hake, BlackShield Jarl Lago, and Prophetess. Seated together in two pews, we spoke in lowered voices that were lost in that huge space.

"There's only one contingency you failed to plan for, Minos," the Metropolitan began without preamble.

"What's that, Your Eminence?"

"Victory."

I wasn't sure what he meant, and my expression must have showed it. He continued, "General Hake and BlackShield Jarl Lago pledged their troops to the cause of defeating Yoshana. She is now defeated."

I opened my mouth, but he forestalled me with a raised hand. "We are left with quite a large army on our hands. Furthermore, for the first time in a millennium, we have a Church that is not only militant but military, and successfully so. And based on what I hear from the events in Stephensburg, we seem to be back in the business of anointing rulers. Under somewhat questionable circumstances."

I didn't even get my mouth open this time before he raised his hand again. "All of this puts us in a difficult position."

This time I got my comment out. "I don't think we would have preferred the alternative."

The Metropolitan's frown made me wish I'd kept my mouth shut. "No one is suggesting that, Minos. But the Church is not prepared for our current circumstances. I suppose that's my fault. However, since you're the author of our victory and the leader of our overgrown army, I thought you should be part of the solution."

I dipped my head. "Sorry, Your Eminence."

"We don't need an army, Your Eminence," Tess interjected. "As you pointed out, Yoshana is defeated. We can return the forces of Rockwall and the Monolith to their homes."

Once again I was cut off before I could speak, this time by Lago. "With all due respect, Prophetess, while my men are loyal to the Monolith, they have found great inspiration in your service. I believe many if not most would prefer to remain here."

"Mine no less," Hake rasped, not to be outdone.

"But there's no -"

"Couldn't we simply transfer the men who want to remain to the Order of Thorns?" I asked. "That way we're not technically retaining Monolith or Rockwall forces."

Father Roric shook his head. "It's not so simple. The Order of Thorns is a third order. Its members are tertiaries of the Church. Certainly for the Monolith troops, as Josephites, it would be canonically difficult if not impossible for them to join the Order of Thorns without conversion to the Universal faith, which I imagine would be problematic."

"Wouldn't it be possible to formally invest the Order as an ecumenical Christian association?" Father Juniper asked. "After all, I strongly suspect that some of its current members are Reborn rather than Universalists. I'm not sure the doctrinal point has dawned on them or frankly is relevant to their faith and duties."

Roric scowled. "Ignorance of doctrine does not excuse heresy. If we have a tertiary order whose members aren't even part of the Church -"

"Isn't the key issue really that Prophetess has brought them to God?" Juniper retorted mildly.

"Brought them to God, or brought them to herself? With no disrespect to Prophetess, an army formed around a cult of personality -"

"There's no need for an army!" Tess protested, voice echoing loudly in the marble hall. She looked briefly embarrassed, but her face fell quickly back into stubborn lines I knew very well. Lago, Hake, Roric, and Juniper all stared at her. The Metropolitan just raised his eyebrows.

We were back to the point we'd debated outside Stephensburg, one we'd set aside. One where I'd hoped her mind had changed, but it evidently hadn't.

I said, "There is, Tess. When Yoshana surrendered to death, it was so you could take up the crusade against the demons and the Darkness unopposed. That war still needs to be fought."

"She said that. I never did."

"She wasn't wrong. Not on that point."

"If you admired her so much, why didn't you take her side?"

"For God's sake, Tess, I picked you! At more than a little personal cost." I jabbed my finger into the wound on my face, which hurt. "In case you forgot, I cut off her head. I think I made my choice pretty clear."

We glared at each other. Everyone else studiously looked away.

As the silence stretched on, I said, "Roshel will send an envoy from Stephensburg to let us know what's going on there. Let's wait until we get some more facts."

At that point everyone, even the Metropolitan, was happy to let the matter drop. Which I guess goes to show that even the most important decisions can be put off if you just make everyone feel uncomfortable enough.

We settled into a routine as we waited for news from Stephensburg. I did the kind of things I thought a military leader was supposed to do, like holding staff meetings with officers and visiting the wounded in the infirmary. In a strange way that was easier now that I was one of them. My limp and scar were less severe than the hurts they carried, but at least I felt I'd shared in some measure in their sacrifice. A kind of red badge of courage, I supposed.

While I'd been in the field with the Shadowed Hand and the Monolith troops, Captain Marek of Our Lady's household guard had worked with General Hake to create a permanent command center in one of the buildings we'd appropriated for barracks. I suppose I could see the Metropolitan's point. The center of the Universalist faith was starting to look more and more like a military base.

Tarc came in one day and looked around the new headquarters. The older Select shook his head and said, "You seem to be getting used to being the glorious general."

There was an edge to his words, as there usually was with Tarc. He'd never fully forgiven me for killing Lalos, his friend, another Select. Select didn't kill each other. Although Lalos had been trying pretty hard to shoot me when I'd cut off his head.

Tarc wasn't wrong. After our improbable victory over Yoshana, I was feeling more and more comfortable as a commander. Most days I seemed to wind up in our headquarters with the senior officers and a handful of others, even if there was no obvious army business to attend to. Well, it was convenient. And Furat would usually go there with his dog, when she wasn't playing outside. I liked to be around the dog. She was uncomplicated.

Tess wasn't uncomplicated. We had once again set aside the argument over the use of our troops, but I no longer had any illusions I had won. The decision was being held in abeyance, waiting for word from Roshel.

Roshel didn't send an envoy. She came herself.

She found me in the command center. We had the windows open in the vain hope a breeze would cool the sweltering summer air. Sam was breathing heavily, her tongue lolling out, even though she'd been doing nothing more than lying on the floor. The shaggy dog didn't like the heat.

It didn't look like Roshel liked the heat either. She stomped in, dusty and sweaty, hair and blouse plastered to her body. I carefully kept my eyes focused on her face. Even without the aura of seduction the Darkness had projected around her, she was a little too appealing to look at. Somewhat unusually, Tess was with us, watching a little knot of officers play cards. Even I knew that staring too much at the dark-haired Overlord would be hazardous to my health.

"That ride's a lot less fun without the Darkness," Roshel complained, her eyes darting around the room. "I'd forgotten what being saddle sore felt like."

Tess opened her mouth, closed it, then asked mildly, "No regrets, I hope?"

Roshel shook her head. "No. At least not most of the time."

"It's good to see you," I said. "How's the situation at Stephensburg?"

"For goodness sake, Minos," Tess chided me. "How was the trip, Roshel? Can we get you some water? You look exhausted."

The Overlord waved her hand absently. "I'm fine. Stephensburg's under control. What's the situation here?"

"Here?" I was puzzled. "Everything's fine here. Although there's a bit of a debate around whether we've got too many troops. We've been waiting for an update from you to understand the status of the Darkness Radiant."

"Too many? Huh." Roshel blinked, as if distracted. "The Darkness Radiant is completely under my control. Melaret has no legitimacy except for what we give her and she knows it. Not everyone was happy with what happened in the battle, but most of the Knights of Resurrection were with us there. They were Yoshana's hard core loyalists. The ones who were going to leave have left. Stephen's men are loyal to the command structure. If he were still alive I don't know what would have happened, but now they'll follow me. And of course by extension you, Minos. Who else is there?"

"No one else," Tess said, meeting Roshel's eyes.

"No one else," the Overlord repeated. "You know what, Tess, you're right. I'm tired. If you don't mind, I'd like to get the men I brought settled and get into something more presentable. Can we continue in more detail over dinner?"

564

"Of course," I said. "Railes, can you get Roshel's troops situated?"

"You got it, boss," my adjutant replied. He turned to her. "How many do you have?"

"Just a company."

"Easy enough. Plenty of room." And the two left together.

I turned to Tess. "Can we go for a little walk?"

It was hot outside in the sun, hotter than in the room. We found shade under a long row of trees. "I'm not the most perceptive guy around," I said, "but even I could tell something was going on there. That was a pretty pathetic report coming from the commander of the Darkness Radiant, and she's way too tough for me to believe it was just because she was tired. You have any clue what's eating her?"

Tess shook her head and made a little scoffing sound. "You really aren't the most perceptive guy around. She was hoping Grigg would be here. And she was very disappointed that he's not."

"Grigg?"

"Oh, for goodness sake, Minos. You told me Roshel had feelings for Grigg, before Yoshana pushed her out of the way. She was hoping that with Yoshana gone, Grigg would be available. You can't tell me that didn't go through your head when you were trying to turn her."

"I mean, I guess…"

"Men may well be the thickest creatures on the face of the earth. It's amazing any of you live to adulthood. Anyway, now Roshel's upset that Grigg isn't here."

I had to admit I wouldn't have minded having the big Select back myself, even if it might complicate our lives - especially if he didn't choose to give up the Darkness. "Do you think he'll come back?"

Tess shrugged. "I don't know. What Yoshana said to him at the end… that hurt him a lot."

I nodded. She'd told Grigg that he was superior to me in every way except the one that counted, supporting his woman. Then she'd died. Tess and I walked on a while in silence. She added, "There's one more problem. Roshel might decide that without Grigg, you're the next best option."

Yoshana's bodyguard Erev had once suggested exactly that. "Well, I might enjoy the competition," I suggested.

"Would you enjoy having Cat skin you alive?" Tess asked with no trace of humor.

There was no doubt in my mind that was exactly what the paleo would do if I hurt Tess' feelings. "I think I'd rather not."

"I didn't think so."

According to Yoshana, Tess was my woman. I was pretty sure the Overlord had gotten the order of ownership backward in that phrase.

The command center doubled as the officers' mess. There was plenty of room in the massive complex of Our Lady for a separate dining hall - seven thousand soldiers weren't easy to feed, but there was more than enough room in the ancient citadel to house them. The space-saving measure was by choice, specifically my choice. The combination of my rank and my wound was allowing me to indulge a previously undiscovered bone laziness. I just didn't want to get up and move around. I was more than half tempted to have my bed brought in.

A lot of the company commanders and all the platoon leaders ate with their men. The group that gathered in the officers' mess was small - the handful of Rockwall's colonels and the Monolith's senior GrayShields, a few captains. Marek of Our Lady's household troops, Tolf as captain of the Order of Thorns, Railes as my adjutant. Hake and Lago, of course. Cat was there because Tess was. River Mist from the Hidden Moon Clan, even though it was just a squad, and Hafnum Furat, even though he didn't command anyone but his dog, because - well, just because. Somehow that pair from the Sorrows had honorary officer rank. Sam lay quietly on the floor like a furry white log, hoping someone would drop food.

Roshel brought a captain she introduced as Teraya. He was a big, dark, quiet man who had come west with Yoshana, one of the terror's soldiers from her time as Warleader of the Shield, before she'd split with the Hellguard. The current general of the Darkness Radiant seemed like her old self again, relaxed and self-confident. She chatted easily with Hake and the Rockwall officers she hadn't met. They accepted her instantly, a tribute no doubt to their mutual professionalism and completely unrelated to her stunning appearance. Right.

Between the main course and dessert she turned to me. "You said before there was some question whether our army was too big. You want to elaborate on that?"

I took a deep breath. "The Metropolitan pointed out that we're housing a mixed force of thousands of Monolith and Rockwall troops in Our Lady, who technically answer to their own sovereigns, not us. He didn't say, but I imagine he was thinking, that seven thousand men also eat a lot. And that's not even counting the twenty thousand plus you've got in Stephensburg."

She snorted, "Well, we're not turning my men over to Melaret. Can you imagine? Anyway, if we released the troops, how would we finish the mission?"

"Thank you," I said.

"There is no mission." Tess didn't shout this time. Her voice was calm and cold. It was more frightening that way.

Roshel gave a little laugh. "Tess, the demons and the Darkness aren't going to defeat themselves. That's what the Darkness Radiant was created for. Yoshana stood aside because she thought you could lead us better than she could."

"You and Minos keep acting like I should care what Yoshana wanted. I don't. I never accepted her conditions. I had one mission from God - to defeat her. With your help, I did that. God never said anything about an endless war against the Darkness and the demons. Evil does not end in this world."

"I actually cannot believe I'm hearing this," Roshel said. "You're just turning away from your responsibilities -"

"Not my responsibilities -"

"Hold on," I interjected, raising my hands. "You said God never told you anything about the Darkness and the demons. Can't you ask him?"

"That's not how prophecy works, Minos. I ask God's guidance constantly. That doesn't mean he always answers. He told me I needed to stop Yoshana. That was it."

Roshel leaned back in her chair. "Wait a minute. That was all God ever told you, and you've been marching around calling yourself a prophet?"

Tess met the Overlord's eyes. There were angry tears in hers, but she didn't blink or flinch. "Yes. It was enough. Saint Teresa of Calcutta had one year of visions from the Lord and then fifty years in a spiritual desert. I can only pray that some day I might be half the servant of God that she was. I trust in him. I answer to him. I don't answer to you."

Roshel turned to me. "Tomorrow I'll give you my latest understanding of the position of Shield and Hellguard forces. We can start planning the campaign."

Tess stood and said to me, "Before you do, read the First Book of Samuel. You can start around chapter ten." And she left.

The First Book of Samuel. The Hebrews had wanted a king to lead their armies, so Samuel the prophet was guided by God to anoint Saul. That went okay until Saul decided he could figure out what God really wanted for himself, and started ignoring Samuel's prophecies. So God picked a new champion. Saul lost a big battle and wound up with his severed head getting passed around the enemy kingdoms as a trophy. After a while his people felt sorry for him and took his headless corpse down from the wall where his enemies had strung it up, so at least the bottom part of him got buried.

The message wasn't subtle.

I sat with the Bible in my lamplit room with my blood pressure rising. First I got mad. Tess had essentially threatened me, in so many words. The parallel was obvious.

Who did she think she was? Without any guidance from God, by her own admission, she'd decided she knew better than I how to conduct a war.

After I got done being mad, I started getting nervous. Whatever exactly you believed about Tess, I'd seen her take a full blast of the Darkness from Yoshana and emerge unscathed. She'd engineered the surrender of two Overlords. One of them now answered to us, the other was dead. Even if God had only spoken directly to her once, she wasn't someone to take lightly.

And that was the problem. She'd won over through purity and strength of character an army greater than the one Yoshana had assembled through seduction and intimidation. But now she didn't want to use it.

I needed to talk to Roshel. She'd understand the full strategic scope of the issue, in terms of both raw force and morale. She might even have a better sense than I of whether we could win Tess over... and if we couldn't do that, how we'd go about leading an army sworn to a prophet who didn't support our mission.

I slipped on a pair of moccasins. The night was warm, and I didn't need a cloak over the light pants and shirt I'd intended to sleep in. My injury gave me an excuse to use my katana as a cane. Not that I expected an attack inside Our Lady, but a certain paranoia had become part of my life.

I limped down the hall toward Railes' room. He knew where Roshel was bunking. I'd just ask him... my shuffling steps slowed and halted. I played out the conversation in my head. "What do you need her for at this time of night, boss?" "Just to ask her about strategy." "Oh, okay."

Cat and Railes were very, very close. She might find out. She might even be in his room and overhear. In my mind, I knocked on Roshel's door and she answered, a thin robe clinging to her curves. And then her eyes went wide as Cat's dagger sank into my kidneys from behind, over and over again, the same way she'd slaughtered Erev. "Strategy, pfft," the paleo sneered.

I turned on my heel and stumped back to my room. Strategy could wait until morning.

Tess didn't join the officers for breakfast, but Roshel did. So I could have my discussion after all. I might have preferred a more private venue, but the images from the night before were stuck in my mind. They suggested I probably shouldn't be alone with the brunette Overlord if I wanted to stay healthy.

I figured it was safe enough to sit next to her in public, though.

"Feeling rested?" I asked.

She shrugged. "Well enough. I may not have the Darkness in me anymore, but I've been on enough campaigns that a little ride up here from Stephensburg isn't a big deal."

"That's good," I said. I stared at the toast on my plate. It didn't have anything to add to the conversation.

Roshel chuckled. "You're terrible at small talk, Minos. What's the point you're dancing around?"

"Okay. To the point it is. What happens if we do what Tess says and declare the crusade is over?"

The new commander of the Darkness Radiant frowned. The sunlight streaming in through the windows played on her skin, highlighting the furrows in her brow. "For starters, the demons and the Darkness rise up and conquer the world, everything the Darkness Radiant fought for was for nothing, and all of us who survive - which won't include you or me, by the way - become slaves."

Her voice rose a bit. "Or if you're asking what happens in the shorter term, a little closer to home, our whole goddamned army falls apart. The Darkness Radiant has veterans from the Shield and the Green Heart serving alongside troops from the Source. None of those three states get along. Your forces right here were literally in the process of killing each other when Prophetess brought them together. Take away the common enemy, and they'll go right back to each other's throats. Without a unifying cause, we're all going to be in the middle of the ugliest civil war since the Age of Fear."

"You can't hold them together?"

The frown deepened, and she glared at me. "Without something to hold them together for? No. I don't think even Yoshana could have done that, and I'm not Yoshana."

I gnawed on the joint of my index finger, hoping the pain would inspire some brilliant plan. It didn't. "Then we've got a real problem, because our prophet thinks the crusade is over."

The Overlord took a deep, shuddering breath. Her voice steadied. "Look, Minos, I spent some time last night thinking about this. Prophetess isn't a soldier. I understand she's intimidated by the thought of taking on the Hellguard. Who wouldn't be? What we need to do is show her a workable plan so she understands it's not a suicide mission. We have the strongest force on the continent at our command. She'll come around once we get the campaign organized."

I didn't think Roshel understood Tess at all, but I just nodded and picked at my food. "Let me spend today figuring out logistics at this end," I said. "Then you can give me that strategic layout you mentioned last night."

Considering that Dee's advice had almost gotten me killed a couple of times, he might not have seemed like the most obvious counselor. But he'd suggested the approach I'd used to separate Roshel from Yoshana. Now that I was stuck between Tess and Roshel's irreconcilable positions, I found myself wanting to hear his perspective.

"Roshel raises a number of valid points," the occultist said. "Firstly, the idea of uniting against a common enemy is well enshrined in history and philosophy. 'Me against my brother, my brother and I against my cousins, my family against the stranger,' as it were. The ancients sometimes expressed it as the concept of the 'repugnant other.' In its most extremely articulated form, the idea was that the most important factor for belonging to a group was to hate the right enemies."

"So Yoshana was the repugnant other for Our Lady's army before, and now the demons and the Darkness are the repugnant other for our united forces."

"Exactly. And Roshel fears that if we allow our hatred for the enemy to cool, we may lose cohesion. It's not an irrational view. Prophetess would no doubt tell us that disapproval of the demons and the Darkness does not require war against them, but the ancients believed that the intensity of the hatred for the repugnant other intensified the cohesion of the group. With such a disparate group as ours, comprised of many nations and faiths, the unifying hatred may need to be intense indeed."

I was back to chewing on my knuckle. It wasn't helping much this time either. "To the point of a war of aggression? I'm not sure Father Roric is going to get behind that, much less Tess."

"I believe you quoted the Hellguard Seven as saying that only the dead have seen the end of war. That aphorism is variously ascribed to thinkers ranging from Plato to Santayana, but I fear the principle remains valid regardless of whoever first articulated it. Humanity is a warlike species."

"You're a big help."

My next stop was Father Roric. That was not a visit I relished. The Advocate for Justice hadn't approved of my use of Seven as a weapon against Yoshana. Not only had that tactic been arguably wrong on moral grounds, it hadn't worked and had resulted in the Hellguard's death. Roric disapproved of most things and most people. I had given him more than the common run of reasons to disapprove of me.

As always, the lean priest was courteous, gesturing me to the chair facing his old, wooden desk.

"Judge Minos. To what do I owe the pleasure of your company?"

"A moral question, Father."

"Indeed? If I recall correctly, the last time you asked my views on a moral question you proceeded without my approval."

I should have just shut up and nodded, especially since I'd fully expected the comment, but instead I retorted, "If I recall correctly, you didn't formally object either."

"Yes, and I regret that. Through my own poor judgment I led you into error and contributed to the death of a man who could not have been in a state of grace at his passing. I have confessed my sin in that regard. I have not heard your confession since we were last together here, but perhaps you availed yourself of the services of another priest."

Heat rose in my face. I hadn't been to confession at all since before I'd gone to the Sorrows to retrieve Seven. I'd killed by my own hand since then, not to mention all the deaths I'd caused indirectly.

"Maybe that's relevant to the question at hand, Father. I understand that confession isn't valid unless it's made with the intention not to sin again. But I think I need to start another war."

Roric and I plowed the ground of just war theory over again. A preemptive strike against an enemy known to be poised to attack might be moral. Manufacturing a threat to hold our forces together certainly was not. I wasn't sure enough of the facts to judge the question honestly. That would have to wait for my strategic discussion with Roshel. But at best, our position would be ambiguous. I didn't leave the meeting feeling any better. I also neglected to schedule a confession. It wasn't a sacrament I enjoyed.

My third interview was one I'd enjoy even less.

"Wow. You really do look like a big, gray sack of crap now," Moya said as I limped into the chamberlain's outer office. The redhead frowned dramatically, wrinkling the puckered scar tissue around her missing eye even more hideously than usual. "Whoever did it had lousy aim, though."

An inch to the right and the gouge torn into my face would have made my eye a match for hers. I wondered if that would have made her like me any better. Probably not. Moya was a generally unpleasant person, but I wasn't quite sure why she particularly disliked me.

"I love you too," I said. "Is he in?"

"For the great, conquering hero? I suppose he'll have to be. You'll want to be careful about your head swelling too much. With that rip in your face it might pop and your brains'll leak out."

While I tried to think of a response, the redhead stood and went through the small door into the inner office, closing it behind her. It opened only moments later and she emerged, followed by Father Doreden's voice. "Minos. Come in, come in."

The warmth in the chamberlain's tone was matched only by the disgust in Moya's expression.

Mindful of my discussion with Father Roric on the subject of confession, I tried to exercise Christian charity and not think of Doreden as a fat, useless windbag. I wasn't very successful in spite of the welcoming smile on his face. Maybe it was because I was getting better at recognizing when that expression was being faked.

The chamberlain's main purpose was preventing people from bothering the Metropolitan. He was the living embodiment of bureaucracy.

Moya shut the door behind us with a bang. Her main purpose was preventing people from bothering Father Doreden. She accomplished that through an exceptionally unpleasant attitude that came as naturally to her as breathing. We might not get along, but I had to admit she was good at her job.

Doreden stood and waddled around his desk to shake my hand. "Amazing, Minos. Simply amazing. I will admit that I myself doubted your chances against Yoshana. I suppose that was a disturbing lack of faith in a man of the cloth, haha. But you proved me wrong and of course I'm glad of it."

"It helps when your enemy decides to hand you her sword and tells you to cut off her head."

"A miracle indeed."

I nodded, frowned, winced, and added, "And all Prophetess', not mine. Or God's through Prophetess, I suppose I should say. But as the Metropolitan has pointed out, it leaves us with the unexpected problem of having a large army and nothing to do with it."

"Ah." Doreden returned to his chair and waved me to another. "Sit, please. This may not be a short conversation."

I sat and winced again. My knee didn't care for standing, but objected to changing position even more. The chamberlain saw my expression but misjudged the cause. He touched his cheek. "Does it hurt much?"

I thought again about my conversation with Father Roric. "Probably no more than I deserve."

The fat priest visibly turned that thought over in his head and equally visibly decided he didn't want to explore it. "So what exactly is it that brings you here today, Minos? I don't imagine you need to go through me to see the Metropolitan these days, heheh."

"I had a logistical question, Father, that I think is more your area. To be blunt, how long can we keep feeding this army?"

"Ah." Doreden steepled his fingers and examined them as if looking for answers. Maybe he was going to count on them. "I suppose that is indeed rather more my area. To be equally blunt, it depends. The harvest both inside and outside the walls should be good, God willing… if there are not late floods, or droughts, or blights. We employed quite a number of General Hake's men to bring all the fields within the walls under the plow this spring. Still, that will likely not be quite enough. Seven thousand sweaty soldiers eat rather a lot."

I nodded. "I imagine we're near the bottom of Our Lady's reserves."

The chamberlain's eyes widened. "Oh, far past. We've kept everyone fed so far only by taxing the surrounding town and farms. Emergency wartime levies. And if we are to continue to support this army, those emergency levies must likewise continue. Of course, the people will only support such sacrifices…"

He trailed off. I finished for him. "…If there's actually a war."

3. The Best Laid Plans

We set up a map table representing the entire eastern half of the continent, with little painted counters showing our estimates of troop strength. Tess pretended it didn't exist.

Roshel and I hovered over it like vultures waiting for a dying man's last breath.

"You need to understand the background, Minos," she began.

"I'm from the Green Heart. I know the basic history. Let's skip ahead to where we are now."

"No. It's not enough to know who, and where. You have to know why. To understand the balance of forces now, you have to go back to when Karst ruled the Shield."

I reached for a pitcher to refill my mug of cider. "I'm getting thirsty just imagining how long you're going to talk."

She glared. "The Shield has always been the plug keeping the Hellguard bottled up inside the Darklands. To the north they're blocked by the Ice Fields, to the east the sea, to the west the Sorrows. And to the south the Shield."

"I do know this."

"Shut up and listen," she snarled, and for a moment she was as terrifying without the Darkness as she'd been with it, and I was forcibly reminded that no one without an iron will could command as much of that hellish power as she had.

"The Shield stood between the world of demons and the world of men, and not just physically. There was almost no commerce between the Darklands and the Shield, but I told you before they trafficked in women and children. The Shield provided the Hellguard with female slaves whose will hadn't been erased like the humans in the Darklands. And if a child was born, and lived, it was returned to the Shield."

The Overlords were those half-demon offspring, conceived in rape and born in death. Roshel had told me no woman survived the birth of a child infected with the Darkness. Most of the children didn't survive it either. I didn't know about the other Overlords, but Roshel, at least, nurtured a burning hatred for the Hellguard.

"The Overlords are the heart of the Shield's army. With our - with their mastery of the Darkness, the Shield could face the Hellguard. And then there are others, with less demon blood but still enough to control the Darkness."

"Why would the Hellguard agree to return those children if it gave the Shield the power to stop them?"

The Overlord smiled. "So you don't know everything you need to know, do you? Be patient. You're getting ahead of the story."

She poured herself some of the cider. "It's a good question, actually. Maybe the key question. I suppose, before Karst took the White Throne, the rulers of the Shield assumed the demons had no ambitions outside the Darklands."

I snorted. "Because their children weren't ambitious at all. Like Yoshana."

Roshel tapped the side of her nose. I'd never seen anyone actually use the gesture. "Ah. Again, you're getting to the heart of it now. Remember, mastering the Darkness requires discipline, self-control. The tradition in the Shield was that no Overlord would rule it, because the ambition to rule wasn't compatible with control of the Darkness."

Ambition and the Darkness had fit together for me like a hand in a glove. Although in the end, I had feared what I was becoming so much that I'd asked Tess to cast it out of me. "But didn't Yoshana -"

"Rule the Shield? Yes. She led a rebellion against Karst, killed him with her own hands, and seized the White Throne for herself. Of course it all turned out to be a lie, what we'd been told. Karst was a master of the Darkness himself, even though he was no Overlord. Who knows how many before him were too."

She took a long drink. "The other thing we hadn't known was that Karst made an alliance with the Hellguard. The Darklands and the Shield would join together and rule the world."

"And Yoshana broke that alliance and the Hellguard turned on her."

"No... Yoshana embraced the alliance."

"I'm confused. I can see her doing just about anything for power. But you - you followed her, and you hate the demons."

Roshel's eyes were shining with unspilled tears. "Yoshana showed me how to use the Darkness. She turned me from a useless monster into... well, I suppose a useful monster." Her laugh was bitter.

"I would have followed her anywhere. I did follow her anywhere. It was Grigg who turned against her. He'd helped her bring down Karst. He'd fallen in love with her, you see, before he knew what she was. But he wouldn't work with the Hellguard. He left and went to organize the Green Heart's defenses. So Yoshana sent me to kill him."

Wow. Talk about a woman scorned. Thoughts chased through my head. I was tempted to do the prudent thing and let them go, but instead I said, "It's, uh, been suggested that you had feelings for Grigg yourself."

She nodded. "Yes. That's why she sent me. If I'd killed him, I'd have been hers forever."

Just as if I'd killed Tess, as Yoshana had planned, I'd have been hers forever. You'd think someone as smart as the white-haired Overlord would have learned from her mistakes.

"But you turned on her instead."

Now the tears pattered onto the tabletop, one by one. "No. I was going to do it. He only lived because the demons betrayed Yoshana before I got to him."

I goggled. Her laugh was awful, a cracking sound like an animal in pain. She gulped more cider and took a long, ragged breath before she went on.

"While I was hunting Grigg, she sent a mercenary force to cause an incident between the Source and the Green Heart. It worked, but it was a suicide mission. The captain of the mercenaries was a woman named Jylen. She was maybe Yoshana's only real friend, from when Yoshana had disguised herself as a normal human. But Yoshana needed to sacrifice a pawn in her game… and Jylen was a pawn."

I remembered Roshel telling me that in Yoshana's world, you were either a player or a piece. I shuddered.

"So the Green Heart and the Source were skirmishing and I was stalking Grigg. With the Heart distracted on their northern border, the Shield started pounding them, crushing their defenses, with the Hellguard in reserve. The Heart couldn't hold, fell back, fell back again. Seafields fell without a fight, and for the first time Yoshana had access to a port west of the Rat Shoals. It was all going perfectly." A smile as fragile as ice crossed the brunette's beautiful face.

"And then the demons told Yoshana to push across the Paint."

It was my turn to swallow hard. My gut clenched in a knot of dread. I had grown up in Goat Hill, on the western bank of the Paint River. My parents had sent me away before Yoshana's legions arrived. I'd reached my thirteenth birthday, and the custom of the Select was for children to leave home at thirteen. Spreading out made us harder to exterminate, and the Select were not a popular race.

I didn't know if my parents had fought at the Paint, but all Select trained in the martial arts - again, it made us harder to wipe out. I didn't know if they'd fought, or if so, if they'd lived.

"Were you there?" I asked. It came out as a kind of croak.

"Everyone was there." She hadn't noticed my reaction. Her eyes were turned inward. "The demons wanted Yoshana's troops to ford the river. Which was heavily defended. Yoshana is - Yoshana was ruthless, but not wasteful. She didn't throw her armies away. She wanted to consolidate her gains, plan some new trick. But the demons weren't interested in preserving the Shield's armies. They saw us as shock troops, to be used up. When Yoshana refused to advance, they found another tool they liked better."

She took another long drink of cider, saw her mug was empty, and refilled it. "There was another Overlord, Rakat. Yoshana thought she'd killed him getting to Karst, but he'd survived. We're hard to kill, you know." Again that brittle smile.

"A lot of the Overlords held a grudge against Yoshana from the coup, even though she was one of us. Maybe because she was one of us, and we'd been taught for generations to avoid ambition. When the demons put Rakat in command, half the army turned and followed him. And that's when we found out the demons hadn't been turning over all the Overlords to the Shield. They had their own half breed troops. More than we did."

She was completely lost in the past. I doubted she could even see me. "So there we were, camped on the Paint. Grigg and the Green Heart defenders on the other side, half of our own army and a company of enemy Overlords behind us, pinning us up against the river. So what does Yoshana do?"

If it had been me, I probably would have seen how much of the army I could smuggle down the Paint on rafts under the cover of darkness, but that wasn't Yoshana's style.

"She changes sides. Goes and makes up with Grigg, all is forgiven, and suddenly it's the demons facing two armies simultaneously. Neat as if she'd planned it all along. You should have seen it, Minos. Grigg, well, you've seen him fight, and his men loved him. The only warrior more impressive than Grigg, who could outfight him and had troops even more devoted, was Yoshana. The two of them together... they were like fire and storm."

Roshel's eyes were shining as she continued. "Grigg's troops forded the Paint in the night and took the demons' army from behind. Rakat's forces were butchered - not to mention Rakat himself, because even we can't recover from being chopped into little pieces. There was only one problem."

Only one?

"Maybe Yoshana hadn't totally trusted me to get rid of Grigg. So she'd sent a crew of veterans along with me. In the confusion, not all of them got the message that the mission had changed. One of them stabbed Grigg in the back."

"Well, like you said, you can heal from a lot with the Darkness in you."

"But not quite from this. When Yoshana found him, he was dying. It took everything she had to save him."

"There's an 'and'..."

"And while she was doing it, one of Grigg's partisans found his leader dying on the ground with an Overlord kneeling over him, so he did what any right-thinking soldier would do."

"He stabbed Yoshana."

"He stabbed Yoshana. Put a spear right through her heart. Well, like I said, we could survive a lot of things, but not that."

"Except..."

"Except she did. We didn't realize. It was chaos. There were Grigg's partisans, Green Heart regulars, Shield troops loyal to Yoshana, Shield troops loyal to Rakat, Darklanders. The losses were staggering, on all sides. The Darkland Overlords didn't go down easy."

My stomach clenched again. Would she even know about two Select serving in a different army? Of course not. I suddenly realized that Grigg very well might. But Grigg was gone.

"Then, on the third day, she rose again."

"You're not serious? The third day?"

"Actually, it was about a day and a half, but in the official version it was the third day." And now Roshel's familiar, knowing smile was back. "She was always good at symbolism."

The Overlord went on. "She came to us in a white robe, not her armor. Who knows where she found it. She said God had raised her up to be his sword against the demons and the Darkness. That God could use anything, even the Darkness, even her, to do his will. We believed her. At that point, we had to believe in something."

I nodded. I understood the power of belief.

"She called the ones who followed her the Darkness Radiant, because even the darkness is radiant in God's sight. But the soldiers most devoted to her called themselves the Knights of Resurrection, because they served a messiah who rose from the dead."

"And then you came north."

She shook her head. "West, first. We weren't really sure where to go. The demons' army was shattered, but they had more men coming. Some of the Green Heart soldiers and partisans joined us, but most didn't, and some were carrying a grudge. We had thousands of hardened, loyal veterans, but no state to provision or house us. Grigg thought we should go west of the Monolith, beyond the Barrier Range, and gather strength. We recruited as we went. But before we got to the Muddy, we started to hear how weak Stephen was."

"And Yoshana decided you could take over the Source."

"You pretty much know the rest. So now that you've got the background of who hates who and why, we can start looking at the pieces on the board."

The pieces on the board. Tens of thousands of living, breathing men and women, reduced to counters on a map. Roshel had perhaps learned the lessons of her messiah too well.

"Let's take a break for today," I said. "I need to let it all sink in."

I sat and stared at the Ermel Clock. The floating hour hand was a bit past three on the golden, outer track. In a few hours it would be at six, where the golden outer circle of day met the silver inner circle of night. And we would pass back into darkness.

How had Grigg and Roshel and Yoshana ever managed to work together? It must have been the most volatile love triangle in human history. I shivered. I was lucky to have traveled with them and lived. God really must watch over fools.

I looked up to the sky and mouthed, "Thanks."

Time passed. The clock ticked on toward four. Time was indifferent to my plans, or lack thereof.

I smelled Father Juniper's pipe before I heard or saw him. He settled on the bench next to me. "Something up?" he asked.

"Just thinking that I've been part of something huge and terrifying and I'm only now realizing how little I understand it."

"Ah. As your friend John Dee might say, that's the beginning of wisdom."

We sat in silence for a while. I said, "I've just heard more of Yoshana's story from someone who was there. I still don't know if she believed she had a vision from God, or if it was just a cover to mask her ambition."

"I don't know if she knew. I would have bet pretty heavily one way right up until she gave you her sword to cut off her head. I suppose there was no conflict between those motives, until the very end. She was complicated. But then, humans generally are, and whatever else she was, she was human."

I nodded. "That's true enough, but it isn't helping me with the question of whether to launch a campaign against the Hellguard."

"I believe you've discussed that with Father Roric?"

"I did, yes. That wasn't very helpful either. Prophetess is dead set against it. Roshel, who's probably the top military leader we've got, insists we have to. And I'm the idiot stuck in the middle. I don't like going against Prophetess, but from what Roshel says, the Hellguard will hit us eventually. At a minimum, we're going to need a defensive alliance with the Green Heart. But the longer we sit around, the more likely our army's going to fall apart. I think Roshel's right. I think we need to hit the Hellguard while we can."

The bearded priest blew a cloud of smoke. "It sounds like you've decided, then. Hopefully the honor and prestige of being commander in chief of this vast legion isn't weighing too heavily on your thinking."

"What? No!"

"Good."

Honor and prestige? Honor and prestige had gotten me a limp and an ugly scar across my face. But somebody needed to lead a united army against the Darklands and the Shield before they took another shot at us. By luck, fate, or the will of a truly whimsical God, that someone was me.

Tess and Roshel were standing on opposite sides of the map table when I walked into the headquarters room the next morning. The air between them was so charged that I nearly turned around and limped back out.

Tess left instead, without saying a word.

"She doesn't understand," Roshel said.

"I should talk to her."

"What are you going to say?"

What indeed? Maybe Roshel was right. Maybe Tess would be easier to convince once we had a strategy. In any event, I had no case to make that I thought she would accept, and so I took the easy path. I let her go.

I heaved a sigh and plopped into the chair next to the Overlord. "Fine. Let's talk troop deployments."

Roshel poked a green rectangular tile with a long pointer. "Good. Now, understand everything I'm about to say is out of date. But let's start with what we know about the Green Heart."

"How is that relevant? We're not planning to attack them."

She sighed and shot me an exasperated look. "I can't believe Yoshana lost a war to you. They're the key to this campaign. If they keep the pressure on the Shield in the south, we have a chance. If they turn on us, we don't. Look."

She rapped the green rectangle again. It was near the border between the Green Heart and the Source, just south of the Shining River that divided the two states and flowed into the Muddy.

"That force shadowed the Darkness Radiant the whole time we were in Green Heart territory, and it didn't stop when we crossed into the Source. I guess they weren't sure what our intentions were. Our best guess is it's due south of Stephensburg now. That's about three thousand men."

A brigade, more or less. Slightly smaller than the units Hake and Lago had brought to the Battle of the Cleansing. I saw Roshel's point. The force wasn't large enough to seriously threaten Stephensburg or Our Lady, but it could wreak havoc with our supply lines once we moved against the Darklands.

She continued, "Most of the Green Heart's troops are still in the southeast, though, drawn up along the Paint, facing down the Shield's troops."

She rapped more green tiles. "The Heart had over thirty thousand regulars at their peak, but they took heavy losses in Yoshana's campaign against them, and some defected to us after the Battle of the Paint. I'd guess they've got no more than twenty thousand effectives left. Minus the three thousand up here and another three thousand or so in garrison and at border defense posts, that's no more than fifteen thousand facing the Shield. They had almost twice that with their militias for the battle, but they can't have kept militia troops mobilized this long. Those guys will have gone home. So figure three thousand on our border, fifteen thousand on the Shield's. You see why it matters now?"

"I get it. They're tying up the enemy for us - unless they decide to make a run at us instead. How many Shield troops are they facing?"

"Good question. Since neither side has made a move in two years, let's assume they're pretty evenly matched. The Shield started with a bit less. Took fewer losses in the campaign, but we took more into the Darkness Radiant. I'm guessing the Shield's total troop strength is less than twenty thousand, plus whatever the demons are bringing to the party. Most of them will be massed on the Paint."

"And we need to keep it that way."

"Exactly. Also don't assume for a second that Gurath's stupid or lazy. He's a three hundred year old military commander with total mastery of the Darkness. We were counting on Yashuath's assassination setting him back and I think it did, but he'll have his own plans. And he'll know Yoshana's dead."

A shiver ran down my spine. For the first time it really sank in that I'd beheaded humanity's best defense against the Hellguard.

"Suddenly this is all feeling a lot more urgent."

"Good. Because Gurath's sitting somewhere doing the same thing we are, except I bet he knows a lot more about us than we do about him."

We decided to send BlackShield Jarl Lago as ambassador to the Green Heart. As a convert to Tess' mission, he was eloquent on its importance. He was a senior military man, a figure who commanded respect. And the Monolith didn't share a border with the Green Heart; he would appear more disinterested than General Hake or a representative of the Source's military.

We decided that a company of his troops would make a good showing and serve as an adequate guard, without looking like an invasion force. Fortunately, he still had the cavalry company that had made my life miserable at the Battle of the Cleansing. They'd make better time than infantry.

"I am honored, Judge Minos," he declared. "Then Prophetess has given her blessing to this venture?"

I really thought about just lying to him. It would make him feel better. Instead I said, "She hasn't said no." Which was true, more or less, in the sense that I hadn't asked her. But how could a peace mission be a bad idea?

"How could a peace mission be a bad idea?" I said to Tess that evening as we walked under the trees.

"It's not, obviously."

"So you agree that Lago should go speak to the Senate of the Green Heart and propose an alliance."

She stopped and shot me an exasperated look. "How about you stop treating me like I'm an idiot. Proposing a peace treaty between the Source and the Green Heart isn't at all the same thing as proposing that we gang up together on the Darklands."

"What about a mutual defense treaty..."

"Minos."

"Tess, the demons will invade again. It's in their nature."

"You know that?"

"I saw what they did to their slaves in the Darklands. I know how they use women. I know what Roshel told me about their plans and before you ask, yes, I believe her."

Tess sighed. "I never said I didn't. Although you might keep in mind this is a woman who tried to murder me in my bedroom. But I don't doubt the demons and the Darkness are a threat. What I'm saying is that my mission wasn't to stop them."

"Let's sit." There was a stone bench nearby. We sank down onto it. "Couldn't your mission change?"

She put her hand on mine. "Of course it could. But it hasn't. Not yet, anyway. And I'm not going to start a crusade that could kill thousands without the Lord's guidance."

A dozen angry, unhelpful retorts bubbled up and mercifully died before reaching my lips. Was her original mission really a message from God, or just a hallucination that had somehow sucked in thousands of followers desperate for a cause? Was she going to just abandon those desperate followers now, so they could go back to slitting each other's throats? Would God finally get around to sending her another message after the Hellguard had butchered their way through the half the human nations?

I said nothing and squeezed her hand instead. The beginnings of wisdom, Dee would say.

"What?" she demanded.

"What? I didn't say anything."

"Exactly. And you don't agree with me. So what are you bottling up?"

So much for Dee's wisdom. I chose my words carefully. "If we do nothing, the Hellguard may attack. I don't know that will happen soon, but I expect it will. Roshel pointed out they'll see an opportunity with Yoshana gone. What'll happen even sooner is our alliance will start to fall apart. Without a purpose, Lago's men and Hake's and Roshel's won't stay together, and they were all fighting each other not long ago. They could be again tomorrow."

"And what do you want me to do about that?"

It was my turn to heave a deep sigh. "I need you to be Prophetess for them."

"So you can hold them together."

"Somebody has to, Tess. I guess that's me."

"I'm not going to endorse this crusade, Minos."

"Can you at least not condemn it?"

Her eyes hooded as she retreated into her own thoughts. After a time, she offered, "I won't say anything against it, Minos. But I'm not saying anything for it, either."

"That's all I'm asking."

"You're asking a lot."

Lago and the cavalry company were on their way. Roshel and I were planning our attack on the assumption his embassy would be successful. Despite knowing what "assume" makes out of "you" and "me."

"I don't understand why you're insisting on a southern approach," I complained. "It puts us up against the Shield's biggest concentration of forces, and the Green Heart isn't going to love twenty thousand of our troops tramping across their territory. If we hit straight through the Sorrows into the Darklands we have surprise, we don't even engage their main force, and we can burn down some of those goddamned Darkness-infested woods while we're at it."

"It's a question of numbers, Minos."

"Numbers? We can leave five thousand men in garrison at Our Lady and another five thousand in Stephensburg and have twenty thousand to deploy. What am I missing? How many men does it take to burn some trees?"

"To start with, we can't indiscriminately set the Sorrows on fire, appealing as that might be. First, because they could burn for months and completely block our advance. And second because it might make the Darkness flee into inhabited areas."

"Okay. Fine. Stipulated. We can still hack our way through safely enough. That place is a pit, but there's nothing in there that can take down twenty thousand men with swords, guns, and torches."

"What about our supply line? We can't live off the land in there. And supply caravans will get torn to shreds going through."

"Fine, so we leave a force behind to secure a passage."

"And that's where the numbers come in. The Sorrows is two hundred miles wide. Assume we need to leave a squad of half a dozen men every hundred feet to secure the path and reinforce each other. Do the math."

I did. About sixty squads of six men each, every mile, times two hundred miles... "Oh." It would take seventy thousand troops just to secure the supply corridor. Even stretching the intervals past the point of safety, we just didn't have the manpower.

I understood her, but I still protested, "But if we join up with the Green Heart on the Paint and push across, we're going to have a hell of a fight on our hands, even if we outnumber them two to one."

"You're not wrong. And don't forget they'll command the Darkness and we won't. Not a lot of Overlords survived the Battle of the Paint, but if they bring up Hellguards, we'll need some kind of counter or they'll go right through us."

I remembered the effect Pious had produced on my troops when he'd been infected - and he hadn't even known what he was doing. I thought of my own success against the Monolith. A Hellguard would be far more terrible than Pious or me - and there were hundreds of them.

"Maybe I'm starting to see why God hasn't been telling Tess this is a good idea. It's not going to be easy."

"And stopping Yoshana was? It's not going to be easy, but it needs doing."

"I do think it needs doing, Father. Don't you?"

For reasons I didn't quite understand, I was once again meeting with Father Roric. The lean priest drummed his fingers on the wooden desk and locked his eagle stare on me.

"Just to be clear, I take it this is not a confession?"

I swallowed and shook my head. I still hadn't arranged for the sacrament.

"Some of the saints confessed daily," he went on. "I can't imagine what they got up to on such a regular basis. But perhaps they were guilty of uncharitable thoughts toward those under their spiritual care. I suppose I could confess to that more frequently myself."

His eyes narrowed further. I felt like a mouse must feel right before it gets seized in a raptor's talons and has its head bitten off.

Roric leaned back. "This is a very ambitious plan of yours. Justified in your mind, I suppose, by the suffering it will alleviate?"

"Or the suffering that will occur if we do nothing."

He steepled his fingers, then rummaged through his books. He seized a thin volume bound in black leather and flipped pages. "Ah. Here."

He looked down at the page, then met my eyes. "The great failing of progressives is a lack of humility. The great failing of conservatives is a lack of compassion. Both are grave sins."

I wasn't sure what he meant, or how it was relevant, and said so.

He pointed a thin finger at me. "Within almost every person, and certainly every society, there are two warring forces. A movement toward change, what we could call progressivism. And a desire for things to remain as they are, which we can call conservatism. Your enterprise, a bold assault on evil in its very citadel, goes to the core of the ancients' progressive tendency. The idea that man can perfect himself on earth through his own efforts. That man can eliminate suffering. A profoundly arrogant view. But a profoundly compassionate one. The conservative view, that suffering is inherent in our condition, and that precipitate action may worsen the situation, shows far more humility. But it can also show a complacent lack of compassion for those who are suffering. Lack of humility is a failure to love God above ourselves, while lack of compassion is a failure to love our brothers as much as ourselves. Each is a violation of one of Christ's two great commandments."

Roric paused to see if I had a response. I didn't. He continued, "I understand that to alleviate suffering is a worthy goal - indeed, among the worthiest. And the Hellguard have indeed caused much suffering, and may yet cause more. But as you walk the line between a failure of humility and a failure of compassion, perhaps you should consider the task you propose to take on. Good and evil are so intertwined in this world that we cannot pluck out the weeds without destroying the grain. So intertwined that the line between good and evil passes through each human heart. Yours, mine... even Yoshana's. Even Gurath's, because as you've pointed out, the Hellguard are themselves human. Looking always and only at the evil that is outside us means not wanting to recognize the sin that is also inside us."

I had to object. "You're saying I should do nothing in the face of evil? Didn't someone say the audacity of the wicked feeds on the cowardice and omission of the good?"

He blew out air in exasperation. "Yes. Pope Leo the Thirteenth, among others. I am not advocating inaction in the face of evil. But to launch a crusade to eradicate the enemy without, while ignoring the enemy within... to see the speck in our brother's eye while ignoring the plank in our own... to seek to purge the world of evil while ignoring its presence in our own hearts... that is an error of which Jesus himself warned us. Repeated over and over, throughout the centuries, by Pope Francis the First and Alexander Solzhenitsyn before the Fall, by Saint Siles after. It's a basic idea that proves frightfully difficult for people to grasp."

I scratched my chin with my index finger, then chewed the knuckle. Inspiration failed to come. I ventured, "So what you're saying is that I'm lacking in humility."

The priest shrugged. "As I said, most people show a mixture of progressive and conservative tendencies. I believe Prophetess disagrees with you on this matter. Perhaps in this case she is excessively conservative, and is lacking in compassion."

"There's just about zero chance of that."

He shrugged again. "Then perhaps you should indeed consider the alternative."

"It's a priest's job to make you feel bad about yourself," Roshel growled. "It's a general's job to win wars. So how about you get back to doing that?"

I glared at the beautiful Overlord. She was still stunningly attractive even without the aura of glamor the Darkness had given her. She was also an opinionated pain in my neck, much like another woman of my acquaintance. They were both effective leaders, and being stuck between them was no fun at all.

"If you're going to back down every time someone accuses you of arrogance, you're never going to accomplish anything."

"I'm never going to be a factor, you mean? The last time you used that line on me I wound up infected with the Darkness as part of a secret plan to kill Prophetess."

She had the decency to look away.

"I didn't know about that," she said softly. Then the fire was back. "But the fact remains, Yoshana got things done. I get things done. You get things done when you show some spine. So are we going to get things done or not?"

I took a long, ragged breath. I'd agonized over Father Roric's words all night. But the fact was, I hadn't cobbled together our unlikely coalition and pressured Tess into supporting it - or at least not opposing it - just to throw it all away. Roshel wasn't wrong. Rallying against the Hellguard was something that needed doing, and I seemed to be the one to do it.

"We are. But we need some option besides forcing a crossing of the Paint at Goat Hill. I'm not going to be responsible for slaughtering thousands in the biggest battle since the Fall. We lost too many men at the Cleansing and Darkness Falling. I'm damned if I'm going to set up an even bigger, bloodier round of that if I can avoid it. Maybe we should try to gather more forces, an army overwhelming enough to force a surrender. I'll admit it, what you said about facing the Darkness scared me. We could send Hake to see if he can drum up support from Rockwall. Maybe after Lago comes back, we can send him to the Monolith."

"It'll take far too long, Minos. And you told me that when you tried bringing the Monolith and Rockwall into your war against the Darkness Radiant, they preferred to sit it out. What makes you think this time would be different?"

I opened my mouth and shut it. She was probably right. "Fine. But we still need a better option. Maybe if we sailed a fleet down the Muddy and swung around the coast, and came up behind them east of Seafields?"

Roshel made a face. "I don't think there are enough ships left in the world to transport twenty thousand men, and again, we're looking at too much time to build them. But crossing the Paint doesn't mean we have to cross at Goat Hill. There's two hundred miles of that river between Heartfield and Seafields. We can cross just about anywhere."

"Fair enough. And the Sorrows aren't as infested with the Darkness that far south. We could maybe even cross through north of Heartfield."

"Maybe. That's dangerous, though. Heartfield has a decent sized Shield garrison in it last I heard. Threading the needle between that and the Darkness would be tricky."

I stared at the unit counters on the map. "We need to understand the situation on the ground better. Is there anyone with you who knows that territory well?"

She frowned. "Maybe. But I don't want to widen our planning circle too much. The more people know, the more likely it is our plans will get back to Gurath."

That was like a punch in the gut. "You think there are spies in our army?"

Roshel laughed bleakly. "I've never seen an army so loyal that it didn't have a traitor or two in it. You of all people should know that - you turned me and Grigg against Yoshana."

I didn't have much to say to that, except, "Let's find some experts on the terrain down there. As few as possible."

The planning circle widened accordingly, then widened some more. As the discussions began to look more interesting, more of the senior officers became involved, and we could hardly keep them away from a map table set up in the middle of our headquarters. And with every new participant came at least one new opinion. Every option Roshel and I had considered was debated again, repeatedly.

Other approaches were brought up and discarded, including marching the entire army north through the Ice Fields and striking the enemy from the least expected direction. It didn't seem like the most terrible of ideas, since the heat of summer rendered the frozen north almost inhabitable. Until someone pointed out that it would also make the uncharted ice floes on the frozen lakes too thin to reliably support a man's weight - much less twenty thousand men's weight. The thought of losing our entire force into a freezing, watery grave shut down that plan.

Days dragged into weeks as decisions got put off, but it was still sooner than expected when a soldier burst in gasping, "Emissaries to see you, Judge Minos!"

I looked around the room. "It's early for Lago to be back, isn't it? Unless things went badly."

The soldier stammered out, "It's not BlackShield Lago, Judge Minos."

4. Uninvited Guests

"Well, whoever it is, I suppose you'd better show them in. And somebody had better go get Tess. They may want to see her too."

"I'm here," she piped up. I'd been so engrossed in the map I hadn't seen her come in. But she, her brother Kafer, Furat, Mist, and a number of others were sitting around a table in the back. Roshel's comment about spies came back to me, and I made a mental note to set a stricter policy on who was able to wander into headquarters.

"It's you we're here to see, Judge Minos."

The voice was oddly sibilant. The four expressionless men behind the speaker wore dark leather armor I'd seen before - but not on this side of the Sorrows. The speaker's tunic seemed impossibly white for someone who'd traveled any distance over dusty roads.

Sam launched herself at the emissary, planted herself six feet away, and burst into barking so loud, deep, and furious that her sides shook.

The man recoiled, then lunged forward and hissed open-mouthed at the dog. Sam yelped, backed five steps, and growled deep in her throat. Her lips pulled back to show teeth I'd seen snap a man's wrist.

The emissary's bared teeth were sharper than the dog's.

"Get her out of here, Furat," Roshel snapped. "She can't stop that thing."

"What is he?" a junior officer demanded. The man was now standing perfectly quietly, a slightly mocking smile on his face.

"It's a Darkness wraith animating a human body," the Overlord said. I had no idea how she'd reached that conclusion, but the man certainly must have been infected to produce that reaction from Sam.

Tess stepped forward. "We'll speak to your ambassador but not to the Darkness. Cast it out of yourself so we can talk. I'll help you."

The man laughed, again showing pointed teeth. "There is no one in this meat to cast me out, girl. The half breed knows better." It leered at Roshel.

"I've exorcised darker powers than you," Tess retorted.

The creature laughed again. "When the meat had a will, perhaps. There is no volition in this shell but mine."

Furat had hooked a leash to Sam's collar and was dragging her back. In a total breach of protocol, the big man had been wearing his pistol. He had it in his hand. "There's more than one way to get you out of there."

The embodied wraith grinned. "That's no way to treat an ambassador."

"Ambassador of what, exactly?" I demanded.

It chuckled. "You know, Judge Minos. You recognize my attendants. Lord Gurath sends his greetings."

I shivered violently despite the summer heat. The wraith's guards hadn't moved once since they'd come in, not when the dog had rushed them, not when Furat had threatened them. Slaves of the Hellguard, their will circumcised, as Yoshana had put it. They would follow orders but had no initiative of their own, not even an instinct for self-preservation. The wraith must have taken over one of those empty bodies.

"Your master might have come himself instead of sending something like you," I said.

It shrugged. The body was tall and healthy, its hair long and sleek and black. But the Darkness had been at work in more places than the teeth. I noticed the ambassador's fingernails had lengthened and thickened into claws. The host brain evidently gave the creature a human intelligence, but I had no doubt it was as feral and vicious as any cloud in the Sorrows.

"Why would my master make such a long trip for such an unpleasant reception? I was created to serve that purpose in his place." Something that might have been resentment flashed across the creature's face and was gone.

How would an intelligent wraith think, with no human will behind it? I imagined it would be an ugly mass of basic instincts, desires to feed, to grow, to dominate. Overlaid with the fear of something powerful enough to destroy it, like a Hellguard.

I didn't know what the thing or its master wanted, and I found myself reluctant to ask. I bought time while I calmed my thoughts. From the corner of my eye, I saw Furat dragging his angry dog away.

"What should I call you, then, Ambassador?"

"Ambassador will do."

"You have no name?"

It chuckled again. "Name. An individual distinction, as if your collection of cells were unique. What I am now, I was not before. I will become more than I am now. But if you must name me then I am Legion, for we are many."

Prophetess crossed herself. So did many of the officers present.

Roshel made a rude noise. "Don't give yourself airs, wraith. You're no demon. I've controlled more of the Darkness than you are."

"You are wrong, half breed. And the one who may have done so is gone now."

Roshel's eyes narrowed, then she waved her hand contemptuously. "Bark out the instructions your masters gave you, little dog."

The creature that called itself Legion snarled. I wondered if it would attack the Overlord. In a room full of our veterans its human body wouldn't reach her alive, but we didn't have the means on hand to stop a cloud of that size.

Instead it shook itself, its mouth twisting back to a mocking grin that still showed fangs. "My message is for Judge Minos, unless the half breed now commands."

"I'm right here," I said.

"My master's wishes are simple, Judge Minos. He asks that you accompany me to see him, so that the two of you may speak. And so avoid this war."

"Who says I'm planning a war against your master?"

"Are you not?"

The wraith cocked its head to the side, the smile never leaving its face. I'd underestimated the thing. Whatever else it was, it was clearly more than a collection of instincts with the power of speech.

"You want me to go to the Darklands."

"My master wishes it, yes. I will escort you."

Roshel snorted out a laugh. "Gurath should know better than to think we're idiots."

I held up my hand. "We'll need some time to consider his proposal. We'll set up a pavilion in the main field where you and your men can rest. Under guard. You understand, of course."

The ambassador dipped its head.

Now it was Prophetess' turn to object. "You can't be serious, Minos! House that - thing - in Our Lady?"

I turned to her. "You think it would be better to turn a wraith out into the town, unguarded?"

She opened her mouth and shut it again. Her face was set in grim lines of disapproval, but she didn't say anything.

"Captain Railes," I continued, "escort our guests to the center of the drill yard. Have a pavilion set up with food and facilities. And have the Shadowed Hand stand guard. All of them. With torches."

My adjutant saluted. "Yes, sir."

I thought the expression that briefly flitted across Legion's face was naked hatred, but I couldn't be sure.

"Prophetess, Minos," Roshel snapped, "come with me."

She added the word "please" as an afterthought, but I knew an order when I heard it. Even though I was her superior officer, I went.

Roshel led us up to the third floor of the command center, to a small room with no windows. My leg was killing me by the second flight of stairs and she must have known it, but she didn't slow down. She took a torch from the wall in each hand as we went. When we were in the room and she had shut the door behind us, the Overlord waved the burning brands through the air, poking at every corner. I winced as the flames surged perilously close to two ancient, faded paintings on the wall. Finally satisfied, Roshel left one torch on the floor to block the crack under the door and kept the other in her hand.

"Kill it," she demanded.

"Huh?" I said stupidly.

"Kill it with fire. We can take it by surprise. I'm pretty sure you or I would notice if it infiltrated us, and I assume Prophetess can repel its probes. It'll have infected almost everyone else around it. But if we hit it fast enough, we should be able to destroy it before it kills too many of the guards."

I thought about how Yoshana had insinuated the Darkness into Lord Brom's men, so she could use it to kill and cripple them at her will. Would Legion have done the same thing? Why wouldn't it?

I held up my hands. "You're right, it's dangerous. And I know how you feel about the Hellguard. But first off, maybe we should think about Gurath's offer."

Before she could interrupt, I went on, "We've been planning long enough to know we don't have the forces for an overwhelming victory. And second, it's really bad etiquette to murder an ambassador, even an obnoxious one."

"That thing's a provocation, Minos. And I don't just mean it's intended to offend us, although obviously it is. I mean it in the literal sense. There are humans in the Darklands who still have will, and Overlords who can pass as human. Gurath could have sent one of them. Instead he sent that wraith to provoke a reaction, observe that reaction, and report it back to him. Every nuance of what we said and did will be information for him. So even if you want to negotiate with Gurath - which is idiotic, by the way - don't give him more knowledge of us than you have to. Go to him if you must, but leave that thing here as a pile of ash."

"That'll tell him something too."

"Yes, it'll tell him we're not to be trifled with. I don't mind if he learns that lesson."

Once again, I was reminded that Roshel hadn't commanded a third of the Darkness Radiant because of her aura of seduction. She had a sharp, ruthless mind and an iron will.

Still, that didn't mean she was right. "We're not murdering a guest, much less an ambassador."

"That's not even a person, much less an ambassador."

"Maybe not. But I've met folks who don't think Select are people either. For that matter, I don't think I thought paleos were people, until one of them turned into one of my best friends. We're not killing Legion."

"That thing isn't going to become one of your best friends."

"I didn't say it was."

The Overlord blew out an exasperated sigh. "Fine. Does that mean you're going to be an idiot and follow an embodied wraith into the Darklands?"

I shot Prophetess a quick glance. "That part I haven't decided yet."

The room Roshel had secured was too small for the group I had in mind. We moved to a conference room on the second floor. And Railes made sure the ambassador's pavilion was set up at the far end of the drill yard, a quarter of a mile away.

"I don't think even a Darkness wraith can control probes from that distance," Roshel said. "But I really have no way of knowing for sure."

She had a torch in each hand again and was prowling around the chamber with them. She even waved the flames toward each person that entered the room - Hake, Railes, River Mist, Tolf, Cat, Tarc, the occultists John Dee and Aharon son of Malak, the priests Father Roric and Father Juniper. Hafnum Furat was the last, along with his dog. Sam trotted around the room sniffing at everyone and wagging her tail, happily collecting pats on the head and scratches behind the ears. After completing her circuit, she retired to a corner, turned around twice, and sank to the ground doing her impersonation of a furry, white log.

The Overlord looked at the dog with narrowed eyes. "Good enough," she decided. She closed the door and set both torches on the floor, warding the crack. Sam sniffed at a drift of smoke, then closed her eyes and went to sleep.

"Good enough," Roshel repeated.

What little chatter there had been died down and all eyes turned to me. "Railes, how are our guests doing?" I asked.

The tattooed captain dipped his head. "They're just sitting there, boss, quiet-like. We've got half of the Shadowed Hand watching them now. I was figuring two twelve-hour shifts. Normally either Mist or I would be with them, but you wanted us both here."

I nodded. The twelve warriors of River Mist's Hidden Moon Clan who'd survived the Battle of Darkness Falling were part of my special forces unit now. They knew even more about the Darkness than the two dozen living veterans of the company I'd led in the campaign against the Monolith. Half the company would be eighteen men. It should be enough.

Thinking about the Shadowed Hand crystalized something in my mind. At our peak, there had been forty soldiers in the Shadowed Hand. The Hidden Moon Clan had brought twenty warriors to the fight against Yoshana. Of those sixty, thirty six remained. They were the best troops in the army, and they'd been at the forefront of every engagement. And now nearly half of them were dead.

I wasn't going to throw them into that meat grinder again if I could help it.

"I'm going to see Gurath," I said.

"What?" Prophetess blurted. Half a dozen throats echoed her.

"When did you decide that?" Roshel demanded. "Half an hour ago you hadn't decided yet. I thought the point of this meeting was so everyone else could talk some sense into you."

"It was. And then I started thinking about how many soldiers we've lost over the past year, and that made the decision for me."

General Hake cleared his throat. "It's good that you're worried about the men, Minos. It's one of the reasons they follow you. But throwing your own life away isn't going to save anyone else's. Everyone knows the demons are treacherous. It's pretty obvious they're just planning to kill you so you can't lead us against them."

All the soldiers in the room nodded vigorously.

"Still, the possibility of peace should never be ignored," Dee mused.

That phrase chilled me more than Hake's blunt declaration. I was pretty sure Dee had used those exact same words when he'd argued in favor of my mission to accompany Yoshana into the Darklands. That journey had seen me infected with Darkness. Under its influence, I'd nearly killed Tess and half the people in this room.

"That's what you said last time, and look how well it worked out," Tolf snapped, echoing my thoughts.

But, in the end, that mission had set in motion a series of events that led to Yoshana's defeat. God really did work in mysterious ways. "Yes, Tolf. Look how well it worked out. Yoshana is defeated. I know this is risky, but I'm not stupid enough to make the exact same mistakes twice. I'm not going to let Gurath convince me that I can control the Darkness."

"No, he's just going to rip off your head and stick it on a pike," the guardsman shot back.

Railes chimed in, "Look, boss, I don't think this is a great idea either. But if you're really going to go, we'll send the Shadowed Hand with you."

I had to smile. The whole point of the exercise was not to get any more of the men and women under my command killed. "Thanks, but what good would it do? If Gurath's really interested in negotiating, I won't need them. If he's going to kill me, he'll just kill them too."

Railes opened his mouth to protest, but I held up a hand. "They're the best special forces on the continent. Man for man, I'd back them against the Knights of Resurrection. No offense."

Roshel shrugged. The Knights had been Yoshana's personal corps, not hers.

"But what are thirty of them going to do against three hundred of the Hellguard?

Railes looked stubborn, but didn't argue.

Furat made a grumbling noise deep in his throat, sounding almost like his dog. He said, "Fine, I'll go with you. You can't tell me you don't need a dog that can detect the Darkness."

I shook my head. "That's exactly what I'm going to tell you. We know the Hellguard are filled with it. For that matter, we know the ambassador is a Darkness wraith. We couldn't keep Sam within fifty feet of it. Thanks, Furat, but no."

The look on his face was just as mulish as Railes', but he didn't say anything either. The objections seemed to have run their course.

"So it's decided." I stood.

Tarc barked out a little laugh. "One more chance for Prophetess to upgrade to a smarter Select protector when the current one gets himself killed." A smirk played on his gray face.

"I'm going too," Tess declared.

The chorus of objections was louder than when I'd announced my decision. I realized that I'd reflexively contributed "Like hell you are" to the general tumult.

"I should have gone with you the first time, when you went with Yoshana," she continued. "You said you won't make the same mistake twice. Neither will I."

"Everyone needs you here, Tess."

"You really don't listen, do you? I have no mission, now. I have no guidance from God. I can't lead an army, or even act as its figurehead. But I can go with you. Maybe that's my mission."

In my mind's eye, Yoshana's sword was at Tess' throat again. "I can't have you get hurt, not now."

"Not hurt, her. With her, me," Cat stated.

"Oh, sure. A girl who doesn't weigh a hundred pounds soaking wet is going to protect Prophetess against the demons," Tolf retorted. The paleo bared her teeth at him in a snarl that rivaled Sam or Legion. The guardsman flinched back.

If anyone could protect Tess, it was Cat.

"I'll go too," Roshel said. "I know the demons better than anyone here."

Tess scowled. Possibilities flitted through my head. The likely outcomes of having Tess, Roshel, and Cat together at close quarters didn't look good.

"You will not," I said. "If this goes badly, we need someone getting us ready for war. That's you. Like you said, you know the demons better than anyone. You've fought them before."

The Overlord glared, but didn't object.

Then, to my infinite amazement, Dee stood. "I'll go," he said.

When I gaped at him, he said, "When else would I have the chance to observe the Hellguard up close? The opportunities for study are limitless."

Tolf muttered, "If this doesn't work, we may all be seeing them up close sooner than we'd like."

Railes caught my shoulder as the planning session was breaking up. "I'll go too," he said quietly.

"Should I flatter myself into thinking you want to protect me, or be more realistic and think you want to protect Cat?"

"You really want me to answer that?"

I shook my head. "Not really. And I'm sorry, but no. I need you here. Roshel can take care of herself as well as anyone, but she's going to need bodyguards, and that means the Shadowed Hand. And I need you in charge of them." The irony of the Hellguard possibly trying to assassinate Roshel in Our Lady wasn't lost on me, since she'd tried to do the exact same thing to Prophetess.

"I get it." Somehow his grimace managed to make even the skull tattooed on the side of his face look anguished. "Just - take care of her?"

He didn't mean Tess. I was about to reassure him that Cat could take care of herself just as well as Roshel when my mind was invaded by the image of her little body crumpled on the ground at Yoshana's feet.

"I will," I said.

I think he would have said something else, but Father Juniper was returning, an acolyte trailing him nervously. "The Metropolitan wants to see you," he announced.

Even with a trip to the Darklands looming, a summons from the Metropolitan was something to take seriously.

"Go on in," Moya grunted. She didn't bother with her usual insults, and even seemed a bit less surly than normal. Maybe my impending doom was raising her spirits.

I passed through Father Doreden's office. The fat priest gave me a vague, worried smile, and gestured toward a door in the back. "Go on in," he repeated.

It was the first time I'd visited the Metropolitan's suite. The room was frankly less impressive than I'd expected for the highest remaining official of the Universal Church left in the known world. It wasn't much more than a dozen feet on a side, with a pair of desks, a small table, and a scattering of chairs. There were paintings on the wall and religious objects on shelves, but none of the gilding or elaborate decoration that made the basilica so impressive.

The Metropolitan stood in front of the sole window when I entered. His back was to me. The view of the lake and fields was pleasant, and I took a moment to enjoy it.

"I find it relaxing to look at God's work," the Metropolitan said as he turned. He was a small, trim man. The close-cropped hair that remained to him was white, but I couldn't be sure of his age. He had the vigor and controlled energy of a man no older than fifty, but a gravity that suggested decades more.

I nodded. "Yes, Your Eminence."

"You're going to see the demon," he went on without preamble. He didn't sit, or invite me to do so. I rested a bit more weight on the shirasaya katana that these days served primarily as a cane.

"Yes, Your Eminence."

"You lived near Redstone for a time, yes?"

I nodded.

"They have a phrase there. It translates roughly to, 'the devil knows because he's the devil, but he knows more because he's old.'"

"I hadn't heard that one."

"Gurath is very old. You've faced Yoshana, but the demon lord is a being of another order."

I frowned. "I understand, but I knew a Hellguard. In the end he was just a man. He helped us against Yoshana, and she killed him."

"I've heard about the Hellguard called Seven. Gurath will not be the same." The others were stronger, Seven had said. And didn't regard unmodified humans as people.

I shivered, but said, "I've been down this road before. I've faced evil. Comes to that, Your Eminence, I've been evil."

The Metropolitan stared directly into my eyes. I wondered what he saw there. What he said was, "I believe Father Roric is fond of quoting Aquinas to you."

I nodded. "And making me read him."

"I don't especially care for Aquinas. He's a little too logical and more than a little too pedantic for me. I prefer to go a thousand years farther back to Saint Augustine if we're going to look to the ancient Doctors of the Church. He said, 'The enemy had my power of willing in his clutches, and from it had forged a chain to bind me. The truth is that disordered lust springs from a perverted will; when lust is pandered to, a habit is formed; when habit is not checked, it hardens into compulsion.'"

I tried to make a joke of it. "If he died two thousand years ago, how did he know me so well?"

The Metropolitan didn't laugh. "He knew himself, and so knew us all. You know temptation, Minos. That doesn't make you immune to it. Perhaps even the opposite, as Augustine suggests. Gurath will know where you're vulnerable, and that's where he will apply pressure. Do not be afraid of those who kill the body but cannot kill the soul; rather, be afraid of the one who can destroy both soul and body in Gehenna."

I shivered again. "Prophetess said that to Yoshana. Yoshana suggested she could do both."

"But she couldn't. Neither can Gurath. But it doesn't mean he won't lead you to the one who can. Fear what Gurath can do to your body, Minos. But fear more what he can make you do to your own soul."

"We have to plan for the chance Gurath's going to betray us," I said to Roshel. We were alone in the vast map room. "Capture Tess and me to hold us hostage, or just kill us."

"I don't think that's a chance, Minos. I think that's pretty close to a certainty."

"You're a real ray of sunshine. I have to believe he doesn't want this war either. At least, not right now. Maybe he's just buying time." Or maybe the Metropolitan was right, and he intended to turn me. If that was the case, I'd disappoint him. The Metropolitan's concern for my soul notwithstanding, I was more worried about the thousands of lives under my command. I continued, "Whatever he's planning, we have to keep getting ourselves ready."

She shrugged. "I'll keep the troops drilling. The Shadowed Hand can start teaching everyone else the basics of how the Darkness works, and how to deal with someone that uses it. Lago will get back from the Green Heart whenever he gets back. At least this little venture of yours should probably hold everyone together until we find out what happens, one way or the other."

One way or the other. "I don't know how long this will take, but do send envoys to Rockwall and the Monolith too. Now that the demons have showed their hand, maybe it'll prod someone in power to actually get off their fat butt and do something useful."

"Maybe. I'll try." She didn't look convinced.

"If we're not back by winter... well. You should probably assume you're looking at a spring campaign. It'll be a pretty good bet that they've murdered us, and that should justify a preemptive strike. Hit them with everything we've got. And keep someone close to Melaret. She's probably still feeling vulnerable and if she thinks Gurath's going to back her more than we've been doing, she could turn."

She nodded. "Go teach your grandmother to suck eggs. I've got your authorization to do what I think is needed, then?"

The look on her face was so intense that I hesitated for a moment. "Give us until winter. And then yes. Do what you think is needed."

Silence stretched uncomfortably. Her dark eyes were on me, her brows slightly raised. "So…" I continued. "You've killed a Hellguard. Gurath's lieutenant. Just in case the need should arise, how exactly did you manage that?"

The brunette Overlord leaned back in her chair and put her booted feet up on the map table. Though the two weren't physically similar, she looked so much like Yoshana in that pose that I struggled not to stare.

"Demons die like anyone else. Of course, it helps if you outnumber them three to one, command the Darkness, and shoot them in the back at extreme range when they're not expecting it."

"In other words…"

"There's no chance you'll be able to defeat Gurath. If the issue comes up, you'd better hope you've made peace with God, because you're going to be seeing him soon."

"Yes, Minos?" Father Roric asked as I stepped into his office.

"Father? I think I'm ready for that confession."

5. Down the River

We let Legion sit until the next morning. I'd made up my mind, but I wasn't in a rush to get going. Nor did I particularly care to start my travels with the wraith at night.

There was daily mass in the basilica. I usually went just once a week, but this seemed like a time to make an exception. Tess went too, of course. So did Dee, though I noticed he didn't take communion. I wasn't sure the occultist worshipped any god but his own intellect.

The Metropolitan himself offered the mass. So at least we were being sent off in style. With my confession of the day before, the eucharist felt somehow more potent than usual. I could hope, anyway. Because we really were going to be walking into the valley of the shadow of death.

Railes had set up small tents for the ambassador's party under a huge tarp stretched across poles. There was a little table with benches in the center. Legion and its guards sat on the benches, utterly still. The Shadowed Hand surrounded them, each soldier holding a bared sword and a burning torch. The Hidden Moon Clan in particular looked as tense as wolves circling a bear.

If the embodied wraith was disturbed by the surrounding troops, it hid the fact well. Its usual, slightly mocking smile remained pasted in place. When we approached it stood languidly, inhumanly gracefully, a characteristic I'd seen before in the possessed.

"And so, Judge Minos? Will you be joining me to visit my master?"

"Yes, Ambassador, I will. So will Prophetess, her bodyguard, and Doctor John Dee." I nodded to the three of them.

The wraith frowned. "The paleo and the occultist are not necessary."

"They will still be coming with me. Unless your master is afraid of them." Interesting that the wraith hadn't objected to Tess.

The smile was back. "My master fears nothing, of course."

"Of course. Although he seems to have feared war enough to have desired peace, and feared personal violence enough to send you instead of coming himself."

Legion gave me a hard look. "My master will not be pleased by insolence."

"Don't take us for idiots, Ambassador. Your master has his own agenda, and I'm certain human welfare doesn't figure highly on it. The welfare of humans in general, or specific humans in particular, like for example mine. I'll go with you. So will Prophetess. That puts two leaders of Our Lady's armies in his power. But Roshel is staying behind to command those armies, and she doesn't like the Hellguard. If Prophetess or I fail to return, she'll roll through the Darklands like a plague."

The Overlord's smile was pure malevolence.

Railes spoke up. "If any of them don't make it back, wraith, I promise you this - whatever else happens, you won't survive."

Had Roshel's expression been frightening before? Now her grin would reduce small children to tears. I thought I was glad she was on my side. I dissected that idea for a second - I thought I was glad, or I thought she was on my side? Maybe better not to examine the notion too closely after all. A very dangerous person was about to step out of others' shadows and put her own mark on the world.

A range of emotions played across the ambassador's face. Rage and hate were certainly there, but for just a moment, I thought I also saw fear. Then it controlled its expression again. Legion was very sophisticated for a cloud of the Darkness, and again I reflected that it was a mistake to underestimate the creature.

"Shall we go, then?" the ambassador asked brightly.

It wasn't quite that simple, of course. We still had to pack - and what we packed depended on where exactly we were going and how we were getting there.

"We will ride south to Eeltown and take ship on the Shining River, down the Big Muddy River to Delta City. I have arranged passage there to my master's territory."

That presumably meant sailing around the continent's southern coast from Delta City to Seafields, formerly in the Green Heart, now under the Hellguard's control. I did some quick calculations in my head. We would be sailing downriver, and along the coast the wind would be at our backs. It would still take weeks. Going the opposite direction would have taken far longer. And Legion had known Yoshana was dead - almost certainly before the creature began its embassy.

"That's not the way you came here."

The ambassador's smile widened, showing fangs. "No. The way I came is not a way you can travel."

That probably meant the wraith and its guards had passed through the Sorrows. I didn't know how the wild Darkness of the forest would react to a semi-tamed cloud like Legion, but there would likely be risk to its guards at least. Which might imply that the Hellguard had discovered a relatively safe route. That was worth knowing.

How many troops could the Darklanders filter through the Sorrows? Were we at risk of being hit from behind, perhaps after Roshel deployed our forces south? If so, the wraith had let slip an important piece of information. Which wasn't likely. Still...

I exchanged a glance with Roshel. The significance wasn't lost on her. The Overlord's grasp of the tactical considerations was almost certainly better than mine.

"We'll pack accordingly then, Ambassador," was all I said. "We'll rejoin you here in two hours and we can be on our way."

I waited until we were nearly back at our headquarters before I spoke to Railes. "You got that, right?"

"That they've got a way through the forest? Yeah. Not a surprise."

"It was to me. We've been counting on the Sorrows being a barrier to them."

Roshel repeated my own musings back to me. "I doubt they can get very many men through at a time, or they would have done it already. And that thing wouldn't have let such a big secret slip. It's not stupid."

"Agreed, but not my point. Railes, I was worried about assassins before. I'm more worried now." I turned to Roshel. "You might want to sleep with one eye open. And a lot of oil lamps around you."

Cat had thrown an oil lamp at Roshel to stop the Overlord from murdering Prophetess in her bed, back when we'd been enemies. Roshel's eyes widened, then she laughed. "That would be a really ironic way to go."

"I'd say you have it coming, but still, let's try to avoid it, shall we?"

"Oh, no argument here."

Kafer made such a pain of himself that I nearly had Railes lock him up. His first words to Tess after finding out about our journey to the Darklands had been, "You're not going." After she explained to her brother in no uncertain terms that she was in fact going, his next argument was - predictably - that he was coming with us. Tess wasn't having any of that either.

I choked back the urge to shout at him, or better still throttle him. He was just worried about his sister. Instead I told him, "I need you here. I need someone I can trust to keep a close eye on Roshel."

Kafer's face lit up. There weren't a lot of adult males who wouldn't be happy to keep a close eye on Roshel. He nodded eagerly. "You can count on me."

"Tricky, you," Cat declared as Tess' brother headed off to make whatever preparations he thought necessary for guarding the brunette Overlord. I wasn't entirely sure whether it was an accusation or a compliment. Knowing the paleo, it was probably a bit of both.

"You ready?" I asked her. True to form, she carried only the glassy knife I'd given her, a thin cloak, and a water skin. I traveled light, but Cat took it to extremes. It wasn't that she couldn't carry more; there was an amazing wiry strength in her slight body. She just didn't believe in owning things. The curiosity that had earned her the name "Cat" had taught her to read and set her apart from her people, but in many ways she followed their traditions. At least she'd stopped trying to eat people.

"Ready, me. Always." She patted the blade at her hip.

"Worried?" I spoke softly. Tess was just out of earshot.

"No." I was more relieved than I'd care to admit. The paleo's instincts were good. She continued, "Die now, die later. Die sometime, everyone."

Not so relieved anymore. I studied her, looking her up and down. She stood just a little taller than five feet and couldn't have weighed much more than a hundred pounds for all her toughness. Her hair was long and dark, her skin strangely light for someone who got as much exposure to the sun as she did. I didn't know exactly how old she was and suspected she might not either, but I guessed it wasn't more than sixteen.

"Railes is worried about you. I told him I'd take care of you."

"Good man, him." She'd said it before. I supposed it was true in the ways that mattered. Cynically, I imagined that was especially the case if you were a woman who listed "murder" as the top skill on your résumé.

"Minos!" Dee was bubbling with enthusiasm, which was pretty much his normal state, often at wildly inappropriate times. The lanky occultist was in many ways the polar opposite of Cat - tall, verbose, and utterly useless in a fight. He would be invaluable in chronicling the events to come, if we survived them. He wouldn't be helpful at all in actually helping us survive. Although he was extremely adept at saving his own skin by running away.

"Are we ready to go?" he asked.

"I suppose we are."

There was no particular ceremony to our departure. We just met up with Legion's group and set off. But as we followed the wraith and its bodyguards through the inner gate that led out to the lake and fields beyond the rectory, we found what seemed like every inhabitant of Our Lady lining the sides of the path. Someone had found a bagpipe, and as we walked by the assembly burst loudly into the strains of "Amazing Grace."

"Amazing Grace, how sweet the sound, that saved a wretch like me. I once was lost but now am found, was blind but now I see."

My heart swelled. "You see that?" I challenged the ambassador. "You really think you and your master can stand against that?"

"'Twas grace that taught my heart to fear, and grace my fears relieved. How precious did that grace appear, the hour I first believed."

Legion seemed taken aback, though its bodyguards were as impassive as ever.

"If we could live ten thousand years, bright shining as the sun, we've no less days to sing God's praise, as when we first begun."

Only when we'd passed through the outer gate and the music had faded behind us did the wraith answer. "Yes. Of course we do."

And even though we were still within the calm streets of the surrounding town, and the summer sun shone down warm on us, I shivered.

There were horses again. It was more than a day's walk - or ride - to Eeltown, and I supposed I should have been grateful I wasn't going to be limping along for sixty miles. But my knee didn't really appreciate being in a saddle, either. After a few hours, neither did my backside. Like Roshel had said, riding was more fun when the Darkness healed the saddle sores.

Of course neither the embodied wraith or its unspeaking bodyguards showed any sign of discomfort. They'd provided their own mounts, and I didn't want to ask where they'd come from. I doubted those horses had crossed the Sorrows. I had to believe it would have been easier for the ambassador to buy them in the Source than to murder their previous owners and steal them. Hell would have plenty of currency to provide its servants. Or so I told myself.

Legion set a steady pace, brisk but unhurried. The road was straight and flat, and the horses were happy enough to amble along it. Tess and I trailed behind the wraith and its soldiers, content to be by ourselves. "It reminds me of the old days. When the two of us first came up here," she said.

"Except the paleos we met were trying to kill us, instead of just sticking to you like a burr." Cat's mount was a few paces behind and to Tess' right. Her knife was sheathed, but it would come out faster than thought at the first sign of danger.

"And Dee didn't have anyone else to bother." The occultist was up ahead, chattering away at the ambassador, apparently completely unfazed to be addressing a human body animated by a cloud of the Darkness. The wraith, in turn, seemed perfectly happy to answer Dee's questions.

"The masters call these creatures the soulless," Legion was saying, waving its hand to encompass the dark-armored guards. If they were offended by that term, they gave no sign. There was nothing to suggest they even knew they were the topic of conversation. Dee said as much.

"They understand my words," Legion replied. "But they have no will of their own and so they do not react. They do not feel indignation, or anger, or even fear. Even the instinct of self-preservation is gone. They are like machines. They follow orders, no more."

I shuddered. We'd killed some of them when I'd crossed into the Darklands with Yoshana, Roshel, Grigg, and Erev. Yoshana had captured one, then killed him. The man had remained impassive even as he died.

I shuddered again, remembering other events from that journey. I'd left Erev crippled when I'd fled Yoshana's company. He'd hunted me down and shot me in the leg so he could finish me off at his leisure. Cat had stabbed him to death from behind instead. The paleo girl's ferocity could be disconcerting, but I wasn't sorry to have her at my back.

My knee twinged in memory of the bullet.

"You okay?" Tess asked.

"Eh. Not the most pleasant topic of conversation up there." Which was true enough, even if it wasn't the whole story.

"So they're born that way?" Dee was asking.

"No. Not born. Made. The Darkness is thick in our home. When the soulless are of a certain age, their minds are circumcised with the Darkness. The will is removed. It is inconvenient in many ways. They must be given strict orders for even the most basic tasks. If they are not told when to eat, they will starve. But it keeps them free from the Darkness."

"I don't understand. Then the body you inhabit...?"

"One of the soulless, yes. It is different. Small clouds of my substance are attracted to the will. They seek out a master to serve, but most humans are too weak to control us, because the human will is too weak to control itself. We follow the deep, strong instincts, rather than the conscious mind. The host turns, follows its darker thoughts. But in many ways, with a small cloud, the host remains the master."

That had been true for me, when the Darkness had been in me. It was hard even to formulate in my mind the right words for it. Had I commanded it? Had I been infected with it? Yes, to both, and no. It had been part of me, usually yielding to my will, but sometimes it had seemed the larger part.

"Such a pairing is dangerous," Legion went on. "A weak host controlled by its darkest drives is a danger to itself and those around it."

I'd seen that, with the first person Tess had freed from the Darkness, a girl in a village called Brambledge. Later I'd experienced it much more personally.

The wraith continued, "Clouds are not attracted to the soulless, for they have no will. But there is a second form of possession. True possession. When we are larger, and stronger, we have enough will of our own to control the shells of the soulless. That is what you see here."

It grinned and spread its arms. "This is our destiny. As we grow and add to our substance, we become greater, and can control more. One day, this accumulation of us that you see here, this I that you may call Legion, will be strong enough to control the uncircumcised as well, and eradicate their will. So I may move to a greater shell, with more potential. You, perhaps."

All its sharpened fangs were visible in the smile it showed Dee. The occultist finally looked perturbed.

"Or even a Select." It turned and leered at me. "One day, this accumulation will be strong enough to control one of the masters."

For a moment, the naked lust on the creature's face reminded me of Stephen before Melaret had killed him. The wraith's self-control was better, and the expression passed quickly. It still felt like a cloud had shadowed the sun.

"How much farther to Eeltown?" Tess wondered aloud.

The days were long at the height of summer, and we made good progress. Still, we'd be at least one more day on the road. I'd seen no signs of a town or even an inn. Farms lined the road, corn growing about to the height of the horses' bellies. The farmhouses stood off in the distance down narrow dirt lanes. I wasn't going to impose Legion and his men on anyone's hospitality.

We pulled off into a wide, flat place at the side of the road as twilight was coming on. This spot was an established campsite; there was a small fire pit and a lean-to that would help cut the wind in winter, though it wasn't necessary at this time of year.

While the others unsaddled the horses, I scrounged for brush and fallen branches. Stacking them in the fire pit, I used flint and steel and a bit of oil to kindle a blaze.

"Are you cold, Judge Minos?" Legion asked.

"No." Although the sun was setting, the air was warm. It wouldn't be chilly even in the dark of night.

"Do you have some food to cook, then?"

"Nope." We had the usual, sad collection of travel provisions - pemmican and hard bread. There was enough water in our skins to reach Eeltown and no need to boil more.

"Then I have to wonder… you don't think such a small flame can protect you from me, do you?"

"Ambassador, I'm shocked. I wouldn't begin to suspect treachery from the Hellguard, or entertain even the remotest possibility that you'd try to murder us in our sleep. But, since you mention it, it might be useful to be able to set you on fire if the need arises."

Cat grinned.

"I assure you, Judge Minos, it will not." The wraith smiled.

"And I'm very grateful for that assurance." I turned to Dee. "You and I will have the first shift. Tess and Cat will take the second. Needless to say, if our friends here make any move toward us, or you feel even the slightest tendril of the Darkness, kill them all and burn the remains."

I returned Legion's smile. "Good night, Ambassador."

For all my bluster, I had my doubts about our ability to deal with a wraith of Legion's size plus four soldiers. So it was with a profound sense of relief that I woke up the next morning to find our throats uncut.

The ambassador smiled blandly. "I trust you slept well, Judge Minos. During the shift you permitted yourself."

"Like a baby, Ambassador."

"Ah. So you woke up crying every few hours? I'm sorry, I didn't notice."

That wraith was much more sophisticated than a cloud of Darkness had any right to be. It didn't help that Tess chuckled at the creature's joke. I'd gotten used to losing battles of wits with a self-educated farm girl who'd grown up on the edge of a garbage dump. Now I was losing to something that wasn't even human.

Cat's expression was so artificially innocent that I shook my head. "Don't you start too." The paleo tried and failed to suppress a snicker.

It figured. I was trying to save the world and my allies were enjoying jokes at my expense by the forces of hell.

It took another full day of throbbing knee and sore backside to reach the town, but there was still plenty of daylight left when we made our way to the open gate in a low barricade that was more fence than wall. Eeltown had a defensive perimeter, unlike the unwalled town surrounding Our Lady, but it was more notional than functional. It wouldn't do much to slow down an army, or marauding Darkness clouds, or even a band of paleos. This deep into the Source it was relatively safe. It also might have helped that Eeltown didn't look like it had anything that anyone would want.

"Eel Creek joins the Shining River here and increases its flow," Dee volunteered. "This is the first point where a large boat can reliably navigate down to the Muddy even when the river's low. So it's a port, more than anything else."

And apparently not much even of that. Eel Creek must have been the stream just past the fence, spanned by a wooden bridge just wide enough for a single wagon. The gate, in addition to being open, was completely undefended. I didn't see many signs of activity in the town beyond.

"It's getting late. People are probably at dinner," Tess said. But she didn't seem very impressed with the place either. Eeltown was a metropolis compared to the farming country near the Flow where she'd grown up and I'd met her, but she'd seen real cities since then, Oldtown and Our Lady and Stephensburg. It had been an eventful couple of years.

"Dinner is a charming notion," Dee volunteered. I'd been contemplating the same thing myself, but the thought of taking the wraith and his soulless troops into a tavern weighed heavily against it. It said something about our present company that a Select and a paleo weren't even close to the most socially unacceptable members of the group.

"I'm not sure it's such a great idea," I said. "We might attract the wrong kind of attention, and the last thing we want is to get into a fight. It's still light out, and the river rafts run day and night. Let's go down to the waterfront and see if we can find someone who's willing to take us out."

Tess shook her head. "That's stupid, Minos. We have to stable or sell the horses, pick up provisions, and find a captain. You want to do all that before it gets dark, and skip the last chance we'll have at a decent meal for weeks?"

"I'm just saying…"

"Come on, let's go find somewhere to eat."

"Dammit, Tess…" I muttered under my breath, but I knew I'd lost the argument.

Legion leered at me. "I had been told you commanded in Our Lady. Evidently I was misinformed."

I snapped, "Evidently you don't really know anything at all about humans. At least not the female kind."

A narrow, paved path wound its way from the gate down to the river. One and two-story wooden buildings ringed with low fences crowded up to the side of the road. Much like Eeltown's outer wall and the farms around the Flow, these barriers were more symbolic than real, usually just two horizontal slats stretched between posts. I wasn't sure whether the structures beyond were houses or shops, or perhaps served double duty as both.

A block into the town, a tan and black dog charged up to a fence rail and barked furiously at us. Either it was generally bad tempered or it didn't need to be a spirit dog to sense the Darkness animating the ambassador's body. Legion's troops marched on impassively, but the wraith recoiled.

I touched its shoulder. "Don't." The last thing we needed was a repeat of the ambassador's confrontation with Sam. Legion looked surprised to see my hand on its body, but nodded and kept walking. The dog continued yapping long after we passed it. I noticed, however, that it could easily have passed through the fence but had chosen not to. So it was smarter than it looked.

Probably smarter than me.

Halfway to the river we came to an unfenced building, larger than most. A freshly painted sign showed a white sailboat on a clear blue river, with neat letters announcing "The Wind Drift" and "Food, Drink, and Lodging."

"Here?" Tess asked.

I shrugged. "Why not?"

There was a stable, but no groom in evidence. I dismounted, staggered as my bad knee took my weight, and passed my reins to Dee. I was only beginning to lurch toward the front door when a big man came out, nearly as tall as Furat or Grigg, and wider.

"Sorry, stable boy's sick," he said. "I'm Karsten Vadlo, I run the place."

Vadlo stopped in his tracks as he took in my gray skin, white hair, and black eyes. "Oh, uh, you're..." His eyes ran across my companions and widened further. "You're not Judge Minos, are you? And... and Prophetess?"

I nodded.

"That's - well, it's an honor to have you, sir. My cousin's in the army, he was at Darkness Falling."

It was my own turn to do some figuring. Our Lady's troops at the battle had all been from the Monolith, except for my Shadowed Hand special forces. Vadlo's cousin would have been with the Darkness Radiant, one of Stephen's men.

"I hope he was pleased with the outcome."

"Lord yes, sir. He's loyal to the Source and he goes where he's told, but he's happy as a clam not to be wondering anymore if he's working for the devil herself." Then, as if he might be having some doubts on that score, the innkeeper stared hard at Legion and his four expressionless soldiers. "Who are your friends, sir?"

Before I could open my mouth, the wraith said, "I am Legion, Ambassador of the Darklands, servant to the Hellguard. Now that Judge Minos has graciously removed our greatest enemy, we are seeking to reach an understanding."

Vadlo looked like he'd swallowed a pickle whole. I glared at the ambassador.

"Will you, uh, be wanting to stay the night? Judge Minos?" By his tone, the big man was clearly hoping the answer was no.

I nodded. "Yes. We'll need a room for Prophetess and her bodyguard, and Doctor Dee and I can share another. The ambassador and his companions can all sleep together." I was more than half tempted to suggest they could do it in the stable, or maybe behind the outhouse.

"I'll go get my wife started on that, then, and get back to see to your horses." And he hurried inside.

"You're a real help," I snarled at Legion.

"Why, Judge Minos," the wraith protested, its voice full of wounded innocence. "You don't mean to suggest that you had intended to conceal the truth from your people? I would not have thought your faith approved of governing by deception."

Vadlo was in a hurry to escort us to our chambers, guiding us through the common room as he said, "I'm sure you'll, uh, be more comfortable dining in private with your party than down here in the crowd." The crowd stared at us as we went by. There was plenty of space for us, but the looks we got ranged from curious to hostile. The innkeeper must have said something about our group. I wondered what.

"I'm starting to regret not letting Roshel burn that thing," I grumbled when Dee and I were behind closed doors.

The occultist raised his eyebrows. "Do you mean that?"

I sighed. "I'm trying to be a nicer person so no, I don't suppose I do. Irritating as it is, it's still an ambassador. And it's some kind of intelligent life, even if it's not human. So no, I'm not going to set it on fire just because it annoys me. But if it gives me a good reason…"

Carefully wrapped at the top of my pack was a pair of oil grenades, modeled on the ones Furat had used against the Darkness and a herd of possessed swine in the Sorrows. He'd managed to kill a wraith. I figured I had a decent chance of taking care of this one, too, if it came to that.

"Minos," Dee said seriously, "Be careful. Physically, of course. I don't know how strong Legion is, but I have no doubt he's a being of some potency. When he said Roshel could not command him, I don't believe he was bluffing. But also, don't forget that he is our adversary. His comment to the innkeeper was not made casually, or merely out of spite. Roshel was quite right. He is a deliberate provocation in every sense."

I'd told Dee about my conversation with Roshel and Prophetess. But I was tired and grumpy and wasn't following his point. "You want to be a little clearer on that?"

"Legion is deliberately undermining your support among the people. As you've observed, he's more sophisticated than you would expect of a Darkness cloud. And those behind him are very, very sophisticated indeed."

"Weren't you the one who thought going to see Gurath was a good idea?"

"Oh, yes. Pursuing the option of peace is almost always preferable to war. But if I had to place money on the outcome of this mission, I'd bet against you." Dee spoke quite cheerfully, as if discussing an academic problem and not the fact that we were going to die.

I remembered the Metropolitan's warning against Gurath. I'd once been something of a dark power myself, and by luck or the grace of God - call it what you liked - I'd faced Yoshana and lived. Turning public opinion against us had been one of her techniques, but the demon lord would have three hundred years' worth of additional tricks up his sleeve. Yoshana herself had told me, *"The Hellguard deceived me, and I'm not easily deceived."*

It was beginning to come home to me that I really had no idea what I was getting into.

Cat greeted me with a bared blade when I knocked on their door the next morning. I didn't mind. I liked that the paleo was careful - not to say paranoid. It had saved Tess before.

Inside the room, the object of that protection yawned and stretched in bed, under the covers. Tess was determined, energetic, and driven. But she liked her sleep. Cat, by contrast, hardly slept at all, and when she did she kept one eye open.

Traveling with "my woman" wasn't going to be as much fun with the paleo stuck to her like a shadow. On the other hand, this trip wasn't shaping up to be much fun anyway.

"Let's get moving?" I said.

"Give me five minutes to get dressed." I considered suggesting that I could stay and watch, but thought better of it. Tess would just turn bright red and throw a pillow at me. Cat might stab me.

I gave Tess her five minutes, then knocked again. Legion and its guards emerged from their room just before my fist touched the door, almost as if the wraith had been watching. Hah. Of course it had. Something like that didn't need eyes to spy on us.

We all trooped downstairs together. It wasn't early, but the common room - which had been so full the night before - was almost empty. A tall woman stood up from her chair. There was a thickset man with her, who stayed seated. Aside from them we were alone.

She smiled brightly and marched up to me. "I'm Losywa," she announced, sticking out her hand.

I shook it. "I expect you're looking for passage down the Shining?" she continued. She was as tall as Prophetess, and broader. She looked like she could be Hafnum Furat's sister - big and blonde, though her eyes were brown rather than blue.

"How -"

"It's really the only reason people come to Eeltown, so it's not hard to figure out. Certainly anyone as important as you and Prophetess, Judge Minos. It's an honor to meet you, and the ambassador too. I'm sure you're doing the right thing, whatever Vadlo says. Did he defeat Yoshana? I don't think so. So do I care what he thinks? Anyhow, what I mean to say is that of course Ram and I will take you down the river. I'm afraid none of the other raft captains is going to. So you're sort of stuck with us."

She kept smiling, the entire matter apparently resolved in her mind. The words had come out in a continuous stream. I wasn't sure when she breathed. I couldn't have interrupted if I'd wanted to.

"Bad idea, Loo," the seated man grunted.

"Did I ask you, Ram? Don't be rude. We talked about this already. Don't mind my brother, Judge Minos. He helps pole the boat, and he makes sure the passengers behave."

"What -"

"He throws them overboard if they don't. You'd be amazed what you see on the river. Some people think their passage buys all kinds of other things. Not that you'd think that, of course. And it's not too wide or too deep here, so if someone goes overboard, they generally get out all right. You wouldn't want to get thrown over the side on the Muddy. Ram, come say hello."

He rolled his eyes and stood. I could see the family resemblance to Losywa, but though his frame was massive he was no taller than his sister. I still would have given him good odds in a wrestling match with Railes or Furat. He certainly wasn't someone you'd want to annoy in a confined space, like on a boat.

He shook my hand, too, then made the rounds of the others. Unlike Losywa, he showed no qualms about touching Legion and the soulless. Despite what she'd said about being pleased to meet them, she hadn't approached the wraith or its party.

"Well, then, I suppose I'm happy you're willing to take us, Losywa. Ram."

"Like I said, I'm honored, Judge Minos. Now of course there is the question of the fee. That'll depend on how far down you're going. I assume it's all of you? I hope you aren't planning on taking your horses? There isn't really room and they don't travel well."

Again the bright smile. So she wasn't so honored to serve Tess and me as to take us for free. That was fair enough - she had to eat too. All that talking must consume a lot of energy.

Legion hefted a small pouch. The contents clinked when the wraith bounced the bag in its palm. A claw-like fingernail teased open the drawstring knot, and Legion showed the captain a ten-weight gold coin. "Ten of these. To Delta City."

Losywa's eyes widened, and she was momentarily speechless. But only momentarily. "That's very generous, Ambassador. Yes, totally acceptable. See, Ram, I told you this was a good idea. But I do hope you'll leave the horses? Like I said, horses and rafts really don't mix. I'll buy them from you, if you give me an advance on the fee. That'll be very clean and neat. And I'll give you a fair price. I hate to say it, but if you sell them to Vadlo, he'll probably cheat you. I mean, he's a good man, don't get me wrong. But I'm afraid he was really spooked by the ambassador. You know how people are."

Even the wraith found it hard to get a word in edgewise. Taking advantage of a brief pause, it said, "One coin as an advance to purchase our horses. The other nine are yours when we reach Delta City."

The captain nodded briskly. "Done. Do you have provisions for the trip down? It doesn't seem like it. Don't worry, I'll take care of that for you. Included in the price. Ram, can you go stock up on food and water? I'll talk to Vadlo about the horses and get them squared away."

"We -"

"I know, you haven't paid him for the lodging. Don't worry, I'll take care of that too. It's the least I can do, you know. We'll get everything organized faster than you can blink, and then we'll have you on your way."

The reason for Losywa's generosity with the provisions and lodging became obvious half an hour later when we made our way down to the docks and she proudly showed us her vessel. It was a wooden raft a little over twenty feet long and maybe eight wide. A small lip around the edge kept water from sloshing over the deck. Or at least limited the amount.

Any one of the ten coins Legion had offered her would have bought the boat outright.

"No sail?" I asked.

The blonde gave me the kind of look usually reserved for halfwits. "The wind blows the wrong way, Judge Minos. We pole down to the Muddy, then it's oars. The current does most of the work. Oh, you're thinking about that sailboat on Vadlo's sign, aren't you? That's, um, what do they call it, artistic license. You can't sail on the Shining."

"How do you get it back upriver?"

"We pay a steamship to haul it, or hire a wagon in a caravan. Sometimes both. There are plenty of ships up the Muddy, not so many that come all the way up the Shining."

So at least some of her profit would be consumed getting the raft back home. Still, I had no doubt the ambassador had grossly overpaid. Would that have been from ignorance? Not likely, given how clever the wraith had shown itself to be. Then... demonstrating that the Hellguard could be generous masters.

I turned to Legion. "All this I will give you if you will bow down and worship me."

The wraith grinned and dipped its head. "My masters have much to offer."

"I'm sure they do. Just look how happy your guards are to be in their service. Practically bursting with joy. Let's get on our way, shall we?"

Losywa looked confused, but she and her brother began shifting the gear aboard. She had been right about the horses, if clearly self-serving; there was no way we could have brought the animals onto the raft.

I had no real experience with boats, but this one was simple enough. It was simply a set of logs lashed together, kept afloat by nothing more than the buoyancy of the wood. Once Ram cast off from the dock, he and Losywa began shoving the raft out into midstream with long poles, and the current quickly caught it. There was some maneuvering to make sure the clumsy craft was pointed end-first, and then the water did the work.

The shore crept by at a walking pace, perhaps fifty feet away on either side. "How long does the trip usually take?" I asked.

"Ten days or so. On a good day we can make a hundred miles, if we use the poles and the oars. We're not going very fast, but we go all day and all night. Why, are you in a hurry, Judge Minos? Because you didn't say so, but -"

"No, no particular hurry." And there wasn't. I had no reason to rush to my encounter with Legion's masters. But I wasn't looking forward to ten days in a little boat with the wraith and its soulless bodyguards, either. I sighed. "No. No particular hurry."

Dee, Tess, Cat, and I took up a position at the front of the raft. Legion and its men gathered at the back. Ram poled at the front left corner, Losywa at the right rear. There wasn't much to do. Tess and I watched the shore go by, sometimes holding hands, and that was pleasant. Cat eyed Ram intently, as if trying to decide if he was edible. The paleo seemed oddly fascinated with him. If being stared at bothered him, he gave no sign.

Dee, however, quickly grew bored. He drifted to the back of the raft and struck up a conversation with the captain, with nightmarish results. Between the two of them, the buzz of voices was nonstop. Literally. You would have thought that at some point one or both would run out of either air or topics of conversation, but apparently not. Tess and I glared at them, with no more effect than glaring at rocks.

Legion strolled up to us. "I could silence them," it suggested. "Permanently."

I looked up at the wraith. "Here's the thing, Ambassador. We don't kill people for being annoying, or you wouldn't be around anymore. And in case you think it's your guards keeping you safe, let me assure you that Cat could gut them all before you even thought of giving them a command. As for you? Well, let's just assume you're beyond my power to control. I have no doubt Tess can hold you, and I have other ways to deal with the Darkness. So let's not have you threatening any of my people."

Its face went very still, but I could sense the thoughts behind the mask. I'd had something like Legion inside of me, or maybe I'd been something like it. Maybe at our darkest core, all of us were something a little bit like the wraith.

The ambassador pasted a smile back on, though fangs showed through its parted lips. "Of course." And it returned to its own end of the boat.

Ram turned to me. "That thing wants you dead, you know."

He hadn't lowered his voice. And it occurred to me that just because Losywa did all the talking for the pair of siblings, that didn't mean her brother was slow.

When night came we slept in shifts. Ram or Losywa stayed awake to guide the raft. Tess, Cat, or I joined them, to make sure our guests from the Darklands behaved themselves. Dee didn't take a shift, since he likely would have fallen asleep and certainly would have been useless in a fight even if he was awake.

The dark water of the river glowed in the moonlight. Ram poled occasionally, ripples spreading and fading. "Quiet out here," I said softly.

He nodded. "Mm hm." He didn't seem to feel a need to talk, and to be honest, neither did I. The rest of the group dozed silently, except for Prophetess, who snored. Despite the unpleasant company at the far end of the raft, it was one of the most peaceful moments of the past two years. Until we reached our destination, there was nothing for me to do. I smiled a little to myself. Like I'd said to Losywa, I really wasn't in any particular hurry at all.

Night turned to day. The river flowed on, farms and occasional towns lining its banks. We drifted by. Dee and Losywa never seemed to run out of topics of conversation. I didn't mind anymore - I'd learned to ignore them. There were little notches along the side of the raft, and Losywa set simple fishing poles into them. Every now and then we caught something big enough to eat. The captain assembled a small metal tripod in the center of the boat, with two bowls in it, the lower one filled with charcoal. The roasted fish made a nice change from our dried provisions.

Late that night it rained, but it wasn't one of the torrential downpours that sometimes scoured the plains, and it stayed warm. I don't think anyone minded being wet - although of course the water ran off Legion as if the ambassador were coated in oil.

The next day Tess and I were sitting together, watching the water slide by and enjoying the sun when the raft abruptly ground to a halt. Ram and Losywa had sunk their poles into the riverbed. I couldn't see why. We seemed to be safely in the center of the channel. We were just beginning to pass under a bridge arcing over the river, but it seemed no different from a dozen others we had floated past.

"Toll," Losywa explained.

"Toll? For what? It's not like anyone's maintaining the river."

"No, but it's also not like we want to be shot with fire arrows or have our boat sunk with rocks. And that's what happens if we don't pay the toll, you see. It's really... well, it's a toll, isn't it?"

"It sounds more like robbery," Tess said.

A tin bucket came down from the bridge on a rope. A pair of heads peered over the edge. One of the men smirked at me and hefted a bow.

"It really isn't a problem," Losywa said. "You see, there's a system, we just put a coin into the bucket, and -"

The bucket clanked onto the floor of the raft. The bowman tipped over the side of the bridge and fell wordlessly, splashing into the river five feet from the boat. A dark stain spread on the water.

I knew instantly what had happened. I'd seen it before.

"Dammit, Legion!"

"You're welcome," the wraith said, its little smile firmly in place.

"You do not murder citizens of the Source!"

"No? Even ones who are robbers that prey on commerce? That is not the sign of a well-ordered society. Your ancestors theorized that the first necessary building block of society was safety against threats both external and internal. The second was rule of law. You appear to be lacking both. You will find that my masters are not."

"The third building block in that particular theory, if I recall, was liberty," Dee said. "Which I believe your masters' society rather lacks."

"But the first two are essential precursors to the third. The third, in the absence of the first two, leads to a failed state. Do you preside over a failed state, Judge Minos? Do you aspire to nothing more?"

My hand itched to draw my katana. I was seething with fury, and I couldn't have honestly said whether it was at Legion, the murdered robbers, or myself. Losywa was staring in horror as blood drifted down the current, surrounding the bowman's bobbing corpse.

"Um, what just happened? Because I really -"

"Pole on," I snapped.

"Well, no, we're not going to do that. Because if we do they'll shoot us from the bridge like I said. And I really -"

"They're all dead, Losywa," I said. "No one's going to shoot at us because they're all dead."

"How -"

"The ambassador here infiltrated the Darkness into them and, I can't be sure, but I'm assuming probably broke down the cell walls of their carotid arteries. Maybe severed some nerves too so they couldn't get off a shot while they were dying. Depends how careful our guest here was being."

The wraith's smile widened. "You are very familiar with the technique."

"Of course I am. You know what I've been, and who I've been with." In my defense, I'd usually used the Darkness to choke my enemies into unconsciousness, rather than killing them. What Legion had done was much more Yoshana's style, both in methods and motive. She hadn't liked being robbed either.

But, to be fair, I'd killed plenty of people too.

I think for the first time, Losywa realized what she was transporting, and for the first time, words failed her. Tears started from her eyes.

Ram gave the raft a push with his pole, nudging us downriver again. He carefully set the long stick on the deck, went to his sister, and put his arms around her. "It's okay, Loo."

She snuffled and whispered, "I think this was a bad idea, Ram."

He replied, "I told you so, Loo," but he smiled when he said it. She smiled back.

The raft drifted on, leaving death behind.

"Don't do that again," I said to Legion.

The wraith hadn't stopped grinning. "As you say, Judge Minos. But I fear my masters will be disappointed in you."

"I certainly hope so."

Provoking. Testing. Collecting information it could pass on to the Hellguard. Roshel had been absolutely right about what Legion was doing. I stared at the sleeping ambassador and wondered again if I'd been wrong when I'd refused her suggestion that we kill it.

Ram and I were again the only ones awake. The heavyset man followed my gaze to Legion, then looked back at me. He opened his mouth but closed it again without speaking.

"What?" I asked.

He just shook his head. I didn't press the point.

The river meandered through a series of long, slow switchbacks. Ram steered us around sandbars with his pole. Then, almost from one moment to the next, the banks to either side disappeared in the distance and we drifted into what seemed like an infinite expanse of black water.

"What just happened?"

"We're on the Shining now. The eastern fork of the Muddy."

The border between the Source and the Green Heart, my childhood home. As Ram guided us into the center of the channel, I could make out flickering lights in the distance.

Losywa came up next to me. She must have sensed the change in the river. "There are towns on both banks. But they're walled. And sometimes it's really a pain to get customs permits to dock and trade. Especially if there's fighting between the Source and the Heart. You know, like a few years back. We can stop, but we'll waste a lot of time on paperwork. And, uh, they may not like your guest."

That was a good bet, especially on the Green Heart side, where they'd suffered an invasion by Yoshana and the Hellguard. If people were suspicious of the Darkness - and rightly so - in the Source, where the Darkness Radiant had taken over the local military, then we'd certainly get an unfriendly reception in the Heart. Which made me wonder what Legion expected us to do in Delta City.

I asked the wraith the next day.

"We have agents in the city," the ambassador said smugly. "They will take us the rest of the way to the Darklands. Loyalty is easily purchased in a port such as Delta City - another weakness of your human regimes."

Sometimes the best answer is none at all. And sometimes you just can't think of a good response. I let the wraith's comment pass.

In daylight we could see the towns we passed. On both sides of the river they were heavily fortified with high, brick walls and cannon emplacements. It was another sad commentary on the lack of unity in the human nations that the Source and the Green Heart were more worried about defending against each other than the threat of the Darkness or the demons. Legion didn't comment, but it seemed to me that it smirked even more than usual.

Steamboats began to appear on the river, huge things like leviathans, driven by paddle wheels at the back or sides of the ship. The river was wide enough that we could stay well away from their churning wakes. It was also too deep now for the poles to work, so Losywa and Ram paddled with oars instead.

A day later the eastern fork of the Muddy met with the northern branch, and the river grew wider yet. "We've made good time," Losywa announced. "More than halfway there."

Tess moved a little closer to me. "Remember when we came up this way?"

I nodded. It had been a simpler time, before there'd been armies to command, before I'd even dreamed of being what Roshel called a factor. Of course, we'd been chased by paleos and drelb, and then an angry Reborn preacher had nearly unleashed a mob on us, and we'd had to cross this river on a bridge that really wasn't meant for humans to walk on, and then we'd nearly frozen to death...

Simpler, yes. Better, not necessarily.

"Who would have thought, huh?" Tess asked.

"That people would be looking to us as leaders? Or that we'd be alive?"

She chuckled. "Both. And that we'd be together."

"Well. That part I was definitely hoping for, even back then."

She smiled, then turned serious. Very softly, she said, "I'm not sure we're doing the right thing now. Going with that... thing."

I shrugged. "I'm not sure either. But I'll say this - after all the people I've killed, and all the others I've sent to their deaths, I'm not going to pass up a chance to avoid a war."

She squeezed my arm and at that moment, at least, I was convinced I had in fact done the right thing.

6. The Road to Hell

Four days later we drifted into the massive, sprawling harbor at Delta City.

The Muddy and the Whitewater came together into a messy tangle. The main channel of each river emptied out into Brown Bay, but upstream little rivulets and creeks spun out into a sweltering, mosquito-infested bog between the two. Delta City sat on a low rise on the eastern bank, the shops and warehouses and residences rising high enough that they didn't flood when the river spilled over its banks. At least, not very often.

Docks spanned the range from rickety gangways that probably got swept away in the current every few years to massive structures on thick pilings, big enough to handle the Muddy's largest steamships and sailing vessels from around the coast of the Warm Sea.

It was unpleasantly hot in the late afternoon sun, but the wharfs still swarmed with activity. I'd never been to Delta City before, but it bustled like a kicked ant hill compared to other ports I'd seen. In addition to thousands of humans jostling each other and shouting in half a dozen different accents, there were bleating sheep, lowing oxen, and hordes of raucous seagulls circling overhead scanning for scraps.

"Lots going on," I said to Losywa.

"It was quiet for a couple of years," she replied. "Well, you know, first there was the Shield invading the Green Heart. That dried up most of the traffic from Seafields. And then the Monolith's mercenaries were attacking shipping on the Whitewater. But it's all pretty much back to normal, right now. And normal here really means there's quite a lot going on. Look over there. That's a steamship from way up the Whitewater, west of Oldtown. And just look at that ship there with the sword design on its mainsail…"

I stopped paying attention. There certainly wasn't peace on earth. As far as I knew, Rockwall and the Monolith still hadn't settled the status of the disputed land between them. And Roshel had made it clear that the Green Heart and the Shield were still glaring at each other across the Paint. But for the moment, commerce was thriving. And that meant a chance for human progress, if we could prevent another outbreak of war.

"Dock at Pier 26A," Legion commanded. "We will transfer to another vessel for the next stage of our journey, and I will make the rest of your payment."

Losywa shook her head. "I literally can't dock at 26. It's a deep water pier. We'd have to tie on to a piling and climb up it. And I really don't think you want to be climbing up a wet piling with no handholds. I can bring us into Pier 18, and then it's just a short walk to 26. Most of the rafts dock up here, farther upstream, and then the steamboats farther down, and then the big sailing ships from the Warm Sea. Some of it's a question of depth. The water's shallower here and the deeper draft ships can't make it this far up. And really I guess some of it's just custom, too…"

Again she continued to talk, but I'd learned to filter the words out. The unending flow of conversation didn't keep her from doing her job any more than his virtual silence kept Ram from doing his. We glided to a low dock and Losywa threw the painter rope to a man standing there, who quickly wrapped it around a low post.

"Couldn't you have just done that yourself?" Dee asked. "Seems inefficient for someone to just stand around to tie up boats."

"I could. But that's a dockworkers' guild job. And if I did it, I'd get sideways with the dockworkers' guild. And if you want to work in Delta City, you really don't want to be sideways with the dockworkers' guild." She tossed the man a small coin, which vanished into a pocket in his tunic. Whatever the amount, it seemed excessive for thirty seconds worth of winding a rope, but I understood her point and kept my mouth shut.

"Come on, I'll take you down to Pier 26," Losywa said. She turned a big smile on Legion. "After we settle up the remainder of the fee, of course."

"Of course," the wraith smiled back. It counted out nine gold coins that shone in the sunlight. The dockworker's eyes bugged out. Losywa was a big woman, and Ram was built like an ape, but I wondered how safe they would be on the docks with that much gold in their pockets.

Dee and Losywa kept up their conversation as they walked, and Tess went in front with them, two tall women and a tall man breaking a trail through the crowds. Ram and Cat followed behind, guarding Losywa and Tess. Cat was perhaps half Ram's weight, but almost certainly the more dangerous of the two. Legion walked with me, trailed by its silent, soulless guards.

"Soon the final leg of our journey begins, Judge Minos." The wraith sounded far too happy about that.

"I can hardly wait."

"This is Pier 26, Ambassador," Losywa announced. There was nothing there. The wraith abruptly looked far less pleased.

Losywa and Ram had gone to ask around. The rest of us stood on the pier, attracting the occasional stare. Even in this cosmopolitan port, we were an odd group. My stomach was beginning that long, slow, never-ending descent I associated with upcoming battles. If we got into a fight, things would get very ugly very quickly.

It was amazing how happy I was to see the siblings again. At least until Losywa started explaining.

"So, here's the thing," she said. "Apparently the captain of the Sea Star - that's the ship that was here - I guess that was your ship, Ambassador? Well, apparently he got drunk and started bragging about the important connections he had to the Darklands government. Which really wasn't a good idea. Because it's one thing to trade with the Darklands and the Shield. But the Heart is still at war with them. So shooting off your mouth about being an agent of their government? Not a good idea."

"What happened?" Legion demanded.

"They burned him alive, sold the crew into slavery, and sailed the ship out into the bay and sank it."

Wow. Not a good idea at all. Apparently the Green Heart was still taking the Shield's invasion very personally. "Was it a lynch mob that did that, or the authorities?" I asked.

"Hard to tell. If it wasn't the authorities doing it, they really didn't do anything to stop it."

"Unacceptable!" Legion roared, its face twisting into a snarl that didn't look human at all. The wraith whirled and slammed its fist into a piling. Wood and bone splintered. The creature's next cry was wordless, inarticulate, and it smashed its other hand into the piling. The beam, nearly a foot in diameter, cracked down the middle.

I had seen enough combat to know the second blow had pulped not just the bones in the wraith's fist, but its wrist as well.

Legion's face was perfectly controlled when it turned back to me, although the ambassador's lips were parted just enough to reveal its fangs. The Darkness was visibly at work in its hands, closing torn skin and rebuilding fractured bones.

I was sickened, more by memory than by the wraith's inhumanity. I'd done something similar once when the Darkness had been in me, except my target had been a human being's face rather than a post.

"Well," Legion said calmly, as if nothing had happened. "It seems we need another alternative. I will find us another ship, or passage overland."

"You're insane," I retorted. "A Select and a paleo are going to draw attention. And once people figure out what you and the soulless are, they're going to kill us all. Weren't you paying attention, wraith? They burned a man alive just for being associated with you. In the Source, Tess and I are respected enough that we could get you accepted, even when you pulled something stupid like you did back at Eeltown. This isn't the Source. If you try to book passage with a ship or a caravan, we aren't going to last ten minutes."

"I have an idea," Losywa volunteered. "Depending on how much more gold is in that bag."

There was a lot more gold in the bag. And that's how we found ourselves the owners of a forty foot, two-masted sailboat.

"It's a coast runner," Losywa explained. "Not big enough to handle a storm out in the Warm Sea. But if we stay close to shore, it should get us to Seafields. That's where you're headed, right, Ambassador?"

Legion nodded.

"And you can pilot this in open water?" Dee asked. "Because I'm given to understand that a sailboat on the sea is rather a different thing from a raft on a river."

"Of course," Losywa assured the occultist. He didn't seem completely convinced. I had no idea. As far as I was concerned, a boat was a boat. As long as I stayed on the inside and the water stayed on the outside, the rest of the details weren't my problem.

The same dockhand who had helped tie up the raft appeared to unmoor the sailboat. It seemed odd to me that one man would cover so much of the waterfront, until he spoke quietly to Losywa. "Seems like you and yours are in quite the hurry and spending quite the cash, missy."

"My passengers really are in a bit of a rush, yes."

"I'd hate to think that's 'cause they're doing something illegal. Like something a patriot should report to the militia. Unless they're just real generous? In which case, I'm sure they won't mind sharing."

Losywa sighed. "And you had in mind?"

"A hundred weight in silver."

It was a ridiculous sum, more than a month of a laborer's wages... although only a tenth the value of one of the gold coins Legion had been so free with.

"My passengers are generous, but not idiots. Ten weight."

"Ten weight'll get you a fine rush job with the painter, no lie. But to keep my mouth sealed tight shut when the troops come walking by? That's worth ninety more, sure."

"And yet there are easier ways to ensure silence," Legion drawled.

"No," I said. "We discussed this."

"You said I was not to murder citizens of the Source. We are not in the Source any longer, Judge Minos, so this man cannot be its citizen. Nor do you have anything resembling authority to give orders here."

"I said no. Get it out of him."

It was finally beginning to dawn on the dockhand that in his greed he might have bitten off more than he could chew. But he masked the fear beginning to cloud his face with a stubborn set of his jaw. "Don't think you can threaten me, blackeye. I've got friends."

"Who will never hear your call before Legion stops your throat, and who would only die if they heard and came to help. The Darkness is in you. You've been infected. Take your ten silver and go. You could tell the militia what's happened here... but then they'd burn you alive to get it out of you. Whereas after we leave peacefully, it will trickle out and away... in time. Long after we're gone."

The dockworker looked from me to Cat, who was grinning like a fiend, and then at Legion's four utterly silent guards. When his gaze landed on the ambassador, the wraith smiled wide enough to reveal all its fangs.

Losywa handed over a single silver coin and the man fled.

"My way is better," Legion said.

I shivered. "I've done things your way. I've been to hell and back. I'd rather not visit again."

The wraith chuckled. "Then you might want to walk back home now."

Dee had been right. The sailboat wasn't the raft, and the sea wasn't the river. The waters of the Brown Bay were calm enough, and Losywa seemed competent with the sails. Ram didn't look happy, but I attributed that to the idea of another week with Legion.

Once we cleared the bay, though, the wind picked up, and gentle swells turned into violent waves. Losywa fought to keep us moving parallel to the coast. Ram didn't seem to have much more idea of how to trim or tack than I did, although at least he knew that sheets and shrouds were ropes and not, as I would have assumed, some part of the sails - which looked more like sheets and shrouds to me.

In a moment of calm, I asked our captain, "How likely is this thing to capsize?" That was a nautical term I'd figured out pretty quickly.

She shook her head. "Not really likely at all. The wind's fierce out here, but the boat's stable. It's built for this, you know. So unless a hurricane blows up... Now, if there's a hurricane, well, then I guess we'd really better start praying. Because -"

"You can stop talking now." I made my way over to Prophetess. "I know you said it's usually not a two-way conversation between you and God, but if you wanted to mention to him that we'd rather not drown, it couldn't hurt."

She glared at me, and I thought she was going to say something about how inappropriate it was to treat the Lord like some kind of wishing well. But then she crossed herself, closed her eyes, and began murmuring under her breath.

"You might also tell him how sorry I am for all the awful things I've done. And said. And thought."

She opened her eyes. "You can tell him that yourself."

Yeah, great. Wasn't that her job? She had the direct line to God. My skill set these days seemed to mostly center around killing people, and getting myself smacked around. I was doing my part - I could use some collaboration on hers in the areas that were outside my expertise.

The wind came up again, harder than before. Tess' hair streamed and tossed in the gusts. The sea heaved and swelled like something alive. Or like the wrath of God. It came to me abruptly that against a living opponent, even one like Yoshana or Gurath, there was something I could do. Or at least imagine I could do. In the grip of the angry ocean, there was nothing. The wind and waves would throw us over, or they wouldn't.

I closed my eyes and stood in the spray, humbled before the divine. There was an arrogance in the Select. Or at least in me. We considered ourselves better than other men, and in some ways, we were. I realized that I had always thought myself superior - intellectually, physically, even morally. A huge part of my self-image was wrapped up in what I could do. But against the vastness of the ocean, of the universe, of its Creator, I was very small indeed.

"Forgive me my pride, Lord. Have mercy on your servant, a sinner." I didn't say the words out loud, but maybe for the first time I felt that I meant them in my heart.

There are no atheists in foxholes, the ancients had said. Or, apparently, in storms at sea.

Losywa shouted at Ram. "Reef the mainsail! More!" Whatever else she said I didn't hear. The two of them fought the sails and the rudder, and the rest of us tried to stay out of the way and not go overboard. Gusts of wind tore at our clothes, and a hard rain like a thousand pebbles battered at us.

And then it was over, and the sails slumped limp in the sudden calm.

"Well, that was exciting," Losywa said. "Ram, ease the sheets."

Her brother let out line, but there was no breeze to catch. "The weather out here really is the darnedest thing," she said.

"There's a reason we work on the river, Loo," Ram grunted.

"Where's your sense of adventure, Ram?"

"Pretty sure I left it back at Eeltown. How about you drop me off on shore and I'll go back for it?"

Two years past, I'd said almost the same words to Doctor John Dee on the way to Our Lady. I clapped Ram on the shoulder. "One of these days I'll tell you what adventure really looks like." And if he had any sense, he'd never leave Eeltown again after hearing that story.

"Tell us now," Losywa demanded, excited as a child.

I looked over at Legion, still dry as a bone despite the soaking the rest of us had taken, and still with the little smirk on its face. I wasn't sure how much of my tale I wanted to tell in front of the wraith.

"Ah, where to begin?" mused Dee. "Our friend Minos met Prophetess while he was salvaging garbage a few hundred miles west of here in Rockwall, but I met the two of them in a village called Brambledge. And I suppose that's as good a place to begin as any, because that -" he paused for effect, "is where Prophetess first cast the Darkness out of a person, and truly came into her own. And I'm pleased to be able to say that I was present for the event itself…"

And he was off. There was as much chance of shutting him up as there was of putting the sea into a bucket.

The breeze didn't come back as the hours - and Dee's story - dragged on. The sea was perfectly calm, but there was a reason why "becalmed" was a bad word in sailing. We weren't going anywhere. I considered suggesting that we could put the windbag occultist behind the sails - all that hot air coming out of his mouth had to be good for something.

I practiced humility and kept my own mouth shut instead.

It was twilight by the time Dee wound down, and there was still no wind. Losywa looked around at the flat, empty ocean in concern. "If it stays like this for too long, we're in trouble. I didn't really pack enough provisions for all of us to just sit here for weeks."

"We can adjust easily enough," Legion said.

With a lightning stroke of one long, sharp claw, it tore out the throat of one of its guards. The body flopped to the deck, twitched, and was still. "I do not require their services any longer. Now this one does not need to eat and can instead be food."

Losywa clapped her hands to her mouth and ran to the far end of the boat. Ram followed her. Tess and Dee had seen plenty of death before, but both stared at the wraith in horror before turning away.

Legion grinned at me. "They have no soul or will, Judge Minos. They are not human in a meaningful way. They are just meat."

The other three bodyguards remained utterly impassive, unmoved by what had happened to their comrade or the thought that they might be next.

"Yeah, that's what the last person who murdered one of them in front of me said. I didn't like it when she did it either, and at least they were her enemies."

The wraith's fanged grin widened. It pulled a knife from its belt and knelt next to the corpse. "Then shall I take it you won't be eating?"

"No, we won't."

"A pity. There's too much for me and my remaining guards to finish before the meat spoils. A shame for it to go to waste."

Cat met my eyes. Alone of us, she hadn't looked disgusted. She looked hungry. Of course, when we'd first met, she'd been planning to eat me.

"No, Cat," I snapped. "We don't eat people. Not even soulless ones, or soulless bodies possessed by Darkness wraiths."

"Waste," she grumbled, and turned away with one last long glance at the body Legion was starting to butcher.

We kept to the bow of the boat after that, with Legion and its surviving guards in the stern. Unfortunately that meant Losywa had to go to their end to steer. Ram and I went with her, because she wouldn't go alone. I didn't blame her at all.

The wind came back in irregular fits and starts. It never left us becalmed again, but twice more it grew violent enough to tip us and spray water across the deck. I didn't mind. It washed away the blood of the dead guard.

On the fifth day, Losywa said, "If we keep up this speed, we should get to Seafields tomorrow."

"Bet you won't be sad to see the last of us."

"I really won't. That's for sure. Not you, Judge Minos. It was an honor, helping you and Prophetess. My duty as a citizen." Although of course she'd profited from it hugely - or would, if she survived. "But I don't ever want to see the ambassador again. I really don't."

"You and me both."

"Do you really have to go with him? Once you're in the Shield, or the Darklands, who knows what he might do?"

I sucked in a long breath. "That thing's not a 'he.' It's an 'it.' And I'm sure it hates me, but it's following the orders of something more powerful."

"And you're really sure whoever's giving the orders wishes you well?"

I was almost completely sure Gurath did not. When you put it that way, what were we thinking? It wasn't too late to destroy the Darklands' monstrous ambassador and turn back... but it would be soon.

I sighed. "Nope. But I'm hoping he might not want a war, at least not right now. And that makes it worth the risk to talk to him."

She surprised me by giving me a hug. "You're a good man."

"In a whole lot of ways I'm really not. But I'm trying."

The next morning there were green sails on the horizon.

"Green Heart patrols," Losywa said. "I'd heard about this."

"News to me. I don't remember patrols from when I lived here." Not that I'd spent much time near the sea back then.

"Well, there wouldn't have been a need, would there?" Dee chimed in. "Before they took Seafields, the Shield couldn't have launched a naval assault unless they sailed around the Rat Shoals, and I'm told that's positively suicidal."

I nodded. East of Seafields lay a sunken peninsula. When the seas had risen in the Last Days, a spur of land hundreds of miles long had been covered by water. But it was far too shallow to navigate, and broken shards of buildings thrust up out of it. To go around was to risk the even fiercer winds that blew farther from shore.

But now, with Seafields in the Shield's hands, the Hellguards' forces could reverse the route we had just taken to strike deep into the Green Heart.

We passed between two of the patrol ships. They were huge, with massive square-rigged sails, many banks of oars, and steam-driven propellers. Cannons poked out above and below decks. They had none of our boat's simple elegance - they looked more like some mad child had screamed, "Make it go faster! And give it more guns!"

They didn't even hail us as we passed.

"Really don't care about anything going this direction, I guess," Losywa said. "Or anything our size."

Commerce continued. And where there was trade, there might be progress, and hope for the future. If we could keep the peace. I kept telling myself that as we sailed out of the Green Heart's waters, past the mouth of the Paint, past the new border where my parents might or might not have fought and might or might not have died. Into the territory occupied by the Shield. Into the lion's den.

"What is it?" Tess asked, seeing something in my face. I just shook my head and didn't answer.

I'd been to Seafields before, before the Overlords and Hellguard took it. It had changed.

The Shield didn't have patrol boats out. But they'd fortified the harbor beyond recognition with thick walls of stone and wood. Each side was wrapped in its own paranoia - the Green Heart with a blockade against a Shield armada that didn't seem to exist, the Shield reinforcing against an attack from an adversary that seemed more interested in defense.

But how to be sure? The Shield was now controlled by ancient horrors even more devious and ruthless than Yoshana, whose plots could mature over centuries. The fact that I saw no assault force didn't mean there was none. And on the other side, the Heart's defensive warships could bombard a city just as well as they could blockade against attackers.

Peace was a fragile thing. And possibly an illusory one.

"I will guide you in," Legion told Losywa. She almost objected, but realized the wraith knew where we were going and she did not. Still, she flinched away every time the creature came close to touching her. Again, I didn't blame her a bit.

The ambassador seemed amused, as usual. But why wouldn't it be? It was home, and we were about to be completely in its power.

Tacking inside the harbor was harder than keeping the right general bearing on the sea, or for that matter poling a raft. When we got close enough to the quay Legion indicated, Ram threw the painter. A pair of men in black and red uniforms hauled us in.

These weren't dockworkers. We were mooring ourselves to a military pier.

"You made good time, skinwalker," one of the soldiers called. "But this isn't the boat we were expecting. What happened, you lose the first one?"

The wraith hissed at them, and they laughed. Maybe Legion wasn't quite as at home as I'd thought. Somehow that didn't make me feel any better.

As the soldiers strained to bring the ship to the dock, Dee said quietly, "The term 'skinwalker' may be taken from ancient lore involving evil sorcerers who could take the appearance or inhabit the bodies of others. If that's the case, the term is likely pejorative. You'll notice the dagger emblem on the uniforms. That's a Shield insignia, whereas our friend Legion is an agent of the Darklands. Perhaps the alliance is not an entirely happy one."

That wasn't hard to imagine. My Rockwall and Monolith troops didn't get along terribly well, and the Shield and the Darklands had been just as much at each other's throats over the years.

The ambassador's hearing was unnaturally acute, not surprisingly. "Some of these humans don't yet understand who they answer to," it growled. "They will in time. One day when my hand is around their throat they'll understand."

"What's that, skinwalker?" asked the nearer Shield trooper as he lashed the boat fast. "Not trying to scare your guests, are you?"

He held out a hand to Prophetess. Both soldiers had the air of casual competence I'd come to associate with the disciplined veterans of the Monolith or the Knights of Resurrection. The pier was slightly higher than the boat's deck, but the man easily pulled Tess up. "There now. Better up here on land with real men than down on that nasty ship with a wraith and those walking dead, eh, missy?"

Cat leaped up to Tess' side and grinned at the soldier. "Better."

"God," the other man gasped. "That's a paleo!"

"Yes she is," I said. "A little help here? I took a bullet to the knee last month and I don't jump like I used to."

The first soldier met my black eyes squarely and grasped my hand. "A Select and a paleo. That's not a pair I would've expected to see together."

"You and me both, buddy. I'll tell you the story sometime if I live."

"You really Minos? The guy who bumped off Yoshana?"

I raised an eyebrow. "That depends. Is that a good thing or a bad thing around here?"

The soldier chuckled. "Good question. It's an impressive thing, no doubt about that."

"Less impressive than you might think. That's another story I'll tell you if I live."

"Man, those sound like two good stories. It's a shame you're going off with the skinwalker, 'cause I probably won't get to hear 'em. I don't expect to see you again. At least, not with your own mind behind your eyes." The man's bantering tone had gone deadly serious at the end. "You watch yourself up there. If I was you, I'd leave the women here with us. I promise we'll get 'em home safe. If they go where you're going... I wouldn't take that bet."

The summer day was warm and bright, but I shivered as if a cloud had blotted out the sun. The second Shield trooper was glaring at Legion and his guards, who had clambered up onto the pier by themselves.

"Good luck, Judge Minos. We'll wait for you here," Losywa announced. "For when you return."

"Better if you go home," I said. "I don't know how safe it'll be."

"A damn sight safer than you're going to be," the soldier who'd been doing the talking put in. I'd gotten his point already.

Legion was grinning again. "As agreed," it said, and tossed seven coins at Losywa, one at a time. The gold flashed as each coin flew through the air. "And now, Judge Minos, your chariot awaits."

"Chariot" wasn't the word I would have chosen. The vehicle at the end of the pier was an ugly, rectangular box on wheels. More than a chariot, the image that came to mind was a giant, mobile coffin. There were no horses to pull it.

The box had six doors, three on each side. Inside it was divided into two sections, the back a large area with two pairs of facing benches accessed by the four rear doors, and the front a smaller cabin with three seats. One of Legion's guards opened the rear doors for Tess, Cat, Dee, and me as we clambered into the back, then joined us. There was plenty of room, and no one had to share a bench with the soulless.

The interior was stark and not especially comfortable, all metal with minimal padding and small windows protected with thick wire mesh. It was dark and smelled old. The impression of a coffin was even greater on the inside.

"Some sort of ancient troop carrier, I imagine," Dee concluded. I supposed he was probably right, although how the Hellguard had kept the thing running for three centuries was a mystery to me.

The vehicle abruptly lurched into motion and a low, rumbling vibration filled it. After the initial jolt I found it more comfortable than riding a horse or even sitting in the bed of a wagon, and it certainly beat the soaking, swaying terror of a sailboat on the sea. But I couldn't say that I was enjoying the experience.

We picked up speed imperceptibly, but soon I could see the town passing outside the little windows far faster than the fastest horse could run. Tess was sitting next to me, and she gripped my hand. I felt better at the contact.

"The soldiers back there..." Tess' words trailed off, but I knew where she was going.

"Those were Shield regulars. The Second Expeditionary Legion, by their uniform." I'd developed a passing familiarity with the Shield's military forces growing up in the Green Heart, especially the First and Second Expeditionary. It came from knowing that they were glowering at us from across the border. "They didn't seem thrilled with Legion or his troops."

I shot a glance at the soulless who shared the compartment with us. He remained as impassive as ever. "Maybe there's a possibility... if their forces are as divided as ours..."

"Don't they say loose lips sink ships?" Tess said sharply.

"I'm not saying anything Gurath doesn't already know," I snapped. But she was right. It was foolish to talk strategy in Legion's presence – and disturbing that she needed to remind me of it. I nodded and shut up.

Despite the troop carrier's shuddering and the unpleasant company of Legion's guard, Tess quickly fell asleep leaning against my shoulder. Dee slumped in his seat and snored quietly. Cat's eyes narrowed to slits, although I was sure she would jolt instantly to full alertness at the slightest danger. She slept like her namesake.

I dozed fitfully, usually waking when the vehicle slowed to negotiate some obstacle or jounced through one of the gigantic potholes that cratered the roadway. We continued on into the night. A dim, red glow with no particular source illuminated the inside of the cabin, providing just enough light to see my companions without blinding me to the darkened landscape outside. Mostly that was just trees. That their shadows seemed somehow twisted and menacing must have been my imagination.

We stopped only once, when the sun was edging over the horizon and dew was on the grass at the side of the road. We all stretched painfully and staggered out of the car to relieve ourselves. My knee had stiffened during the night and hurt more than usual to move.

There were no signs of civilization, no facilities except the privacy afforded by the trees. I limped off behind one, then limped back.

"Where are we?" I asked Legion as one of its guards did something complicated to the vehicle involving large metal canisters.

"Inside the Darklands. It won't be long now." I was getting even sicker of the wraith's perpetual smirk. The deeper we were brought into the thing's domain, the more unsettling it became. But I had to admit I was amazed at the distance we'd traveled. We had passed out of occupied Green Heart territory and crossed all of the Shield in a single day. That would have taken us weeks on foot.

"Come on, time to get moving again," the ambassador said.

"Can we at least stop to eat?" Tess demanded.

"You are welcome to eat in the truck. But we should not keep my masters waiting now that we are so close."

I had exactly the opposite reaction. The closer we got, the more inclined I was to keep his masters waiting as long as possible.

The next time the vehicle stopped was the last. There was an unnerving sense of finality as it shuddered to a halt and the vibration ceased. I found I'd gotten used to it. Or maybe it was just that I understood what it meant to have reached our destination.

We shaded our eyes as we emerged from the dimly lit interior into the bright blue skies of noon. But if the heavens above gave no sign that we were in the Darklands, not so the earth below. The ruins of a devastated town surrounded us. We were near the sea - a few miles away to my right, I could see a forest of skeletal buildings, the tallest I'd ever seen, poking out of an expanse of gentle waves. Some were so huge that their tops vanished into the clouds. A monument to man's pride – and the Fall that came after.

Directly in front of us stretched a tall, black iron fence much like the inner defenses of Our Lady. And the resemblance didn't end there. Behind the fence rose a cathedral like Our Lady's basilica but far larger, grander, and more beautiful. From the outside, at least, it was in perfect repair, an island of order in the decrepit waste around us.

"My master's citadel," Legion announced. Its annoying little smile had widened into a grin as we goggled at the building.

Soulless guards in their dark uniforms lined the perimeter. Two of them pulled aside a heavy gate, and we followed the ambassador across a courtyard paved in marble so white the reflected sunlight hurt my eyes.

The great central doors of the cathedral stood open and the wraith strode in without pausing, wordlessly passing two more unmoving soldiers. They made no attempt to take the shirasaya katana I used as a walking stick, or Cat's knife. Their indifference to our weapons only made me more nervous.

I whispered to Dee, "If I don't make it, let Roshel and everyone else at Our Lady know what's happened."

The occultist nodded. Somehow neither of us had any doubt that he would live, even if I didn't. Some things in the world were constants, like Dee's survival skills. I only wished I felt nearly as good about my own.

Inside, even illuminated only by the light filtering through the stained glass windows, the structure was even more breathtaking. Rows of columns marched toward the altar, each so wide two men couldn't circle it with their arms and stretching up dozens of feet to a painted ceiling. The pews had been removed, making the space seem even more vast.

Legion continued, confident but unhurried. We trailed along in the creature's wake until it stopped twenty feet from where the altar should have been and prostrated itself before a huge throne.

Light blossomed from a hundred sources simultaneously. The dark shape looming on that seat resolved into a gigantic man rising smoothly to an inhuman height. His hair was long and black, his skin the color of mahogany. Like Stephen, he wore his shirt open to reveal his muscled chest. I was sure that, unlike Stephen, the massive physique was real. Although far more of the Darkness filled this body than the dead lord of the Source's.

Piercing sapphire eyes bored into me.

His voice grated, deep and ominous as a stone door sealing a tomb. "So you're the one who helped assassinate my lieutenant, got my friend Seven killed, and cut off my daughter's head? You've got some nerve showing up here. I thought Select were supposed to be smart."

7. The Dark Lord

My daughter. Those eyes. I tried to swallow but found my throat was too dry. We'd truly stepped in it this time.

"Lord Gurath?" Once the words were out of my mouth, I regretted the honorific as much as I regretted the tremor I could hear in my own voice. But the Hellguard was terrifying. Bigger than Seven, more terrible than Yoshana. "Your ambassador invited us to speak with you and discuss peace."

Gurath boomed out a laugh that echoed in the huge church. "And you believed anything that lying sack of crap said? You really are an idiot."

It was as if the demon's words entered my body and sank into my stomach as lead weights. "You mean you didn't invite us?"

The sapphire eyes locked onto mine. Even in my fear, I couldn't look away. I didn't know if the awe and terror flooding me were a natural reaction to that huge, ancient monster, or an effect of the Darkness. Gurath replied, "I invited you. But the wolf doesn't discuss peace with the sheep."

A black cloud formed beneath Tess, rising up around her legs. She stifled a scream.

"The prophetess who can resist the Darkness," the master of the Hellguard continued. "I wonder if you imagine you can resist me."

Cat's knuckles were white on the hilt of her dagger.

I found my voice. "Stop. That. I can't stop you from destroying us. But I can make sure you have to. You can kill us, but we won't be your toys."

The huge demon laughed again and sank back onto his throne. The Darkness vanished. "Now you sound like someone worth having a discussion with." He turned his piercing glare on Legion, still face down on the floor. "Get up and go do something useful while real people talk."

The wraith climbed to its feet and slunk away.

"Disgusting things," Gurath muttered. Only when he rested his hand on it did I notice the double-headed ax leaning against the throne. Next to him it seemed to be of a normal size. I wasn't sure I could have lifted it. On his other side rested a rifle, a complex thing of sculpted black metal that bore little resemblance to the simple carbines we could still make.

The weapons were incongruous in the church. Except for them, and the demon lord's seat in place of the altar, it still looked like a house of worship, majestic and immaculate.

Tess had noticed the same thing. "Beautiful," she whispered under her breath as she looked around, no longer mesmerized by the Hellguard's awesome presence.

Gurath chuckled. "What, you expected it to be smeared with blood and feces, maybe with some half-eaten corpses lying around? Why would I do that? I live here."

Those eyes focused on me again. "And so here you are in my home. My enemy, his pet prophet, a paleo bodyguard who might weigh a hundred pounds dripping wet, and what? Some half-educated windbag that thinks he's an occultist?"

For all his bantering tone, this was not Seven, an incredibly dangerous man constrained by his own decency. This was a being still more dangerous, constrained by nothing. "I wasn't joking before," he continued. "You have a lot to answer for, Minos. You can start with my daughter."

"I didn't have the impression the two of you got along," I said carefully. Of course, I also hadn't realized they were related. I wondered if Yoshana had known. She'd never mentioned it, but the similarity was striking. But for her white hair, she had been the demon lord on a smaller scale. "She did kill your lieutenant."

Gurath smiled, a hard twist of the lips with no humor behind it. "Yes. Yashuath was becoming an annoyance. Demanding that we press our attack before I was ready. Three hundred years old, and he had no patience. I could have killed him myself, but why? He was strong enough that fighting him would have been risky, and I don't take unnecessary risks. And having him killed by my disgraced Overlord daughter? Plausible deniability, and any of my men who figured it out were impressed at how cunning it was." The smile turned still more vicious. "She was useful to me in so many ways that she never suspected, my Yoshana. And now you've taken away my favorite catspaw. I'm not pleased."

"She let herself be killed so humanity could stand united against you, Gurath," Tess said. "Maybe she suspected more than you think."

The Hellguard's eyebrows went up. "Maybe she did. She was a clever girl. I'm still not pleased."

"So you invited me here to kill me?" I asked. Maybe it wasn't bright to push that point, but I was already tired of the demon's games. He had his malevolent sense of humor in common with his daughter, as well as his appearance. It hadn't been one of her more appealing traits.

"That's one possibility, yes," he said easily. "Who did you leave in charge back at Our Lady?"

I hesitated, wondering if there might be some advantage to be gained by silence.

Gurath chuckled again. "Wraith. Come here."

Legion hadn't gone far. It was back at its master's side in seconds. The demon stretched out his massive hand and Darkness streamed out from the ambassador. The empty shell slumped to the ground. The black cloud that had inhabited the body swirled around Gurath for a dozen heartbeats, then returned, and Legion regained its feet.

Gurath stroked his chin. "So, Roshel. She doesn't like my kind. And she's probably the most competent commander you've got. If you don't come back, she'll launch a war against me for certain. A reasonably clever insurance policy, Select. Well then, killing you isn't my preferred option. And with that being the case, I brought you here to talk."

"We've been talking. So far you've mostly insulted and threatened me. Couldn't you have just sent a nasty letter?"

The demon laughed again, with something like real humor this time. "No. I want to talk, but you need to see something to understand what I have to say."

"I just spent close to a month with your ambassador. I think I understand you well enough."

"You really don't, Minos. You really don't. But come with me and you will."

"Where are we going?"

The cruel smile was back. "That would spoil the surprise."

"I've found I don't generally like surprises."

"No. You probably won't like this one either."

There were more Hellguards, and more soulless. I had seen none of them as we'd approached the throne, and I hadn't heard them enter. They were just abruptly there. Given what I knew about the Darkness and the demons' mastery of it, they could either have been there all along cloaked in virtual invisibility, or entered in total silence.

Seven hadn't liked being called a demon. I'd stopped applying the word to him. For these beings it seemed only appropriate.

Every one of them was larger than my friend had been. Gurath was one of the biggest, nearly seven feet tall, inhumanly broad across the shoulders, layered in muscle. When he moved it was with the grace of a cat. I'd never seen a lion or tiger in person, but I imagined those huge predators must have been something like the demons… if lions or tigers had superhuman intelligence and could rip you apart at the cellular level without laying a hand on you.

They were all some shade of reddish brown, some as light as Gurath, others as nearly black as Seven. Their hair was universally dark. I remembered Seven had told me the Hellguard had been created as military special forces. I supposed their dark complexions were intended to make them stealthier at night. With the Darkness blurring their outlines, they would be virtually invisible in shadow. Walking nightmares brought into the world, a curse of our ancestors' arrogance to torment generations to come.

There was a bit of the pot calling the kettle black there. My gray skin, black eyes, and white hair were the physical marks of that same arrogance, when my forefathers had tried to perfect their children. In Seven's telling, the Hellguard were no different than the Select - only a more advanced version.

The soulless followed orders with the mindless precision of automatons. At Gurath's command they brought out massive tables, which they installed where the pews would have been. Chairs followed, and then food - a steaming array of hot meat and bread, fruit, vegetables. As uncomfortable - no, terrifying - as the setting was, my stomach rumbled.

"You desecrate the house of God," Tess protested.

The Hellguard chieftain barked out a laugh. "It's not like I brought my horse in. You people used to eat the flesh of your crucified God in here, at least according to your superstition. This is just the meat of animals. And it hasn't been the house of your dead God for a long time. Like I said, it's mine now. I've been eating here for hundreds of years. So you may as well join me."

He cocked his head and stared at her. "Unless you think this is like Hades, and if you eat or drink here you'll be damned. But that's a pagan belief, isn't it? Didn't your crucified God say it's not what goes into your mouth that defiles a man, but what comes out of it?"

Tess blinked, taken aback, briefly at a loss for words. We shouldn't have been surprised. Yoshana had freely quoted scripture. It only stood to reason that her father would be familiar with it as well.

The other demons talked among themselves as they waited for the meal. They were openly and rudely curious about us, staring and even poking. One lifted Tess' long hair. She stood very still. My jaw clenched.

"I told you they wouldn't have bred out the diversity of appearance yet in the wild," the Hellguard said. "They've still got blondes."

"Okay, sure, if you call that blonde," one of his companions rumbled. "But for how many more generations? I'll admit I'm surprised there are still Select, though. That appearance should breed out immediately."

The first shrugged. "Probably not much opportunity for it. Who'd want to mate with one of those things?"

He continued to play with Tess' hair. I thought of Roshel, and what the Hellguard did with human women. My hand tightened on the hilt of my katana. It was still doing duty as a walking stick, but these days I was steady enough on my feet to use it for its true purpose.

Cat was clearly having similar thoughts. She glared at the demon with naked hatred, and I could hear a low growl from deep in her throat.

Another Hellguard came up behind the paleo and lifted her in a single massive hand.

"Look at this, though. Speaking of things you'd think would go extinct. I mean, paleos, for Christ's sake. They're actually getting smaller." He tossed her lightly and caught her in the other hand. "Bunch of malnourished, inbred idiots."

All three Hellguards laughed, and the demon who'd caught the girl dropped her back to the ground. Cat's eyes were wide with terror, her lips thin with fury. I couldn't tell which emotion predominated, but she'd controlled both well enough not to scream or lash out.

Which was fortunate, since I had no doubt that if she'd drawn her knife, they would have killed her with no more concern than swatting a fly.

It was a measure of how upset Cat was that when Tess rushed over to her, the paleo girl allowed herself to be enfolded in a hug.

I summoned up my nerve and glared at our host. "Not my idea of hospitality."

I got a contemptuous smile in return. "If you bring your dogs into my house, my brothers might want to play with them. Or kick them. Hopefully they don't bite or pee on the floor. Come on, let's eat. I'll even let you and your pets sit at the table."

Dee was already seated, eyeing the food. He looked up at me. "It would after all be rude to refuse Lord Gurath's hospitality, Minos."

The occultist's adaptability was matched only by his spinelessness. Actually, his lack of a spine almost certainly helped him adapt, like some kind of invertebrate that could squirm through the smallest of openings. Erev, Yoshana's bodyguard, had said something similar about me. With my pulse pounding angrily in my temples, I found I wasn't in the mood today.

"Like I said, this isn't my idea of hospitality. Stand up, Dee. I said it before, Gurath. I can't stop you from killing us, but we won't be humiliated."

The demon lord smiled lazily. "I'm pretty sure you're wrong there, but I did ask you here to talk, and not to amuse my companions. Gentlemen," he went on, addressing the other Hellguard, "Let's be respectful, please."

Although his tone had become entirely serious, I was pretty sure we were still being mocked. But I wasn't going to stand on my honor to the point of suicide. "Thank you," I said. And sat.

The demons helped themselves to the food. They weren't dainty eaters, but their table manners were no worse than most of the soldiers I'd traveled with. Dee joined them enthusiastically, as did Cat. I noticed Tess eyeing the meat suspiciously. I hadn't tried it myself.

"Like I said, it's just the flesh of animals. Beef, specifically," Gurath said. "Trust me, it's not human. You don't taste that good."

Cat grinned. "Depends. Who."

Gurath laughed. "I like your pet, Minos. I might keep her."

The paleo's smile vanished.

I tried the meat. It was excellent. The demon continued, "I do have to admit, I'm impressed you had the guts to come. Stupid, but gutsy."

I met his piercing blue eyes. "I dare to stand every day as a sinner before the Lord God. Why should I be afraid to stand in front of you?"

The demon's eyebrows lifted in surprise, then he laughed again. "How long did it take you to come up with that one?"

"I've been working on it since I got here," I admitted.

He chuckled, then the huge, reddish face grew serious. "Do you actually believe that garbage the Universal Church says? Like what came out of your mouth just now?"

When I didn't answer immediately, he continued, "Because that's a big part of what we need to talk about."

8. Thus Spake Gurath

Demons began to get up and leave, without ceremony. Some of them seemed to fade away, passing just beyond my line of sight and then vanishing. It was disconcerting, to say the least, which must have been the intention. They had no reason to use the Darkness to mask their coming and going in their own citadel, except to intimidate us. It worked. I found that, while the food was the best I'd had in as long as I could remember, I'd lost my appetite.

One of the soulless appeared and approached Gurath. Before it could speak, the demon said to me, "The horses and gear are ready. It's time to go. Unless you and your friends want to stay a while longer? Maybe spend the night?"

Of course none of us did. There was no need to ask the others. I hadn't slept much, and none of us had slept comfortably. The meal we'd just eaten was a reminder of how terrible food on the road would be. But I could tell by the way my companions' eyes darted from side to side that no one, not even Doctor John Dee, wanted to spend a minute more in the beautiful, terrible cathedral that Gurath called home.

I wasn't thrilled about the horses. "Can't we take that truck wherever we're going?"

"No. The roads get bad up north. And by bad, I mean sometimes nonexistent. We'll be lucky if we don't have to walk half the way."

North. The Hellguard's capital was near the Ice Fields. I didn't know exactly where we were, but I thought we were well south of that. For one thing, it was warm.

"We're going to Imperium?"

"No. Farther than that. You don't think we maintain the roads to our own capital?"

If Select could blush, I would have. "I thought maybe from a defensive standpoint…"

"You think I want to conquer the world, but I'm so afraid of it that I'd hide my capital behind impassable terrain. I thought you were supposed to be some kind of general. You should stop talking before you say something else stupid." He paused for a moment. "Or is this another part of your insurance policy? Convince me you're so dumb that I'd be doing Our Lady a favor by knocking you off and leaving Roshel in charge? Because that would be kind of clever. I'm going to choose to believe that."

The ancients had a saying, better to be silent and let people assume you're a fool than to open your mouth and confirm it. Applying that wisdom, I shut up.

Gurath and I rode up front. I wasn't comfortable riding alongside him, and not just because my knee hurt. I wasn't even comfortable around his horse, a massive beast able to carry the demon's immense weight. It had a look in its eye like it would enjoy stomping me to bloody fragments and then disproving the notion that horses were herbivores by eating the remains. But I could hardly have the discussion the Hellguard wanted from the other end of the column.

At that other end rode Legion and its three surviving guards.

"Thought you might want a friendly face along," Gurath had said, and laughed. He could have been under no illusion that we enjoyed the wraith's company. From his earlier comments, he didn't enjoy it either. The demon wouldn't be relying on the ambassador and the soulless for protection from us, or even to keep watch on us. He was more than capable of that himself, even in his sleep. So I had no idea why he had brought the wraith. Whatever the reason, I was sure it would prove to be one I didn't like.

Outside the iron fence surrounding the cathedral were only devastated ruins, long since stripped of anything valuable. In the distance I could see the gigantic, crumbling towers poking up from the sea. The horses' hooves echoed on the abandoned streets. This would have been one of the ancients' seats of power. Nothing was left but one huge, old church, converted to a demon's palace. I was seized with a vast melancholy. Our forefathers' grand dream was dead, and there seemed to be no one who could breathe life into it again.

"Son of man, can these bones live?" I muttered.

I'd said it softly, under my breath, but Gurath's head spun and his eyes locked onto me. "That depends. Do you understand reality, Minos?"

I didn't know what to make of the question. I had no better answer than, "What do you mean?"

"In reality, there is only nature and the will. What is, and what you want. If you can't impose your will on nature, impose what you want on what is, then you tell yourself lies about what is, or about what you want. Those lies are religion and civilization. They're the construct and comfort of weaklings. Failure to understand that is the reason the bones of the ancients are drying in the sun. And the reason your Universal Church's cause is lost."

We continued for a while in silence broken only by the echoing hoofbeats. After a time I said, "That's a pretty dark philosophy."

"That's the truth. The question is, do you understand it?"

I retorted, more snappishly than was safe, "I understand that's what you say is the truth. I'll even give you credit for really believing it, instead of just finding it a convenient excuse for tyranny."

The pain in my knee was making me cranky, and crankiness looked a little bit like bravery. The demon chuckled tolerantly.

"And what do you believe in, Minos, a white-bearded sky god that grants wishes to good little children who say their prayers?"

"That's a pretty gross distortion of Universalist beliefs and I'm sure you know it. God isn't an old man with a beard, or even a corporeal being of any kind. God is the first principle, the origin. And beyond my comprehension, or even yours."

"Been reading Aquinas?"

"I can't sit around planning war against you all day. The more interesting question is, have you been reading Aquinas?"

Gurath laughed again. "I can't sit around planning war against you all day. I've had three hundred years longer than you to get bored enough to read dusty old philosophers. And I find it's helpful to understand what my enemies believe. Even if it's stupid."

The sapphire eyes drilled into me, just as his daughter's had. "So I'll ask you again, do you really believe all that garbage you're spouting?"

"If not God as a first principle, then what?"

The Hellguard waved his hand, encompassing the ruins around us. Crumbled piles of bricks and concrete that had once been buildings were making their slow return to the dust from which they'd risen.

"Chaos. Random chance. Accident and entropy. Life growing out of a soup of chemicals that happened to combine the right way after billions of years. Hundreds of millions of years more of evolution that eventually spat out beings intelligent enough to wonder why they existed, and too fearful of death to admit that it was for no reason at all - it was just because they did. Nothing special, just apes with bigger brains and existential angst. Over time they developed rules to live by. What worked to preserve their society they called good, what didn't they called evil. They made up stories of gods and devils to teach the difference. Boring stories, mostly."

I rode on a while in silence, ignoring the demon's eyes on me. "God is dead, huh?" I said after a time. "I've read Nietzsche too."

"Did you understand him? He didn't mean the old man in the sky had stopped breathing. He meant the myth had stopped being useful. It carried no awe anymore, couldn't shape behavior or culture. There had to be new myths, created by those with the will to reach into the abyss beneath civilization and pull out a new essence, a new soul to animate the world's rotting corpse."

"Created by an *Ubermensch*. A superhuman."

The demon smiled. "Just so. The ancients followed Nietzsche without understanding him or considering the implications. They made things like you to be the most a human could be. Then they made things like me to be more. What didn't occur to them is that to the superhuman, our creators look subhuman."

The mocking expression that was so often on Legion's face was only a pale shadow of its master's. I shuddered.

We bedded down at the side of the crumbling road, perhaps twenty miles north of Gurath's cathedral. The whole area was a vast, continuous sprawl of weed-choked ruins being overtaken by nature. Here as well, anything of value had been long since stripped away.

This wasn't the haunted forest of the Sorrows, but trees grew thick and tall around us, casting long shadows as the sun set. In other parts of the world I might have feared attack by bandits or paleos. Here we were under the protection of the demon lord. There was no worse threat to us than Gurath himself. And if he'd wanted us dead, we'd be dead already. So I kept telling myself.

"Did you have to spend all day with him?" Tess demanded as she settled on the grass. I staggered around in little circles, trying to decide if working the stiffness out of my knee was worth the pain that shot through me every time I took a step.

"That was the point of the whole exercise, wasn't it?" I snapped. "And it didn't seem like a healthy idea to offend him."

"All that talk about his philosophy isn't healthy either."

"I'm not going to argue about it, Tess. Especially since he can hear every word we say when we're within two hundred yards of him."

The Hellguard met my eyes at that moment from where he sat fifty feet away and gave me a broad grin. Cat looked jumpier than usual and began suspiciously scanning the air for the Darkness - even though she knew as well as I that the probes Gurath was using wouldn't be visible.

The demon lord rose, stretched, and lazily strolled over to the larger of the two sumpter horses the soulless had been leading. He unstrapped a long, black case, big enough to hold a twin to either the rifle or ax that he carried. I tensed as he opened it.

Inside was a guitar. The demon adjusted the tuning pegs, walked over to us, and settled in the grass. The melody he began to pick out was marvelously complex and beautifully executed.

"Magnificent," Dee murmured.

"Nietzsche believed that the creation of art was part of the measure of the superior being, and that music was the expression of the collective soul. Like I said, I've had a lot of time on my hands." The Hellguard grinned.

"Not everything evil is ugly," Tess said tightly.

I tensed again, but Gurath merely said, "And not everyone agrees with your definitions of good and evil, little prophet."

Legion had come up behind the demon. "Wasteful," it said. "Noises like that provide no food or shelter. A meaningless, obsolete pastime."

In a movement so fast I couldn't follow it, Gurath spun to his feet, pulled his ax free, and severed the wraith's head. He still held the guitar in his other hand.

Tess bit down on a knuckle to keep from crying out. Cat's hand was on her dagger, but she didn't draw it.

A thick cloud of Darkness flooded from the stump of Legion's neck. It hovered for a moment, then swiftly descended onto one of the soulless. The man's eyes momentarily turned as black as mine as the possession was completed.

The newly embodied wraith hurried to Gurath and prostrated itself at his feet. "I apologize, master."

"I don't tolerate insolence from your kind," the demon growled. "And get rid of that."

Legion - in its new body - and one of the soulless hauled the corpse into the trees.

"You have to make sure your creations know their place. My creators were careless in that respect," Gurath said with a smile. He inspected the ax critically. The Darkness in Legion had kept the blade free of blood, but I saw black particles crawl over the edge, smoothing away nicks made from splitting bone. Satisfied, the demon lord returned the weapon to his belt and resumed playing the guitar.

We didn't sleep well that night.

The order of march was the same the next day. Tess glared at me, but I continued to ride in front with Gurath while she, Cat, and Dee took the middle of the column, followed by Legion and what I now thought of as two spare bodies. The soulless were like sumpter horses for the wraith. The idea was physically revolting but I couldn't put it out of my mind.

The Hellguard and I rode for a long time in silence. I was the first to speak. "So you're Nietzsche's perfect being? Warrior, artist, philosopher? Like some sort of samurai ideal?"

Gurath just smiled.

"It doesn't trouble you that your source of inspiration was not, to the best of my knowledge, much of an artist... and was certainly no kind of warrior?"

The demon chuckled. "Why would that trouble me? Nietzsche was not himself the superhuman he knew that the world needed. Does that mean he was wrong? It does not. He had the intellect to grasp the truth, if not the characteristics needed to fulfill it himself. Maybe he couldn't even live with the implications of his own philosophy, and that's what drove him mad. Or maybe his madness was just the result of a disease contracted from a woman he paid because that was the only way he could obtain female companionship. His weakness as a man doesn't make his conclusions invalid."

"Surely it makes them suspect."

"The opposite, Minos. A truth that is hard to stomach is more likely to be true than one that is comforting. Your mind recoils from the abyss like from a wall, and so it bounces off into other philosophies that are softer and more easily digested. Silly sentimentalism about the brotherhood of man, as if such a thing ever existed or will ever exist. Idiotic religions with no basis in reality, like the one preached by your little prophet."

Gurath turned and gave Prophetess a broad grin. She ignored him.

"That's interesting," I mused. "So religion is for the weak-minded."

"When Marx called it the opiate of the masses that was probably the only intelligent thing he ever said."

"And yet Yoshana declared herself the prophet of, what was it Dee called it? A syncretic, pan-Abrahamic religion? Was your daughter weak-minded?"

The Hellguard laughed again. "Ah. Clever, but superficial. Why would you think that what Yoshana preached and what she believed were the same thing? She was not weak-minded, but how many of her followers were as strong as she?"

None. "But why preach the religion of a God that you say is evidently false? If she was a superhuman herself - and you must think she was - why not a religion with herself as the supreme being? She had the power for it."

Until the end, Roshel had very nearly worshipped the older Overlord as a god. And Roshel was no weakling.

Gurath paused only for a moment. "Two possibilities. The simplest answer is that it's easier to just steer believers into a slightly different path than to convince them of an entirely new belief system. Sheep are more easily guided to the left or right than turned around entirely."

"Sheep."

"Baaah. Aren't they mostly sheep? When we took away their will," the demon turned and leered again, this time at the soulless, "We didn't take very much. Nietzsche said the teeming masses were no more relevant than so many animals in terms of the meaning they could add to the world, and he wasn't wrong."

Gurath turned the grin on me. "The second answer is that when you set yourself up as a god, it's no one's fault but your own when you lose battles. Which implies you aren't much of a god. When you're a prophet, you can blame it on the worshippers not being sufficiently devout. You quoted the Old Testament yesterday. You know what I mean. Every military loss the Israelites suffered was because they'd turned away from their God, worshipped graven images, whatever. It's a hell of an excuse."

And seemed like the kind of thing that would occur to Yoshana. "But you don't feel the need to have a god backing you up. You're willing to set yourself up as one yourself. By your own logic, isn't that risky?"

The demon chuckled. "Only if you lose. I don't."

I could have made a comment about spending three hundred years bottled up in the Darklands, or an offensive stalled at the Paint River after his catspaw turned against him. But I didn't. Instead, I said, "So the only thing that matters is the exercise of your own will? Your own success, imposing what you want on what is? There's no higher, objective good?"

"That's right." He nodded, like a man whose dog had finally learned a basic trick that had eluded it.

"Then tell me this. Why did your daughter let herself be killed to unify humanity against you?"

Gurath's eyebrows went up and, for the first time, he had nothing to say.

It was only as the silence stretched on that I realized my face hurt. And only after contemplating that for a while that I realized the scar was no more painful than usual - it was just that it was usually masked by the greater pain in my knee. Which had now faded.

I stared at the demon. He stared back, blue eyes piercing into mine.

"Have you been healing me?" I demanded.

A little smile. "It's annoying, watching you limp around. And we may need to move quickly in the days ahead, and I can't have you slowing us down. So yes, I have."

My blood froze. I had thought I could sense and deflect the Darkness penetrating my body, even when controlled by a master like Gurath. "Get that stuff out of me!"

And now a mocking chuckle. "So now you're so offended by the Darkness you won't even let it heal you. You who once controlled it."

Through my anger and fear, I still noticed he used our world's term for the Darkness, instead of calling it the prant as Seven had. "Yes. I know what it did to me before, and I won't have it in me again. The Church is right. There's no good in it. Get. It. Out."

"And so you presume to know good from evil. And you call my philosophy arrogant." The demon chuckled again. "It's gone now. Unless you'd like me to take a moment to reverse the repairs I've already made?"

I glowered at him. "No."

"Good and evil. You're a funny thing, aren't you?" Gurath continued to smirk at me for miles.

We stopped late in the afternoon at the foot of a huge bridge, sixty feet wide and miles long. The river beneath was as wide as the Muddy, but its banks were steep, rocky cliffs rather than a gentle floodplain.

"We'll cross tomorrow," the demon said. "Stay close when we reach the other side. The land's strange there."

"What do you mean?" Dee asked. "Isn't it all part of the Darklands?"

"It's our territory, yes... but we don't cross that river except when we have to. There are worse things than the Hellguard in the world."

I recalled Gurath's comment that we might need to move fast. My leg was still stiff and sore, but nowhere near as much as it had been the day before. I had a hard time cataloging exactly how I felt about that. "I don't think I want to meet anything worse than you."

"Then you're definitely not going to enjoy this trip." The demon laughed, and pulled out his guitar. He played long into the night, complex melodies of haunting beauty. And, once again, we didn't sleep well.

The river flowed below us. Gurath resumed our conversation as we crossed. "I've thought about what you said about my daughter. It was beneath her, but self-sacrifice is a perversion of mastery that can have a certain appeal. Especially when you've lost your ability to impose your will on others besides yourself. As she apparently had."

I couldn't have imagined I would ever be indignant on behalf of the Overlord. "She'd hardly lost the ability to impose her will. She had Prophetess under her blade, and there was nothing anyone could do to stop her."

"But she'd lost control of her lieutenants. She'd failed in her own mind. So she took the coward's way out. When you can't impose your will on others, you impose it on yourself. How does it go? 'In every ascetic morality man adores part of himself as God and to that end needs to diabolicize the rest.'"

I snorted. "You're actually saying that self-denial is weakness."

"Of course it is. 'I'm a fine person because I refuse myself some pleasure.' What a steaming pile of mediocre hypocrisy. At least Yoshana had the strength to take it to the logical extreme."

I turned that over in my head as the horses' hooves rang on the bridge, taking us to see something worse than demons.

Gurath spoke again. "Reality, and the will. What is, and what you want it to be. Now that you've become so fond of the Universal faith, here's another thought for you. Once the ancients came to believe that they understood the reality of what they were, you and I became inevitable. Once they could make themselves, they could remake themselves as they chose. Whatever their wills demanded, they imposed on reality – even immortality."

The demon smiled. "According to the Book of Genesis, your God threw man out of Eden after he ate the fruit that gave him knowledge of good and evil, but before he could eat the fruit that would make him immortal. Because if he ate both, he would become a god himself. Not long before the Second Fall, one of the ancients said that man has become a product of our own action, that can be selected according to the exigencies established by ourselves. Man knows how to clone men, knows how to use men as a store of organs for other men, and so he does it, because this seems to be an exigency of his freedom."

His smile widened as he stared straight into my eyes. "Your kind, the Select, are the very essence of a product selected according to the exigencies established by yourselves. And who do you suppose I was quoting just then about the exigencies of human freedom?"

I thought Nietzsche, Gurath's philosophical hero, had died before the age of human cloning and organ storage. I shook my head.

"Pope Benedict the Sixteenth," he said. "He didn't live long enough to see your race, but he anticipated you. Give the man credit for understanding, anyway."

"I doubt he said it approvingly."

"Well, no. But he wasn't wrong. His interpretation of the facts was just warped. He had an archaic vision of good and evil, like you."

"'In the days before the Son of Man, the Gentiles worshipped many gods. But in the Last Days, man worshipped no one but himself.'"

"Ah, good. The First Book of the Fall. I enjoyed Saint Arvan. I never actually met him, but I'm sure he would have been even more entertaining than you." Gurath laughed again. "Although I prefer chapter four: 'Let the Hellguard go forth! Let the demons and the Darkness reclaim what we have lost. For are we not masters of every power?'"

"Again, not said approvingly. Arvan was describing the Fall."

"Your fall, not ours. You fell once when you ate from the tree of knowledge. Then came the Darkness, and you ate from the tree of immortality, and you fell again. And we rose in your place. It's all a matter of perspective. That's what you insist on failing to understand. You said it yourself - God is dead. Arvan and Siles might have tried to breathe some life back into that myth. Your prophetess is making a valiant effort too, I'll give her that. But that corpse is still and cold. No amount of artificial resuscitation is going to make it live again. Your kind and mine have moved beyond fairytales of absolutes handed down from heaven on stone tablets. Sometimes you choose to forget because those stories make you feel better when you're eyeball to eyeball with the void. To be fair, it's a little easier for me to see past that, being undying."

"Seven died. So did Yashuath."

"They made mistakes I intend to avoid. But you miss the point. It's not the possibility of death that terrifies your kind - it's the inevitability of it. So there has to be something greater, or you despair. But there isn't. All dogs don't go to heaven, and neither do all humans. In fact, not even one."

"You keep acting like you're something completely different. Seven called himself human."

"Seven had serious issues. There's a reason he lived alone in a forest for three hundred years, you know." We turned onto an overgrown path as we left the bridge, picking our way down toward the river's edge and the ruined town that stretched along it. It reminded me in a way of the Sorrows, and I tried to figure out why.

"Not looted," I said after a minute.

"No. I told you, we don't come here unless we have to. The radiation was bad here. It wouldn't kill us, not with the Darkness in us, but it wasn't pleasant. Long gone now, but somehow… not even the Hellguard are totally rational, you know. A little superstition can be healthy. Even a touch of supernatural dread."

"What does the *Ubermensch* fear?"

"You said it. We can be killed. And Nietzsche was no rationalist. He saw through the sterility of that. Even my kind needs myths. We've just made better ones than your kind did."

"Make up your mind," I growled. "Am I the creator or the created? According to you, am I human or not?"

"Ahhh. That depends. What do you want to be?" Gurath flung an arm wide, and a wave of the Darkness lashed out at a nearby tree. The trunk shattered in an explosion of fragments. One of the largest floated back to him, buoyed on a wave of particles. By the time it reached his hand, it was shaped into the image of a man.

The demon laughed at my open-mouthed amazement. "Didn't know it could do that? It's just hydrostatic shock inside the trunk that ruptures the wood. As far as the levitation, the Darkness can't carry much weight, but it looks impressive, doesn't it? And the carving, well. We've established the importance of art. If it makes you feel better, I doubt Yoshana knew how to do those things either. Seven might have taught you, if you'd spent some time with him instead of dragging him off on your fool's errand and getting him killed."

I couldn't think of a response. He continued, "Creation, creator, that's another meaningless distinction. You are what you make yourself. You, in particular, could make yourself more than you are."

There it was. The hook, dangled in front of my mouth, waiting for me to bite.

"I've heard that offer before. I accepted it last time. I didn't like the results. Not again."

Gurath shrugged. "I know what you've done. At least Yoshana picked herself up and tried again after the first time she got her ass kicked, even if she did give up after the second time. But then, you're not Yoshana."

I should have been pleased that he said that. So why wasn't I?

We made our way inland, though the river remained in sight. This place seemed more ancient even than other ruins from before the Fall. There was something disconcerting about it. Maybe just Gurath's words playing on my nerves.

The Hellguard noticed, of course. He might have been using the Darkness to read my mind, or maybe, as the Metropolitan suggested, he was simply tapping the experience of centuries.

"The stories say this place was haunted even before the Last Days," he said. "Seven hundred years of ghosts here."

We passed by the weathered headstones of a cemetery that looked older than time. The trees on either side of the road rose impossibly thick and tall, spaced with unnatural regularity, yet each one of them twisted in a way that made my gut clench. I shivered in their shadow even though the air was warm.

Gurath smiled, but it seemed forced. "Yeah. Everyone feels that here. I told you there are worse things than the Hellguard in the world."

"What's out there?" I demanded.

The huge man's laughter was real, but I thought it betrayed the slightest hint of nerves, and one massive hand was on his ax. "Not so scrupulous about the Darkness now, are you? I don't sense a thing here. Not a damn thing. Never have."

"But...?"

"But I wouldn't sleep on this stretch of road in exchange for the keys to Our Lady."

The morning and afternoon and two dozen miles had passed before we camped, and it still didn't feel long enough. I didn't ask if my companions had felt the same effect when we passed between that double row of trees. Tess was quiet in the way that meant she was angry with me.

I supposed I understood. She'd come to support me, and I was spending all day with the monster I'd sworn to fight. She'd be feeling abandoned. She'd be worrying that Gurath might turn me. But even though I understood, I was still angry that she was angry.

Worse, I wasn't entirely sure her fears were unfounded. I remembered what the Metropolitan had said. *Fear more what he can make you do to your own soul.*

You would have thought that having been down this path once before, I wouldn't be tempted to walk it again. I'd certainly assumed that. I'd been wrong.

There was no talking to Tess when she and I were in our respective moods. We'd just fight. I pulled Dee aside instead. Not surprisingly, the occultist wanted to know everything I'd discussed with the demon lord.

"Imagine that, Minos. It's a rare privilege, the chance to discuss philosophy with someone who actually lived through the Last Days. A contemporary of Saint Arvan and Saint Siles. A being actually named in the Books of the Fall."

"They didn't name the specific Hellguards."

"You know what I mean, Minos. He wasn't just there, he was a protagonist. And to have him share his beliefs with you... an honor indeed."

"He's not talking to me because he enjoys my company, Dee. Or because he respects me." Although I realized I hoped that ancient terror did respect me, a little. "He wants something."

"Well, of course. But as long as you know that..."

"The problem... the problem is, I'm not sure he's wrong."

"Ah."

"What he's saying... I wouldn't have put it the same way, but it's maybe not too different from what I thought before I met Tess."

"Ahh. 'We do not suspect that he is acting in us, because he follows the current of our inclinations.'"

"Oh God. I've been quoted at by a demon for the past three days. Who said that?"

"Jacques-Benigne Bossuet, about eight hundred years ago. Referring to the subtlety of the devil."

"Gurath's persuasive, Dee. And I can feel him picking at me. 'Surely you're smart enough to understand what I'm saying. Surely you're the kind of person who could be superhuman. You don't need to believe silly stories like those sheep, do you?' If I know he's doing it, why is it working?"

The occultist smiled. "The appeal to vanity is a strong one. I believe Roshel and Yoshana used it quite effectively as well."

"And what am I?" I'd asked. "That depends on what you want to be," Roshel had answered. "You, in particular, could make yourself more than you are."

"So, again, why the hell does it keep working?"

"'For pride is always seen to be the essential base of the diabolic.' It's as old as sin itself."

"And that one was?"

"Simone Weil. About four hundred years after Bossuet, from the same part of the world."

"Where do you get all that stuff? I think you make half of it up."

Dee laughed. "The secret of appearing educated is knowing one more obscure quotation than the person you're talking to. The secret of *being* educated is knowing when to use them."

"Yeah, good to see there's no pride at all in you."

His grin widened. "I never claimed to be a saint. Or even a good Universalist. I'm far too open-minded for that. What I will say is this. You read that book of Lovecraft I gave you, yes?"

I nodded.

"The horror of the universe Lovecraft describes isn't the presence of powerful malevolence. It's the absence of God. Shub'nigurath is the representation of Nietzsche's uncaring universe, a mindless living protoplasm endlessly copulating with itself and spewing out new life, some of which is devoured, some of which thrives, but none of which has purpose. Azathoth, the mindless nuclear chaos at the center of the universe, is Lovecraft's answer to Aquinas - what if the prime mover exists but has no goodness, no will, nothing but awesome power? The demon flutists that serenade Azathoth are a parody of the hosts of the seraphim."

"Hold on. You told me Lovecraft was an occultist. Was he describing things he thought were real, or writing allegory?"

"Why do you think there's a distinction? Lovecraft drank deep of that same atheistic, Nietzschean nihilism that you find so persuasive when you speak to Gurath. It was thick in the air then, and stayed that way until the Fall. The ancients understood just enough of the universe to decide there was no need or room for God in it. And yet... there are interesting details in two of Lovecraft's case studies, 'Dreams in the Witch House' and 'The Haunter of the Dark.' In those accounts, Universalist rituals and sacramentals that Lovecraft himself dismisses as superstition proved effective against the monsters of the abyss. The protagonists of those cases were rationalists, as was Lovecraft himself, and yet they were consumed. But those icons of faith proved effective where reason did not. And so... the rationalist made a case for faith, perhaps. There was more to Lovecraft than there seemed."

"Gurath said even a Nietzschean needed myth. Are you saying faith is nothing more than a way of strengthening the will?"

"No, that's not what I'm saying at all. That's what Gurath would say. Aquinas, whom you've been attempting to use against Gurath, would say that faith is no more or less than a comprehension of eternal truth. Me personally? As I said, I'm far too open-minded to choose a side in that debate."

I snorted in exasperation. "You're no more use against Gurath than you were against that drelb two years ago."

"If you're expecting me to tell you what to do, or swat some Darkness-infested bear with a stick, then you're doomed to disappointment, my friend. But I'll say one more thing, since you seem to feel that Aquinas is losing the battle against

Nietzsche, and you'll have to forgive me for quoting again, in this case from the Angelic Doctor himself. 'There are, therefore, some points of intelligibility in God, accessible to human reason, and other points that altogether transcend the power of human reason. For there are some so presumptuous of their own genius as to think that they can measure with their understanding the whole nature of the Godhead, thinking all that to be true which seems true to them, and that to be false which does not seem true to them.'"

I held up my hand. "Hold on." I turned the words over in my head in the hope that there was more to them than there seemed. "All you're saying is that God is beyond humanly comprehensible proof, and it's arrogant to think otherwise. That answers Gurath how? He's just going to say I've admitted that he's right and I'm making up things I can't prove because it makes me feel better."

"You didn't let me finish. 'But because we cannot see his essence, we are brought to the knowledge of his existence, not by what he is in himself, but by the effects which he works.'"

"I still don't get it."

Dee smiled tolerantly. "Perhaps you should spend more time with Prophetess."

9. Heart of Darkness

I took Dee's advice, even if I didn't understand his point.

"Remembered you have a girlfriend?" Tess asked when I fell back next to her in the column the next day.

"You're more fun to be around than Gurath. Better-looking, too." Although in fact the demon lord was as exotically handsome as his daughter had been beautiful, each in their own terrifying way. "Plus I figure you're less likely to disembowel me when you get mad."

"True. I've got Cat for that." The paleo gave me a feral grin.

"Hardly seems right. She was my friend first."

"You keep telling everyone how she tried to kill you and eat you when you first met. It only seems fair to let her finish the job."

"Wow. With friends like you, who needs all-powerful, immortal enemies?"

Tess' face turned serious. "Not all-powerful or immortal, Minos. Strong, yes. But he too shall pass."

Legion left the surviving soulless behind and trotted past us to join Gurath. In a stage whisper easily loud enough for us to hear, it said, "The Select is stubborn, master. If he doesn't turn when we reach our destination, give his body to me. I'll make better use of it."

The Hellguard glared at the wraith. Legion flinched, but the smirk didn't vanish from its face. When it turned to wink and grin at me, I saw the new body's teeth had already lengthened and sharpened.

We followed the river north on a road that sometimes led inland, then returned to the shore. At times the land met the water in a gentle beach, but more often it rose in rocky cliffs a hundred feet above the swift current. A fall from that height would quite possibly be fatal, and I didn't care at all for the way the asphalt was sloughing away at the edge and slowly crumbling into the water below. On some of the higher, curving sections of road, my horse and I hugged the cliff to my right so closely that Gurath laughed openly.

"If you think this is bad, just wait," was all he said. If he was offended that I no longer rode with him, he gave no sign.

The next morning we swung east, away from the river, and continued that way for days. The land grew as thickly forested as the Sorrows, but the road was mostly intact. Sometimes we would come to a bridge that had collapsed and we would need to lead the horses down the banks and ford the stream below. The path didn't seem dangerous - at least not in the company of Gurath and Legion. I didn't like to think too much about what horrors might lurk deep in those trees. Lovecraft's stories had been set in this part of the continent. When I'd read them on the flat prairies of the Source, the notion of evil, alien gods hidden in the woods had seemed vaguely ridiculous. Here in the midst of those woods, the idea didn't seem silly at all. When we camped at night, Dee, Cat, Tess, and I crowded around the fire.

And not just because of the unknown terrors in the dark. It was getting cold, although by my reckoning it was still late summer. Gurath took heavy fur coats from packs on the sumpter horses and distributed them. I was so grateful for mine that I wasn't inclined to question whether I should be taking gifts from the Hellguard.

"You'll need it - we're getting close to the Ice Fields," Gurath said, reading my thoughts. "You'll understand soon enough."

He kept saying that. It didn't make me feel better.

The demon lord seemed content to ride by himself at the head of the column. Of course, Dee couldn't leave well enough alone. One day he rode up to join the Hellguard. I looked at Prophetess, who shrugged. I nudged my horse closer to eavesdrop.

"…but there is a far greater sweep of philosophy to consider and debate than merely the dichotomy of Aquinas and Nietzsche, Lord Gurath. One need hardly believe that uprooting a supernatural god from the garden of ethics leads inevitably to a rejection of objective standards of good and evil. Consider Mill, for example -"

"Let's not," the demon snapped. "Mill, Russell, Rawls, any of your humanist philosophers. They start with the truth that there is no God, and then recoil from the conclusion. They were all incoherent moral cowards, unwilling to follow through to the end that there is no right except what's made by might. At least Aquinas and the rest of his bleating Universalist flock are internally consistent. If you start with the false premise of a living God, you arrive at the false conclusion that he has established an order of righteousness. If you start with the correct premise that there is no such God, but still arrive at the same false conclusion, then you're just an idiot or a weakling."

"Nominalism hardly implies nihilism," Dee objected mildly.

"Of course it does. Or what you mean by nihilism, anyway. Either you believe in some mythical natural law, or you believe that all morals are set by convention. If you believe all morals are set by convention, who sets the conventions? The strong. To pretend anything else is childish. Your philosophers yanked away the pillars of religious superstition on which society rested, then tried to pretend that society could float along on its own without support."

"I hardly think -"

"Exactly. You hardly think. And yet you open your mouth and sounds comes out anyway. It serves my purpose to make Minos understand truth. It doesn't serve my purpose to do the same with you. I'd rather teach a dog to play the guitar. It would be easier, and the resulting noise would be less annoying."

"But I don't see how you can simply discard the evolutionary basis of the social compact -"

"The social compact boils down to this, human - what rights do the strong need to grant to the weak, to keep you pacified so we may rule you more easily?" His huge hand swept behind him, encompassing the soulless. "In the present case, the answer is none at all. Once we've done away with a mythical creator, there is no one to endow my subjects with inalienable rights. And I have no need to grant any."

"But the principle of harm -"

The demon had reached the end of his patience. His voice cracked like a whip. "Keep spouting principles, and I'll harm you. Spare me your voice, and I'll spare you my ax."

Say this for Dee - he knew to shut up when his survival was at stake. He hauled back on his mount's reins and dropped back as Gurath continued on.

The occultist's eyes were bright with unshed tears when Tess and I caught up to him. Annoying windbag that he was, it was easy to forget that he had feelings that could be hurt.

Tess guided her horse over to Dee's and set her hand on his. "He's just a jerk," she said, oblivious to the danger of insulting a monster that could reflexively use the Darkness to both hear and kill us. "Don't listen to him. He thinks because he's strong, he can treat other people like garbage."

"Actually," I said, "he thinks because he's strong, he *should* treat other people like garbage."

"Like I said. He's a jerk."

I spent the rest of the day waiting for the blow to fall. I was under no illusion that Gurath hadn't heard Tess' comment. But there was no retribution. When we settled down for the night, the demon sat some distance away from us, but that was his usual habit. Apparently he tolerated insolence from humans better than from Darkness wraiths.

Dee had perked up and was back to his usual, talkative self. I might have wished for a bit of a break from his chatter, but he had been a friend to me over the years. So instead I rested and let the flow of words wash over me.

I turned to Tess and said, "You really are a good person."

She grimaced. "For an egomaniac leading a cult of personality."

"That's not what Roric meant."

"I'm pretty sure I heard the words 'cult of personality' come out of his mouth. Right after 'no disrespect,' which always means someone has something unpleasant to say about you. Father Roric tends to say what he means."

"Father Roric can be a little too direct in saying what he means," I said.

She shook her head. "The thing is, Minos, I'm not sure he's wrong. You and Roshel both said you needed me as some kind of rallying point for everyone. That's not what I should be at all."

"You're a prophet. You're supposed to be a signpost pointing to God."

"I'm a prophet with no prophecies. And if people are still looking at me as a leader, they're looking at the wrong thing. We're supposed to be transparent as glass, so people can see God shining through us. People shouldn't be looking at us instead of looking at God."

I frowned. "You started out saying 'me,' but then that changed to 'us.' Are you saying people are looking at me when they should be looking at God, too?"

And in that incredibly irritating way she had, all she said was, "You're the one who needs to decide that, Minos."

I tried prayer. Along with confession and being a general, it didn't seem to be something that came naturally to me. After a quick recitation of the standard supplications, I murmured, "Lord, if you're listening, now would be a good time for a sign. A lightning bolt hitting Gurath would be great…"

I trailed off. I wasn't entirely sure what I was asking for. "I guess… it would be nice to know you exist. To know the right thing to do. Because this is hard, and I can't do it alone."

There was no reply. Roric had told me salvation had to be on God's terms, not mine. That I had to surrender to him, to understand that the world didn't go my way. But right then, a little more direct help would have come in handy.

Several nights later we camped at the outer edge of a great city. It was as completely fallen into ruin as any I'd seen, but it had clearly been a massive thing in its day, larger than Acceptance or Stephensburg. To the northeast, a glow lit the sky.

"That's where we're going?" I asked.

Gurath nodded.

"So this is another Hellguard citadel, all the way up here? Why?" It was noticeably colder now. I couldn't imagine why the demons would establish an outpost in this godforsaken place.

By the firelight I could see Dee's eyes widen in alarm. "I say. This isn't -"

"Shh." The Hellguard held a huge finger in front of the occultist's lips. "Don't spoil my surprise. Let him see for himself."

"I must admit, I've always been curious," Dee went on, "but perhaps it would in this case be more prudent for me to master my curiosity and stay behind. To observe with the greater objectivity of distance, as it were."

Dee's attack of cowardice filled me with more dread than I'd experienced yet. His instincts for self-preservation were unsurpassed, but we'd just seen how they existed in constant tension with his insatiable desire to stick his long nose where it didn't belong. If he didn't even want to approach our destination, I didn't either.

"Ah, but you've come so far," Gurath said. "So you'll come the rest of the way too." His words were gentle, nothing like the harsh tone he'd used with the occultist days before. But they were just as absolutely final. Dee nodded reluctantly.

I'd been serious when I asked the occultist to get a message back to Our Lady if I didn't make it. I wondered now if anyone would make it back alive. I lay awake long into the night, after the others had gone to sleep. Could I get my companions away from here?

I couldn't begin to see how. I felt sure we could overpower the soulless, and probably Legion. But there would be no defeating or escaping Gurath. I had barely managed to slip Yoshana when I'd turned on her. And that had been in the confusion of battle, when I'd commanded the Darkness myself, and didn't have three other people to worry about. Gurath was centuries older and stronger than his daughter, and we were deep in his territory.

A trembling shiver that had nothing to do with the cold ran up my body as if spiders were crawling on my skin. I'd believed I could at least sense the Darkness, if not turn it. But Gurath had wormed it inside me to heal my leg and I hadn't noticed. He'd have a web of it wrapped around me now. I stifled the urge to beat wildly at my clothes, or roll into the fire.

I jumped when Tess sat down next to me.

"Hey, it's okay," she said. Apparently she couldn't sleep either.

I wanted to say something reassuring - I owed her that much, at least - but I couldn't. "I'm not sure it is. Wherever we're going, it scares Dee. And I'm d-" I stopped and rephrased, considering the circumstances. "I can't think of a way to get us out of here."

"It's okay," she repeated. "We had a good run. We beat Yoshana. You commanded an army. You had the Darkness in you and threw it out. I had dinner with the Metropolitan of Our Lady. Not bad for a farm girl and a garbage miner from the Flow."

"I don't think it's right for a woman under twenty to be saying 'I had a good run.'"

"I did what God asked me, Minos, and a lot more besides. Everything of this world passes away. Me, you, even him." She jerked her thumb at Gurath, apparently asleep. "Our kingdom's not of this world. But I'll say it again. We've had a pretty good run while we've been here."

"You know, I love you."

Her eyes widened. "Do you really? Well, that's something to live for. I love you too."

She settled her head on my arm and curled up next to me for warmth. And to my surprise, we had no trouble sleeping that night.

We'd been riding the better part of the day through the dead city, our horses' hooves sending up long echoes in the cold air. We'd seen nothing move except for distant gulls that drifted our way when the wind came from the east, bringing the smell of the sea. I started in my saddle every time one of them called.

Then abruptly we emerged from weed-choked ruins into a devastated no-man's-land at the edge of a river. Gurath flung his arms wide. "And here we are. As the Prophet Siles said, 'The bones of the great civilization that went before the Fall lie scattered like the shells left behind by the retreating tide. Or, though the image be not so pretty or so flattering, like the slime left behind after the snail has withdrawn once more into his shell. What remains of that which went before but hollow monuments to vanity, towers so tall that no man would dare now to ascend them? Truly we are but ash and dust.' Humans, I give you the remains of your world."

Dee visibly cringed. Legion laughed out loud.

The air was frigid, and small sheets of ice glided by on the river's sluggish current. That was despite the fire. And the fire was everywhere.

For a hundred yards on our side of the river, nothing grew and no building stood. Tall, dark poles rose in that waste, thick cables trailing from them back toward us. Metal towers loomed at the edge of the devastated strip. Fires burned inside them. Pits and trenches filled with fire dotted the waste. And fire burned in the weapons of the giant figures patrolling it. If that concentration of flame perturbed Legion, the wraith didn't show it. Something like lust shone in its eyes.

"Cocytus," Gurath proclaimed. "The largest concentration of Darkness in the world. On this continent, anyway. Trapped between the Ice Fields, the river, and the sea. What's in here makes the wraiths in the Sorrows look like fluffy kittens."

One of the patrolling Hellguard approached and saluted Gurath. The demon wore a sword and heavy pistol at his belt, but his principle weapon was something like the naphtha-throwers of Rockwall's fire wardens. This device was far larger and looked much more sophisticated.

"Anything new, Bal?" Gurath asked.

This demon was smaller, almost compact by the standards of the Hellguard, though he still bulked as large as Seven. He looked even bigger in the heavy parka he wore against the cold. He threw back his hood and answered, "Nossir. Pretty quiet. There was a breach two weeks ago in the northwest quadrant. Tunneled under our sensors and came up behind us. That was entertaining for a while."

"Serious thrust?"

"Nah, just a probe. Screwing around. Seeing if we were paying attention."

Gurath turned a mirthless smile on me. "Balmalek here is second in command at Cocytus. It's a crappy job. I've got almost a hundred men keeping that stuff contained. Oh, look. It's noticed us."

Among the buildings on the far side of the river, something was growing. A dark cloud boiling up that looked like smoke, but didn't move with the wind. It swelled huge, larger than the largest building.

"A wraith that size..." I murmured.

"What? Is more intelligent than a human? Yes. Is far too strong for anyone's mind to resist? Yes. Could suck up the Darkness in the Sorrows into a juggernaut beyond your imagination? Yes. Would roll over your world like the angel of death? Yes." The demon barked out a laugh. "So, you're welcome."

"But you're not keeping it bottled up as a favor to us, are you?" Tess asked.

Gurath laughed again. "Give the little girl a prize. No. It would come after us, too. Maybe not at first - you'd be easier prey. But eventually, after you were all eaten or controlled, it would come back for us. We're too much of a threat for it to let us live."

The dark mass on the other side of the river was roiling, thickening.

"It looks pissed," Gurath muttered.

"Well, we know it doesn't like you, boss." Balmalek tapped the side of his jaw and spoke into the air. "All troops, black alert status. Possible full frontal assault on my position, all reserves deploy. All troops in the field hold current position, repeat alert status black."

He turned back to Gurath. "My bet is it's just a diversion. If it breaks out anywhere, it'll be somewhere else. Been wrong before, though."

His eyes went to the cloud. "It definitely looks pissed."

Dee was staring, unblinking. Cat had grabbed Tess' hand. It didn't seem right to call what we were facing a wraith. The word did no justice to its huge, awesome malevolence. If that vast cloud of Darkness came over the river, what could we do? There would be no outrunning it. In my heart, I didn't believe even Tess could resist it.

Thudding feet were all around us, and dozens of armed Hellguards swarmed the riverbank, flamethrowers aimed at the cloud. A tentacle thicker than my body lashed across the river. At once it was struck by bolts of lightning from the poles, arcs of fire from the towers, more flame from the Hellguards in the waste. And just as quickly it dissipated and retreated, and the huge mass thinned and vanished.

"Guess it was just saying hello," Balmalek muttered, but his voice was shaky. He tapped his jaw again. "All troops, assault on my position has ended. Reserves to barracks. Other quadrants, watch for another push."

"Sometimes it waits until the adrenaline has leeched away, then tries again somewhere else," Gurath said. "But not often. It doesn't spend its substance lightly."

I stared across the river. The buildings there were lower than in the rest of the city, but stately. They reminded me of the ruins around the library in the dead city of eternal lights.

"You drove it out of the Darklands to imprison it here?"

"No. What got loose in the Darklands is mostly still there. We don't have enough manpower to round it all up. That's why we circumcise the minds of our slaves, so it doesn't possess them. Well, one of the reasons." Gurath turned to his lieutenant. "Give me your flamethrower for a minute."

The smaller Hellguard unstrapped the weapon from his back and passed it over. Gurath turned the bulky device in his hands, studying it. Absently, as if his mind were far away, he went on, "This cloud was already like this when we got here. A huge concentration, even back then. We're pretty sure it ate some of the locals who didn't get out. We tried to control it at first, but it was too strong. We lost men in that first fight with it. That's when we came up with these."

He patted the flamethrower and continued. "When we couldn't kill it, we blockaded it. I mean, I suppose we could have nuked it - and that's still a last option we've got. But we've learned to live with the stalemate. We set up the defenses you see here. It's a huge commitment of resources to tie up Hellguards watching this river, so at first we mostly used slaves to patrol. That's how we found out that when it gets strong enough, it can even possess the circumcised. Turns them into things like Legion, here. Speaking of which..."

The big Hellguard whirled and bathed the wraith in flame. Legion screamed. Tess, Cat, Dee, and I scattered like rabbits to avoid the burning droplets spraying from its flailing limbs. Gurath kept the stream of fire trained on his former ambassador, destroying what tried to come out.

I would swear the screams went on after the blackened host body had stopped moving, as the last of the Darkness burned away.

The demon lord handed the weapon back to Balmalek, who calmly strapped it in place.

"Like I said," Gurath continued impassively, "You have to be careful with your creations, or they turn on you. We learned how to make those things, and they've got their uses. But you can't trust them."

Dee was staring in open horror at the charred corpse on the ground. Tess looked physically sick. Only Cat seemed unperturbed. In fact, I thought there was the smallest hint of a smile on her face. But then, the paleo's morality was uncomplicated, and didn't include mercy toward people she didn't like.

I hadn't liked Legion either, but the wraith had been a thinking, feeling being. Not a cockroach to be crushed because it was inconvenient.

Gurath looked down at the smoldering body, then out over the fire-scarred no-man's-land between us and the river. His eyes were somewhere far away.

"They used to call me the Flame, back before the Fall. And I have to admit, there's something satisfying about watching things burning. Certain things, anyway. Things that need to burn."

Legion's body twitched, but that was just a reflex in the corpse. I'd seen enough of those not to be surprised.

Gurath went on, "You see, we all have enemies. Yoshana was your enemy, but she stood between you and me. Do you really want to stand against me, when you can stand with me? You think I'm your enemy, but I stand between you and this."

The demon lord jerked his thumb over his shoulder, at the ruins where a gigantic mass of the Darkness lay waiting. He stepped close, looming over me, transfixing me with those piercing blue eyes. "Now you understand, don't you?"

10. The Last Choice

I fought hard not to step back. The Hellguard was twice my weight, and one thing I understood very well was that he could split me in half before I had a chance to blink. And for all our philosophical discussion, what Dee had foolishly thought of as a conversation between equals, Gurath wouldn't hesitate to do just that if it suited him.

I lifted my eyes from the demon's massive chest to his face. "Understand what, exactly? You think that because the Darkness is worse than you, that what you're doing to humanity is right?"

The blackened body of Legion's most recent host twitched once more in mute accusation.

The Hellguard shook with laughter. "Right? 'You know as well as we do that right is a question that only has meaning in relations between equals in power. In the real world, the strong do what they will and the weak suffer what they must.'"

Anger was getting the better of fear. I snapped, "So you decide what needs to be burned because your will is the strongest. Enough Nietzsche."

He just laughed again. "That wasn't Nietzsche. That was Thucydides, almost three thousand years ago. He understood the truth, way back then. But humans keep forgetting that truth, or trying to, until it forces its way back into your little worlds. And then you understand reality, and that what you want isn't the same as what is, and all your prayers to your dead god won't make it so."

That bleak vision was hard to argue with in the devastated waste between the Darkness and the Hellguard. I watched the fires burn in the pits scattered through that field of death.

"So let's say I understand. Why did you bring me here, exactly?"

"Good. Let's get to the point." The demon smiled. "The point is that you could be a valuable ally to me, Minos. Or to be just a bit more accurate, a satrap."

"You want me to be your vassal? What exactly are you saying, Gurath? I don't rule the Source, and if I did, I sure as hell wouldn't want to answer to you."

His grin broadened. "But you could rule the Source. And why shouldn't you? You wouldn't be better suited to it than that treacherous, murderous whore, Melaret? If you don't believe that, then you aren't the man I think you are."

It was hard to disagree with that proposition. But I looked over my shoulder at the two remaining soulless. "And in exchange, what? I give you a land full of mentally circumcised slaves?"

Gurath waved his hand dismissively. "No. Rule them as you see fit. Give them whatever freedom makes you happy. You've seen that we didn't burn the will out of the soldiers in the Shield. Our authority doesn't need to extend to the rest of the world in exactly the same way as it does in the Darklands, as long as it's not challenged."

The Hellguard commander's eyes bored into mine. "We want the same things in the end, Minos. A unified world. Or at least a unified continent. A beginning of a return to the civilization the ancients had. The benefits of peace and commerce. Together, with your forces and mine on two sides of the Green Heart, we can bring them to the negotiating table. Install an allied government there too. Then we can burn the Darkness out of the Sorrows. Imagine one nation from here to the Muddy River. With you administering a quarter of it."

"All this I will give you if you will bow down and worship me," I said. Gurath's offers were no more subtle than Legion's had been.

The demon just chuckled. "Well, sure. Easy to take a pass on what the devil's offering if you're the son of God, or you think you are. But you're not. You're one more little human that's going to fade away into dust. But you don't have to. 'Those then that do know and apprehend perpetual being as such, desire the same with a natural desire.' That was your Aquinas, by the way. I can give you perpetual being. Real perpetual being, not the bullshit promise of a nonexistent afterlife."

"So you'll fill me with the Darkness again? No thanks. Like I said, I tried that before, and it didn't go well last time."

"No, and to be blunt, that's because my daughter did a lousy job of it. She didn't train you properly. Seven could have done better. I can certainly do better. Plus she lied to you through the whole process. I think you'll have to agree that I've been painfully honest with you."

I nodded reluctantly.

"Not to mention that she wanted you to kill your woman. I have no interest in that. You can marry your prophet and set her up as your queen for all I care." He smiled again. "My yoke is easy and my burden is light."

Christ's words in the demon's mouth were repellent, but I turned the offer over in my head. I had no desire to serve Gurath. And I'd given up on that particular kind of eternal life when Prophetess cast the Darkness out of me. But the Hellguard's proposal could prevent a war that would almost certainly kill thousands. And removing Melaret would be doing the Source - and all mankind - a favor.

"Why me?" I demanded.

"Well, for starters, because you're available. And since I've been honest so far, I'll continue now. You're ambitious enough to want to be my governor, but smart enough to know you can't overthrow me and take the top spot for yourself. That was the problem with Yoshana - a little too much ambition, not enough humility or common sense. As a war hero, you've got some legitimacy with the people, but as a Select, you're enough of an outsider that it would be hard for you to rally them against me. We both know you can control the

Darkness, but not enough of it to make you a threat to me personally. You're just about perfect for the job."

"I think I like my current job well enough."

Gurath's expression hardened, just a bit. "And how long do you think that will last? How compatible do you suppose you really are with your prophet's Universalist twaddle? I'll give you another one from Aquinas, since you're so fond of him. 'Where there is a definite nature, there must be definite activities proper to that nature. Now it is certain that men's nature is definite. There must therefore be certain activities that in themselves befit man.'"

"I don't -"

"Don't follow what I'm saying, Select?" the demon demanded. "If man's nature is definite, then what are you? Nothing that God created, certainly. So what are the activities that befit you? Are there any? So do you just let yourself be put away, an abomination allowed out on occasion, when there's something worse to be fought? Or do you embrace the truth, which is that you create yourself? You could be a greater being, one who shapes myth and convention. Or... you could just be an abomination on a chain, like I once was. You can surrender to the imagined will of a god that doesn't exist and wouldn't care about you if he did... or you can make your will into a true god. Which do you prefer?"

Fear more what he can make you do to your own soul. The Hellguard's attempt to turn me was transparently obvious... but was he wrong? If the option was war... not only war now between Our Lady and the Darklands, but the stupid, perpetual war that had engulfed the world since the Age of Fear... if I could bring peace... shouldn't I?

I glanced at my companions. Tess' face was full of horror, as I'd expected. There was no compromise in her on this sort of issue. Cat was impassive. She loved Tess, but she respected strength. In part she loved Tess because Tess was strong. Universalist morality was meaningless to the paleo.

I found myself searching for the answer in Dee's eyes, but the occultist wore his usual bland expression.

"Minos, you can't be seriously considering this!" Tess blurted.

"Dammit, Genia!" I snapped. "Can you shut up and let someone else think for once? If there's a chance for peace - if I can be the person who brings that peace - then shouldn't I do it? Am I thrilled at the idea of being a demon's viceroy? Not really. But I don't see a better option, and like he said, I'm here, and maybe this really is what I'm supposed to do."

Her face went very still, and very softly she murmured, "Who else is fit to rule here but me?"

My cheeks heated as if she'd slapped me. Stephen had said that, in his fit of mad rage, as the Darkness had taken control of him. Just before Melaret had stabbed him to death. Anger boiled up.

"What, you think I'm like Stephen? You think I'm some nasty little tin-pot dictator with delusions of grandeur?" The woman was ridiculous. She couldn't ever stop picking at me, couldn't ever trust me to do the right thing. Here, with the wreckage of the Last Days around us and the Darkness gathered at our doorstep, she thought I was trying to make myself feel important? "After all that I've done? For you and for the Church? I've done the best I could, Genia, and even if you've never been willing to see it, it's been pretty damn good, thank you very much! I'm a hundred times the man Stephen was, and a hundred -"

My eyes went back to Dee's face, and I sputtered to a halt. *We do not suspect that he is acting in us, because he follows the current of our inclinations.*

I drew a long, shuddering breath, and turned back to Gurath. "No."

"No? Just like that you're picking her dead end over my open path to freedom? She's just asked you to deny yourself. All that I ask is for you be true to who you are."

"Yep. The problem with what you're asking is that who I am is very frequently a selfish asshole."

The demon's smile was thin. "Or at least not very smart. A superior being is offering you a kingdom, and you're spitting in his face."

"Jesus said his kingdom isn't of earth. And neither is mine. I'm not buying what you're selling, Gurath. You know the last thing your daughter said to a Hellguard? Hear, Israel. The Lord is God. The Lord is one. There is no God but God." I met Gurath's piercing eyes. "And you're not him."

His smile twisted mockingly. "And where is my daughter now? Dead. Just like your God."

"Nietzsche took that as an axiom. He never bothered to prove it."

"And you can prove he's wrong? You can prove your God exists? Because smarter men than you have tried, and I have to say that so far you've utterly failed to persuade me."

I remembered Dee's words, which finally made sense to me. "'But because we cannot see his essence, we are brought to the knowledge of his existence, not by what he is in himself, but by the effects which he works.' I can see how God works, through people like Tess. And I can see how you work. And I know which I like better."

The demon took a step back, laced his fingers together, and cracked his knuckles. "So. We're enemies, then?"

I chose my words carefully. Not just because the Hellguard was so very, very dangerous, but because I wanted to be understood. I'd experienced a strange clarity.

"We're certainly not friends, or allies. But if you're asking whether I intend to make war against you? No."

The big face smiled a bit. "Then you did understand, at least a little."

"I don't think I understood what you meant me to. I understood what she meant me to." I nodded at Tess. And I remembered my conversation with Father Roric. "Is gardening one of your talents, Gurath?"

"No."

"Mine either. But my father was good at it. I remember before the war, him telling me about a big pine tree that grew in our yard. He said sometimes he was going to prune a branch he thought was sick or dead, and he'd find green shoots coming out of it. He said sometimes you risked taking the good with the bad if you pruned too much. Sometimes it was better to just let what was dead or rotten fall under its own weight."

The demon scowled.

"I find your philosophy dangerous and evil," I went on, "And I think what you've done to your people is revolting. But it's not for me to wage war because of that, or because I think I can do better. This isn't the kingdom of heaven where we'll see perfection. It's just earth. And I'm certainly not God to judge, any more than you are. Maybe I'm the one who's wrong, or maybe there's some good in you, or if there isn't… one of these days, you'll fall under your own weight."

Gurath stroked his chin. "Well. That's insulting. I'm not worth killing?"

"No. Not that. It's that this isn't Heaven, it's earth, and here man is made of crooked timber. We're not going to invade the Darklands even though you've turned them into outposts of evil. I'm not going to start a war and kill whatever green shoots there might be."

The Hellguard chieftain barked out a laugh. "Funny. In the end, you renounce war, not because you understood truth, but because you rejected it."

"I understood your truth, Gurath. It's just that I also understood a better one. I could believe what you do. Or I can choose to believe in something better. I choose better. We'll go now. If you don't bother us, we won't bother you."

I turned away, putting my back to Cocytus and its devils. *Get thee behind me, Satan...*

An iron grip closed on my shoulder and spun me around. Gurath's other hand wrapped around my throat and lifted me off the ground like a doll.

"There's one question we haven't answered," he growled. "I follow your logic why you won't join me. And I follow your logic why you won't kill me. What we haven't addressed is why I shouldn't kill you."

I found that somehow his grip left me just enough air to croak out a response. "You said you hadn't lied to me -"

"What, about safe passage? I never promised you safe passage. That did -" he gestured contemptuously with his other hand at Legion's corpse, "But I told you it was a liar. Really? No better answer than pathetic whining about deception? Is it all just too unfair?"

The demon's voice dripped sarcasm. His grip was tightening.

"Roshel," I choked out.

"Yes, she's more of a military threat than you, I agree. But I wasn't just flattering you when I said you'd be a good ally. Which also means you'd be a bad enemy. You and your prophet might be more effective than Roshel at unifying your people. Why would I take that chance, when I can end the threat right here? No, I don't think you're going anywhere after all."

Air wasn't coming anymore. I caught sight of Tess' face. Her eyes were wide with horror, but her hand was locked on Cat's arm.

Anger flashed, feebly. So she wouldn't even let Cat fight for me?

And then clarity returned. The paleo would just get herself killed if she intervened. Tess understood that. She was letting me go, as she had to. As I had to. With or without the Darkness in me, I was proud, and selfish. That was my human nature.

When Yoshana's blade had been at Tess' throat, Tess had recited the *Anima Christi*, commending her soul to God. Not the famous psalm saying she wouldn't fear the shadow of death, because she had been afraid. As I was now. Instead, the prayer putting herself in the Lord's hand at the end. I looked at her and forced a smile. I could do no less.

Gurath's grip tightened. "And so it ends, Minos. 'In the world, of course, destructive capacity is still the real proof of power.' That was Benedict the Sixteenth again. Despite being a priest, he wasn't a fool. If you'd studied him, you might not have found yourself here."

Dee spoke up. "A bit out of context, Lord Gurath. More completely, Pope Benedict said, 'After all, the tenor of our faith is that God's distinctive greatness is revealed precisely in powerlessness. That in the long run, the strength of history is precisely in those who love, which is to say, in a strength that, properly speaking, cannot be measured according to categories of power. So in order to show who he is, God consciously revealed himself in the powerlessness of Nazareth and Golgotha. Thus, it is not the one who can destroy the most who is the most powerful - in the world, of course, destructive capacity is still the real proof of power - but, on the contrary, the least power of love is already greater than the greatest power of destruction.'"

I had to smile at the most cowardly man I knew confronting the most terrible being I'd ever encountered. *Eius in obitu nostro praesentia muniamur. May we be strengthened by his presence in the hour of our death*

The last thing I managed to say in the demon's grip was, "John the Baptist said, 'he must increase, but I must decrease.' I understand now. The Lord has conquered death. We can't do that alone. But if we die with him, we will live with him."

The demon smiled back. "People keep saying that. Let's see if it's true."

11. It Is Finished

"And then what happened?" Roshel demanded.

"I'm sorry," Dee said. "I appear to have run out of water, and exposition is thirsty work, especially in this heat. Might someone bring another pitcher?"

The headquarters of the Order of Thorns was indeed uncomfortably hot in the early fall afternoon, which didn't contribute to the Overlord general's good humor. Although she would have been furious with the occultist even in more comfortable conditions.

If I still had the Darkness in me, I'd wring the truth from his scrawny body, Roshel fumed. A dozen thoughts chased through her head. What had happened to Minos and Prophetess? Why was the loudmouthed occultist here alone, and why for the love of God wouldn't he answer a simple question? Was she now the ultimate military authority in Our Lady?

The satisfaction of that last idea warred against nebulous rage and dread of the unknown. Her feelings for Genia Carter were mixed, but Minos was a friend.

A friend who wasn't quite the general that most people thought. Not the general that Roshel was. The thought was disloyal, and she hated herself for it.

Nearly as much as she hated Doctor John Dee in that particular moment.

But before Roshel could voice her frustration, Railes was at Dee's side, his dagger at the occultist's throat. His snarl distorted the skull tattooed on the side of his face into a ghastly shape.

"You're thirsty, you stupid bag of wind? How about I open your veins and you try drinking your own blood? That's my commander that's missing, and *my woman!* She's been too patient with you." He shot a glare at Roshel. "But I'm done! What the hell happened?"

"Minos was quite explicit that I should tell his story if he didn't return, and I am attempting to do justice to that request," Dee sputtered. "And I must hasten to add that if you were to slit my throat, I could hardly finish that story, now could I?"

"I can cut pieces off you that'll still leave you able to talk, you -"

"Captain Railes. Stand down!" The authority in the Metropolitan's voice lashed at Minos' adjutant. Blinking, Railes dropped the knife. It clattered on the stone floor, throwing echoes into the sudden silence.

The Bishop of Our Lady, Father Roric, and Tarc the Select stood in the doorway. It seemed to Railes that Tarc wore a hint of that irritating little smirk he so often had. *Sure, you treacherous bastard,* Railes seethed. *You always had it in for the boss, and he put up with you 'cause you're Select, and 'cause he felt bad about killing your buddy. And now you're happy he's gone. Well, guess what? You're not going to enjoy life without him around to protect you.*

But he braced to attention and addressed the Metropolitan. "Sorry, Your Eminence." There would be time to settle up with Tarc later.

"I suppose," the Metropolitan continued, "that in some ways I'm fortunate that Doctor Dee has taken his time, since he won't have to repeat himself for me. But now, Doctor, let's get to the point. What has happened to Judge Minos and Prophetess?"

The Metropolitan was an old man who had seen a lot of the world. He understood the look that Railes tried to hide. "And Cat, of course," he added.

"I must say," Dee began, "that when I've visited the paleos, I found they showed much more respect for my narrative skills than some of the supposedly more civilized denizens of Our Lady. But I do understand that perhaps it's time to hasten the tale along, as art must sometimes take a back seat to -"

"Dee!" the Metropolitan snapped. "Four people went out. Only one came back."

"And not the one any of us would have preferred," Railes growled, picking up his dagger.

"Ah. Well. Then, to get to the point, as it were -" Dee eyed the weapon, "Gurath let us go."

"What?" Everyone said it at once.

"Yes. He set Minos back down and said we were free to leave. Gurath explained that he hadn't been certain whether Minos was lying about his intentions in order to escape with his life. He thought Minos might be able to deflect the Darkness probing his mind. But when Minos was facing his death, Gurath could read his intentions clearly. And so, realizing that Minos was telling the truth, he released us, apparently content to let his plans mature at their own pace."

Railes' knife slid again from a hand weakened with relief and stuck point-first in a crack in the floor.

"I must say," Dee went on, "That I do wonder whether that explanation was entirely true, or whether Gurath was just toying with us for his own amusement. He's not a pleasant fellow, you know, and his sense of humor can be rather perverse. For example, I have only repeated his vile slanders against my own person out of a strict sense of narrative accuracy."

"Then where are they now?" Roshel demanded. "Why are you the only one here?"

"Ahh. Well, you see, something happened on the road."

"For God's sake, Dee! What happened on the road?"

"Ah. Well. I'm not sure exactly how to put this -" Dee realized that Railes was stooping once again to retrieve his knife and opted for brevity. "Minos and Prophetess decided they weren't coming back. At least for now."

"What about Cat?" Railes demanded.

"To hell with Cat," Roshel snapped. "What do you mean they decided they aren't coming back? Sorry, Railes, but the future of the Source takes precedence over your love life. I don't care what's turning blue."

Dee considered which question to answer first. Roshel was by far the senior commander, but Railes was closer, and was the one who had pulled a weapon. "I believe Cat will be along shortly. She just wanted to be sure that Minos and Prophetess, or should I say Miss Carter, got where they're going. And as for that, you see, the corollary to Minos' decision that there is no need for war is that there is no need for a warrior."

That wasn't exactly his strong suit anyway, Roshel mused. Although she hadn't seen him when he'd been leading the Shadowed Hand in the service of Rockwall, which had arguably been the high point of his military career. So maybe she was being a little unfair. He certainly wasn't much of a general, though. The idea of supreme military command, without Minos having to die for her to get it, was very appealing. She fought to keep down a smile that would be inappropriate.

"That's fine, but we need a prophet," Tolf burst out. The captain of Prophetess' personal guard had been silent to that point, but was now visibly distraught.

"Well, again, no," Dee said. "Miss Carter, who has become quite insistent that she no longer be referred to as Prophetess, also felt rather strongly that her particular calling had come to an end. At least for now. One never knows when God may call her to that task again, after all. You see, they both felt they had become central foci for rallying the people to war, and that war was no longer the answer. They debated for some time the notion that some kind of struggle against a common enemy was needed to maintain unity. But Miss Carter persuaded Minos that, whatever the historical precedents, a new approach was needed. An order based on love rather than shared hatred."

Dee cleared his throat. "As Christ himself said, 'A new commandment I give you, love one another as I have loved you.'"

Tolf said in an anguished tone, "But why leave us instead of leading us?"

"Because Jesus' public revelation is already quite clear on that point, and there's nothing to add to it. No need at this point for more prophecy or, for that matter, prophets. Miss Carter felt she could be seen as competing with the Metropolitan's authority, which is not what she wanted at all. And Judge Minos believed that you, Roshel, would be better suited to peacetime military leadership than he."

No argument there, Roshel thought, but kept it to herself. The Metropolitan's face also remained carefully blank.

"Minos, ah, did caution rather strongly against military adventurism. Such as mounting a crusade against the Hellguard, for example. Or, ah, any temptation to depose Melaret and take a position as military dictator of the Source."

Roshel had to allow the smile out. Whatever Minos' flaws as a general, he understood her well enough.

"But... I don't..." Tolf didn't seem to be capable of forming a coherent sentence. "What are we supposed to do without them?"

Dee smiled at the guardsman. "Ah. Proph - er, Miss Carter, did have some specific advice on that point."

"What did she say?" Tolf demanded.

Dee's smile widened. "Have faith."

12. Epilogue

"It was nice of Losywa and Ram to wait for us. And then give us a ride," Tess said. The wagon swayed gently as we rattled along up the road. The Paint wound by on our right. The wagon's bed was nearly full of barrels of beer and flour shipped from the Source, bales of tobacco from the Shield, and a variety of stranger and more exotic goods whose provenance I couldn't guess. There was room for Tess, Cat, and me to sit on the tobacco bales - but only just.

"Yeah," I said. And it had been nice to see a pair of friendly faces when we'd finally returned to Seafields. The trip south had taken far longer than the journey north. Gurath had let us keep the horses, but they were nowhere near as fast as the truck had been.

Of course, I'd overheard more of Losywa's conversation with Ram than Tess had.

"Why aren't we just going home, Loo?" he'd complained. "We've got more than enough money to just quit while we're ahead."

"You heard what Judge Minos said," she'd retorted. "The Source isn't going to war against the Shield and the Darklands. The Hellguard aren't in a position to try anything themselves, not with two possible fronts against the Source and the Green Heart. The Heart is sick of war. And Yoshana's gone and her crusade with her. If the peace holds, there's a lot of profit in trade. And with Legion's money, we've got the capital to be right at the front of it. We just need to widen our circle of contacts. Find some folks we can trust, get our network set up. Goat Hill's as good a place to start as any."

So our friends weren't taking us north entirely for altruistic reasons. I didn't mind. Losywa might be more than a little bit calculating, but merchants like her could help bring back trade, and the progress that went with it.

I was more grateful to Tess. "Thanks again for agreeing to come this way."

"I already told you I'm not in a hurry to get back to Our Lady. Frankly, all the attention always made me uncomfortable. And you've been worried about your parents as long as I've known you. Why wouldn't we go look for them now?" She glanced at me sidelong. "Um... I suppose I should ask... how do you think they're going to feel about you having a girlfriend who isn't Select?"

I'd been wondering the same thing. After the Fall, the Select had formed a separate community that didn't intermarry with others. We were, after all, genetically superior. And of course, there wasn't really a long line of people beating down the door to mix with a race of gray-skinned, black-eyed aberrations. So the issue only rarely came up.

I didn't know the answer to her question, so I gave her the only answer that mattered to me. "I don't especially care. I really want to find my parents, but if they don't like you... I don't especially care."

That wasn't a question for me alone. "What about your folks? How are they going to feel about you and a Select?"

Her smile was radiant. "I don't especially care either."

Hesitantly, I added, "Well, I suppose Gurath gave us permission to get married, so who else's opinion really matters?" I grinned.

"You really care about a Hellguard giving us his blessing?"

"Look who's talking. You decided you were my girlfriend after Yoshana said it."

"Hmm. Touché. It's still hard to believe she's gone. In the end, I can't help but think that at least some of her intentions were good. Trying to bring humanity together. Even if she did go about it the wrong way."

I thought a bit, choosing my words before I continued. "About that... why do you think God called you to stop Yoshana but not Gurath? Granted there's a mix of good and evil in every human – and Hellguard. But isn't Gurath the more evil of the two?"

She took even more time before she answered. "I've wondered the same thing. And I've wondered if I understood wrong. I suppose... I think Yoshana's lies were more insidious because they were closer to the truth. She called people to a greater good, but it was a false good, and it had to be refuted. In the end, Gurath's not calling anyone to anything but selfishness. That evil's obvious."

"And seductive," I said. "I'm not sure I'd say it's evil, exactly. The desire to define yourself is natural to humanity. It made me and my kind what we are. Surrender to God's will doesn't come easily, Tess. Not to me, and Lord knows not to our ancestors before the Fall."

She nodded. "I know. But that's a battle everyone has to fight inside their own soul. No one can fight it for us. Believing in ourselves as gods goes back to Adam."

Father Roric had said the same thing, more than once. The front line between good and evil passed through every human heart, and that war was fought every minute of every day.

Cat yawned and stretched in the sun. The paleo was smart but had little use for philosophy. Sometimes I envied her.

"It does seem like a shame about Yoshana," I said at last. "I think it was G.K. Chesterton who said the reformer is always right about what's wrong - she's just often wrong about what's right."

Tess glared at me. "I swear, the next person who quotes anyone is going to get slapped. Between you, and Dee, and Gurath, I can't even begin to tell you how sick of it I am."

I laughed. "I get it. As Machiavelli said, a man who uses other men's words is no - Ow! Hey! I was just making that one up."

She hadn't slapped me, which I'd almost been expecting. She'd punched me in the stomach instead. She had a heck of an arm.

She glared. "You still had it coming."

Cat grinned at me, laughing soundlessly. Cat could be a bit of a sadist. I stuck out my tongue at her.

I reached over and took Tess' hand. "Safer this way," I said. "Now you've only got one hand free to hit me."

We sat in silence for a while watching the world roll by. The land was mostly given over to fields of cotton. Ranks on ranks of bright clouds stretched overhead, thinning the sunlight and making the afternoon pleasant and cool.

"Do you think Dee made it back to Our Lady?" Tess asked.

I'd wondered the same thing, not without some twinges of worry and guilt. If something happened to the occultist and Roshel concluded we'd all been killed, it could mean war. But I said, "If there's one thing I'm confident of, it's Dee's survival skills. He made it."

And I was sure of that. We had booked him passage on a boat back to Delta City, and I really was certain that the gangling windbag could make it through anything the journey might throw at him.

Tess nodded. "I feel that too. It seems strange… not having any responsibilities."

I stared out over the river.

"What's wrong?" Tess asked after a time. "You're a million miles away."

"I was just thinking… speaking of responsibilities…" I was having trouble getting it out. "What do you think of what Gurath said?"

"About what?"

"About us."

She squeezed my hand hard. "Minos, what exactly are you asking?"

"I'm a better person when I'm with you, Genia. You save me. I can't get to heaven without you. And I can't think of a better reason to want to be with someone forever. So… I guess… I'm… I'm asking you to marry me."

She pulled her hand away and hit me again. There were tears in her eyes. "You're doing a lousy job of it! You should at least be down on one knee!"

I laughed nervously. "What in all the time you've spent with me would make you think I'd be good at this? And my knee hurts, remember?"

But I struggled down onto one knee between the bales and barrels, wincing at the ache that Gurath's Darkness hadn't fully banished. I looked up into her gray eyes and asked, "Genia Carter, will you marry me?"

The tears ran down her cheeks. "I couldn't be who I am without you. You make me a better person too. So yes, you unromantic gray jackass, I'll marry you."

And that's how it was decided.

Acknowledgements

I started this series with the notion of a dialog between faith and reason. In *Freedom and the Role of the Artist*, Terry Teachout said:

> The artist whose chief goal is not to make everything more beautiful but to enlist his audience in a cause - no matter what that cause may be - is rarely if ever prepared to tell the whole truth and nothing but. He replaces the true complexity of the world with the false simplicity of the ideologue. He alters reality not to make everything more beautiful, but to stack the deck. This is what Oscar Wilde meant when he said that no artist ever tries to prove anything, though I'd put it another way. Great art doesn't tell - it shows. And this act of showing is itself a moral act, a commitment to reality.

I tried to keep the action and dialog intellectually honest, but as Teachout says, there's a danger any time you write fiction with the goal of making a point.

Pontius Pilate infamously asked "What is truth?" We can only look into our hearts and try to find the answer to that question. These five books reflect my attempt to do that as best I can, for myself if not for anyone else. The faith journey here is mine. Your mileage may vary. It took me seventeen years of intense exposure to Catholicism before I converted - so Minos was a much quicker study in that respect than I was. While I can't imagine these novels have persuaded anybody one way or the other, maybe they've given a few readers something to think about.

For those already starting from a position of faith, I'd suggest that the best way to convince others of the truth of God is by example, as I was myself convinced - not by preaching, but by letting God's light shine through your actions and interactions.

***

Emerging from the darkness of sin into the light of grace is an idea woven throughout the Abrahamic religions. The series title was inspired by the design of the Dead Sea Scrolls museum in Jerusalem, which is reached through a tunnel so that you have to literally pass through darkness to reach the light.

When I looked for the specific phrase "passing through darkness," I turned up Albert Pike (the lead quote for Book One). Pike was... let's say "interesting." He was an eminent Freemason who authored a guide to the Scottish Masonic Rite. He is the only Confederate soldier to have an outdoor statue in Washington, D.C. According to the Smithsonian Institute's Civil War studies program:

> *Carved at the base of Albert Pike's statue at Third and D Streets in Northwest Washington are the words, "philosopher,*

*jurist, orator, author, poet, scholar, soldier." Some of his
contemporaries could accurately add, "libertine, traitor,
glutton, incompetent, murderer."*

Pike fought for the Confederacy but sympathized with the Union. He wrote important treatises on morality but left his wife to have an affair with a woman forty years younger.

And for a series of novels about the moral ambiguities of the human condition, who could ask for a better muse?

***

Simone Weil was an early 20th century French philosopher, activist, and mystic. Born Jewish, she converted to Catholicism - sort of (she was never baptized). She believed that detachment from self was necessary to approach God. A better-elaborated version of the quote "Evil is the form which God's mercy takes in this world" (lead quote for Book Two) might be:

> *Misfortunes leave wounds which bleed drop by drop even in sleep; thus
> little by little they train man by force and dispose him to wisdom in
> spite of himself. Man must learn to think of himself as a limited and
> dependent being; and only suffering teaches him this.*

Another wonderful quote is, "Bourgeois society is infected by monomania; the monomania of accounting." I love that one because in my day job, I'm a certified public accountant. I think she means we only value what we can measure, which generally isn't very valuable.

***

The philosophy of Edmund Burke (lead quote for Book Three), as articulated in *Reflections on the Revolution in France*, could perhaps be boiled down to, "You aren't as smart as you think you are." He was conservative in the deepest sense, and had a wicked, sarcastic tongue that I appreciate:

> *I do not deny that, among an infinite number of acts of violence and
> folly, some good may have been done. They who destroy everything
> certainly will remove some grievance.*

Burke was skeptical of much of the Enlightenment philosophy coming from France. And yet, he was not a reflexive reactionary. A conservative English Protestant, he supported Irish Catholic emancipation. Deeply suspicious of democracy, he was sympathetic toward American independence.

He probably would have known better than to go messing around with the Darkness.

***

I took a social psychology class in college, many years ago. The class was given the MACH-IV test, which measures the respondents' Machiavellianism. When the instructor asked for a show of hands as to how many people had scored in each category, mine was the only hand that went up for the highest.

To which I responded, "Yeah, sure, because anyone who scored higher than me would lie about their results."

The interesting thing about Machiavelli's quote that all armed prophets are successful and all unarmed prophets are destroyed (Book Four) is that it's wrong on its face. While Muhammad was certainly an armed prophet and founded the world's second most successful religion (by number of adherents and geographic extent), Jesus was an unarmed prophet and founded the world's most successful religion by the same criteria. Buddha was another unarmed prophet. And in the modern world we have the leadership examples of Mohandas Gandhi, Martin Luther King Jr., and Nelson Mandela. The example of Jesus would of course have been obvious to Machiavelli - so it's interesting that such a clever man would have said something so obviously false.

On the other hand, we have the also self-evidently untrue aphorism that "violence never solved anything." As Robert A. Heinlein famously responded, "I'm sure the city fathers of Carthage would be glad to know that."

The trick, I suppose, is navigating between those two untrue statements.

***

Much of the final book I imagined as a discussion between St. Thomas Aquinas and Nietzsche (the lead quote for Book Five). The main problem is that they were both a lot smarter than I am. So it's really just an argument between my understanding of Aquinas and Nietzsche. The other problem with that debate is that Aquinas and Nietzsche start with opposite, unprovable propositions - God lives, or God is dead.

Alan Bloom seemed to think that without a belief in a higher power, philosophy tended inevitably toward the will to power in Nietzsche's void, "beyond good and evil." Bertrand Russell instead regarded Nietzsche as a nasty little back alley of modern thought (although Russell was unable to refute Nietzsche, calling his philosophy "internally consistent").

Through much of my early life, my world view was probably Nietzschean, although I'm not sure I would have framed it quite that way. As Minos said, it's a pretty dark philosophy. I spent a fair amount of time reading Nietzsche while writing this book, and it perturbed me - largely because his views still resonate with me. My wife suggested that I should focus on reading Aquinas instead, and she was right.

***

Speaking of Aquinas, Books Four and Five refer extensively to his *Summa Theologica*. In fact, almost all references are from the more relevant (and much shorter) *Summa Contra Gentiles*. I choose to assume that the edition that Father Roric gave Minos combines both works. The *Summa Contra Gentiles* is a masterful work of philosophy, but it's about 800 pages long. The *Summa Theologica* is almost four times that. They are both quite dense, and I have to admit that I did not finish the *Summa Theologica*. To quote Yoda, "page-turners they were not."

Some notable fiction from which I've probably "borrowed" unconsciously, and which I'd whole-heartedly recommend: Walter M. Miller's *A Canticle for Leibowitz*; Glen Cook's *Black Company* series; C.S. Friedman's *Coldfire Trilogy*.

The phrase "radiant tide of light" is blatantly lifted from the name of a character in Glen Cook's *Garrett, P.I.* series. Glen, if you're reading this, I just want to state for the record that no, Ken and I did not knock over a liquor store that time at ChamBanaCon twenty-five years ago.

All bad puns (generally put in Prophetess' mouth without her knowledge) are entirely my fault. A particular apology to the United Negro College Fund - a mind *is* a terrible thing to waste. I'm not going to apologize to Blizzard for the Diablo III pun. They have enough bad puns in their games - they deserve it.

Thanks to Andy Prieboy for allowing me to appropriate the lyrics of "Tomorrow Wendy," performed by Concrete Blonde.

The phrase "monsters from the id" is a shout-out to the 1950s movie "Forbidden Planet," which has aged surprisingly well - my kids still enjoy it. Like Frankenstein and so many other works of fiction since, it sets out the dangers of playing God.

The quote "the almighty gave us our lives, and I suppose he meant us to defend them" is from H. Rider Haggard, whose character "She" may be the archetype of the dark, tragic, immortal sorceress deep in the ancestry of C.S. Lewis' White Witch, Glen Cook's Lady, and Yoshana.

Seven paraphrases John Jay from the Federalist Papers and quotes George Santayana in Book Four. Demons are pretentious that way. Father Juniper quotes Dom Augustin Guillerand. Apparently priests can be pretentious too. Yoshana cites Reverend Arthur Liebscher (as quoted in Daniel Burke's "The Pope's Dark Night of the Soul") when she says prophets were fine, but their adherents were hard to take.

The horror author H.P. Lovecraft needs no introduction or explanation. To the best of my knowledge, he never intended any of his fiction to be viewed through the Nietzschean lens that Dee ascribed to it. And as a supreme rationalist he

Acknowledgements

might have been offended by Dee characterizing him as an occultist. I prefer to believe that wherever he is, he's taken both ideas with the humor with which they were intended.

Among the ridiculous number of attributed quotes, there's an unattributed paraphrase from Peggy Noonan. The original was, "But you go forward accepting the simple tragedy at the heart of life, that this isn't Heaven, it's earth, and man is crooked timber. You wouldn't invade the Warsaw Pact countries even though they've been turned into outposts of evil." I found it to be a powerful statement from one of the speechwriters for the president who called the Soviet Union an "evil empire."

If I've borrowed the words of others liberally throughout this series, it's because others have done a better job than I could of expressing thoughts that I found to be critically important.

Speaking of plagiarism, there would have been some really funny lines worked in from Paul Simon's *The Sound of Silence* if either (1) US copyright law for song lyrics were a little less weird (apparently you don't need permission to cover a song, but you need permission to quote the lyrics), or (2) I were persistent enough to get through the layers of bureaucracy shielding Mr. Simon from people like me, so I could get permission to quote them. As it is, use your imagination.

***

I have to admit that I hadn't figured out Prophetess' first name until the third novel. When it finally came to me, it was obvious. It's a variation on the middle name of the person who inspired the character, and the first name of the person I'd wanted to edit the series for me. The latter is Eugie Foster, a Nebula Award-winning author and a friend of mine from high school. The fact that she died of cancer at forty-two is a pretty good argument for inventing the Darkness, and she might have thought messing around with it wouldn't be such a bad idea after all. I didn't have a chance to ask her. You should read her books.

It seems only appropriate to acknowledge the great debt I owe to Kevin and Barbara, my guides in the Rite of Christian Initiation as an Adult. All errors in understanding and doctrine are entirely my own.

A quick but important shout-out to Karl Popoff, my unofficial (and very much unpaid) West Coast publicist, who entirely out of the vast goodness of his heart tried to promote this series. Karl has been a great friend and a great inspiration - thank you.

Finally, another shout-out to Richard, Gabriel, Duncan, and Lucia, who have been both inspirations and critics. But first, last, and always, this is for Veronica.

www.ingramcontent.com/pod-product-compliance
Lightning Source LLC
Chambersburg PA
CBHW071329020726
47502CB00001B/15